"This is definitely a story that needs to be told; a clear and poignant example of the economic age that we live in, in which corporate profits are more important than human and environmental health and well-being."

Dr. Ann López
Director, Center for Farmworker Families

"In a saga filled with elegant prose, Mary Flodin takes on the existential crisis of our time — global climate change. Set against the backdrop of a lovingly-rendered California Central Coast, *Fruit of the Devil* weaves elements of mystery, romance and fantasy."

Vinnie Hansen
author of *the Carol Sabala Mystery Series*

"Using mesmerizing descriptive language in an eco-thriller rich with scientific rigor and local history, Mary Flodin comments on corporate greed, the plight of the environment, and the human condition. Mystical and romantic. A breathtaking read that will restore your hope."

Nancy Lynn Jarvis
author of the *Regan McHenry Real Estate Mysteries*

"An organic school garden — oasis for both teachers and students, yet located beside commercial strawberry fields using toxic pesticides — exemplifies the complexity and contradictions at play in *Fruit of the Devil*. Author Mary Flodin weaves an important tale about committed teachers doing their best to bring environmental justice to their community, based on her own life experiences. A tribute to teachers who teach with their whole hearts."

Roberta Jaffe
Founder and Emeritus Director
Life Lab School Garden Project

"With a fine eye for her characters and the details of place, Mary Flodin deconstructs the pernicious evils of our toxic food system. The spirit of resistance and renewal illuminate the pages of *Fruit of the Devil*, showing us a better future is possible."

Mark Lipson
Molino Creek Farming Collective
U.S. Organic Agriculture Policy Advisor 2010-2014.

"Some people think that we no longer exist — that our people, the California Costanoan Ohlone — were swept away through colonization and genocide. But we are still here, in the Land of Our Ancestors. We are very proud that Indian Canyon is part of Mary Flodin's novel, *Fruit of the Devil*. The history of our people goes back to the beginning of time, and the world needs our healing stories now, more than ever. *Noso'n*."

Anne Marie Sayers
Beloved Elder — Tribal Chairperson
Ohlone Indian Canyon

"For those of us who live on the Central California Coast, Fruit of the Devil ticks all the boxes of relevant issues facing our community. Mary Flodin artfully interweaves the plight of our native runs of salmon and steelhead with passion and mysticism. A must read."

Barry Burt
Founder and Emeritus Educational Director
Monterey Bay Salmon and Trout Project

Fruit of the Devil

Mary Flodin

An excerpt from this novel was originally published as
"The Game Warden" in *Santa Cruz Weird*
by Good Read Publishers

Published by Paper Angel Press
paperangelpress.com

ISBN 978-1-949139-73-0 (Trade Paperback)

10 9 8 7 6 5 4 3 2 1

Regions of California

1. Northern Coastal Region

2. Central Coastal Region

3. Southern Coastal Region

4. Central Valley Region

5. Mountain Region

6. Desert Region

Watersheds Flowing into the Monterey Bay
National Marine Sanctuary

1. North Coastal Watershed
2. San Lorenzo River Watershed
3. Byrd River Watershed
4. Salinas River Watershed
5. Carmel River Watershed

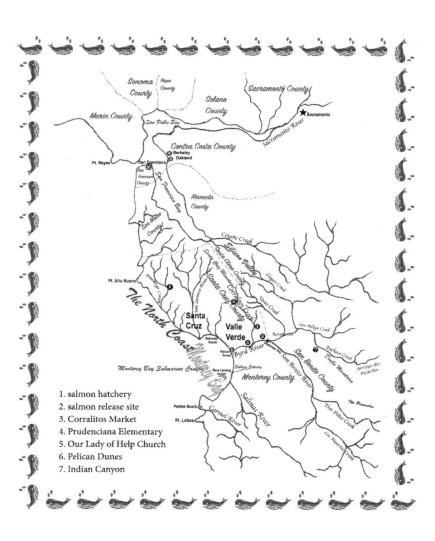

1. salmon hatchery
2. salmon release site
3. Corralitos Market
4. Prudenciana Elementary
5. Our Lady of Help Church
6. Pelican Dunes
7. Indian Canyon

This is a true story about Salmon Boy and the strawberries.

Or anyway it's how I recollect what happened, best as I recall. Though I can't say for sure how much of what I remember got changed by the dreams, or by the Water Oma.

I jus' hope that, if any of them people UpRiver as saw Salmon Boy back then hear this tellin', and if they recognize themselves in the tale, well then I jus' hope I got it all close enough to true that nobody gets too bent outta shape. But knowing the way things are UpRiver, chances are somebody's gonna get pissed off, no matter what.

Here in the Village on the River that flows Underneath the River, we survivors gather close together 'round the lodge fire in these last days, tellin' our stories, tryin' to understand what happened, how we let it all slip away, tryin' to make sense of who we are and what we mean to each other. Like baby wolves, our eyes are just beginnin' to open. I pray it ain't too late.

For all my relations, from my heart spirit, and for the Water Oma, and Wilghtnee, the Salmon Queen, and Her People, and for the children, I offer this story. May it be worthy. May all beings benefit.

Noso'n. In Breath so it is in Spirit.

IN MOUNTAIN POOLS

"The water cycle and the life cycle are one."

— Cousteau

1

B LACKBERRY VINES TANGLED AROUND THE LITTLE GIRL'S ANKLES. She stumbled, squeezing the infant tighter as she struggled for balance. Falling forward, she rolled so she wouldn't squish her baby brother. The infant's wail cut through the dark like a flare. Another scream, eerily like the baby's, answered from deep in the forest. *Mountain lion.*

"*Shhhh,*" the girl whispered close to the baby's face. .

Sharp pricks of dried tan oak leaves and redwood needles poked through her thrift store T-shirt and pants. The swaddled baby on the ground next to her was silent. *Is he dead?*

The little girl lay still, listening. Her heart pounded so hard she was afraid those men would hear.

The flowing creek, the sound she'd been following downhill through the night, shushed a warning.

1

The girl shivered in the dank cold. Small and skinny for her nine years, she was exhausted from carrying the baby. Mama said he was big for a four-month-old. The little girl groped through the baby's blankets until her hand found the warm pulse on his neck, under his chin. The baby gurgled and turned toward her hand, wanting to suck — wanting mama. She wanted mama too. Swiping at the tears wetting her cheeks, she kissed her baby brother's face.

She didn't have the strength to carry him anymore. She'd drop him if she tried. She barely had enough energy to keep her own legs moving. She had to leave him here.

Hastily, she wrapped the baby's blanket tighter and pushed leaves and redwood duff around him, making a nest so he wouldn't roll.

"Be brave," she whispered. "I love you. The angels will watch over you. Stay quiet."

Trembling, she pushed herself to her feet, and brushed the twigs and redwood needles from her clothes and hands. She took a tentative step. And then another. Her feet found a path. She blinked. The path ahead glowed slightly brighter than the surrounding forest floor. Dawn was coming.

She started to run.

*　　*　　*

SATURDAY, JULY 23, 1998 – 6:30AM
FOUR MILE BEACH
THE NORTH COAST, NORTH SANTA CRUZ COUNTY

Four miles north of Santa Cruz, Aurora turned her ten-year-old Toyota pick-up across the two-lane Pacific Coast Highway and eased into an isolated North Coast parking pullout.

The rutted dirt sparkled with broken safety glass from years of land sharks trolling surfers' parked cars for valuables. Aurora left her truck unlocked and empty.

She slipped her ignition key into the security pocket of her wetsuit, reached behind her back for the long string and zipped up. Hoisting her board out of the truck bed, she tucked it under her arm

2

and hustled along the Ohlone Bluffs Trail to the edge of the Brussels sprouts fields. She wove through the acrid-smelling fields and crossed the railroad tracks, then startled a family of Mallards out of the tules as she trotted around Baldwin Creek Marsh to the beach.

On this wild coast north of town — beyond the sheltered waters of the Monterey Bay — the full power of the Pacific Ocean pounded the shore. Here, Aurora always experienced a profound and ineffable sense of the spiritual. This was her church, her temple, her mosque, her holy place. She shaded her eyes with her hand and squinted into the dawn. Water and sand shimmered like abalone shell with reflections of pink and gold sunrise.

An Aleutian freight train of six-foot swells rumbled in from the northwest. The right point break, often compared to Hawaii's legendary Waimea Bay, was firing! Waves walled up and barreled through the inside bowl in perfect glassy tubes.

There was no one out in the lineup yet but a sea otter and a few pelicans.

A black fin cut through the water; Aurora's heart skipped a beat. *Shark?*

Aurora anxiously scanned the water. Hopefully, this morning all of the Great Whites hungry for seals and sea lions would stay in their usual hunting grounds, about fifteen miles up the coast at Año Nuevo. Aurora had been surfing Four Mile for years. Perfectly safe, right? What could happen? A Pacific white-sided dolphin leapt all the way out of the water!

Aurora shrugged of the fear she'd been holding like a duck ruffling its feathers.

She Velcro'd her leash around her ankle, dropped her board in the water and paddled out, diving under icy cold waves that avalanched over her.

Once outside the break zone, she straddled her board, faced the shore, and peered over her shoulder. She didn't have to wait long for a perfect wave. Easing onto her belly, she started pulling through the water ahead of the swell. At its peak, the wave grabbed her. She carved diagonally down its face. At the bottom, she dug in her heels in a roundhouse cutback and charged toward the powerful whitewater rushing at her. She turned with the whitewater, pumped to gain speed,

3

and raced up to the lip of the wave, then crouched down and floated into the tube — into that timeless, ethereal world she sought in her dreams at night, the state of being that kept her coming back to the ocean.

Stalling with weight on her back foot, she stuck her hand in the face of the wave to slow down and stay in the tunnel. Hissing thunder filled her. She rode through the pipeline as the crest of the wave broke continuously overhead. Rapture. She was pitted for what seemed like an eternity.

When the wave spit her out, Aurora carved back up the face and kicked over the top. As the sun rose, she went flying through a steaming rooster tail that sprayed off the wave's humped back. Misty rainbows shimmered all around her, sizzling like fireworks. Beads of water scattered like jewels over the ocean's surface. Throwing her head back, she yelped with joy.

*   *   *

SATURDAY, JULY 23, 1998 – 6:30AM
UPPER CORRALITOS CREEK, SANTA CRUZ MOUNTAINS
BYRD RIVER WATERSHED, SOUTH SANTA CRUZ COUNTY
CENTRAL MONTEREY BAY COAST, CALIFORNIA

In the middle of the creek, the priest stood on a large boulder, naked.

A spectral aura of mist surrounded him. Mountain-cold water swirled around his bare feet. His copper skin glistened in the early morning twilight. The pendant at his throat seemed to waver in and out of existence. His black braid shimmered with luminescent highlights; loose strands of hair feathered around his face in the wind that rushed down the canyon. Biceps inked with tribal tattoos flexed as he reached above his head, his priestly hands grasping a magnificent Rainbow Trout.

On the sandy bank of the wooded creek, Old Joe stood at Detective Charlie Rosa's side.

"What the hell?" Charlie gaped at the naked priest. "I feel like I'm watching a documentary about some Native American fisherman from hundreds of years ago."

Old Joe laughed. "My son walks to the beat of his own drum. His mother claims he's a throwback from my Ohlone Indian blood. But when he was in college, her Spanish genes kicked in. He took up the Art of Swordsmanship and we joked that we had Zorro for a son."

"What's he doing?"

"Catching fish with his bare hands. Trout tickling. It's Old Ways. You enter the water without making a ripple, get your hands under the fish's belly and rub its sides. Fish goes into a trance, and you can pick it up. Not many have the knack, these days."

"Trout tickling?" Charlie cleared his throat. "That's a first."

The priest returned the fish to the stream and climbed, dripping, out of the water. Charlie averted his eyes, but not before he noticed that, as fit as he was, Father Francis was the stronger man, and would probably be able to best him in combat.

No wonder the cholos respect him. Charlie tried to act natural, but he had to admit he felt more comfortable after Father Francis had pulled back on his faded jeans and T-shirt.

"Sorry if I threw you a curve, Charlie," said Father Francis. "Sometimes I just have this feeling that the fish are calling to me. I can't resist getting into the water with them."

Charlie laughed it off. *This is going to be an interesting fishing trip.*

He pulled his jacket collar up around his neck and poured himself a cup of coffee from his thermos. Hugging his arms in close to his chest, he huddled over his cup and blew steam off the surface. The dawning sun had not yet cleared the redwood trees. The air was cold and damp, with a distinct fresh and not unpleasant fishy smell.

"Ready for some fly-fishing, boys?" Old Joe called over his shoulder as he waded into the water with his gear.

A flash of iridescent silver glittered in the rising sun and a fish broke the surface. Old Joe braced his legs in the rushing stream, leaned back, and played in the tugging line. Working his way backward toward the bank of the creek, he stepped deftly over slippery rocks.

Father Francis, wearing a rag wool glove, grabbed the tail of the thrashing fish. It struggled, splashing wild-eyed in the cobbled shallows, then stilled. Father Francis cradled the salmonid in his hands. Keeping the fish under water and facing into the current, he murmured something under his breath.

Old Joe used his hemostat to flip the hook out of the Rainbow's jaw. Then he pulled a ruler from one of his pockets and measured. "Fifteen and three-quarters."

Father Francis smiled and nodded. Working quickly, they weighed the fish and recorded the data on a card. Breathing hard, brows wrinkled in concentration, they called out numbers over the hush of wind in the trees, the rush and splash of water.

Once the trout had been measured and examined, Father Francis continued to hold it facing into the current. Charlie got a good look, marveling at its beauty. Slowly, the priest opened his hands, freeing the fish's belly and tail. The trout remained suspended in place, only its gills moving. Then, with a sudden flare of rainbow colors, it flashed away into the deep green.

"That boy's gonna have some stories to tell." Old Joe's smile deepened the creases in his tanned face.

Disturbed water striders skated across reflective surfaces to an upstream eddy. A sapphire blue dragonfly circled low over the water, alighting on a horsetail fern.

The men hauled themselves onto the dry tarp they'd spread on the bank and flopped down. Charlie yanked off his waders and wiggled his toes in the warmth of the sunlight now filtering through the trees. He pulled a paper sack full of donuts out of his backpack and passed it around.

"Hey, Padre, I think I like fishing," Charlie said between bites of jelly donut. "Feels like getting away, out into nature, even though we're only a few miles outside of town. Thanks for the invite."

"Our pleasure. Dad and I get out fishing regularly. We'll let you know next time we plan a trip."

"That was a funny-looking hook you were using," said the detective.

"Barbless," father and son answered as one.

"Huh?" Charlie wasn't sure he'd heard right, over the water that was falling and riffling around a natural dam of boulders upstream.

Father Francis laughed. "Didn't read that reg book you got with your license, Detective?"

Charlie grinned. "Too busy catching bad guys."

"So, you're probably planning to fry up some tasty Rainbow Trout for dinner tonight, huh?" The two fishermen's eyes twinkled.

Charlie's brow furrowed. He didn't yet get the joke.

"We're using barbless hooks so that after we catch them, we can release them without damage," explained the priest. "We give the data we collect to the state fisheries monitoring project."

"I figured it was something like that."

"It'd be foolish not to," said Old Joe. His white hair and beard gave him the appearance of a rugged sage, despite the boyish baseball cap that shaded his eyes. "Salmon and trout have lived for at least two million years along the Pacific coast. When I was a boy, there were so many Coho in this creek that you could walk across the water on their backs. And Steelhead, what we locals call Rainbow Trout, were as plentiful as weeds. Now the Coho are nearly extinct in this watershed and Steelhead are disappearing too."

"These fish serve as our canary in the coalmine," said Father Francis. "We need to take care of them."

A kingfisher's bubbling call washed down the wooded canyon. A Great Blue Heron glided high above the meandering channel toward the coast.

"Like the old days, huh?" Old Joe smiled at his son, crinkling the well-eroded laugh lines around his eyes.

"Yeah," said Father Francis. "It's still pretty good up here on the Corralitos. But you know, Dad, downstream on Byrd River there's somethin' wrong. None of the sensitive water bugs left. No striders, no mayflies or stoneflies, no caddis ... nothin' alive for the fish to eat."

"Probably the latest chemicals those ag boys are spraying on the strawberry fields."

The three men spread out along the creek, each fishing solo in his own timeless blue-green world.

Drifting westward, the afternoon sun chiseled deep shadows into boulders and fallen logs.

Father Francis' shout broke the stillness.

"Charlie! Hey! You'd better come over here."

The fishermen stared at a dilapidated lean-to covered with spray-painted gang tags, cowering at the edge of the creek. Trash and garbage littered the ground — rotten food, old clothes, plastic trash bags, filth-encrusted dishes, glass jars, empty packages of cold tablets.

"Watch out." Father Francis pointed to a heap of rubble partially hidden under an old blanket.

With a stick, Charlie lifted a corner of the filthy blanket and the men stared into evil's underbelly: used needles, broken glass pipes, razor blades, cans of acetone, drain cleaner, paint thinner, spilled bags of lye and fertilizer.

"Jesus, Mary, and Joseph," said Old Joe. "Smells like death and cat piss."

The men held kerchiefs over their faces, coughing and trying not to gag.

"Careful," said Charlie. "We've got a meth lab here."

Father Francis nodded. "Somebody ransacked this camp recently. What a mess."

"Charlie, over here," said Old Joe. "Think this is blood?"

"Yeah. It's all over this sleeping bag too."

"Christ. There's blood everywhere. Some of it's still tacky."

"Don't touch anything," said Charlie. "This is a crime scene."

"Recognize these tags?" asked Father Francis.

"Not any of our local gangs," said Charlie.

"Over here!" Old Joe's shout came from a lopsided tent cabin slumped behind the lean-to.

The three men peered into the tent.

"Kids' toys," said the detective, pointing to a doll dressed like a princess.

Old Joe nodded toward an opened suitcase covered with pink butterfly tattoo decals. "Little girl's stuff."

"Oh, no," said Father Francis. "Diapers. Dear God. There was a baby in here."

2

T HE DAWNING SUN PAINTED A WATERCOLOR WASH ACROSS SKY and ocean. Aurora spirited up Coast Highway north from Santa Cruz in her new red Miata MX-5 with the top down and wind in her hair.

The tang of early morning ocean air hit her face and she felt as if she were flying. But a pang of guilt dampened her elation.

No reason to feel guilty for buying this Miata, she told herself. The old Toy is perfect for hauling all my fun stuff: surfboard, bike, kayak, art and gardening things, but I definitely needed a more reliable car for commuting to work.

When the speedometer topped 80 mph, she eased off on the gas and glanced in the rearview mirror, relieved not to see the Highway Patrol on her tail.

Stop stressing about being late to the hike. Be present.

Her artist's eyes took in the waves catching sun diamonds as they crashed on deserted beaches along the open ocean north of Monterey Bay — beaches too windy and wild for the tourists who flocked to the town's seaside and boardwalk. Flying past Four Mile cove, she turned up the volume on her CD player. The foreboding lyrics of Jackson Browne's "Before the Deluge"— warning of a future Earth devastated by climate chaos — wrung her heart.

She was so in love with this coast — this "injured coast". She longed to become one with everything she could see and sense, to wrap her arms around all of it — sky, birds, ocean, forested coastal mountains of uplifted marine terrace, rocky coves and wild salmon streams. She ached to hold it all, take it into her, until she and the spirit of this place became one.

But underneath her exultation, a familiar loneliness scratched at her heart.

What's wrong with me? I've got everything I need. A fulfilling job. A sweet little cottage of my own by the beach. I love my independence. I should be happy.

She downshifted when the two-lane highway threaded through the historic whaling village of Davenport Landing. Past the highway marker that read "San Francisco 73 miles," she picked up speed again. A bittersweet memory welled up, of drives along Coast Highway as an only child with her mom and dad. They would have loved coming with her on this hike today. If only they hadn't stopped for drinks on that last drive down the coast.

It's more than ten years since they died. You're not twenty anymore. Grow up.

The CD player switched discs and Grace Slick's voice unfurled like ribbons in the wind. "Find somebody to looooooove."

When Aurora approached the lagoon where Buckeye Creek empties into the Pacific, she turned her roadster away from the coast onto a narrow, winding country byway and cranked up the volume on her CD player. Vivaldi's joyful "Spring" concerto made her heart soar as she followed a flock of sky-dancing swallows up into the coastal mountains.

*   *   *

TUESDAY, JULY 26, 1998
LOWER CORRALITOS CREEK, SANTA CRUZ MOUNTAINS
BYRD RIVER WATERSHED, SOUTH SANTA CRUZ COUNTY
CENTRAL MONTEREY BAY COAST, CALIFORNIA

At the passing scent of vole, Bella's whiskers twitched. Her head was growing heavy in the late morning sunshine. Her eyelids drifted shut against the flickering shadows under the huckleberry bush where she'd made her nest.

Bella was a good dog. She had certainly been told it often enough, and she knew it was true. She was an excellent friend, companion and protector of her beloved human family. And she was also an excellent mother. Over the years, she'd successfully raised many litters of healthy, happy, well-bred pups. At this point in life, she'd reached the place where little could cause her to lose her equanimity.

However, four dawns ago, when she'd trotted through the ranch fence and started her patrol along the creek, she'd felt that something was amiss. As she'd sniffed for scents, her black and white husky hackles had stood up in a thick ruff around her neck. Mountain lion. That unmistakable musky smell. The cougar had passed nearby in the night.

Sitting on her haunches, Bella had lifted her nose to the morning breeze, assessing the movement of the cougar, still too close for comfort. Then she'd sensed something else in the air. Smelled it before she'd heard it. A faint sound. Human pup? A cry. Jumping to her feet, she'd run toward the sound.

That was four long days ago …

The pup stirred underneath her. Instantly alert, Bella shifted to her side and put down her muzzle to investigate. Snuffling her way through blanket folds, she touched the furless skin of the human pup with her wet nose, and sniffed. Alive, but far weaker than when she'd first found it. A wonder she had found it first, and not the mountain lion.

11

The pup whimpered.

Sorrow. Many salmon moons had passed since she'd weaned her last litter. No milk to give this poor hungry baby.

At least she was keeping it warm. Once, she had felt a pup grow cold and lifeless under her. Her first litter. Never again. But there wasn't much time left for this one.

She raised her head and pricked up her ears. The creek's song. Steller's jay scratching in the leaf litter. Deer eating lichen. No human voices. Someone should be searching for her by now.

Bella nuzzled the pup, then walked a little distance and squatted, marking the edge of the boundary she would defend. With strong hind claws, she scratched a neat covering of duff over her mark. Then she returned to the pup, circling above it until her nest was arranged just right.

Carefully, she lowered herself on top of the babe. She prodded the pup with her muzzle to make sure it was warm, comfortable, and breathing. It cooed and pressed a fist to her belly, much as one of her own pups would do. Satisfied, she settled back into her vigil. When would they find her?

3

TUESDAY, JULY 26, 1998
Physics-in-Nature Hike
Buckeye Creek
North Coast Watershed
Santa Cruz County, California

A URORA HAD BEEN TO THE SALMON HATCHERY BEFORE, so she recognized the way the buckeye trees clumped just before the bend, and how the smell of the air changed from salt spray to the pungent scent of California bay leaves. The unmarked driveway was identifiable only by a wooden fence and a sign stating "Private Property. No Trespassing."

Her Miata's tires crunched gravel as she eased, in second gear, past a horse pasture and pulled into a dirt parking area next to several other cars.

She slid out of her roadster, settled her daypack on her shoulders, and joined the other hikers gathered at a trailhead at the edge of the forest.

A woman with a little boy at her side handed Aurora paperwork on a clipboard: a standard hold harmless agreement that released the property owner from liability in case of accident. Aurora signed, and passed the clipboard to the next person in the circle.

"Good morning, everyone," said a tall, ruggedly tanned man with untamed Albert Einstein hair and white moustache. He wore faded khaki shorts, a "Solar Saves Salmon" T-shirt, and thick glasses taped at the corner of the broken frame.

"Welcome to the Magic of Physics in Nature. I'll be your guide today. My name is Dr. John Stevenson, but most people call me 'Cosmic John'."

He made eye contact with everyone as he spoke, welcoming them into his magical adventure. Aurora counted about twenty hikers in the circle. Good vibrations. This was going to be a perfect way to spend one of her last precious days of summer vacation.

"As we hike along the creek," "Cosmic John" explained, "we'll be looking for waves and rainbows, bubbles and crystals, whirlpools and shadows, echoes and mirages, and discovering new ways to see and appreciate the natural world. Along the way, we'll learn some local history and visit a fish hatchery. At lunch, I'll answer questions about my research at NASA on the ozone hole. And then we'll have a swim under a waterfall. But first, I'd like to start in a circle with introductions so that I, and also all of you, can get an idea of who's here, and what you hope to gain from this adventure."

Aurora pulled her braid over her shoulder to inspect the split ends in the morning light. As usual, all those glorious days of surfing and gardening in the summer sun had streaked her hair with deep gold. She should make an appointment to get a trim before school started.

A retired librarian finished her introduction. Then the man standing next to her flipped his styled, side-parted, blonde hair out of his eyes. "Name's Billy Baker," he said. "From Valle Verde City in South County."

He flicked an imagined speck of dirt off his tan slacks, adjusted the collar of his Lacoste polo shirt — red with a gold crocodile appliqued over his heart — and shuffled his tasseled loafers.

"Why am I here?" With a smart-alecky grin, Billy held up his hands, palms out, in an off-putting gesture. "Hey, I'm only here because my girlfriend made me come."

Everyone laughed politely.

The girlfriend, about as tall as Billy, leaned on him with her hand on his butt. Bulging over the top of a spandex tank, and out the bottom of fire-engine red short-shorts, she introduced herself with a little wave of her hand. "Name's Misty. I work at Blue Fin, near Cannery Row, at the other end of the bay." She wiggled her hips as she spoke. "Billy and I were up here in Santa Cruz partying over the weekend and we read about this magic in nature thing in the *Santa Cruz Good Times*. I just looove rainbows, bubbles and crystals, don't you?"

The woman standing next to Hot Pants was slender and healthy looking, with shiny brown hair cut in a clean, smooth bob. Her shorts and green T-shirt looked neatly pressed.

Glancing around the circle, she smiled pleasantly. "My name is Kelli Cavanaugh. I guess you could say I'm here on a busman's holiday. I'm a State Fish and Wildlife Warden. I've heard a lot of great things about this hike John does so I'm happy I was free to come today."

"Well, thank you, Kelli," Cosmic John said.

He turned to Aurora and nodded.

I'm next.

She blushed. It was never easy speaking to a group of strangers — unless they were children.

"My name's Aurora Bourne. I live in Santa Cruz near the university, and I teach fourth grade in the south part of the county, at Prudenciana Elementary in Valle Verde."

As the introductions continued, Aurora focused on remembering everyone's name. A software engineer from Silicon Valley finished speaking, and Aurora's attention skipped to the next person in the circle. Her breath caught.

The man radiated a compelling power. She couldn't stop her eyes from tracing the lines of broad shoulders and ripped chest under his white T-shirt. His skin glowed with a red-brown cast the color of redwood bark. A peek of ink banding his biceps made her itch with curiosity to see the whole design. His black braid caught subtle iridescent highlights in the sun. Aurora skimmed down his canvas shorts, along the utterly masculine sinewy legs of an athlete, to his river sandals.

Taller than everyone else in the circle — surely over six feet. Probably almost forty.

He smiled with an easy grace as he made eye contact with each person around the circle. For an instant, his eyes met hers, and an electric jolt shot through her, all the way down to her toes. He was so stunning, with so much animal magnetism, she couldn't breathe until he looked away.

Even after his attention moved on, she continued to gape at him, her heart pounding. She imagined softly running her finger over his clean-shaven cheek, tracing the fine black shadow of his beard, the hard contour of his jaw and chin. Her body throbbed in time to a pulse emanating from him. She hoped no one noticed her reaction to this man, least of all him. Aurora dropped her gaze and studied the ground.

"My name is Father Francis Hilman." At the sound of his voice, she shivered. "I'm a priest at Our Lady of Help Catholic Church in Valle Verde. I volunteer at the hatchery and I've heard good things from other volunteers about Dr. John's 'Physics in Nature' hike."

Oh, no. A priest.

*   *   *

Aurora fell into the end of the line of hikers. Patterns of light and shade flickered on the dirt trail. It was early enough that the ocean breeze still bit with morning chill, but the maple syrup aroma of pearly-everlasting flowers already warmed in the rising summer sun. While she walked, Aurora found peace in the hum of life waking in the forest and the hush of creek water flowing over stones. She hadn't learned everyone's name yet, but she'd probably get to know more of the people as they hiked.

The group stopped in an open area on the trail — a sunny spot near a log cabin, under a radiant blue sky. Aurora joined the circle, standing between four university students, and well away from the priest.

Father Francis was speaking to three Latino teens he'd brought with him from the continuation high school basketball team he coached: Victor Lopez and his friend Pato, and Victor's little brother Johnny. Johnny looked like a handful. Victor Lopez had a sweet face with a coal dust of mustache smudging his upper lip. A gold crucifix hung around his neck and a crystal earring pierced his left earlobe. Gang tattoos graffitied his arms and the knuckles of both hands.

Aurora took notes while Cosmic John gave a fascinating explanation of why the sky is blue, and insights into the physics of light and color.

Johnny picked up a rock to throw. Father Francis stopped him with a raised eyebrow and subtle shake of his head. Johnny opened his fist, pointedly letting the rock drop to the ground, and brushed off his hands. Johnny's older brother, Victor, said something to Father Francis, then snatched the red baseball cap off Johnny's head and tousled his hair.

"So who built that log cabin?" asked Johnny in an obvious ploy to reclaim his dignity.

"Good question," said Cosmic John. "In the late 1800s, a young whaler from Massachusetts fell in love with the California coast. After the whales had been hunted to the brink of extinction, he homesteaded this watershed and built this cabin for his bride with redwood from the property."

"Save the whales!" one of the university students blurted. Aurora smiled and nodded, as did several others in the group.

"Well now, saving the whales is another story," said Cosmic John. "But to finish answering Johnny's question about the cabin, after World War II, the homesteader's son and grandsons returned to the land from overseas duty, and founded Buckeye Creek Lumber Company. That original family still owns the company, and this property. A number of endangered and threatened species continue to thrive on Buckeye Creek that are extinct in other parts of the watershed, including Coho salmon and an interesting bird called the Marbled Murrelet."

"We studied Marbled Murrelets last semester," said another of the university students. "The only place they can reproduce is in old growth redwood forests, and this is some of the last old growth left on the planet."

"That's right," said Cosmic John. "Most virgin redwood was logged in the 1850s, but thanks to the work of generations of local forest conservationists and Buckeye Creek Lumber's stewardship, old-growth trees can still be found here — some over 1,200 years old. We'll be hiking through a unique ecology — one of the few places on the planet where you can still experience an intact old growth redwood forest ecosystem. Ready to move on?"

The group unwound from its circle and moved like a snake, side-winding up the trail. As they followed the creek, Cosmic John stopped from time to time to demonstrate physics phenomena at play in the water.

*   *   *

The fish hatchery was a small operation. One low, rectangular building made of corrugated metal huddled by the creek. The sound of running water echoed from inside it. Situated next to the building, a tent of fabric netting shaded three large above-ground Doughboy Pool fishponds. The damp forest air held a pleasant fishy smell.

A formidable older man, large and heavyset, waited in front of the pond tent. With a shaggy beard and greying auburn hair that curled to his collar, he reminded Aurora of a grizzly bear.

"This is Dr. Daniel Scott," said Cosmic John. "Dan is the only paid employee at the hatchery. All the other workers here are volunteers. This hatchery is unusual because of its size and because it's on private property, although it's overseen by Cal Fish and Wildlife. They keep the operation small so they can closely monitor and manage the genetics of the wild population."

"Each creek that weaves together the vast watershed of the Pacific Northwest Coast has its own distinct tribe of salmon," said Dr. Dan. "My job is to preserve the unique biodiversity of the salmonids specific to the creeks in this region." Dr. Dan's voice sounded like deep water flowing over gravel. "I grew up fishing the waters around here. When I was a boy, I used to ride with my grandpa in his horse-drawn buckboard up the creek at spawning season. I'd help him pitchfork the carcasses of hundreds of spawned-out Coho — the ones that the birds, raccoons, bobcats, cougars, and other critters hadn't eaten — into the back of the buckboard until they were piled up high, and then we'd take them down to the ranch to slop to our hogs. But now, I'm sorry to say, Monterey Bay Coho are almost gone."

From under bushy eyebrows, the biologist examined the group. He exchanged a nearly imperceptible nod with the priest, a look that conveyed friendship and mutual respect.

When he spotted Aurora, he smiled. "Nice to see you again."

"You too." Aurora blushed and tried not to stammer under everyone's interested stares. "I'm excited to see the hatchery again before school starts."

"I recruited Aurora three summers ago to be a teacher for STEP, the Salmon and Trout Education Project," said Dr. Dan. "She's been doing a great job with her elementary school students. If anyone wants more information on our education and conservation projects, volunteering, or anything else, just ask me as we go through the tour. Now, let me show you inside, where we keep the eggs."

After the hatchery tour, Cosmic John announced a short rest stop. "Feel free to look around on your own. The outhouses are over there. Ahead, we have a creek crossing. On the other side of the creek, we'll stop for lunch at a nice spot with picnic tables. While we're here, please remember to take only photos and leave only footprints."

The university students asked Aurora if she would take their picture. They composed themselves: four jolly, ragtag, outdoorsy, twenty-somethings who smelled like pine sap and campfire smoke, and appeared as if they'd spent the summer rafting the California rivers and backpacking the Sierra without ever changing their clothes. They reminded her of herself at that age. Aurora snapped the photo.

Two couples who'd driven over the coastal mountains from Silicon Valley sat together on the bench near the fish tanks and chatted with a local graphic artist and her husband, a nurse. Each of the Silicon Valley couples had a child. A hatchery volunteer handed fish food to the two children — a boy and a girl, both about eight years old — and they threw the pellets over the surface of the water. A hundred shining silver daggers sliced through the green-shadowed liquid, and then Steelhead fingerlings broke the surface, splashing and feeding in a frenzy.

19

Aurora found a comfortable log near the creek and rummaged in her daypack for a snack.

The priest appeared with the Fish and Wildlife Warden, Kelli Cavanaugh. They sat down nearby in front of a large, concave boulder that amplified their voices — a natural echo chamber like the one Cosmic John had demonstrated earlier. Aurora didn't mean to eavesdrop, but she could hear them clearly.

"Lucky we found it when we did," said Father Francis. "The Sheriff's Office got a forensics team and a hazmat drug task force out there right away."

Kelli had a notebook open. "What did you say your friend's name was?"

"Rosa. Detective Sergeant Charlie Rosa. Santa Cruz County Sheriff's Office. The camp had been ransacked. There was blood all over the place — a meth kitchen tossed upside-down."

"Gang tags?" asked Kelli.

"Yes, but not any of our hoods. We think it might be the work of a skinhead group from San Jose."

Kelli tapped her pen on her notebook and stared at the creek. "Someone's facing serious prison time just for the Fish and Wildlife violations. Those chemicals contaminating the creek are going to wreak havoc on our salmon."

"That's not the worst of it, Kelli."

"What else?"

"We found evidence that a little girl, or girls — maybe more than one — and a baby had been living at the camp. The Sheriff's Office has mounted a search for the children."

"A baby in a meth kitchen?" Kelli snapped her notebook shut and stood up.

The priest and the game warden walked away, still talking.

Aurora shivered, despite the warmth of the summer morning.

Cosmic John signaled the hikers to assemble, then led them up the trail at a leisurely pace. Although the day had warmed, the ground and air in the temperate coastal rainforest remained moist, creating a perfect habitat for slimy yellow banana slugs, gentle salamanders, and earthy-smelling mushrooms of fanciful shapes and colors. Tall redwoods filtered the light like stained glass in a cathedral. Cosmic John demonstrated why light shining through irregular spaces in the leaves overhead cast perfect sun circles on the shadowy trail.

Aurora counted more than twenty shades of green before she lost track. Giant fallen trees lay where they'd crashed during winter rainstorms, slashing diagonal lines through the landscape. Woodpeckers and Steller's jays scolded from the treetops. Layers of flora and fauna laced and crisscrossed all the way up to the canopy of the tallest redwoods, piercing more than three hundred dizzying feet into the brilliant blue sky.

Prehistoric ferns reached curling fingers down to tap the top of her head as she passed. Scraggly Old Man's Beard hung from branches like Halloween decorations. The gruesome image of the bloody meth camp leapt into Aurora's mind. *What happened to the children?*

The trail led to the water's edge. Across the creek, it re-emerged and snaked off into the forest.

The teenage boys and two of the university students had already crossed to the other side. One of the tattooed teens had taken his high-top tennis shoe off and was pouring water out of it.

The two dads from Silicon Valley, their river-sandaled feet braced ankle-deep in the rushing cold stream, balanced on slippery, uneven cobbles and helped wives and children pick their way from boulder to boulder.

Aurora approached the retired librarian, Louise Daniels, who stood squinting forlornly at the water.

"Would you like some help getting across?" Aurora asked. "I can hold your hand and help you keep your balance."

"Here," said Kelli. "I'll take your other hand."

"Thank you, dears. I'm a lifelong member of the Sierra Club, so I've crossed my share of creeks, all over the world. But at my age, I could use some help balancing. All this moving water makes me dizzy." The three women picked their way without mishap to the other side.

Only three people still needed to cross. Hot Pants blinked anxiously at the water. She put a hand on Billy's shoulder, pulled off one of her sequined sandals, and rubbed her bare foot. Billy rolled up his pressed khakis, then glanced around with a desperate glint in his eyes.

Father Francis spoke to Billy, then took off his sandals and traded them for Billy's tasseled loafers and socks.

Wearing the priest's sandals, Billy hoisted Hot Pants off her feet and carried her into the water like a husband bearing his bride over the threshold. She squealed, squirmed and kicked her legs. Billy's foot slipped, but he regained his balance and yelled at Hot Pants to hold still, shaking her as if she were a sack of potatoes. Father Francis followed closely behind them, carrying Billy's socks and loafers. Aurora cringed at the thought of the priest walking barefoot across the uneven creek bed awash with sharp stones and sticks.

Once back on dry ground, Billy released his burden with a grunt. Hot Pants stumbled like a drunk as she landed, giggling hysterically. The priest handed Billy his loafers and socks. Billy sat on a rock and put them back on while Cosmic John congratulated everyone for their daring and successful creek crossing. There was a picnic area ahead, the scientist said, with tables and benches, where they could rest and have lunch. Afterward, they'd hike to a hundred-foot waterfall.

As the group followed Cosmic John up the trail, Aurora glanced over her shoulder. The priest's sandals lay on the ground by the creek, where Billy had thrown them without saying thank you.

Father Francis knelt by the water. He seemed to be singing, or talking to himself.

The drumbeat she heard was her own heart pounding.

4

Corralitos Creek
Byrd River Watershed, South Santa Cruz County
Central Monterey Bay Coast, California

"Bella! Here girl! Bella!"

Bella's ears twitched. She opened her eyes and sniffed the air. Her family was coming!

"Daddy, we've got to find her."

Bella jumped to her feet. She didn't dare leave the pup. She had to get them to come to her. As hard as it was for her to disobey the "Come" command, Bella stood her ground. She raised her head and howled.

"Daddy, it's Bella! She's singing! Listen!"

"This way," said the boy's father. "It's coming from over here! Bella!"

The human pup began to cry. Bella howled louder.

"Bella! Here you are!" said the man. "What is this? Oh, my God. A baby. What in the ... No, wait. Don't touch it, son. Let me. Get Bella's leash on her."

The boy threw his arms around Bella's neck and hugged her, then clipped the leash to her collar. "You must be hungry, poor, brave Bella."

Bella barked and licked the boy's hand. She couldn't stop wagging her tail. The human pup would live.

"How is this possible?" The man lifted the baby from the nest. "Come on, little one. We've got you. You're going to be okay. Hurry, son. We need to get this baby back to the house fast and call 911."

*   *   *

TUESDAY, JULY 26, 1998
PICNIC LUNCH
BUCKEYE CREEK, NORTH COASTAL WATERSHED

Aurora settled in next to the children on the bench at the redwood picnic table and unwrapped her tuna sandwich. Kelli, the wildlife warden, was talking with Cosmic John. At the far end of the table, Father Francis handed out sandwiches, apples, and bags of chips he'd brought for the teenage boys.

After a few minutes of eating and conversation, Cosmic John stood. "This morning, I promised you some 'true tall tales of the universe' over lunch. We can talk about astronomy, cosmology, current events in atmospheric science. Who has questions?"

"What exactly do you do?" asked Billy. "I mean to earn a living?"

"I've worked as an atmospheric scientist at NASA, over the hill at Moffett Field in Silicon Valley, for the last twenty years or so, on various projects. These days, I'm involved in research on ozone depletion."

"Let's talk about astrology," shouted Hot Pants.

"I don't know much about astrology," Cosmic John answered. "Astrology and astronomy are totally different. I'm an astrophysicist."

"I'm a Virgo," Hot Pants quipped. A few people laughed.

"We've heard there's a meteor shower coming up," said one of the university students. "Can you tell us about that?"

"The Perseids! One of my favorites," said Cosmic John. "The Perseid shower peaks every year in mid-August. They often have long, dramatic tails that linger in the sky like fireworks."

Cosmic John answered everyone's questions about meteors, stars and planets, our location in the universe, the relative scale and arrangement of solar systems and galaxies, black holes, the many worlds hypothesis, string theory, dark matter, gluons, and what he called "the whole shebang".

"But my favorite thing to share with people," the scientist continued, "is that we are all made of stardust."

"What do you mean?" asked the little boy.

Aurora was delighted by Cosmic John's explanation, through Socratic questioning, of how it happens that much of the matter in the universe, including humans, is composed of atoms that originated in stars.

I'm definitely adding this to my astronomy curriculum. My students will love it.

"Star dust my ass," Billy whispered to his girlfriend, who was freshening her mascara in a compact mirror.

"What about your ozone hole research?" asked the Silicon Valley engineer wearing a T-shirt with an Apple logo.

"The ozone hole project has been very interesting to work on," said Cosmic John. "Partly because there are both scientific and political-economic aspects of the problem. We're well on our way to a solution, now. Are any of you familiar with *The Montreal Protocol*?"

"Yes," the retired librarian spoke up. "It's an international treaty to protect the ozone layer around the Earth, by banning chemicals that cause the ozone hole."

"Exactly." Cosmic John pushed his glasses up his nose. "It's been hailed as perhaps the single most successful international environmental agreement we humans have managed, to date. A cause for real hope about the fate of the world."

"So the ozone hole is real?" asked the graphic designer.

"The ozone hole is real, and very dangerous to life as we know it on the planet. Certain man-made chemicals, including CFCs and halons, destroy stratospheric ozone. These chemicals are widely used in fire extinguishers, refrigerants, solvents, aerosols, and blowing agents for plastic foams."

Cosmic John related how his research group at NASA had discovered the "smoking gun" that drives ozone depletion. "The hole in the protective ozone layer allows not just the good sunlight, but also harmful ultraviolet rays to hit the Earth. This increased UV-B hitting the planet," the scientist warned, "has already caused crop damage, massive havoc to ecosystems, and threats to sensitive species."

"Threats to humans too," said the nurse. "Ozone depletion is causing serious health issues. Cataract-induced blindness, malignant melanoma, autoimmune disruptions, and the spread of infectious diseases are up worldwide."

"It's also affecting wildlife," said Kelli. "All over the world, amphibians — newts, salamanders, toads, frogs — are declining in numbers, even going extinct. The prevailing theory is that it's a combination of increased UV-B from depletion of the ozone layer, coupled with climate change. Frogs are an indicator species, a canary in the coalmine, like salmon. We should be paying attention."

Another one of the students spoke up. "My professors say that if ozone depletion goes unchecked, it will cause the decline of the oceans' plankton, which could disrupt all of Earth's food chains. Scary stuff."

"So, now we have an international treaty in place banning the chemicals that deplete ozone?" asked the software engineer with a silver streak through her ponytail. "That's good news."

"Yes," Cosmic John answered. "Manufacture and use of CFCs is finally being phased out worldwide. But the CFC industry didn't give up easily. As late as 1986, the so-called Alliance for Responsible CFC Policy, an association funded by the corporation that manufactured CFCs, was still arguing that the science was too uncertain to justify any action. They supported their claims with 'junk science' written by unqualified people on the company payroll."

"Our professor says those false reports are still being circulated. Even though there's no longer any debate at all in the peer-reviewed science, industry is still intentionally misleading the public."

Billy Baker stood up, upsetting the balance on the picnic bench. Aurora nearly fell off the other end. Ignoring the people trying to right their balance, Billy squeezed his girlfriend's ass. She wriggled as he escorted her into a hazelnut thicket at the edge of the clearing.

"So, are we out of the woods yet, with the ozone hole?" the retired librarian asked.

"Nature does have the capacity to repair itself, over time. It's believed that if the international agreement is followed, the ozone layer should substantially recover by 2050."

"So we can fix this?" One of the engineers looked at her daughter, then at her husband.

"Well, the big hole in the ozone layer over the Antarctic is on the mend, with the phase-out of CFCs. But not as fast as anticipated. That's possibly because other ozone-depleting chemicals listed in the protocol aren't being so successfully phased out. Our greatest worry at this point is methyl bromide."

"What's that?" asked one of the students.

"Methyl bromide is a fumigant used in agriculture. In California, it's used to sterilize the soil in strawberry fields. Strawberry growers are using more methyl bromide now than when the chemical was banned."

"If it was banned by an international treaty, how can they get away with that?" asked another of the university students.

"The U.S. government continues to grant exemptions to the agricultural lobby for methyl bromide use even though we're now years behind the stipulated phase-out."

"Exemptions? Why?" asked the nurse.

"*Cha-ching*," said another student, carving a dollar sign in the air.

A red baseball cap flew over Aurora's head and landed on the table in front of her. Johnny reached over Aurora's shoulder and retrieved his hat.

"What about the greenhouse effect — global warming?" asked the graphic designer.

"Oh, now that's a different story," the scientist explained. "The ozone hole and global warming are both problems disrupting the Earth's atmosphere, but the causes, as well as the chemistry and physics, are different — although some of the ozone-depleting chemicals, like methyl bromide, are also greenhouse gases."

At the far end of the table, Johnny, his red baseball cap back on his head, shoved his big brother, Victor. The boys laughed. Father Francis leaned over and whispered something to them. They sat up straight and put their hands on the table, struggling to control their laughter. Father Francis' eyes met Aurora's. He smiled. She looked down at the knots in the picnic table, feeling her face flush.

"But," said Cosmic John, "we should be moving on. We've got a waterfall to visit."

While people packed up, Aurora lingered at the picnic table to finish writing the notes she'd been making in her journal. Her mind was full of ideas for a new unit on the ozone hole and climate change she planned to include in her science curriculum this year. She might get some pushback from administration, but the content was definitely in alignment with state standards. Her students and their parents needed to know about this.

A branch cracked nearby. Billy Baker, holding his belt buckle, emerged out of the trees. His girlfriend stumbled into the clearing behind him, redwood needles in her hair and red lipstick smeared across her cheek.

*   *   *

"I hear the waterfall!" The children danced excitedly around their parents as the hikers followed Buckeye Creek along a meandering trail. The distant roar of the falls grew louder. Finally, Aurora clambered around a large boulder and the path opened, revealing a forest grotto.

Water pounded over a hundred-foot cliff, dampening all other sounds. Aurora felt as if she'd arrived inside the beating heart of the forest. She lifted her face to the cool mist rising from the waterfall.

At the foot of the falls, a natural rock pool — its diameter as wide as the waterfall was tall — shimmered emerald green in the filtered light. Reflections of ferns, endangered orchids, and dogwood trees wavered on its surface. Around the edge farthest from the tumult, the water calmed in mossy shallows. Aurora watched a salamander wriggle under a submerged boulder.

The darkest green center of the pool appeared infinitely deep and very cold. In the shadow of the cliff closest to the falls, serpentine black waves rippled across the water. At the base of the fall, white water thundered incessantly into the pool, churning frothy turbulence.

"We have about forty-five minutes here," Cosmic John shouted. "Enjoy yourselves, and be safe. Now, if you don't mind," he said, pulling his T-shirt over his head and laying it on a rock with his hat and glasses, "I'm going for a swim!" With that, he turned and dove from the boulder into the forest pool.

Behind a thimbleberry thicket, Aurora dropped her pack onto the redwood duff and slipped off her tank top and shorts, stripping down to her bikini. She adjusted a strap, hitching her breasts more comfortably into her top, then tiptoed to the edge of the water, took a few squishy steps, and dove.

Ten fast laps, stretched out and kicking hard, and then she turned onto her back and relaxed, letting her vision soften. Wavering lines of blue and green water waves reflected trees and sky. She floated outside of time, suspended in a magical medium.

"Dude! This is hella dope!"

Aurora rolled in the water and peered toward the shout. The teenage boys, Father Francis, Cosmic John, and the university students were dog paddling in front of the waterfall.

In a few fast overhead strokes, Aurora joined them. They were taking turns diving under the fall. She fit herself into the circle and watched one of the students go under. It seemed like a long time before he burst back to the surface, gasping for air.

"Awesome!" he shouted. "Fuckin' awesome!"

"I'll go next." Aurora took a big breath and dove.

Sudden, stark silence enveloped her.

The water forced her down, down, twisting and pulling.

She opened her eyes. Nothing but white bubbles.

Chest on fire. My lungs are going to explode.

She pulled hard for the surface.

Her hands smashed into the bedrock at the bottom of the pool, fingers tangling in the slithery weeds.

A great rushing sound filled her skull. Her mind went black.

5

AURORA STARED INTO A FIELD OF BLUE-GREEN, swirling with flecks of gold — Father Francis' eyes, inches from hers. Struggling against the current pulling her to him, she stepped back. An aura of colored lights whirled around him. When she regained her balance, she took in her surroundings.

She stood on the bank of a stream, different than the one where she'd been hiking. Each plant and rock shimmered with a radiance that merged with the auras of everything around it, including the energy emanating from the man, and her own body. Every leaf, twig, and spider's web vibrated to notes that harmonized with the music of the flowing water.

Father Francis stood before her, but there was no sign of the other hikers. Aurora touched her head. No pain or bumps. As she moved, she felt as if she were pulling through water. Yet her hair was dry and so was her clothing. Her heart raced.

"What's happening, Father Francis? Did someone pull me out of the water? Where are we? Where are the others?" She shivered so hard her teeth clacked together. "Am I hallucinating? Did I — did I drown?" She fought to control the panic surging through her.

Father Francis wrapped his hands around hers. *Warm, strong, comforting.* "Take some deep breaths, Aurora." He held her with his eyes until her shivering subsided. "You did not drown. You're safe here, and you're not hallucinating. That is, not exactly. No one pulled you out of the water. We are in *Naadaayi Héen a Tayee.* Some call it *Río Abajo El Río,* the River Under the River."

A wave of vertigo swept over her. Father Francis held her by the shoulders to steady her.

"What do you remember?" he asked.

"I dove under the waterfall. I ran out of breath, and then I was sucked into some kind of hole."

"We call that hole Frog Woman's Pond. It's a vortex, a portal into this world."

"What?"

"There are many worlds in the Universe, existing side-by-side. *Naadaayi Héen a Tayee* is, in a quantum sense, tethered to the UpRiver world we just came from."

"I don't understand."

"The two worlds push and pull against one another much like two row boats moored together, bouncing on the waves. Here, we are more aware of the culture UpRiver than that world is of us. We hold to an ancient path here. We try to influence UpRiver culture in positive directions, but our way of life here in *Naadaayi Héen a Tayee* is also affected by what happens UpRiver."

Aurora wrinkled her forehead and shook her head.

"Look around you, Aurora."

A light emerald glow tinged the air. Sun filtered through the tree canopy, dappling the ground with circles of white gold. The chill breath of the stream smelled fishy, and fresh green. The music of clear mountain water sang over cobbles and played in counterpoint to the song of wind in trees.

"Over there." The priest pointed.

In the shallows, hundreds of bright red salmon wallowed and writhed in a mating frenzy. The intense vermillion of the fishes' scales glittered with a million subtle colors — radiating, it seemed, from a light within.

Aurora held her attention on one large fish. It wriggled over a patch of pea-sized gravel, carving out a trough. As the fish hovered above, translucent red eggs floated down into the nest. In a heartbeat, another fish swam over the redd, leaving a milky white stream in his wake that settled over the eggs. The female swished her tail, covering the eggs with gravel.

Father Francis, his face clouded with sorrow, turned to Aurora. He spoke in barely more than a whisper. "There used to be so many more of them. If they disappear UpRiver, they will disappear here, too."

Aurora reached up to push aside an alder branch so she could step closer to the water.

"Wait," Father Francis whispered, putting his arm out to block her way.

On the opposite bank stood a grizzly bear.

Should I be frightened?

Strangely, she felt no fear. The bear seemed uninterested in them. It kept its eyes on the waterfall. Suddenly, it pounced into the falls, came up with a salmon flapping in its mouth, and threw it to a bear cub waiting on shore. The cub devoured the fish with happy chortling sounds.

As they watched, the mammoth adult grizzly wavered and became transparent. Around the nearly invisible bear was a perturbation, a kind of sucking in the fabric of space itself, as if a guitar string were being stretched through a plastic bag. The bear vanished.

Aurora blinked. The creature was solid again, and lumbered away into the trees with her cub. Wide-eyed, Aurora turned to the man by her side.

He nodded. "There are places here where the — ah — membrane between the worlds has grown very thin."

She stared at him.

"Sorry," he said. "I know this doesn't make sense to you yet. Let's go a little farther downstream, where we can sit and talk."

They came to a small beach where dancing light dappled the sand. There was a sense of peace by the river beyond Aurora's experience or understanding, the beauty almost too much to bear. Crystal-clear water seemed animated with infinite loving intelligences — each dazzling, swirling molecule singing its own pure tone, and all the notes blending into a vast and swelling harmony so joyous Aurora felt her heart might burst.

"*Rumm'e,*" Father Francis whispered in her ear. His breath tickled, pulling her fully into the present.

"Sorry?"

"*Rumm'e,*" he repeated. "It's an ancient word. There is really no English translation, but its meaning conveys … all of this." Father Francis' expansive gesture embraced everything Aurora could see and hear and feel.

"*Rumm'e* means this sound of the living, moving waters, the very movement itself, and the creek that contains and is one with and inseparable from the water. It is a sacred word, that points to the many different dimensions of Being in Creation — dimensions like ripples in the flowing water, dimensions that the sound of moving water helps us to access, to travel within. Water is the blood of Mother Earth. *Rumm'e.*"

He leaned down and picked a smooth cobble of green jade from the water.

"Here," he said, opening her hand and pressing the stone in her palm. He folded her fingers around it. "I know you're feeling disoriented. Probably frightened. Release the fear and confusion from your emotional body and feel it flow into the rock. Take as long as you need. When you're ready, wash it here in the stream. Then we'll walk to a sunny place where you can set your medicine stone out to dry. Keep it with you always, to remind you of *Rumm'e*, and of me."

She emerged from the creek with the cobble in her hand feeling refreshed, more like herself, at ease and centered.

"Ready?" he asked.

She nodded.

"Good. This way."

Aurora followed Father Francis along a path uphill into an open meadow. In the warm afternoon sun, they mounted a rise shaded by an oak tree and stopped to gaze over the wide expanse of the bay.

Then Father Francis led Aurora off-trail to a patch of grass dotted with poppies, buttercups, and sweet-smelling lupine. Butterflies of astonishing color gave the appearance that some of the flowers had taken flight. At a flat-topped boulder large enough to make a bench for two, he gestured with a gracious bow for her to sit.

She perched on the sun-warmed boulder and placed her river rock next to her. He stood before her.

"Father Francis," she said before he could speak. "Please explain why I'm here. What is this place?"

"I'm sorry. I can't, exactly ..." He raised his face to the sky, where two eagles circled. "Think of this land as a parallel dimension. We're in a different time and space modality. The world here is eternal and exists *all at once*, so to speak. It is not temporal or linear. It's interesting that you remember where we came from. That's not always the case when people arrive here."

Aurora frowned and shook her head. The air felt heavy, as if she were breathing underwater.

"I recall how it was for me long ago, when I first found myself here," said Father Francis. "I refused to believe it. I was angry and struggled against it. Please, Aurora, just trust me. Even though you clearly do not remember, you have been here before. We are in a world that exists alongside what you think of as the 'normal' world. There are doors — portals, one might say — from this world to that other. And this is not the only alternate dimension. There are many, like the many different musical notes in a symphony."

"Why are you here? Did you follow me into the Frog Woman's Pond?" asked Aurora. "Do you know how to get back — UpRiver? Do you remember — when we're in the, when we're UpRiver ... Do you remember everything you're telling me now?"

"I've been back and forth so many times that, in a sense, I'm able to be in both places at once. And yet, when I'm embodied UpRiver, I never completely remember my life here, in *Naadaayi Héen a Tayee*. Like most people, I have feelings ... dreams, hunches, premonitions, visions of this world ... but not a clear memory, not in the same way that I remember the UpRiver world when I'm here."

Father Francis leaned in close to study Aurora's face, his brow wrinkled in concern. "You look pale. Are you alright?"

The sky spun around Aurora's head. Her vision blurred; her mind felt dull.

"I don't feel well, Father Francis."

She stood carefully, afraid she might faint, and tucked the medicine stone into her pocket.

"Please, Father Francis, can you help me get back home?"

*   *   *

Lungs on fire!

Aurora frog-kicked with the last of her strength in a direction she hoped was sideways.

The churning pressure pushing down on her suddenly released. The white haze of bubbles cleared. She could see the murky bottom of the pool. With a hard kick off the bottom, she propelled herself toward the surface.

The roar of the waterfall filled her. She gasped for air. "Oh, my God!"

She blinked and tried to focus her eyes. Her head was spinning. *Did I almost drown?*

The swimmers in the circle cheered and whistled. Others dove and returned.

Eventually, everyone found new entertainments to explore. The sun moved behind the treetops and shadows lengthened.

People climbed out of the water and disappeared behind bushes and boulders to change. Aurora scrambled out of the pool over slippery rocks and submerged tree roots.

In her private bower behind a large thimbleberry bush, she squeezed water out of her braid, feeling invigorated. The air was still warm. Her skin tingled as it dried. She rummaged in her pack for the new blue and green sarong she'd bought earlier in the summer, on her birthday surf trip to Hawaii. Covered in the sarong, she wriggled out of her bikini bottoms, then let the cloth slip down to her waist so she could pull off the wet bikini top. From out of the bikini top tumbled a small green stone. She picked it up, wrapped her fingers around it, and closed her eyes, holding it to her heart. Sensations of peace and comfort flooded through her. Inside her mind, she heard a word. *Rumm'e?*

Where'd that come from? What does it mean?

She shook her head to clear the water from her ears, then examined the rock. *Jade.* She dropped it into her backpack and finished dressing underneath her sarong's modest cover.

As she bent to pick up her ball cap, she heard a branch snap. Through the dense green matrix of forest growth, she caught a flash of gold. Crocodile gold. *Billy Baker.*

*   *   *

When Aurora reached the creek, most of the hikers were already on the other side. Victor and Pato flanked Louise Daniels. Holding her hands, with very serious expressions on their faces, the teens helped Louise navigate from rock to slippery rock.

Aurora stepped into the rushing stream and began picking her way toward the other side. A noise behind her made her turn and lose her balance. Hot Pants, in Billy Baker's arms, was squealing and flailing her legs. The two-headed, eight-limbed beast lurched toward Aurora. As she teetered on the boulders, Billy and his burden blundered into her.

Aurora fell hard on the sharp rocks. Pain sliced through her. Her very essence seemed to shatter into a million pieces and float downstream in a trail of bloody water. She couldn't move.

Strong, sure arms lifted her, carried her to the stream bank, and tenderly placed her on a blanket. She looked up and tumbled into the priest's eyes. Her soul was naked.

Her eyelids fluttered. Gently, he released her, leaving her craving more of his touch. Her body throbbed in swirling pleasure-pain.

"She's bleeding pretty bad. Do you think anything's broken?"

Someone was patting Aurora's left leg. It hurt so much she held her breath so she wouldn't cry out.

She opened her eyes. One of the students was using Aurora's beautiful new sarong to daub at the blood streaming out of cuts on her hip and thigh.

"Let me see. I'm a nurse."

People moved aside and the nurse examined Aurora, put pressure on the worst cuts, and, with the first-aid kit that Cosmic John produced, cleaned and wrapped the wounds. Aurora's throat was so dry she couldn't speak. Wordlessly, she longed for water.

"You're thirsty," said the priest. He lifted her head and helped her drink from his water bottle.

"Think you can stand up?" asked Kelli.

"Yes." Aurora wiggled toes, feet, fingers, hands. Pain shot through her in every direction.

Slowly, she got to her feet. Everyone applauded.

"I don't think anything's broken," she said.

"You should get x-rays just to be sure, and your cuts will definitely have to be stitched up. You need to go straight to the emergency room when you get back to town," Cosmic John stated firmly.

Oh great, thought Aurora. *That's sure to be tons of fun.*

She limped down the trail, flanked by Warden Kelli and the nurse. She could feel the priest walking behind her.

When the group reached their cars, Cosmic John asked Aurora if she was okay to drive. Aurora insisted she was, apologizing for all the trouble.

"In my professional opinion, you should not drive," said the nurse. "I will drive you to the E.R. in your car. My wife will follow in ours. The hospital's on our way home."

As Aurora climbed awkwardly into the passenger seat of her car, she sensed the priest's eyes on her. The remembered pleasure of his hands on her body merged with the searing pain of her wounds, burning, throbbing, beating, beating, beating.

6

Prudenciana Elementary School, Valle Verde City
Byrd River Watershed, South Santa Cruz County
Central Monterey Bay Coast, California

A URORA WAS STILL LIMPING TWO AND A HALF WEEKS LATER when
she walked across the parking lot of Prudenciana Elementary
School in Valle Verde. Her left side was bruised and scraped. The
worst cut on her thigh had needed seven stitches, but nothing was
broken, and the wounds were healing.

"Aurora! Hello!"

A friendly voice flew like Mary Poppins across the parking lot on
the rush of an onshore breeze. Threadbare ghosts of fog scuttled across
the sky toward the distant coastal mountain range. The person
shouting held onto the brim of her straw hat. Exuberant silver curls
framed her face. She smiled and chuckled a little under her breath, as
if the world were a funny, wonderful place and Aurora must share the
delightful joke.

"Ruth. It's so good to see you. Are you ready for another year?" Aurora and Ruth hugged.

Ruth Redding, bilingual first grade teacher, chuckled some more, kind eyes twinkling. "Oh yes, yes. I'm ready. I came in a few times over the summer. And you?"

"I did all my classroom cleaning and organizing at the end of school last June," Aurora answered. "Worked a couple of weeks solid. What a job. Yuck. How do classrooms get so dirty? Promised myself I wouldn't come back until the first paid teacher work day. I needed a good rest. But now I'm ready. Excited, a little nervous as usual, and totally looking forward to another year."

"Two weeks of unpaid work in the classroom over the summer. That's more than enough. We'll be putting in plenty of unpaid hours during the school year, as always."

"Labor of love," Aurora replied.

Ruth chuckled and nodded. "Labor of love."

"Speaking of which," said Aurora, "I've got a stack of incredibly beautiful sea otter watercolors my students painted last year, waiting for me on my desk. I talked to Friends of the Sea Otters in Monterey over the summer and they're interested in framing and selling the kids' paintings as a fundraiser for sea otter protection. Maybe even turn them into prints or notecards to sell in the aquarium gift shop. I'm going to take the artwork down to Monterey this week. The children are really excited."

"Excellent. Shall we go?"

Like soldiers heading into battle, the teachers squared their shoulders, lifted their chins, and marched through the front door into the school office.

"Miss Redding. Miss Bourne. Have you heard the terrible news?" Bushi, the petite and efficient Japanese-American school secretary, was uncharacteristically flustered and breathless. "Salvador — our little Salvador Luna — was shot last night, at a laundromat near his cousin's house." She tugged a handkerchief out of her sleeve and wiped away tears. "He's gone. I'm so sorry."

Stunned, Aurora froze. Tears rilled down her cheeks. *Salvador Luna? One of my best fourth grade students last year. So serious, so eager to do the right thing.*

Salvador stood before her, his eyes wide, his sweet forehead wrinkled in puzzled concern. Aurora lifted her hand to pat his shoulder, and shivered. Nothing there but the feeling that she'd dunked her hand in ice water. Salvador stared up at her with frightened eyes.

Other teachers arrived and the news about the shooting spread. No one else seemed to notice the child. Everyone talked at once. "Salvador was one of the most promising students in the school." "Awards at every honors assembly since kindergarten." "Never met a sweeter kid. Everybody loved him." "Why? He was only nine years old. No way it could have been a gang killing." "This just doesn't make sense."

A woman Aurora had never seen before shoved her way into the room. "We must not have a crowd in the front office!" she shouted. "Clear the area immediately and go to your rooms. Work on your own today. Our first staff meeting will be Monday morning, at 8:00 am, sharp. See that you are prompt."

"That must be Deana Wagner, the new principal," whispered Ruth. "I heard this is her first principal job. Word is that the superintendent recruited her personally."

"Too bad Dr. Rozini retired," said Aurora. "He was one of the best."

Ruth nodded. "He trusted us, and treated us like professionals."

Teachers spilled out of the office and flowed down the hallways toward their classrooms.

*   *   *

As soon as Aurora opened the door to her room, she sensed that something was wrong.

All the desks and chairs were pushed to the far corner of the room, half of the desks turned upside down and piled on top of others.

That's good. The custodians had time to wash and wax the floor over the summer. I'll have to remember to thank them.

Aurora limped across the cave-like, musty room, climbed painfully around the stacked furniture, and wrestled the broken venetian blinds open. Stepping back to survey the now day-lighted classroom, she gasped.

Everything's been stripped from the walls.

She took a mental inventory of what was missing: the California missions poster; her poster on scientific method; the stages of the writing process poster; her topo map showing the streams and rivers of California with a "We Are Here" arrow pointing to the center of the horseshoe of coastline surrounding the Monterey Bay; the water conservation poster she'd hung over the sink, reminding that "every drop counts" with a picture of a water spigot and Planet Earth, like a drop of water, coming out of the tap; the "friends come in all colors, shapes and sizes" poster; the "all feelings are okay, it's what you do with them that counts" poster showing kids' faces in various emotional states, the emotions labeled.

What else?

She surveyed the room, wild-eyed.

"Aurora! Are things missing in your room?" Helen and Harriet, the two fifth grade mentor teachers, stood just inside the door.

"Yes! Everything's gone. What happened?"

"Apparently the new principal ordered the custodians to 'clean' the walls of all the classrooms. Everything went into the trash."

"What? It took me years of going to workshops and buying things to get those materials. Some of the posters are irreplaceable."

"Everyone lost things they won't be able to replace. We're so sorry."

"My number line! It went all the way around the room, above the chalkboard. I had to special order one that went to positive *and* negative 100. And my adorable wild animal cursive handwriting strip. That's gone too."

"It's devastating." Helen put her arm around Aurora's shoulders. "We know you're going to want to replace what you can, but be careful about how much you spend out of your own pocket. Remember, the district cut classroom budgets again this year so none of what you spend is reimbursable. We all do it, spend too much of our own money on our classrooms, but don't go overboard."

"We'll be okay," said Harriet. "We're teachers. We've seen worse. We can handle anything, right?"

Aurora scrunched up her face.

"We're going to have a great year," said Helen.

"Teachers never give up," said Harriet.

The mentors hugged Aurora and left.

Gasping for air like a stranded fish, Aurora forced herself to take deep calming breaths. She visualized her energy grounding deep into the core of the Earth, the way her *Tai Chi* teacher had taught her. She imagined letting go of all the things she'd lost, allowing them to fall back into the arms of Mother Earth. They were gifts, given to her temporarily.

Breath out. Let go. Draw in another deep breath, allowing Mother Earth's strength and wisdom to flow up, into your center.

Reaching into her pocket, she wrapped her fingers around the jade pebble she'd found on the waterfall hike. Warmth and comfort washed through her.

Balance restored, Aurora studied her classroom. Her heavy old wooden desk had been shoved into the farthest corner. The desktop was clear. What had she left there?

The paintings! The children's beautiful watercolors of sea otters! They're gone!

She pulled a child's chair off a stack and slumped down in the seat, covering her face with her hands. Her leg throbbed. Her head hurt. She had a metallic taste on her tongue.

A cold chill tingled down her spine. She glanced up. Salvador Luna stared at her, holding his sea otter painting. It had been one of the best.

Aurora rubbed tears away from her eyes and blinked. The child was gone.

She rummaged in her bag for her water bottle and took a long drink. Standing, she stretched and pulled her shoulders back. Then she began un-stacking the desks and chairs and arranging them in clusters of five, instead of in the traditional straight rows. She'd start this year with cooperative learning groups.

*   *   *

By mid-morning, Aurora had all the furniture arranged and her computer and printer set up. She needed a break. Her head ached, her left side was screaming, her throat was scratchy, and she felt dizzy. She sat down in her off-kilter swivel office chair and pulled up the cuff of her shorts to inspect the wound. No blood oozed through the dressing. The stitches must still be intact. She grabbed her water bottle and a snack, and limped out of her classroom.

Head down, deep in plans for the coming school year, she bumped into a woman passing along the corridor. The woman dropped the books she was carrying, and Aurora stooped to help her pick them up.

"I'm so sorry," said Aurora. "Are you okay?"

"I'm fine." The woman smiled, straightening, with a stack of books in her arms up to her chin.

Aurora smiled back at an attractive younger woman with a light caramel complexion. She wore the kind of flimsy cotton shirt and slacks you'd find in a thrift shop. Yet even though the woman's clothing almost defiantly proclaimed poverty, her bearing projected an air of pride and dignity.

"I'm Katie Cooper. New teacher. Fourth grade bilingual."

"Welcome to Prudenciana Elementary, Katie. I'm Aurora Bourne. Officially, the non-bilingual fourth grade teacher, but I'm learning Spanish *poco á poquito*. I guess we're the fourth grade team this year. I was just going to the teachers' room."

"Me too," said Katie. "Let me drop off these books at my classroom, and I'll go with you."

They stopped two doors up the corridor at Katie's room, then walked together through the covered hallway along the edge of the recently mown playing field. On the far side of the field, Monterey Pines lined the school perimeter like sentries, green spears piercing the bay blue sky. Behind the trees, a cyclone fence separated the school from strawberry fields covered in sheets of plastic, shimmering like a lake in the sun.

*   *   *

Aurora and Katie sat at a table in the center of the dreary, cluttered teachers' room and talked while they ate. Aurora took a bite of sticky almond butter and honey spread between toasted slices of whole grain bread. She washed it down with green tea, and started on her apple.

"Organic?" asked Katie.

"Nothing but," replied Aurora.

"Me too," Katie crunched on a celery stick.

"So, how did you end up here at Prudenciana?" asked Aurora.

Katie related that she was from a poor mixed-race family in the Central Valley. "People called us 'trailer trash'," she said with a laugh. "I loved school. I had great teachers who helped and inspired me, and I did well. So much so that, when I graduated from high school, I got a full scholarship to Stanford. First in my family to go to college. Graduated with honors and received a fellowship to Berkeley's Bolt Hall School of Law. I wanted to be a lawyer and help the poor. Fight for social justice, liberty for all … you know."

Katie dipped a carrot in hummus, popped it in her mouth and continued. "My first week, one of my law professors said, 'I know many of you are here because you're interested in justice. This is the only time we'll use the word 'justice' in your four years of law school. *Justice*. That's it. Now, let's talk about law.'"

"Really?"

"Yep," said Katie. "I lasted a year. My grades were okay, but my heart wasn't in it. I dropped out of law school and decided to become a teacher. Went the two years of grad school at Cal, earned my Masters and credential, and then, just this summer, got married and started my first teaching job here, in Byrd Valley. I taught a mixed-grade bilingual migrant summer school class called 'Write for Success'."

"Great!" said Aurora. "So, how'd it go?"

"It was a disaster."

"Oh no. What happened?"

"First we brainstormed possible topics. That part went well. The kids were surprised that I wanted to listen to them, wanted to know what they were interested in. Turns out, of course, that they're interested in themselves, in their own lives, and in what all of their families do — work in the fields. Most of them are *freseros* — strawberry workers. They talked about their families and the work. They had a lot of questions, so I started getting guest speakers to come in and discuss various aspects of farm work — including the history, safety, everything. The kids brought in articles, Spanish and English, and references, and photos and stories from their families."

"Sounds perfect. Then what?"

"A clear picture emerged, Aurora. These people are so vulnerable. They have no protection, no rights. A lot of farmworker families would rather be home, in their own country, but they were forced off their lands and away from their villages by U.S. trade policies. By NAFTA."

Aurora nodded and sipped her tea. She'd had suspicions about NAFTA since she'd first heard about it.

"We found out that farmworkers' health is terrible in this state," Katie continued. "California is the deadliest state in the U.S. for Mexican workers. The longer they're here, the sicker they get, due to poverty, poor nutrition, overwork, pesticide exposure, and lack of access to health care."

"I've been kind of worried about pesticide exposure myself, since I started working in the Byrd Valley. But I don't really know anything about what goes on in the fields, so most of the time I just try not to think about it. I figure this is the United States of America. We have federal regulations that protect us from being poisoned at work and school, right?"

Katie smiled. "You might want to examine that assumption."

"What do you mean?"

"One of my students brought in an amazing quote by Cesar Chavez. He said that in the old days, miners would carry canaries with them into the mineshafts to warn against colorless odorless poison gas seeps, knowing that in the event of a toxic gas leak, the birds would die before the miners. If their canaries stopped singing and died, the miners knew they had to act fast to save their own lives. Chavez said that these days, farmworkers and their children are society's canaries. They demonstrate the effects of pesticide poisoning before anyone else."

"I thought Chavez and the UFW changed things. Is it still that bad?"

"Oh yeah. My students and I discovered that every year, two billion pounds of licensed pesticides are used in the U.S. The EPA estimates that pesticides poison about three hundred thousand farmworkers each year nationwide. But since many cases are never reported, it's probably a lot higher than that. Many of my students had stories of family members who were sick from pesticide exposure, but too afraid to say anything. When we found out that *freseros* die at an average age of only forty-nine, my kids were outraged."

"Forty-nine years old? That's horrible."

"Yep. When my students found out all that, they were totally motivated to write. They wrote, and talked with each other and read and helped revise and edit each other's work. The writing they produced was outstanding — stories, poems, songs, essays. They wanted to publish all of the writing in a class book. I promised them that no matter what it cost, I'd get the book printed and give each of them a copy, which I did end up doing. But a lot of the kids also wanted to write letters to someone about stopping the pesticides, so I suggested they could write letters to the editor of the local newspaper."

"Uh oh." Aurora set down her mug of tea and leaned forward.

"Yep. The kids wrote their letters, and I mailed them to the *Valle Verde Register*. All the letters got published on the editorial page of the Sunday paper. Next day, you'd have thought the whole town of Valle Verde was on fire and burning to the ground. So many phone calls! I thought for sure I was going to get fired."

"I'm glad you didn't. I'm happy you're here, Katie. You're obviously a great teacher. You learn along with your students, teach your kids to do research, think for themselves, and use their knowledge to make a difference in the world."

"Um, unfortunately, it's not over yet. I kind of brought the situation along with me to Prudenciana."

"What?"

"Local agribusiness put a lot of pressure on the school administration about the letters. So the superintendent and the school board demanded that the Prudenciana students who were in my summer school class be given a 'balanced perspective'. Since each of the Prudenciana fourth and fifth grade teachers have some of my students, the board decided that all Prudenciana fourth and fifth graders are going to have a mandatory assembly about the benefits of chemical-based agriculture."

"Seriously? You're kidding, right?"

"Nope. I'm really sorry. But it figures. Know what the *freseros* call strawberries?"

Aurora shook her head.

"*Fruta del Diablo.* The Fruit of the Devil."

7

Pebble Beach, Monterey County
Carmel River Watershed
South Monterey Bay Coast, California

M ALONE SAT AT A TABLE ON THE TERRACE and twisted the 5-carat Tiffany diamond solitaire on her finger from side to side, watching the lights flash off its facets. Beyond the green of the 18th hole, scattered diamonds sparkled on the bay. She reached for the long-stemmed crystal wine glass. Streaks of light shimmered through pale gold liquid. She put glass to lips, breathing in the terroir of the wine as she sipped.

A man approached across the Mediterranean-tiled terrace. Moving in and out of the shadows of patio umbrellas, he appeared to flicker, as if caught in a transporter beam short-circuiting him in and out of this dimension. His spiked golf shoes struck the tiles with a sound like sparking electrical wires.

Malone studied the approaching figure and smiled to herself. Sean Stark, CEO of CalGreen. A very private, mysterious man. Operating an illusive empire with virtual impunity and no competitors. CalGreen: the only game in town; the one pivotal link between multinational chemical producers and agricultural users of methyl bromide. Not accountable to stockholders. A man with so much power he tells the state and federal pesticide regulators when and how they can monitor his operations. A builder of corporate coalitions, with controlling financial interest in at least thirteen different multinational corporations.

He loomed above her, blocking her sun. From under his tan golf hat, he pinned her with his eyes.

"Well, if it isn't the Strawberry Queen herself. Good afternoon, Malone."

"Strawberry Queen? What's that supposed to mean, Sean?"

"Come on, Malone. You must know everyone's calling you that." There was an elegant touch of silver in Sean Stark's black sideburns and goatee.

Malone raised her eyebrows, lifted her chin, and pursed her lips in a faux pout. "Tell me more."

"Everyone knows that when your husband introduced soil fumigation to the industry, he made strawberries the most lucrative crop in California. But William's just a farmer. It's no secret that you're the one holding the reins of the Baker Strawberry Farm. You, Malone, are master of the checkbook, the calendar, the networking, and the politics. You are the Strawberry Queen."

Malone held her glass to the light and swirled the liquid affectionately, a smile turning up the corners of her mouth.

"What have you got there?" Sean leaned in close. "Chardonnay?"

"Please, Sean. Do you think I'm that predictable? This is Sones Cellars Cancion del Mar. A new California Coastal blend. Fresh and crisp. Delicious. Care to try a glass?"

"Love to, but I'm due to tee up in a few minutes. Just wanted to say hello. Where will you be later?"

"I'm going to the spa this afternoon for a pedi and hot stone message. This evening, William and I are meeting for dinner at Bitterwater. Join us?"

Sean checked his Rolex, then swooped up an empty glass from the table, plucked the linen-wrapped bottle out of the ice bucket and poured a splash of wine. He rolled the liquid in the glass, inhaled to savor the bouquet, and tasted.

"Jasmine, warm spice, grapefruit, peach, tropical fruit. Very nice."

He squinted out across the greens to the bay for so long Malone wondered if he would answer her.

Finally, he spoke.

"I'm meeting some people at Bitterwater tonight. Perhaps we can all have a drink after." He set his glass down. It rang with the *cha-ding* of fine crystal as he walked away.

Malone watched Sean's red polo shirt retreat across the links. Beyond the greens, a lone Monterey cypress leaned over the cliff edge. Wild waves battered the rocks below, leaping up to grasp at overhanging roots of the gnarled tree.

Malone reached into her bag and slid out a glossy brochure: *CalGreen Annual Report.* She ran her hand over the slick cover of Sean Stark's company prospectus. *Strengthening Industry Leadership through Corporate Coalitions.*

Malone flipped open the glossy booklet and read the first page: *Interlocking Directorships & Industry Partners.* She ran her red lacquered fingernail down the list.

And all these industry partners are here at The Grove this weekend for the annual international coalition directors' meeting. Malone tapped her nail against her lips and gazed into the distance. *This should be a very interesting weekend.*

A waiter refilled her glass with filtered ice water. With a silver handled brush and dustpan, he swept away the quiche crumbs and removed her empty salad plate.

Malone raised her cut glass tumbler to the sunlight and turned it this way and that, watching rainbows scatter over the table. Her thoughts turned to her son. Under Stark's mentorship, the boy was doing well on the CalGreen staff.

The day had grown pleasantly warm. Malone sipped her lemon ice water with satisfaction.

8

F ATHER FRANCIS HILMAN HAD BEEN WORKING in the organic
garden behind the rectory all afternoon with his homeless group.
Hopefully, the skills these men were learning would help them find
management jobs in local community gardens, or on one of the small
organic farms that were cropping up around the county. With jobs,
they'd eventually be able to transition to more permanent housing
than he could offer them here at the church.

After weeding, double digging two new rows, tying beans to a
trellis, and turning compost, they harvested. Then, amidst jokes,
laughter, and poignant conversation, Father Francis and the homeless
gardeners cooked a stir-fry and enjoyed their meal together. After
supper, more than one man expressed gratitude not only for the food,
but also for the simple pleasure and dignity of being able to prepare
his own meal and wash his own dishes.

*   *   *

In back of the church on a knoll shaded by eucalyptus and live oak, the priest watched the sky as sunset layers of green, yellow gold, and salmon pink washed over the distant bay. Below him, plastic spread out over the strawberry field like a lake, reflecting the sunset colors.

Two small dark figures picked their way across the field toward the church. The silhouetted hikers climbed the hill past the graveyard, to the knoll on which Father Francis stood.

"*Padre, por favor. Ayúdanos. En el nombre de Dios. Por favor.*"

Father Francis led the couple along the path toward his parish office as if they were Mary and Joseph and the bundle the man cradled in a dirty pink blanket were Jesus. The couple's eyes darted back and forth, in the manner of small animals afraid a hawk might swoop down any minute and snatch them. A wide-eyed girl about nine years old who'd been wrapped close inside her mother's silhouette stepped out from the shadow of the woman's skirts, still holding tightly to mama's hand.

The priest, who towered over them, stood aside as they passed through his office doorway. The man and woman were stocky, with dark coffee-brown skin, obsidian black eyes, and straight hair as blue-black as the priest's. The woman wore colorful ribbons woven into her braids. The man's hair swept his shoulders; a strip of red cotton banded his head. *Husband and wife made from the same mold.*

The priest settled them in chairs and gave them water.

"Your daughter is missing?" The couple spoke no English. Father Francis confirmed, in his fluent Spanish, what they had just revealed to him. He wrinkled his brow. Spanish was not their first language.

Mayan, he thought. *Probably from the Yucatán, forced off their ancestral lands by a Mexican government hostile to the indigenous.*

The woman explained they'd last seen their fifteen-year-old daughter — their oldest — when the family was picking in the strawberry fields the day before.

The mother and her husband had finished a row, stood up, and looked for their daughter. She was gone. They asked people, but everyone said they had not seen the girl; said they had seen *nada*. The girl had just vanished.

The woman cried. The man explained that they'd searched for their daughter until dark, slept in the fields overnight, and then had taken up their search again this morning. They could see the steeple from the fields all day long while they looked for their daughter. This evening, they'd walked up the hill to the church, because they didn't know what else to do.

"*Ay, Reina del Cielo, ayúdanos* (Queen of Heaven, help us)," the woman prayed as she wept.

"We need to phone the police," said Father Francis.

The man and the woman both became wild-eyed. "Oh, no! That is impossible. *La Migra! No! Por favor, Padre!*" The little girl clung to her mother like a drowning animal. The baby in the pink blanket started to cry.

That the couple was undocumented and feared deportation, Father Francis had no doubt. He could only imagine the horrors they must have endured to get here, and the unbearable suffering that would have driven them to make such a dangerous border crossing in search of asylum.

He spoke with them a while longer, trying to reassure them, encouraging them to come back to the church in a few days. He gave them directions to a shelter, gave them food and a little money, and prayed with them. Then he escorted them back to the knoll and watched them make their way downhill and across the fields, until they disappeared in the darkening twilight.

9

FRIDAY, AUGUST 12, 1998
The Nineteenth Hole Bar, Pebble Beach
Carmel River Watershed, Monterey County

S EAN STARK RATTLED THE ICE IN HIS SCOTCH GLASS, then took
another sip. At the Nineteenth Hole Bar, the last of the afternoon
sun poured through panoramic windows, infusing everything inside
the room with the quiet glow of old gold.

"A private security company, Sean?" The silver-haired gentleman
in summer-weight silk slacks focused fire blue eyes on his son-in-law.
"Trained, high tech, top-secret former military men? Aren't you
getting just a little too carried away, too James Bond, about this whole
situation?"

Stark didn't flinch. He glared back, taking his father-in-law's
measure: Lawrence Evermal II, President and CEO of Evermal, Inc.,
married to the only daughter of BioGenesis' founder. A blue silk shirt
open at the collar complemented the old man's yachting tan. For a
man pushing eighty, he looked remarkably vigorous.

Sean tapped his crystal tumbler on the counter, and nodded to the bartender. The bartender poured three fingers of Dalwhinnie single-malt into his glass.

He could get the Board to approve this new operating expense without the old man's backing, but it would go much smoother with his father-in-law's blessing. "It's the future, Lawrence." Sean stroked his goatee. "You've always been on the forefront of change. You agreed with the Board last year that it was time for Evermal to go through a major restructuring, remember? Time to reverse the expansion, acquisition, and diversification phase that you and your father so brilliantly led."

"My father had a hell of a set of balls, Sean." The old man drew together his bushy brows. "Don't you forget, he started with just a little paper mill in Louisiana, and ended up pulling off the largest leveraged corporate buyout ever completed at the time."

"Your father's acquisition of Ethyl is legendary, Lawrence. He transformed a backwater little paper company into a player at the table with the giants of global finance. That was a risky move in '62."

"That's right. And since then, never forget it was me who kept pushing the envelope. Diversified into energy, pharma, real estate, financials. I acquired conglomerates, created holding companies." The old man threw his head back and downed the rest of his scotch, then rapped his glass soundly on the bar. "It was me who maneuvered our family into the inner circle that controls today's global marketplace."

"You've led the charge for thirty years, Lawrence." Sean finished his scotch. "Guts and brains. No one could have done better. But now we're heading into the twenty-first century. The New World Order is falling into place, as planned." Sean met the old man's eyes directly. "It's time to divest ourselves of distracting assets and streamline operations. Focus on CalGreen and methyl bromide. They're the keys to the BioGenesis family's future."

The bartender refilled the men's glasses.

"Yes, yes. Methyl bromide. I know that," said the old man. "But, Blackriver, Sean? Our own secret military? That seems like overkill, to me."

"It's the future, Lawrence. Blackriver only hung their shingle a year ago, and they're already so busy they hardly have time to return my calls."

"If it's the UFW vote you're worried about, I still think Arturo Rodriguez will hang himself on his own," said the old man. "Just give him enough rope. He may be Chavez's son-in-law, but as everyone says, 'He ain't no Cesar Chavez.' Rodriguez and Huerta don't have any base — any rank-and-file farmworker leadership to help them organize, the way Chavez did in the old days. Their attempt to unionize the strawberry workers will be a fiasco. You'll see."

The server placed a bowl of peanuts on the bar and the old man helped himself.

"Things have changed since Chavez built the UFW," said Lawrence. "These days, field bosses recruit friends and family from their home villages in Mexico. The workers obey their field bosses, and the field bosses answer to us. We have better ties, more loyalty than Rodriquez and Huerta do. We've got 'em by the balls. Chavez is dead and buried. They're not going to bring back those days. There won't be any more serious UFW problems in Valle Verde. You don't need a private military to ensure that, Sean."

"I know what you're saying. Just the same, that UFW lawsuit against Strawberry Bay Berry last year cost us. There's going to be a vote, Lawrence. We can't avoid it. It was stipulated in the settlement. We can't afford to take chances. When it comes to strawberries, migrant laborers trying to unionize cut into our bottom line. We've got enough to deal with over this methyl bromide phase-out situation."

"Look, Sean. Both of our sons have been doing an excellent job with our lobbying efforts in D.C., shaping the public mind about strawberries and methyl bromide. The way your boy is handling the debunking of the ozone hole is brilliant. The Founder would be proud. Let our sons worry about buying us more time on the phase-out."

"True, but we don't need to rock the boat with a tide of public sentiment for the 'poor Mexican laborers' in the press right now. Not when our critical exemptions are up for review. And we don't need the UFW snapping at our heels. Blackriver will keep an eye on things. They are discrete. No one will know that they're there, much less that they work for us. If problems do develop, Blackriver can help us in a variety of ways. We need them, Lawrence. It's the New World Order."

"I guess I can drink to that," the old man said, lifting his glass.

Sean tossed back his scotch and left some folded bills on the bar. "Dinner?"

*   *   *

FRIDAY EVENING, AUGUST 12, 1998
BITTERWATER BAR & GRILL, PEBBLE BEACH
CARMEL RIVER WATERSHED, MONTEREY COUNTY

Malone entered the Bitterwater Bar and Grill at The Grove on the arm of a pampered-looking bad boy with a wayward blonde lock curling over one eye. Malone and her tanned, blonde escort paused at the entrance to survey the room. Almost everyone in the Bitterwater tonight wore a CalGreen affiliate lapel pin. Malone assessed the people at the tables, and their positions.

Although Malone was nearing sixty, she was well aware that she still commanded a presence that was sexy, powerful, and compelling. Heads turned. From the other side of the restaurant, her husband, William, caught her eye. He was at a table in the far corner, speaking with two men who had that up-and-coming captains-of-industry look about them.

With her knight at her right hand, Malone glided over the floor, a queen moving across her chessboard. She heard snippets of conversations as she walked through the room.

"… and then he was appointed to a presidential commission on agriculture and water. A sitting member of the World Trade Organization. And he has that banking connection. Definitely a useful contact."

Malone stopped at a table to kiss the cheek of a plump woman in purple silk. The woman's husband, Mosie Blumberg — one of the overseas bromine reps — dipped crabmeat in red sauce. He acknowledged Malone with a nod, then turned to the man on his right. "Dead Sea Bromine isn't associating itself with any of the Israeli-Palestinian rhetoric. That's our policy. But … you know where I stand."

Malone and her escort continued their soiree.

"I thought all Catholics were Kennedy Democrats," said a stout man with a comb-over and a red, bloodshot nose. He rattled the ice in his whiskey glass while he spoke. As Malone walked by his table, he grabbed her hand. He smelled like cigars. "Malone. The Strawberry Queen herself. Nice to see you again. Stop a minute and try one of these oysters. Hog Island Sweetwaters from Tomales Bay. They're amazing." The man lowered his voice. "Let's get together before the weekend's over. I want to share with you how you can significantly lower your distribution costs if you switch to my new broker."

Malone and her escort sampled the oysters while the table conversation continued.

"All Catholics are Kennedy Democrats? Ha," said a man who resembled Tiger Woods. "Kennedys be damned. This is the New World Order. Democrat, Republican, Catholic, Protestant, Atheist, Arab, Jew — none of that matters anymore. The only thing that matters is your bottom line, your net worth."

"I agree," said a tall man with long white fingers. "Wealth is the new political party, the new religion. Hell, for that matter, it's the new nation. Who gives a damn what country you're from? In the New World Order, national boundaries don't matter. The WTO guarantees a free global marketplace. Any government regulation of any country that interferes with our bottom line, we sue. And our pockets are deep enough to ensure that we can always hold out until we win."

"You're right." An olive-skinned woman at the table helped herself to a slithery oyster, and brought the conversation back to the original topic. "Anyone can be bought. And I'd say that once or twice over the course of things, we've managed to persuade the Church to serve our interests."

Someone poured Malone a splash of champagne. She and her escort lingered, enjoying the sparkling wine with more oysters.

"I have a high-placed connection in the Church back East," said the olive-skinned woman. "Maybe we should consider having the Agricultural Workers Committee bring a few East Coast priests out to Valle Verde before the Bay Berry union vote. Mexicans are Catholic. They'll do what the priests tell them, right?"

Malone thanked the table and moved on, gleaning more scraps of conversation along the way.

"If your crews can't — or won't — work, it's like you've got hundred-dollar bills lying out in the fields getting rained on. We can't afford a UFW strike."

"I feel like an endangered species. We're being forced out by urban sprawl, inheritance taxes, unions, and poor commodity markets. How do we make them understand that by keeping farming viable with generous federal subsidies, you preserve farmland? We can't feed people if we pave over the land."

"Malone." A diamond-tennis-braceleted wrist tapped Malone on the arm. "Care to join us for a few minutes? They've just delivered this wonderful platter of calamari."

Malone and her escort squeezed in at the table. Malone filled a small plate with calamari and accepted a glass of wine.

"I understand you and William are interested in purchasing a new fleet of tractors." The woman's diamond bracelet flashed. "Why don't you give me a call next week? You can tell me what you're thinking about and we can talk pricing and availability. Let me get you my card."

The woman opened her purse, and Malone glimpsed a concealed handgun.

"How do you like your Sig Scorpion?" Malone asked.

The woman raised an eyebrow and appraised Malone with a sideways stare. A slow smile oozed across her face. "The slide is easy to rack back. I like the way it fits my hand, and I love the way it looks. What about you, Malone?"

"William bought me a Colt .38 Diamondback last year for my birthday. We occasionally go out to the Rod and Gun Club practice range. Why don't you and your husband join us sometime?"

"We'd love that. Call me." The woman handed Malone her card, then lifted her empty glass to the waiter.

Malone's attention turned to a well-dressed man with shifty eyes holding forth at the table.

"How did Joystone get into the mix? Joystone Capital was my father's idea." Paul Cooke, one of the Cooke brothers' sons, took a long pull on his dirty martini.

"Christ, when my father created Joystone and handed me the reins, the ink was barely dry on my Harvard MBA. To make a long story short, the UFW sued Bay Berry last year, and BioGenesis Agrochem, the parent company, had to dump it. BioGen needed a way to disappear from the Bay Berry ledgers while maintaining a controlling interest. So my father created Joystone Capital, we stepped in, acquired Bay Berry as a holding company, and made a secret 'sweetheart' deal with UFW, AFL-CIO. We conceded that Bay Berry would be publicly 'friendly and supportive' to the UFW, and agreed to allow the farmworkers a union vote." Paul Cook swung his hand to reach for the breadbasket and knocked his dirty martini onto the floor. He signaled the waiter to bring him another. "Of course, we're taking measures to assure that the union vote goes our way."

Malone and her escort rose and thanked the table, Cooke's voice hanging in the air as they walked away. "Sold the Pearson in Nantucket," Cooke bragged. "Sailed my new Hinckley Sou'wester 61 to Morea last Christmas. Tacks on a dime. When I leave Pebble, I'm taking her out for a long solo cruise."

Malone paused a moment to enjoy the view with a group of CalGreen associates sitting at a table by the window. Outside, moonlight cut a golden path over the ocean out to forever.

When Malone and her escort approached Sean Stark's table, Sean was introducing a stunning Japanese woman to his father-in-law, Lawrence Evermal II. "This is Shibu Yayoi."

Old man Evermal leered approvingly. Stark nodded to acknowledge Malone and her escort.

"Shibu works for Arita Chemical," Stark said. "One of our subsidiaries in Japan. She's designing a new product for us, in case we don't manage to overturn the Montreal Protocol and we actually do have to come up with a methyl bromide alternative. Her product is already being used experimentally in medical research, to induce cancer in lab rats. Of course, if we bring the product to market as a methyl bromide alternative, we'll have to keep that little piece of information quiet. Ms. Yayoi calls her new baby methyl iodide."

Two men in black suits stood against a wall nearby. They didn't seem like waiters; more like military men. Malone reminded Sean they were getting together after dinner for cocktails, and then she and her escort moved on.

At a table in the far corner of the room, Malone's husband and his two companions stood as she drew nearer. All three men eyed her with a testosterone-enhanced glint she found quite satisfying.

"Very nice to meet you, Malone." A man exuding charisma extended his hand. "I'm Blair Evermal, Laurence's second son. Just flew out from D.C. for the weekend. This is my big brother, Lawrence the Third. He's the one with the brains. Number One Son, and soon-to-be new Chairman and CEO of Evermal."

Laurence Evermal the Third, heir apparent of the multinational methyl bromide industry, acknowledged Malone with well-schooled courtesy. Hand extended, he turned to Malone's escort.

Malone suppressed the urge to push that lock of hair away from her escort's face.

"And you are ...?"

"This is my son," said Malone. "William Baker the Third."

Malone's escort flipped his hair out of his eyes and extended his hand. "Call me Billy."

10

SATURDAY, AUGUST 13, 1998
Our Lady of Help Church, Valle Verde
Byrd River Watershed

AURORA HATED FUNERALS. She was not fond of churches, either. But she'd loved Salvador Luna, and wanted to be here for him. She flicked on her left turn signal and waited in the center lane of Highway 152 for an opening in the traffic.

Farm trucks barreled toward her from the direction of Mount Madonna and the fields surrounding the county fairgrounds. Flatbeds packed with crates of fresh-picked produce and trucks laden with tanks of mysterious substances roared by, reckless cowboys stomping pedal to the metal.

To banish the gloomy thoughts chasing their tails around in her mind, Aurora studied Our Lady of Help Catholic Church from a painter's perspective.

The sand-colored building with a red clay tile roof, surrounded by green fields, raised its simple cross into blue sky. A eucalyptus grove rose behind the west end of the structure, with an atmospheric hint of the bay in the far distance.

On the north side of the church, under the shadow of Mount Madonna, sprawled a two-hundred-year-old cemetery. Between church and cemetery, a large altar of piled rocks sheltered a statue of the Virgin of Guadalupe. *Holy Mother, Lady of Help.*

The road cleared and Aurora made her turn.

Only a few parking places remained in the large lot. Throngs of mourners poured into the church. Salvador had been well loved.

Why so many police and sheriffs' cars?

Flowing with the solemn crowd, she made her way up the stairs, through the middle arch into the narthex, where people dipped fingers into a giant white clamshell filled with holy water. Aurora's senses flooded with the aroma of incense and flowers, and with the peculiar odor of the church itself — like some ancient holy place she dimly remembered, or perhaps had only dreamed of. She followed the crowd into the sanctuary and found one of the last spaces on a bench, making herself small to squeeze into it.

In every shade of skin color, and every style of black clothing — expensive suits, thrift shop, gangbanger baggie dickies and beanies, and campesino hand-woven cloth — people of all ages packed the pews and overflowed into the aisles. Aurora recognized Prudenciana teachers, families, and Salvador's classmates — children too young to be touched by this senseless violence. Lips moved in silent prayer while fingers counted rosary beads.

Police officers in dark uniforms blended into the sorrowful sea of black. A large man with the physique of a quarterback knelt on the tile floor, head bowed, praying with a rosary and swaying as the crowd pressed against him. *Never Forget Salvador Luna* was scrawled in white cursive across the back of his black hoodie.

Quiet weeping and whispered prayers wafted around the church like ghosts. Aurora wiped tears from her own cheeks. It took her by surprise to feel the wound of her parents' death open anew. That car crash had happened ten years ago. She'd thought she was finished with all the stages of grieving. She searched her heart, trying to find an invisible god to pray to. She was not going to bow her head to the god of Christian patriarchy.

Bells rang, a deeply resonant, angry peal. Everyone stood. Swelling waves of liturgical music filled the sanctuary.

As the poor little casket, supported by strong men in ill-fitting black suits, floated down the central aisle, Aurora wiped tears off her cheeks.

Pallbearers placed the casket in front of the altar and retreated.

The music ended abruptly on an ominous chord, and the people in the pews sat down on wooden benches the color of aged brandy polished smooth by almost a century of service. Once seated, Aurora moved her head from side to side until she could see through the spaces between those in front of her.

A shock of recognition quaked through her body.

Behind the casket stood a priest in embroidered vestments, upraised arms opened in a magnetic gesture that enfolded everyone in the church. He seemed larger than life, glowing with an aura of unearthly radiance.

She had thought of him hundreds of times since the waterfall hike. Now, seeing him in front of her in his full priestly regalia, she struggled to control the disturbing sensations rushing though her. She could still feel his touch as he'd carried her from the creek. She squirmed on the wooden bench until she found the off switch that disconnected her body from the rest of her. Once she'd settled, she craned her neck to see him again. The priest was gone.

Everyone was singing, accompanied by a single acoustic guitar. "We send your child home to a place of everlasting love to join there with the angel choirs and blessed saints ..."

A lecturer at the podium read from the Old Testament. The serpent in the garden promised Eve that if she ate the forbidden fruit, she and her husband would control the world, and all would serve them.

The lecturer stepped down and the priest appeared again in front of the altar. Blue starlight shimmered over his black braid and all around him.

"We know," Father Francis said, "that temptation comes our way not only in our gardens of delight, but also in the deserts of our lives. At times of great sorrow such as this, when a terrible injustice has been committed, we may be tempted to turn away from God, to try to take control and exact our own revenge. But this morning's reading reminds us that absolute power is God's domain alone. No matter how much you may be tempted to take matters into your own hands, instead look to God and to one another for redemption, for solace, and for strength. If you loved Salvador and want to honor his memory, then find forgiveness in your heart for his killers. Work for peace. Vengeance is not the way. Trust God. Love your enemies."

Five burly men hooded in black rose from the pew in front of Aurora. Menace in their posture, they pushed their way to the center aisle and stalked toward the priest.

A communal gasp issued from the congregation. Aurora could barely breathe. The church itself seemed frozen in the moment.

Like snarling panthers poised to attack, the men loomed over the little casket separating them from Father Francis. Black hoods shadowed their faces; hands thrust into pockets suggested concealed weapons.

A deathly silence filled the sanctuary.

Golden rays streamed from Father Francis and poured over the angry men.

An eternity passed.

Suddenly, all five men threw back their hoods revealing their faces, whipped around and rushed out through a side door.

A collective intake of breath.

"Peace be with you."

Aurora joined in as everyone stood and hugged their neighbors. Music played, and people began lining up for communion.

Aurora remained at her seat, her mind and heart racing. "This is my body, broken for you."

She closed her eyes and focused on her breathing.

People received communion while the choir sang, "May angels speed you to paradise. The lord is my light. Before whom should I tremble in fear?"

Breathe in, breathe out.

"This is my blood, shed for you."

Anxious, confused feelings welled up: grief for her parents and for Salvador, fear for the priest's safety, her unexpected and inappropriate attraction to a Catholic priest, the discomfort of being in a religious environment she'd rejected long ago as oppressive, rigid, and misogynistic. To still her mind and calm her heart, Aurora closed her eyes and began the meditation practice she'd learned in yoga class. As anxious and sad thoughts arose, she imagined placing them in a basket on a river and letting them float away.

*   *   *

NAADAAYI HÉEN A TAYEE

The hiss of rattlesnakes seeped through the air with evil foreboding.

Oh no. Am I dreaming?

Aurora hiked along a marsh trail, Father Francis at her side.

"Where are we, Father Francis? How did I get here?"

Father Francis turned to Aurora and smiled. "Welcome back to *Naadaayi Héen a Tayee*. What do you remember, Aurora?"

"I remember getting pulled through Frog Woman's Pond to this place — and all the things you told me when we were here before." Aurora shivered as she spoke. "And I remember everything about my life back home, back 'UpRiver', as you called it." Aurora's brow wrinkled. "But I don't remember … *this* place … when I'm home, 'UpRiver'."

Father Francis nodded. "Do you still have your river rock?"

Aurora reached into her short's pocket and closed her fingers around the water worn cobble the priest had given her last time she'd found herself in this "alternative dimension".

Grey mist swirled damp and cold around them, sticking to the tules, enveloping them.

Aurora zipped up her sweatshirt and pulled the hood over her head. Father Francis showed no sign of chill, even though he wore only shorts and a T-shirt.

The marsh water was black. Tules and cattails moved in the mist as though large creatures crept among them. Thorny brambles along the edge of the trail wrapped around Aurora's ankles as if trying to trip her.

An eerie, high-pitched howl echoed through the fog. Aurora moved closer to her companion.

Suddenly, a terrifying thrashing disturbed the marsh. Predatory grunts, growls and squeals made the hair on the back of Aurora's neck stand up.

From the swamp, a black amorphous form rose, dripping algae and slime. A foul wind filled with invisible forces rushed at them. Enormous sharp-clawed appendages reached for them. Snapping jaws, fanged and poisonous, exuded evil putrescence.

Aurora screamed.

Five fletched arrows pierced the dark.

The primordial beast wailed, jerked and twitched on the path before them, bleeding out in deathly convulsions.

Stinking black blood, mucus, and steaming pus oozed onto the ground around a beast as big as a large boar. It had the skin of a slug — slimy, soft, and covered with poisonous tentacles. Its face was almost human, though grotesque and wicked. From the fanged mouth hissed a foul purulence and a drool of ichor — putrid, bloody, and so acrid it stung Aurora's eyes. Malevolent orange flames flared behind the monster's terrifying glare, then dulled and went out.

Aurora clung to Father Francis, trembling. He pulled her close, so close she felt his heart beating. Bare footfalls thudded on the dirt path, quickly coming nearer.

Five loin-clothed warriors peered at the dead demon. Father Francis spoke with the warriors in a language Aurora did not understand. The hunters threw an animal skin over the carcass and carried it away.

Tears ran down Aurora's cheeks. With his broad thumb, Father Francis wiped them away. He held her until she stopped shaking. Then, hands on her shoulders, he looked into her eyes and spoke carefully.

"As I was saying, the membrane that separates the worlds is growing dangerously thin in places. That — *thing* — is not from *Naadaayi Héen a Tayee*. It doesn't belong here and should never have been able to enter. But the Pattern is breaking apart, Aurora. As the world UpRiver is damaged, desecrated, and defiled, so it is also injured here. We are doing everything we can to hold together and heal the Sacred Geometry, but I am worried."

"What was that creature? What could cause such an imbalance?"

"The entire human species UpRiver is undergoing a metamorphosis, a catastrophic molt, so to speak. The human spirit has reached a turning point, a spiritual bottleneck, and must rapidly evolve. This has caused a critical instability in all the worlds. Out of the discarded skins of practices and beliefs that no longer serve, dark entities are emerging, bent on wreaking havoc. If they prevail, the consequence could be eternal annihilation of all we love."

*   *   *

SATURDAY, AUGUST 13, 1998
OUR LADY OF HELP CHURCH, VALLE VERDE

The congregation was rising. Aurora glanced around, then stood. She joined in singing the final hymn as the priest lead the procession of pallbearers with the casket down the aisle.

The casket was gone before the music ended. Aurora let herself be swept along with the tide of people flooding out of the church.

Once outside, she turned to the parking lot, separating from the funeral procession that wound toward the cemetery. She could not bear to watch the little casket be lowered into the ground.

She found her car and exited the church parking lot as quickly as possible. She needed to be alone, on her surfboard, in the pure sacred ocean.

*   *   *

The parking lot was beginning to clear. From the top stair of the church entrance, Father Francis scanned the crowd. He spotted Detective Charlie Rosa among the sea of people heading for their cars.

"Charlie," the priest called as he caught up to him. "Do you have a minute? There's something I want to talk with you about."

"Of course, Padre."

"Let's go to the kitchen. I think there's still some coffee that might not be too stale."

*   *   *

Father Francis took the coffee cup out of the microwave and handed it to Charlie. "Sugar?"

"No thanks. Black's fine. Listen, Frank. The way those *cholos* reacted when you preached about forgiveness and not taking things into your own hands has me worried. I thought they were going to shoot you or shank you right there in the church. If those mad dogs don't chill out, this could be the beginning of a long, bloody vendetta." Charlie shook his head. "*Es malo, amigo. Muy malo.*"

"Those 'mad dogs' are all friends and relatives of Salvador Luna, Charlie. Of course they're angry and want revenge. I'll reach out to them. Maybe I can help them find a better way to heal."

"Watch yourself, Padre. Don't get hurt."

"I hear you, *hermano*. No need to worry. Tell me, are you still thinking Salvador's murder might be mixed up with that Salinas coke bust last month?"

"Maybe not. I'm starting to feel like there's something far more sinister going on."

"What do you mean?"

Charlie rubbed his temples. "It's just a gut feeling, maybe far-fetched, but I'm wondering if the Luna murder could somehow be connected to that tossed-up meth camp you and I found on our fishing trip."

"A meth kitchen on a creek and a child murdered in a laundromat? What possible connection could there be?" Father Francis bowed his head and steepled his hands in front of his face. "But I'll tell you, Charlie, I just can't seem to get those pink butterfly tattoos off my mind."

"Butterfly tattoos?"

"In the tent at the meth camp. The suitcase full of little girl's clothes. Remember? It was plastered with pink butterfly tattoo decals."

Charlie nodded. "I remember. By the way, forensics confirmed that besides the baby there were two little girls living there, maybe twins."

"Twins? Any closer to finding them?"

"Nothing yet on the girls or their mother, but we found the baby."

"I read about that in the papers. Figured that must be the baby from our meth camp. What a miracle. Four days in the forest, kept alive by a dog." Father Francis' eyes narrowed. "What about all that blood?"

"We sent blood samples to the Department of Justice DNA lab in Sacramento and they fast-tracked us to the top of their queue, but results aren't back yet. Someday DNA testing will probably be more efficient. But at this point, it's slow going."

The priest nodded. "And the gang tags?"

"Thanks for the information from your Norteño and Sureño homies. That helped. But none of our local gangs want to own it, and neither do the San Jose skinheads."

"Somebody new in the 'hood, then?"

"It looks that way." Charlie drained his coffee cup and set it down on the kitchen table. "What was it you wanted to talk with me about, Padre?"

"I had a visitation yesterday evening from a family of new arrivals — Mayan, from Chiapas. Their teenage daughter disappeared while they were working in the strawberry fields just down the hill from here. They came to the Church for help."

"Young women are raped and disappear out of the fields all the time, *mi amigo*," said the detective. "We don't have reliable statistics on it, because the friends and relatives of the victims are usually afraid to involve the authorities. But we know it happens all too often."

"Is there anything you can do to help this family find their daughter, Charlie?"

The detective unwrapped a stick of gum, popped it in his mouth, and shoved the wrapper in his suit jacket pocket; then he took a deep breath and sighed. "There can be no official investigation unless the parents file a police report. If a case were opened, the incident would fall to the sheriff's office, making it within my jurisdiction. But I know how scared undocumented immigrants are about talking to the cops. They won't talk to the police."

"Their daughter is missing. Can't you find some way to help them?"

"Tell you what. I'll go out and speak with Yudas Medina when I get the chance. Informally, of course. He's the field boss at that property, so he might know something. Meanwhile, next time your Mayans show up, give me a call. I can 'just happen to drop by for coffee'. If they'll open up to me, I can file a missing persons report for them and set the ball rolling on an investigation. But don't get your hopes up that we can find the girl. Most of the time, there's nothing we can do. Collateral damage, *mi amigo*. It's simply part of the price of agriculture in the Byrd Valley."

11

SUNDAY, AUGUST 14, 1998
(Perseid Meteor Shower)
Moss Landing Harbor, Monterey County
Salinas River Watershed
Central Monterey Bay Coast

P AUL COOKE RELAXED ON A DECK CHAIR ON HIS YACHT. He sipped
a dirty martini and watched blue and orange shooting stars arch
across the sky, leaving trails like fireworks. The Perseid meteor shower.
He'd almost forgotten.

This past week at Pebble Beach had been a nice recreation, and a
fruitful investment of time from a business standpoint. But now,
finally, he was almost ready to sail. He swirled the olive in his glass and
watched another shooting star leave a trail across the sky.

Martini glass in hand, he ducked below decks to inspect the cargo.
Wooden boxes of California champagne and brandy had been stowed,
along with his favorite wines and delicacies from the Monterey Bay.
There was just one more thing to load.

Setting down his martini glass on a wooden chest, he swung himself back up topside and surveyed the harbor. No one near. It was time.

He hustled down the gangplank to the black van that had been parked and left for him earlier this evening. Someone would return later to pick it up.

He opened the van's back doors. There it was.

Straining, he hoisted the covered wire dog crate, about German Shepherd size, out of the van. Duck-walking under the weight, Cooke carried the awkward cage up the gangplank, wrestled it below deck, and settled it beside the other commodities he'd collected.

He took a sip of his martini, then unzipped and removed the cage cover and peered inside.

The sedated child was sleeping, curled in a fetal position on a fleece dog mattress. She might begin to stir before long.

He would administer more sedative before he got underway. Some of his acquaintances, those who shared his exotic tastes, preferred it without the sedative — enjoyed the struggle, the screams, the face of terror and pain. But he liked his children quiet and docile.

He picked up his martini glass and stirred the tooth-picked olive, considering the crated girl.

Exclusive rights to an untouched child was massively expensive, but well worth it. He did appreciate the fact that his appetite for this particular delicacy was a bit perverse. But after all, he thought with a mental shrug, he was entitled. With all his responsibilities, the pressures of wielding so much financial and political power, he needed some exceptional outlets. Yes, he was entitled to indulge himself once in a while. There was certainly no shortage of this throwaway commodity. The poor bred like rabbits.

The child shivered in her sleep, goose bumps developing along its exquisite skin.

He'd be sure to feed it this time, so he could enjoy it longer than the last one, get his money's worth. When it had become too damaged to be of further interest, he'd be far out to sea. It would simply go overboard. Shark food.

The little girl stirred and rolled onto her back. She stretched out her arm, exposing a pink butterfly tattoo.

12

A URORA'S MORNING COMMUTE from Santa Cruz to Valle Verde took about forty minutes. She turned off Highway 1 at Freedom Boulevard and drove north toward Prudenciana Elementary, drinking in the landscape of the Byrd River Valley as if savoring the terroir of a good wine.

The little school nestled at the base of coastal mountains that had been thrust and twisted up from the sea geologic eons ago. An upraised scar on the face of the land, the mountains bore evidence of the epic clash of monumental tectonic plates. The continental shelf forced the Pacific plate down, and the Pacific shoved back, punched up from underneath, and caused the continent's skin to buckle and fold.

Through a deep gash in the scar, rains washed off the hills, down Corralitos Creek to the Byrd River. For millennia, Rainbow Trout had been migrating downstream on spring storms, over the willow-lined bedrock of Corralitos to the Byrd, pushing out through the swollen

77

rivermouth into Monterey Bay. And for millennia, adult Coho and Steelhead had been miraculously navigating by moon, stars, and scent from the vast Pacific back to that one thin, precious thread of their home stream, bringing the rich gift of nutrients from the sea to the plants, animals, and people up river.

Aurora parked and slid out of her car with only a little stiffness and pain. Her stitches had finally mostly dissolved. She rubbed the red, raised scar on her leg and stretched, pausing to appreciate her last moment of summer vacation.

Shreds of summer morning fog clung to the coastal hills. The bell tower of the original one-room schoolhouse peaked over the roofline of the modern elementary school. Pioneers had built that first school near the creek in about 1880 on land donated by Señora Prudenciana and her daughters. Just a small gift from Señora Prudenciana, whose rancho had been one of the most extensive and beautiful of the *Californio* ranchos granted to favored elite by the new Mexican government after the closing of the missions.

The old schoolhouse had served the children of Italian and Portuguese fishermen and farmers. And the children of Mexicans, displaced by Yankees from their regal status as *patróns* of vast rancheros to become landless peasants. Children of the all but invisible indigenous people, and of the industrious and prosperous Japanese, so adept at farming and fishing, attended the one room schoolhouse. Filipinos came to fish, and Croatians turned apple blossoms into gold. The Chinese came, hoping for gold. But forbidden by law to mine the yellow metal, instead, they built the railroad that connected East to West across the continent, and they settled in camps around the Monterey Bay called China Beach and China Town, to fish and sell, and raise children more American than Chinese. The English, Dutch, and Irish brought their food, their customs, their gods and myths, and their children. And so the one-room school served the children of every immigrant group, from every continent, of every creed, color, and culture who washed onto the shore in wave upon wave, hoping for a better life.

Around the schoolhouse, these pioneers fished the rivers, the streams and the bay, and planted apple orchards, broccoli, Brussels sprouts, and artichokes, flowers, berries, and salad greens in the fertile alluvial soil, the black gold, gifted by the river gods of the abundant and generous River of the Birds.

In 1947, the parcel of land with the historic one-room schoolhouse was sold to a family who restored and preserved the building. On an adjoining parcel, also part of Prudenciana's original gift, a modern elementary school was built. Heritage apple orchards surrounding the school were torn out to make way for more lucrative strawberry fields. Otherwise, not much had changed in the hundred years since the schoolhouse first opened its doors to the children of Byrd Valley.

Aurora hefted her book bag over her shoulder and set her course across the parking lot to the school library and the first faculty meeting of the year.

Teachers were milling, chatting, pouring coffee and tea from big urns, and filling paper plates with pastries and fresh fruit, provided courtesy of their union. A few people talked about the Salvador Luna funeral, and several teachers discussed the article in Sunday's paper about a baby found in the woods.

An excellent selection of shelved books lined the room. Many of them, from beautifully illustrated kinder books through fifth-grade chapter books, from remedial to very challenging books for the gifted, in Spanish and English, had been acquired through teacher-written grants. This was the only elementary school library that had survived the district's drastic budget cuts. Aurora expected that the ongoing battle to keep their library open would be one of the items on today's agenda.

"Quiet. Be quiet! Take your seats!" An authoritative voice cut through the warm buzz of the collegial hive. Deana Wagner, the new principal, clapped her hands for attention as if she were addressing six-year-olds rather than experienced professionals with advanced university degrees.

"It is eight o'clock. The meeting will begin. You will find agendas on the tables."

Aurora picked up her thick agenda packet and thumbed through the pages. Every teacher had been assigned a supplemental duty. She scanned the list. As usual, she would coordinate the after-school Gifted and Talented Program. This year, her GATE students were going to design and paint a mural depicting the history of the school, working with the Byrd Valley historical society and a local Native American muralist.

"What is this?" Principal Wagner's voice sounded like a fist coming down on a table.

A very pregnant Dora Lockhart, the bilingual resource teacher, stood in the doorway with a horrified expression on her face. Behind her, morning sun glinted off the plastic covering the strawberry fields. Dora's hand rested protectively over her belly.

"You are late! That will not be tolerated. Everyone must understand this right now. I am a stickler for timeliness. I will be watching for your arrival every morning. Your contract stipulates that you must be on campus by 7:28 am. If I catch any of you arriving even one minute late, I will write you up. You are reminded that your so-called 'tenure' does not mean you can't be fired. As long as I build documentation in your file of your infractions and incompetence, any one of you can be removed, and your union won't be able to help you."

The woman standing at the door looked at her feet. "I'm so sorry," Dora said. "I wasn't feeling well this morning."

"Take your seat," said Deana Wagner. "We will begin with the first item on the agenda. Blood-borne pathogens."

Harriet leaned over and whispered, "She's wrong about the Union. We're strong."

The school nurse rose and smiled at the teachers apologetically. "I know most of you have been through this training many times."

Aurora made a note to herself to buy first aid supplies for her classroom. Having taught at Prudenciana for over five years, she knew all too well that cuts, scrapes, and bloody noses were a regular occurrence in elementary school. The school nurse roved between all the schools in the district. But, because of budget cuts, she was only at Prudenciana one day every other week on an irregular and mysterious schedule. It was up to the teachers to administer routine first aid. Sick children were only sent to the office in the case of serious illnesses or injuries that necessitated a phone call home.

When the nurse sat down and the school counselor, Nathena Hamilton, rose to speak, Aurora tuned back in.

"… must remember that you are all Mandated Reporters." Tall and imposing in a boldly colored caftan, like a tribal African queen out of the pages of a picture book, Nathena's gold bangle bracelets shone against her dark chocolate skin. Aurora was deeply involved in her visual brain modality, working out the geometric pattern, like music, on Nathena's dress, and only partly listening to the presentation she'd heard many times before.

"If you have the slightest reasonable suspicion that one of your students is in danger, or being physically or emotionally abused or neglected, you must inform Child Protective Services. If you failed to do so, you would be criminally liable, and your teaching credential could be revoked. Following are some indicators to watch for."

When the counselor finished her presentation, first grade teacher Ruth Redding raised her hand.

"Yes, Ruth?" Nathena smiled.

"What about some kind of emotional support for our students who were close to Salvador Luna? All our kids are bound to know about the shooting. I noticed quite a few of them at the funeral and …"

"Check your agenda." Principal Wagner shot out the words before Nathena could respond. "We must follow protocol. That is Item 17. Next is professional evaluation procedure."

There followed a mind-numbing several hours of committee assignments, furniture and equipment inventories, yard duty and lunch scheduling, new rules for using the copy machine, and a discussion about whether the red balls could be kicked or must only be used for throwing.

When the vote to cancel the library program came up, as it did every year, no discussion was necessary. Because class size and student-to-teacher ratio was such a clear determinate of student success, keeping classes small was more important to the teachers than their own salary. Yet the teachers voted unanimously to each take a few extra students on their roster in order to free up a full-time credentialed teacher to work in the library and coordinate an interdisciplinary literacy program articulated across the grades. It was only because of their strong union that Prudenciana teachers had been able to implement this exemplary teaching model.

Deana scowled.

"Where is our librarian today?" Aurora asked Helen.

"She's out sick. We're afraid it may be something serious," Helen whispered.

Deana flipped the page of her agenda packet. "Next item. I have received a report from your union representative, Tom Olsen, regarding the use of pesticides and herbicides on the school grounds. You all have a copy of the report in your packets. Mr. Olsen, please summarize."

Tom stood. "Teachers and parents in our school district have been concerned for some time about the use of pesticides and herbicides in and around our schools. Pesticides are used on a regular basis even when no insects, rodents or other pests are present. WeedRangler is being applied on the athletic fields, and even on the grass directly under outdoor picnic tables, where children eat lunch. Rat and insect poisons are used in the cafeteria, school offices, in the classrooms and even in school buses."

The principal tapped her foot.

"In recent years," Olsen continued, "six Prudenciana teachers out of our small staff of just over thirty have been diagnosed with cancer. And our area is gaining a reputation on Stanford Hospital's pediatric oncology ward. We've applied for a grant with the California Environmental Protection Agency to develop a model pilot Integrated Pest Management Program to reduce school pesticide use, which we hope can be disseminated throughout the state."

"I haven't had any word yet about a grant," the principal said. "But I was informed over the summer that you teachers all signed a letter, which your union sent on your behalf to the superintendent and the School Board, regarding the use of herbicide around the picnic tables and in your Life Lab garden. WeedRangler can most efficiently eliminate the weeds in those difficult-to-reach areas. The district grounds maintenance staff has been reduced to a minimum due to budget cuts. We do not have the personnel to cut the grass by hand."

"Principal Wagner," Olsen said. "I've volunteered to bring my own lawn mower from home on Saturdays to take care of it."

Deana Wagner glared at the union rep for a heartbeat. "Very well. Everyone knows that WeedRangler is perfectly safe. But I have been instructed to let you try this your way. However, if the grounds are not maintained to my satisfaction, I will inform the superintendent."

Aurora felt stiff and her head throbbed. A metallic taste bit at the back of her tongue and she felt nauseous. Item 16 was next on the agenda: Dora Lockhart's update on the ever-evolving and contentious bilingual education program.

"Is this about that anti-bilingual education ballot initiative — the 'Unz' initiative?" Aurora whispered to Katie.

Katie nodded. "Yep. The latest wave of anti-immigrant legislation brought to us by millionaire racist nut-job, Mr. Unz. They're never going to stop scapegoating immigrants."

Dora Lockhart rested her hand on her baby belly while she addressed the staff.

"So, the initiative would require schools and hospital emergency rooms to refuse anyone who could not produce a valid green card. If the initiative passes, most bilingual classes will be dismantled. The initiative would make it illegal for teachers to speak Spanish to students in non-bilingual classes, even if the students can't speak any English."

Teachers shook their heads and muttered among themselves. "This is the craziest thing I've heard of yet," said a teacher at Aurora's table.

Dora looked pale and didn't deliver her spiel with her usual energy.

"Ah, Detective Rosa from the Sherriff's Office! Just in time." The principal beamed at the law enforcement officer walking through the door. "Item 17. Follow-up on the Salvador Luna shooting. Detective Rosa?"

Detective Charlie Rosa explained the new gang prevention awareness program they would be introducing at Prudenciana — a collaborative effort jointly funded by the city, county and state agencies, and the school district.

"Do you think this will work?" Aurora whispered to Katie.

Katie rolled her eyes.

"In addition," Detective Rosa said, "the County Family Services Agency has collaborated with the school district and the Sheriff's Office to provide mental health support for any children at your school who were close to Salvador, or who show signs of emotional trauma associated with the shooting. Just give the names of students you'd like to refer to your counselor, Mrs. Hamilton. And here is my card. Please get in touch with me if you or your students have any information at all pertaining to the shooting."

Tom Olsen helped the detective pass around his business cards.

"Thank you for your time and attention. There's just one more thing. I've been authorized to inform you that we are investigating an incident that occurred near here, on Corralitos Creek. The situation was most likely violent, and involved a methamphetamine lab. A baby was found abandoned in the woods near the crime scene."

There were gasps and murmurs of alarm from the teachers.

"This is what I was telling you about," someone near Aurora whispered. "I read about it in the papers."

"The baby is under protective custody and is receiving medical care. I understand he's doing well. But there may have been more children, possibly two little girls. So, we are asking all personnel at the nearby schools to keep eyes and ears open. Look for anything you think seems suspicious or might be related to our investigation, such as parents or children new to the school who appear to be traumatized, abused, battered, paranoid, or under the influence. You all have my card."

There was a crash and a commotion. Aurora turned around to see petite, pregnant Dora Lockhart lying on the floor next to her overturned chair.

"She fainted! Move back, give her space. Let the nurse through."

13

The Life Lab Garden, Prudenciana Elementary School
Byrd River Watershed

T WO DAYS AFTER THE HORRIBLE FACULTY MEETING, Aurora had finally completed most of her preparations for the new school year. Her students would arrive tomorrow. She was eager to get out to the school garden, Prudenciana's outdoor classroom.

She opened the Torii garden gate and entered a world that seemed enchanted. She half expected to find that the flower fairies from Cicely Mary Baker's exquisite 19th Century watercolor illustrations had come to life here.

The organic student garden flourished, with squash and pumpkins, salad greens, carrots, tomatoes, and onions overflowing its raised wooden beds. Butterflies fluttered around her head. Flowers lined the paths; pole beans climbed up tipi trellises. Aurora touched the damp soil, happy to find that the garden had been watered over the summer by volunteer parents and children.

Blinking as she moved from the shade of the trees into full sunlight, she made her way to the compost bins. Most of the plant material tossed into the bins last spring had decomposed. She scooped up a handful of compost, smelled it, and crumbled the fragrant humus with her fingers.

I'm holding the soil food web in my hands.

Thin white threads of beneficial fungi, hungry soil microorganisms, and wriggling red worms had turned the compost into sweet-smelling black gold. Rich with billions of beneficial microorganisms in each handful, this humus would provide live nutrients for the new plants this fall, as well as excellent soil structure for holding oxygen and moisture. The compost was ready to be turned, shaken through a sieve and put onto the beds.

Is the garden toad still in his usual spot?

Aurora pulled opened the lid of the water turn-on valve box. It was cool and wet inside, and smelled earthy, like a root cellar. There he was, *Bufo boreas,* fat eater of slugs and other plant enemies! He croaked at her and winked his bright, jewel-like eyes.

Once she got to work, swimming through the flowerbeds, selecting blooms and trimming off spent blossoms, Aurora came across numerous ladybugs, a green lacewing, predatory damsel bugs, and an enormous garden spider poised in the center of a perfect orb web. Her new students were going to love discovering these beneficial garden critters. In about fifteen minutes, she'd harvested three colorful bouquets: one for her classroom, one for her new friend Katie, and one for the front office.

A high-pitched scream.

Aurora turned her face to the sky. Two golden eagles, the pair who nested every year in the Monterey Pines at the edge of the playground, slowly circled above. Aurora watched the eagles soar higher and higher, until they disappeared into the blue radiance.

She buried her face in the fragrant armful of flowers. The eagles whistled again. A haunting sound.

*　　*　　*

NAADAAYI HÉEN A TAYEE

Aurora blinked. She still felt shaken by the slaying of the demon, as if it had happened only minutes before. Yet, she remembered all the details of time's passage in her UpRiver life, since she'd last been here, in *Naadaayi Héen a Tayee.*

Where is Father Francis?

She found him nearby, engaged in conversation with a very old man. Both men turned toward her as she approached.

"Aurora, this is Xigmacse. He is my, ah, doctor, and one of our beloved elders."

The old man's face reminded Aurora of eroded sandstone cliffs. His long white braid glittered as if made of stardust. Wearing nothing but a deerskin loincloth wrapped around his hips, and a mountain lion fur cape draped over his shoulders, Xigmacse's full physique shone forth — remarkably muscular and robust for an elder. Leaning on a walking staff decorated with shells, feathers, colored string and deer antler, the old man studied Aurora, his eyes the color of a glacial mountain lake.

"Hmmph." He nodded, a hint of a smile on his lips.

He turned and put his hand over the priest's heart. "Tomorrow. You come see me."

Then the old man strode away, as straight and tall as a young warrior.

"I feel like I've met him before," said Aurora.

Father Francis frowned as he watched Xigmacse disappear into the mist.

"Where to now?" Aurora asked, hoping there wouldn't be any more demons.

"This way." Father Francis led Aurora out of the marsh, down a hill to a sandy beach. A small wooden pier jutted out into the water, a rowboat moored to it.

Aurora slipped off her sandals and walked barefoot across white sand to the edge of the lapping waves. Icy water bit her ankles.

Anchored in the middle of the wide channel, a dozen fishing boats and sailboats gently rocked. The water, glittering brilliant aquamarine in the sun, reflected quick white brush strokes of boats and sails. On the far shore, a dizzyingly crooked structure perched above a dock, defying gravity. As precarious as a child's stack of blocks, built too high and almost on the verge of tumbling, its pointy gabled roof jabbed at the sky like a witch's hat. Behind the cockeyed building rose a mass of lush green foliage, a rainforest. A large owl called and circled above.

Unusual to see an owl in the daylight.

Aurora watched the owl disappear into the trees, then bent down, scooped water into her hands, smelled it, and tasted a drop with the tip of her tongue.

"Brackish," she said.

"Yes." Father Francis raised an eyebrow. "The river is slightly salty here. We're near the rivermouth, close to the sea, and subject to its tides."

Aurora shivered. *This is definitely not the Byrd River.*

"This way," said the priest.

They ran side-by-side over the sand, following the river downstream. Around a bend, the water roared and thundered into a bay far larger and wilder than Monterey Bay. In the middle of the wide rivermouth, pale pink islands floated in the mist.

They slowed to a walk as sand gave way to rocky tidepools.

"Hey, Sagrado!"

Aurora turned to see a stout man in jeans and a sleeveless T-shirt waving an arm overhead in greeting. His long black hair was tied at the nape of his neck, a red bandana wrapped around his forehead.

"Ah! An old friend," said Father Francis.

The man wore a patch over one eye; a scar slashed diagonally across his face. The arm he'd waved was burly, but the other was shriveled, less than half as long as his healthy arm.

Father Francis and his friend slapped one another on the back. "Aurora, this is Yáahl. He's a Seer, and one of our best storytellers. Yáahl, you remember Aurora, of course?"

Yáahl met Aurora's eyes with openness and love. "Welcome home, Aurora. It makes my heart glad to see you again."

Aurora blushed. His words confused her, but his voice sounded familiar. She pictured herself sitting by a fire, listening to him.

But when? Where?

The men spoke for several minutes in a language Aurora didn't understand. Then Yáahl disappeared as quickly as he'd arrived.

Father Francis smoothed a wisp of hair out of Aurora's face, tucking it behind her ear. His fingers lingered lightly on her cheek. She froze, aware of nothing but his touch.

"Yáahl tells me there's been trouble here since I've been gone." His voice was husky. "People are worried. The Council meets tonight. I must attend."

A tumult of questions flooded Aurora's mind.

"Let's keep walking." Father Francis took Aurora's hand and they set off up the beach, trudging through dunes covered with wild rye grasses, beach lupines, and fragrant coastal sage. Aurora rubbed the pungent smelling sage leaves between her fingers. She stooped to pick up a black flake of chert from the sand.

"Is this worked stone?" she handed the glossy rock to the priest.

He held it up to examine it, his beard shadow catching the light like finely ground gemstones.

"Yes, it's an arrowhead. We're walking through an ancient midden — a place where my people have been disposing of their kitchen remains: shells, bones, broken pottery, stone tools for … a long time."

A piece of abalone partially buried in the sand caught Aurora's attention. She bent to pick it up and, as the sand fell away, she found it was attached to a large animal bone that had been covered in tar and inlaid with abalone shell.

"What's this?"

"Ah! This is a significant find. A ceremonial object used for powerful healing. Very old. Sometimes things that have been buried for eons get unearthed when they're needed again. I'll take this to our elders." Father Francis wrapped the object in his kerchief.

"I've read about middens and seen a few, long abandoned," said Aurora. "This one appears to still be in use."

"Yes. Our traditional village is up there." He pointed to a cluster of tule huts on a rise above them.

In a clearing in front of the huts, blue smoke curled into the air from an open fire. Fish hung from a rack made of bent branches, drying above the smoke. People, some naked, some wearing loincloths, others in deerskin clothing, sat and stood near the fire. A creek meandered past the village. On granite boulders along the creek, women sang while they ground acorns in the hollows of the rocks.

A path led from the huts uphill to a longhouse. Behind the longhouse, a massive wooden totem pole, carved and painted with orcas, eagles, salmon, and bear jutted into the sky. Far above the village on the ridgeline, wind rushed through a stand of pine trees with a hushed, otherworldly sound. Wind turbines scattered along the ridge turned silently.

"Wind turbines?" Aurora's brow furrowed.

"As I've said, vast changes are taking place in the order of things. We believe it's not sufficient just to slay demons and fight against evil. During this Great Turning, it's vital that we imagine and manifest the details of a peaceful, abundant new world to nurture future generations. In the hope of influencing culture UpRiver, our scientists, artists, and craftspeople here in *Naadaayi Héen a Tayee* are experimenting and innovating system change in every area of life, including food, medicine, transportation, education, housing, water management, energy ..."

Father Francis led Aurora up a path that meandered along cliffs above the ocean. He gestured animatedly as he spoke, his face aglow with passion.

"We've developed wind, small hydro, tidal, and solar power, and we're currently working on a project to create renewable hydrogen bioenergy through photo-conversion. Some of us have chosen to build hybrid Smart Haus homes, like mine, and to grow food in organic permaculture gardens. A group of our young families have even designed dwellings using biomimicry."

"Yet with all this innovation," said Aurora, "you still have a traditional village?"

"Yes, we believe it's important to keep the Old Ways alive, so some of our people choose to live traditionally, without electricity, by hunting and foraging. Later, if you'd like, we can visit the village. But for now, come this way."

They took a fork in the path and headed inland, startling a flock of birds that burst into the air with a *whoosh* of wings.

At the end of the path, they came to a red dirt road. Up the road to the west, some children played with a dog in front of a row of houses. Down the road toward the east stood a two-story Craftsman-style house surrounded by a cottage garden. Overhead, two golden eagles circled.

✳   ✳   ✳

THE LIFE LAB GARDEN
PRUDENCIANA ELEMENTARY SCHOOL

The eagles called. Aurora raised her face to the sky, blinded by the sun. She blinked, and awoke to the fragrance of the flowers in her arms.

She returned to her classroom, and arranged the flowers in vases, then delivered one of the bouquets to Bushi in the front office.

"From our school garden," said Aurora. "Thank you for all you do for us, Bushi. I hope you have a great year."

Bushi accepted the gift with thanks and a bow.

"Have you heard any news about Dora?" Aurora asked. "How's she doing?"

"Ah, a miscarriage is always very difficult both physically and psychologically, especially so late in the pregnancy."

"Miscarriage? Oh, no! Do they know what caused it?"

"I understand that she became violently ill as soon as she arrived on campus Monday morning. Perhaps, if she had just taken a sick day, gone right home instead of staying for the meeting. But, we will never know."

"How is she now?"

"We hear she is doing as well as can be expected. Her husband has informed us that she plans to return to work after Labor Day. What is very strange, though, is that the custodian's wife had a miscarriage this week, as well. It was her second. They live across the street from the school and he's been going home at lunchtime to take care of her. I would suggest that you do not say anything to him about his wife's miscarriage, however, Ms. Bourne. He's been very touchy. He definitely does not want to talk about it."

Aurora left the front office the back way, through the staff room, and stopped to check her mailbox. She met Katie Cooper there and they walked to their classrooms shoulder-to-shoulder along the outside corridor next to the playground.

"Did you hear about Dora's miscarriage?" Aurora asked.

"Yep. Horrible."

The women walked in silence, each in her own thoughts.

"My throat feels scratchy," said Aurora. "Don't know why I can't seem to shake this thing. I've been talking vitamin C and Echinacea all week, but it doesn't seem to help."

"Have you noticed that plastic out on the fields?" asked Katie.

Aurora squinted across the playground toward the strawberry fields on the other side of the cyclone fence. "Of course. Sometimes it's there, sometimes it isn't. I guess I've always just assumed they use it for weed control, right?"

"They cover the fields with plastic after they fumigate."

"You mean spray pesticides?"

"No, they don't spray. They inject a poison gas called methyl bromide into the soil before they plant the strawberries. The gas is so deadly, it literally sterilizes the earth. Nothing lives, not even the beneficial microorganisms or worms. The strawberries aren't grown in a nutrient rich, living earth. They're grown in a dead, inert substrate. The growers mix the methyl bromide with a chemical called chloropicrin."

"Chloropicrin?"

"It's tear gas. Chloropicrin was developed for chemical warfare. Exposure to the stuff causes severe inflammation of the eyes, skin, and respiratory system. It can even cause pulmonary edema, which is potentially fatal. And it's been linked to cancer."

"I learned about methyl bromide and the Montreal Protocol when I was on a hike last month," said Aurora. "It's an ozone-depleting chemical. I thought it had been banned by international treaty."

"Yep. It's supposed to be completely phased out of agricultural use in the U.S. by the end of the century, about a year and a half from now. But Congress keeps giving strawberry growers so-called special exemptions from the ban."

"So they're injecting these deadly poisons into the soil, right on the other side of the fence from our school?" Aurora stared. Across the asphalt foursquare and basketball courts and the grass soccer field, on the other side of the cyclone fence, acres of plastic shimmered like a lake in the sun.

"Yep. And methyl bromide is a volatile gas. The soil outgases for ten days to two weeks after they fumigate. The plastic is supposed to keep the poison gas from contaminating the air. Ha ha."

"You're saying the gas escapes in spite of the plastic cover?"

"Yep. Farmworkers who apply the gas and lay down the plastic get a big dose. And there are always leaks along the edges where the gas escapes. The industry itself admits that fifty percent of the gas escapes into the air."

"Then we're breathing it now?"

Aurora stared at the plastic-covered strawberry fields. The usual prevailing wind was blowing from Monterey Bay across the plastic and into the school grounds. The ocean breeze felt cool on her face, but it no longer seemed refreshing.

"I've had a headache all week," said Aurora. "Watery eyes, scratchy throat, itching in my inner ears. I've even been feeling dizzy. It was intense on Monday, during the staff meeting. Think it could be from tear gas?"

"Yep. They fumigated last Thursday morning, about six days ago — the same morning we all came in to work in our classrooms."

Katie stopped at her door, turned and faced Aurora. "I think the methyl bromide and chloropicrin are making us sick, Aurora. Maybe even caused Dora's miscarriage. I heard she was working on campus Thursday and Friday, right after the fumigation."

"That just seems impossible. We have laws protecting us, don't we? Schools are supposed to be safe places. Dora's miscarriage has got to be just a coincidence."

"I hope you're right."

14

THE PACIFIC OCEAN

D AWN ILLUMINATED INFINITE SKY AND OCEAN, stretching out around Paul Cooke in all directions to forever. The yacht gently rolled under his legs on a calm sea. He stirred his Bloody Mary with a celery stick, squeezed the lemon wedge and dropped it into his glass. As he took a sip, he squinted against the glare, staring out to the horizon.

Just the right amount of Worcestershire and Tabasco, but it could use another splash of vodka.

The rubber sole of his deck shoe squealed as he turned and ducked back inside the cabin.

He spread out the charts and checked again. He was in the mid-Pacific, far from any shipping lanes or commonly traveled cruising routes, in an area known for Great Whites. And the trench below was deeper than any diver could go. The cage would never be found. He finished off his Bloody Mary and went to the galley to fix another.

He took a long pull on his fresh drink. Last night was something of a blur. He'd lost control of himself. Dangerous, when you're sailing alone. Today he had some housekeeping to do. He wasn't looking forward to cleaning up the mess. His little toy was ruined, so soon.

He felt himself tightening and stirring again at the thought of last night's games. Such a delightful little girl. He was already hungry for another. Should have bought two. Maybe he'd try a boy next time. A delicious warmth spread over his groin. Yes. A boy and a girl. He swirled his celery stick in his Bloody Mary, pulled it out and thoughtfully licked off the thick red juice, considering the possibilities. Well-fortified with vodka, he went below deck to fetch the ruined garbage. Shark chumming should be an interesting way to pass the morning.

*   *   *

AURORA'S COTTAGE
SANTA CRUZ, THE WESTSIDE
SAN LORENZO RIVER WATERSHED
NORTH MONTEREY BAY COAST

Orion, "the ghost of the shimmering summer dawn", shone through Aurora's skylight. A shooting star silently arced like an arrow from his bow.

The silk of Aurora's new back-to-school teacher dress felt like ice water slithering over her. The navy blue and white polka dotted dress was pretty, yet professional. She brushed her hair to a shine, then pulled it back and gathered it at the nape of her neck, winding it into a neat chignon. Mascara, light lipstick, and a spritz of an expensive Hawaiian floral scent. She stepped into new, low-heeled, sling-back sandals comfortable enough to stand in all day and then put on gold-backed pearl earrings. Around her neck she fastened the string of pearls her parents had given her, feeling their love surround her. Tomorrow she'd dispense with these artifacts of her privileged upbringing and wear something more relatable, but today she wanted to set a professional tone that honored her parents, her students, and the memory of Salvador Luna.

"That's it, Blue. I'm ready. First day of school. Here we go again."

The big black cat rubbed Aurora's leg and purred.

*   *   *

She stood outside her classroom door, extending her hand to each child as they arrived. Some of her new fourth graders scrunched up their faces and wouldn't make eye contact; they didn't know how to shake. Aurora took each small, sweaty, sticky, awkward, timid hand in hers and smiled.

"I'm your new teacher, Ms. Bourne. Welcome to fourth grade. Your desk is all ready and waiting for you. Please go in and find your nametag. Once you get settled, you can start your worksheet. I think you'll have fun doing it."

A buxom woman wearing jeans, T-shirt and hiking boots offered her hand. "How do you do, Ms. Bourne. I'm Destiny Dore. This is my daughter, River."

A beautiful child with high cheekbones and a mane of pale blonde hair rippling over her shoulders stared at Aurora. The woman gently pushed at the child's back, urging her to step forward and greet her new teacher.

"I really wanted my daughter to be in your class. I was born here in the Byrd Valley and went to school right here at Prudenciana. But we've been out in Oklahoma for the last few years. We're Cherokee, and I wanted River to experience life on the Rez. She's very connected to nature, Ms. Bourne, and I know you do a lot with the garden and animals in your class. I'm a full-time stay-at-home mom, so I'm available. Please let me know how I can help."

Aurora welcomed River, and sent her into the classroom, then turned back to Destiny. "We'll surely be needing your help, Mrs. Dore. I'll be in touch."

A boy who introduced himself as Caleb presented Aurora with an apple. "My family has been growing apples in the Byrd Valley for generations. My grandfather told me to tell you that you won't find this kind in the grocery stores. It's a heritage apple. I hope you like it, Ms. Bourne."

The bell rang and Aurora followed the last student into the classroom.

Aurora had organized the desks into six groups of five. Above each group hung a photo of a local endangered animal. Most of the children were engaged in completing the worksheet on "My Favorite Things". One child was picking up crayons that had spilled on the floor. Another was giggling at something the child next to her had said.

In the red-legged frog group, a stocky little boy wearing a backward red baseball cap hunched over a teetering stack of crayon boxes, his arms surrounding the stack. A puppy guarding a bone. The other students in the group glared at him; he glared back.

Aurora leaned close to his ear and glanced at his nametag. "Oh dear, Rico," she said confidentially. "Your teammates need their crayons so they can finish the self-portraits that go with this assignment. Please give everyone back their crayons."

The boy stared at Aurora, wide-eyed. She smiled at him. Like a young dragon uncoiling from its prey, Rico unwound from the stack of crayons and began returning them to his disgruntled group mates.

When all the crayons were returned, Aurora smiled brightly, said, "Thank you, Rico," and moved on.

All of the seats in the desk groups were filled. A pale, thin boy stood stiffly in the back of the room in brand new slacks, a white dress shirt, and an argyle sweater vest. Salvador Luna's ghost hovered beside him. Aurora approached the boy she didn't recognize, ignoring Salvador.

"Hello. What's your name? Can't find your name tag?"

The boy scowled, his brow wrinkling.

"*Cómo te llamas?*" Aurora repeated the question in Spanish.

"Antonio Medina."

Aurora skimmed her class roster. "Well, Antonio, I don't see your name on my roll sheet. Are you a fourth grader?"

He nodded.

"Hummn. I think you're supposed to be in Ms. Cooper's class, Room 10, down the hall."

"*Sí, pero mi padre,* my father, he tol' me come to here, *no en la otra clase,*" said the little boy in Spanglish.

"Oh. Well, I understand that you want to do what your father tells you to, and that's usually the right choice. But, today, we need to follow the instructions the school gives us. Do you think you can find Room 10 by yourself? It's just down the hall."

The little boy reluctantly nodded yes.

"Alright then." Aurora escorted him to the door. "It was nice to meet you, Antonio. Have a wonderful day. I'll find you later, and make sure you're doing okay."

Salvador Luna followed Antonio out of the door. She shivered as she watched them go, and wondered if Antonio also saw the ghost.

Aurora continued her sashay around the room, then took her place in front of the white board, under the welcome banner. She stood quietly and calmly, hands at her sides, centering and grounding her energy while she watched the room.

Gradually, students started shushing one another. The room was quiet. All students' eyes were on their new teacher.

"Good morning. What an excellent class," Aurora said. "Thank you all for coming in on time, getting right to work, and giving me your focused attention. Well done." All of the students sat up straighter. "Welcome to fourth grade. I know every one of you is going to have your best year ever. I'm your new teacher, Ms. Bourne." She pointed to her name, printed on the board, and spelled it. "You may call me either Ms. Bourne, or Ms. B, as you wish."

Several students giggled.

"I want you to enjoy this year and this class, because I really care about every single one of you. I'm here to help you succeed, and I will not allow anyone or anything to interfere with your positive learning experience this year." Aurora smiled and made eye contact around the room.

"Now, everyone, please put your worksheet and your crayons inside your desk, but keep your pencil out."

The old-fashioned desktops lifted, and students gazed with curiosity and awe inside the cavernous space that now belonged to them. After a certain amount of opening, closing, and shifting, most children sat at clear desks with pencils ready, looking at Ms. B.

"Well done, boys and girls. Oops, I notice that a few of you are still wearing your hats. If you haven't already, please take your hat off now, and remember to do this whenever you come into the classroom, as a gesture of respect for our learning environment."

Rico, the only child still wearing a hat, glanced furtively around the room, removed his backward red baseball cap, lifted the desktop, and tossed the hat into his private cave.

Aurora led the class through a discussion of the "three R's" — respect, rights, and responsibility — that would guide class behavior for the year. Then, in cooperative groups, each student shared three things about him or herself.

"I'm excited to get to know you," said Aurora. "Please write me a letter now, with the three things that you just shared in group about yourself."

Aurora watched her students work. One child bit his tongue in concentration. Another dropped his pencil and spent some time crawling around on the floor trying to find it. A very tiny girl sat up on her knees on her chair so she could write at her desk. Her nametag said Nikko. Aurora made a note to ask the custodian to raise Nikko's seat. She learned a great deal about her new students by watching them put their names on their papers. One child just sat and stared. Alice. She was dirty, pale, and appeared to be malnourished. Aurora made a mental note to keep an eye on that one.

"I see it's almost recess. Remember, your first priority at recess is to use the restroom, and then eat a snack if you brought one. Then try to make at least one new friend."

The bell rang. Aurora collected the papers and dismissed the children, group by group.

When all the other students had gone, one child remained seated — the bedraggled girl who hadn't managed to write much other than her name on her paper. Tears wetted the child's pale cheeks.

"What's the matter, Alice?"

The girl shook her head.

"Are you feeling ill? Hungry?" The child lifted her head at the mention of food.

"Would you like some graham crackers and juice?" Aurora offered.

The child consented, with a weak nod. Aurora went to her cupboard for cookies and a small, boxed juice.

"It's a beautiful morning, Alice," Aurora said. "How about if you go outside and enjoy this in the sunshine? There are picnic tables right out there on the grass."

Once Alice had gone, Aurora gathered her own snack, locked her door and hustled to the faculty room. A ten-minute recess was not very long.

While Aurora waited for her turn to use the only women's restroom in the school, someone started shouting. Aurora spun around to see the principal yelling at Katie Cooper.

"... Mr. Medina in my office all morning insisting that he doesn't want his son in your class. He says he's calling the superintendent to get his son out of your room. This wouldn't be happening if your summer school students hadn't written those letters!"

Katie's hands shook and unshed tears glistened in her eyes.

"Excuse me, Principal Wagner," said Ruth Redding. "But this isn't about Katie and the letters. I had Yudas Medina's son in my first grade. Mr. Medina has been fighting the bilingual placement since kinder. He wants his son in an English-only class. He just doesn't understand that, until a child achieves fluent English proficiency, academic instruction needs to be in the primary language. As we all know ..."

Aurora's turn in the restroom came up.

When she greeted her students on the playground after recess, she found Melody in tears. Blood ran from a scraped knee. Her pretty new back-to-school dress was stained with grass, dirt and blood.

"She fell playing jump rope," River offered. "It's weird, 'cause she's got really good balance. She said she just got dizzy."

Aurora put her arm around Melody and surveyed the rest of her group. Two of her boys, Ryan and Steven, had nosebleeds. Heads back, they pinched the bridges of their noses. Blood streamed down their chins.

"What happened?" Aurora wrinkled her forehead.

"Dunno," one of the boys replied nasally. "Jus' started bleedn'."

Aurora sent the boys to the office. Several children were scratching their arms, legs and necks, raising red welts. A few had scratched so hard they'd drawn blood.

Petite Nikko got out of line and slipped her hand in Aurora's. "Ms. B, I don't feel good," the little girl whispered.

Just then a stiff on-shore gust tore the plastic on the other side of the playground fence. An acre of thin plastic sheeting billowed like a sail in the wind, flapping and flying fifteen feet off the ground.

Holding Nikko's hand, with her other arm around Melody, Aurora led her students back to class. Like a row of ducklings, they followed her, some hopping on one foot, two limping, one walking backwards, another whistling happily.

The "Welcome to Fourth Grade" sign on Aurora's classroom door, which had seemed so bright and cheery this morning, now felt tinged with irony. As her students entered the room, she reminded them to get started on their Bell Ringer cursive handwriting activity. Then she led Melody to the sink to wash the skinned knee.

"I'm so sorry, sweetheart," she said, squeezing green soap on sterile gauze. "This is going to hurt."

15

FRIDAY MORNING, AUGUST 26, 1998
Corralitos Creek, Byrd River Watershed
South Santa Cruz County, Central Monterey Bay Coast

"**I** FOUND THE ARM."
Fish and Wildlife Officer Kelli Cavanaugh ducked under the crime scene tape. With a gloved hand she reached into a brown paper bag and pulled out a human arm with a good deal of flesh still attached to the bone.

Dr. Ahern, a forensics specialist from the Department of Justice, looked up from the body still partly covered by a pile of redwood duff, sticks, and tan oak leaves.

"The arm was mostly buried under forest litter, just like the body," said Kelli. "Mountain lions typically cover their food. And I found scat and tree scrapes near the remains. A forensic deputy took photos and secured the area. He cleared me to bring you this, to bag with the rest of the remains." She dropped the arm back in the paper bag and handed it to a forensic tech.

Detective Rosa leaned down for a closer inspection of the mangled body that sheriff-coroner deputies were meticulously uncovering, using tweezers to lift each leaf and twig off the gruesome remains.

"I see why the hikers who found this body were so traumatized. This is not pretty."

"How often do mountain lions eat humans?" Dr. Ahern asked.

"Cougars have attacked only eleven humans since 1890," said Kelli. "And most of those attacks did not result in a kill."

"Then, was this man already dead when the cougar ate him?" asked Detective Rosa.

"Most likely," said Kelli. "But he probably hadn't been dead for long. Cougars like their meat fresh."

"We'll know more once we get him back to the lab," said Dr. Ahern. "But my preliminary assessment is that his heart had already stopped pumping when the mountain lion found him. It looks like he probably bled out from these stab wounds."

"Time of death?" asked Detective Rosa.

"Judging from the level of decomposition, I'd say the remains have been out here for several weeks. Too bad the liver's gone. That'll present some forensic challenges."

"The liver is missing?" Detective Rosa rubbed his forehead.

"Liver, heart, and lungs," said Dr. Ahern.

"Mountain lions tend to eat the chest-area organs of their prey first," said Kelli. "They'll chew a hole in the ribs and go straight for the tastiest, most nutritional morsels."

"Sir." Young, redheaded Deputy Jamison stepped through a tangle of poison oak and blackberry vines to join the group. "I found the place where the cougar made contact with the victim. A small clearing near the creek. Plants are crushed down. Lotta blood. No signs of a struggle, though. Lion tracks and drag marks made it pretty easy to follow from there to here."

"Good work, Jamison," said Detective Rosa. "Now, who is this guy? Keep searching the area for a wallet, some form of ID. Where did he come from? Who stabbed him and why?"

"Judging from the condition of his teeth," said Dr. Ahern, "he was a serious meth user."

"I'm guessing some of that blood we found at that meth camp might match our victim's," said Kelli.

"When I get back to the DOJ lab, I'll make sure my technicians cross-check this man's DNA with your meth camp blood samples," said Dr. Ahern.

Sheriff Rosa pulled a small notebook out of his chest pocket and flipped pages. "I wonder if our victim here is the father of the baby they rescued in the woods."

"My lab should be able to determine that as well," said Dr. Ahern.

"Kelli," said Detective Rosa. "How about if you and Deputy Jamison go back to where the cougar first made contact with the deceased? If he was stabbed at the meth camp and fled, there should be a blood trail. See if you can track him from where the cougar found him back to the meth camp."

*   *   *

The flickering dance of alder leaf shadows and sunlight over the ferns made the dark blood stain on the ground hard to see. Kneeling, Kelli put her nose close to the earth and sniffed. The smell of blood, death and decay was faint, but unmistakable. Jamison scooped up some of the bloody soil into an evidence bottle.

Within an hour, Jamison and Kelli had followed the dead man's tracks back to the meth camp. The sheriff's office had recently released the site to the county HazMat team for clean-up. This was Kelli's last chance to find any evidence that may have been missed.

She squinted and gazed around the abandoned camp. Last time she'd been here was nearly a month ago. She'd been called in to the investigation because of her reputation as an ace tracker. But even after hours of searching, she hadn't been able to find a track from the meth camp to the found baby site.

"I can't stop thinking about that baby," said Kelli.

"Me either," said Deputy Jamison. "I actually didn't expect he was going to make it. When I arrived at the Wycoff ranch that day, the baby's eyes were sunken and his skin felt tight."

"Dehydration and extreme hypothermia," Kelli nodded.

"Exactly. Lucky the ambulance and the EMTs responded fast and got that baby to the hospital in time."

"Yeah," said Kelli. "And good thing Mr. Wycoff and his son went searching for their dog. Another day in the forest and that baby would probably have been a goner."

"I hear he's out of ICU and doing pretty well now. They're planning to place him with a foster family soon."

"Who could possibly have left a baby alone in the woods?"

"It had to have come from this camp," said Deputy Jamison. "His pajamas were the same size and label as clothes left in the tent."

"Whoever abandoned that baby, it wasn't our dead man. After he was stabbed, he ran upstream from the camp. The baby was found downstream."

Deputy Jamison glanced at his watch. "I'd better report back to Detective Rosa."

"You go ahead," said Kelly. "I know the trail is a month old, but I want to take one more look at that nest where the dog kept the baby alive, before HazMat erases all linkages. Maybe we missed something."

∗   ∗   ∗

By midafternoon, Kelli was down on her hands and knees examining the remains of the nest under the huckleberry bush. Something wet and cold slid up her triceps.

Kelli jumped, rolled in the duff, and came up in a defensive squat to face her assailant.

A happy bark and a wagging husky tail made her laugh.

"Well, hello there. You're Bella, aren't you? Do you have any idea how that baby of yours got here, girl?"

Bella wagged her tail, pounced on the pile of redwood needles that had sheltered the baby, and began digging. A cheap blue rubber flip-flop, size 4, flew into the air and landed at Kelli's feet.

"Well. This is helpful. Good girl, Bella."

Kelli turned the child's sandal over in her hands. Dried river mud was caked between the ridges of the sole. She secured the sandal in an evidence bag, then tromped through a thick stand of Bracken ferns to the edge of the creek, the dog at her heels. She followed the sandy bank upstream, climbed over a fallen madrone, and found herself standing at the edge of a little beach of dried clay.

There it was. A perfect imprint of a size 4 flip-flop. And the other footprint. And another. The isolated location and dry summer weather had preserved perfect clay casts of tracks leading downstream toward the found baby site.

Kelli took photographs of the tracks and tied a strip of yellow plastic police tape to a nearby branch. Hopefully it wouldn't rain any time soon, and the tracks would still be intact by the time forensics could get back up here to make plaster casts.

Bella barked again, drawing Kelli's attention upstream. A scrap of yellow and green flannel torn from the baby's blanket clung to a wild rose bush.

From here on, following the trail from the baby drop point back to the site of the meth hooch was going to be a cakewalk. Apparently, the person carrying the baby was a child with a size 4 foot.

16

T HE CAMPFIRE SMELLED OF CEDAR AND SAGE. Flames danced above
the logs inside the stone fire ring. Smoke swirled, carrying sparks
toward the stars. The crack and pop of burning wood punctuated the
distant drum of the waterfall and shush of wind in the forest.

Father Francis sat on a log near the fire and basked in the heat.
He raised his eyes to the stars and watched Sagittarius rise over the
trees. The Milky Way boiled out of the constellation like steam out of
a teapot — ancient light from the center of the galaxy. Father Francis
let his body disintegrate, become the stardust from which he was
made, and he flowed with the smoke into the endless universe.

"Is this how you do it?" One of the young men sitting nearby
broke into the priest's reverie.

Father Francis examined the prayer tie, the offering for the *Inipi*,
which the young man held. Small squares of colored cotton cloth, each
square bundled into a pouch containing a few pinches of tobacco, were

tied along a string. He turned to the ceremonial leader of the purification and healing lodge. The elder nodded approval.

"This is a good start." Father Francis returned the prayer tie to the young man. "You'll need forty bundles on each strand; thirty-five more to go on this one. But don't be in a hurry. Each pouch you tie is a prayer. Focus your mind and spirit as you work."

One of the young men in the circle pushed the hood of his black sweatshirt away from his face. Angry flames burned in his eyes. "How do we know this is going to work?"

Is this going to work? thought the priest. *Will I be able to lead these young relatives of Salvador Luna out of their hatred and grief, away from their desire for violent retribution for Salvador's murder? I've known these boys since they were kids but they mad-dogged me at the funeral because I preached forgiveness and peace. It's a miracle I persuaded them to come here to the canyon with me. Will they find peace and balance in the Inipi — a vision of love and life, rather than death, fear, hatred, and revenge?*

"Spirit knows what you're seeking by seeing into the sincerity of your heart," the ceremonial leader addressed the young men. "Humble yourself. Offer thanksgiving and gratitude for all of existence. Feel the blessing inherent in each moment of being. Give thanks and praise for all the gifts of life, even the pain and suffering. All things flow from One Source, and all things return back to that One in their own time."

Waves of energy spiraled around Father Francis and the others huddled near the fire, binding them together, melting doubt and fear.

"Pray for vision. The truth is here." Father Francis touched his heart. "You won't feel the same when you come out of the sweat as you did when you went in. The *Inipi* ceremony is a rebirth, a renewal. Something happens that goes beyond physical form and takes you into the reality of the nonphysical world, the spirit realm, where the real healing takes place."

"*Noso'n.* (In breath so it is in spirit)," said a man sitting in the shadows.

He began beating a rhythm with clapper sticks and singing a slow, haunting song in a language unknown to most of the listeners. Someone played clear, pure notes on an elderberry flute. When the last note wafted with the smoke up toward the stars, a woman spoke.

"That was a beautiful song, Gabe and Luis. Thank you. I could feel the ancestors dancing. I've brought you all water. You don't want to be dehydrated going into the sweat tomorrow morning, so you should drink."

"Thank you, Marie Christine." Father Francis took the cup offered. He'd known Marie Christine since they were both children, and he loved her as if she were an elder sister.

As he sipped the water, he recalled the first time his father had brought him here, to Indian Canyon. On that day, he'd learned that the loving couple he thought of as his grandparents were actually his father's *adopted* parents. His DNA grandparents — his father's birth parents — were Native Americans of the Costanoan Ohlone band. Displaced from a failed mission system, their traditional indigenous culture extirpated, Father Francis' young grandparents had been unable to care for their baby. So, like many other Indians in California at the beginning of the twentieth century, they'd given him up, into the care of the priests at Our Lady of Help Orphanage in Valle Verde.

Francis Hilman and his dad — and countless other displaced indigenous people seeking to find their way home — had found sanctuary here in Indian Canyon, in the heart of the Gabilan Mountain Range. Marie Christine, her mother, and generations of ancestors before her had been born and raised on this ancestral Ohlone land hidden in a remote canyon. She welcomed indigenous people from all over the world to her canyon for ceremony, healing, prayer, dance, storytelling, and a reclaiming of their cultural traditions.

"Thank you again for hosting us, Marie Christine," said Father Francis.

"It is my honor, Frank." Marie Christine smoothed her long skirt and sat down on a boulder near the fire. "My mother used to say that 'When ceremonies, singing and dancing stop, so will the Earth.'"

"What's that thing you've got in your hand?" asked one of the boys.

Marie Christine held an object about the size and shape of a human tibia up to the firelight. It seemed to glow with great power.

"This is an artifact unearthed a few weeks ago at a new construction site in Silicon Valley. Since I'm the legally designated ancestor of record in our region, the object was given to me to determine how it should best be reburied. It's a ceremonial object. Very old and very sacred. I've been sitting with it, praying over it, waiting for Spirit to reveal the proper reburial place to me."

"What's it made of?"

"The back leg bone of a grizzly, covered in tar and inlaid with abalone chips." Marie Christine wrapped the object in a cloth and put it away in her bag.

"What tribe are you?" asked one of the boys.

"We are Ohlone of the Mutsun band. 'Costanoan' is what the Spanish called us, and all of the indigenous peoples who have inhabited the coastal areas of Central California since the beginning of time."

One of the boys looked up from his prayer ties and spoke. "My auntie says our family were Mission Indians."

"Mission Indian isn't a tribe," said Marie Christine. "The Spanish developed missions to spread Christianity to the 'heathens' and to give Spain a military claim on California before English, Russian, American, and French adventurers could do so."

Luis, the man who had played the clapper sticks, put another log on the fire. Flames surged and lit the faces of the listeners.

"In 1776, when the Spanish Empire established Mission Dolores in San Francisco, there were twenty thousand Indians living in over fifty different villages and tribes, speaking at least eight distinct dialects, in Ohlone territory: the land that extends along the coast from San Francisco to Big Sur, and inland from the Pacific Ocean to the Gabilan Mountains. Very quickly, thousands of Ohlone were either enslaved at the missions, murdered, killed by infectious disease, or forced to flee their ancestral homeland. By 1810, the Ohlone people in the Bay Area numbered less than two hundred."

"How did your tribe survive?" asked one of the young men.

"Ohlones who escaped from nearby Mission San Juan Bautista ran toward these hills, up here into Indian Canyon. As you saw when you drove in, the head of the canyon is lowland swamp. Nowadays, the surrounding vineyards have drained down the water table and it's drier, but in the time of the missions, the land was covered with water, tules, and sedges. Once runaways got into the swamp, they left no trace. The Spanish thought there was a spell on the land. They thought the Indians just disappeared, vanished into thin air. 'Indian magic', they called it."

"How come your people didn't starve up here?"

"The watershed provided abundant fresh water, and the creek was full of salmon. We trapped deer with snares made from nettle rope. There were berries, acorns, tubers. Plenty of food. The weather was always comfortable. We were happy, healthy, and very blessed, here in the canyon."

"But outside the canyon," said Gabe, "in California at large, Mexico ended the mission system. Native people were forced out of the missions into the world, stripped of their culture and lacking basic means of survival."

"Ninety-one million acres of Indian land were taken," said Marie Christine. "Most of the California tribes were never recognized by the new government."

"Federal treaties were never ratified by the state," said Luis. "In fact, the new state of California put a bounty on native people."

"Five dollars a scalp," said Gabe.

"Newcomers wanted California gold," said Father Francis. "They wanted our land and water."

"They wanted to exterminate us," said Luis.

"Cold-blooded Indian killing was considered honorable, Marie Christine continued. "Shooting Indians, murdering even women and children who were 'domesticated', was done without reason or a moment's warning."

One of the boys swore and jabbed at the fire with a stick.

A dog who'd been sleeping by the fire got up and put his head on Marie Christine's lap. She scratched his ear. The fire cracked and flames danced, making long ghostly shadows on the surrounding trees.

"Tell us more, Marie Christine," one of the boys urged as he reached for another square of cloth for his prayer tie.

"California law in the 1850s resulted in a profitable and lively Indian slave trade. Our children went for fifty dollars each. Over ten thousand

Indians were legally sold for work and sex. I've read reports by federal Indian agents from that time documenting the transport of Indian children in cages." Marie Christine looked into Father Francis' eyes.

"They've been taking our children for a long time," said Father Francis. "Genocide and child sex trade started on this continent with Christopher Columbus."

"That's fucked up," said a boy with a scar through his eyebrow.

"To admit you were Indian in California in the 1850s was suicidal," said Gabe. "Out of self-defense, many indigenous people claimed to be Mexican. They married Mexicans and their descendants eventually forgot their indigenous ancestors."

"Dude, we speak Spanish and English at home, but one of my *abuelas* talks some freakin' language that only some of the other grandmas understand. Maybe I'm Indian."

"Me, too," whispered a boy shrouded in a black hoodie. "I wonder what tribe we were."

Marie Christine smiled. "Maybe someone in your family still knows."

"I'm gonna find out!"

"Me too," several voices vowed in the dark.

A ribbon of fire hissed along a log.

"Noso'n." A loud crack issued from the fire. A log split and fell into the flames. Luis stirred the coals and added more wood.

"But that's enough looking back," said Marie Christine. "It's important to honor our ancestors by knowing our history, but we should not dwell on it. You are here because of the murder of Salvador Luna, for purification and healing, and to help his spirit find peace. We all have many things to overcome that confront us in our lives. Holding on to our wounds, feeding them with regret and hatred, makes them fester. To seek revenge only makes the sickness grow. Wounds need to be cleansed. Then they will heal. Open your mind to understanding. Hold only love in your heart."

The elder spoke. "Fasting, prayer, song and the sweat lodge can help us heal and get our balance, so we can be at peace within ourselves. When we are in silence and we pray in the lodge, then we can see in a different way some of the things that have crossed our paths. We can review the past and how it happened with a clear heart. Grasping onto fear and anger keeps us back. When we let those things go, we become stronger."

"What exactly is going to happen tomorrow, when we go into the sweat lodge?" asked one of the young men.

"If you come to the lodge in a good way," said the ceremonial leader, "you may hear or see things that will amaze you. If you hear voices or see visions, remember them. If you want to talk afterward, you may seek out any of the elders here for counsel. Things you never noticed before in nature, like seeing a spider's web, or hearing a bird, really hearing it, will seem like miracles. The land knows you're here, and will talk to you if you listen. When I'm on this sacred land, here in Indian Canyon, my heart jumps with joy. I feel free. I feel home."

"You'll reconnect back to Nature," said Gabe. "Grandmother Earth and your ancestors will speak to you. You'll feel like you've come home to a place you hardly knew your heart was missing. You'll feel physically and emotionally stronger. You'll finally truly know who you are, and you'll feel more like a whole person than you ever have."

"So, is this kind of like a religion, or what?" asked one of the boys.

"No. It's not a religion. People from many different religions come to the Lodge to sweat and pray," replied the elder. "Some form of the Sweat Lodge, what Lakota people call *Inipi*, is practiced for purification all over the world. In our Lodge, we honor all things because all beings are sacred, bound together in a living web of earth, air, fire, and water. Earth is our Grandmother, and we are all relations. When we bring the heated rocks into the Lodge, we greet them as our Grandfathers."

"Once we let go all the areas of negativity we're holding onto, and work them out," said Marie Christine, "we receive love and wisdom. Then we see where and how we can serve, how to take responsibility for the effects of our actions seven generations into the future, how to help Grandmother Earth and her children, all our relations. That is what sustains us. That is why we have survived."

The pure notes of Gabe's flute faded into the night. Now silent, the drum and clapper sticks continued beating in the listeners' inner ears. It was their own hearts beating in time to music dissolving into the starry sky. Only a few flames flared and ran along the charred logs in the fire circle. Under the fire-eaten logs glowed a bed of red coals.

The young men went off alone into the woods, each to his own private place of power for the night. The elders left quietly, one at a time.

Father Francis sat by the fire, sipping from his water bottle, watching the stars move around the dome of the sky and listening to the music of the creek, the wind in the trees, until all the wood burned. Waves of red and black plasma rippled over the glowing fire pit. An owl screeched from a tall redwood. Finally, he stood, stretched, banked and secured the coals, and hiked up the mountain to a place he had known, had been drawn to, for most of his life.

On a ridge top, on a flat outcrop of marble, Father Francis had left his backpack earlier in the day. Now, on crystalline marble rock under the stars, he spread out his mat and sleeping bag, stripped off Levi jacket, T-shirt, and jeans, and slipped naked into his bag. He rolled his jacket into a pillow, lay on his back with hands under his head, and watched the sky.

His thoughts were erratic — circling from the tossed meth camp to the missing girls and their mother, the baby found in the woods, the teen missing from the strawberry fields, and Salvador Luna. A thin glowing crescent appeared at the top of the distant mountain. The ghostly white object became an enormous circle; it burned a hole in the dark sky, and set the silhouetted trees on the distant ridge into sharp focus. The moon rose higher and seemed to grow smaller. Father Francis rolled on his side, closed his eyes, and fell asleep.

He dreamed a phoenix flew toward him, its feathers streaming a fiery borealis. The bird landed at his feet and became a beautiful woman. Naked, she cast her eyes modestly to the ground.

As he reached for her, she became a mountain lion, standing upright on hind legs. They embraced, and danced together over the mountaintops and into the sky, until she spun away into the darkness. He fell down and down, into a pit, filled with caged animals and children, and snake-like venomous demons, thrashing and snapping.

Warriors dressed in animal masks rushed in and vanquished the demons.

"Clan Brother," the warriors said. "Soon you must return to the River Under the River and rejoin the Camp of the Formless Warriors. Prepare yourself for the Great Turning that is to come."

*   *   *

Father Francis opened his eyes with a start just as the dawning sun flared emerald green over the mountains. Another flash, brilliant gold, and the sun rose above the far ridge. Father Francis stretched inside his sleeping bag, scrubbed his hands over his face, and rolled onto his back.

A mountain lion crouched on the rock ledge just above him. Two huge yellow eyes stared at him.

Father Francis froze. As still as a statue except for a slight flick of the tail curled around her enormous paws, the puma watched the man.

Suddenly, she sprang toward him, her underbelly arching over his face. The musky scent of the beast overwhelmed him.

The mountain lion cleared the priest's head by inches and landed at the far edge of the marble slab. She looked back over her shoulder, directly into Father Francis eyes, and flicked her tail. Then, in a heartbeat, the creature bounded away.

17

YUDAS MEDINA WONDERED IF HE SHOULD REFRAIN from taking Communion today. Things he had done were weighing heavily on him. A good man should go to confession before he received the Body and Blood, the Holy Eucharist. He was unclean; he had sinned. He should have gone to confession yesterday. Now, he'd have to wait another week.

Yudas stared at the statue of Our Blessed Lady next to the altar, while Father Ruiz gave his sermon in Spanish. She cast her eyes down upon him and shook her head. A tear glistened on her cheek. *La Virgen* was not happy with Señor Medina this morning. He did not blame her.

He was angry with himself. And he was irritated by this sermon. The English language service would be superior to this Spanish one. It would be better for his *familia* to mix with the important *anglos* who came for English mass, especially good for his son, Antonio. The boy was struggling in that new bilingual teacher's class at Prudenciana.

But it was no good that Father Francis was the one who presided over mass *en inglés*. Yudas hated that priest, Father Francis. They should not have a *moreno*, a dark-skinned man, offering the English mass.

No, he must take Communion today even if he was unclean. If he did not receive the Body and Blood with everyone else, it would not look good. *Holy Mother, intercede for me. Dios mío forgive me, for I have sinned.*

Soon, he would go to confession. Soon.

*   *   *

FRIDAY MORNING, SEPTEMBER 2, 1998
PRUDENCIANA ELEMENTARY SCHOOL, VALLE VERDE
BYRD RIVER WATERSHED

"First, let me ask you a question. What is a chemical?"

A distinguished-looking man sporting a black and silver goatee faced the audience as if he were addressing a congressional hearing. He checked his Rolex and waited for a response.

One hundred and thirty children on rows of benches in the Prudenciana Elementary School multipurpose room sat politely, staring at him. Fourth and fifth grade teachers Aurora, Katie, Tom, Helen, and Harriet accompanied their students. They were here to listen to the "pro" side of the pesticide debate.

Aurora leaned toward Katie, sitting next to her on the bench, and whispered, "Who is this guy, again?"

"Sean Stark. He's president or something of CalGreen. We couldn't find out much about the company, but I do know that they run the soil fumigations for nearly every strawberry grower in Central California."

"Superintendent Spieler and I read those letters Ms. Cooper's students wrote to the *Valle Verde Register* this summer." Stark glared at Katie. Her face flushed red.

"We thought that you needed some — ahem — some additional information," said Superintendent Spieler, a tall man standing next to

Sean Stark. "You need a chance to ask questions from people who represent — that is, ah, some scientists who have expertise and knowledge about pesticides." The superintendent gestured toward Stark and a man standing to Stark's left, adjusting his bow tie.

Aurora cringed. These men obviously didn't know how to talk to a group of nine- and ten-year-olds with mixed English language skills.

She leaned forward and squinted along the row, checking on her students. Salvador Luna was squeezed in between Rico and Caleb. Aurora's brow furrowed.

Why is Salvador's ghost here?

Rico, his red baseball cap on backwards, squirmed and punched Jessie in the arm. Aurora caught Rico's eye and smiled. Rico grinned back and slowly removed his cap.

"To Mr. Stark's left is Dr. Ringer, Director of Santa Cruz County Public Health. He's here in case you have questions about our own bodies and, uh ... that is, when we use pesticides."

Aurora rubbed the scar on her thigh, which had started to throb, and leaned over to whisper to Katie again. "I've hardly ever seen the superintendent on campus. Why are these important men skipping their golf game and power lunch to talk to a bunch of little kids?"

Katie rolled her eyes and shrugged. "I think there's something wrong with the superintendent, don't you? He's so pale, kind of wooden, and his eyes just look dead."

"Frankenstein?" Aurora whispered.

"No — zombie." Katie covered her mouth to stifle a snorting laugh.

Dr. Ringer smiled an oily smile and adjusted his bow tie. "If you have an interest in some of the health risks from the foods we eat, since I see so many people from your, er, *background* in my medical practice, poisoning is my area of expertise, so I can answer any of your questions."

Aurora turned around to quell a disruption on the bench behind her.

"Hey," she whispered to Katie. "Who are those men in black suits and sunglasses standing in the back of the room?"

Katie glanced over her shoulder to see. "Oh, my God. I have no idea who they are, but they look like the Division 6 agents in *Men in Black,* only more sinister."

"I loved that movie." Aurora giggled.

"I'm going to be talking about three different subject areas," Mr. Stark continued. "Number one, the procedures you have to go through to use pesticides in the United States. Number two, how methyl bromide is used. Number three, the current regulatory situation concerning methyl bromide."

Aurora wondered how the superintendent could condone such an inappropriate use of instructional time. *My kids are missing their math instruction for this.*

"I'm so sorry I brought this debacle with me to Prudenciana," Katie whispered.

Stark continued. "So once again, I ask you, 'What is a chemical?'"

Sarah, a large blonde fifth grader in the back row, raised her hand.

"She was one of my summer institute students," whispered Katie. "Very bright, but dyslexic, a struggling reader. On the autism spectrum. She's thirteen, so she should be in middle school, but she was held back."

"Yes?" Stark pointed a long white finger at the girl.

"A chemical is what you use to kill weeds," Sarah answered.

"Well, ah, that's something chemicals can do. Anyone else?" The students sat still.

"You!" He pointed at a non-English speaker in the front row. The boy jumped. "You are chemicals. And you, and you and you!" He jabbed his finger wildly at the children then took a step back, looking as if he'd just jumped all the pawns on the chessboard and captured the queen.

"That's right, we're all made of chemicals. And most likely, you actually drink some chemicals. What's the most common chemical that's, ah, in your body?"

Several students called out, "Water!"

"That's right. And you probably had some water this morning, or something with water in it. What makes one chemical, like water, a pesticide and another not?"

"One kills and one doesn't!" Sarah waved her hand in the air and shouted the answer.

"You're on the right track," said Stark. "But it really has to do with the amount of chemical it takes to kill. If it takes a very small amount of chemical to kill something, then it has the potential to be a pesticide. If it takes a huge volume of chemical to kill, then it's not useful as a pesticide. You see, all chemicals can kill, even water."

Dr. Ringer launched into a lengthy technical explanation that sounded to Aurora like a cascade of bleats.

"Now, let's talk about methyl bromide," said Stark. "It's gone through almost all of those regulatory steps. It's cost us nearly ten years and eighty million dollars, and the testing still isn't quite finished."

"If the testing isn't finished yet," Sarah called out without raising her hand, "why are they allowed to use it?"

Stark glared at the girl. "Methyl bromide has been in use in the U.S. for over thirty years. We know it's safe. The tests are only a formality. We just need some new data required by a California citizen's ballot initiative — legislation passed a few years back."

"You mean the *Birth Defects Prevention Act*?" Sarah shouted.

Stark cleared his throat. "What kind of data do you think scientists collect, in order to get a pesticide approved?"

Several hands went up. All of the hands belonged to Katie's summer institute students.

"Watch this," Katie whispered to Aurora. "My kids really know their research."

As Stark pointed to the students, they called out symptoms and consequences of pesticide exposure.

"Pesticides poison our food and water, and our earth."

"They make *freseros* sick."

"Skin rashes. Asthma."

"Blurry vision. Dizziness."

"Hallucinations."

"Nosebleeds, throwing up, headaches."

"Panic attacks. Seizures."

"Miscarriages."

"Birth defects, lowered IQ, learning disabilities."

"Cancer."

"Yes, well, *ahem*. Those are all *alleged* consequences of so-called pesticide poisoning. But there is no data to support any of that. I knew that some of you already had some ... information. But, it's very complicated. Remember, a little knowledge is a dangerous thing. As I said, scientific *experts* have been studying this in depth for years, and we have spent millions on the research. Once the U.S. EPA has determined that this chemical can be used safely as a pesticide — that is, when we've satisfied that one, ah, 'birth defects' issue with the State of California then, well, that is how a pesticide is approved." Stark frowned as he scanned the audience. "In the *United States of America*."

Aurora leaned toward Katie and whispered, "Who's paying for this research?"

"Conflict of interest." Katie whispered back. "The fox is guarding the hen house. They fund the very studies that certify the safety of their own products. A terribly expensive proposition for poor them to do all that 'research'."

"But quite a profitable bottom line."

Stark pushed on. "Now, many people think we *spray* methyl bromide on crops, but they are mistaken."

"It's a gas," a student called out.

"Yes." Stark straightened his tie. He frowned as if someone had just beaten him in telling the punch line to his favorite joke. "Because methyl bromide is a gas, it has to be handled in a closed system, like your propane tank. It can't be touched, because it's too poisonous. So it's applied through 'shanks', which are sunk ten inches into the soil. Our tractors have a special nozzle that injects the methyl bromide gas down through the shanks at the same time that polyethylene rolls off the tractor, covering the field. Only five well-trained professionals are actually involved in the fumigation process: the tractor driver and the Mexi—, ah, *workers* on each end of the field who walk alongside, burying the edges of the plastic."

Aurora whispered to Katie, "How many people driving along roads next to plastic-covered fields realize they're breathing poisonous gas?"

Katie rolled her eyes. "How big a dose do you think those field workers are getting in their face, while they walk alongside the fumigation truck burying the edges of the plastic?"

"My dad is one of those guys who covers the plastic," a fifth grade student waved his hand in the air while he shouted. "It makes him really sick."

"Yes, well, the tarps are left on at least a week to kill the pests living in the soil," Stark continued. "No crops can be planted in the field for two weeks after the fumigation, so none of the crops themselves are ever exposed to the pesticides, just the soil."

A student raised his hand and Stark pointed to him. "Where does the methyl bromide go?"

"Fifty percent reacts chemically with either the pest that it's going to be controlling or with other organic debris that happens to be in the soil. And fifty percent of the gas escapes through the tarp and goes into the atmosphere."

"Other organic debris?" Katie's whisper oozed sarcasm. "Such as worms and beneficial microorganisms?"

"Excuse me! Let me get this straight," Sarah jumped to her feet and called out. "Half of it goes into the air? So, how does that affect people when it gets in the air? Doesn't it poison us when we breathe it?" The girl's face was unusually pale, with bright red blotches on her cheeks. "Just tell me one thing: Is methyl bromide going to give me cancer?"

"Oh, oh," Katie whispered. "Sarah's escalating."

Stark answered with barely disguised annoyance. "Remember what I said earlier about what makes a chemical a pesticide? I explained that it takes a very small amount of it to kill. It's the concentration that determines whether it's going to have an impact on you or not. Very few instances of *acute* poisoning have been documented. Now, this gets technical, boys and girls, so it's going to be over your heads, but we need to consider the data. It's virtually impossible to determine the effects of *chronic long-term exposure*. Too many other variables."

"Let me talk about buffer zones." Dr. Ringer stepped forward, straightening his bow tie. "After reviewing all of the data, county agricultural commissioners determine what are the safe levels of exposure. Then they set buffer zones, 'no spray zones', between fumigated fields and sensitive areas such as schools, homes, and hospitals."

Alice and Nikko asked to be excused because they felt like throwing up. Aurora sent them to the office. Salvador Luna's ghost went with them.

Aurora whispered to Katie, "Did they fumigate the field next to the school today?"

"Yep. And there is no buffer zone."

A chubby boy waved a hand in the air. "My family lives right next to a strawberry field," said the boy. "You said there are buffer zones to protect us from fumigations, but my dog was out there when they were putting the plastic down, and he died."

"Well, now I don't know what the circumstances were that you're talking about," said Mr. Stark. "But your parents should contact the agricultural commissioner if they have questions. He will be the one in charge of enforcement, so he would come out and identify the situation. His job is to make sure all of the rules are followed and everything is done safely. We have given his card to your principal, and enough cards to your teachers so that each of you will have one to take home. Your parents should feel free to call the commissioner anytime, if you have questions or concerns."

"Just remember," said Superintendent Spieler, "there's no reason that we should be fearful of things we can find out about. It's good that you found out about this subject or any other subject that has concern for you. Just make sure you get all the facts and listen to all sides before you make up your mind. And one more thing ..."

There was a commotion coming from the back row. Aurora jumped to her feet.

"It's Sarah! She's having a seizure," Tom shouted. "Someone call 911!"

18

FRIDAY AFTERNOON, SEPTEMBER 2, 1998
Prudenciana Elementary

RYAN AND STEVEN STOOD AT AURORA'S SHOULDER, bloody noses dripping on their shoes. Seated at her advanced math center, Aurora wrote an office pass for the boys while her math group waited patiently. An eraser went flying by her ear.

My kids are falling apart. Deciding to go ahead with the math centers that got bumped for the morning pesticide assembly: bad choice. I should have stuck with our usual after-lunch reading routine.

"Give me all your blocks, now!" Rico stood on his desk, red hat on backwards, and waved a sword constructed of plastic snap-together blocks at the other students in his math group.

From behind her came a loud crash. Aurora swung around to see a tower of wooden base-ten blocks tumble to the floor around the feet of the gleeful Long-Toed Salamander demolition crew.

Taking a deep calming breath, she sent the bloody noses to the office with extra tissues. *Maybe the roving school nurse will be in today.*

127

At that moment, Alice, who the office had sent back to class after the assembly, threw up all over her desk, herself, and the floor. Action stopped; everyone stared.

Odor of vomit oozed around the room. Alice started crying.

Aurora went to the intercom to ask Bushi to contact the custodian. She was standing with the intercom handset to her ear when the principal opened the door.

Principal Wagner's lips were thin and tight. Her nostrils flared in disgust as she stood at the door taking in the scene.

"Ms. Bourne, step outside with me a moment."

Aurora shot Rico a look. He took off his hat, jumped off his desk, and began picking up the toppled wooden blocks. Other students followed suit. Aurora slipped out and closed the door behind her.

Principal Wagner glared.

"Ms. Bourne, Mr. King has been in my office for the past hour, complaining about you. It seems that last year, when his son was in your class, you portrayed Christopher Columbus as a blood-thirsty conqueror who stole from the Indians, enslaved, tortured, and killed them. That is a terrible story to tell children."

Aurora kept her face in neutral and suppressed the impulse to defend herself. The Project Interact Social Studies simulation she'd used for that lesson was exemplary experiential learning curriculum aligned with the goals, objectives, and best practices of the California Social Studies Standards. After prearranging with one of her students, she'd pretended to sail around the classroom on Columbus Day and land at the student's desk, where she'd proceeded to unpack and claim the student's belongings, exclaiming about all the wonderful things she'd discovered.

The class had expressed outrage. "You didn't discover that stuff! It belongs to Leanne!"

The students' response had led to an excellent, academically rigorous discussion about Columbus and colonialism. But Aurora knew there was no point in trying to explain all this to the principal.

"Mr. King was taught that Columbus is a hero," said Principal Wagner. "He feels that elementary school children are too young to hear otherwise. You have his daughter Lizzie in your class this year and Mr. King wants to be sure she is taught the inspiring Columbus story he learned as a boy."

Niño, the custodian, arrived with a bucket of industrial-strength sudsy water, a mop, and a can of sawdust. The chemical smell of the water made Aurora's eyes tear and her throat constrict. Niño threw open the classroom door and pushed his bucket inside.

Alice returned from the office wearing fresh clothes from Bushi's emergency box, with a note from Bushi stating there was no one at home who could pick her up early, so she would be staying until the end of the day. Aurora ushered her into the classroom.

"I don't want the Kings in my office about this Columbus business again this year," said Principal Wagner.

Niño emerged, pulling his bucket of toxic pink cleaning fluid. He wheeled it to the storm drain in front of Aurora's classroom and dumped it.

Open-mouthed and wide-eyed, Aurora turned to the principal. *Isn't she going to say something to the custodian about dumping toxic chemicals down the storm drain? That storm drain flows to the bay, to the National Marine Sanctuary!*

"You may go back to your class now," said Principal Wagner. "Remember to watch what you say about Columbus."

Aurora reentered her classroom feeling numb. Her students had put away all the math manipulatives perfectly. They were sitting at their desks with library books out, engaged in sustained silent reading, their usual after lunch "Drop Everything and Read" activity.

"Oh, what a wonderful class you are!" she said. "I think you must be the best class I've ever had. I'm so lucky and honored to be your teacher."

All of the children sat up straighter, and held their books with even more commitment. They couldn't sit any taller if they tried.

Aurora glanced at her watch. "Tell you what. Today's schedule has been pretty discombobulated. Raise your hand if you'd still like to have a few minutes of our usual Teacher Read Aloud before we go out to P.E.

Every student's hand went up. Aurora reached for the book on her desk and held it up so everyone could see its exquisitely illustrated cover — a watercolor illustration of a lovely grey-haired woman kneeling on a wild coastal hillside, planting lupines.

"*Miss Rumphius*, by Barbara Cooney," Aurora began. "This is a story about Alice Rumphius. When she's young, she tells Grandpa that when she is grown, she wants to travel to faraway places and then settle down in a cottage by the sea. 'That is all well and good,' said Grandfather. 'But there is one more thing you must do. You must find a way to help make the world more beautiful.'"

Aurora studied the rapt faces of her students. "Please turn to the person next to you," she said, "and tell them what you think Miss Rumphius might do to help make the world more beautiful." When her students had finished sharing, she asked, "Now, raise your hand if you'd like to share what will you do to help make the world more beautiful?"

Hands flew up. "Yes, Melody?"

"I'm coming to the beach clean-up this weekend!"

19

MONDAY, SEPTEMBER 5, 1998
(Labor Day)
Annual Beach Clean-Up
Pelican Dunes, Byrd River Watershed
South Santa Cruz County, Central Monterey Bay Coast

"HEADS UP, MS. B!"

Aurora was walking along the sand at Pelican Dunes Beach, looking for trash. The fog had already cleared and the morning was beginning to warm.

Teams of Prudenciana students and family members combed the beach, each team with an official trash bag, a bag for recyclables, and a pencil and data card for the California Coastal Commission's annual Adopt-a-Beach event.

On Aurora's team were Rico, River, Paloma, Caleb, and Melody Escobar. They wanted to carry all the stuff, so Aurora walked empty-handed.

"Heads up, Ms. B!" Rico's voice got through to Aurora, and she turned around just as he let fly a Frisbee.

The disk came whizzing toward her. She reached up, but it was a little too high. She ran backwards to catch it. Stretching. It was going to be close.

The back of her head smacked into someone as hard as a rock wall. Fireworks exploded behind her eyelids.

A strong red-brown arm reached above her, caught the Frisbee, and threw it back to its sender. At the same time, a matching arm clamped around her waist.

"Smooth, Ms. B!" Rico called.

Two large hands gently turned her and held her by the shoulders at arm's length, as if there were concern that she might not be able to keep her balance.

She stared at the man holding her, the man built like a rock wall. Recognition seared through her core.

His eyes. As blue-green as the sea. She held her breath, a mouse under the spell of a hawk.

She forced herself to look away, down at the sand between their feet. Could he tell how her body reacted to him? He was a Catholic priest. He probably didn't understand such things.

She met his waiting eyes. *He knows.*

"Are you alright?" He lifted his hands off her shoulders tentatively.

"Yes." Aurora rubbed the back of her head. "Sorry to bump into you like that. Are you okay?"

"Didn't feel a thing." The priest's eyes twinkled. He picked up Aurora's baseball cap, dusted off the sand, and handed it to her. "I remember you from Cosmic John's waterfall hike. Aurora, right? I'm Father Francis. Frank Hilman. From Our Lady of Help in Valle Verde."

"I remember you, too." *As if I could possibly ever forget.* "Thank you again for helping me when I fell in the creek. Don't know why I keep acting like such a klutz. I usually have pretty good balance." She replaced her hat, trying to control her chaotic feelings.

"Looks like you've recovered from your injury. I — we — were worried. No broken bones, I take it?"

"No, but I did need stitches. All better now." She pulled up the hem of her shorts and rubbed the raised scar on her thigh.

He inclined his head to inspect the scar. His eyes narrowed and he swallowed.

She blushed. *Why did I do that? My thighs are too fat. I'm an imbecile. He probably thinks I'm disgusting.* Her throat was dry. *Say something.*

"I went to the funeral for Salvador Luna at your church," Aurora stammered. "I — I saw you then. Salvador was a student of mine."

"We hate to bury children, especially victims of violence," said Father Francis. "Thank you for being at the funeral. It meant a lot to Salvador's family to see all the people there who loved him, from so many walks of life. It helped heal the wounds in the community, too, I think."

"I'm afraid the community's going to need a lot more work to heal its wounds." Aurora recalled the black-hooded hoodlums who'd threatened Father Francis during the funeral.

Just then, the very same hoodlums appeared.

"Yo, Padre. My dog an' me gonna hang wid our homies up ahead. You wanna take our stuff?"

Father Francis accepted the nearly empty trash bag and data card. "So you two are going to team up with Victor's group?"

"You got it, *vato*. We'll let'cha know if we fin' any buried treasure. Later, Padre." The young men sprinted away down the beach.

"Aren't those the angry young men from the funeral who ..."

"Salvador's relatives. Yes. They craved revenge at first. They were poisoned with grief and rage. It's taken time to help them find peace." Father Francis shrugged his shoulders and smiled. "Looks like they just left me holding the bag."

"My team's gone off without me, too." Aurora pointed toward her team far down the beach, recognizable by the dot of red that had to be Rico's baseball cap.

Father Francis' eyes caught flecks of sunlight glinting off the waves. "We've got a bag here. Shall we?"

Aurora's first impulse was to make an excuse and run. But that would be childish ... and rude.

They walked in silence.

"I don't think there are as many cigarette butts as last year," Aurora said after a while. "The Coastal Commission's educational campaign must be working."

"You do this every year?"

"I've been the beach captain for my school for a few years. I think it's really important for my students to get involved."

"This is my first time. I brought the basketball team I coach, plus a few of the other, ah, black sheep in my flock. I wanted to show them how great it feels to make a positive difference in the world." The priest picked up a scrap of red plastic that had once been part of a disposable lighter and dropped it in the bag. "I hope today's experience will give them a way to connect with their community that's more socially constructive than tagging." He watched the boys running toward the rivermouth. "They seem to be enjoying themselves."

"I noticed the tattoos. Are they gang members?"

"Some are," answered the priest.

"I've got a student — a little guy who wears a red baseball cap," said Aurora. "I think he's interested in — what's the gang that wears red?"

"That would be the Norteños. You think he's at risk? I'd be happy to meet him."

"His grandma's raising him. She's at the tables back at the beach entrance with a few of my other parents, preparing a picnic. If we get a chance, I'll introduce you to her and Rico."

A pod of dolphins offshore kept pace with them as they walked. Like a swimmer caught in a rip tide, Aurora felt swept up in the priest's power.

"What's this?" She reached down and tugged at a piece of frayed plastic rope. Sand fell away as she pulled.

"Here, let me help." Father Francis took hold and they leaned their weight against the buried line. A fishing net began to emerge from the sand. They tugged again. It was heavy. Aurora fought the urge to fall into the man's arms.

A few of Father Francis' basketball players ran up to help. Several of Aurora's students and some parents joined in. It turned into a game of tug of war between the sand and the humans.

"Puulll!" yelled a burly tattooed basketball player.

Suddenly, the whole net came loose and everyone tumbled into a pile on the sand, shouting and laughing.

Father Francis had gracefully sidestepped the pile. He looked serious as he gathered the net into a big bundle. "Miles of this kind of netting are adrift in the ocean, killing senselessly. Well done, everyone."

The net pullers scattered like sandpipers, but one young man stayed back. He had a coal dusting of mustache, a sweet face, gang tattoos on neck and hands, a crystal earring, and a gold crucifix around his neck. *In memory of Salvador Luna* scrolled in white cursive letters across his black hoodie. One of his arms rested protectively across the shoulders of Paloma. His other hand grasped the shoulder of an angry-looking boy about fifteen wearing a red baseball cap.

"Ms. Bourne? I met you when Father Francis brought me an' my friend and my little brother Johnny, here, to the hike at the waterfall," said the young man. "Do you remember me? I'm Victor Lopez."

"Of course I remember you, Victor. It's good to see you again."

"I just wan'ed to say hello 'cause you're my little sister's teacher and our parents are — well, I'm kinda like the father for my little brother and sister. So, I just wan'ed to say hi, and thank you." Victor shuffled his feet in the sand. "Paloma likes you, a lot, Ms. Bourne. I was sorry when you got hurt on the hike. I saw what that *puto* did. He ran into you and pushed you down, and didn't even say sorry. I'm glad you're okay, and I'm glad you're my little sister's teacher."

"Thank you, Victor. I'm really happy that Paloma's in my class. She's a wonderful student. I look forward to working with both of you."

Paloma broke free from Victor and wrapped her arms around Aurora. Johnny, the younger boy with a red hat like Rico's, shook his brother's hand off his shoulder, kicked the sand, and stomped away.

Victor turned to Father Francis. "Hey, Padre. I'll take the net up by the cans where they gonna collect all that *basura*."

He hefted the heavy net onto his shoulder and set off across the sand. Paloma limped down the beach to join her classmates.

Aurora turned to Father Francis. "So, Victor's raising his brother and sister?"

"The grandfather is legal guardian, but he speaks very little English, and doesn't read or write." Father Francis answered. "Victor is the one who's kept the family together. He's been the younger children's liaison with their teachers and the schools for years."

"May I ask where the parents are?"

"Their father is in Soledad for life. Heavy duty Norteño. Mom OD'd a year and a half ago. Victor was determined to keep his brother and sister together, out of foster care. He was just sixteen. Got off drugs, out of gang banging, got himself back in school. Even though he's been working full time, he's still managed to continue his education."

"That's a huge burden for a person his age."

"He's doing a great job. He'll be graduating from Oceanview Continuation High School this June and has a full scholarship to UCSC's Agroecology Program. He's been tapped by ALBA to join their Small Farmer Education Program. And he's already made connections with California Farm Link."

"Farm Link?"

"A new non-profit that provides farmers with the tools they need to lease and purchase land, access capital, and grow their business. I'm confident Victor will have his own organic, fair-labor farm one day."

Aurora wondered how much of Victor's success had to do with the priest's influence. "His little brother seems to be struggling," she said.

"Juanito is in a dark place."

Aurora nodded. It wasn't hard to recognize the signs of an at-risk adolescent. "Why does Paloma limp?"

"Birth defect."

In the blue-on-blue distance a gull flew toward Byrd River, an eerie cry trailing in its wake. They started walking again.

"Our school hasn't issued the annual confidential health reports yet, but it seems to me the rate of birth defects and other health issues in our district is rising," said Aurora.

"Any theories about what's going on?" The priest dropped a plastic bottle into his recycle bag.

"Lately, we've been wondering about the effects of pesticide exposure." Aurora told Father Francis about the events of the past weeks at Prudenciana: the CalGreen assembly, and the teachers' conversation in the lunchroom afterward. "Just about every teacher in the lunchroom confessed to be struggling with some sort of illness. Katie Cooper has made us aware of the fumigations going on in the strawberry fields around the school. It seems far-fetched, and I can't imagine how you could prove it, but we're starting to wonder if all the seemingly unrelated health issues at Prudenciana could be connected to pesticide exposure."

"I'm concerned about the pesticides too, Aurora. Not only their direct effect on human health, but also on the water quality in our creeks and rivers — in our watershed and on the fish."

Aurora met Father Francis' eyes. Something ancient looked back at her with a light both terrifying in its power and at the same time so pure, kind, and gentle it made her want to weep.

Whitewater from the incoming tide surged toward them. Aurora and the priest both abruptly sidestepped, and bumped into each other. He held her for a moment, lines creasing the corners of his eyes. His T-shirt smelled of fresh laundry and the ocean. The stark white of his shirtsleeves stretched tight around red-brown biceps, encircled by tattooed bands of swimming fish. Aurora's heart rocked to the pulse of the waves beating against the shore.

"Sorry," said Father Francis, releasing her and taking a step back.

"No, it was my fault. I'm truly not usually this clumsy."

They laughed and walked on, combing the beach in silence. A line of pelicans flew low over the water.

Father Francis stopped to pull a short length of yellow plastic rope out of the sand. "This should be useful for something." He coiled the rope and stuffed it into the back pocket of his jeans.

"One less thing destined for the Great Pacific Garbage Patch," said Aurora.

Father Francis shook his head. "Floating islands of plastic the size of Texas polluting our oceans."

"I've heard that some of it's decomposing into clouds of micro beads that fish are mistaking for edible plankton. They're calling the plastic plankton "mermaids' tears"."

"The human race needs to confront its plastic problem, soon," said Father Francis. "But I think it could be a great opportunity for innovation — an economic bonanza for whoever figures out how to reclaim all that material and remanufacture it into products we need."

They approached a group of Aurora's students, gathered around three dead seabirds tangled in a pile of seaweed.

"Ms. B! Why do you think they died?" Rico kicked at one of the birds. "Should we put it in the trash bag?"

"Remember what we talked about in class, Rico? Many of the things we find on the beach are natural. Natural things we respect, and leave alone, right?"

"Yeah, but maybe it ate a piece of plastic and got poisoned, or got covered with oil. It's all black."

"Black is the actual color of their feathers," said the priest. "These are Sooty Shearwaters. They died of natural causes. Death is as natural as life. It's all part of the journey."

Rico eyed the priest with suspicion.

"Rico, I'd like you to meet a friend of mine," said Aurora. "This is Father Francis. He's a priest at Our Lady of Help Church."

"You don' look like no priest."

"Well, Rico, things are not always as they appear to be," Father Francis winked.

"My teacher says that too." Rico glanced sideways at Ms. Bourne, then back at the priest.

Father Francis offered Rico his hand. "Pleased to meet you, Rico."

Rico sized up the priest a moment longer, then thrust out his hand and shook.

"So," Rico said, "how come these birds died, then?"

"Every year in late summer, the Shearwaters arrive in the Monterey Bay in enormous flocks," said Father Francis. "They're on a spectacular long-distance migration. They're flying from their breeding colony near New Zealand north to the Aleutian Islands, and they get very hungry. When they encounter the huge schools of anchovies in the bay, they go into a feeding frenzy. Some break their necks and drown."

Rico wrinkled his brow and studied the dead birds. "I hope I never get that hungry."

"Race you to the river," Melody shouted.

The children ran down the beach, Paloma limping behind the others.

Aurora and Father Francis caught up with the children at a rope fence cordoning off a wildlife closure area in the dunes.

"Stop! Stop!" A woman in uniform waved her hands.

Aurora recognized the warden, Kelli Cavanaugh, from the waterfall hike. Warden Cavanaugh stood in front of the wide-eyed children, her arms crossed over of her chest and a very stern look on her face.

"River, Melody, Paloma, Caleb, Rico. Did you forget what we learned in class?" asked Aurora.

"Oh," said River. "The Plovers?"

"Exactly," said Warden Cavanaugh. "Endangered Western Snowy Plovers. Hi, Aurora. Father Francis. Nice to see you both again." She turned to the children and pointed at the sand, sprinkled with bits of shells, dried seaweed, and pieces of driftwood. "Look there."

"Oh my gosh," River whispered. "It's so beautiful."

A tiny, fluffy bird the color of the sand — variegated white, tans, browns, and black — nested in a slight depression in the dune. The mother bird had pulled a few shells close, and camouflaged her nest with dried seaweed and bits of wood. Bird, nest, and eggs were nearly invisible, astonishingly beautiful, and fragile. As Aurora stared at the sand, several other nesting plovers came into focus the way stars first appear in the twilight. Some of Father Francis' young warriors, including Paloma's older brother, Victor, joined the group. They all hovered in awe before the tiny birds.

One of the plovers left her eggs and darted around, one wing dipping in the sand as if it were broken. "She's trying to lead us away from her nest," Kelli explained. "If we don't move away from the area now, she might keep doing this until she dies of exhaustion and her eggs get too cold to hatch."

Father Francis led the group out of the dunes. Aurora turned to follow, but Kelli stopped her. "Aurora, how are you doing? That was a bad fall you had at the creek."

"Thanks for asking. I mended pretty well."

Kelli nodded.

"Thank you so much for helping me that day, and also for being here," said Aurora. "Will the plovers be alright? I hope we didn't disturb them too badly."

"Sadly, these little birds are on the brink of extinction. This is one of the last viable plover nesting habitats on the coast. We have the closure ropes and signs up all summer, but on a high-use weekend like this, we need a warden on site, to explain the dune closure to people face-to-face. Thanks for helping raise awareness by bringing your students today."

Leaving Kelli at her station to defend the nesting plovers, Aurora hurried to catch up with her group.

The group had almost reached the river when they discovered a truck tire partly buried in the sand.

"Let's dig it out!"

While Aurora was watching the tire excavation, a slight movement in the dunes farther down the beach near the rivermouth caught her attention. Like a teacher on playground duty, she marched off to investigate.

She walked along the wet sand, then turned up into the dunes that insulated the exclusive gated Pelican Dunes Estates community above the dunes from the public beach below. She threaded her way through maze-like clefts between hills of sand that loomed over her head, until she was no longer able to see the ocean or her group.

Around the next bend, the narrow trail opened onto an illegal campsite. Aurora was shocked by the presence of three swarthy men squatting by a fire. They turned toward her in surprise.

Yellow bloodshot eyes with dilated pupils took her in. Rotten-toothed grins spread across the leathery, predatory faces. Aurora felt something slimy flow over her body.

The men's foul odor overwhelmed the wild fragrance of sea spray and coastal sage.

One of the men slowly stood. He gripped his cooking knife. His hands were black with dirt.

"*Hola, Chica,*" he leered. "*Venga aquî. Quiero comer tu panocha.*"

Another of the men made kissing sounds. A smear of grease glistened on his lips and chin. "*Quiero follarte,*" he sneered.

The third man pulled a stained blue cap down to shade his eyes and slowly rose to his feet. He put his hand on his crotch. *"Venga conmigo, coño. Quiero hacerte."*

The men hissed and grunted in mocking laughter.

Blue Cap rubbed his hand up and down his fly. His lizard tongue darted in and out through dry lips.

Aurora froze, skin tingling, pulse racing.

She didn't know what to do. If she screamed, she doubted anyone would hear her beyond the dunes, over the roar of the surf. If she ran, these men would surely catch her.

Time stood still as she stared at the three men, hyper-aware of a yellow crust lining the corners of Greasy Lip's mouth. She felt weirdly immobilized.

Suddenly, he lunged toward her. On pure instinct she turned to run. Greasy Lips grabbed her by the hair, dragged her toward him, and caught her in a strangling rear headlock. She gasped for breath and tried to pry his arm away from her neck. The man in the blue hat clawed and tore at her shorts, forcing them down below her hips.

She struggled, screamed, and kicked. Suddenly she landed a hard knee between Blue Hat's legs. He doubled over. She twisted in Greasy Lips headlock, tucking her chin into the crook of his elbow and grabbing his arm. He cursed at her in Spanish and tightened his hold. She worked her fingers into the space between his arm and her chin and gained some breathing room.

Blue Hat seemed to be reviving. She didn't have much time before he was on her again. She bent her knees, dropped her weight, and swung her foot back behind Greasy Lip's calf. He lost his balance, releasing his hold. She ran.

The man with the cooking knife rushed at her.

She scrambled backward, stumbled and fell, her hand coming down hard just inches from three plover eggs.

Seeming to appear out of nowhere, Victor Lopez loomed like a bear between her and her assailants. Victor had thrown off his baggy black sweatshirt. His sleeveless tank revealed the musculature of a body builder.

"*Ya basta. No chingues, putos. (That's enough. Don't mess with her.)*" Victor's clear male voice boomed over the dunes. He clenched a knife in his white-knuckled fist.

Aurora sprawled on the sand, hypnotized by the confrontation.

"*Y Qué? (What are you going to do about it?)*" The man with the blue hat taunted.

"Send you home to your mother, *paisa*. So you can fuck her again." Victor hefted his knife.

"*Rifamos, pinche cabrón. Bailamos.*" Blue Hat flicked open a switchblade. Aurora heard the click of the blade as if it were inside her head.

Someone was helping her up — Victor's angry little brother, Johnny.

A shadow like a large wild cat brushed by her. *Father Francis.*

She blinked. The man who'd been holding the cooking knife was on the ground, empty-handed, unconscious. Blood ran from his nose and mouth.

Victor and Blue Cap circled each other, knives carving the air in slow motion.

A high-pitched screech crazed the dome of sky. Aurora turned toward the sound. Mask-like and disembodied, a leathery face hung in the air, greasy lips twisted in a soul-piercing wail. An ornate broadsword fiercely stabbed up into the heavens, then arced down, slicing across the priest's chest. The priest pulled back like a Flamenco dancer, spun, and kicked the weapon out of Greasy Lip's hand.

In one smooth motion, Father Francis caught the blade as it rolled in the air, and hurled it into a distant dune. The steel sheathed up to its hilt in sand and Father Francis grabbed Greasy Lip's arm, twisting it hard behind the man's back.

Greasy Lips howled again — a haunting sound, barely human.

Father Francis forced him face down in the sand. With a knee in the attacker's back, he bound hands and feet with the yellow rope from his back pocket.

Victor held his side, doubled over and panting. Blood soaked through his shirt. A man lay on the dune at Victor's feet, unmoving.

Partially buried in the sand next to the unconscious body was a bloody blue cap.

"Johnny!" Father Francis commanded. A ragged slash split open the priest's white T-shirt. Bright blood arced across his chest and ran down his torso.

"Go get Ms. Cavanaugh, the game warden, *mi'ijo!* Tell her to radio dispatch for backup. Have them send a squad car and an ambulance around the back way, through the Pelican Dunes Estates. Be quick, and don't make a fuss about it. Take Ms. Bourne with you. Go!"

SWIMMING UPSTREAM

"What is the Northwest? Anywhere the salmon can get to."

— Timothy *Egan, A Year Without Rain*

"I doubt there is an area in the world that identifies itself with a species to the extent that the people and the landscape of the Pacific Northwest identify with the Salmon. The long-lasting marriage between the Salmon and the Northwest is made of the stuff of legends."

— Luisa Molinero, University of Alcalá, Madrid

20

T HE NEARLY SPENT MOON SHONE ON THE BLACK WATER of Moss
Landing Harbor. Red nightlights, reflected from boats and dock,
danced an eerie tarantella across rippling shadows. Wind waves pushed
and slapped the moored vessels. The sad, soft ping of halyard clips
betrayed a breeze sneaking down the dark channel with the changing tide.

Standing lookout at the bow of his dad's boat, Father Francis
Hilman shivered. He usually enjoyed fishing trips with his dad, but
this predawn, the darkness seemed to harbor something evil.

The sexual assault of Ms. Bourne weighed on his heart. He
couldn't shake a feeling of foreboding and dread.

Old Joe Hilman, at the helm of the *Maria Estrella,* navigated out
of the harbor, past murky shapes of sleeping otters and sea lions.
Father Francis pulled his watch cap over his ears, shoved his hands in
his jacket pockets, and leaned into the wind.

"This is spectacular, Frank."

The priest turned toward Charlie Rosa, who was hunkered down on a bench just outside the cabin, gripping a mug full of steaming coffee. Hopefully, Charlie would enjoy this — his first deep-sea fishing trip.

"Think you'll need that Dramamine, Charlie?"

"Naw. I'm feelin' okay, thanks. This is really something." Charlie gestured toward the East.

The rising sun hid behind cumulous clouds, casting strong shadows. Brilliant spears of light thrust through the spaces between clouds, setting the ocean afire. Pink, purple, gold, and orange splashed onto sky and water.

When the colors dissipated, the boat floated in an infinite field of luminous blue and white above and below. Old Joe idled the engine, stepped out of the cabin, and nodded to his son.

"My sonar's finding some good-sized fish about fifty feet down," said Old Joe. "How's about we set up the rods and troll along the edge of the canyon here. That way, we'll have our hands free to grab a little breakfast."

The skipper and his son set about rigging the rods for salmon fishing.

Charlie peered nervously over the rail of the boat. "Fifty feet is pretty deep."

"That's nothing," said Father Francis. "We're just at the edge of the Monterey Submarine Canyon. The bottom here is about two hundred fifty feet down."

Charlie gripped the rail tighter. His knuckles were white.

"Once we're well over the canyon," Old Joe winked, "it can get to a depth of twelve thousand feet, over two miles below the surface."

"Damn, that's deeper than the Grand Canyon!" said Charlie.

"That's right," said the priest, baiting another line. "The canyon's the reason we have so much life in the bay. Seasonal currents bring cold water upwelling from down deep, loaded with rich nutrients."

"I see you're using barbless hooks again, like we did on the creek," said Charlie.

"For salmon, always. Anything less than twenty-four inches, we'll release. And we look for tags on each fish we catch. If we find a tag, we report to Cal Fish and Wildlife. That's important data for the restoration project. If we hook a Coho of any size, we have to release it. It's the Chinook — King Salmon — that we're after today."

When the rods were baited and set, Old Joe led the way into the cabin. He pulled food out of a small fridge and various cabinets, and arranged breakfast on the boat's drop down table: fresh fruit, bagels, cream cheese, smoked salmon, orange juice, and a thermos of hot coffee. Charlie added his bag of donuts to the spread, and the men helped themselves.

"How's that knife wound on your chest healing up, son?" asked Old Joe.

"It was superficial, Dad. Just a scratch. That knife shouldn't have touched me, though. I'm out of practice. Haven't trained with a blade in quite a while."

"Your mother was worried."

"Honestly, I'm fine."

Old Joe patted his son on the shoulder. He picked up an apple, returned to the helm, and headed the boat along the edge of the canyon, toward open ocean.

The engine changed tone as their trolling speed increased. Father Francis leaned over the side and squinted into the sun. The crusty salt spray around his eyes cracked like dry fish skin. He rasped his thumb along his jaw, enjoying ocean's breath on his face, and watched the bait and flasher dance.

"Dad, kick it up another knot," he shouted above the noise of the engine and the water splashing against the vessel.

Satisfied with the trolling speed, Father Francis settled in the stern with Charlie. The sun was well up in the sky and the men had stripped down to T-shirts and jeans. Father Francis wrapped a bandana around his head to keep the sweat out of his eyes. The *Maria Estrella* rolled like a gently rocking cradle; water patted the hull. Fishing seabirds called and dove nearby.

"So, Charlie, were you able to question the men who attacked Ms. Bourne?"

Charlie adjusted his sunglasses. "I did a preliminary interrogation when we booked them, but they didn't give up much on the first go around. They were loaded on meth, cocaine, pot, tequila, who knows what else — too high to make any sense. We'll definitely be talking again once they've had time to detox."

"You'll be on the case then?"

"My lieutenant assigned me to be the lead investigator. I've assembled a solid inter-agency task force: the crime scene team that worked with us at the Corralitos Creek meth lab site, the Medical Examiner, a narc and gang enforcement specialist, and Warden Cavanaugh. FBI wanted in too — and INS, of course."

"Impressive. Any leads?"

Charlie shook his head. "I can't shake the feeling that there's a nexus between those three *pinches* in the Pelican Dunes who assaulted Ms. Bourne, the meth lab you and I found on the creek, and the Salvador Luna murder."

Father Francis raised an eyebrow. "Feels like quite a stretch."

"At this point, we're throwing the net wide," said Charlie. "We'll see what turns up."

"How can I help?"

"Glad you asked, Frank. You're already so involved with the local gangs and the whole situation, I'd like to formally bring you onto the team. I've talked with my lieutenant about deputizing you, and he's cleared it. What do you think?"

Father Francis gazed out to sea, as if listening for an answer.

Finally, he turned back to Charlie. "I accept. What do I do?"

"You'll have to come by the office sometime in the next few days to be formally sworn in, but for now just let me bring you up to date, then we can start tossing some ideas around."

"I'm listening."

"Hikers found a body partially eaten by a mountain lion not far from the meth camp. The M.E. confirms that our victim died before the cougar got him. Bled out from multiple stab wounds."

"I'm glad he wasn't eaten alive."

"Copy that. His wounds appear to match a blade we took from one of Ms. Bourne's assailants, possibly the same knife that cut you. DOJ is crosschecking blood samples on the knife against the cougar victim's DNA. I suspect we'll also find that some of the blood on the knife is yours. We'll need to get a swab from you into evidence."

"Of course. Makes sense. Have you identified the victim?"

"The lab confirmed that his DNA matches blood spatter we found at the meth camp. He didn't have a wallet or any I.D. on him, but Warden Cavanaugh followed his trail back to the camp. We think he might be the father of the baby found in the woods. We're still waiting for results on that."

"Do you have his name?"

"Yeah. It wasn't easy. His teeth were so destroyed by meth that dental records were impossible. But one of our best techs managed to get prints from what was left of his hands. He's in the system. Vince Reilly. A low life with a drug and petty theft record across five states."

"What about the baby?"

"Warden Cavanaugh located tracks that confirmed one of the little girls left camp carrying the baby and abandoned him in the woods where the dog found him."

"How's he doing now?"

"Doctors were concerned that, given where the baby came from, he could be addicted to meth, but he tested drug-free. He's out of ICU and prognosis is good."

"*Qué milagro.* And the girls?"

"DNA confirmed that the two girls whose stuff we found at the meth camp are twins, about ten years old. Definitely the baby's sisters."

"Did you get anything on the blood yet?"

"CSI identified blood at the camp from two different victims."

"The man eaten by the cougar and ...?"

"The baby's mother."

"The mother?"

"DNA confirms it. The blood is from a drug-free female, and genetic markers show a maternal relationship to the baby and the little girls. CSI found no baby bottles or formula at the scene, so we assume the baby had to be surviving on mother's milk."

"A nursing mother." Father Francis shook his head. "To keep herself drug-free in that environment would take tremendous determination. She must have loved her children very much. And then, to be violently separated from her baby ... That poor woman."

"Judging from the amount of blood she lost," said Charlie, "she was hurt pretty bad. Must have put up quite a fight."

"We need to find her." Father Francis gazed out to sea. "Where is she? And where are her daughters?"

"Sorry to say, *mi hermano*, at this point, they're in the wind."

A reel chattered and spun. Father Francis grabbed the bucking rod and lifted it out of its holder. He leaned forward and took in the slack, dropped the rod tip a foot, and sharply snapped it up. The fish tugged on the line. The hook was set.

Charlie pulled the other lines out of the water so they wouldn't tangle. The fish ran to the port and the skipper cut the engine.

Father Francis let the Chinook run. A dance of man and fish. Reeling in. Running back out. Under his breath, the priest spoke to the salmon. He could feel the fish growing tired. Still, it fought. Time melted away. The priest, the fish, the boat, the other men, the ocean itself — all floated suspended in a timeless, eternal blue.

"Now!"

In one motion, Father Francis pulled up on the line and Charlie slipped the net in front of the fish and lifted, trapping the salmon against the side of the boat. The Chinook thrashed, churning water.

Father Francis stripped off six more feet of line and secured his rod in the holder. The men hauled the shimmering fish into the boat.

Old Joe used a club to still the struggling King.

"Twenty-six pounds. What a beauty," said Father Francis.

"Good work with the net, Charlie," said Old Joe. "You're a fast learner."

The men hoisted the fish off the scale and slipped the catch into the ice-filled box.

"Radio chatter has a good bite on — over the deep canyon fishing grounds, at the Black Can Hole," said Old Joe. "What do you think about stowing the trolling gear and heading out there?"

"Sounds great, Dad. Let's go."

Once the gear was secured and they were underway, Old Joe opened the throttle and they sped toward open ocean.

As the boat bucked across the surface of the water, Charlie waved his hat overhead and cheered. "*Adelante, amigos!*"

21

TUESDAY, SEPTEMBER 6, 1998
Black Can Hole, Monterey Bay

O LD JOE SLOWED AND STEERED A STEADY COURSE for the deep
canyon fishing grounds, while Father Francis and Detective
Rosa sat at the stern, out of the wind, to continue their conversation.

"I've been thinking — you might be onto something with your
nexus theory," said Father Francis. "What else have you got that connects
the attack on Ms. Bourne with whatever happened at that meth hooch?"

Charlie took his notebook out of his pocket and thumbed through
the pages. "You're not gonna like this, Frank. In a backpack we took
from Ms. Bourne's attackers, we found a little girl's underpants, same
size and label as the kid's clothing from the meth camp."

Father Francis looked out to sea, crossed himself, and said
something under his breath.

"Here's something else, Charlie continued. "Shoe prints at the
meth camp match shoes worn by one of Ms. Bourne's assailants. That
puts at least one of the three men we have in custody at both crime

153

scenes. Also, one of the chapetes who assaulted Ms. Bourne had a pack of Deltas in his pocket. Delta cigarettes are hard to get here in the States, but popular in El Salvador. We found Delta butts at the meth camp, Pelican Dunes, and the laundromat where the Luna boy was murdered. The DOJ lab is running DNA on the butts from all three crime scenes."

Charlie turned a page. "Here's more connecting the incidents at Pajaro Dunes and Corralitos Creek: The Salvadoreños who attacked Ms. Bourne at the dunes had baggies of crystal meth in their possession. Some of the baggies contained bits of redwood duff that matched the material on the ground at Corralitos Creek, and the meth crystals in the baggies had the same chemical signature as meth recovered from equipment there."

Charlie turned several more pages. "Oh, and one of the chapetes we arrested at the dunes had a kerchief in his pocket with bloodstains on it. The DOJ lab is testing for a match with the blood found at the creek site."

"Sounds like you have solid evidence to make a case that Ms. Bourne's attackers are the same ones who stabbed the man at the Corralitos meth hooch."

"The evidence is stacking up. I think we're close to having enough to keep those *chapetes* locked away for a long time. But there are still plenty of questions hanging fire."

Charlie took off his ball cap and wiped the sweat off his forehead, then resettled his cap to better shade his eyes.

"What are the charges against Ms. Bourne's attackers at this point?" asked Father Francis.

"Assault with intent to rape, assault with a deadly weapon, and attempted murder. And of course, on top of the criminal charges, they're facing federal prosecution by INS for illegal immigration."

"Do you think they walked here all the way from El Salvador?"

"They confirmed it," said Charlie. "They hiked from El Salvador through Mexico along the Sierra Madre Mountains, crossed the border into Arizona somewhere near Agua Prieta, climbed through the Chiricahua Mountains, and then made it across the Sonoran Desert to California. From L.A., they followed the coast up here to Monterey."

"Why such a brutal route? I thought most of the illegal border crossings from Mexico into the western U.S. were made near San Diego or El Centro."

"That used to be the case, but now that they've tightened security along California's borders, more and more people are attempting to cross through Arizona, over desert mountains that were once believed to be nearly impenetrable. Arizona's national wilderness has so much illegal foot traffic at this point, it's not even safe to go into many of the parks."

"I've heard that parts of the Organ Pipe National Monument are closed to the public. That's the reason?"

"*Sí.* The *coyotes* bringing people across are armed and extremely dangerous," said Charlie. "Not the kind of people your average tourist wants to meet on a trail. And sex is part of the price they expect to be paid to guide refugees across the border, even after they've extracted the family's life savings. Married women, grandmas, little girls ... few escape the *coyotes'* rite of passage. I've seen the rape trees — trees in the desert with women's underwear hung on the branches like trophies."

"People have to be desperate to subject themselves to that kind of predation."

"Looking into the eyes of Ms. Bourne's attackers, *mi hermano,* it was hard to find any humanity left in them at all. I've got to say, I kind of felt sorry for them. That tortuous trek through the mountains and desert would be enough to break most men. And El Salvador — that country's been a terrifying place for the last two decades."

"I've seen it first-hand," said Father Francis. "When I was newly ordained, I traveled in Central America. I had the great honor to meet Archbishop Óscar Romero — champion of the poor and outspoken critic of injustice — a year before he was murdered inside his church in San Salvador while saying mass. It sickens me that the U.S. poured billions of dollars into that war to defeat peasant rebels fighting for justice, in order to maintain an oppressive regime that protects our business interests. We put military assault weapons into the hands of child soldiers. Priests, nuns, labor organizers, teachers, doctors, anyone trying to help the peasants were tortured and murdered. Over two million people fled the country."

"I was aware, back then, of some of what you're saying. But at the time, it wasn't reported much in the news," said Charlie.

"Who knows what those three men you have in custody may have lived through," said Father Francis.

"They seemed insane to me when I interrogated them," Charlie wrinkled his forehead. "PTSD for sure."

"Maybe there's an angle we're not seeing yet — something bigger going on."

"Something's changing. The routes people use to cross the border illegally have always been infested with gangsters trafficking drugs, arms, and humans," Charlie said. "The Mexican Sinaloa Cartel controlled trafficking for years, but the power structure is shifting."

"Who's in charge now? Who or what is pulling the strings?"

"According to the FBI, the Mara Salvatrucha has allied with the Sinaloa Cartel. Together, they now control most of the illegal traffic being smuggled over the border."

"I don't know much about the Mara Salvatrucha. Fill me in."

"While El Salvador's civil war was going on in the '80s, many Salvadorans were granted political asylum here in the U.S. A lot of them ended up in L.A., where they — and especially their children — were pressured and harassed by the Mexican Sureños, who felt that their turf was being invaded. The Salvadoreños formed their own gangs in self-defense. Mara Salvatrucha — also called Maras, Truchas, and MS-13 — was one of the first of the Salvadoran gangs to emerge. Young Maras did bad things and wound up in prison, where they developed more sophistication in terms of their illicit pursuits. Many eventually got deported, took their newly acquired American-style gang culture with them, recruited new members from their home villages, and came back to the U.S. armed to the teeth with civil war weapons."

"Weapons provided to El Salvador courtesy of the U.S." The priest rubbed his temples. "This is an international mess."

"A complete snafu. Imported American-style gangs, like MS-13, are now a major part of the social fabric of El Salvador, and spreading all over Latin America."

"So you think the *chapetes* who cut me could be affiliated with the Mara Salvatrucha?"

"Remember the gang tags we found around that tossed meth lab at the creek? I've been researching FBI photos of MS-13 tags, and they match. It appears that the Mara Salvatruchas have arrived in Central California, Padre."

"That's really bad news. Where do we go from here?"

"We've just got to keep asking questions and connecting the dots." Charlie took off his sunglasses and palmed his eyes.

"I have a bad feeling," said Father Francis, "the way children are involved in all of this."

"Me too. It would be helpful if we could locate a witness to at least one of the crimes."

"How can I assist with that?"

"Our Sureños here in the Monterey Bay are rivals of MS-13. Sureños will most likely be keeping a close watch on their new enemies; they'll probably know what's going down. It might be helpful to check in with your homies on the south side as soon as possible, Padre."

"I'll do that." Father Francis pulled his water bottle from the cooler and took a long drink.

Old Joe cut the engine and the *Maria Estrella* floated over the deep canyon fishing grounds known as Black Can Hole. Flat blue ocean reflected intense midday sun.

Father Francis tied a mooching slip rig and bit off the tag end of the nylon knot, relishing the salty taste in his mouth.

By three in the afternoon, the boat had caught its limit: two King Salmon per licensee. Father Francis and Charlie cleaned and gutted the fish and put them on ice.

"The flesh is so red," said Charlie.

"Feeding on krill gives the fish that color," Old Joe explained.

"Charlie," said Father Francis, "if it's alright with you, I'm going to take a third of our catch down to Corralitos Market. They'll smoke it for us. I'll bring you your share when it's ready."

An enormous, wing-shaped fin, black and striated, reached out of the water alongside the boat. The behemoth attached to the fin rolled slowly, exposing its huge belly and then its back. Righted, the beast snorted a blast of saltwater out of the blowhole on the back of its head.

"Humpback!" Father Francis grinned so hard he felt like his face was going to split.

The whale slapped the water with his fin, then rubbed against the side of the boat.

"Uh-oh. Is this a problem?" asked Charlie.

"Don't worry, Charlie. It's friendly behavior. Even though they were hunted in these waters to near extinction just a hundred years ago, this new generation has never known aggression from humans. They're starting to avoid us less. They seem to be playful by nature, and curious about us."

The whale tilted its head toward the men.

"I'd swear he just looked me straight in the eye," said Charlie.

"I've gotten that eye-to-eye myself. A little unnerving, isn't it?"

The Humpback circled the boat. It lifted its tail high into the air, lobbed the water, and dove.

Charlie stared at the slick whale footprint wavering over the water's surface. "Humpbacks are migrants, aren't they?"

"Right. We see humpback whales in Monterey Bay from late April to early December. Then, from December to May, the California grey whales migrate through here."

"Ironic." Charlie polished his sunglasses with his T-shirt. "Migration is so normal in the animal world, yet we criminalize it in humans."

About twenty feet from the boat, the humpback surged straight out of the sea with a great whooshing of waters, its whole body airborne, then landed on the surface of the water with a thundering clap and prodigious spray.

When the boat stopped rocking from the whale's wake, Father Francis and Charlie settled down on a bench in the stern and Old Joe set a course toward the harbor.

"When you think about it," said Charlie, "I guess we're all migrants."

"That's right," said Father Francis. "All life forms continually move around, adapting to changing conditions. Humans have been migrating over the face of the Earth, searching for food and shelter — for a better life for our young and ourselves — since our species began. I believe that the closer we humans come to appreciating — I mean really *feeling* — our kinship to all other beings, the closer we'll come to solving a lot of our problems."

22

TUESDAY AFTERNOON, SEPTEMBER 6, 1998
Prudenciana Faculty Room, Valle Verde

F INALLY, THE LAST BUS DROVE OFF. Aurora shuffled into the
teacher's room.

She slumped onto the old stained couch, elbows on knees, face in
hands. The room smelled of stale coffee, communal refrigerator
science experiments, and crushed crayons. She felt nauseous.

"Are you okay?"

Aurora opened her eyes. She recognized the dark chocolate legs
sprouting out of arty shoes, and the hem of a boldly colored skirt. She
didn't trust herself to answer. She shook her head and looked up into
the compassionate face of Nathena Hamilton.

"Not so good." Aurora's eyes welled with tears.

"Would you like to go into my office where we can talk in private?"

Aurora nodded. Nathena led her through a door off the teacher's
room into the counseling office and settled her on a comfortable couch.

"Now what's going on?" Nathena asked.

Aurora began to sob. Nathena sat next to her on the couch, put an arm around her, and rocked her as if she were a child. When the sobbing subsided, Nathena handed Aurora a box of tissues.

The whole story about the assault at Pelican Dunes poured out.

"I feel so pathetic," said Aurora. "A weak, helpless victim. If Father Francis and Victor hadn't come along, who knows what would have happened to me? How stupid could I be? It never occurred to me to hesitate before going into those dunes. Father Francis and Victor were both injured because of me."

"You're being pretty hard on yourself, Aurora." Nathena held Aurora's hands. "Weak? Pathetic? Stupid? A helpless victim? No. You are most certainly not any of those things. Where is your anger, your rage toward those men for what they did?"

"I was taught as a child that anger is a personality flaw — that I should take responsibility for what happens to me and never judge or blame others."

"That's a good rule of thumb to a point, but sometimes anger is justifiable, Aurora. Suppressing your feelings and blaming yourself is unhealthy. It seems to me that you're wrestling with some low self-esteem issues. Why is that, do you think?"

Aurora shook her head. "Don't know. I've always felt like I'm not quite normal, like I don't fit in, don't really belong to the human race the way other people do." Aurora couldn't believe she was confessing her secret feelings out loud. But she continued. "Maybe it has something to do with my parents' drinking problem, or that I'm well into my 30s, single, and don't have children. I just don't feel the same as other people."

"How about if you start by taking some deep breaths. That's right. Now, let's see if you can find poor little frightened Aurora — your 'inner child' — and let her know that everything is alright, that she's going to be fine."

"What do you mean?"

"Sometimes when we have a bad scare, a trauma, part of our self disassociates — kind of runs away. It seems to me that you've been psychically shattered by the experience you had with those men. With a little work, I think I can help you reintegrate, rebalance yourself. Would you like to try?"

Aurora nodded "yes". Her eyes still brimmed with tears.

The psychologist engaged Aurora in a process of conversation with the various parts of her adult self and inner child, followed by a series of positive self-affirmations. Aurora agreed she'd be more wary about walking into potentially dangerous situations. She promised she'd take a self-defense class for women, and finally attend that Al-Anon meeting for Adult Children of Alcoholics she'd been meaning to go to for years.

"Thank you, Nathena. I feel much better. There's something else that's been bothering me, though. Can I tell you? I'm afraid you'll think I'm crazy."

"Nothing you say to me will ever be judged."

"Okay." Aurora took a deep breath. "Ever since I was a child, I've — um, I've *seen* things, that other people don't see. Lately, I keep thinking I see Salvador Luna. I suppose it must be just a grief response thing. My brain's way of coping with his death. But he seems so real. Sometimes I feel that he needs something from me. I just don't know what to do for him."

Nathena took Aurora's hand. "I think it's more than a grief response, Aurora. This is my personal opinion, now, not a clinical assessment, but I've seen him too. It seems to me that he's not yet at rest. Often, in the case of violent death, a spirit can't pass into the light until justice is served and balance restored."

"You've seen him too? Is there something we can to do to help him?"

"Sometimes, our only role is to witness, to let the child know we see him and we care. I've experienced this before, in the death of children. School is often a place their spirits will haunt until they pass over. It may be that all we can do for Salvador at this time is open our hearts, send him love. Watch and listen. And pray."

23

THURSDAY, SEPTEMBER 15, 1998
Prudenciana Elementary Playground

"T HE WIND IS REALLY BLOWING THIS MORNING." Parent volunteer Beth Verdot pointed to the tall Monterey Pines swaying at the perimeter of the playground.

"Look there," said Destiny, her face lifted to the sky. The pair of golden eagles carved slow circles in the updrafts.

"They seem to be enjoying the wind," said Aurora.

"Golden eagles have been nesting in the Prudenciana pines ever since I went to school here." Destiny shaded her eyes to watch the soaring raptors. A sudden gust blew her hat off.

"Winnie the Pooh would call this a 'blustery day'," said Beth.

"Oh, no. Over there." Destiny gestured toward the recently fumigated strawberry field.

The wind had found its way under the plastic sheet covering the field. As the women watched, gusts worried the plastic until a corner came loose. It rose into the air, billowed, snapped, and fluttered.

A little girl ran up to the women with a nosebleed. Destiny stuffed a handful of tissues in the child's hand and helped her clean up, while Aurora wrote an office pass.

"There is really something wrong here," said Beth, once the nosebleed had been dispatched to the office. "I have a scratchy throat, a metallic taste on the back of my tongue, my eyes are watering, and my ears itch deep inside. I think whatever they're using on the fields is harming us."

"Welcome to the club," said Destiny.

"We're new to the area," Beth continued. "But I'm wondering why it hasn't occurred to all of you before now that the strawberry pesticides are making people sick."

"When I grew up here," said Destiny, "there weren't so many strawberry growers, and I don't remember them laying down all this plastic. I don't remember there being so much asthma and cancer, either."

"Most of the Prudenciana teachers know nothing about agriculture," said Aurora. "And teachers tend to be very isolated from other adults at work. We stay in our classrooms, and don't have time to interact much with each other, except over school business. Most of us deal with personal illness very privately. We're just starting to be aware of how many crazy health issues people are experiencing at Prudenciana, and realizing that all of it might be related to pesticides. Katie's helping us connect the dots."

"What happened to the girl who had the seizure? Is she going to be alright?" asked Destiny.

"They held her at the hospital a few days for observation," said Aurora. "She's back in school now, and seems stable, but all of the teachers are keeping an eye on her. Her doctor is still running tests, trying to figure out what's going on."

Beth shook her head. "I have a friend whose kids go to that new school across the county line in Monterey. It's surrounded by strawberry fields, too. Before the school was built, the district promised they would create a buffer zone between the strawberry fields and the school to help minimize pesticide exposure, but the buffer zone was never put in. The school health report shows a much higher than normal incidence of asthma, but the administration denies that there's any connection between pesticides and health. The parents are outraged. They just had a meeting about the dangers of using pesticides so close to the school and over a hundred and fifty people showed up."

"My kids and I get sick every fall when school starts," said Destiny. "Runny nose, sore throat, drippy, itchy eyes, cough, wheezing, dizzy. The doctors don't know what's the matter. They thought it might be pollen allergies, but none of the allergy medications work. They've run tests for Strep, and tried antibiotics, which don't do anything either, except give me yeast infections. The symptoms last for months, usually until about Thanksgiving or Christmas break, then clear up. But it always starts again in the early spring when the plastic is back on the fields. It's got to be connected to the pesticides. It's wearing me down."

"I'll tell you something else." Beth glanced over her shoulder. She lowered her voice. "I volunteer at the Valle Verde Community Hospital, in the oncology ward. You wouldn't believe what's going on. We're seeing young Mexican men who should be strong and healthy coming in from the fields weak and in pain. They're being diagnosed with a rare bone cancer. Not just one or two men, but a stream of them. And — this one really gets me — babies are being born to mothers who work in the fields with — well, not only with defects, but with cancer. Babies are actually being born with cancer, right here in Valle Verde."

"What can we do?" Aurora asked.

"Give me that agricultural commissioner's phone number, Ms. B," said Destiny. "I'm going to give him a call."

*   *   *

After lunch, Aurora took her students to the Life Lab garden to hunt for insects, signs of insect activity, and seeds. Each child had a clipboard with several sheets of drawing paper, a data sheet, a zip lock bag with drawing tools, and a magnifying glass on a yellow string.

Paloma, Dana, and Lizzie King examined seedpods under their hand lenses. Nikko and River sat together, cross-legged on the ground, drawing a praying mantis. Rico and Caleb hopped along the garden path like frogs.

Melody Anna Escobar stood amidst a brilliantly colored swale of native wildflowers, looking as if she'd just stepped out of a Diego Rivera painting. An Oaxacan peasant blouse with bright, hand-embroidered flowers along the bodice set off the child's olive-skinned face, framed by thick black braids. This morning, Melody had breezed flawlessly through a ninth-grade reading assessment, the music of her mother tongue singing through the English. Melody represented the crowning achievement of one of Prudenciana's most cherished educational goals: a fluent, high-functioning bilingual. Aurora was looking forward to meeting her parents.

Ben, Panchito, Steven, and Salvador Luna sat along the edge of a raised bed like birds on a wire, watching a group of girls stalk a butterfly.

Skinny little Alice sat in the sun, shivering, while she drew a flower.

Aurora rang her bell, and the students gathered in a circle to share what they had found on the hunt. When Alice's turn came, she shyly held up several remarkable drawings, like scientific illustrations out of a textbook, of plant parts, seeds, seedpods, flowers, and bees.

River and Nikko showed their drawings of a praying mantis. To Aurora's surprise, Alice whispered, "That's not right."

"Alice," said Aurora, "Would you be willing to explain what you mean?"

"The arms. They go this way." Alice put a fresh piece of paper on top of her clipboard and drew a flawless, detailed praying mantis. "And the head, it's shaped like this. It has big eyes, like this."

"Alice has a photographic memory!" Rico shouted.

*   *   *

PRUDENCIANA ELEMENTARY LIBRARY

The principal droned on. The monthly afternoon faculty meeting was almost over. The librarian was out sick again. With heavy eyelids, Aurora stared through the open door. Outside, plastic sheeting lay over the fields, shimmering in the Indian Summer sun.

"Final item on the agenda," said Principal Wagner. "The phone calls you have been making to the agricultural commissioner about the fumigation of the fields surrounding our school. Apparently, you've been encouraging parents to call him as well. This harassment must stop. Commissioner Grumond and I had a long conversation, and he informed me that he sent agricultural inspectors out here yesterday afternoon. They detected no trace of pesticide over the allowable limits. But they did find that the Monterey pines around the perimeter of the playground had a pollen release this week. Commissioner Grumond told me to assure you that what you are experiencing is simply pollen allergies. There is nothing to worry about. The fields surrounding the school are perfectly safe at all times, even during fumigation. We are concerned, however, that you all have a case of hysteria."

The principal paused and glared directly at Aurora.

"It is giving our school a bad name, and reflects badly on me, as your principal. The commissioner and I have therefore agreed that, from now on, no one from this school is to make any attempt to contact him. You are not to discuss pesticides with the parents. That topic is outside the bounds of what is educationally appropriate. From now on, if any of you have a concern about the pesticides in the fields near the school, you are to bring your concerns to me. I will decide whether or not there are sufficient grounds to bother the agricultural commissioner."

Aurora felt her face flush with frustration and anger.

Katie leaned over and whispered, "Did you know that the federal allowable limit for farmworkers' exposure to methyl bromide is significantly higher than it is for homeowners who get their houses fumigated for termites?"

"Oh, so homeowners are more sensitive to poison than farmworkers?" Aurora responded.

Katie rolled her eyes.

The meeting adjourned, and Tom Olsen stood. "All those who would like to stay may join us for a union meeting." The principal fixed a menacing scowl on Olsen, gathered up her papers, and stomped out.

All of the teachers stayed. When the principal was out of sight, someone closed the door.

"This is a violation of our civil rights!" Helen said.

167

"I agree. What an outrage," said Katie.

"So," said Harriet, "the agricultural commissioner is dismissing us as a bunch of hysterical nitwits?'"

"This is the United States of America, not some fascist dictatorship," said redheaded third grade teacher Corkie Duncan. "What about the Bill of Rights, our freedom of speech?"

Everyone started talking at once. After a few minutes, Tom called the meeting to order.

"It may be that ed code allows the principal to restrict what we say to parents on campus. And if the ag commissioner has said he doesn't want to hear from us, well … I need to talk to the union officers about this. Until I've been advised as to what California Education Code stipulates about the legalities and our rights, I can't say more. I'll contact the union this afternoon and get back to you all as soon as I have any information."

The teachers left the library shaking their heads in disbelief.

24

D URING LUNCH BREAK ON THE DAY AFTER the faculty meeting, Aurora stayed in her room to prepare her afternoon literature lesson: a Salmon and Trout Education activity that integrated Native American legend with art. A few minutes before the bell rang, Tom Olsen came by.

"I didn't see you in the lunchroom. I wanted to be sure to connect with everyone today about the union's response to the principal's gag order."

"Thanks, Tom. What did they say?"

"Our attorney determined that admin has the ed code behind them. So don't try to contact the ag commissioner, Aurora. And do not talk to parents about pesticides. And for God's sake, don't mention pesticides in your classroom."

The bell rang and Tom hurried away.

Feeling her outrage growing to a boil, Aurora took a deep breath, then let it go. She wanted to give one hundred percent of her best self to her students.

*   *   *

"This afternoon, boys and girls, I'm going to play a tape recording of a Native American legend from the Pacific Northwest, from the region that native people call Salmon Nation. As you listen, imagine seeing pictures of what you hear. When the story ends, you'll be using watercolors to illustrate your favorite scene."

Aurora especially loved this story and had shared it many times over the years with her students. She couldn't remember where this cassette tape had come from. After so many years of teaching, she'd accumulated boxes and boxes of wonderful resource materials. The handwritten label on this cassette, partially rubbed away by years of use, read, "Tape 1. Na...ator: Yáahl, a st..yteller from *Na...dayi Héen a Tay*, the Village on the R... Under... Riv.r." She pressed 'Play'.

*   *   *

Long ago in a village on the River near here lived a boy who was taller, stronger, and more handsome than any of the other children. But his heart was twisted and dark. The boy's mother made him a talisman for healing and protection — a powerful totem. She hung the medicine charm on a cord and placed it around his neck.

Other children feared this boy. He was a thief, a liar, a bully.

The Elders taught the villagers that when they took the bodies of the Salmon People from the River to eat, they must give back even the smallest bones to the River with Prayer and Gratitude. Otherwise, when the Salmon People returned to their home in *Naadaayi Héen a Tayee* — The Village on the River Under the River — and changed into their human shape, missing their bones, they would be horribly deformed. But the boy never gave back Salmon People's bones to the River. Instead of honoring the Salmon People with *Oma*, he poisoned the water and the land.

170

One day in the Month of First Rain, when the River swells and the Salmon People pass by, village children walked down to the River to swim. Respecting River's power, all the children swam close to shore. All except the boy with the twisted heart. He swam out to the middle of the River to show off.

A giant whirlpool caught him and spun him around, around, around, around and pulled him down, down, down, and down into the deep dark, black, without sound or light. Out of the dark, a gleaming blue spiral swirled toward him. Inside the spinning blue, a point of light opened like a flower and out emerged forms — silver and luminal.

Quicksilver Salmon People circled the boy.

"You will come with us," they said.

And they took the boy to *Naadaayi Héen a Tayee*, the Village on the River that Runs Underneath This River, where the Salmon People live.

When they arrived at their village, the People climbed out of their salmon skins and stood on two legs in human form.

They were kind to the boy. They gave him a new heart, and a new name. They called him Salmon Boy.

His new heart beat in beauty, and he wept for the pain he had caused in his village UpRiver.

Salmon Boy was taught the way of Ceremony — how to Sing, Dance, Pray, and Listen. He became an Impeccable Hunter, capable of caring for Mother Earth and her children with Gentleness, Respect and Love. He learned to plant, tend, build and mend, and to use the power of words, and of thought itself, never to wound, but only to move Spirit in the direction of Truth, Peace, and Compassion. He learned to see Light dancing through the golden threads of the Web of Existence that unite all beings.

When the Elders recognized that he was ready, they led him to the Healers' Lodge and initiated him into the most Secret Mysteries of the Ancient Ones. Salmon Boy's heart cracked open and the Source of All was revealed to him. He became a Great Healer, a Formless Warrior-Priest.

Many cycles spun on the Wheel.

One day, the Old Ones let it be known that it was time to return UpRiver. Salmon Boy and his People dressed in their fish skins and prepared for the Journey. They were not as many nor as mighty as they once had been, because the power of *Oma,* the spirit flowing to them from the people of the village UpRiver, no longer ran generous and clear.

As Salmon Boy swam past his old village, his mother stood by the shore holding her net. Salmon Boy swam into it.

His mother saw the totem shining around the fish's neck and she knew it was her son. The villagers helped her carry the heavy salmon back to her hut. She held the fish in her arms and rocked him and wept, prayed and sang, for eight days.

On the first day his mother held him, the head of a man pushed out of the fish's mouth. On the third day, the fish skin split and peeled back, revealing Salmon Boy's strong warrior shoulders, arms, and heart. Salmon Boy's mother rocked him, prayed and sang. On the eighth day, Salmon Boy knelt barefoot before his mother and father, in the perfect body of a man. He cried salty tears over their hands, kissed their feet, and begged forgiveness.

The People in the Village by the River saw Salmon Boy's Transformation and Celebrated his Return. He lived with them, as Teacher and Healer, for many Cycles. Salmon Boy helped his People remember the Old Ways and how to return the Water Blessings of *Oma,* making the People whole and complete once more.

In the ripeness of time, Salmon Boy dreamed the Call for him to Return to the Lodge at the Center of the Circle within the Circle.

On a clear day in the season when the creeks swell and Ceanothus flowers release their fragrance, everyone gathered by the River to say goodbye. With tears in their eyes, Salmon Boy and the villagers sang the Salmon People close to shore. The current was swift. A Shadow thrust its spear into Salmon Boy's heart. He fell into the River and was swept into the center. A whirlpool formed around him, and pulled him down, down, down, down.

When Salmon Boy returned to *Naadaayi Héen a Tayee,* his *Ña' táayaa,* was waiting for him there. He looked into her eyes and remembered that he had loved her forever.

He has journeyed to many worlds, where he is known and belovéd by many names. It is said that every few lifetimes, Salmon Boy returns UpRiver to a village by the River near here.

*　　*　　*

In the silent classroom, Aurora watched her students paint watercolor images from the story.

Sunlight filtered through breeze-blown bougainvillea outside the open window. Shadow bands rippled along the white walls of the classroom. Aurora felt as if she were underwater.

The gentle *ding* of the timer brought her out of her reverie.

"Time to clean up, boys and girls. Ten minutes until recess."

The students swished their brushes in a bucket of clean water in the sink, then set them in the brush holder. Neat bristles pointed straight up like a basket full of new fishing spears.

When the children had all left the room, their colorful illustrations rested like butterflies in the drying racks.

"Good," Aurora said out loud.

Then she sighed, her breath catching on that bittersweet loneliness, that quiet ache, which she was always trying to keep at bay.

Out of the corner of her eye, she sensed movement, and turned. Salvador Luna stood before her, holding a watercolor of a Native American warrior wearing a loincloth and grasping a fishing spear, his arms inked with tribal designs — patterns that were tattooed on her heart.

25

Stark Ranch, Valle Verde

FIVE PRIESTS GATHERED UNDER THE OAK TREES near the ranch's long barbeque grill. All five men wore black, with white clerical collars that proclaimed their vocation, and each had a whiskey glass in hand, as did the other men in the group.

Aurora studied the priests from her vantage point behind the crowd milling around the hors d'oeuvre table. She didn't admit to herself that she was hoping Father Francis would be one of them, until she spotted him.

Even from this distance, his power pulsed over her in waves. The way his black polished cotton shirtsleeves wrapped tight around his biceps made her want to wrap herself around him. Her eyes stroked down his forearms to large hands, and the long, expressive fingers holding his whiskey glass. Her inner editor rushed to suppress thoughts of what those fingers might do.

He rattled the ice in his glass, and brought the whiskey to his lips. Subtle. Sensual. The tendons in his neck tightened as he swallowed. She imagined touching his face, his lips, caressing the rough shadow along his jaw.

Her hands reached around his broad shoulders. She spread her fingers behind his neck and lifted his thick black braid. Her breasts lightly touched his shirt. The desire in his eyes flared through her. Slowly, she loosened his braid, breathing in his scent — smoke, sea salt, whiskey, musk of aroused male.

His arms tightened around her. His kiss was hard, urgent. Her lips parted. His hand slid over the curves of her back. He pulled her hips firmly against his. A stab of pleasure shuddered through her core.

Stop it! You'll probably go to hell for thinking thoughts like that about a priest! Never, ever read another romance novel.

Aurora turned her back on the priests. Feeling disoriented and angry with herself, she stomped off, and nearly bumped into another kind of man in black, a CIA-looking guy, like the ones who'd been at school during the pesticide talk.

"Excuse me," she said, brushing by him. He was as unresponsive as a rock.

Why had a man like that been at an elementary school assembly? Here, at a political fundraiser for a U.S. Congressman, his presence seemed more reasonable.

Aurora skulked in the shade and considered her surroundings on this beautiful, impressive ranch. Classic California country. On a stage under the oak trees, a bluegrass band played. Field rows made a "V" toward the purple hills of Mount Madonna. Horses grazed on distant pasture; a windmill turned slowly. Beyond, a fringe of willow and buckeye trees marked the riparian corridor of the Byrd River, meandering toward the sea.

People sat on hay bales and listened to the music. Some balanced plates of barbequed steak, garlic bread, and various kinds of salads on their laps.

Aurora snuck one more glance over her shoulder toward Father Francis. Partly obscured by barbeque smoke, he appeared to be deep in conversation with … that man from the pesticide assembly, Sean Stark! And oh-my-God — the creep from the waterfall hike. Billy Baker.

Aurora made her way to the bar, set up in front of a rustic barn. A collegiate-looking bartender poured wine for a dyed-blonde bombshell of a woman who leaned on the bar, twisting an enormous diamond ring on her finger and flirting with him.

"What can I get you?" The bartender smiled at Aurora. She surveyed the many wine bottles lined up on a table behind him. "We have a full bar, but if you're interested in wine, this is a good chance to taste some of the best of the Santa Cruz Mountains without having to spend the weekend driving winding roads. The best boutique vintners in the region all donated wine to this fundraiser."

Aurora wrinkled her forehead in indecision.

"Bargetto is always a great choice," said the bartender. "The Bargetto family has been producing outstanding hand-crafted wines in the Santa Cruz Mountains since 1933. May I pour you a taste?""

"I'm drinking the Bonny Doon *Ca' del Solo Albariño*," said Bombshell, smiling in Aurora's direction. "It's light and vibrant."

She swirled the wine, put her nose to the glass and drew in a long breath, savoring the bouquet.

"Lemon blossoms, white ginger and sage, citrus, green almond. Crystalline." She took another sip, closing her eyes. "Beautiful. I know you're supposed to pair red with steak, but on a hot, Indian Summer day like today, I like a crisp white with any meal."

"Sounds good. I'll try it. Thanks," said Aurora.

"We haven't met. My name is Malone."

"I'm Aurora. Nice to meet you."

"What do you do for work, Aurora?"

The blunt question, and the way Malone was checking out her jewelry and clothing, threw Aurora off balance. Had she been gauche to pair diamond earrings and her heirloom gold bangle with gaucho jeans? Was her red camisole too low cut? Aurora buttoned the middle button of her white blouse to cover her chest, shifted her sandaled feet in the oak leaf litter, and reached for her wine glass.

"I'm an elementary school teacher here in Valle Verde."

"A hundred dollars a plate is pretty stiff on a teacher's salary, isn't it?"

Aurora laughed. "Yes, but I'm a big supporter of Congressman Carson. He's a staunch defender of our Monterey Bay National Marine Sanctuary. He's beaten back the oil companies every time they've made a move to get leases for offshore oil drilling. I'd give just about anything to protect our coast from oil drilling, wouldn't you? I definitely want to see Carson re-elected. I love how accessible he is."

"We appreciate that about him, too." Malone's smile was enigmatic.

"I heard that President Clinton's new Secretary of Agriculture, Michael Fespy, is going to be here. I'm hoping to speak with him."

"That's him, over there." Malone gestured toward a scholarly looking black man with glasses and a moustache, in a suit and tie. A dozen more suits and ties crowded around Fespy like ants to a drop of honey.

"How about you?" Aurora turned back to Malone. "What do you do for work?"

"My husband, William, and I are farmers. We own the property on either side of Highway 1, on the Santa Cruz County side of the Byrd River. William's family has farmed that land for three generations. We grow strawberries."

Aurora's eyes got big. She held her tongue and sipped her wine.

"So, how did you find out about this event?" Malone asked.

"I've supported Congressman Carson before, so I'm on his mailing list. This is a beautiful ranch. I wonder who's actually hosting this fundraiser. Do you know?"

"Yes. The Monterey Bay Strawberry Growers Association. The ranch belongs to a friend of ours: Sean Stark," said Malone.

Aurora put her nose in her wine glass and inhaled deeply. She tried to keep her face neutral, and collect her thoughts while she sipped.

"I wonder what those priests are doing here?"

Malone eyed the group like a cat watching mice. "One of them is local — the gorgeous one who looks like an Indian. The others came out from the East Coast. I hear they're going to be speaking at an Agricultural Workers' Committee rally. Something to do with the fieldworkers' union vote."

Malone's diamond ring caught the light filtering through the oak trees, and scattered a rainbow into the apple-yellow wine she swirled in her glass.

"Well," said Aurora, "I think I'll go see about getting some food. Nice to meet you, Malone."

After filling her plate, Aurora sat on a hay bale to enjoy the music while she ate. She had the whole hay bale to herself and was using part of it as a table. The beef was tender, charred on the outside, medium rare inside, juicy, full of flavor. She didn't often indulge in red meat, and she was enjoying her meal immensely.

She watched for an opening with Fespy, waiting for the right moment to approach him. He was the country's first African-American Secretary of Agriculture, and he'd grown up in Mississippi during the Civil Rights Movement. He'd attended Harvard as an undergraduate, and had earned his doctorate in law from the prestigious Catholic Santa Clara University in Silicon Valley. Surely, with that background, he would understand the issues of rural agriculture and the plight of minority farmworkers. He was probably smart, hip to California's special ways, ethical, and sensitive to the rights and needs of the poor and people of color. Aurora looked forward to meeting this man. Another glance in his direction told her he was still surrounded by an impenetrable wall of suits.

She felt someone standing over her. The presence created a palpable pressure that took her breath away. She looked up. The priest smiled down at her, eyes twinkling.

"Ms. Bourne. Nice to see you again."

Aurora abandoned her empty plate on the hay bale and stood to face the man.

"Father Francis." She offered her hand. "Please, call me Aurora. I never got a chance to thank you for ... for helping me, again."

"Don't mention it." When the priest took her hand, a pained look crossed his face. Slowly, she slid her fingers out of his grasp.

She forced herself to make eye contact. It was like falling into a whirlpool. She almost lost her balance.

"I ... I'm so sorry for all the trouble I caused. It was stupid of me to walk into a situation like that, and endanger other people."

"You had no reason to expect any danger. Pelican Dunes is generally a safe place. Don't blame yourself."

"You were wounded. Are you alright?" Aurora asked.

"I'm fine. Just a superficial scratch. I heard you visited Victor in the hospital, and insisted on taking care of his medical bill. That was very generous of you."

"It was the least I could do, especially when I learned that the family doesn't have health insurance. You and Victor saved my life."

"I'm grateful that Victor and I happened to be there."

"Well, thank you again, Father." Aurora paused a moment, before her curiosity overcame her sense of propriety. "I have to say I'm a little surprised to see you here today. I didn't know priests got involved in politics."

"I'm playing host to some visiting colleagues from the East. I was, ah, *asked* to escort them here today."

"I noticed you were talking to Sean Stark from CalGreen earlier. He's the person I told you about, the man who came to our school for that strange pro-methyl bromide assembly."

"Stark is responsible for … *inviting* my colleagues out to California," said the priest. "There's a big *fresero* union vote coming up. Stark and his associates seem to think they're going to persuade us to speak at a rally in Valle Verde *against* the United Farm Workers."

The priest grinned, creasing the laugh lines at the corners of his eyes. "It's absurd, Aurora. They obviously didn't do their homework. We marched with Chavez when he was organizing the UFW, during the grape boycott. And participated in his Fast for Life in '88." The priest laughed out loud. "What brings you here?"

"I want to support Congressman Carson," she answered. "But I'm also hoping to get a word with Secretary of Agriculture Fespy. I want to remind him that, while the farmworkers here in California are growing food that feeds the world, their own children aren't getting enough to eat. That's unacceptable. And I want to ask him to stop granting strawberry growers exemptions to the methyl bromide phase-out that was mandated by the Montreal Protocol."

"Good luck with that. You have a just cause, but do you know who's throwing this shin-dig?"

"Yes, I just heard," said Aurora. "The Monterey Bay Strawberry Growers Association. But, this is a fundraiser for Congressman Carson. He has a great record on the environment. And, judging from Fespy's background, I assume he'll be sensitive to the needs of real people."

"I wouldn't be so sure about that. Look who's surrounding him. Those men control a huge amount of California's agricultural wealth. They're all worth millions."

"But it shouldn't be about wealth. The Secretary of Agriculture should be interested in what's best for the nation, for the people and for the Earth."

Father Francis looked at Aurora the way adults look at children who are too innocent to understand the ways of the world.

"Father!" one of the suits called to the priest. "Please. Join us."

"Excuse me, Aurora. Nice to see you again. Good luck with Fespy." The priest walked away, leaving Aurora dizzy and breathless.

She regained her equilibrium and returned to her vigil. Fespy was standing at the bar with only one other man. This was her chance.

Drawing closer, she overheard the man in the polyester blue suit say something to Fespy about cigars. "… after-party up at the house. Sean and I want you to try one of our Royal Habaños, with a glass of damn good brandy. I'm fond of the Hoyo de Monterey Regalos, myself. If you find you enjoy them, we'll be sure to ship you some."

Blue Suit's back was to her, blocking the Secretary of Agriculture from her view. Blue Suit was a big man. Aurora might as well have been invisible. But she could hear every word.

"By the way, at your hotel room tonight, you can expect a little, em, surprise guest. Just another token of our … appreciation. We're sure as hell glad you could make it out to our celebration, Mike. We want to make goddamn sure you enjoy yourself. Tomorrow, we'll drive you down to Pebble so you can try out your new clubs. Our illustrious governor, the Honorable Pat Wilton, plans to join us."

"Excuse me, Mr. Fespy?" Aurora spoke up. Blue suit's back went rigid, but he didn't move. Aurora walked around him, planting herself in front of the two tall men.

"Mr. Fespy? My name is Aurora Bourne. I'm a local teacher." Aurora put out her hand. Fespy took it with less than complete focus.

"Mr. Fespy, I'm sure you must be aware of the plight of farmworkers' children in this state. Although many of them labor in the fields along with their parents, a vast number of these children suffer from malnutrition. I'm sure you would agree that something should be done to correct this. I'm hoping that, as Secretary of Agriculture, you will be able to find a way to make a difference for these kids."

Aurora watched his face the way she watched the faces of her fourth graders when she was teaching a new concept. There was a problem here. What she'd said didn't appear to have registered. She sensed she didn't have much time.

"Also, Mr. Fespy, I am very concerned about methyl bromide." She thought both men jolted slightly, yet their faces revealed nothing. "I teach at a school here in Valle Verde that is surrounded by strawberry fields. We believe the methyl bromide is making our kids sick. I want to ask you to end the critical-use exemptions to the Montreal Protocol phase-out for methyl bromide, and help strawberry farmers transition to organic methods."

It seemed as if Fespy was trying to suppress the giggles.

"Mike, you haven't had a chance to eat yet. There's a steak over there on the barbeque calling your name. Shall we? Excuse us, Miss." Blue Suit's Sunsweet lapel pin flashed in the sun as he took Fespy by the elbow and escorted him away.

Incredulous, Aurora watched the men depart.

"Excuse me, Señorita?"

A young Mexican man in a white jacket offered a bowl of strawberry shortcake. "You like dasurt?"

She contemplated the offering. It looked wonderful — just like the kind her mother used to make. It smelled delicious, a quintessential summertime aroma.

She hesitated. There was no way these were organic berries, not at Sean Stark's home. Yet, everybody on the planet ate these berries. They were marketed globally and prized around the world. Could these berries really be bad for you, if so many people ate them? Aurora accepted the strawberry shortcake.

She went back to her hay bale to eat her dessert. It tasted as delicious as it looked and smelled. No wonder these picture-perfect strawberries were such a lucrative crop.

Was it feasible to grow commercially successful strawberries without pesticides? Aurora knew, from the many failures in her own backyard garden, that growing food organically without insect damage was extremely challenging. But was a pesticide-perfect strawberry worth the price that farmworkers and those who lived and worked near the fields paid with their health?

Sean Stark had claimed at the assembly that, without methyl bromide, the multi-billion-dollar California strawberry industry would suffer complete economic meltdown. Was that true? Who actually benefited from the strawberry profits? Did the strawberry industry really create jobs for a significant number of Californians, and produce income available to everyday people? Or was it only the wealthy growers and CEOs of the agricultural corporations, like Sean Stark, Blond Bombshell, and Blue Suit of Sunsweet, who benefited from the enormous strawberry profits?

Aurora thought about agricultural jobs as she scraped the juice and whipped cream off the sides of her strawberry shortcake bowl. It was a complicated business. Aurora realized how little she actually understood about agriculture. From now on, she should probably just follow her employer's orders — forget about trying to interfere where she didn't belong and concentrate on teaching. That's what she was trained to do — what she was getting paid for. All these big questions about how to best run the state's multibillion-dollar ag industry should be left to the experts. Whatever made her think she could make a difference?

She felt stuffed, and depressed about the way her meeting with the Secretary of Agriculture had gone. She sat on the ground, leaned back against her hay bale and let the music rock her. It was a very warm afternoon. Her eyes fluttered shut.

Salvador Luna stands in front of her, hand-in-hand with Alice. No, it's not exactly Alice; there are subtle differences. A large crystal teardrop hangs in the air between Aurora and the children. A monkey, like the ones in Frida Kahlo's paintings, clings to the little girl's shoulder. The girl's feet are bleeding. A wire dog cage with an open door floats next to the children. Sharks swim around the children's feet. Salvador reaches out his open hand, which holds an enormous red strawberry.

26

ON THE MORNING AFTER THE BARBEQUE FUNDRAISER for Congressman Carson, resident and visiting priests sat at a table in the large, sunny kitchen of the church rectory. All wore comfortable clothing, and had cups of freshly brewed coffee in hand. Several of the priests read sections of the Sunday papers. One had his nose in a book.

The table was set. Sourdough bread and crusty browned country potatoes warmed in the oven. Father Francis was cooking breakfast.

"Haven't had a chance to ask how your tour of the farmworkers' labor camp and the fields went." Father Francis turned the bacon sizzling in his pan.

"Deplorable working conditions," said the priest from St. Louis. "Sanitation is non-existent. Where there are any portable restrooms provided at all, they aren't maintained. In the fields, the bathrooms are far from the workers, and, for hours at a time, workers are not allowed to leave the strawberry picking."

"There is blatant harassment of women," another of the visiting priests chimed in. "Many women told us they'd been assaulted, even raped. They're fired if they complain."

"We saw clear child labor law violations. These people work twelve hours a day doing backbreaking stoop labor. They are denied water, even on the hottest days. We heard about a young woman who recently died from dehydration and heat exhaustion."

"Injuries and illness related to pesticide exposure are rampant, but the workers don't have access to health care. Anyone too hurt or sick to work gets fired."

"At best, they make about $8,500 a year, far below minimum wage. Who can live on that in the U.S.?"

"And sometimes the paychecks bounce."

"Living conditions are unspeakable," another of the visiting priests offered. "We saw people in the camp sleeping in shelters made of pesticide-contaminated plastic tarps from the fields. Three families camped under one lean-to, with no running water. And those who have a place in a camp consider themselves lucky."

The priest with the book took off his reading glasses and studied the faces of his companions. "We heard reports of some field workers sleeping under bushes by the river, and in caves. Caves, for God's sake. Is this America?"

"Chavez made gains back in the '70s, but things have been slipping since his death. Today's *freseros* need a strong, revitalized union."

"What did you think of the barbeque?" Father Francis sautéed organic onion, garlic, green and red bells, serrano chilies, and zucchini in his omelet pan.

"That man Stark cornered me," said the priest from Connecticut. "He told me he knew that I have political aspirations in the Church; that I want to go to Rome. He claimed he has influence and could make it happen if I would speak against the UFW at his rally. It was insulting."

Father Francis added fresh spinach to his pan, poured beaten eggs over the sauté and grated grainy, sharp cheddar over the mixture. Good smells filled the kitchen.

The priest who'd been reading closed his book. "Some character in a blue suit cornered me," he said. "Told me he knew that my mother needs an expensive operation my family can't afford. Offered to pay for everything if I would speak at their rally, tell the fieldworkers to choose the Agricultural Workers' Committee, not the United Farmworkers' Union. It was obscene. What's the matter with those people?"

"Seems as if we were all propositioned at some point during the barbeque, Frank. When we got back last night, we wrote a letter to the archdiocese. We've decided to leave early. We will definitely not be speaking at any rally. Do you think you can drive us to the airport this afternoon?"

"Anytime after the 11:00 mass," Father Francis replied. "Breakfast is ready, brothers. Come help yourself."

The priests filled their plates and sat down to enjoy their Sunday morning repast. After a simple shared prayer of thanksgiving, they ate companionably, without another word about the anti-UFW rally and temptations offered.

*   *   *

TUESDAY EVENING, SEPTEMBER 27, 1998
OUR LADY OF HELP CHURCH, VALLE VERDE

From his contemplative vantage point on the knoll behind the church, he recognized them, silhouetted though they were in the twilight. In silence, Father Francis continued his evening prayer as the Mayan family drew closer, trudging up the hill by the cemetery.

When they reached the top of the hill, he welcomed them, and invited them to accompany him into the rectory. The sitting room in the priests' living quarters was spacious, with old-fashioned over-stuffed chairs and couches, a Georgian mahogany secretary desk, Edwardian library and tea tables, wall-to-wall bookshelves, and a fireplace.

The priest settled his visitors on a comfortable couch and told them again, sincerely, how glad he was to see them.

"I'll be right back with some refreshments," he assured his guests.

In the kitchen, Father Francis went straight to the phone and dialed Charlie Rosa's number.

"Charlie. What a miracle that I reached you. The Mayan family whose daughter went missing from the fields just showed up here at the church. Yes, I'll do what I can to keep them here until you arrive ... You're sure this won't cause them any problems with immigration, right? Okay. See you in a few."

The priest returned to the sitting room with sandwiches, cookies, and coffee. A glass of milk for the little girl. The child ate her sandwich as if she were starving. The parents were more restrained, but clearly hungry. The baby slept, snuggled inside the mother's *rebozo*. The priest thought about what food he had in the kitchen that they could take with them.

"You've got shelter in a *fresero* camp nearby?" Father Francis spoke with his visitors in Spanish.

"There was no room for us there, Padre. We have not yet found lodging, but we have hope."

"Then where are you sleeping?"

The man and woman exchanged a glance, then the man spoke. "There is a small cave in the hills nearby. We can see the steeple of the Blessed Mother's church watching over us from there."

"And your daughter, Iztli, you have enrolled her in school?" asked the priest, noticing that the child carried a public school library book.

"*Sí*. She is in fourth grade at Prudenciana Elementary," answered the mother proudly.

"That's excellent." The priest turned to the child with the milk moustache. "How do you like school?" he asked.

"*¡Me gusta mucho!* I love it."

"And who is your teacher?"

"*Maestra* Cooper." Iztli's face lit up. "Our class is reading *Charlotte's Web,* and *Maestra* Cooper took us to the County Fair with *Señora* Bourne's class."

"Padre, we are very afraid about the vote that is coming," said the Mother. "There is talk in the fields about the Unz *Iniciativa*. They say that the vote would make it impossible for our daughter to go to school here in California. We came to *Los Estados Unidos* hoping for a better life for our children, Padre. But now we are afraid."

When Charlie Rosa arrived, both men pretended that Rosa's visit was just a coincidence. The detective, wearing casual street clothes, sipped his coffee and made small talk in Spanish until the Mayan family seemed relaxed.

"Have you made any progress finding your daughter?" asked the priest.

The man and woman stared grimly at their hands. A tear rolled down the mother's cheek.

"My friend Charlie here is a detective. He may be able to help you."

Both the man and woman went rigid, their eyes darting to one another.

"I promise you, nothing said here tonight will put you in danger of being deported. I urge you to talk with Detective Rosa, tell him what happened. He may be able to help you find your daughter."

In the silence that followed, Father Francis watched the woman's stoic face, a face carved in stone, erode and crumble. It was like watching an earthquake destroy Mount Rushmore.

The woman's shoulders shook. She sobbed. Her husband held her and rocked her, patting her back. The baby cradled between them wailed. After a while, the woman dried her tears. The infant hushed. And the parents began to talk about their missing daughter, Sacniete.

27

**SATURDAY AFTERNOON, OCTOBER 1, 1998
(ROSH HASHANAH)
UCSC Harvest Festival, Santa Cruz**

H E HAD A SPLIT SECOND TO GET OUT OF HER WAY, but he didn't.
A small sin.

When he caught her, the smell of her hair — *saltwater, honeysuckle, cinnamon, woman* ... Electricity ran through him. His pulse quickened. He tightened.

He inhaled another deep breath of her. She wriggled like a fish in his arms. Reluctantly, he released her.

Just a small sin?

"Oh, no! Father Francis! Not again. I'm so sorry! Are you okay? I wasn't watching where I was going. I was looking at those chickens. All the different colors and patterns on their feathers. Aren't they beautiful! The way the feathers turn iridescent in the sunlight. I'm surprised to see you here, by the way."

He laughed and jammed his fists in his pockets.

"Nice to see you again, Aurora. My housemates wanted to take the workshop on permaculture gardening. I'm glad we came. There's a lot going on here …" Before he could stop himself, his eyes raked her over from head to toe. "Even more than I expected."

"I didn't know priests had housemates, Father Francis."

He faced into the sun, squinting down at her. Wisps of golden hair made a halo around her face. He swallowed, and cleared his throat.

"We maintain a small transitional homeless shelter at Our Lady of Help. I work with the shelter residents in our garden, and sometimes in the kitchen when our cook, Mrs. Garcia, permits it."

"What a good idea to bring your, um, housemates. You're right. This event is amazing. I've learned so much today."

"Mind sharing the highlights?" He stepped to the side so he didn't have the sun in his eyes. She moved with him, and they faced one another, their toes nearly touching. He felt her heat run up his legs.

"I went on a medicinal and culinary herb walk earlier." Aurora's cheeks were flushed. "And I just came from a panel with Vandana Shiva and Winona LaDuke on sustaining biodiversity."

"I wanted to get to that panel, but it was my Saturday to hear confessions. What did I miss?"

"LaDuke's main message is that it's crucial for us to hold on to resilient food seeds that can adapt to climate change. We need to bring back the practice of saving seeds, instead of relying on BioGen's non-fertile GMO seeds."

Her eyes are infinite, and changeable, like the ocean when you're far at sea …

He felt a flush spread across his chest. *Snap out of it.*

He pulled two guavas out of his pocket and offered one to Aurora. "Speaking of preserving food diversity, I picked these up at the heritage fruit tree booth. They're wonderful. Care to try one?"

"Thanks," said Aurora. "I'll save it for later." She dropped the fruit in her fanny pack.

With his thumbs, Father Francis split open his guava. He scraped the bittersweet pulp out of its skin with his teeth. Juice ran down his arms.

Aurora blushed and her pupils expanded like black holes.

He pulled a kerchief out of his back pocket and wiped off the sticky juice. "What did Vandana Shiva have to say?"

"She says our current agricultural system alienates people from the Earth and each other. All humans on the planet need to reconnect with one another as members of Mother Earth's family. We need to reclaim control over what we eat and how it's produced if we're going to survive as a species. Shiva predicts that the fossil fuel era will soon collapse into chaos."

"I agree," said Father Francis. "Our industrial food system based on cheap oil is unsustainable. We need to adopt the agroecology model that the university farm here has developed: cooperative, resilient, just communities; equitable, environmentally sound, local food systems; and energy interdependence based on renewables."

"Yes, and water. Water's going to be the oil crisis of the twenty-first century. I've heard that in the Byrd Valley, agriculture is pumping so much water out of the aquifer, they've got saltwater intrusion."

Father Francis nodded.

Aurora glanced at her watch. "Two rounds of workshops left." She pulled a brochure out of her back pocket and opened it. "It's always so hard to choose. Which ones are you going to?"

Father Francis held a corner of the schedule so they could read it together. "Let's see." He ran his finger along the page. "I'm interested in this one for the second round."

"Open Space Alliance?" Aurora leaned in closer. His heart pounded in his ears —a tribal drum circle that almost drowned out Aurora's voice as she read. "A nonprofit formed by local citizens. We have already set aside more than 1,500 acres of wild coastal lands, redwood forest, and wetlands. Our current focus is protecting the agricultural lands of South County from strip mall and tract home development now threatening to pave over some of the most fertile soil on the planet."

"I've met the environmental attorney who's serving as legal counsel for the Alliance," said Father Francis. "Mrs. Petrakis, a Greek woman. She's tough-minded. Very effective."

Aurora took a step back and refolded the brochure. "So, at the same time that we need to radically transform agriculture in the Byrd Valley, we also need to save it? That's ironic."

"Aurora! We've been looking for you." With silver grey curls sprouting out from under the brim of her straw hat, a woman in a flower print dress threw her arms around Aurora. "I thought you'd be here. Corkie said she saw you earlier."

A young redheaded woman nodded and laughed, jiggling a baby on her back and a large pumpkin in her arms.

"Father Francis," said Aurora, "I'd like you to meet Ruth Redding and Corkie Duncan — colleagues from Prudenciana Elementary."

Ruth shook the priest's hand. "Yes, of course. I remember you from Salvador Luna's funeral, Father Francis. Such a tragedy."

"I've heard about all of the good work you do in the community," said Corkie. "It's an honor to meet you."

"Thank you. And you as well," said the priest. "I have great respect for you teachers."

Ruth smiled, then turned to Aurora. "Did you try that hand-pressed apple cider? And the pies. Oh, my! Oh, and I just met Corkie's brother. He's an organic strawberry grower, a very successful one! Isn't that fabulous!"

"Corkie, is your brother Jay Duncan, the pioneer in organic strawberry farming?" asked Aurora. "I heard him speak earlier today."

"Did he mention that he's helping to train a new generation of farm interns in his organic methods?" said Ruth. "What a revelation to talk with him."

"Thanks to him," said Aurora, "we know for a fact that there *are* economically feasible alternatives to methyl bromide. Organic agriculture is not a fantasy, or a communist plot, despite what the Valle Verde strawberry growers say."

Corkie frowned. "If you listen to them, you've got to believe organic agriculture can't be done on a commercial scale. But it can! It just has to be approached differently. My brother isn't a millionaire like some of the Valle Verde strawberry growers, but he makes a decent living for his family, he's fair to his workers, and he grows really good berries without poisoning the planet."

"I'm familiar with his work," said Father Francis. "His berries are a little smaller, but they taste better than the ones grown with pesticides."

"My brother says that big monoculture crops, like year-round strawberries, require so much artificial fertilizer, water, and pesticides they'll inevitably destroy our ecosystem."

"Exactly," said Ruth. "Jay's gone back to the traditional practice of rotating multiple crops and diversifying production over the seasons to care for the fertility of the soil. I've learned a lot about agriculture today."

"And he's collaborating with the agroecology department here on campus," said Corkie. "They're experimenting with natural soil fumigants like brassica plants."

"We're heading over to the Pesticide Action Network workshop next. PAN sent people from their headquarters in San Francisco to help us get organized here in Santa Cruz County." Ruth looked at her watch. "It's starting in a few minutes in the gatehouse."

"I was planning to go to that one myself," said Father Francis. "Shall we walk over together? Ms. Bourne told me about the pesticide situation at your school. I share your concerns. I've decided to make it a personal priority to help move forward the transition to sustainable organic farming in Valle Verde."

The foghorn blew. Father Francis shivered, an inexplicable chill. He gazed down the hillside of golden native coastal grasses, the land of his Ohlone ancestors, to the wide vista of the bay.

Silent white sailboats dotted the sea. The sky was cloudless, and Mediterranean blue. Far off on the horizon, a bank of fog loomed, waiting to roll back over the bay like a blanket pulled up in the chill of the night. The breeze carried a hint of a tropical storm far out at sea. The sun was coming in at that oblique angle that saturated everything, including her skin, in warm golden light, and signaled that fall had arrived in the Monterey Bay.

Aurora lifted her eyes to meet his. He fell in, adrift. Her hair shimmered like silk. He battled with an urge to touch it. He took a deep breath, a step back.

The foghorn sounded again, like a ram's horn *shofar*.

*   *   *

SUNDAY AFTERNOON, OCTOBER 2, 1998
OUR LADY OF HELP CHURCH

The priest chanted in Latin. Clouds of incense smoke rolled in the stained-glass morning light of the church. The pews of Our Lady of Help were full.

Yudas Medina posed with his *familia* on a bench near the back. On his right, Yudas' son, Antonio, sat stiff, thin, and straight in his new Sunday clothes. The little girl, younger than Antonio, perched in her pretty, flouncy dress at papa's left. The mother sank into the wooden bench as if she would like to become one with it, offering no resistance.

Across the aisle, closer to the front, huddled the dark skinned, poorly dressed Mayan family.

Señor Yudas Medina, *Jefe de Campo*, cast a poisonous glare into the backs of *los indios*. They were troublemakers. Just this week, a detective had come to see him during the workday about the missing daughter of these people. As if he had time to worry about such *problemas*.

Father Francis was offering the mass in Spanish today. Usually it was Father Ruiz. Maybe Padre Ruiz was ill. Yudas had bad feelings about this Father Francis. Rage boiled through his blood. He tried to calm his thoughts.

Of course, all priests serve God, and I love God more than anything. My faith is strong. But this Father Francis, he gives too much attention to los campesinos, *to the poor and low class. Your church is supposed to help lift you up. How is a man supposed to get ahead* en Los Estados Unidos *if he never leaves the barrio?*

Yudas watched clouds of incense roll in the stained-glass light. Well, Father Francis or no, starting next week, Yudas Medina, *Jefe de Campo*, would begin taking his family to the English language mass. *Sí*. It would be better for his children to hear the mass *en Inglés*. And it would give him an opportunity to worship with *los personas de mejor clase* — a higher class of people.

196

28

SUNDAY, OCTOBER 9, 1998
Baker Ranch, Valle Verde

M ALONE BAKER SOPPED UP THE REST OF HER MAPLE SYRUP with a last bite of blueberry pancake, then leaned back, and savored her dark pressed coffee.

The scent of chrysanthemums in a vase on the table mingled with aromas of cinnamon and maple. Sunlight drizzled through the beveled glass of the old farmhouse windows, splashing rainbows around the tabletop.

Malone's husband, Will, sat across from her, absorbed in the business section of the newspaper. The maid cleared away his empty plate, leaving him his unfinished glass of fresh squeezed orange juice. Will wrapped his fingers around the glass as he read.

Billy sat next to his father, indulging in a slice of pumpkin pie and a fried egg along with his pancakes, and reading the real estate section. He'd broken up with his latest "mistake", and had temporarily moved back home. Malone didn't mind. She loved having her only child close to her. She'd do anything to assure her baby's happiness. Maybe this time she'd finally be able to guide the boy into finding an appropriate mate. A smart young woman of quality, a good girl who'd love Billy and this land as much as she and William had; a girl who'd help Billy farm the property for years to come and make babies to pass the land on to.

Kitchen windows framed the orchard that surrounded the old Valle Verde ranch house. Leaves coming into their autumn colors rustled in the breeze. The apple trees were heavily laden. Hundreds of fire-orange fruits covered the persimmon trees.

Malone surveyed her kitchen with pleasure. Will had grown up in this house, and so had his father. His grandfather had built the place. And she'd come here as a young bride. The recent remodel had gone well. They'd updated all the wiring, lighting, plumbing, insulation, and cabinets, and added the most efficient and top-of-the-line appliances money could buy, but they'd still retained all the charm of the century-old ranch house.

Will turned the page of his newspaper, burrowing into the stock report. He was an astute businessman, no doubt about that. His decision to take out the heritage apple orchards and go into strawberries, being the first grower to adopt the new fumigation technology, had placed them at the top of the most lucrative ag industry in the country. Risky at the time, but it had turned out to be a brilliant move.

Will was tough and shrewd about money, but it wasn't money he loved. At heart, Will was a farmboy — her farmboy. A good man. He loved his family, and he loved this land he'd been born onto. The man actually still liked to get his hands dirty. It was her head for politics and networking that had earned them their place at the top of the California strawberry empire, not his. They made a great team.

As she watched her husband, Malone felt her body open. Remembering last night in their bedroom, her mouth turned up at the corners. Will wouldn't be needing any of that Viagra that had just come onto the market. Now that she thought of it, though, her generation of aging baby boomers was probably going to go crazy for anything that helped them keep it up as long as possible. Biotech was likely to go big. She'd ask her broker about it next time they talked.

Billy looked up from his real estate section. "How's the market doing today, Dad?"

"Bullish as hell," Will replied from behind his paper.

"I've been talking with some of the guys at the gym about stock trading, Dad. Day trading. Interesting stuff. I just bought a book about it."

Will put down his paper and looked his son directly in the eye.

"Stay away from that crap, Billy. Stock trading is just glorified gambling. Last thing we need in this family is a son with a gambling habit. Forget about day trading. You have a good job with CalGreen, an honest way to make a living, son. Stick with that, and you'll do fine."

"Real estate's going through the roof," Billy said, ignoring his father's comments. "The dot-com boomers in Silicon Valley are planning to turn Valle Verde into their bedroom community-by-the-bay. From what I hear, the town fathers are carving up the Valle Verde map in the back room, making sweetheart deals, getting into position to fill their pockets. Out-of-towners — hell, even international developers — are lined up at the door, their dicks in their hands, bankrolled to the max."

"Billy, don't talk like that," said Malone.

Billy ignored his mother. "Look at this," he pointed at an article in the paper. "LAFCO's approved development of that property on the north end of the Struve Slough, on Main. The Overlook Development, they call it." Billy laughed. "Ha. Overlooking what? That stagnant old swamp? What a joke. Light industry, commercial and residential. They even got a gas station approved, right on the edge of the slough. I never thought they'd get that one past the environmentalists. And there's going to be a fancy new hotel. Sounds like we're expecting visitors, with money to spend. They've even included some low-income housing in the deal — the tickler that lures our bleeding heart liberals, and gets them to swallow the fly. And of course, the developers are promising jobs, and revenue for the city. There's big money to be made in real estate, Dad. Now's the time to get into the game."

"Hmnph." William squinted at his son over the top of his newspaper. He finished his orange juice and burrowed back into the financial pages.

"There's also talk of a huge development on the ocean side of the highway. They'll have to slip that one past the Coastal Commission, but I hear there's plenty of high stakes money and politics in hand to get those ducks lined up. You could make a killing if you sold off some of this old ranch land, Dad. Developers would jump at the chance to add a piece of our land to their portfolios. Even twenty acres could net you millions right now."

Will looked over the top of his paper. "Told you already, Billy. I'm not interested. We're sitting on some of the most fertile and productive farmland on the planet, boy. This land is priceless. It would be a crime and a sin to pave it over."

Billy threw down the real estate section, picked up the sports pages, and left the table.

Malone helped herself to the front section of the paper and skimmed through the stories. On the third page, a photo caught her eye.

"Oh look, Willie. That teacher I met at Congressman Carson's fundraising barbeque is a local celebrity. The Monterey National Marine Sanctuary and Association of Monterey Bay Area Governments nominated her Teacher of the Year for her work with children and salmon restoration. Why can't Billy go out with a nice girl like this?"

"Hmnph," said William, not looking up.

Malone turned the page.

"Jesus, Mary, and Joseph!"

Will raised his head. "What's the matter?"

"Listen to this, Willie! 'A luxury yacht was found yesterday drifting out in the middle of the ocean, in an area they call the Great Mid-Pacific Gyre. NOAA climate change researchers, who made the discovery, found pieces on the deck of an adult male body, desiccated from weeks of baking in the sun. A Great White Shark's tooth was embedded in the cervical spine of the torso. In a freakish, nearly unprecedented attack, the Great White apparently leapt on board the yacht and devoured the skipper-owner.'"

"Christ Almighty. Never heard of anything like that before."

"It says that only one body was found, but two different blood types were identified on the deck and in the cabin of the unmanned yacht. 'According to the ship's log, the victim, whose name is being withheld pending further investigation, sailed solo out of Moss

Landing Harbor in mid-August. The vessel's prior port of call was a private mooring in Pebble Beach.'"

Malone put the newspaper down and took her husband's hand, "Willie, I think this could be one of the people we met at Pebble! The man who spilled his martini. He talked about his yacht, about how he was planning to spend some time alone at sea after the Pebble Beach gathering. Paul Cooke, as I recall."

"I remember him. A real smooth dresser. Shifty eyes. He drank a lot. I thought the guy might be queer. Didn't like him much. Hell of a way to go, though. Hell of a thing. Hmnph." Will put his nose back in his paper.

"I just can't imagine. A Great White Shark. How strange …"

Malone shivered.

29

MONDAY, OCTOBER 10, 1998
(Columbus Day)
Prudenciana Elementary, Valle Verde

AURORA STOOD IN THE CENTER OF THE PLAYGROUND on recess duty with the usual two volunteer mothers, wrestling with herself about courage and academic integrity. She'd decided not to even mention Columbus Day to her students today.

But if we submit to random censorship and the rewriting of history, the next thing we know, they'll be burning books.

"Did you notice the plastic tarp on the field down the street when you drove in this morning?" asked Beth Verdot, her baby asleep in the carrier on her back.

"I sure did," said Destiny. "And I saw kids waiting at the bus stop right at the edge of the plastic. Some of the children were sitting on it, poking it with sticks, and sticking their fingers into holes."

"This isn't right," said Beth.

"I phoned the ag commissioner as soon as I got to school this morning," said Destiny.

203

"Didn't you hear?" asked Aurora. "We aren't allowed to contact the ag commissioner any more."

"What are you talking about?"

"At our last faculty meeting, the principal told us the ag commissioner felt we were harassing him. Now only the principal is allowed to contact him."

"He's a public employee. It's his job to respond to our concerns. I'll contact him if I want to. It's my right," said Destiny.

"We thought so too, but our union rep checked it out with the union's legal counsel. They said the administration can do that."

"Well, I don't care what your principal said," replied Beth. "She doesn't have any authority over me. This is a free country. I'm calling the ag commissioner about that torn plastic at the bus stop as soon as recess is over."

"Screaming!"

"It's coming from the play structure in the sand box!"

The three women went running.

A crowd of shrieking children made a wall Aurora couldn't see through. She pushed her way into the writhing ball of kids to find Rico mounted on top of a boy kicking and struggling for breath, with his face smashed into the sand.

Aurora lifted Rico off. She helped the beaten boy stand up, brushed away the sand, and gave him a once-over. His lip was split and blood ran from his nose.

Angry tears welled in Rico's eyes. He puffed out his chest, clenched his fists, wrinkled his red face, and gasped like a distressed pug puppy.

Speechless, Aurora stared down at Rico. The bell rang.

"We'll take them both up to the office," said Beth. Her baby was crying. She put an arm around the injured boy.

Destiny took Rico by the collar and said, "March."

*   *   *

VALLE VERDE STRAWBERRY FIELD

Can't breathe. Too hot.

Sacniete wasn't sure how long she'd been in the van.

She pushed her tongue out, touching rough cloth, and gagged. Nostrils flaring, she struggled to inhale quick desperate breaths.

So *thirsty.*

She tried to swallow but couldn't. Panic shook her.

Rills of sweat ran down her neck onto her breasts, stinging open scratches and bite wounds.

Pain. Terrible pain everywhere. Ooooh. Especially down there.

She blinked, trying to see.

Too dark.

Her head pounded. *Spinning.*

She fought to keep down waves of nausea and vertigo. Sharp knives slashed through her chest. Her heart boomed and roared in her ears.

The hump of clothes piled against her arm stirred, and moaned.

My friend, Cecelia.

Sacniete held her breath; listened.

It's quiet. Where's that other woman? The white lady who cries all the time for her baby and her little girls? They said they'd take her to Mexico if she didn't shut up.

She must be gone. Will she ever see her kids again? Will I ever see my mama?

Tears rolled down her cheek.

My arm's asleep. Need to turn over.

In the dark, Sacniete contracted her muscles to roll over. Pins and needles prickled across her arm.

Can't move! They tied me again.

Panic boiled through her. *Please God don't let them take me to Mexico.*

Her bladder released. The warmth of the urine spread over her groin; the white-hot sting singed her abraded genitals.

So cold.

30

MONDAY, OCTOBER 17, 1998
Parent Teacher Conferences
Prudenciana Elementary

"I APOLOGIZE FOR BEING SO DRESSED UP." The woman was as sophisticated and urbane as a New York executive, her tightly sculpted body clothed in a superbly fitting, expensive pinstriped suit. Her silky dark hair shone in an immaculate bob that curved gracefully around her face and swung in an elegant line above her shoulders.

"I've just come from a pediatric conference in San Francisco. I'm sorry my husband can't be here today. He's in England on business."

"I'm glad you could make it, Dr. Escobar. I see that your family is new to our school district. I've observed that your daughter Melody is a fluent bilingual. Do you speak Spanish as well?"

Dr. Anna Escobar tossed back her head slightly as she laughed. It was natural, unaffected laughter. "I absolutely speak Spanish," she said, without a touch of an accent. "Spanish is my first language. I was born and raised in a small rural village near Mérida. My parents still don't speak a word of English."

"How old were you when you came to the US?"

"When I was five, my father forded the Colorado River with me on his shoulders. I'll never forget how frightened I was. One false step and the river would have swept us away. Every step of the way, he kept saying, 'Never go back. Never give up. Keep going forward. Always keep going forward.'"

Aurora's jaw dropped open. This woman broke all the stereotypes of an "illegal immigrant". "How ... how did you ...?"

"How did I get from there to being an MD delivering professional papers at an international pediatric health conference in San Francisco?" Dr. Escobar's eyes shone. "Since you're a teacher, it's probably a story you should hear." She glanced at her watch. "Shall I tell you?"

"Yes, please."

"Well, even as a small child, I was painfully aware of how much my parents had sacrificed to bring my sister and me to the US, and of the importance my parents attached to a good education. But there were no bilingual classes in the school, and I still wasn't speaking or reading English by third grade. One afternoon at the beginning of third grade, I stayed after school to talk to the teacher. I tried to explain, in my broken English, that I wanted to learn to read. I wanted to *learn*. The Holy Mother herself must have been watching over me that day, because the dear teacher invited me to stay after school every day for one-on-one tutoring. With personal attention, I learned quickly. By Christmas, I was speaking English and reading fluently. By the end of the year, I was reading at grade level in English, and I was ahead of my grade in math. I've always heard my father's voice in my head, saying 'Keep going forward.' I graduated from high school with highest honors and was class valedictorian. I got a full ride to Stanford for pre-med, graduated *magna cum laude*, and was awarded a graduate fellowship to Johns Hopkins. No one in my family before me had ever been to college. If not for that third grade teacher, I would probably have never graduated from eighth grade. She retired last year. I still visit her when I can."

Aurora was crying. "Sorry," she said, drying her eyes. "I guess I never really realized what a difference one teacher can make."

"Never doubt it for a minute," said Dr. Escobar. Her eyes held Aurora's.

"What was your paper about, the one you presented today at the conference?"

"The health issues of immigrants — particularly children of migrant farmworkers. The paper I delivered today was based on my book. And on that note, I do have a health-related concern I wanted to discuss with you today."

"Is Melody unwell?"

"Not at all. And we want to keep it that way. I've noticed the constant fumigations around the campus since school started in August. This pesticide exposure concerns me."

"My colleagues and I, and other parents, share you concerns, but we aren't sure what to do. Parents are organizing. Here's a contact number for our group. We've tried working with the ag commissioner, but he told our principal he doesn't want us to bother him anymore."

"So you are aware of health issues here at Prudenciana that may be pesticide-related?"

"We think so, but we don't know how to prove that the symptoms we're seeing are actually caused by pesticide exposure. The ag commissioner and the school administrators tell us there's no data to support our fears."

"Oh, but there is data. Just read my book. I'll make sure you get a copy. Many studies both in the US and in Europe have verified statistically significant correlation between pesticide exposure and disease. Pesticide exposure is particularly dangerous to young children, whose bodies are still developing."

"The thing is, there are so many different symptoms," said Aurora. "It seems crazy to claim they could all be related to pesticide exposure."

"Not necessarily. Remember, pesticides are poison. Multiple pesticides are used on these fields, each with a specific target, including the endocrine, immune, neurological, respiratory, and reproductive systems. Many of the chemicals were developed as weapons of chemical warfare. The endocrine disruptors are especially dangerous to children because the endocrine system regulates and coordinates every aspect of the body's development: formation of the brain's social-emotional functions as well as the intellect, determination of height, insulin production, and development of the reproductive system."

"We should finish our conference about Melody's school work today," said Aurora. "But I do want to talk with you further at another time about this pesticide situation, Dr. Escobar. I look forward to reading your book." Aurora opened Melody's student folder. "Let me show you some of the remarkable work your daughter's done so far this year. Melody tells me she wants to be an anthropologist when she grows up."

*   *   *

Rico's grandma, Mrs. Perez, faced Aurora from the other side of her round reading table. They were going over the suspension letter Rico's grandma had received from the principal.

"I don't understand it," said Aurora. "He's improved so much, both academically and in terms of his social skills. Why the meltdown on the playground today?"

"I'm sorry this happened, Miss Bourne, but I think I know why. Rico's father is in prison, in Soledad. I was planning to take Rico to visit his father this coming weekend, but we got a phone call yesterday letting us know that my son got into a fight and lost his visiting privileges for the month."

"That would certainly explain today's behavior. Does Rico's father have gang connections, by any chance?"

"Yes. It breaks my heart to say it."

"I have a thought, Mrs. Perez. Do you remember the priest who was at Pelican Dunes with a group of teenagers for the Beach Clean-up Day?" Aurora suppressed a shiver as she recalled that day.

"Yes, I do remember someone pointing him out to me. But he must have left before our picnic. I didn't meet him."

"That was Father Francis from Our Lady of Help Church. He' s doing very effective gang intervention and prevention in the community. He generally works with older kids, but he did meet Rico that day at the beach, and Rico seemed to connect with him. Father Francis may be able to help your grandson stay out of the gangs and stay on track in school."

"Thank you. I'll go see him." Señora Perez shook her head. "My grandson has always had trouble getting along. And he can't sit still. We've talked to the doctor. He says maybe Rico should take medicine."

"Before you put him on medication, I'd like to go ahead with a referral to our Special Services Program, with your permission, Mrs. Perez. Our school psychologist and Special Services Team can evaluate Rico, and then we can determine together how to best serve him."

"Yes, please. I've been asking the school for that ever since kindergarten, but teachers are always too busy to do the paperwork. *Gracias*, Ms. Bourne."

"Let me show you Rico's current math and reading scores, and his writing samples. The growth in just two and a half months is exciting. He's very bright. But I do agree that his social-emotional development is problematic. Not to alarm you, but that may be a sign of mild autism. Do you mind if I ask, was he by any chance exposed to pesticides *in utero*?"

"*Sí*. His mother was working in the fields when she was pregnant."

31

FRIDAY, OCTOBER 21, 1998
Downtown Valle Verde

DETECTIVE SERGEANT CHARLIE ROSA TURNED SOUTHEAST on
Main and cruised through the center of town, past Valle Verde's
historic Mexican colonial park plaza.

Valle Verde was a funny city. There'd been a lot of changes in this
town since he'd graduated from Valle Verde High about twenty years ago.
Look one direction and you might as well be in Mexico. Turn your head
another direction, or drive another half block, and you had Anglo yuppies,
gentrified *shiatsu* massage, and fancy cappuccino shops in your face.

Charlie maneuvered his unmarked black '96 Mustang GT
through downtown traffic and continued southeast toward the river.

He glanced at the white paper bag next to his holstered service
weapon on the passenger seat and thought about eating that last jelly
donut. He decided against it. Didn't want to chance spilling red jelly
on his clean pressed slacks or his nice sports shirt. Instead, he popped
a stick of gum in his mouth.

Proud of you, boy. You've sworn off. Whiskey and cigarettes for life. Women for a year. Twice burned. Need some distance, recovery time. Still eight months to go on the year. Someday ... maybe I'll meet a nice lady ... Aye, angelita. Such a pretty schoolteacher ... Down, boy. Don't go there. Thank you, Holy Mother, that she wasn't raped.

Charlie blinked hard, and took a long, deep breath.

Focus on the Luna case.

Rosa cruised down Main past the ornate old Wells Fargo bank building. An interesting building, he'd always thought, constructed in the '30s WPA era. Somehow, it had survived the '89 quake. Valle Verde had done a great job of rebuilding after that devastating earthquake — better than the rich *anglo* city of Santa Cruz.

Charlie passed women pushing baby carriages, men wearing cowboy boots, silver belt buckles, and sombreros, and a couple of seedy bars where the police were frequently summoned. He stopped at the light on Second Street, then eased by one of his favorite *taquerias.*

As he approached the river, traffic thinned. Here, mostly *campesinos* and *paisas* owned the street.

Next to Los Venenos Night Club was the laundromat where the Luna boy had been shot.

Finally, he'd gotten something back from ballistics. Striation marks on the bullet proved the murder weapon was a FN P35, Browning Hi Power handgun. Single-action, 9mm semi-automatic. Same type of pistol furnished by the U.S. to Salvadorian military. The Luna murder weapon had been smuggled in from El Salvador.

Rosa took the Main Street Bridge over Byrd River. The river was just a stagnant trickle at this time of year, its banks overgrown with vegetation where homeless and *pandilleros* could hide.

*   *   *

PAJARO *BARRIO,* VALLE VERDE

On the other side of the bridge, in the unincorporated *barrio* known as *Pajaro* — the poorest of the poor side of town — *campesinos* and *freseros* crowded together in little shacks along the river, several families more often than not sharing one small *casita*.

Detective Rosa's unmarked black 'Stang rolled passed the gas station, the Mercado de Carnitas butcher shop, a tattoo parlor, Inez Auto Parts, and a wrecking yard.

Graffiti covered every building.

The walls are the gang newspapers. Tags are a language, if you know how to read them. Specific from gang to gang, place to place, and constantly changing.

Rosa noticed some new tags. *Salvadorian Pride. MS-13.*

Not good.

Shop windows were broken and boarded up with plywood. Trash piled against the curbs and blew down the street.

He turned east onto San Juan Road, which ran along the edge of the riverside housing tract. Then he hooked another left up Gonda Street, and took it slow as he threaded around the wooden shanties by the river.

Paint peeled off weathered siding that was once brightly colored. Dogs, junk cars, men leaning on stacked crates drinking out of brown paper bags, broken glass, hanks of rusting barbed wire, hub caps, piled up truck tires, more graffiti. Here and there, red, yellow, orange and purple flowers bloomed in improbable containers. There was a spicy feel to the neighborhood. It was full of noise, piss stink, rotting garbage, laundry flapping on makeshift lines, good cooking smells, music, babies crying, kids shouting, life.

*   *   *

Charlie sat at the Formica-covered table in the tidy little kitchen. Ristras, strings of dried chilies, hung from the kitchen ceiling. On the wall, a framed print of the crucified Jesus blessed the room. A pot of pinto beans simmered on a back burner of the old gas stove. The aroma of the bubbling *frijoles* reminded Charlie of his childhood home. A baby cried in a back room. Somewhere in the house, a TV was on.

A small, plump, grey-haired woman wearing a flowered print dress and a white apron sat across the table from Charlie. She clutched a rosary.

Both Detective Rosa and Señora Ramirez spoke in Spanish. As she spoke, the grandmother gulped back sobs, wiping away tears with a corner of her apron.

"I didn't want to tell anyone what I saw, Agent Rosa. I'm afraid they will kill me if they find out I told. Maybe they will murder everyone in my family."

Sniffling back tears, the grandmother fingered her rosary. Her lips moved silently. Detective Rosa waited.

"I know to remain silent, it was a sin." Old, dark eyes searched Rosa's face. "When I went to confession and told the priest what I saw, he said I must go to the police. He gave me your name. Sorry I waited so long to call you. But, Agent Rosa, I am afraid."

"You did the right thing by phoning me, Señora Ramirez," Detective Rosa said gently. "Can we start at the beginning? Please describe what you saw."

The woman fingered her rosary a moment more.

"After dinner, my grandson helped me put my family's laundry in our car. Then I drove across the river to the laundromat."

"What time was this, do you remember, Señora Ramirez?"

"It was starting to get dark. Maybe, eight o'clock. I parked on the street, at the side of the laundromat. I could see in through the big windows. Only one small boy was inside. Good, I think. Because then I will have enough machines to do everything before they close. I open my purse to count my quarters. I do not want to have my purse in the laundromat. I always hide it in the car, and lock it. The car has tinted windows so no one can see in."

The detective nodded.

"While I counted my quarters, I saw two men go in without any laundry. They had tattoos all over their faces, necks and arms. They were like monsters in a movie. They give me a bad feeling. I do not want them to see me."

"How old do you think the men were?"

"I think maybe twenty, twenty-two. They were skinny. Their pants were too big, and came down too far so you could see their underwear. Their heads were shaved. One, his ears stuck out very far, like a monkey. I watched him smile at the little boy. Not nice, not a good smile. Skinny

216

lips, a big, big mouth, some missing teeth. His lips and eyebrow were pierced. The other one, he had a silver tooth. Spikes in his ears and in his eyebrow. The tattoos made it seem like he wore a mask."

"Can you describe the tattoos?"

"Yes. The lights in the laundromat were very bright. Then one of the men lighted up a cigarette and the flame around his face made him look like the devil. I will never forget. The tattoos were everywhere you see skin. Face, neck, arms, hands, fingers — like a painting. Bad things. Skulls with devil horns, spider webs, bleeding naked women, crossed rifles, gravestones. Both men had a black teardrop tattooed in the corner of their eye."

Señora Ramirez started to cry again. Detective Rosa made notes in his casebook. When the grandmother's sniffles subsided, Rosa asked her to please go on.

"I could tell these are bad men, Agent Rosa. I stayed in my car, very quiet. They didn't see me. I knew the little boy was in danger, but I could do nothing. I knew if they saw me, they would hurt me."

"Other than the tattoos, why did you think that?" asked Detective Rosa.

"The day before, I heard my grandsons talking. They think I do not listen. I am just old grandma, in the kitchen. My grandson, he saw men with tattoos at the 7-Eleven across the street from the middle school. They threatened some Sureño boys that they must join the Mara Salvatrucha, or they and their families would be hurt. While I watch the men in the laundromat from my car, I think these must be the same ones my grandson saw. The Salvatruchas are very bad men, Agent Rosa. You have heard about them, yes? They are sick animals. Monstrosities."

"I understand, Señora Ramirez. I'll talk with my team at the sheriff's office. We'll increase our patrols around the school. Please, can you tell me what else you saw the evening of Wednesday, August 10th at the laundromat?"

"I watch them talk to the boy. They try to give the boy some candy. He shakes his head no. The man with the silver tooth holds out some bills to the boy. The little boy shakes his head and backs away. The skinny man with the monkey ears, he throws down his cigarette and grabs the little boy. I think the man will drag the boy to the door. The boy struggles and slips away from the man, and runs for the front door. The silver tooth man has a gun. He shoots. Ayyyyyeeeee. The boy falls. The tattooed men run out the door, past my car. I don't move. I don't breathe."

"What happened next?"

"People from Los Venenos Cantina next door heard the shot and came outside. They saw the men running down the street, but no one followed. They found the boy. I drove home. I told no one.

"The next day, I took my laundry to another place. I have been so afraid. I read in the newspaper that the boy died. I did not go to the funeral. I have bad dreams. Soon, it will be the Day of the Dead. I see the little boy sometimes here in my kitchen, standing over there, in that corner, staring at me. He seems so sad. Thank you for coming to my house and listening to me. I believe that God and the little boy will forgive me now for my silence. All this time, I have been praying for the child."

Suddenly, the sound of gunshots shattered the air. The woman screamed and threw her apron over her head.

Car tires squealed.

Rosa jumped up and rushed to a window, hand on the Glock at his hip.

"It's okay Señora Ramirez. It's alright. It was only a car backfiring."

Once Rosa's words got through to the woman, her screams subsided into sobs.

Detective Rosa sat back down at the kitchen table across from Grandmother Ramirez. He quietly reviewed his case notes while the grandmother's sobs sank into hiccups and finally into silent fingering of the rosary.

As soon as it seemed decent to do so, Rosa thanked Señora Ramirez, reassuring her that she had made the right decision by calling him. He promised that he would do all he could to keep her and her family safe. Then he took his leave.

As he drove back up Main, across the river, Detective Rosa reflected on the interview.

Time to sit down and do a complete case work-up. Work with the unknowns. Hours of overwhelming paperwork loomed before him.

But first, I need to pay a thank-you visit to a friend.

32

FRIDAY, OCTOBER 21, 1999
Parent Teacher Conference Week
Prudenciana Elementary

P ARENT-CONFERENCE AFTERNOONS BLURRED TOGETHER. Autumn spiced the air, the days grew shorter, and Halloween drew near. Wind flurries blew colored leaves across the playground. Aurora met with Rosie and her Filipino grandfather, Destiny and River, Christina's Portuguese family, Maverick's black and white family, Giang Son's Viet Nam War refugee father, and the "Watch What You Say About Columbus" parents. The twins' two gay mothers, who worked in tech over the hill in Silicon Valley, offered to help with Net Day. Jessica's young parents, covered with gang tattoos, were distracted by their squalling baby and out-of-control toddler. Ben and his parents, both marine biologists who taught at the university, brought a big box full of class supplies, and offered to chaperone on field trips.

*　　　*　　　*

Friday finally arrived. Panchito's father looked as if he'd just stepped off the bus from Mexico. Big hat, big belt buckle, cowboy boots.

Panchito's mother had two swollen purple, yellow and black eyes, a deep red oozing gash along one cheek, a split lip, and numerous scrapes and scratches on her face.

Aurora rose to welcome the couple and introduce herself. She wasn't sure how to begin with these people. Should she have arranged for a translator to be present, or maybe a counselor?

Their son, Panchito, was a wonderful student. He'd been reclassified as Fluent English Proficient this year. He was bright, working hard, and holding his own, but Aurora knew he still struggled with the deep cognitive structures of the English language.

"I want to let you know, *Señora y Señor* Vargas, that if you would like a translator to be present, I can arrange that. We can either reschedule the conference, or go ahead and meet now, but also meet again later with a translator if you have questions."

"*Gracias, Señora Bourne. Entendemos.* I understand," said Panchito's mother. "*Es difícil* to have time from work, for us, even so late in afternoon. We are *freseros*. We work in the strawberries. *Pues*, let us meet today, and if we have questions, then another time with translator. *Muchas gracias.*"

The husband spoke rapidly in Spanish and the woman laughed.

"My husband say tell you he no hit me. Please, let me explain my face."

"It looks very painful," Aurora said. "Were you in an accident?"

"*Sí y no.* We live here, *en Los Estados Unidos*, and work in the fields for many years. We pick strawberries at Baker Farms. Soon we will vote to choose which union represents us. My husband and I have been with UFW all our lives. When we were children, our parents took us to march with Cesar Chavez. So, of course, we vote for UFW. But it's no same anymore. The Baker's *Jefe de Campo*, Yudas Medina, says AWC is better, but we know AWC is no good for *freseros*. Señor Medina he work for growers, no to help us. He bring new people from Mexico, from his own village, to work here. He give them jobs, instead of hiring experienced *freseros* who live here in *Los Estados Unidos* for long time. My husband and I, we go to UFW organizing meetings. One night at a meeting, Medina's AWC workers raid our hall. They surround us. Someone hit my face with a wooden strawberry box." Panchito's mother put her hand to her face. "*Policía* came and the attackers went *loco*. The *policía* used pepper spray to stop riot."

Aurora studied the woman's face more closely. *She needs antibiotics.*

"Mrs. Vargas, I really think you should have stiches for that cut," Aurora said. "You need medical attention."

"*Sí*, but we can no afford doctor. I have herbs from a *curandera*."

"Just a minute." Aurora went to her filing cabinet. She located the folder containing information on community resources and returned to the table. "Here," she copied agencies, contact names, addresses and phone numbers onto her yellow tablet. "There are free clinics. Salud Para la Gente is here in Valle Verde. They have doctors who will help you, and you'll be able to afford it, I'm sure. They speak Spanish. They may even be able to help you get some legal assistance."

The woman took the paper with tears in her eyes.

"Thank you, Señora Bourne. We have been so afraid. The union vote, and also the vote on immigration that is coming soon. The Unz *Initiativo*. We have our green cards, but many of our friends and *familia* no have. We fear if we speak for UFW, we no get hired next season. The work is very dangerous. My husband gets sprayed in his face with pesticides when he laying tarps. Now he has headache and *problemas* with his eyes. He can't see so good. But if we say something, he will lose his job. We work very hard, Señora Bourne. Our Panchito is a good boy. We only want for him a better life."

$$* \qquad * \qquad *$$

Victor, serious and formal, attended the conference with his little sister Paloma. They were accompanied by the sullen fifteen-year-old brother, Johnny, and the grandfather who spoke no English. Paloma presented Aurora with a pretty gift-wrapped box. Inside were abalone shell earrings and a beautiful abalone shell necklace that Victor and Johnny had made for their little sister's teacher.

Steven's and Ryan's parents were concerned about the frequent nosebleeds. Ryan had been having headaches and an inexplicable rash that wouldn't go away. Steven was having vertigo and vision problems. None of the doctors the boys had seen had been able to diagnose the problems.

Defying the district's gag order, Aurora told both families that she thought the nose bleeds and other issues might be caused by pesticides. She shared what she knew. When the parents asked what they could do, Aurora passed them Destiny's phone number.

Caleb's parents, Mr. and Mrs. Trask, brought Aurora a bag of apples. "Our family has been growing apples in this valley for over a hundred years," said Mr. Trask.

"We have one of the last heritage apple orchards remaining in the state," said Mrs. Trask. "These are what apples are supposed to taste like. You can't buy them in grocery stores anymore."

Nikko Kioku's parents arrived with an armful of flowers. Nikko's father was a fisherman. "My daughter is excited about your Salmon and Trout Education Program. If you'd like, I'd be happy to come into your classroom and teach the children how to tie flies. Maybe tell them some stories about the 'old days' — my childhood fishing the creeks and rivers around here, when you could walk across the water on the fish's backs."

"We'd love that. Let's plan on it."

"We've heard you're concerned about the pesticides on those strawberry fields surrounding the school," said Mrs. Kioku. "We believe our daughter is especially sensitive to the chemicals, possibly because she's so petite."

"I'm the fifth generation to be born and raised in Valle Verde," Mr. Kioku said. "I can tell you something about growing strawberries. We Japanese introduced strawberries to the Byrd Valley. My grandfather went to school here, in the original one-room Prudenciana schoolhouse. He was fighting for the U.S. Army in WWII when the government took our farm and interred the rest of the family at Manzanar. After the war, my family returned to Valle Verde and we got our land back. I didn't want any part of farming. I work for the Water District. But my brother still farms the way we were taught by grandfather, seasonally rotating brassicas with the berries. Brassicas are a natural fumigant. My brother has never had to use pesticides on his strawberries."

*   *   *

Finally, the last conference. Aurora had been working fourteen-hour days in order to accommodate all her parents' scheduling needs. She was exhausted.

The woman who arrived for Alice's parent-teacher conference looked nothing like Alice. And she seemed hardly more than a teenager.

"Oh, I'm not Alice's mom. My name is Miss Smithy, Casey Smithy. I'm on the day shift at the Group Home."

Aurora felt like Alice in Wonderland falling down the rabbit hole.

Salvador Luna walked through the door hand-in-hand with a girl who was almost Alice, but different. The two children watched and listened.

"Group Home?" Aurora repeated.

"Well, actually it's called a Family Child Care Home. Alice will probably be placed in foster care eventually, when they can find her a family. But she only just entered the system about three months ago. They wanted to keep her at the FCC Home for observation for a while, before putting her in a private placement."

"But why is she in a Family Child Care Home? Did she do something wrong? Where are her parents?"

"Oh, I don't think she did anything wrong. I don't know where her parents are. I'm just a day worker. And anyway, even if I did, I wouldn't be allowed to discuss those kinds of details."

"Why didn't the agency inform me earlier that Alice has special circumstances? I should have been told."

"They usually don't do that. I guess they want our kids to have a chance to find their way in school at first without being sti— astima— um, marked as having a problem. If Alice had had any problems in your class, and you'd tried to phone the parents earlier, someone from Child Protective Services would probably have talked to you."

"Alice does have issues. I've been looking forward to meeting her parents so we could discuss some things."

"What kind of issues? Is she disruptive?"

Aurora studied the young woman. What good would a conversation with this day worker do for Alice?

"No. She's not at all disruptive. But she is listless. Her head is down on her desk most of the time. Can you tell me anything that would help me understand her and better meet her needs?"

"Honestly, I know almost nothing about her. Sorry. I just got this job a few weeks ago. It's only temporary. I'm going back to school next semester. I only see Alice every once in a while. It's not like I really hang out with her or anything, you know?"

"What will you do with the information I give you? Do you report back to anyone about what we've said at this conference?"

"Not really. If there are problems, I tell my supervisor, and he might call you. That's it. I don't write down anything that goes in a file, if that's what you mean."

"Can you give me your supervisor's name and phone number?"

"I'm not really supposed to do that, but I can have him call you if you want."

"Yes, please. Here's my home number. Do you know when they plan to move Alice into private foster care?"

"We never know."

"Would she stay enrolled in my class at Prudenciana, if and when she goes to foster care?"

"Sorry, but you just can never tell."

Aurora glanced around the room. Salvador and almost-Alice were in the class library sitting on big floor cushions, reading.

"Can you tell me if she's healthy?" Aurora asked. "She seems not to eat enough. She's very skinny."

"All our kids receive good health care and good food at the FCC Home. But I know what you mean. Alice does seem like, you know, wherever she was before, she didn't get enough to eat. She is in counseling. I know that. She sees a therapist once a week. They're evaluating her before they put her in foster care. I guess to decide what kind of people she should be with or something. I don't really know why she needs counseling."

"Well, thank you very much for coming, Ms. Smithy. Please do remember to ask your supervisor to give me a call."

Alice's day worker walked out of the door. Salvador and almost-Alice departed as well.

Aurora felt as empty as the room.

33

FRIDAY, OCTOBER 21, 1998
Our Lady of Help Church, Valle Verde

FRIDAY AFTERNOON, STILL THINKING ABOUT HIS INTERVIEW with Señora Ramirez, Charlie found Father Francis working in the homeless garden in back of the church.

"Charlie, *mi amigo*. What brings you here today?" The priest got a devilish gleam in his eye. "If you're coming for services, the next mass isn't until seven o'clock tonight."

"Thanks anyway, Padre. I was hoping you might have a few minutes to talk."

Father Francis picked up the bushel basket of squash and beans he'd harvested. "Follow me. I need to drop this off in the kitchen. There's fresh coffee, and our cook, Mrs. Garcia, made oatmeal raisin cookies this morning. We can take some with us to my office."

*   *   *

Charlie licked cookie crumbs off his lip and set his coffee cup down on a table next to his chair. "I interviewed Mrs. Ramirez this afternoon. Thanks to you, we've finally got a witness to the Luna shooting."

"Thank God. I wasn't sure she'd call you. She's frightened, Charlie. Did I do the right thing, encouraging her to come forward?"

"The Luna case really needed this break, Frank. Mrs. Ramirez saw everything. She can I.D. the killers."

"But now that she's come forward? Can you protect her?"

"I wish it was like on TV, and I could just arrange for her to be put into witness protection. But the real world isn't as easy as that. Too expensive. Too complicated. Too much paperwork. For witness protection, someone would have to go to the DA, find funds, personnel." Charlie rubbed a spot between his eyebrows. "Who has time for that? And even if it happened, it would only be a short-term thing. If these guys are as bad as I'm thinking, the real danger for Mrs. Ramirez will be after their trial."

"What do you mean?"

"Once they're in prison, if they find out who she is, they'll most likely send some of their brothers on the outside to do her."

"Dear God, Charlie. If I'd known …"

"Look, Padre, we will do our absolute best to keep the Ramirez family safe, for as long as we can. And, hell, all that's assuming we ever even find these scum bags."

"Alright. What are the next steps?"

"We need Mrs. Ramirez to come in and work with our forensic artist. Maybe you can encourage her to do that, Padre."

"She'll be afraid to go to the Sheriff's Office, but I can pick her up and drive her. Even if someone's watching her, driving somewhere with her priest shouldn't raise any alarm bells in the community."

"Good. Once we've got sketches, we'll give the drawings to the newspapers and TV stations. My team will hand out fliers around the hoods with descriptions and composite sketches. We'll visit the jails, talk to the jailers."

"Jails?" Father Francis' forehead creased.

"The perps might already be in custody, or have come through the system on some other charge."

"There can't be that many men wandering around the county who match the description Mrs. Ramirez gave. I understand they're slippery, but I'd think that anyone who sees them is bound to remember."

"We'll keep searching and following every lead until we find them, *hermano*. With the help of Valle Verde PD, we'll canvas the neighborhoods. We'll talk to those kids from the middle school. Maybe even turn up some other witnesses. The FBI is hunting too. MS-13 is high on their list. Eventually, we will nail Salvador Luna's shooters."

"What about that meth lab we found. Any traction there?"

"My gut still tells me there's a nexus, but I don't have enough evidence yet to connect the dots. El Salvador. MS-13. Drugs. Blood. Delta cigarettes. Dead and missing kids."

"I'll keep reaching out to my communities. I'll do all I can to help."

"Good. People are terrified. We need help with public outreach. We're talking with school and church personnel, shelters, hospitals, other law enforcement agencies. We start where the killers were last seen and work our way out. We need to restore peace and calm, a sense of safety in the neighborhoods."

"Speaking of safety, what about the three men you have in custody for assaulting Ms. Bourne? Last time we talked, you were waiting on DNA results from the cigarettes."

"DNA from the Delta stubs at the creek and the dunes matched, but not the laundromat. Scumbags we nailed at the dunes didn't shoot the kid."

"That's what we were thinking anyway, right? The men at the dunes and the meth hooch attacked with knives; the Luna killers used a gun." Father Francis eyebrows drew together. "Besides, just because they all smoke the same cigarettes doesn't necessarily mean they're working together."

"True, but I still have a hunch that Ms. Bourne's assailants are somehow connected to the Luna shooting, even if we can't place them at the crime scene. We've got to crack their silence, make them tell us what happened at that meth hooch. I'm going to interrogate them again as soon as possible."

Charlie took his notebook out of his pocket and wrote something, then tapped his notebook with his pen. "The DA arraigned Ms.

Bourne's assailants on felony assault charges. They're being held with no bail set. The case is in discovery, so I assume they'll be brought to trial soon. I've requested that my lieutenant convene a cross-force briefing, ASAP."

"Good." Father Francis rubbed his chin. "What else do you need from Mrs. Ramirez?"

"When we do bring in suspects, we'll have to pull Mrs. Ramirez in for a line-up."

"That will terrify her, Charlie."

"We could do a 6-Pack instead. A photo line-up. She'd just have to look at pictures in a book."

"Go with that. Much less traumatic. She has good reason to be scared. What kind of person would murder an innocent child?"

"From the way Señora Ramirez described that night, what went down at the laundromat could have been a child abduction gone bad. Maybe that's the *why* of it? The men tried to grab the kid. He was getting away. They shot him."

Father Francis nodded. "Connections?"

"Again, the meth lab. We found Mara Salvatrucha tags, and signs that young children had been there."

"Speaking of children," asked Father Francis, "what about the infant found in the woods?"

"The baby's going to be fine. A family in Hollister is fostering him. I think they may adopt him."

"Good news. What else?"

"Nothing so far on the little girl who left the baby in the woods, or the mother and other twin." Charlie thumbed through his notebook. "Oh, but this is interesting. Forensics found that there was no match between the baby's DNA and Mr. Reilly — the vic the cougar ate. Vince Reilly was not the baby's father."

"Anything else from the forensics team?"

"There wasn't any point in trying to pull prints at the laundromat. Public place like that, there are just too many irrelevant prints. But we do have prints from the meth hooch that match the prints of the three would-be rapists we have in custody. Once again, that connection is tight."

"What about the Mayan girl who went missing from the strawberry fields?" Father Francis asked.

"Sorry, my friend. At this point we have no clue."

34

Prudenciana Elementary

K ATIE AND AURORA SAT AT A REDWOOD PICNIC TABLE in the Prudenciana Life Lab garden after school, heads bent together over plan books and papers. They were collaborating on a lesson about native plants that integrated science, social studies, and art.

Sheaves of dry corn stalks stood watch at the garden Torii gate. Orange and black Monarch butterflies danced around a patch of tall sunflowers. A few forgotten pumpkins peaked out from under tendrilly masses of leaves as large as Green Man's hands, mottled with grey splotches of decomposition. Pale, dry ghosts of sweet pea plants rattled in the light breeze, and a few shriveled tomatoes clung to leafless vines. A huge zucchini, brown at the ends and pecked by birds, lay where it had been tossed on top of the compost pile. Near a hay bale, a scarecrow stared forlornly at the teachers.

In the distance, toward the bay, low, slanted rays of golden light diffused over the landscape. Katie squinted into the marine haze on the horizon. "Aw, crap."

"What?" said Aurora, following Katie's glare. "Oh, no. They're getting ready to do it again."

"Yep."

The field on the other side of the school fence had been plowed. A man walked along the burnt umber field rows, far enough away that he was not much more than a black dot with a touch of crimson for his hat.

"Wonder who that guy is," Katie said. "I'll bet he's the strawberry grower. I really, really don't want them to fumigate again. I want to have healthy children someday. I'm going to go talk to that man. Right now."

Before Aurora realized what Katie intended to do, she was gone. She was running across the grass playing field toward the cyclone fence, climbing up and over, loping like a young coyote across the plowed furrows toward the man.

Aurora watched from the school side of the fence. Katie and the farmer stood face to face, talking. It seemed to be an amiable conversation, judging from the body language.

Aurora gathered their things and left the garden, with a silent prayer to the Mother of All Beings.

*   *   *

About fifteen minutes later, Katie burst into Aurora's classroom.

"He wants to meet with us! He's really nice. I told him how I felt about the pesticides, how sick everyone is getting. He actually listened. He wants to come here, to the school, and talk with us."

"Slow down," said Aurora. "Who are you talking about?"

"The strawberry grower. His name is Pete Choate. Bobby's uncle — you know, Bobby Choate in your class."

"And he wants to meet with us about the fumigations? When, where?"

"Yep. He is getting ready to do another pesticide application, just like we thought. But he said he'd be willing to meet with us first, here at the school, if we can do it soon. We need to tell everyone, right away."

"This is incredible, Katie. Let's see. Tomorrow's probably too soon to get people together. How about if we find out who's available day after tomorrow, Thursday afternoon, about 3:30?"

"Perfect."

"I guess we'll need to kind of, you know, let the principal know." Aurora pulled at her braid.

"We should ask Tom Olsen to tell her. She'll probably go ballistic. It's safest for him, since he's the Union rep."

"I'll check with him right now," said Aurora. "I'm pretty sure he's still here. Call me at home tonight. Okay?"

"Yep. Sounds perfect." Katie gave Aurora a hug, gathered up her plan book and papers, and rushed away into the light pouring like warm cider through the open door.

*   *   *

Thursday afternoon, thirteen Prudenciana Elementary School teachers crowded around the round conference table with strawberry grower Pete Choate. As the union had advised, none of the untenured teachers had shown up, except Katie.

"Thank you so much for meeting with us this afternoon, Mr. Choate," said Katie.

"Well, the things you told me the other day, out in my field, really moved me, Ms. Cooper. I have nephews here at the school, you know. My own kids are still toddlers, but they'll be coming to Prudenciana in a few years. I certainly don't want to be responsible for causing any harm to the children here at the school, or to the teachers."

Bobby's uncle exuded stability, maturity, responsibility. Aurora studied his large hands, folded on the table, chapped, with dirt under the fingernails — hands you could trust to hold a newborn infant or gentle an injured animal, as much as to fix a tractor or build a barn.

"We respect what you do, Mr. Choate," said Tom Olsen. "We're very aware of Byrd Valley's agricultural history, and we honor your important work."

"Thank you for your appreciation. My family came here from the Azores over a hundred years ago, and we've been farming this land ever since. My father worked for a pesticide company when I was a kid, and I think I'm none the worse for it. But the Valley has changed. So many more people live here now. These days, too many fields are surrounded by houses and schools that didn't used to be here."

"Actually," said Helen Rice, "Prudenciana was here before the agriculture. It's one of the oldest schools in the Valley. It was founded in the 1850s, long before the strawberry fields were put in."

"We understand that you intend to fumigate again soon, on the field right next to the school," said Ruth Redding. "Is there any way we can persuade you not to do that, Mr. Choate?"

"My pesticide advisor from CalGreen has told me that methyl bromide doesn't drift. They've run tests. It should be perfectly safe."

"We know it drifts," said redheaded Corkie Duncan. "Whenever there's a fumigation, our eyes water. We get a metallic taste on our tongues. Our kids get nosebleeds and throw up. We know when there are pesticides in the air, even without seeing the tarps, Mr. Choate. Your field is in direct line with the prevailing coastal winds. The wind blows off the bay, across your field, straight into the school. If there are pesticides in your field, we get them at the school. We have no doubt about it."

"Well, I ..."

"We've been experiencing a confusing array of physical issues, Mr. Choate," said Harriet. "We don't know which, if any, of our symptoms may be caused by pesticides, but we do know the pesticides are drifting into the school."

"Anyway," said Aurora, "the methyl bromide you strawberry growers are using is supposed to be phased out in the U.S. by next year, by international law. Methyl bromide is one of the worst of the ozone depleting chemicals and it's also a greenhouse gas. What are you guys doing about the phase-out? Aren't you supposed to be trying to find alternatives to methyl bromide?"

"Yes, I know about the phase-out. We've increased our fumigations this season because of that."

"What? You mean you're using even more methyl bromide than usual?" Katie looked stunned.

"Well, yes, that's what CalGreen and the Monterey Bay Strawberry Growers Association have recommended. It's been very expensive, I have to say."

"So, how about if you just skip this fumigation?"

Deep furrows formed between Pete Choate's eyebrows. He steepled his large hands in front of his face and closed his eyes for several heartbeats before answering.

"To be honest, I have been thinking about going organic for some time now. I've done some research on my own. But I just don't see how it could work. Even if it's possible to produce strawberries on a commercial scale without chemical soil fumigant, which I'm not sure about, the cost of converting to organic is prohibitive for a small farmer like me. I have a family to provide for, and workers who depend on me for jobs. I have to be prudent."

"My brother is successfully growing strawberries organically, Mr. Choate," Corkie said. "His name is Jay Duncan. He has Townsend's Berry Farm up on the North Coast, near Davenport. I'm sure he'd be happy to talk with you."

"I'm willing to talk. But, like I said, from what I can see at this point, the costs of conversion to organic make it out of the question. To get certified, you have to forgo chemicals on your ground for three years. That's three years of fallow ground, or growing a crop in limbo, where you can't sell it at organic produce market prices, but you're still bearing all the extra expense of growing organically. Organic fertilizers are more costly, and it's far more labor intensive. I just don't see how I could compete."

Pete Choate took off his John Deere cap and scratched his head. "The economy of agriculture is shifting more and more toward multinational agribusiness. Valle Verde used to be known as the frozen food capital of the world, but in the last few years, since NAFTA, the big frozen food plants have shut their doors and moved to Mexico, with massive job losses for our workers here. Strawberry growers have picked up the slack, keeping Valle Verde farmworkers employed."

"Didn't you just say that organic is more labor intensive? If you went organic, you could employ even more workers," said Ruth.

"True, but right now, I couldn't afford to hire any more people. The big growers, with thousands of acres, can afford to put aside a few hundred acres for three years, and write it off. But at my scale, as a small family farmer, putting even ten acres of land in transition — getting paid low commercial prices for high-cost organic produce while I wait for organic certification — could ruin me."

"It sounds like what we need," said Mrs. Chang, "is subsidies for small farmers to help them go organic. Big agriculture gets all kinds of federal subsidies. Why can't our government help small farmers transition to organic?"

Pete Choate laughed. "Sounds great. Let me know when that happens. But, frankly, I won't be holding my breath waiting for reforms in the federal farm bill. Truthfully, if we get too much pressure over pesticides, a lot of small farmers, myself included, aren't going to last. The small family farmer is an endangered species."

Aurora was worried about another endangered species — the salmon, threatened because of all the water that strawberry production used, not to mention the pesticides running off into the creek. But she kept silent, not wanting to derail the conversation.

"We're already getting squeezed out by the big agribusiness concerns," said Pete. "Add to that the pressure from new people who move into the Valley because housing is affordable and then complain about our farming practices, and — well, more and more small family farmers are deciding to just get out, let developers have the land."

"We definitely don't want to see that, Mr. Choate," said Tom Olsen. "That's happening all over the country, we know. We don't want to see our fertile valley get paved over. Farmland needs to be preserved. We want to work with you, not force you out of business."

"Maybe we could do some research, look into writing a grant to help Byrd Valley farmers transition to organic," said Dora Lockhart.

"We managed to protect our coast from oil drilling," said Aurora. "The people of California persuaded Congress to designate a National Marine Sanctuary in the Monterey Bay. It seemed impossible, but we did it. Why not a model sustainable organic National Agricultural Sanctuary in the Byrd Valley? We should dream. A new century is coming. We need to envision the most positive future we can."

"It's been so informative speaking with you, Mr. Choate," said Helen. "I understand a little more about your point of view now. And I think you hear us, and understand our concerns. This feels really positive."

"What if we had a community forum?" said Esteban. "A teach-in about organic versus chemical agriculture. We could host it here, at Prudenciana, and invite everyone — *freseros*, growers, parents, pesticide reps. Kind of like that new Watershed Council — a forum where all points of view would be respected. Maybe we could move closer to understanding one another and finding mutually beneficial solutions. What do you think Mr. Choate? Do you think the growers and farmers would come?"

"It might be worth a try. I'd be willing to talk to some of my friends and associates, as long as it was respectful, on both sides."

"There may be more than just two sides to this," said Tom Olsen. "We may find there are many points of view, here in the Valley, that we need to respectfully consider."

"Um, what about the fumigation?" asked Katie. "Are you still planning to fumigate your field again soon, Mr. Choate?"

"I'm going to have to think about it. I have to make a living. I have a farm to run. People depend on me for their jobs, so I can't be rash. But I will think deep and long about all this."

35

SATURDAY, OCTOBER 29, 1998
Santa Cruz, The Westside
San Lorenzo River Watershed, Steamer Lane

AURORA FLOATED IN LIQUID IRIDESCENT PINK, fire orange, and abalone green. Shimmering water mirrored flaming sunset sky.

The harvest moon shone like a pumpkin. She moved her hand through the seasonal bioluminescent algae bloom, painting a streak of glowing blue-green-violet fireworks across the water.

She'd been surfing for hours in ecstatic timelessness. She pulled her hands through the water and they felt encased in cement.

Time to go in.

Dark rollers thundered over the black boulders of the breakwater along the cliff. Between crashing waves, she scrambled with her board over treacherous, sharp rocks to the stairs. With her last reserves of strength, she hauled her board up slippery, moss-covered steps to the parking lot.

Standing by her truck in the Steamer Lane lot, teeth chattering, she could barely peel the sticky black neoprene off her arms, pop it over shriveled blue hands, and roll it down away from her chest. She groped with numb fingers to pry the lid off a plastic bucket full of hot water she'd brought from home, then wriggled the rest of the way out of her wetsuit and poured the fresh water over her head. Even though it had cooled to lukewarm, the water stung as if it were scalding hot.

She wrapped in a big towel, peeled off her bathing suit, rubbed down, and slipped into dry sweatpants, hooded sweatshirt, and fleece lined boots. Once her body was no longer sending out hypothermia alerts, she walked over to the grassy knoll next to the lighthouse, where fire dancers were practicing for Burning Man.

Beyond the fire dancers, a swath of moonlight twinkled across the water. An occasional night surfer cut a fiery streak through the waves.

The Lighthouse beacon, flashing out to sea in its registered period, kept time with the dancers' drums. Behind Aurora's back, the beam of light swept along the edge of the fence, illuminating two men crouched in the shadows with faces like Halloween masks, inked with spiders, horned skulls, gravestones, and a black tear drop in the corner of each man's eye.

*   *   *

SUNDAY, OCTOBER 30, 1998
AURORA BOURNE'S COTTAGE

Sunday afternoon, Aurora sat at her kitchen table, fingers wrapped around a mug of Earl Grey tea. A plate of warm oatmeal raisin walnut cookies sat within her reach, filling the kitchen with their just-baked aroma.

Blue had draped himself over a cushion at the kitchen window seat. A hanging crystal fractured the Indian Summer light and scattered rainbows around the kitchen walls. The cat gave the rainbows a glance, but had tired of batting at them.

Aurora's students' illustrated final drafts of their scary stories sat in a stack on the table before her.

The kids had been working on the stories all month. Narratives about the scariest experience you've ever had — real or imagined.

Aurora planned to have her students read their scary stories out loud tomorrow, with the lights off and a candle burning like a campfire in the middle of the classroom. She had face paint and some fun Halloween decorations, cookies and apple cider for the class party, and the Disney version of *Legend of Sleepy Hollow* to show in the afternoon, after the school-wide costume parade.

She reached for the next story on the stack. Alice's. Alice had refused all help during the writing process. It was going to be interesting to see what she'd come up with.

NIGHTMARE AT THE CREEK

A little girl was living beside a creek with her mom, her twin sister, and her baby brother.

The creek was magical and beautiful, with lots of deep blue green pools, shallow gravel bars, and little bubbling waterfalls, tall trees and ferns, interesting birds, dragonflies, water striders, salamanders, and little silver fish. The creek made music that sang to the sisters.

There was a man living with them in their camp by the creek. He fought with mama and hit her a lot.

One night, when everyone was asleep, Alice woke up and remembered that she'd left her favorite doll in her and her sister's secret hideout under some bushes. She put on her T-shirt, pants and flip-flops very quietly, then snuck out of the tent to get her doll. The moon was bright and the hide-out was close by. She crawled inside and found her doll. Then the screaming started.

Mama and sister screamed and screamed, the scariest screams she'd ever heard. Men were shouting. The little girl peeked out through holes in the bushes. In front of the campfire, Mama's boyfriend was fighting with three strange men. The firelight made their knives shine

243

red. Mama's boyfriend was bleeding. He ran away into the dark, holding onto his side.

One of the bad men pushed mama down on the ground. He held her by the neck and bumped up and down on top of her. Mama screamed and cried.

Another man grabbed sister by the hair. He pulled her over to the campfire, pushed her down in the dirt, and stood over her laughing. She wasn't wearing nothing but a T-shirt.

The third man searched all around camp, taking things, smashing everything, and tagging everything with spray paint. The baby was screeching.

Then the men made mama and sister go away with them. Mama could hardly walk. She stumbled, and fell a few times. The men poked knives at her to keep her moving.

The little girl in the hide-out waited a long time. She was so scared she couldn't breathe. When she felt sure everyone was gone, she snuck back to camp, picked up her baby brother, and started walking, following the creek.

When the moon went down, it was so dark it was hard to walk without falling. The baby got so heavy. She didn't want to leave him, but she couldn't carry him any more. She put baby brother down in a hiding place where she thought she could find him again, and kept going.

When it started getting light, she was on a road that ended by a market. The market smelled good, like barbeque. The girl was so cold and hungry and tired, she lay down in a little grassy place across the street from the market and fell asleep. When she woke up, she found out that it had all been just a scary nightmare. The End.

Aurora's hands shook. She turned the page. The illustrations leapt out at her.

"Oh, my God. Oh, my God."

Snarling at her off the page was a colored pencil drawing, so accurate it could almost have been a photo, of the three men, knives in their hands, who had nearly raped her at the Pelican Dunes. The next illustration was of a lean-to by a creek, with an assortment of things scattered around in front of the lean-to that gave the place the aspect of an old-time illegal still. The last illustration was of Alice, hand-in-hand with her twin. The girls were peering into the creek, with a salamander staring back at them from under the water.

It's her. Alice is the child they're looking for. It has to be her. How could I have been so dense? I should have seen this a month ago.

Aurora dialed the number Detective Rosa had hand-written on his card. Cold prickles crawled down her back. Phone to her ear, she turned. Salvador Luna sat at the window seat, Alice's twin beside him. The children stared at Aurora wistfully.

"Detective Rosa here," came the answer through the phone line.

"Detective Rosa. This is Aurora Bourne, one of the teachers from Prudenciana Elementary School. I'm so glad I reached you."

36

SUNDAY, OCTOBER 30, 1998
Valle Verde City

P ALOMA'S FIFTEEN-YEAR-OLD BROTHER JOHNNY dropped the spray
can on the pile of trash and squinted at his fresh tag on the alley
wall.

Be afraid, pinche Truchas. This is our turf.

He could hardly feel his broken nose or cracked ribs anymore.
Only when he moved, or breathed — and then he kind of forgot about
the stabbing pain as soon as it stopped.

Yo, I be Norño Watson now for reals. I'm jumped in.

Johnny puked on the trash piled up against the alley wall.

Beer and tequila shooters all day, for the last two days. Yeah. Wait.
Maybe it's three.

Someone clicked a lighter and held it under the bulb of the small
glass pipe in Johnny's hand. The yellowish crystal ice in the bowl
snapped and sizzled as it melted, and he took a long pull. His face
melted. The fresh tags on the wall behind him bled. The wall melted.

247

He couldn't find his hands. His stomach came out through his mouth and grabbed his dick, like in some weird cartoon.

"Hold it in, Dawg, Hold it in. Twenty-nine ... Thirty. Now!"

Johnny gasped for breath.

Oh, shit that's good!

He barely remembered getting jumped in. It was behind a shit stinkin *baño* in some fuck ass park two nights ago.

His homies came at him with pipes, bats, rubber hoses, kicks, other shit. *Ha, ha, ha, ha.* The pain was a burning red light scream. Then he couldn't see. Must've passed out.

Next thing, his homies was all hugging him, patting him on the shoulder, giving him love 'cause now he was one of them and they had his back and he had theirs, forever. Unless he ever fucked up or crossed 'em, some *pinche* way. *Serio.* Like he was ever gonna do dat.

His eye throbbed from being nearly swollen shut. He sucked in another hit of the sweet, hot ice. Some homie was taking the pipe away and putting somethin' hard and cold in his hand, wrapping his fingers around it. He could barely feel his fingers, like they weren't his.

"Wa sis?" Johnny mumbled.

"Waz a matter wid ya, ya stoopid ass bitch. S'a *cuete, puta.* Fuckin' *coño.*"

Johnny made an effort to grip the gun. Holding it loosely, he waved it over his head and giggled on a high-pitched, crazy note that echoed through the night.

The revolver went off. The bullet ricocheted overhead, bouncing against the walls of the buildings on either side of the narrow, dark alley where they'd been tagging. A thread of pale blue smoke with a funny smell curled upward like a ghost.

Johnny sat stupefied on the ground, his ears ringing like a cathedral bell inside his head.

"You crazy ass mutha fucka. *Ese, Morito. Tu eres loco. Vato Pura loco. Vamanos.* Let's go."

"Yeah, we gotta snuff us out a fuckin' Trucha bitch."

"Yeah. Let's go find us some fuckin' ass Salvatrucha cunts and bomb on their ass. *Ese. Vámanos, vatos.*"

248

As they stumbled out of the alley, Johnny came face to face with some people in masks. The masks floated in the air.

One of them turned into his mother's face. The blue face he'd found planted on the kitchen table when he'd come home from school, and she was dead. OD'd. Fuckin' snuffed on smack, eyes all bugged out. Tongue all black. His mother's face floated in front of him. He crossed himself.

Someone was pulling him down the street. He kind of knew he was stumbling. He couldn't find his feet. Did he still have feet? *Ha ha ha.* He had a gun. But where wazit? And whad'he hav'ta do ta make it go off? Or not. *Ha ha ha ha.*

He looked down. He was taking a piss, the yellow stream falling on his father's face. Motherfucker. Where were you? *Tú eres basura.* He shook off his dick and put it back in his pants. Or did he? *Ha ha ha.*

Someone pushed him in the back an' he was moving again. *Ha ha ha ha ha. Ha ha ha ha ha.*

37

MONDAY, OCTOBER 31, 1998 (HALLOWEEN)
Prudenciana Elementary School, Valle Verde

T HE SUN HAD NOT YET RISEN OVER THE GABILAN MOUNTAINS. A few stars still shone above Byrd Valley when Aurora downshifted and steered her roadster over the Corralitos Creek Bridge. In the misty grey shadows of pre-dawn, an old bag lady stood by the bridge railing. Like an illustration of La Llorona out of the bilingual Tales of the Supernatural, the hag fixed her glowing yellow eyes on Aurora and cackled.

Aurora shivered and turned up the heater.

Once she arrived at school, she traipsed back and forth along shadowy hallways from her car to her classroom, unloading all the things she'd brought for the day's festivities. Soon, parents would be dropping off their children, in elaborate costumes, balancing trays and bowls full of sticky treats for class parties.

With just enough time left to change before kids arrived, Aurora slipped into the faculty restroom and donned her ankle-length white dress with lace trim, high Victorian collar, long sleeves, and old-fashioned covered buttons. She slid her feet into sparkly silver shoes, glittered her face and hair, and fastened her angel wings. Aurora was Glinda, the Good Witch of the North.

She negotiated her wings out through the door of the faculty lounge and stopped to check her mail cubby.

From the cubby, she extracted a schedule for the costume parade, various flyers, and a piece of white copy paper folded in half with the word "*Important*" handwritten in red pen across the front.

It was a note from Tom Olsen addressed to the teachers who'd been at the meeting with Mr. Choate last Thursday.

Dear Colleagues,

I reported to Deana on our meeting and I phoned Len to get his take, as Union President, on our idea of having a community forum on pesticides. Both Len and Deana called me at home this weekend, on orders from Superintendent Spieler's office and the School Board. I was told to pass on to you the following urgent directives:

1. All discussions and contact between the staff of Prudenciana Elementary and neighboring strawberry growers must cease immediately.

2. You are reminded that teachers may not discuss the topic of pesticides in their classrooms, nor may they discuss the topic with parents of their students.

3. Teachers are directed to focus strictly on providing instruction in the district approved curriculum, and may not use class time or district resources, including class lists, phones, fax, or copy machines for any purpose other than authorized educational activities.

The Union attorney strongly recommends that we comply with these directives. Therefore, DO NOT pursue plans for a community teach-in on pesticides or use district resources to research agricultural grants or related topics. *DO NOT have any further contact with the strawberry grower, Mr. Choate.*

You will receive an official memo from the superintendent by this afternoon. I'll try to touch base with each of you personally today, in case you want to talk.

Tom O.

Aurora felt herself changing colors: red, purple, white, blue — like one of those cuttlefish at the Monterey Bay Aquarium.

How could the Union support such an ultimatum? Teaching elementary school on Halloween was something akin to surfing fifty-foot walls at Mavericks on the back of a Great White. It took every bit of energy she had. This memo knocked her completely off-balance.

She closed her eyes, put her hands in prayer pose at her heart chakra, lifted her right foot and placed it against her inner thigh just above the knee. *Vrksasana*, Tree Pose. Breathing slowly and deeply through her nose, she centered and dropped her energy down into the Earth.

"Ms. Bourne!" The force of Principal Wagner's voice was like a punch in the solar plexus. "What's going on here?"

Aurora held her balance as solidly as a deep-rooted tree.

"You're blocking the mail cubbies with those wings. You need to get to your classroom right away. Hurry. Students are already arriving. Make sure you read my memo about today. And talk to Mr. Olsen about that nonsense over the meeting you were involved in last week. We'll have no more of that. See that you keep your mind on your teaching."

"Yes, I …"

Like the Wicked Witch of the West (even without a costume) Principal Wagner disappeared around the corner, spine straight as a broomstick.

*   *   *

At recess, Aurora stood yard duty with the usual parent volunteers, Destiny and Beth. Beth was dressed as Snow White. In the baby carrier on her back was a diminutive dwarf. Destiny was a hilariously plump Humpty Dumpty. On a leash, she had a pot-bellied pig.

"This is Rosebud," Destiny introduced the pig to Aurora. "She lives on our ranch. River and I can bring her in to meet your class next week, if you'd like."

"My kids would love that." Aurora glanced over her shoulder. With a lowered voice, she told the mothers about the teacher's meeting with Mr. Choate, and the district's response.

"This has gone far enough," said Snow White. "You teachers are bound by your contracts. You have to do what the district says. But they can't tell parents who we can and cannot talk to! Prudenciana parents are already organizing. They can't stop us."

Aurora watched two non-school adults walk toward her across the playground. They appeared strangely out of place amidst all of the Draculas, Batmans, Frankensteins, Harry Potters, Hermiones, and Cinderellas. Aurora stepped away from Destiny and Beth, who were talking animatedly, and approached the detective and his companion, Fish and Wildlife Warden Kelli Cavanaugh.

"Ms. Bourne," said Detective Rosa. "The office said we could find you out here. I think you've met my colleague, Warden Cavanaugh? She's been assisting on the Corralitos Creek case."

Aurora and the visitors shook hands.

"We've come for the little girl, Alice," said Detective Rosa. "I thought it would be best to have a woman with me for this. I understand that Warden Cavanaugh and the girl met at the Pelican Dunes beach clean-up."

"We thought Alice might be more comfortable leaving school with someone she knows. We've already cleared it with the office. Here's the paperwork." Warden Cavanaugh handed Aurora a signed Student Release Form.

"We've also notified CPS and the Family Care Home. We'll be taking the girl downtown for a while this afternoon."

"A counselor will be there while we talk with Alice, and also an attorney from the Child Care Advocacy Program, to look after Alice's interests," said Warden Cavanaugh.

"Would you please get us the story she wrote, and those pictures she drew that you told me about? The secretary in the office said it would be a good idea to find the girl during recess, so she won't be embarrassed by being taken out of class."

"Yes, of course. Meet me in front of Room 8. I'll be there in just a minute with Alice. And Detective Rosa, if Alice really is one of the missing girls you're searching for, I'm so sorry I didn't figure this out sooner. I just hope you can find Alice's sister and mother before it's too late."

"We'll meet you in front of your classroom, Ms. Bourne."

*　　*　　*

Alice was sitting on the ground under a mulberry tree near the Life Lab garden with her twin. Alice was drawing in the dirt with a stick. As Aurora approached, the twin jumped up and ran behind the tool shed. Although she was certain that no one would be behind the shed, Aurora couldn't help taking a peek.

No one.

"Hi, Alice. I read your story. It was well written, but pretty scary."

Alice didn't look up. She continued drawing.

"There are some people here who'd like to talk with you about what happened at the creek."

"I know. My sister told me."

"They're waiting for us over by the classroom. Shall we go?"

Alice stood, dropped the stick, and brushed the dirt off her hands and clothes. Without a word, she slipped her hand into Aurora's. They walked together to the classroom, where Detective Rosa and Warden Cavanaugh waited.

Aurora unlocked the door, helped Alice gather her things, and handed Alice's story folder to Detective Rosa. With her backpack hung on her skinny little shoulders, Alice put her hand in Kelli Cavanaugh's. She left the room between the detective and the warden, without a backward glance.

38

JOHNNY WASN'T LAUGHING ANYMORE.

"Jesus, Father, it hurts. Oh. It hurts so bad. *Aghhhhh.*"

Johnny vomited again into the steel hospital pan the priest was holding for him. His broken ribs were wrapped, and his cuts washed and bandaged.

What am I wearing? Some kinda white gown. Where's my clothes? There's a cop guarding the door.

Father Francis wiped Johnny's face and mouth with a clean, warm cloth.

Water.

Johnny took some of the offered water in his mouth, swished it, and spat it into the puke dish. Then he took a drink. And almost lost it again.

"What's going on, Father?"

"What do you remember?"

257

Johnny's head was pounding. "*Nada.* I don't remember nothin." He turned his face away, on the white pillow. *Jesus, how'd they even get sheets and pillows as white as this?* "Awwwwwo. Fuck. I wanna die."

"You came pretty close, Juanito," said Father Francis. "And you almost took some innocent people with you. Johnny, I need to talk to you. Can you listen to me?"

Johnny turned toward the priest, then closed his eyes.

"Look, Johnny. You are in some pretty serious trouble. Your homie Oso is in critical condition. He may die."

Johnny's eyes popped open wide. "Oso? No way. *No es possible.* Oso has a kid, Padre. He's got a little baby. He can't die."

"I'm sorry, *m'hijito. Es verdad.* The man behind the counter at the liquor store had a gun. When you guys tried to rob him and waved that *pistola* at him, he defended himself. Oso got hit. We don't know if he's going to make it."

A cracked cry broke through Johnny's lips. A tear rolled down his cheek. He turned his head away from the priest again.

"What happened to everybody else? Where's all my homies? How come no one else is here?" he asked the wall.

"From what we could learn, all your friends scattered as soon as there was trouble, Johnny. No one's tried to come see you, or even asked about you."

"No way. My homes' got my back, Padre. *Serio.*"

"Sorry Johnny, not them. But we're here. We've got your back. Believe it," said the priest.

"Juanito. *Hermano.*" It was a different voice. "Johnny. We gotta talk." Johnny's big brother, Victor.

Oh, Jesus. What's he doing here?

"Johnny," said Victor, "You little asshole. What the hell were you thinking? I've told you over and over again to stay the hell away from those *sucios.* Why can't you listen to me? You really fucked up this time. As soon as you get medical clearance, the cops are taking you out of this hospital. They're putting you in Juvie. This ain't no shit, bro. *Serio.* You fucked up, bad, dude. They're gonna *process* you. Fingerprints, photographs, take your clothes, put you in some prison suit."

"Fuck off, V. Shut up. Jus' leave me alone. *Aoow.*"

"I'm telling you, little brother. They're gonna take your *life* away. Listen to me, please. I've tried so hard to keep us together. Our *familia*. We're family, bro'. But now, even if they let you go, they'll probably put you on probation, and send you away to live in some foster home, with strangers." Victor's voice choked. "Johnny, you gotta listen to what Father Francis is gonna tell you. Please, *hermanito*."

Johnny moaned and tried to sit up. The priest raised the bed and fixed his pillows.

"Johnny, this is what's going to happen. They're going to take you to the Juvenile Hall on Graham Hill Road, all the way up to the north end of the county. They'll hold you there until your case goes to the DA."

"How long will that take?"

"We don't know. You'll just have to wait. At some point, you'll have a detention hearing. A judge will review your case. You won't have a jury, just a closed hearing, with the judge, the DA, your intake officer, maybe a probation officer. They may let me attend, as your pastor."

"I thought everyone gets a trial by a jury in America," Johnny mumbled.

"If they lock you up and throw away the key, it's what you deserve, you little *pendejo*."

"Hang on, Victor. Take it easy." Father Francis put a hand on Victor's shoulder. "Johnny, the thing is, most likely, the judge will find sufficient merit for a criminal complaint. That means they'll probably hold you at Juvenile Hall for a trial. You'll be charged with attempted robbery, Johnny. Armed robbery. Assault with a deadly weapon. If Oso dies, you'll also be charged with murder, even though you didn't pull the trigger. You'll be charged with first-degree murder in process of a felony. In that case, they'll most likely try you in as an adult, with a jury."

"Do you even get how much trouble you're in, *hermanito*?" asked Victor. "If they try you as an adult, you could actually go to the penitentiary. Do you really want to follow in our dad's *pinche* way? You wanna be a gang banger in the Penn the rest of your life? Really?"

A nurse came into the room and took the puke pan away.

"Look, Johnny," the priest said, "the point is, even if they don't try you as an adult, the Juvenile Court Judge can send you up to the

California Youth Authority if he wants. They can even send you out of state. You've got some big choices to make in the days ahead, my friend. I know this is a lot to lay on you, all at once, but there's a lot at stake. You'll need to pay attention and keep your wits about you, Johnny."

Johnny curled up in the fetal position and threw his bandaged arms over his head.

"Listen to us, Johnny." Victor loomed over the hospital bed and pried Johnny's arms away from his face. "Listen, bro'. They've got you. They can do whatever they want to you, Juanito. It's their game. If you go down as a juvenile, you'll be completely at the mercy of the judge. There's no jury. The judge, he's got all the *cajones*. You got *nada*. He and the DA — they're gonna decide the rest of your life."

"So what. Who cares?" Johnny rolled over to face the wall. "My life is over."

"Your life is not over. We care, *m'hijito*," said Father Francis. "The CYA is a pretty nasty place. We don't want to see you end up there. But the odds are not in your favor."

"Just don't do anything to piss off the Judge, Juanito. Don't make him mad, please. Get him on your side. And the DA, and anyone else who talks to you. You gotta suck it up. Be polite. Be smart, for once. You can turn this around. You can get outta this. I love you, bro'. I want you to be okay."

A tear escaped through Johnny's closed and swollen eyelid. He turned from the wall to meet his brother's grief-wracked face.

"Today is All Souls Day, Johnny," said the priest. "I have to go. I'm offering mass in the cemetery this morning, in an hour. Just, please, think about what we've told you, *mi'ijo*. I'll pray for you."

"And Oso?"

"Yes. And Oso."

39

WEDNESDAY, NOVEMBER 2, 1998
Día de los Muertos (**Day of the Dead**)
Valle Verde Plaza

A T HIGH NOON, THE FIFTH ANNUAL PEACE AND UNITY MARCH
wound through town toward the Plaza. Leading the march, the
Azteca Mexica Ixtatutli — the beautiful White Hawk dancers, all in
feathers — blessed the *barrios* and the *pueblo* in an indigenous,
ceremonial way, with smoky copal incense and the haunting tones of
a conch shell horn. The blessing felt like strong medicine. Victor,
wearing a brown t-shirt and brown beret, was up at the front of the
march with other similarly uniformed young men and women.

The community of Valle Verde had organized and come together
today, on el *Día de los Muertos,* to honor those who had died in
violence, to listen to the family members of those who had been
murdered, and to pray, bless, rally, sing, dance, and support El Pueblo
de Valle Verde with peace.

Victor felt very uplifted and salved in his heart to be a part of this
gathering. These people, his *communidad*, had *Ganas* — they had the

261

will, the spirit, to affirm life and peace, in the face of so much personal tragedy. That's what he needed today, just to keep it going, to keep on believing.

The marchers wound through the city and returned to the plaza. Victor watched all the *familias* setting up memorials to loved ones lost to violence, placing mementos, photos, flowers, and even favorite foods and personal effects of the departed on the altars. People were remembering their *muertos* for all the community to see.

The rally started. A woman up on the stage spoke through a microphone. She was a small woman, but her voice sounded like it could shake down mountains.

"This *violencia* is going to stop," she said. "I'm here today because I lost my son at the hands of gang members. Too many of you know about the pain I am feeling. We all need to work together to end the violence and bring peace to our community. The cops try, but they can't do it by themselves. We need the families to get out and show support. The answer isn't just more law enforcement. It's about parental involvement and community building, education, and faith at a time when it's clearly hard to come by. I pray that all this violence will stop. But prayer isn't enough. This is our community. We need to take it back, for the sake of our children."

The crowd cheered and applauded. Another speaker took the podium — one of the founders of the Valle Verde Brown Berets, a guy named Vallejo.

"We are proud to be here today. Proud that the Brown Berets could play a part in organizing this Peace and Justice rally. We're tired of the injustices in our community, and tired of not having a voice or political representation in our own town ... We're young and brown, so they don't want to listen to us. But we will be heard."

Victor had a lot of respect for Vallejo and his message of courage and self-determination. He'd met Vallejo at Indian Canyon with Father Francis, and had heard him speak at the weekly Brown Beret meetings in the Bike Church downtown, across the alley from the Adult School. The guy was a natural-born leader.

Victor ambled around the fountain in the center of the park-like plaza. Art, tradition, and culture surrounded him. The *Folklorico* dancers were swirling their colorful skirts in beautiful, traditional dances of Mexico. Women and children were giving out treats for free: candies, skulls made of sugar, and *pan de muertos,* bread of the dead.

On the stage where the woman had spoken earlier, *Teatro Campesino* was getting ready to put on a performance. Victor sat on the grass to watch and drink his *champurrado,* a thick and delicious Mexican hot chocolate. The Father of *Teatro Campesino,* The Farmworkers' Theater, introduced the play. Luis Valdez was a distinguished-looking man with a silver moustache. He related the story of how *Teatro Campesino* had gotten its start out in the fields on flatbed trucks, among the grape and lettuce pickers, back in Cesar Chavez's day. It had been born on the strike lines of the Great Grape Strike of 1965 — *Chicano Comedia Popular,* revolutionary guerilla street theater.

"When I produced my film *Zoot Suit,* I made enough money to purchase a *teatro permanente* down in San Juan Bautista. If you haven't already, I hope you will come to see us there. But we don't forget our roots. We will always show up for the people, right out in the open air, whenever we are needed, like today. We hope you enjoy the show."

As usual, the actors wore wonderful, crazy costumes, and talked in a mixture of Spanish and English, street slang, and even a little bit of barely intelligible Azteca and Mayan. The play was an exciting and surreal story full of regular people getting mixed up with strange, supernatural characters and happenings, surprises for both the living and the dead, and very funny lines with lots of double meanings and satire that made the audience split their sides laughing. Victor's heart was hurting real bad with worry for his little brother. But still, it felt good to laugh.

After the play, children in skeleton costumes with black and white painted faces gathered in the center of the plaza, next to the fountain. Victor's little sister, Paloma, was not among the children. He'd insisted that she stay home with Grandpa tonight. She was too upset about Johnny.

As evening's shadow descended, people began lighting the candles they held in their hands.

Several *compañeros* from the Brown Berets stepped out of the dark and surrounded Victor. "We're here for you, *hermano*. We heard about Johnny," said Pato. "He's gonna be alright."

A large *mariachi* band assembled. Wearing cleric's collars and black robes, a couple of priests from St. Patrick's — the big red church in town — said a blessing. Acolytes passed through the throng with smoking incense censers. Pretty soon, everybody was moving, following the children on a procession to the community arts center a few blocks away. There, they would have a grand fiesta, with elaborate *altares* made by community groups, more food, music and dancing until midnight, when all of the souls went home to rest.

Victor moved along with the crowd, following the eerily lit skeleton kids and the priests with their thuribles of swirling, ghostly copal smoke. The procession wove along Main Street and up toward the *Galleria del Arte*. The *mariachi* band, with its full-blown brass cacophony, sent evil spirits flying off ahead of the revelers into the night.

In the bruised, dark purple twilight, Father Francis suddenly appeared at Victor's side.

The priest, clothed in jeans and a light nylon jacket, threw his arm around Victor's shoulder and sang to the *mariachi musica* at the top of his voice.

Victor joined in, lifting his voice, his heart, and his spirit, up into the night.

40

FRIDAY AFTERNOON, NOVEMBER 4, 1998
Detectives' Bullpen, Santa Cruz County Sheriff's Office
County Government Center, Ocean Street, Santa Cruz

DETECTIVE CHARLIE ROSA RUBBED HIS TEMPLES, then shuffled again through the stack of paperwork. It was quiet in the small office known as the "bullpen" that he shared with three other detectives. Everyone else was out in the field working their cases.

Elbow on desk, he dropped his forehead into his palm and shook his head. Frustrating. That little girl, Alice, shouldn't have fallen through the cracks.

How did we miss it? There'd been a shift change. The officers responding to the abandoned child pick-up call from Corralitos Market were a fresh team. The weekend team that investigated the creekside meth lab and the found baby had all gone home.

Too much paperwork in the office. We're understaffed. Things got buried. The connection between a lost child in front of the Corralitos Market and a baby found in the woods was simply missed.

Charlie took another sip of cold coffee. He looked at the stiff, stale half-donut sitting on a grease-stained napkin on his desk. His stomach turned. He fumbled in a drawer for a pack of gum.

Alice and the baby are siblings. That's confirmed.

Charlie pinned the lab report, along with photos of Alice and the baby, on the bulletin board behind his desk.

Concentrate. What's next? Where is Alice's twin, and the mother? Once DOJ runs Alice's DNA through the Missing Persons Database, maybe we'll get a hit.

Charlie folded the stick of gum and popped it in his mouth, then unfolded the gum wrapper and smoothed it out on his desk, staring at it as if it were a map. He opened his notebook and made a note to cross-check Alice's DNA through CODIS, the FBI's new Combined DNA Index System. It was a new database, so it wasn't complete, but he might get lucky. He turned the pages of his notebook.

He needed to talk to those Salvadorans from the Pelican Dunes assault case again.

Maybe after all these weeks in jail, they're ready to tell us where to look for Alice's twin and her mother. Maybe they even know where to find those pinches with the tattoos who shot Salvador Luna.

Charlie picked up the phone and dialed the county jail.

"What? What do you mean they're no longer in the system? The INS? Deported back to El Salvador? Jesus! Tell me you're kidding!"

Charlie slammed the phone down, stood up, and kicked the metal trashcan across the room.

41

SUNDAY, NOVEMBER 6, 1998
Aurora's Cottage
Santa Cruz, The Westside
San Lorenzo River Watershed
North Monterey Bay Coast

"**D**ID YOU RESET YOUR CLOCKS?"
"Spring ahead. Fall back. I love this time of year," Aurora sighed. "But I could do without the days getting shorter, and night falling earlier. This gloomy sky isn't helping, either. I think it's going to rain."

The woman on the other end of the phone laughed. "It's already raining here in Davis. So, Coz, are you coming for Thanksgiving?"

Blue rubbed around Aurora's ankles, purring loudly. His black fur shimmered with violet highlights. Just outside the kitchen window, a busy flock of pine siskins covered the thistle seed feeder and pulled at the white birch catkins, making it snow catkin fluff. Brilliant golden leaves from the birch tree scattered across the green hot tub cover and the red patio bricks.

Aurora took a sip of her sweet, spiced chai.

"I don't think so, Kath. Not this year. Davis is a three-and-a half-hour drive, even without traffic. On Thanksgiving weekend, it'll probably be more like five. Besides, I've got too many papers to grade. It's just too hard to get away."

"Well, then, Christmas. We'll be at the cabin at Squaw Valley. It would be such fun to have you there, to ski together like in the old days. The kids miss you. They want to introduce their Auntie to snowboarding. And we can spend some time at the Resort, sit in the steamy hot tub in the snow, get hot stone messages and manicures at the Spa."

"Sounds good. I'll think about it. Thanks."

"I'm worried about you, Aurora. I worry that you isolate yourself. You don't seem to have any close friends, and you spend too much time at work. Do you ever think about anything besides serious stuff?"

"You know I've never been good at small talk, Kath. Gossip, celebrities, fashion, sports … all the things normal people talk about don't interest me at all."

"I only want you to be happy, Aurora. Anything new in the love department? Have you met anyone?"

"I'm just not ready yet. There was that miserable thing with the keyboard player from the reggae band a few years ago, and then there was that hot contractor last Christmas who turned out to be a such a jerk. He showed me I still have lots of work to do on myself before I can even think about being in a relationship. You know — being an adult child of alcoholics really screws a person up."

"Alcoholics? Don't call them that. Your parents weren't alcoholics, Coz. They were lovely people. Highly educated, successful professionals, cultured, giving back to the community. They just enjoyed life, and their milieu of social drinkers. And your dad shouldn't have been behind the wheel that night in that fast car of his."

There was a crash, a bark, and a shout on the other end of the line. "Oh, no! Baby Karli and the new puppy got into something. Gotta go. Love you, Aurora."

Aurora hung up the phone and threw open the sliding glass kitchen door, startling the siskins, who burst away in a whoosh. She rolled her mountain bike out of the backyard shed and took off on a long ride up through the coastal hill trails of Wilder Ranch State Park.

That evening, in a church meeting room in downtown Santa Cruz, Aurora perched on a cold metal chair hugging her knees and listening to the rain hit the roof. She stared blankly around the circle at the faces of strangers who had come to the adult children of alcoholics gathering. The moderator led a call-and-response read-aloud of the Al-Anon 'Laundry List'.

"We judge ourselves harshly, and have a very low sense of self-esteem. We isolate ourselves emotionally. We fear and resent authority figures. We often become workaholics to fulfill our sense of abandonment and inadequacy ..."

42

MONDAY MORNING, NOVEMBER 7, 1998
Valle Verde, Byrd River Watershed
South Santa Cruz County, Central Monterey Bay Coast

IN THE MISTY, PRE-DAWN TWILIGHT, Aurora waited at the stoplight on the corner of Airport Boulevard and Green Valley Road. The click-shush of the turn signal and windshield wipers kept time to her sleepy, cloudy thoughts.

Election signs sprouted out of the bare dirt field to her left, catty-corner to the Community Hospital.

"Vote No on Prop. 35 — Farmers, Protect Your Water Rights!" and "Yes on UNZ for Immigration Reform!"

Beyond the field rows that stretched to the northeast, the cross on top of Father Francis' church was just visible at the foot of Mount Madonna. Aurora hadn't seen him since the Harvest Festival, over a month ago. Did he ever think of her?

Green light. Aurora turned left toward school.

It was almost dawn when she pulled into the Prudenciana lot. The light drizzle that had persisted through the night threatened to become a downpour before noon.

Aurora slipped the hood of her yellow rain slicker over her head, and wheeled her black teacher's cart across the bumpy parking lot, threading through hectic reflections on wet asphalt of the arriving and departing car lights.

In the faculty lounge, teachers were talking animatedly.

"All my students' parents are terrified," said Katie. "If it passes, most of them will keep their kids home tomorrow. They're scared INS is going to show up at the schools and just start deporting people, or worse — separating parents from their kids."

"If the Unz Initiative passes," said Ruth, "most of them won't even be allowed to bring their children to school. No public education for undocumented immigrants. No food stamps or free school lunch, even if they're starving. No access to hospital emergency rooms. Not even for life-threatening accidents, childbirth, or infectious diseases."

Nathena held her coffee cup in both hands. Her boldly colored African caftan brightened the dark morning. "If it passes, the District will be required to close all bilingual classes and put all the kids into English only, even if they don't speak any English at all."

"That will never happen," said Tom. "Both state teachers' unions — the CFT and the CTA — plan to sue if this thing passes. The District has already announced that it will not be able to comply with Unz until the end of the school year, even if voters approve it. By then, there will be lawsuits. The thing can't possibly be implemented. It's too poorly written, and completely contrary to good educational practice. Furthermore, it's unconstitutional."

"It's a classic case of scapegoating," said May Chang. "Exploiting crude ethnic stereotypes to incite racist fears and hatred. When the people throw the scapegoats into the volcano, the community will be cleansed. The gods will be satisfied, and the people will prosper. When will we outgrow this superstitious behavior?"

"Society will pay for this idiocy in the long run," said Helen.

"Here's an 'Open Letter from the California Council of Churches' in this morning's paper," said Esteban. "The churches are coming out strongly against the initiative. I'll leave the article on the table for anyone who wants to read it."

Katie pulled Aurora aside. "I'm going to the migrant labor camp after school today to talk to my families. I want to answer their questions and reassure them that, no matter what happens in tomorrow's elections, it will still be safe to send their kids to school. Want to come with me?"

43

MONDAY, NOVEMBER 7, 1998
Our Lady of Help Church, Valle Verde

F ATHER FRANCIS PUT HIS PEN DOWN and rubbed his forehead, then cupped his palms over his eyes to soothe the strain. Sunday's sermon would be a simple homily on gratitude and generosity, in honor of Veterans Day, and to prime the pump for Thanksgiving.

He put his feet up on the heavy oak desk and gazed out of the window. The wavy glass of the hundred-year-old double-hung window made the homeless garden outside appear as if it were underwater.

He reached over to the CD player and switched on a recording recently sent to him by an opera-loving friend, Father John O'Malley, who served at the Wind River Reservation Mission in Wyoming.

Apparently John figures Sarah Brightman will lure me into loving opera?

Father Francis leaned back and closed his eyes. Brightman's voice singing "In Paradisum" surged through the room.

No! Far too romantic. Father Francis hastily switched off the music, before the beautiful female voice led his thoughts some where he did not want to go.

Picking up the phone, he dialed Charlie Rosa.

"*Hola, amigo.* Ready for another fishing trip? Sports fishing season opens November 20th on Río San Lorenzo. That good rain we got last Monday means there will be salmon moving into the rivermouth, ready to run upstream. Any Steelhead with clipped fins that we catch, we can keep. I'm taking the day off to go fishing. You in?"

"Sunday, the 20th? Sounds good."

"It'll be just us this time. Dad and my mom went to Seattle to see my sister and her family. New grandchild and all that. I'll meet you just before sunrise, about five am at the riverside entrance to the big parking lot in front of the Santa Cruz Boardwalk. No problem parking. It's deserted this time of year."

"Thanks, Padre," said Charlie. "I'll be there. But hold on a minute, Frank. One more thing."

"What's up?"

"We've heard that Mara Salvatrucha have moved into the *barrio* on the flats by the Santa Cruz Boardwalk," said Charlie. "If you're gonna be waiting for me in some deserted parking lot by the river, watch your back. Seriously, Frank, these *sucios* have a completely different M.O. than anything we've seen before. We're getting reports from the FBI of mutilations and … beheadings."

Father Francis crossed himself.

"These *diablos* are predatory and completely loco, Padre. INS deported the Salvadorans you caught at the Dunes. They're gone, along with any intel they could have given us. Now our only lead to the Luna shooting is Señora Ramirez. She worked well with our forensic artist and we've been circulating the sketches, but our two suspects are rolling deep. No one's seen them."

"They're bound to turn up."

"That's what worries me, Frank. After the way you took down those three *pendejos* in the Pelican Dunes, I'm betting MS-13 know who you are. We're not sure exactly what we're dealing with yet. Just watch your back, *hermano.*"

*　　*　　*

After school, the downpour still threatened. The sky growled —
a dark, ominous rumble — and cold gusts of wind blew leaves across
the parking lot. Aurora clutched her wool scarf, tucked it and her braid
under her raincoat, hurried across the lot, and climbed into Katie's
ten-year-old Plymouth.

Katie turned the car heater on full blast.

A black sedan slithered onto Green Valley Road and followed the
Plymouth at a well-calculated distance.

"Hey, Katie, how did your first formal classroom observation go?"

"My lesson was great. I taught an exemplary standards-based
activity, and my kids were all on task and completely engaged. It went
perfectly. But Deana gave me a terrible evaluation."

"What? I've observed your teaching. You're outstanding. Why is
Deana so down on you?"

"When I was in law school, I interned for a pro-bono immigrants'
rights law firm, and I managed to make some really important ag
lobbyists very mad. I think my reputation as a social justice activist and
a 'troublemaker' followed me here, especially after my summer school
students wrote those pesticide letters. The superintendent obviously
has strong connections to big ag in this community, and they don't
want me here."

"And Deana Wagner is the superintendent's tool."

"Yep." Katie turned right and navigated downhill onto a steep,
rocky dirt lane obscured by trees.

"I've gone by here hundreds of times, and I've never noticed this
road."

"These camps are always tucked away," said Katie. "There are
nearly thirty migrant labor camps scattered around Byrd Valley. But
they're all located, like this one, up in the hills or down in a swale,
behind fields or stands of trees. They don't want the public to see how
these people live, right here in Santa Cruz County, one of the most
affluent regions in the nation. These are the people who produce our
food, for God's sake."

The teachers pulled up next to a dented car with two flat tires and a broken windshield, in front of a barracks-like building with boarded up windows. Nothing was growing in the hard, bare ground except broken glass, pieces of metal, and abandoned soda cans. Even though the ground was damp, the wind was kicking up dust and debris.

A woman washed clothes at an outdoor sink trough.

"That's the only way they can do their laundry," said Katie. "No hot water. See how red her hands are? That water is really cold."

"Look over there," said Aurora, zipping up a warm fleece jacket under her raincoat. Several dwellings assembled from agricultural debris — corrugated metal, wooden flats, and plastic from the fumigated fields — squatted behind the barracks building.

A door slammed and a man, adjusting his belt buckle, ambled away from an outhouse toward a group of *hombres* in dirt-stained clothes and dusty boots. They gathered near an old truck around a little fire. Three grimy, barefooted children played with a mangy puppy at the men's feet.

As Katie and Aurora stepped out of their car, the men stared. Silently, they watched the women approach.

Katie greeted the farmworkers in Spanish, introduced herself and Aurora and explained why they were there. The men nodded. They pointed in the direction of the barracks building. One of the men walked toward the building, then stopped and gestured, intending that the teachers follow him.

The man held a door open for them and Aurora and Katie stepped through into the dark. Inside, they blinked as their eyes adjusted to the dark. Ahead was a long, narrow hallway with a bare concrete floor. About halfway down the hall, a woman wearing a black dress sat on a broken wooden chair in an open doorway. The old woman watched a diapered baby roll around on a blanket on the cold floor, playing with its feet and cooing. A bare light bulb flickered dangerously overhead.

"At least they have electricity," said Aurora.

"In each of the rooms here," said Katie, "a whole family — five or more adults and children — lives crowded together. Families pay over $800 a month, a large percentage of their monthly earnings, for the one room. The building is condemned, but the city just looks the other way. There are a few government-owned camps in the area that are a little better, but they have their problems too."

The man who had escorted Katie and Aurora into the building spoke to the old woman. The old woman picked up the baby and gestured for the teachers to follow her. Inside the room, two Prudenciana students sat on a couch with Salvador Luna, watching TV. A woman stirring a pot on a stove offered the teachers food. It smelled good, but they politely declined.

The old woman handed the baby to a teenager, who bounced the chubby babe on her hip while she prepared a bottle. The old woman sat down at a table and gestured for the teachers to join her. More people entered the room and occupied all the chairs. Still more people arrived, and stood. The room filled, and people out in the hall leaned in to hear.

Katie asked the people gathered what they had heard about the upcoming vote, and what questions and concerns they had. There was a question, and then another. The people talked and listened intently for nearly two hours.

The conversation shifted. Katie translated for Aurora. "They want to talk about pesticides. This woman says they've heard that we tried to organize a forum about the pesticides, but the school district stopped us. They want us to know there are a lot of people here in the camps who are sick from the pesticides, but they don't know what to do about it. This person has hives all over her body from working in the fields. See the rashes on her arms? And this woman says that her brother died of bone cancer he got working in the strawberries. They really hope we can do something about the pesticides."

Someone spoke rapidly in Spanish. People laughed.

"They're feeling a lot better," said Katie. "They say they understand much more about the Unz Initiative now. They say they're really glad we came to talk with them."

$$* \qquad * \qquad *$$

Katie's Plymouth bumped uphill along the curving dirt road, away from the labor camp.

The rain started to come down, hard.

Through the car window, Aurora squinted into the storm. "This road's going to be impassable before long. Good thing we left when we did."

Katie clenched her jaw and concentrated on maneuvering the Plymouth up the dirt road, around the deepest ruts, rills and mud puddles.

Aurora listened to the swish of the windshield wipers, and thought about the Blesséd Mother, whose image she'd seen on cloth and pottery, painted on walls, and enshrined as statues, all over the camp.

They didn't notice the black sedan following them.

44

Baker Ranch, Valle Verde

H AT IN HAND, YUDAS MEDINA STOOD AT THE BACK DOOR of
Malone and William Baker's Valle Verde ranch home.

Through the screen door, Yudas could see into the kitchen. While
he waited, he watched Señora Baker pull silver things — bowls, trays,
tea pot, pitchers — from the shelves of the glass case and give them to
the Mexican girl who helped at the house. As La Señora's hands
moved, the big diamond on her finger shot sparks like fire. Mrs. Baker
was explaining to the girl how to polish silver.

Billy came to the door, pushing his arms through the sleeves of
an expensive leather jacket. "Okay. Ready, ameego?"

"*Sí, vámonos.*"

"Yeah. Mom, don't expect me home for dinner. After the
CalGreen meeting in Hollister, I'm driving down to Monterey to meet
some friends. Probably be home late. Don't wait up."

"Okay, baby. Remember to tell them at the meeting that your father wants to get one more crop out of the east field. He needs to know if they can work another fumigation into their schedule."

"Yeah, got it covered, Mom. Bye."

*   *   *

From the kitchen door, Malone watched Yudas climb into the shotgun seat of Billy's red Corvette. Just before they sped away, Malone called out, "Billy! Maybe tonight in Monterey you'll finally meet a nice girl! I love you, baby. Drive carefully."

*   *   *

Yudas wasn't comfortable riding in the red Corvette with this *menso*. The dumbass drove too fast on these winding country roads, like a *muchacho* trying to prove his *cajones* had dropped. Yudas's son, Antonio, was more mature at eleven than this *puto*. Such a shame for Señor y Señora Baker. To have such a son. *Qué lastima.* And they could not even see what a *cabrón* they had for a child. Good thing Billy had the radio up loud. As long as the radio was loud, Billy wouldn't ask for any more favors. Yudas felt sick to his stomach about the things Billy expected him to do. As if he, Yudas Medina, was some *alambrista*. Billy. *Qué burro.* What an asshole. *Árbol que nace torcido jamás su tronco endereza. (A tree that grows bent never straightens its trunk.)*

Billy accelerated into the oncoming lane to pass a farm tractor. Yudas held on to the gold crucifix under his shirt and pushed his foot to the floor of the passenger side, as if he were stomping on the brake pedal. The Corvette slipped back over the line just in time to miss a head-on. Yudas said a *Hail Mary* under his breath. The country road stretched on ahead.

Like feeling with your tongue for a loose tooth, Yudas' mind felt for the new credit card in his wallet. A small electric charge of anxiety tickled up his nerves as he thought about the three other credit cards at home that were maxed out. Quickly, he brushed those worries aside. He'd been personally invited to have this new card. The invitation had come in the mail, a VIP gold emblem embossed on the letter. Yudas' chest puffed out at the thought.

VIP Gold. Yudas Medina. A VIP. He sat tall and straight on top of the card in his wallet, like a *patrón muy grande*, sitting his fine stallion. A man of enormous responsibility.

When Señor Baker had approached him and offered him the chance to lease land and become a grower, he couldn't believe his good fortune. Some people called it sharecropping, but that was an old-fashioned and undignified term. He, Yudas, was a subcontractor. He had been chosen, personally selected.

El patrón had made everything very simple, had greased the wheels, so to speak, as if for a close personal friend. A loan to lease the land at $3,000 an acre, a loan to rent the machinery and pay for plants and fumigations. Even a loan to pay the workers. And he, Yudas, was the "employer of record", with sole responsibility for all the hiring and firing.

El patrón, Señor Baker, had generously shared his knowledge about growing strawberries. And as long as Yudas followed the guidelines Señor Baker gave him, *el patrón* guaranteed to buy all the berries Yudas had grown at the end of the season. True, Yudas had to promise to sell his berries only to *el patrón,* and not shop for the best price. And true, the interest rate on all the loans was very high, but then, strawberries were the most profitable fruit crop in the US, other than, perhaps, apples. Annual sales of California strawberries were over $800 million.

Yudas' large losses these first two years as a subcontractor were most unfortunate, but *el patrón* was very understanding. He had arranged for a bank to carry all the debt forward and give him a large new loan for this year. This would be a good year, Yudas felt sure.

He was a VIP. A member of the Club of Patrónes, now. He was not worried. All men of substance carried large debts. It was the way of things in the modern world of high finance. In business, everything depended on credit. And Yudas Medina's credit was gold. VIP gold.

*　　　*　　　*

CALGREEN HEADQUARTERS, HOLLISTER
BYRD RIVER WATERSHED, SAN BENITO COUNTY

The Corvette squealed tires as it turned right on San Juan Road and cruised through the little cowboy town of Hollister. On the far side of town, Billy pulled into the parking lot of an unobtrusive, corrugated metal warehouse building. The multibillion-dollar corporate headquarters, one of only four companies in the U.S. permitted by the EPA to produce and distribute methyl bromide, shrugged back from the road, its muted color and plain rectangular form rendering it nearly invisible to passersby. Only a small sign on the side of the door identified the building: CalGreen.

Billy and Yudas walked shoulder-to-shoulder into the front office, along the tan polyester carpeting of the sterile hallway, passed the pot of burnt coffee and the powdered creamer spilled like a line of cocaine on the countertop.

Yudas breathed in the good, expensive smell of Billy's fine leather jacket, its monogramed satin lining making a rich swooshing sound as they walked. Next to Billy's plush leather, Yudas was uncomfortably aware of the thin cheap feel of his own Sears nylon and fleece work jacket.

The men entered the conference room. Most of the chairs around the long wooden table were already filled. Two men in black wearing sunglasses leaned against the wall.

Señor Sean Stark, CEO of CalGreen, sat at the head of the table.

Yudas took the seat next to Billy. He was the only Mexican in the room with these big shot *gabachos*. A grower in his own right. And also earning Saturday overtime today on double payrolls — field foreman of the Baker Ranch and the only paid employee of AWC, the Agricultural Workers' Committee, his own *freseros* union, backed 100 percent by the growers. *Aye, qué buena fortuna.*

Yudas didn't completely understand all of the complicated ways the many organizations represented around the table exactly hooked up, or just who were all these *señorónes*. But he did recognize the eight men who headed the eight giant shipper-cooler corporations that were at the very top of the strawberry pyramid. These men called the shots for the whole industry, from selecting the types of berries grown, to determining the kind and amount of pesticides used, pesticide application schedules, and the number of acres farmed. Yudas knew that at least one of the shipper-cooler operations represented here was owned by a bigger corporation that was owned and controlled by BioGenesis Agrochem. And he knew that Billy's father, Señor Baker Senior, sat on the board of directors of the biggest strawberry shipper-cooler in Valle Verde.

Most of these men were on many interlocking boards and wore many different hats. The alliances were complex, and most of the connections secret and all but invisible. But that there were *muchos dólares* on the table here today was clear.

The PR man was passing out *gorras* (caps with visors) embroidered with the AWC logo and an emblem of two open hands cupping strawberries. He had a big box of the hats.

"Go ahead, take as many as you want," the PR man urged, tossing the caps to all the men at the table. "Spread them around. Get them out to the fields. Get your field foremen to make sure all their laborers are wearing them." Some of the men in expensive suits put on the caps. They looked ludicrous. "We'll have T-shirts and buttons out for you soon."

Yudas reached for a cap.

"Here, Medina," said the PR man. "I have a whole box for you."

Luckily, Yudas thought, *my cousin is picking me up after the meeting, in the truck. This box would not fit in Billy's Corvette.*

"Make sure all your workers wear them, everywhere."

Oh, yes. My freseros will wear these hats if they know what's good for them.

Yudas had stopped hiring the families who'd been working the Valle Verde fields for generations. Families who'd come to expect the jobs. *Familias* who had marched with Chavez's UFW. Instead, Yudas had brought in newcomers from his own village in Mexico. People who owed allegiance to him and to his father and grandfather. Families whose infants had been christened as his godchildren, whose daughters' *quinceañeras* he had paid for. It was a matter of respect for his laborers to vote for AWC when the union vote came. They would wear the hats. They would march and carry his signs. And they would vote for his union. Their well-being depended on it — and they knew it.

The one woman sitting at the table, the company secretary taking notes, smiled at Yudas. He didn't smile back. He didn't want her, or anyone else, to think she and he were at the same level. She would never be able to lift herself above what she was now. A woman would always be lower. But he, Yudas Medina, was going up in the world. Mexican men in the U.S. could be somebody. Someday, he would wear the fine leather jacket and sit as a true equal with these other men at the table.

"By the way, Yudas." Señor Stark glared directly at him. "We didn't like the negative publicity you brought down on us with the fiasco at the UFW meeting, when that woman was hit in the face with the strawberry case by your AWC people. That kind of thing doesn't look good, at all. That story, and the photo of the fucking woman with blood running down her face was hard to suppress. A real pain in the ass. We're working to gain public sympathy, not alienate people, *comprendes?*"

"Yes, Mr. Stark. I understand. I am very sorry that happened. I will make sure there is no more negative publicity for AWC."

"Very good. Now ..." Yudas breathed with relief when Stark's glare released him. "You all understand that without methyl bromide, the end of agriculture as we know it is near."

Sean Stark stood stroking his black goatee and focused his intense eyes on everyone seated around the table. "For American agriculture to survive the changing climate and an exponentially exploding population, American farmers must be able to produce increasingly more crops on less land. And for American farmers to compete, the crops they produce must look good and taste good to American consumers. I know this, and you know this. But we can't depend on the public to know shit. They need to be educated. Therefore, it is your responsibility to make sure that everyone you speak with, at work, on the golf course, and even at your dentist's office, understands that American agriculture cannot be sustained without pesticides, especially methyl bromide.

"Planting, harvesting, processing, storage, packing, shipping. Every single worker in the industry, at every level, must be clear that a ban on pesticides will bring lost jobs and the complete economic collapse of American agriculture. *Freseros* must have no doubt that, without methyl bromide, the strawberry industry is finished, and so are they. Fear is our friend. Spread your message widely."

A couple of men passed the packets around the table.

"In this packet," Stark said, "you'll find a series of position papers written by the Methyl Bromide Working Group in Washington, D.C. These people know what they're doing. The messages are simple. Memorize them. Even your average housewife needs to be able to defend these positions against environmentalists like those fucking schoolteachers who think methyl bromide should be banned."

Stark folded back the cover page, and everyone around the table did the same. Yudas noted that each sheet was written in the format of "myth vs. fact."

"First myth," Stark read out loud. "'Methyl bromide is a dangerous pesticide.'"

Stark called on each man at the table to read one of the "myth vs. fact items". He skipped Yudas.

Does he think I can't read?

"I just want to add here, if I may," one of the younger men at the table waited for Stark's signal that he could speak. Stark gave him a nod. "The Crop Protection Coalition is committed to rolling back or even repealing the Clean Air Act. Our lobbyists are working overtime on that. One way or another, we'll take the teeth out of that socialist agenda, and get big government out of the way of the free market. Be assured, the CPC knows the Golden Rule. He who has the gold, rules." Everyone laughed. "We're confident our generous lobbying efforts will persuade the governor to override the California Birth Defects Prevention Act. I don't think we'll ever have to worry about coming into compliance there."

"Questions?" asked Stark.

"I have one," said the president of Diablo Mountain Products. "What about the work they're doing up at the university, with — what do they call it — agroecology, those organic methods? What do we tell people who bring that up?"

"Organic, bullshit!" Stark's upper lip curled in a snarl. "Those commies don't know enough to pour piss out of a boot. Tell them they should all go back to Cuba, and fuck themselves."

Scornful laughter rippled around the table.

"So," said Stark, "are we clear on our strategy? CalGreen believes in its products and its service, gentlemen. We are pioneers in soil fumigation, helping farmers to succeed. That is our commitment, and our pride. Thank you all for being on board."

Everyone, including the secretary, applauded.

"Take these packets, memorize the talking points. Duplicate and distribute them widely. We have them in Spanish, too. We want every household in the valley — Spanish- and English-speaking — to understand and believe in these statements, like it's a goddam religion. Any questions?"

"Speaking of religion," said a man wearing a silk tie bearing a BioGenesis logo, "what ever happened with those priests who were supposed to speak out at the AWC rally against the UFW?"

Stark's face darkened; his eyes narrowed in anger. "The plan was sabotaged. Things were going good, and then they pulled out on us. We think that fucking Indian priest with the pigtail screwed things up. The good Father Francis. Something has to be done about that meddling padre, boys."

Yes, Yudas thought. *Something should be done about that priest.*

One of the men in black who'd been standing against the wall shifted his weight slightly. He turned to whisper to a *patrón* in a striped suit.

As the man in black twisted, his jacket opened. For just a moment, Yudas saw a leather shoulder holster and the butt of a Glock.

Yudas' mouth went dry. He broke into a sweat and fear gripped his *cajones*. He looked back at Señor Stark with a different kind of respect.

45

THURSDAY, NOVEMBER 10, 1998
A Cave Near Mt. Madonna and Our Lady of Help Church
Valle Verde

T HE MAN AND WOMAN ROUSED THEMSELVES from under their
hand-woven blankets just before dawn. The ground was hard,
but they had slept rough before. At least the cave provided some
shelter from wind and rain.

The woman nursed the baby while the man made a fire. As she
rocked the baby, she worried about her lost daughter. Softly, she
crooned another prayer to the Blessed Mother.

She woke the little girl, combed and braided her hair while the
man started water boiling for coffee and to reheat the last of the beans.
The man and the woman each had an egg, and some bread. That would
be sufficient to keep them going for the long day of physical labor
ahead. The child would get breakfast and lunch at school.

Morning fog slithered up the valley, its cold, wet tongue licking at
the cave mouth. The woman pulled a blanket around her shoulders. The
family had made their toilet a proper distance from the cave. Once

everyone had completed their morning necessities, the man would shovel dirt over the hole he had dug. His camp was clean.

The girl dressed in the new pants, shirt, and shoes her teacher had bought for her, and packed her books in her new backpack. The man was careful to extinguish his cook fire before the family left for the day.

They made their way across country toward the strawberry field where they had worked the day before. The man worried as they walked. He hoped to be given work again today, but nothing was certain. They had not yet been paid for yesterday's work. Today would be a good day. Señor Medina's crop was excellent, and there were still many berries to pick.

Picking strawberries was a skill, and they were learning fast. Each and every berry had to be judged for ripeness, size, firmness, shape and color. The stem of each berry had to be carefully twisted by hand, so it remained on the berry. Berries with bruises, mold or damage had to be discarded into the bags they wore on their backs.

While they picked, the strawberry runners had to be clipped and weeds removed from the rows and put into the bags on their backs. The bags grew very heavy. The fragile berries had to be arranged attractively in the plastic baskets without bruising, and the cases filling with strawberry baskets had to be moved quickly along the rows as they worked.

On this job they were paid by the hour: $4 an hour, not by the piece. The work had to be done rapidly, or they would not be rehired. If all went well, he and his wife would each earn about $40 for the day, working a ten-hour day with no stops for rest or lunch. But they would not be paid until the end of the month, and they had no money now.

The man worried about the stories he'd heard of *La Migra* raiding fields, rounding up *indocumentados* and deporting them before they were ever paid for their work. Some said that happened especially in fields where workers supported the UFW. And one man had told of working for a *patrón* who paid with checks that bounced.

At a creek running down from the hills, the man filled his plastic gallon milk jug with water. He knew that, even in America, river water could give you a stomachache, but it could get very hot working in the fields all day, and there was no drinking water provided for the workers. Yesterday, he'd seen a girl about the same age as his missing daughter faint from dehydration.

And last week, about thirty young men bending over a strawberry row were hit on the back of the head and knocked unconscious when a big irrigation pipe swung around in the wind. Most were still unable to work. He'd heard from a woman in the fields that her husband, whose job it was to shovel soil on the edges of the plastic right after fumigation, had lost his vision.

Neither the girl who'd fainted from dehydration, the young men hit in the head, nor the man who'd lost his vision, had received any medical attention. Everyone was told to keep quiet about what had happened.

The man knew his wife's back was hurting her, from bending over ten hours at a time, day after day. She carried her baby on her back and he carried the extra weight of her weeding basket on his back. She did not complain. And neither would he.

The man and woman left their little girl at the school bus stop next to the field covered with plastic where other children were waiting. A parent waited with them to keep them safe.

The man and the woman could not read, so they did not understand the small cardboard sign posted at the edge of the field. Stapled to a wooden stake, the sign read: *Danger! Peligroso! Do not enter.*

The sign was limp from morning fog. It curled over at its corner, completely covering the skull and crossbones.

46

FRIDAY, NOVEMBER 11, 1998 (VETERANS DAY)
Downtown Valle Verde

A BEAUTIFUL NOVEMBER MORNING, COLD AND CRISP. Downtown Valle Verde had a relaxed, fiesta-day feeling. Young women pushed baby carriages past the shops along Main Street. A group of teenagers in jeans and baseball caps crossed the street and sauntered toward the library. In the plaza, elders rested on park benches near the central fountain; black and orange butterflies danced around flowers lining the paths. The mouthwatering aromas of roasting carnitas, chilies, and fresh pressed apples from the local cider factory saturated the air.

Aurora drove slowly down Main, searching for the address of the United Farmworkers' Union Office among the rows of historic buildings, each structure playfully designed in reference to a different architectural period. She loved the ornate terracotta facades of these stuccos created by Victorian architect William H. Weeks at the turn of the century.

There it was: a five-story pink building, with parapets like a sandcastle, and fanciful terra cotta bas-relief. She promised herself that

293

one of these days she'd come downtown with her camera, just to photograph these architectural treasures.

The meticulously-crafted Spanish colonial revival opened into a red-tiled courtyard, framed by a wrought iron gate. Inside the courtyard, a young Latina woman stood behind an open Dutch door. She wore jeans and a red T-shirt that bore the UFW eagle logo and an image of a strawberry, with the slogan, *Con Union se Vive Mejor (With Union, We Live Better)*. The woman greeted Aurora and gave her some UFW literature and a button. "Welcome. Looking for the Farm Without Harm Meeting? They're in the room across the courtyard."

Aurora pinned the UFW button on her sweater and stuffed the literature into her scuffed brown shoulder bag. "Thank you for making your offices available to our group. It's very generous of you."

The woman in the UFW T-shirt chuckled. "Not at all."

About twenty people sat around a long table in the narrow room. Several young men and women wore the red UFW T-shirts. Vintage photos of Cesar Chavez and UFW posters dating back to the grape boycott decorated the walls.

Ruth, Helen, and Harriet were among the Prudenciana teachers at the table. Aurora also recognized Cecile, from the middle school across the river, and a teacher from the district's newest elementary school, recently constructed in the midst of acres of strawberry fields.

Aurora took a seat next to Katie and near her yard duty partners, Destiny and Beth. She greeted other Prudenciana parents, including Melody's mother, Dr. Anna Escobar.

People introduced themselves. Louise Daniels, the retired librarian from the waterfall hike, smiled at Aurora. A woman sitting next to May Chang tearfully revealed that her son Danny, a third grader in Mrs. Chang's class, had just been diagnosed with bone cancer. Her family had been living in a house surrounded by strawberry fields since before Danny was born.

A silhouette appeared, backlit in the open doorway. *Father Francis.*

As he stepped through the doorway, she took in all of him in one breath: intense eyes, broad shoulders, washed-out jeans wrapped tight around packed thigh muscles, cowboy boots. She quickly looked away, shocked to discover how much she'd been longing to see him again.

She forced herself to focus on Sharon Lumina, a marine biologist who worked at the Monterey Bay Aquarium.

"Thank you all for coming today," Sharon said. "Since we're a new group and, for some of you, this may be your first Farm Without Harm meeting, I thought it would be useful to give a brief account of how our group formed."

Aurora wished she'd worn something prettier. She was planning to stop by school after the meeting to work in the Life Lab garden, so this morning she'd pulled on faded Levis torn at the knees, a favorite old heather-rose T-shirt, and work boots. Her chocolate-brown cardigan had a hole in the elbow, and her autumn-colored angora scarf smelled of the garden: lavender, straw, cocoa bean hull mulch … She'd brushed out her braid this morning, but hadn't gotten around to re-braiding. A wildly unprofessional mass of curls burst out from under her floppy wool fedora.

"About six months ago," said Sharon, "a strawberry grower leased the property next to my home on Revilla Drive in Aromas. He fumigated his soil without notifying any of the neighbors. That first fumigation killed my dog and her whole litter of pups, and made my family sick. Several of my neighbors are here with me today, including Professor Ron Khurie. He'll tell you a little more about our group."

"Good morning," said Professor Khurie. "I teach hydrogeology at UCSC. I normally tend not to get involved in politics, but when the field adjacent to my ranch was fumigated, my entire flock of sheep died, and all of my neighbors became very ill. Sharon and I tried talking with the strawberry grower and the ag commissioner about our concerns, but we got nowhere. At that point we realized that citizen action was required, that we must organize to demand safeguards from pesticides. So we called a community meeting and founded Farm Without Harm. This is our second meeting. I'm grateful to see you all here today."

Father Francis leaned over to say something to the man seated next to him. He hooked the heel of his boot over the rung of his chair, and moved his arm to point at something in the meeting agenda the man next to him was holding. Aurora noted the white cuff of the priest's T-shirt showing under the short sleeve of his plaid button-down. His T-shirt cuff stretched taut over that hard, carved bicep the color of burnished cinnamon, with tantalizing traces of ink. She remembered the way she'd felt, walking next to him on the beach at Pelican Dunes, his clean laundry and slightly salty pungent male scent. She ached.

"Now," said Sharon, "I'd like to introduce Jenny Merritt, who drove all the way down from San Francisco for today's meeting. Jenny's a professional organizer for Pesticide Action International, which represents a global network of community groups like ours."

Aurora glanced up from her yellow writing tablet and caught Father Francis looking at her. Their eyes locked. She couldn't breathe.

Something shifted in the air. Fire flashed behind his eyes. A slow smile lit his face. The man hadn't shaved this morning. She flushed and looked away.

Jenny Merritt took charge of the meeting. "I'm here to help you file a formal legal challenge of the pesticide use permits issued to growers near Prudenciana Elementary School."

With markers and a large easel pad, Jenny began outlining the steps that would be needed to challenge the strawberry grower's pesticide permits.

"First, research will have to be done to develop a map of agricultural properties in the vicinity of the school. Someone will have to go to the County Assessor's Office to get the parcel numbers of the properties. Then they'll have to go to the Agricultural Commissioner's Office to request copies of the growers' Restricted Materials Permits and Pesticide Use Reports, which are public record." Jenny selected volunteers for each job.

"Next, for each of the permits, a formal challenge against the agricultural commissioner to the California State Department of Pesticide Regulation will have to be written. PAN will provide a template. Any volunteers?"

Katie and Aurora volunteered to write the permit challenges.

"Once written, the permit challenges will have to be taken door-to-door around the Prudenciana neighborhood, in order to gather the required number of signatures for filing with the State Department of Pesticide Regulation. Volunteers?"

All of the Prudenciana teachers and parents sitting at the table volunteered to gather signatures.

A subcommittee was organized to develop educational literature and take on a letter writing and leafleting campaign, in Spanish and English, about pesticides. Volunteers came forward. Several people offered to leaflet at local farmer's markets and in shopping centers. Others volunteered to develop plans for a series of public rallies and to create media packets.

"I have a friend who has access to those giant puppets on stilts they use for festivals," said Corkie. "I'm sure we could borrow them for a rally."

Ruth raised a concern about farmland preservation. "We don't want our work against methyl bromide to negatively affect farming in the valley. We need to preserve our valuable agricultural lands, not force landowners into the arms of developers."

"I've heard that the Open Space Alliance is working on that," said Father Francis. "They're helping Monterey Bay area farmers put their ag lands in trust, through conservation easements. Perhaps Farm Without Harm could assist Open Space with that work."

"Yes," said Jenny. "Great idea. In fact, I met with Mrs. Petrakis. I had already planned to bring this up. She requested that we consider having a couple of volunteers meet with her, to get a list of properties of interest. Our volunteers could then contact the property owners and help persuade them to either donate or sell their land to the Open Space Alliance outright, or create a conservation trust easement that would legally protect the property from development."

Jenny stood at the easel with markers ready. "Volunteers?"

Aurora raised her hand, along with several other people.

Jenny took a moment to consider the raised hands, then pointed. "Great. You, Aurora. And ..."

"You, Father Francis. Perfect. A teacher and a priest. You two should make a very effective pitch team for the farmland preservation committee. Next ..."

Heart racing, Aurora felt like an animal caught in a trap. She couldn't look at him. How could she work closely with the man, when being in the same room with him made it difficult to breath, let alone think straight?

As soon as the meeting was over, she scurried across the patio, escaped through the wrought iron gate, and rushed along the busy sidewalk to her parked car.

She didn't notice the man in the black suit standing in a shadowed doorway down the block. He tossed his cigarette on the sidewalk, crushed it under his shoe, and watched the blonde curls swing down the street, reflecting cold November sunlight.

47

THURSDAY, NOVEMBER 17, 1998
Indian Canyon, Hollister Hills
Byrd River Watershed
San Benito County, Central California

F ATHER FRANCIS TAPPED THE STEERING WHEEL, unconsciously
keeping time to the beat of a far-away drum. His thoughts
meandered along the flickering gold and green field rows of the
winding country road.

He'd visited Johnny every day since the arrest. The boy's cuts,
bruises, and broken bones were healing, but his spirit was not. Johnny,
now being held in Juvie, was despondent, lethargic, and barely eating.
The priest offered another prayer.

Thank God the other boy did not die, he thought, for the sake of
Oso and his young family, and also for Johnny's sake. What will the
judge decide at the detention hearing? Will Johnny be remanded to
adult court? Or — with the grace of God — in six months or so, will

he be out on probation, with an ankle monitor? Then the hard work will begin to get him turned around. He is a child. He needs another chance.

Father Francis clicked on his turn signal and made a right at San Juan Road. He slowed as he cruised along Hollister's sleepy main street, enjoying the warmth of California's oblique November sun on his face and on the bare arm he rested in his open window. A cowboy bar, a feed store, a diner. On the far edge of town, Father Francis steered his Honda CR-V into a gas station. He recorded his mileage on a notebook he kept in the glove box, thinking it might be time to look into getting a more fuel-efficient car.

Hand on the pump, he scanned the landscape. No sprawl here yet. Beyond that corrugated metal warehouse building across the street, nothing but open country. The golden hills of California rolled on and on to the horizon. The pump released with a loud click, like the sound of a gun cocking.

The priest made a turn out of the gas station onto the nearly deserted road just as a red Corvette squealed tires around the metal building and shot out of the driveway across the street, coming straight at Father Francis. He swerved and accelerated, missing the Corvette by inches. In his rearview mirror, he watched the red flash streak away. He'd only had a second's glance, but the driver seemed familiar. *Billy Baker?*

Father Francis turned east, and was soon back in open country.

He wound through golden hills quilted by vineyards. A flock of quail flushed from a thicket by the side of the road. He switched on a new CD by a friend of his, Morten Lauridsen, and the transcendent music of *Lux Aeterna* lifted his heart. Soaring with red tail hawks above ancient oaks, he followed an unmarked dirt road that twisted toward a steep-sided canyon.

At the gate across the narrow canyon mouth he stopped and stepped out of his car. A hand-painted sign read INDIAN CANYON. The scent of sun-warmed Bay Laurel leaves embraced him.

Peace.

He took a pinch of tobacco out of a leather pouch he carried and sprinkled the tobacco under a ten-foot tall quartz boulder, decorated with strings of abalone shells, which rose like an obelisk by the side of the road. With bowed head, he listened to the canyon for some minutes. Steller's jays, thrushes, warblers, woodpeckers, and chickadees chattered in the treetops. Deer shuffled in the undergrowth. The land welcomed him home. Satisfied that all was well, he returned to his dusty green Honda and continued through the gate.

Following accepted protocol, he had informed Tribal Chair Marie Christine that he was coming, but did not plan to visit with anyone while he was here. He was on retreat.

He followed the dirt road curving along the creek. A few teepees, tents, and sweat lodges were set up here and there underneath the canopy of oak trees. A small group of people knelt by a cook fire; the good smell of their bacon frying over wood smoke reminded him he was hungry. He would be fasting for three days.

At the foot of a nearly hidden trail that snaked up the canyon wall, he parked, settled his pack on his back, and began the hike.

His moccasin nicked a wild mushroom — a golden chanterelle — at the side of the trail. It gave off a satisfying earthy scent. Dried oak leaves and acorns on the path pushed on the soles of his feet through his soft moccasins. His toes curled in pleasure at the feel of sacred Earth underfoot, the smell of evergreen and redwood duff. Overhead, through filtered forest light, the red flash of an acorn woodpecker's feathers caught his eye.

Rumm'e — the music of the waterfall next to the trail — filled his senses. Whenever a stray thought bubbled up, he let it drift away, bringing his full attention back to here and now, to the exquisite pleasure of every breath, the peace of each footfall.

As he climbed higher, shady redwood forest gave way to low growing, dry chaparral. He felt years slough off of him, as if he were walking back in time, until he imagined himself no longer on a twentieth-century trail, but in a far earlier age.

A blue belly lizard sunning itself in the middle of the path scurried under Manzanita brush at the rocky trailside. Father Francis stopped to pick and eat some of the small tart Manzanita berries, and to drink from his water bottle. At the base of the chaparral plant, its red limbs like a bloody gash in the side of Mother Earth, he made another offering of tobacco and a prayer.

The lizard cautiously emerged from hiding, found a sunny spot on a rock, and pushed itself up and down on its front feet, as if bowing. The man pulled a red kerchief out of his pocket and wiped the sweat off his forehead, then rolled the kerchief and tied it around his head. Nodding to the lizard, he adjusted his pack and turned up the trail, squinting into the cloudless sky.

The steep trail gave way to deer and bobcat paths. The last few yards to the top of the ridge he scrambled up loose rock. He pulled himself over a ledge and onto a flat, smooth stone slab, the outcrop of marble he'd first discovered as a boy. As far as he knew, no other humans came here. High above the forest, he surveyed the distance. The view seemed to stretch across the blue and purple Gabilan mountain range to eternity.

The priest dropped his pack and kicked off his moccasins. Bare feet grounding down through the ancient marble, deep into the center of the Earth, he lifted his face and his hands overhead.

His sense of self dissolved. He released all sensation of existing as a separate being, and surrendered everything to the vastness. As if filling a chalice, the whole sky seemed to pour into his open arms until the man was no longer. There was only the rolling swirling ocean of now and forever. Seconds, minutes, years, ages passed. The Earth rolled through its circles; the solar system, the galaxy, the universe twisted around its Mobius. There was no time.

Then, in an instant, the priest reappeared. He began to chant as he turned to each of the four corners, singing gratitude, blessing, healing out over the blue and purple distances, down into the dry Earth. Finally, he dropped his hands to his sides, dropped to his knees, and bowed his head.

The sun was low in the west when the man stirred himself. He rose and stretched, drank from his water bottle. A fringe of leathery Yerba Santa grew at one edge of the marble slab, next to the boulder. Father Francis offered tobacco at the base of the plant, then picked a piece of a gummy leaf and chewed the bitter herb. A golden eagle circled above his roost.

Ignoring the twinges of hunger in his belly, he unrolled his sleeping pad and his down bag. He pulled his T-shirt over his head and peeled off his jeans, tucking the clothes into his pack. Naked, he walked down the other side of the marble outcrop, far above a small bowl-shaped valley.

Standing astride the edge of the outcrop facing the setting sun, he took a long, satisfying piss, watering the dry chaparral below him as he considered the view. Shaking himself off, he returned to his roost on the marble slab.

The sky blazed orange and red. Rocks and trees glowed as if splashed with molten gold. Father Francis sat cross-legged on top of his bedding, open hands resting lightly, palms up, on his knees.

The orange sun touched the horizon and flattened as if melting. A small molten piece split off and hovered like a UFO. Just before it disappeared, it flashed brilliant emerald green.

Wind moaned through the treetops far below and raced up the ridge like a tribe of ghosts flying through the mountains. Father Francis shivered and drew a blanket around his shoulders.

He watched stars and planets appear like small holes in the shimmering blue silk veil of twilight. Twilight blue gradually faded to dark indigo. Bright stars arranged themselves into familiar patterns of light against the moonless night. Ceres rose at Orion's feet, twinkling like Christmas lights. There was the backward question mark, the mane of Leo the Lion.

Suddenly, coming straight out of the Lion's mouth, a fireball streaked across the night, so bright the trees cast shadows. Trailing the fireball, a glittering ribbon of stardust lingered, twisting and turning like a serpent in the high-altitude winds.

The priest smiled to himself. This was going to be a truly memorable Leonid meteor shower. Just then, another fireball, brighter than Venus, burned across the sky, leaving a glowing streamer in its wake.

Throughout the night, thousands of fireballs and lesser meteors flew all over the sky. A firestorm! The biggest display of Leonids since 1966. As fireballs whirled and spun over the mountains, constellations glided slowly across the dark dome toward the west.

While he watched, the priest let his thoughts wander through the hallways of his mind. But there was one door he would not open. Behind that door, he felt her waiting.

Fiery claws reached out of the air and snatched the priest from his perch, holding him dangling upside down by his heels over a flaming void.

He swung there, upside down, fireballs lashing and searing incandescent scars across the black back of night.

Out of the darkness, men appeared, naked except for grotesque fish masks covering their faces. They jabbed at him with fiery spears. A spear pierced him in the side, and he bled — the bright red of his blood dripping, splashing, sizzling into the blazing pyre below. His flesh slashed, blood gushing from many wounds, he twisted and writhed in agony, burning above the flames.

Monsters flew at him, devouring him, mocking his pain as they stabbed out his eyes and pecked his liver. Knives flashed. Pain vaporized all thought. His skin was being flayed. As he writhed, the flayed skin peeled away from his flesh, crackling like burning fish skin.

He spun over the endless void, flames licking his raw flesh. Agony beyond measure, without end.

With superhuman effort, he reached out, gathering into himself all the pain of the world. All suffering, all doubt and fear, all hatred, sin, and sorrow, he drew into himself, feeling it flow into his veins, a thick vile, dark venom.

He surrendered completely, and the flames consumed him; all of the darkness he had gathered into himself utterly annihilated in a blinding conflagration of pure light.

Out of the light his brother warriors emerged. They lifted what was left of his charred remains from the sky hook, carried him to the water, and began the work of making him whole again.

*   *   *

AURORA'S COTTAGE
SANTA CRUZ, THE WESTSIDE

She rolled like an otter in the Jacuzzi bubbles, switched off the jets, floated on her back in the hot water, and watched the stars. Another fireball streaked across the sky, leaving a sparkling ribbon of stardust in its wake.

She tried to relax and enjoy the meteor shower, but anxious thoughts bubbled up in her mind.

Alice. She's gone mute since being taken to the police station on Halloween. Nathena Hamilton is counseling her twice a week. What's going to happen to Alice? Will they ever find her mother and twin sister? At least, she's been allowed to visit her baby brother. If they don't find the mother, will Alice be placed with a foster family and moved to a different school? Will she and her brother eventually be fostered together, or separated?

Paloma. Also in counseling with Nathena, distraught about her brother Johnny.

Salvador Luna. His killer still not found. Salvador and Alice's twin are constantly at Alice's side, and Alice's lips often move as if she's having secret conversations with the ghosts. If Alice's twin is appearing as a ghost, she must be dead, too. How could anyone commit such monstrous evil?

The Unz Initiative, outlawing bilingual education. The voters approved it. Not surprising, considering the enormous amount of racist propaganda and money pumped into the campaign. Prudenciana's migrant families all kept their kids out of school for a couple of days following the election, but the work of Katie and others is helping to abate parents' fears. Many are bringing their children back to school now. The District, as promised, is not going to make any changes in its bilingual program until next school year. Meanwhile the Unz Initiative is being challenged in the courts. Hopefully, it will be overturned. But even if UNZ never gets implemented, I'm sure we haven't heard the last of anti-immigrant talk and legislation. And until some other immigrant group becomes the target, Mexicans will serve as our scapegoats.

A fireball brighter than Venus lit up the night. A burst of smaller meteors shot from the huge red star, Regulus. Sparkling meteor trails curled away from the lion's heart like smoke.

Katie and I need to finish writing the pesticide permit challenges by tomorrow night, so people can gather signatures over the holiday. Another late night. There've been so many of these the last few weeks. I'm exhausted.

Aurora let herself sink under soothing the hot water, then came back up for air.

It all seems so hopeless. I'm probably wasting my life. I should just get a life, like my cousin says — stop feeding this self-imposed loneliness. Why can't I find a nice man, settle with the way things are, make babies, have fun like normal people, instead of beating my head against the wall with this compulsion to save the world? Why can't I just be like everyone else?

But, as exhausting as it all is, staying late in Valle Verde last Wednesday for the City Council hearing had definitely been the right thing to do. People packed the Council chambers — others like me, who care about preserving the environment. I'm not that weird. I'm not alone.

Aurora switched on the Jacuzzi jets, leaned back, lifted her eyes to the fiery sky, and reviewed the meeting at City Hall.

*   *   *

A long line of people waited to speak against annexing the wetlands property to the city for development. Father Francis stood at the back of the line.

Aurora sat on the other side of the room, with a group of people from Farm Without Harm and another newly formed conservation organization, Wetlands Watch. Seated next to Aurora, Louise Daniels, the white-haired librarian from the waterfall hike, introduced Aurora to Mrs. Petrakis.

"Nice to meet you, Aurora," said Mrs. Petrakis. "I'm looking forward to working with you and Father Francis on our agricultural conservation trust project."

Part way through the hearing, Aurora had to take a restroom break. When she slipped out to the foyer, a man in a striped suit accosted her.

He moved in so close that the toes of his hard shoes almost touched her soft fleece-lined boots. Oily old-style electric razor overtones in his aftershave scent reminded her of a creepy friend of her father's, who had tried to touch her when she was little.

Mr. Striped Suit, more than a head taller, glared down at Aurora and wagged a finger as thick as a cigar so close to her nose that her eyes crossed.

"I know who you are," he said. "I've seen your picture in the papers." His voice was high-pitched and whiney. "You're that teacher. Better be careful. Keep that pretty little nose of yours out of places where it doesn't belong, or you're going to end up getting it punched down your throat."

Aurora's knees went rubbery.

"What?" She'd never seen the man before in her life. "Sorry. Who are you?"

He turned and walked away without answering.

Back inside the Council chambers, Aurora pointed him out to Mrs. Petrakis. "Do you know that man in the striped suit, over by the curtains, next to those men in black?"

Mrs. Petrakis squinted. "The striped suit? I don't know exactly who he is, but I've heard he's been involved in some really big real estate deals in town. Very pro-annexation. He's pushing hard for the new development project, the one with Wal-Mart and Starbucks right on the border of the wetlands." Mrs. Petrakis seemed agitated. "From what I hear, he's bad news, Aurora. Stay away from him."

He's a bad news rich developer and he knows who I am? I'm nobody. Why would such a man give even a moment's thought to an insignificant elementary school teacher like me?

At the end of the evening, Father Francis stepped to the podium to address the crowded chamber. The auditorium hushed at the sound of his charismatic voice.

"The city is proposing to annex six hundred acres on the fragile coastal side of the highway for development. This proposed annexation stands to obscenely enrich a few people. If the land is re-zoned for development, its value is expected to increase more than tenfold. For certain interests, that's a compelling incentive to develop.

"Proponents make the usual specious claim that annexation and development will bring jobs to our area.

"But studies have shown that so-called growth by corporate developers actually robs communities of the unique, locally-owned economic activities that define a community, while despoiling natural resources — which future generations need to thrive.

"Our vision is to place our prime wetlands and agricultural lands under conservation easements, guaranteeing that they remain pristine in perpetuity, to do the essential work of recharging the aquifer. Water is life. Please help us create the kind of world we all want to live in. Preserve the wetlands. Vote against this proposed annexation."

The next morning, the *Valle Verde Register* ran a front-page story about the Wetlands Watch victory. The City Council voted *not* to allow annexation and development of more unincorporated coastal ag lands. *Finally, some good news!*

*   *   *

Aurora closed her eyes and sank under the hot water. As she came up for air, another fireball exploded through the heavens.

Floating on her back in the steaming tub, she saw Father Francis' face in the constellations. Feelings she'd been suppressing flooded through her. A sparkling fission of shooting stars crisscrossed the sky. She surrendered to thoughts of him.

48

NAADAAYI HÉEN A TAYEE

AURORA AND FATHER FRANCIS WALKED down the red dirt road
toward a particularly intriguing cottage. Father Francis stopped,
opened the gate, and led the way along a garden path to the front door.
With a smile and a bow, he opened the door and ushered Aurora over
the threshold into a foyer.

"That was a long hike. You must be tired and chilled. Your room is
at the top of the stairs. If you'd like, take a hot shower and change into
warmer clothes for the evening. I'll wait for you in the kitchen."

Upstairs, Aurora found a room with an open door. When she
entered, she felt as if she'd arrived home after a long absence.

A window framed the moon rising over the ocean.

Judging by the furnishings, this was the home of a craftsman. A
blanket hand-woven in native patterns draped over the back of a
bentwood rocking chair. On a tea table next to the rocker sat a Tiffany
lamp with a stained-glass dragonfly shade.

An antique vanity with a mirror stood against one wall. Against another wall, a freestanding wardrobe — with an intricate design of fish inlaid on its double doors, in varied colors of wood — emanated a magical vibration. A fresh bouquet of wildflowers on the bedside table filled the room with a sweet and calming fragrance. Two botanical illustrations of native flowers hung on the wall next to the window.

In one corner of the room, a door stood ajar. Aurora investigated. *Bathroom.*

White beadboard wainscoting covered the bottom half of the walls, painted seaglass green above.

A stack of fluffy white towels filled a shelf and a plush white terrycloth robe hung on an ornate, fish-shaped copper hook. Conch and abalone shells were arranged in an alcove above a large sunken whirlpool bath. Behind a glass door was a shower with natural rock walls, out of which grew ferns — creating the impression of a grotto. Behind another door, Aurora found a small chamber with a toilet and sink. Blue and white floor tiles warmed her bare feet.

She stepped into the shower. Stars and moon shone through a skylight above, making her feel as if she were showering in the open air.

Warmed and refreshed, she wrapped in a towel and peeked into the bedroom. Assuring herself that she was still alone, she tiptoed across to the wardrobe.

Recalling C.S. Lewis's magical story, she cautiously opened the wardrobe doors.

To her relief, she found only casual clothes of the sort she usually wore, in her size.

She dressed in drawstring sweatpants, a comfortable T-shirt, a fleece sweater, and fur-lined moccasins, then sat in front of the vanity. Arranged on top was a brush and comb set with sterling silver handles, an ornate fish design surrounding her monogramed initials worked into the silver. She combed the tangles out of her hair, wondering again if she were dreaming.

Delicious cooking smells wafted into the bedroom. Letting her damp hair hang loose over her shoulders, she stood and took several deep grounding breaths to prepare herself for whatever was to come next, then followed the sound of clattering dishes downstairs to the kitchen.

A blanket around his bare shoulders and a wine bottle and two glasses in his hands, he welcomed her with a smile. Fish chowder simmered on the stovetop, and wood burned in the fireplace. The kitchen table was set with salad, sourdough bread and butter.

Being in such intimate proximity to a shirtless Father Francis made Aurora's pulse race. She tried to act nonchalant.

"You can't have done all this in the fifteen minutes it took me to shower and change clothes?"

He laughed and poured the wine. "No. Not me. The tribe is caring for us while we ... *adjust*, and heal."

A spot of bright red blood oozed through a bandage over his heart.

"You're bleeding! I didn't realize you'd been hurt."

"It's nothing. A scratch from the demon."

"Please, sit down Father Francis," said Aurora. "Let me serve the soup."

The man obeyed, wincing slightly as he dragged his chair to the table. Aurora ladled hot soup into stoneware bowls. She looked up to find he was watching her. He reached for her hand and gently guided her to sit close to him.

"Aurora, please don't call me Father Francis. Here, in our home, I'm Frank. You'll hear people refer to me by other names, some of them strange and unpronounceable to you. But please *ñ'a táayaa*," he laughed, "don't call me Father."

"Why? Does that mean that you're not a priest, when we're — here?"

"I'm still a priest, as much in this world as in that other. But when my body passes through the portal, much more ancient promises hold sway."

He rose and paced in a small circle, eyes on the floor. Finally, he stopped in front of her.

"UpRiver, I'm a Catholic priest. But the tenets of all the religions of that world are written on a very small part of the infinite heart of God. Here, I am still a spiritual initiate, still learning the Way from elders far more evolved than I. And a period of chaste service is required for my — *initiation* — here in *Naadaayi Héen a Tayee*, as well as UpRiver. But in *Na'Tayee*, I am not bound by the narrow customs and social conditioning of a given time and place. Here, I'm not constrained to hide my feelings from you. I am, most assuredly, free to be a man." He sat down facing her, took her hands in his, and kissed them.

"I love you Aurora."

Aurora pulled her hands away. When she could speak, she said, "You, I — we don't know each other. I mean, not really. How can you … I — I'm sorry. Please, Father Francis, I …"

"We are not strangers, Aurora. You and I already knew one another very well eons ago, when we chose to be handfasted, to go through the binding ceremony together."

"Handfasted? This is crazy," she said. "If what you say is true, why don't I remember?"

"You sacrificed a great deal to journey UpRiver, to be a Teacher. But I believe you're beginning to rediscover who you are. Trust your feelings."

Aurora's brows pulled together. "How well do we know each other?"

A slow smiled smoldered across his face. "We have not yet mated, *ñ'a táayaa*, but I ache to be one with you."

"Mated?" Aurora blushed. "Do you have these feelings for me when we're together UpRiver?"

He leaned closer and softly brushed her lips with his finger. "Yes. You arouse me."

She thought he was going to kiss her, but he pushed his chair back, rubbed his temples, and swallowed.

"You arouse me more than I can say. When we are UpRiver, it tortures me to hide my feelings from you. But to let you know my desire would be too dangerous, not only for you and me but also for all the beings we're working to heal and protect, and all the worlds we must hold together during the coming chaos of the Great Turning. We must keep our promises and remain impeccable."

"This can't be real." Aurora picked up her spoon. "And yet this spoon in my hand feels so solid." She tasted the soup. "The soup tastes delicious. And I believe that truly is blood seeping through your bandage. I feel like I'm in an actual place, not in some kind of vision or hallucination."

He shook his head. "It's hard to put into words. We are in a sacred, eternal dimension. And yes, it is 'real.' There are laws — codes — operant here, holding the Pattern together, but here, nothing is bound by the same limitations as in the world UpRiver. Here, time itself bends and folds."

Aurora thought it best to remain silent and accept that explanation for now.

As they ate, her mind wandered more than once to the question of who was going to sleep where that night.

As if answering her unspoken thoughts, he said, "I will not be sleeping here at the house tonight, Aurora. I have to go see my ... doctor. After that, the Council meeting will probably continue all night. I might have to be away for ... some time."

She was staying here tonight all alone? Maybe for some undetermined length of time? In a place with bizarre space-time warps and demonic beasts?

"You will be safe. I promise. This house, and everyone within it, is protected, shielded. Nothing will harm you here. I'll return as soon as I can."

49

FRIDAY NIGHT, NOVEMBER 18, 1998
Prudenciana Elementary

AURORA STOOD IN THE CLASSROOM DOORWAY, gazing out toward the empty fields. Dark as obsidian. Socked in and no stars. Shivering, she pulled the door closed.

Nine-thirty.

She stepped carefully around the papers and books spread all over the floor and precariously stacked on the desks. "Katie, do you think we'll really be able to finish these permit challenges tonight?"

"We have to." Katie stretched in her computer chair and palmed her eyes. "People need to have copies by Tuesday so they can gather signatures over Thanksgiving break."

"Alright. What's next?" Aurora rubbed her forehead. They'd skipped dinner and she felt slightly nauseous. She took a sip of her herbal tea. *Cold.*

"Let's see." Katie shuffled through the pages of a stapled document. "Sevin."

Aurora picked up a thick book marked as the property of the University of California Library. "Here it is. Ready?"

"Yep. Shoot." Katie's fingers hovered over the keyboard.

"'Sevin: Trade name for Carbaryl. Carcinogen. Reduces sex hormones. Affects reproduction. Highly toxic when ingested or inhaled. Symptoms of Carbaryl exposure in humans are malaise, muscle weakness, dizziness, hypersensitivity, sweating, headaches, abnormal salivation, nausea, diarrhea, incoordination, and slurred speech.'"

"This is overwhelming," said Aurora. She waited for Katie to finish typing. "There's more on Sevin. Ready? 'Documented chronic health effects: Behavioral and neurological problems. Anemia. Causes respiratory, blood, liver, kidney, spleen and bone marrow damage. Carcinogen and mutagen. Suspected viral enhancer. Known to suppress the immune system. Its ability to drift over seven miles has been documented. Highly toxic to birds, fish, crustaceans, aquatic insects and bees. Has been detected in muddy banks and groundwater.'"

"Bees?" Katie's eyebrows pulled together.

"Right. Seven's just one of many chemicals known to be toxic to bees. No wonder bees are in colony collapse worldwide."

"Yep. Poison the pollinators. Brilliant." Katie pulled on a beanie with pom-pom ears that made her look like an angry forest creature. "Here's the next one. This one's listed on all three permits. Section 18 Myclobutanil."

Aurora shuffled through the stack of papers at her feet. "Got it. 'Can cause damage to the organs. Known to be dangerous to pregnant women. Can cause reproductive damage and birth defects. May be fatal if inhaled, swallowed, or absorbed through the skin. Toxic to aquatic life, with long-lasting effects. Section 18 means the EPA granted a Section 18 emergency exemption to allow its use, establishing a maximum permissible level for residues on food, in spite of its extreme toxicity.'"

Katie finished typing, then squinted at the small illuminated square of the computer monitor and scrolled to the top of the document in progress. "So here's the list. Thirteen different chemicals, classified by the U.S. EPA as Category I Acutely Toxic Substances, are being applied right next to our school. Choate's use permit has all of them. Garritt's has all but Sevin, and Mr. Cowley's has all but Methomyl."

Katie's face glowed green in the light of the monitor.

"Methyl bromide, chloropicrin, Paraquat, Sevin, Guthion, aluminum phosphide, Avitrol, Monitor, Disyston, Trigard, Metasystos-R, Section 18 Myclobutanil, and Methomyl."

Aurora groaned. She looped her wool scarf around her neck and zipped up her jacket.

"Look! There he is again." Katie pointed to a little grey mouse, whiskers quivering, poised like a toy under the bookshelf by the wall. The mouse watched the teachers with eyes as shiny as glass beads. He stood on his hind legs, rubbing his front paws together under his chin.

"He looks so innocent, like a mouse in a fairy tale," said Aurora.

"Yep. I feel like he knows we're trying to stop the poisoning and he's here to encourage us," said Katie. "We can do this. The Choate letter is pretty much done, and we can use it as a template for the other two."

Katie buttoned her thick felt jacket over a sweater and wrapped a green Pendleton scarf around her neck. Even though she was very slender, bundled up in her woolens she reminded Aurora of the prickly hedgehog in *Alice in Wonderland*.

"Do you think the ag commissioner will really take the time to read these?" asked Aurora. "Don't forget, he told us never to contact him again."

"He probably won't," said Katie. "But maybe someone will. I'm pretty sure all the teachers here at Prudenciana will, and everybody in Farm Without Harm. Anyway, it's our Constitutional Right to file these permit challenges, so I don't think we can be fired for doing it."

Aurora tapped a yellow pencil on the school desk. "Even if the ag commissioner doesn't read our permit challenges, he's still legally required to respond within ten days."

"If only people knew what's going on here ... We're waging chemical warfare on our women and children, the people who grow our food, and Mother Earth. We're poisoning ourselves, for God's sake."

"Let's review what we've got. Read the whole permit challenge out loud. If it's okay, we can go home."

"Alright." said Katie. "Here it goes. 'Dear Commissioner Grumond, we are writing to request that you review your action in issuing the Restricted Materials permit #44-97-440482A. Pursuant to

Food and Agricultural Code #14009, we request that you revoke this permit. Prudenciana students, staff, and community members have experienced irrefutable symptoms of pesticide poisoning, including headaches, nausea, numbness of extremities, burning and tearing eyes, blurred vision, difficulty breathing, sore throats, joint pain, auto-immune disorders, inner ear complaints, nosebleeds, itching and burning skin, changes in the taste of food; behavioral abnormalities such as lethargy, agitation, panic attacks, hallucinations, and disorientation; cognitive impairment, miscarriages, seizures, and cancer. Teachers and parents have reported these complaints to the Agricultural Commissioner's Office.'"

"Yeah, we ask him to do his job and protect us, and he calls it harassment," said Aurora.

"He's one of the pesticide 'good old boys'. It's no surprise that he defends his cronies. But it's an outrage that he can get away with it when he's being paid to protect public safety."

"What are the qualifications for his job, anyway? Did someone appoint this guy?"

"I've heard he's appointed and 'serves at the pleasure of' the Board of Supervisors."

"What about the school administration? Why are they aligned with corporate chemical agricultural interests? I know I keep asking this, but it just doesn't make sense."

"Oh, come on, Aurora. *Cha-ching*. Follow the money. Isn't it obvious? Big ag owns the politics and economy of this city. They sit on the School Board, the City Council, the Board of Supervisors. They pour money into elections, pay taxes — huge taxes — fund the high school ag program, and donate millions to the school district. The district is going to need a lot of help funding the new high school. Think about it. It's ag money that makes everything go around here."

"Then why even try to fight it?"

"We're 'mandated reporters', remember? As teachers, we're legally obligated to report any situation we suspect may be endangering our students. You can quit now if you want to, Aurora. But I just have to keep going. It's my responsibility."

"You've put so much on the line for this, Katie. You don't have tenure. They can fire you anytime they want."

"What am I supposed to do? Just bow my head and ignore the poison drifting into my classroom, making my kids and me sick? Just teach boring, rote, repetitive tasks without question, training my students to be obedient little automatons, willing to take their places, when the time comes, as dehumanized consumers and indebted wage slaves, living to perpetuate the growth of an economy that serves the oligarchy? Eating whatever shit, breathing whatever poisons the corporations dish out? I can't do it, Aurora."

"Me either," said Aurora. "I just wanted to be an excellent teacher, live healthy, be happy. Make a positive difference in the world. But this pesticide thing is changing me. I feel like I'm turning into a foaming-at-the-mouth activist."

"I'm just getting angrier. Keep reading?"

"Go."

"'According to Dr. Anna Escobar, a pediatric specialist, children are the most vulnerable to pesticide exposure. One of the largest classes of pesticides is the endocrine disruptors. The human endocrine system is crucial in regulating all aspects of children's developing bodies and brains. Children's body cells are rapidly growing, but their livers and other enzyme systems are not mature. This means that they don't detoxify chemicals as well as adults. Their immune systems are also less mature ...'"

Katie stopped to take a sip of tea. "If you're finished reading Dr. Escobar's book, could I borrow it?"

"You can have it over the break."

"Thanks. The next part is about what each of the pesticides does. Should I keep going?"

"I'll read," Aurora said. "'Methyl bromide is classified by the U.S. EPA as a Category One acute toxin, the most potent class of toxic chemicals. The effects of methyl bromide exposure include blurred vision, twitching and convulsions, numbness of extremities, seizures, psychosis and death. Chloropicrin, a suspected cell mutagen, is commonly known as 'tear gas'. Exposure causes choking, disorientation and confusion, severe panic attack, and can lead to irreversible pulmonary damage and death.

"'Methyl bromide and chloropicrin are commonly used together in strawberry production. Combined, the chemicals are synergistic in killing soil-borne organisms. Combining the pesticides also magnifies their toxicity against humans. No health studies have been done on the degree of increased toxicity as a result of synergistic effects.'"

"I can't believe that there haven't been any studies of the synergistic effects of combining pesticides," said Katie.

"I just saw an article about that." Aurora shuffled through a stack of papers. "Here it is. Listen to this. 'In breast cancer studies conducted by scientists from Tulane University in 1996, when four pesticides were tested for their ability to disrupt the human hormone system, potentially leading to breast cancer and reproductive damage, the pesticides showed only a small effect when tested individually. But when they were combined, they were up to one thousand times more potent carcinogens.'"

"One thousand times more potent carcinogens when combined? How could they just gloss over something so important? The EPA should require that all pesticides be tested for synergistic effects before they're approved."

"There's more. 'Public exposure to these combined chemicals when they are applied in fields near houses, schools, hospitals and businesses is inevitable. In some cases, more than fifty percent of a pesticide application drifts from its intended target.'"

"According to Mr. Stark, methyl bromide does not drift into the school. Remember?" said Katie. "Even though the stuff is being applied right next to our playground."

Aurora frowned and pulled on her braid. "Does he really believe that, do you think? Or is he just a straight-up cold-hearted liar?"

"Who knows. What we do know is, he's wrong," said Katie. "The pesticides are drifting into the school. For sure. We just need some way to prove it."

"We should ask Pesticide Action Network if they know anything about monitoring drift." Aurora made a note on her yellow tablet to follow up on the drift-monitoring question. "You want to read?"

Aurora sat cross-legged on top of a child's desk, surrounded by reference materials, ready to verify the facts on each pesticide as Katie read.

"'Pesticides listed as Category One toxins range in toxicity from substances which cause severe respiratory and nervous system reactions to substances which will kill a person with just one drop on the skin. We find it unacceptable that pesticides listed by the U.S. EPA as the most potent class of pesticides are used near an elementary school.'"

"Did you hear something? I thought I heard a noise outside," said Aurora.

Out of the corner of her eye, she saw Paloma's brother Johnny slouched against the wall by the door. When she blinked, he was gone.

"I have the creeps tonight," said Aurora. "It's so demeaning that teachers aren't trusted to have phones in their classrooms."

"Yep. It's almost the millennium, and they treat us like it's the 19th Century."

"Being isolated out here at night without any way to communicate with the outside world could be dangerous. What if something happened?"

"Yep. Oh, look. There he is again." Katie pointed.

The field mouse was on top of the bookshelf, holding a kernel of yellow and red Indian corn in his paws. He sat up on his hind legs like a little person, taking dainty bites.

Aurora laughed. "Oh no. I guess my kids didn't clean up very well when we made our Thanksgiving corn necklaces."

"Never mind," said Katie. "Ready for more?"

Aurora nodded.

"'Paraquat: A dose of less than a teaspoon can result in death of an adult male. An agent of chemical warfare, it has been implicated in Parkinson's disease. Corrosive to the skin. It's a teratogen, neurotoxin, endocrine disruptor, and a suspected cell mutagen.'"

"Teratogen. Meaning it causes birth defects, right?"

"Yep. And also miscarriages." Katie's face flushed with anger as she turned back to the computer screen.

"'Methomyl: EPA Category 1 restricted use toxic pesticide. A nerve gas and known mutagen. Can cause respiratory, liver and genetic damage. Because of its water solubility and high degree of toxicity, concerns exist for its potential impact on non-targeted aquatic organisms as well as on surface and groundwater.'"

"Neurotoxins." Aurora felt sick. "Children come to school to learn and develop into their full glorious potentials, and we expose them to substances that give them autism, lower their IQs, and cause brain damage."

"Ready for the next one?" Katie asked. "'Aluminum phosphide: Dead gophers that have ingested this poison are typically eaten by eagles and hawks, killing them and moving the poison up the food chain. In humans, causes damage to heart, lungs, central nervous system, gastrointestinal tract, liver, and kidneys. Implicated in congestive heart failure.'"

"Hawks and eagles." Aurora shook her head. "What's next?"

"'Avitrol: A granular pesticide used to non-selectively poison all birds.'"

"Non-selectively poison all birds? Are you kidding me?" Aurora stood and waved her arms. "These agricultural fields are on the Great Pacific Flyway, the major migration route for most of our western migratory birds, many of them endangered. How do they get away with that? Isn't it a violation of the Federal Endangered Species Act?"

Katie rolled her eyes and resumed reading. "'Monitor: A dangerous organophosphate. Exposure can cause hair loss and decreased fertility.'"

"We've blamed ourselves for our health problems for years," said Aurora. "We tell ourselves it's our own fault we're sick; our fault we have weird skin rashes, our hair is falling out, we can't conceive a child. We've convinced ourselves that we just need to eat better, exercise more, get more sleep, do a better job of managing our stress, that it's just another virus going around."

"Now at least we know there is definitely something in the environment that could be causing all of these seemingly unconnected health issues," said Katie.

Aurora shivered and pulled her mittens on. "How do we gather scientifically valid data to prove cause and effect? Classroom teachers don't have time to systematically gather health data. But someone needs to do it. We need to demonstrate with a high degree of statistical probability that the pesticides are making us sick."

"Statistical probability bullshit," said Katie. "How could anyone in their right mind with access to this information honestly have any doubt that the pesticides being used here are dangerous? Look at this list. Besides, the studies have already been done. Think of Dr. Escobar's book. The data is there. But no matter how many studies are done, the industry's public relations people will just discredit the science. And guess who the public's going to believe?"

"I know. People believe the slick wizards of propaganda, not the nerdy scientists. But we still have to maintain scientific objectivity, Katie. We have to be very careful what we say and how we say it. We can't make unsubstantiated claims. You know that people are oh-so-ready to dismiss us. We've got to be able to do the science and cite our sources."

"This is so wrong. The burden of proof should be on the pesticide companies."

"Well, sadly, that's not the way things work right now."

Katie sighed. "You want to read?"

"'Disyston: An organophosphate and reproductive toxin. Guthion: a neurotoxin; damages muscle tissue. Trigard: A suspected feto-toxin. Metasystox-r: Proven to be extremely dangerous to pregnant women and their fetuses.' That's it. All thirteen of them," said Aurora. "What kind of a society creates a food system dependent on poisonous chemicals?"

"They get away with it because the chemical manufacturing corporations are considered people. I learned about it during my year of law school."

"That's ridiculous. Corporations aren't people."

"They are by law. The Supreme Court determined that our Constitutional Rights enumerated in the Bill of Rights apply to corporations as if they're people. So chemical corporations are 'innocent until human members of the public can prove them guilty' of causing harm," said Katie.

"And the federal agencies that are supposed to protect the public rely on research conducted by or for the very corporations whose products are under scrutiny."

"Yep. The fox guarding the henhouse."

"Wait. Did you hear that?" Aurora cocked her head to listen. "Sounds like something's moving around outside the door."

"Maybe a raccoon raiding the trash," said Katie. "Did you lock the door?"

"Don't remember. I'll check." Aurora hurried to the door. With a shiver, she turned the dead bolt to the locked position.

"Almost done," said Katie. "I'll read."

The teachers faced the computer monitor, with their backs to the door. They didn't notice dark eyes framed by a black knit facemask peering through the little window in the door. The man in black watched and listened as he smoothed the skin of his black leather gloves.

"We do not want our staff, community members and students to be the guinea pigs who are harmed before more stringent regulation of these dangerous chemicals is finally implemented. We believe that we all have a right not to be poisoned while working or attending school."

A sound like rapid bullet fire exploded through the room.

The women screamed and ducked, turning toward the noise.

An avalanche of colorful plastic math cubes tumbled from the bookshelf.

The field mouse peeked out from behind a stack of *Magic School Bus* books, whiskers quivering.

"Oh, no." The teachers laughed. "He tipped over the bucket of math cubes."

Katie continued reading.

"'We recognize that Mr. Choate is already taking great and courageous strides in leading our agricultural community toward the transition to sustainable practices. He has voluntarily increased his buffer zones, reduced the amount of methyl bromide he is using, and has begun researching less pesticide-intensive agricultural strategies. We value his leadership enormously. However, with all due respect, in order to prevent any further threat of hazardous exposure to the staff, children, and community of Prudenciana School, we ask that you revoke the restricted materials use permit #44-97-440482A issued to Mr. Choate for the chemicals listed above and eliminate the use of all restricted materials, as well as any substances suspected of being harmful to the environment and/or human health, including all known carcinogens, endocrine disrupters, neurotoxins, immune suppressors, respiratory, cardiovascular, liver, kidney, and/or reproductive toxins on this parcel of land in perpetuity.'"

Katie put her palms to her eyes. "That's it."

"Perfect. I can print all three permit challenges at home and have them ready for Jenny to pick up Monday morning, so she'll have time to make copies and get things ready for the signature gathering."

Aurora ejected the Zip disk and tucked it in her bag. There was another noise outside the door. Wide-eyed, the teachers stared at each other.

"Let's get out of here," said Katie.

"Wait. We should have our keys in our hands before we go out. We don't want to be standing in that parking lot in the dark trying to find our car keys."

The man in black swore silently and settled the teetering trashcan. He barely had time to disappear into the shadows and flatten himself against the wall.

The smell of the classroom poured out through the open door. Crayons, glue, old carpet, chalk dust, stale school lunches.

The teachers burst through the doorway, shoulder-to-shoulder.

Light from the classroom flooded the hall, just missing his black shoes. The blonde turned her head to peer up and down the corridor, then squinted toward the strawberry fields — a sea of darkness.

An owl screeched. The man in black touched the gun at his hip.

50

F OG, A MONSTER WITH COLD, GHOSTLY SHOULDERS, loomed offshore, hiding in the darkness before the dawn. Father Francis waded hip deep into the river, cast his line out and flicked it back, cast, flick, dancing it on the water's surface. Dream-like mists of fog tugged at the ephemeral whip curling around the fisherman's head.

Río San Lorenzo flowed under the train trestle and wound around the back end of the Boardwalk. From there, the rivermouth opened wide and snaked out to the bay. Clammy tentacles of fog probed up the rivermouth, swirled over the train trestle, and wrapped around the intricate wooden scaffold of the roller coaster.

A giant reclining skeleton, the Giant Dipper roller coaster sprawled, rolled, fanned, dropped, arched, and twisted over the landscape. The historic red and white landmark was already one of the oldest roller coasters in the country when Francis Hilman was a boy. The priest had good memories of the classic wooden coaster.

Dawn flamed over the water. Father Francis could feel the Steelhead ripening, eager to scoot on upstream to spawn. A silver fish jumped, making a splash that caught morning's first sunlight. The Steelhead were mobbing into the rivermouth for a good late fall run. The priest lost himself in the dance of fly-fishing, the bright river diamonds, the fish, the flick and pull of the line, the rising, thinning mist, the mewling gulls, the faintly felt pulse of a distant drum.

*　　　*　　　*

On the other side of the river, in a sandstone cave just above high tide line, a tattooed man with a black teardrop in the corner of his eye crouched, bare assed, above a steaming pile of shit. He wiped himself with a torn-off corner of the brown paper bag that held the empty tequila bottle, then dropped the paper on top of the stinking heap. He pulled up his pants and stumbled toward the lump of filthy blankets on the ground.

"Eh, *pinche puto*. Wake up." He kicked his companion until the sleeping man stirred, and swore.

While the sleeper roused himself, the reeking man used the sleeper's blanket to wipe a brown smudge off the back of his hand, then stumbled over to his backpack. He rummaged until he came up with the plastic bag that held his rig and his junk. *La Negra. Chiba. Caballo.* He held the bag of tar up to the dim light of the cave mouth, yellow eyes assessing how much was left. No worries. A continuous supply was a sure thing. His lip curled in satisfaction, lizard-like tongue flicking over silver tooth.

He set out water bottle, spoon, cotton, and lighter on a cloth on the ground. Then he pulled his rig and dope out of the plastic bag. He examined the needle, holding it close to his face and trying to focus. Already used twice. Maybe good for once more.

He placed some of the tarry junk in the spoon and added water. The lighter clicked. He held the flame under the spoon until the tar dissolved. Using the plastic plunger, he scraped bits of *chiba* off the sides of the spoon, stirring a little to make sure he didn't waste any, then cooked the mixture a little longer. When all the skag was dissolved, he dropped a piece of cotton in the spoon. It sucked up the liquid heroin. He used the plunger to press down on the cotton a couple of times, releasing the filtered liquid. Sweating, he drew the heroin into the syringe.

Slowly, he eased the needle into his arm, swearing from the pain. He pulled out a little, hoping to see blood flow. All he saw was air. Missed the vein. Fuck. He pulled out, and shot himself again. This time he hit the vein and pushed the plunger, feeling the delicious flood of warmth run through him like orgasm. Better than. His jaw fell open and his head lolled onto his chest. The rig, blood drying and caking the needle, dropped to the ground. It rolled out of the cave, onto the sand.

The other man gathered blankets and belongings into his pack, leaving last night's trash where it lay. Pack on his back, he kicked at the lolling man. "*Vámonos.*" Reaching down, he pulled his companion to his feet.

The two stumbled out of the cave, scuttled along the edge of the rivermouth, and scrambled up the cliff through wild lilac and poison oak to the train trestle. They picked their way along the trestle over the river, toward the Boardwalk.

Halfway across, one of the men stopped, swaying as he squinted down at the fisherman.

"*Mira. Ese.*" He spat.

The other man looked. "*Oyé. El pinche Padre.*" He drew the gun he carried stuffed under his belt. Closing one eye, he took aim.

"*Padre!* Diiii…"

*   *   *

A shot rang out as Father Francis hit the water. Underwater, he pulled off rubber boots, unhooked the suspenders of his heavy waders and wriggled free. Swimming in zigzags across to the other bank, he came up under cover of a willow, breathing hard.

Another shot pinged the water, inches from where the waders floated. Father Francis spotted the shooters up on the train trestle. Two skinny young Latino men covered in tattoos. They leaned over the trestle looking into the water. One held a gun.

A siren yelped once. An amplified voice seemed to come from everywhere.

"This is the Sheriff! Drop your weapon!"

Detective Charlie Rosa crouched in the parking lot, shielded by his car. Firearm held in both hands, he aimed at the assailants. The Salvatrucha fired at Rosa, then ran along the tracks toward the Boardwalk.

Dripping mud and algae, Father Francis scrambled up the bank and chased the men across the trestle.

Rosa shouted another warning, ran across the lot, and up the ramp just in time to see the Truchas jump a chain link fence and swing themselves onto the roller coaster scaffold.

Father Francis caught up with Detective Rosa. They grinned at one another and nodded.

In seconds, the priest and the sheriff were up on the narrow scaffolding, jumping over air between tracks as they climbed higher and higher above the bay.

The Salvatruchas slipped like monkeys around and through the intricate scaffolding. They kept appearing, disappearing, appearing again.

Rosa and Father Francis pursued, never quite closing the gap. Father Francis was as agile as a sailor in the rigging of a tall schooner during a storm, trying to catch a couple of mice.

Rosa clung like cotton candy to the mast-like struts, not daring to look down at the blue water far below. Fighting back a surge of nausea, he focused on an unmoving object toward the western horizon. In the hazy distance, the wharf held a steady, thin black line. Sirens wailed.

"Here comes the back-up I called for," Rosa shouted to Father Francis across a steep dip.

Rosa glanced over his shoulder to see the Mara Trucha with the gun teetering on the highest arc of the Giant Dipper. The Trucha took a wild shot at Rosa and Father Francis. The pistol kicked back, nearly knocking the shooter off the scaffold.

He swayed, arms out, trying to regain his balance. The gun slipped out of his hand. It clattered against the coaster's wooden skeleton all the way down, spinning to rest on the ground at the entrance to Captain Jack's Pirate Ship ride.

Just as the gun landed, the other Trucha dropped like rotten fruit off the edge of the coaster onto the sand, and rolled behind the bandstand.

The one still on the scaffold disappeared from view. Rosa and Father Francis scanned the structure without success. A thud drew their eyes. They watched the shooter follow the first man onto the sand. In less than twenty seconds, both Truchas had scuttled up the stairs and vanished through Boardwalk Exit #3, the exit that led straight into Beach Flats *Barrio*, a neighborhood of little houses and shops that held its secrets as tightly knit as any border town.

*   *   *

Back on the ground, Rosa and Father Francis examined the weapon lying in front of Captain Jack's pirate ship. A Browning FN P35 Hi Power semi-automatic.

"This is the same type of pistol that killed Salvador Luna." Rosa took a handkerchief out of his pocket, picked up the handgun, and dropped it in an evidence bag.

"Not a bad fishing trip," said Father Francis.

"Too bad they got away."

51

B LUE HAD BEEN CURLED UP ON AURORA'S BED FOR HOURS, fast asleep. Aurora sat at her kitchen table, grade book open, surrounded by piles of student papers: math tests, spelling sentences, Daily Language Skill Builders, book reports ... It seemed like she'd just finished report cards, but the next progress reports were already almost due. She was so far behind in her grading that she'd decided she'd better bring everything home and get it all done over the weekend. What a marathon. Now, Sunday at midnight, she was nearly finished. A few more Daily Language Skill Builders ... Her eyes glazed over. *Just need to rest my head on my arms for a minute ...*

*   *   *

NAADAAYI HÉEN A TAYEE

Aurora stood in the dark, staring out of her bedroom window at the full moon on the water, thumbing the medicine stone. She was alone, yet his presence lingered, filling his house with warmth.

When will he be back?

A cloud floated in front of the moon. She turned from the window and climbed into the big bed, longing for Father Francis to return.

Still alone when she awoke the next morning, she dressed and found her way to the kitchen. A teapot filled with dried herbs stood on the counter, next to a pot of honey. A kettle waited on the stove. She sniffed and examined the herbs in the teapot while she waited for the water to boil. Cinnamon bark, pennyroyal, raspberry leaves, ginger, chamomile. *Women's herbs.*

She carried her steaming mug outside and wandered through the cottage garden, unlatched the gate, crossed the red dirt road, and walked down the trail to the beach. She sat cross-legged on the dock, sipping her tea, and listening to water lap against the side of the moored rowboat.

The water looked inviting. She wanted to swim, but felt cautious, all things considered. She'd wait until she could talk with someone local about the swimming conditions.

On the surface of the water, her own wavering reflection danced with the yellow and red reflection of the rowboat, the shimmering upside-down forest, and white clouds scudding across aquamarine blue sky water. Beneath the surface reflections, dreamy eelgrasses swayed and parted underwater, revealing little minnows and Dungeness crabs.

Where is he?

She felt angry. Angry at him for leaving her alone here. Angry at herself for feeling lost and helpless.

She unzipped her hoodie and spread it out on the planks, stretched out on her back, and basked in the day's warmth. The dock rocked gently. Aurora's eyes fluttered closed.

When she woke, the sun was already low in the sky. A large fish jumped, leaving concentric rings shimmering over the surface of the water. The rings grew, opening and rippling across the inlet until they dissipated. An osprey made slow circles overhead. A breeze rustled through the forest and stirred up wind waves that jostled the rowboat.

"*Rumm'e.* We are, each of us, and every particle of creation, perfect notes in the great symphony of water music." She heard his voice again in her mind, clear and rough, and felt the warm whisper of his lips on the curve of her ear. She reached into her pocket and wrapped her fingers around the medicine stone. Taking a deep breath, she felt at peace.

On her way back to his house, she noticed the children she'd seen the day before. They ran down the road toward her.

With a shock, she recognized them.

"Ms. B! Ms. B!" Salvador Luna threw his arms around her, washing her in sweet, child love. His arms felt all too solid.

"Salvador! How wonderful to see you! But, why are you here? How can you speak to me? I thought you were, were …"

"A beautiful lady brought us here," said Salvador.

"The lady wears a blue cloak, Ms. B," said a girl who looked like Alice, "and she sparkles as if she's made of stardust. She's really, really nice."

"She told us that we're only staying here a little while," Salvador said. "When we leave you, the lady is taking us somewhere to have a peaceful rest."

"Ms. B," said the girl who Aurora assumed was Alice's missing twin. "The Blue Lady told us to give you this." The child handed Aurora a folded shawl.

"We love you, Ms. B," said Salvador. As Aurora unfolded the shawl, fragrant fresh red roses spilled onto the dirt.

The shawl shimmered, translucent as spun light, a pale iridescent blue, as transparent as dragonfly wing. The material almost seemed alive. Aurora turned the cloth over. On the other side, the shawl was opaque, pearlescent, and covered with glowing, twinkling stars.

By the time Aurora thought about the children again, they were far up the road. She refolded the shawl, gathered the roses, and continued down the red dirt road.

As soon as she entered Father Francis' house, she had a sensation that someone had just left. She found a vase in the kitchen for the roses, then set about investigating every room. The house was empty.

Upstairs, she discovered a second bedroom. Shyly, she stepped a little way inside. It was fresh and filled with light, with several large windows, and French doors opening to a balcony that provided a sweeping view of the bay. The room had a masculine feeling — beautiful, yet Spartan and scholarly. The back of her neck tingled with the feeling that any minute he'd appear behind her, perhaps not pleased to find she'd entered his private chamber uninvited.

She closed the door and returned to her room. She was about to place the shawl on a shelf in the wardrobe when she noticed that it smelled strongly of roses. She pulled back a corner of the shawl and found fresh roses enfolded once again in the fabric. Carefully, she placed the shawl on a shelf. A yoga mat she hadn't noticed before leaned in a corner of the closet.

There was plenty of open space on the polished bamboo floor. Aurora unrolled the mat and began her yoga practice. A maritime breeze ruffled the gauzy curtain at the window as she flowed through her asanas.

Eventually, hunger reminded her she had a body. Making her way to the kitchen, she was not surprised to find a covered pan on the stove with hot sautéed vegetables, crispy tempeh, and a green salad. The food was light and fresh, exactly what she wanted.

After supper, a mug of tea in her hands, she wandered through a parlor with original Emily Carr oil paintings hanging on the walls, and on through sliding pocket doors into a formal sitting room with floor-to-ceiling bookshelves.

The rest of the evening, she browsed his library. Physics, astronomy, math, history, anthropology, metaphysics, and botany, poetry, fiction, biology, zoology, ecology, philosophy, Tantra yoga ... Now and then, she pulled a book off a shelf, read for a while, and then replaced the book where she'd found it.

She discovered an old edition of the Kama Sutra, opened it, and flipped through the pages.

The illustrations were beautiful, and startlingly erotic. Her heartbeat quickened. The lovers in the pictures were coupled in a different position on every page, some of them positions Aurora had never imagined. She stared long at each image, absorbing every detail and nuance. She visualized herself with him, imagined she could feel his touch.

Her head nodded. As she began to fall asleep, the book dropped to the floor, startling her awake.

Did he come back? Is he here?

She tiptoed upstairs and peeked into his bedroom.

Empty.

Crestfallen, she shuffled down the hall to her room, undressed, crawled between the sweet-smelling sheets and turned out the light. Soon she had fallen into a deep sleep.

She awoke in the middle of the night, sensing that someone was standing over her bed.

"Who's there?"

"Aurora, I didn't want to wake you. I just needed to see you — to make sure you're alright."

"Father Francis?" Aurora switched on the light on her bedside table and sat up, pulling the sheets to her chin.

A savage warrior glistening with sweat and the blood of battle loomed over her. He sat down heavily on her bed and touched her hair.

"Please, *ñ'a táayaa*, don't call me Father," he laughed bleakly. "I love you, my sweetheart. I love you forever. I promise we will be together soon."

Aurora reached out to touch his face. He disappeared, leaving no trace that he'd been there.

*   *   *

In the morning, Aurora found the teapot in the kitchen again, ready with fresh herbs. She put the kettle on to boil. With her tea, she ate toast and jam, then walked down to the dock again.

Days passed in this way. Breakfast, walk to dock, nap, return to house, yoga, dinner, library. She lost track of time. Father Francis did not return.

52

Prudenciana Elementary

IN AURORA'S CLASSROOM ON THE DAY BEFORE THANKSGIVING, two volunteers from the Surfrider Foundation — a tanned, long-legged young woman and a young man with sun-streaked hair — smiled at Aurora's students gathered around the Watershed Model.

The table-sized plastic model of the Monterey Bay watershed illustrated in bas-relief the coastal mountains, with creeks that sprang out of the mountains to join the national marine estuary and the watershed's salmon rivers: the San Lorenzo — cutting through Santa Cruz at the north end of the bay — Valle Verde's Byrd River — which emptied into the middle of the horseshoe-shaped bay — and Monterey's Salinas and Carmel Rivers at the southern end of the bay. Miniature forests, farms, wetlands, harbors, cities, and villages covered the hills and curving coastline.

The girl Surfrider handed Rico a spray bottle. It was his group's turn to "rain" on the watershed. Students had sprinkled yellow and red

339

bath salt "pesticides" over the farms, dribbled "used motor oil", various colors of "toxic household cleaners", and water laced with "house paint" into the storm drains, and had spread "septic effluvium" into the creeks around houses in the mountains. They overturned a miniature truck carrying "toxic material" on a mountain road, and watched yellow ooze dribble down the embankment into the creek and spread over salmon spawning gravels.

Rico and two other students used their spray bottles to rain on the watershed with great gusto. Students *oo*'ed and *ah*'ed as streams of sickly-looking liquids soaked underground into the aquifer and ran into the bay. The Surfrider volunteers led a discussion of how difficult it would be to clean the polluted watershed and protect endangered wildlife.

Aurora watched the volunteers and her students interact. Like magic, the surfers had infused the kids with an understanding of the watershed concepts that *everything's connected*, and *water is life*. They had instilled in the children a passion for preserving the health of the marine sanctuary. Students signed watershed conservation pledges and were given informational pamphlets to take home and discuss with their parents from the county water district about watershed health and the disposal of toxic waste.

At noon, students and volunteers gathered at the picnic tables in the Life Lab garden where they shared a Thanksgiving potluck that Destiny and Rico's grandma had helped to organize.

Aurora couldn't enjoy it. She was worried. She'd still received no administrative approval for the storm drain stenciling project, even though she'd submitted her lesson plan weeks ago.

She had permission slips from all her kids' parents, and the project was a highly respected centerpiece of the Monterey Bay Marine Sanctuary education initiative. Schools and clubs all over the region were stenciling storm drains to raise awareness about run-off polluting the bay. It had taken weeks to get the Surfrider Foundation volunteers, reserve the watershed model from Save Our Shores, and arrange everything. She couldn't believe the principal hadn't responded to her project request or her multiple notes.

Excusing herself from the picnic, Aurora went to the office to try one more time to check in with the principal. Bushi said Principal Wagner was off campus all day.

Aurora couldn't go ahead with the stenciling without administrative approval. After lunch recess, she let everyone know that the project had to be postponed. The Surfrider volunteers packed up their orange road crew jackets, gloves, paint, and *No Dumping, Flows to the Bay* stencils and said goodbye, leaving the storm drains around campus unprotected.

*   *   *

On her drive home after school, Aurora stopped at the Santa Cruz wharf. She parked in front of the fish market and walked to the railing overlooking Main Beach to enjoy the view.

The famous vermillion and white scaffolding of the historic Giant Dipper roller coaster wound like a bit of scalloped crochet work along the seam between beach and sky. Even though it was a November weekday, the Boardwalk was open, in honor of the long Thanksgiving weekend ahead. Screams drifted across the beach from the Boardwalk, as the thunder of the carts' wheels on the tracks picked up momentum through those final dramatic dips. She could just make out the little dots of color, the happy adrenalin seekers inside the carts, screaming down the tracks of the famous rollercoaster.

Like plankton upwelling from the depths, an image of Father Francis floated to the surface of her mind. She cringed at the memory of the last time she'd seen him. So childish of her to rush away without speaking to him after the Farm Without Harm meeting! She should contact him soon about working together on that ag land conservation trust project.

Fat sea lions barked from their usual station on the wooden decks underneath the pier. In front of the "Please Don't Feed the Sea Lions" sign, a family of tourists threw French fries down to the enormous beggars. A brown pelican and a few gulls watched anxiously from the railing.

"Why are you still here?" Aurora asked the pelican. "Are you mixed up because the climate is changing? You should migrate south, as usual. Get going!"

NOAA climate scientists were forecasting a Super *El Niño* this winter and spring, with heavy winds and lots of rain. They predicted that unusual *El Niño* currents would disrupt the migration patterns of much of the wildlife in the bay. Was this connected to global warming?

The huge prehistoric-looking bird perched on the wharf railing ignored Aurora's question and concentrated on the tourists and their French fries.

"Aurora!" A woman with smooth bobbed hair and an athletic figure rolled up on a bike, startling the pelican and the flock of gulls into the air.

"Kelli Cavanaugh," Aurora returned Kelli's warm smile. "What brings you out to the wharf on this beautiful Thanksgiving Eve afternoon?"

"It's my day off. I'm working tomorrow, so tonight I'm treating myself to dinner at Riva's."

"I'm on my way to Riva's too," said Aurora.

"Want to share a table?"

"I'd love it."

Soon, the women — glasses of chardonnay in hand — were seated at a table by the window, with a view of sunset colors floating on Cowell's cove, framed by silhouettes of seal rock and the lighthouse.

"Do you have plans for Thanksgiving, Aurora?"

"I've been working with a Native American artist on a student mural project, and he invited me to the Indigenous People's Thanksgiving Sunrise Gathering on Alcatraz Island in San Francisco. I leave at four tomorrow morning to catch a ferry to Alcatraz before dawn. The rest of the day, I plan to fast."

"I've heard about the gathering. Giving thanks to Mother Earth with the Indians sounds like a great alternative to pigging out on turkey and watching football."

A waitress arrived to take dinner orders. After she collected the menus and left the table, Aurora turned to Kelli.

"I haven't had a chance to thank you for helping Detective Rosa take Alice to the police station for questioning."

"How's Alice doing?" asked Kelli.

"She's deeply traumatized. She's gone mute. Our counselor, Nathena Hamilton, is working with her, but she hasn't spoken a word since the day you picked her up from school. Have you found out anything about her missing sister and mother?"

"Sorry, Aurora. I can't talk about an ongoing investigation."

Conversation shifted to the environment, fish and wildlife, and other shared interests. After dinner, Aurora and Kelli walked down the wooden stairs from the wharf to the beach and strolled side-by-side along the water's edge, each in the silence of her own thoughts. Reflected ribbons of colored lights from the pier fluttered across the bay waters, dancing with star diamonds and moonlight. Gently lapping waves rocked in and out over the sand, making a soothing *shhhh*.

Happy squeals from roller coaster riders plunging down the biggest dip broke the silence.

"Do you believe in destiny, Kelli?" asked Aurora. "Do you think maybe we make agreements — I don't know — I mean kind of like contracts, before we're ever born, while we're still pure spirits in heaven? You know, to meet and be with certain people, to accomplish certain missions during our time on Earth?"

"What?" Kelli laughed. "No way. Sorry, Aurora. I don't believe in any of that hype. I don't buy destiny, or reincarnation. I don't believe in heaven, or angels or spirits. As far as I'm concerned, all that is just fairy tales we tell the children. For me, what we see is all we've got. I refuse to drink the Kool-Aid. There's only you and me. Just us, randomly here now. Nothing else."

"There's got to be more to it, Kelli. Look around you. Don't you feel the sacredness of this night, of the ocean, the stars? I can't believe we're all there is. There has to be something far bigger and more profound than us."

"You mean like God?"

"Yes, something like that. I mean, I don't believe in a great white father with a beard sitting on a throne in the sky. But I think there is

— well, an ineffable, unnamable, unknowable … I don't know … Force, I guess, like Obi-Wan Kenobi called it. You know, some all good, all knowing, eternal creator and destroyer of all that is, was, and will be. Some higher power that transcends gender, religion, race, even transcends species."

"You have quite an imagination, don't you? As far as I'm concerned, shit all just happens."

Aurora looked out to sea along the moon's shimmering path to the horizon.

"I'm an atheist, Aurora," Kelli continued. "I believe that all of this is simply the result of a random evolutionary process. We humans are no more significant than an aphid on a rosebush. In fact, I think a hell of a lot of other life forms on this planet are more interesting and beautiful than we are, and more worthy of preserving. In my darkest moments, I think humans are a scourge on the Earth, a pestilence. The sooner we're sloughed off, exterminated, the better chance for the other, perhaps worthier, or at least more evolutionarily sustainable creatures, like dolphins and whales, butterflies and songbirds. But it doesn't matter. No master intelligence is watching out for us, directing our destiny, punishing and rewarding us for what we do, guiding our story to a happy ending. There's no one out there. Nothing. *Nada.* No God, or Great Spirit, no Allah, or Divine Mother Goddess, or Corporate Boardroom of the Gods in heaven or on Mount Olympus. No heaven. No hell. It's just us. We are all alone, and we don't mean shit. It doesn't matter what we do, in the big picture."

"But you do believe that the life on this precious planet is worth protecting. Really, Kelli, I know you think we should be doing everything we can right now to help save the Earth. We're causing the greatest mass extinction of plants and animals ever to occur on the planet, what evolutionary biologists are calling the Anthropocene. An extinction event at least as enormous in scale as the Permian."

"Exactly," said Kelli. "And up until now, historic mass extinctions have all had natural causes. But this time, humans are responsible. This extinction event, the Sixth Extinction as scientists are calling it, is anthropogenic — caused by human activity, not by natural phenomenon. The evidence is irrefutable."

Kelli bent down, picked up a rock embedded with prehistoric fossils, and — with a flick of her wrist — sent it skipping over the water. A thousand moon diamonds scattered across the surface.

Hands on her hips, she turned back to Aurora and continued.

"We've fouled the atmosphere around the planet with smoke from clear cutting and burning forests so we can graze cattle for Big Macs. We're destabilizing the climate by burning fossil fuels, and pumping methane into the atmosphere from our meat production. We're poisoning ourselves and everything living on the planet with our toxic chemicals. We've engineered an epidemic of neurological damage in our children, and the neurotoxins we're using in pesticides are causing colony collapse in bees. No pollinators, no food. Soon the total mass of plastic pollution in the ocean will exceed the total mass of fish. We're throwing a monkey wrench in the delicate planetary electromagnetic field with all the electromagnetic smog we're creating. And we're covering over and eroding away our precious topsoils. The ozone hole, climate change, desertification, extinction ... Sorry. Maybe I had a little too much wine. I don't usually rant like this."

Aurora laughed. "Rave on, Kelli. Obviously, you agree that we should be doing everything we can right now to save the Earth."

"Save the Earth?" Kelli snorted. "Are you kidding? The planet doesn't need saving. Think of how many species have overpopulated or somehow or other gone out of balance since life first evolved on this planet. When a population starts consuming more resources than the habitat can support, it becomes unsustainable, and crashes. Over the course of Earth's history, many species have gone extinct, including some early bipedal hominids closely related to Homo sapiens — sometimes due to their own avariciousness, sometimes just because of random events, like the comet that took out the dinosaurs. We're just one more random event."

The sad sigh of the four-mile buoy drifted over the cove.

"Honestly, Aurora, I really don't think we're going to last much longer. Worldwide plagues and famine, nuclear annihilation, climate change — something is going to finish us off pretty soon. We've clearly exceeded our carrying capacity. Good riddance. I'm just sorry that we'll probably take out so many other species with us — elephants,

345

giraffes, gorillas, redwood forests, all of the large fish in the sea —
already nearly gone. But the planet? *The Earth Abides*, as the writer
George Stuart said. Planet Earth is going to just go on doing its
inevitable cycling and evolving until the sun blows up, supernovas, or
dwindles into a white dwarf, or until something really big crashes into
it. That will probably be a very long time from now. Then it's gone. So
what? It means nothing." Kelli skipped another rock.

"If you don't believe in any kind of god," Aurora asked, "then
what guides your sense of right and wrong, of good and evil? What
moral compass do you have to steer by?"

"I believe we make our own sacredness by how we live, Aurora.
A person doesn't need some invisible authority figure watching to
know the difference between right and wrong. As the song says, 'Life
is a carnival.' Each of us buys our ticket and takes our chance. I'm a
results person. If my actions result in making my surroundings more
in sync with the natural world, and more beautiful, functional,
comfortable, peaceful, sustainable, healthy, and safe for me, my loved
ones, and my community — *all* the beings in my community,
including the salmon and the honeybees — I choose to call that 'good'.
That's all the moral compass I need."

53

MONDAY, NOVEMBER 28, 1998
Prudenciana Elementary

T HE NEXT MONDAY, AT MORNING RECESS, Aurora sat in the child-sized chair in front of the principal's office, reading Howard Zinn's *People's History of the United States*.

While she read, her mind wandered to last Thursday's Thanksgiving Sunrise trip to Alcatraz Island, known as "The Rock" during its years as a federal penitentiary.

*   *   *

Wake up to an alarm clock Thanksgiving morning at four. Drive two hours alone, in the dark, along the winding coastal cliffs to San Francisco. Then, in the cold dank fog, catch a ferry packed with American Indians — in full regalia — from tribes across the nation, and with people from all over the world who had come to "Turtle Island" for the annual Indigenous People's Thanksgiving Sunrise Gathering.

347

Aurora had to admit to herself that her real motive for going had been the hope that she might see Father Francis. But even though he wasn't there, she was glad she went.

In the misty, ghost grey pre-dawn, on "The Rock," overlooking the lights of San Francisco, Aurora stood with others, around the huge bonfire. She listened to a woman adorned with a basket hat and traditional facial tattoos tell the Native American version of the Christopher Columbus story — the first Thanksgiving — and the ongoing genocide and desecration of forests, water, wildlife, and sacred places since the European invasion.

While dawn illuminated the silhouetted Golden Gate Bridge and the cityscape across the bay, native children passed baskets of tobacco, and the speaker made a plea that all those present stand with indigenous people and "all our relations" in defense of Turtle Island's precious air, soil, and water. The speaker raised her arms to the sky.

"Mother Earth needs our help. When I look around this morning, I see plenty of Natives, but I also see people of all skin colors, all walks of life. If you're here, it's because Mother called you and you heard her. Thank you all for showing up, because she needs you. She needs us all, working together. As we give our tobacco to the fire, let each and every one of us make a commitment to do everything we can to help protect and heal our Mother. *Noso'n.*"

The sun rose yellow gold over the bay. Aurora went to the crackling flames in the center of the circle, threw her tobacco into the fire, and watched with awe as spirit animals leapt and flew out of the flames — cougars, bears, eagles, dolphins, whales, and salmon. She made her commitment.

*   *   *

"The principal will see you now," said Bushi.

Aurora felt none of the tail-between-the-legs guilty shame and heart palpitations she usually experienced when forced to interact with capricious authority figures. She entered the principal's office with her head held high, and sat up straight in the chair facing the administrator's desk.

"Good morning, Mrs. Wagner. Thank you for your time. I just wanted to find out if you could tell me why you didn't authorize our storm drain stencils."

"What? I shouldn't have to explain! It is an outrage that you would consider painting graffiti around our school! We will not have our campus defaced."

Aurora could still see the looks of disappointment and confusion on the faces of her kids when she'd told them they couldn't go through with the project. She slipped her hand in her pocket and wrapped her fingers around the smooth green stone she'd found on the waterfall hike last August.

"I submitted documentation well in advance, from the National Marine Sanctuary about the project's importance, along with my written lesson plan, documenting its alignment with State educational standards and frameworks, Mrs. Wagner. I tried repeatedly to check in with you about it. When you didn't respond, I thought maybe you hadn't seen the request."

"I do not appreciate all the embarrassment you cause me, Ms. Bourne. If you stir up one more problem, I will place a professional reprimand in your personnel file at the District Office. This conversation is finished."

Deana Wagner rose, ushered Aurora through the door, and slammed it shut.

*   *   *

When Aurora finally got home that evening, the light on her answering machine was blinking.

"Hello, Aurora. This is Father Francis."

Aurora slumped into the nearest chair, heart pounding.

"I'm calling about the outreach work you and I agreed to do for Farm Without Harm. I know you're busy, so I took the liberty of meeting last week with the Open Space Alliance attorney, Mrs. Petrakis. I hope you don't mind my going ahead. I got all the information you and I will need to move forward, including the list of landowners to approach about conservation easements. I think we

349

should to get together soon to plan our strategy. Can you meet in my office at Our Lady of Help, about four o'clock this Friday, December 2nd? Please give me a call and let me know if that works for you."

Aurora checked her planner. She was free Friday afternoon.

She dialed the number the priest had given her, heart racing. A machine answered. Relieved that she didn't have to speak to him in person, she left her message confirming their meeting.

*   *   *

Wednesday afternoon, after the monthly Marine Sanctuary Education Advisory Panel meeting, everyone headed over to Phil's Fish Market in Moss Landing for live music and fresh seafood. People were well into their second bottle of Silver Mountain Pinot Noir. On the big platter in the center of the table that had been piled high with calamari, only a few tentacles remained.

The graphic artist who'd designed the *Storm Drains Flow to the Sea* poster asked Aurora how her storm drain stenciling project had gone.

All eyes were on Aurora. Her face flushed.

"It was a disaster." She brushed away a tear. "I did everything I could to connect with my principal every day for three weeks in advance of our stenciling day. But she just never responded. It felt like she was intentionally avoiding me."

"What happened?"

"The Surfrider volunteers were great. My kids loved the watershed model, learned a lot, and even went home and taught their families about storm drain pollution. I've had really positive feedback from my students' parents. But I had to cancel the stenciling because I never got approval from the principal. Monday morning as soon as I arrived at school, I went to her office and spoke to her. She called the stencils *'graffiti'* and threatened to reprimand me for bothering her."

Everyone started talking at once. More than one person vowed to make phone calls first thing in the morning.

*   *   *

"So you see, Superintendent Spieler," said County Supervisor Marley Warmhardt, "with all the support the Storm Drain Stenciling Program has from so many powerful environmental organizations and alliances around the Monterey Bay — the Coastal Commission, the Monterey Bay National Marine Sanctuary, Surfriders Foundation, Wetlands Watch, Save Our Shores, Coastal Watershed Council — it would be most impolitic to fail to give the Storm Drain Stenciling Program your full support. Speaking as your friend, I suggest you do something right away about the situation at Prudenciana Elementary. As the only public elementary school classroom teacher appointed to the Monterey Bay National Marine Sanctuary Education Advisory Panel, Ms. Bourne has a lot of supporters in the environmental community. I've received at least thirty phone calls so far this morning, from very influential people, about what that principal did. If you want to build your new high school on the edge of the Valle Verde wetlands, you're going to need the full backing of every one of those environmental groups. If I were you, I'd do whatever it takes to rescue that Prudenciana teacher's storm drain awareness project."

Superintendent Jon Spieler put down the phone and buzzed his secretary.

"Get ahold of the local TV news station, and the Santa Cruz, Valle Verde, and Monterey papers. Issue the following press release ..."

When he finished dictating the release announcing the storm drain stenciling project sponsored by the Surfriders Foundation and the Valle Verde School District, taking place next Monday afternoon at Prudenciana school, he phoned Prudenciana principal Deana Wagner.

54

Santa Cruz County Juvenile Detention Facility
San Lorenzo Valley, San Lorenzo River Watershed
North Santa Cruz County

ALL OF HIS TEACHERS AGREED THAT JOHNNY HAD POTENTIAL. If only he'd show up at school more. And if only he could get a hold of his attitude, control his temper.

But he hadn't listened.

Now, Johnny was in solitary confinement at Juvie. It wasn't fair.

Alone, Johnny awaited his detention hearing. He stared at the walls. Why hadn't any of his homies helped him? What was the point? Even if he ever got outta here, his life was shit.

Johnny Lopez, in his solitary cell, wasn't going to wait forever. It was over.

He wound a thin strip of bed sheet around the bars in the window and tied it around his throat.

353

Like a dead insect, a chair lay on its back under Johnny's dangling feet. All alone in his cell, at midnight, Johnny Lopez hung by his neck.

A swollen purple tongue stuck out of a blue mask with bulging red eyes.

Johnny Lopez was almost sixteen. He had potential.

55

FRIDAY AFTERNOON, DECEMBER 2, 1998
Our Lady of Help Church, Valle Verde

W *HAT AM I DOING, watching at the window for her to arrive like*
a lovesick teenager?

Frank Hilman rubbed his chin, smooth from a fresh shave.
Besides his Honda, there were no other cars in the lot.

It's quiet. The office ladies must have already gone home for the
day.

He went back to his easy chair and resumed reading the book that
Cosmic John had sent him: *The Complete Briefing on Global Warming*
by John Houghton.

While he read, threads connecting each vital pulse, each vortex of
meaning, shimmered in a weave he could trace. He could see the
complex web of life on Earth unraveling. Yet, despite the urgency to
change course or annihilate itself, the world continued to do business
as usual. He closed his eyes and prayed for the wisdom and courage to
help humanity awaken. His prayers reached out to a spiritual Ocean

that was the birthplace of all religions, all faiths. His heart opened, one note in a great tidal symphony, and loving waves of universal systole and diastole surged through him.

Tires rolling over gravel.

Through the window, Father Francis watched the red Miata glide into a parking space in front of the parish office.

He opened the front door of the Residence to welcome his guest.

Ms. Bourne's shirt was red, tight, and cut too low.

The priest flushed in discomfort. He cleared his throat and tried to keep from looking.

"Hello, Father Francis. I hope I'm not late," she said, offering her hand.

When he took her hand, he felt the connection ping through him. She cast her eyes to the floor and pulled away.

He cleared his throat again. "Not at all. Right on time, Ms. Bourne. Please, come in."

She passed so close that a fission of electricity sizzled between them.

Her hair smelled of ocean and flowers. He recognized her natural scent, but there was something different today.

Father Francis ushered the teacher toward the sitting room, walking behind her. Her black pants were skintight. High-heeled boots pushed her bottom up in the air. He tried to look away.

This was a mistake. God, grant me strength.

They settled at the library table and he offered her tea. She accepted, with milk and honey, as he'd anticipated.

When she took the fine old porcelain teacup and saucer from him, their fingers touched. Her sharp intake of breath made him tighten. He poured himself a cup of tea, hoping she wouldn't notice that his hand trembled.

He offered a plate of lemon bars and smiled at her. She met his eyes. Her pupils were dilated. His throat constricted.

"I want to apologize for meeting with the Open Space Alliance attorney without you, Ms. Bourne. I tried to reach you and, when I couldn't, I decided to go ahead and get things started, at least get the information we need."

"I appreciate the time you've already put into this, Father Francis. I apologize for being hard to reach. But please, call me Aurora."

She took a bite of her lemon bar. A dusting of powdered sugar clung to her upper lip.

Grant me strength.

Her tongue darted out and lapped up the sugar, leaving her lips wet and glistening.

Breathe.

"These are delicious. Thank you, Father Francis. And thank you so much for following up on this project."

Frank Hilman took a sip of tea, and shifted in his chair.

"Good. Well then, Aurora, here's a copy of the notes I took when I met with the attorney, Mrs. Petrakis. And your list of the owners of prime agricultural land in the valley who are known to be facing development pressure."

Aurora took the papers the priest slid across the table, and their hands touched again. She jerked away, knocking a pen off the table.

It rolled across the floor. She stood, her scent rising around him. Musky. Luscious.

Dear Lord. The woman is in heat.

She turned her back to him as she bent over to pick up the pen.

Tight pants carving the curve of her ...

His eyes involuntarily slid around the twin rise of her buttocks, to the sweet forbidden v between her legs, down along her thighs to the crease at the back of her knees, slipping lower to the perfect calves disappearing into boots with push-up heels.

God help me.

He sipped his tea as he watched her resettle herself in her chair and smile at him. She said something self-deprecating about dropping her pen. He could barely make sense of her words.

"So," she said, "As I understand it, we're supposed to contact these potential land donors and introduce them to the Open Space Alliance and the concept of conservation easements and agricultural land preservation trusts, get them interested, and answer any questions we can. Then, when and if they are ready to actually speak with the Open Space Alliance attorney, we arrange a meeting?"

She tapped the stack of papers on the table to straighten them, then rearranged them just so beneath her chest. She leaned forward on her elbows, deepening her cleavage.

"Yes," said Father Francis, silently counting backwards in Sanskrit.

"Do you see anyone on this list of land-owners you already know?" asked Aurora. "I've met this woman. Malone Baker. I talked to her at that political fundraiser for Congressman Carson, the barbeque at that ranch."

"I know her slightly myself. She and her husband attend Our Lady of Help once in a blue moon," said the priest. "If I see them, do you mind if I go ahead and approach them, even if you aren't there?"

"Of course not," said Aurora. "I think if either of us run into any of the people on this list we should speak with them about the Open Space Alliance."

"I agree. Strike while the iron is hot."

Aurora blushed.

"I'm going to be really busy until school gets out for Christmas vacation. But during winter break I can try to make contact with some of these people."

"Let's stay in touch," said the priest. Aurora blushed again. "Ah, keep each other informed about the connections we're making."

"I can do that," said Aurora. There was a gritty rasp to the timber of her voice.

The room is very warm. Maybe I should open a window.

Father Francis glanced through the frosted window at the cold grey December sky.

Focus on the work.

"Did you read Pesticide Action Network's *Barons of Bromide* pamphlet?" the priest asked.

Aurora took a bite of her lemon bar, then licked her fingers, one by one, with little wet sucking sounds. He felt like whimpering.

"Yes," she said.

"Yes?" the man tried to remember what they were talking about.

"I did read the pamphlet," she said. "I think Pesticide Action Network did a brilliant job of explaining how the multi-national petrochemical industry that's behind CalGreen works to control agriculture. It's all there."

She touched her fingertips to enumerate her points.

Concentrate.

"How they discredit their critics by trivializing and demonizing them, spin junk science to confuse the public and call into question the real science, delay meaningful action by requiring yet another prolonged study, and frighten growers and workers with the threat of job loss and economic ruin."

"I've seen those strategies applied time and again to derail social justice movements," said Father Francis.

She rolled her shoulders and took a deep breath. He watched her chest rise and fall.

"I think the people behind CalGreen and its subsidiaries are buying our politicians with legal and illegal campaign contributions and lobbying," said Aurora. "I think they're influencing our democratic process, blatantly subverting the federal laws that are supposed to protect people and the environment."

Aurora reached up to touch the nape of her neck. "Who are these people — the actual, real people running the big corporations, anyway? They have to live on this planet, too. Right? Eat the food, drink the water, breathe the air. Why are they ruining it? Do they think there's another planet somewhere they get to go live on? Are they just blinded by greed, or do you think they really believe their own PR, really think their poisons are beneficial and desirable?"

"Whatever their motives," said Father Francis, "the Montreal Protocol will eventually prevail. Methyl bromide will be forced off the market and we'll have to come up with another way to grow strawberries." He rasped his thumb along his jaw.

"Yes, but then the chemical manufacturers will do what they've always done. They'll just remarket the poisons under a different name, or for a different use, or sell the stuff in a different country. Their continued profitability is dependent on keeping us addicted to their chemicals."

Aurora reached over to pull the red *Barons of Bromide* booklet out of her bag, releasing another cloud of musk, deeply earthy — the scent of forest and chanterelles. As she leaned forward, Frank Hilman had a clear view down the front of her shirt.

Red silk with something lacey underneath.

Under the lace, the top of her black bra pushed up her breasts.

He forgot to breathe. If she leaned over any farther, they would surely tumble out. He shifted in his chair to ease the distracting weight between his legs.

The sun coming through the hundred-year-old window glass made ripples of light and shadow shimmer over her skin. What would that red silk feel like between his fingers? The pleasant fullness had become an uncomfortable pressure.

Was this electricity flowing two ways, or was he deluding himself? Did she want him as much as he wanted her?

He watched her, bent over the table, writing.

Yes.

He was experienced enough with women to trust his instincts. He was comfortable with his own sexuality, had explored down the mysterious and ecstatic path of physical intimacy with several beautiful women as a young man, before he'd entered the seminary and taken his vows.

No, he was not unfamiliar with these physical feelings. Although it had been a long time since he'd had to deal with involuntary arousal. Never, since his ordination, had he been seriously tempted to break his vow of chastity. He'd worked all that out long ago. But this was different. Not just physical.

What is this? Love?

The ache was almost as painful as it was pleasurable.

Can I resist?

Aurora scribbled on the paper, her mouth opened slightly, forming an "O". She was breathing rapidly, her chest swelling as it rose. He throbbed.

She stopped writing, put the blunt end of the pen in her mouth and sucked.

A tsunami of hot blood surged through him.

No. He could no longer let this thing go on under the surface, something they both sat here pretending they didn't notice. His heart drummed in his ears. He had to bring this out in the open. He didn't want to alienate her. God knows he didn't want to hurt her. He studied the outline of erect nipples under red silk.

He cleared his throat.

She raised her eyes to meet his.

I could drown in those eyes.

Summoning all his will, he forced himself to speak.

"Ah, Ms. Bourne. Aurora. Before we go any further, there's something we should talk about. It's an awkward subject, yet I feel I need to bring it up. May I?"

"Yes, of course." He met the young woman's guileless eyes and almost wept. Her hair framed her face with golden mist. An angel. Sacred ripe flesh.

With my body I thee worship.

"I don't want to embarrass you, Aurora, but … well, I can't help noticing that you — that is, I think you seem to be physically attracted to me."

Aurora sucked in air as if she'd been hit. She blushed and looked down at her hands, folded on the table. Her eyes welled with tears.

She raised her face, met his gaze.

His heart broke, but he had to be strong, for both of their sakes. They were in dangerous waters.

"Please forgive me if I'm mistaken. But I feel as though there is an unspoken question between us. I think it only fair that I give you an honest answer. I believe we have important work to do together, Aurora. I feel that our work together could make a difference, could benefit humanity. I respect you and see you as a powerful ally. I would hate to spoil our effectiveness because of this … situation."

"I'm sorry, Father Francis. I'm so ashamed."

Tears brimmed over and rolled down her cheeks.

"Honestly, I don't know what's wrong with me. I've been trying to control these feelings I have for you. I know you're a priest. I would never want to interfere with your devotion, your spiritual practice. I'm very passionate — I mean, very serious, about finding a way to deal with the pesticide issue, and about preserving the wet — wetlands and the farmland. I want to work with you on this, as a professional. I'm sorry. I'm so, so — embarrassed. My body — no. More than my body. All of me, just — *reacts* to you. I don't understand it. I can't seem to help it. And today, I—I guess I just … I thought — I don't know what's wrong with me. I feel grotesque. I'm so sorry."

"Please, Aurora. Don't punish yourself. You are a lovely woman. You honor me. I must be truthful. I find you attractive as well." He paused an extra beat, regretting her startled expression.

"I've spent years counseling people. I'm no stranger to human sexuality, so I know that physical feelings sometimes come up, whether we want them to or not." He watched her eyes cloud in confusion. His mind was in turmoil.

Forgive me.

"But speaking professionally, as a counselor, I do think you may have some unexplored issues that have led you to become attracted to a priest, to someone inaccessible for a romantic relationship. You might want to examine that."

He shifted to ease the pressure of the monstrous erection pressing against his jeans.

"You and I can never be in a sexual relationship, Aurora. I hate to be so blunt, but there it is. I have taken a vow of chastity, as a Catholic priest. My ordained vows are a sacrament. As long as I live in this body, I will never dishonor my vow of celibacy."

"I understand, Father Francis." Tears were streaming down her cheeks. "I'm so sorry, so ashamed. I apologize for disturbing your peace."

He watched her curled fingers rub slowly up and down the side of her teacup, and swallowed, thinking about how her hands would feel touching him.

"No need to apologize, Aurora." His tongue stuck to the roof of his mouth. He was painfully swollen, pulsing, desperate for release.

Excruciating, delicious torture.

"You haven't disturbed my peace," he lied. He despised the deception, hated his weakness, his arrogance and poor judgment. He took a deep breath and prayed for guidance.

"You shouldn't in any way feel ashamed." He almost reached out to take her hand.

Don't touch her.

If he gave her the slightest opening, she would pursue him. He might not be strong enough to resist. "I know someone is out there waiting for you. In fact, I'm surprised you don't have someone already."

"I don't want to talk about it, Father." For a split second her eyes flared with anger. A tumult of emotions crossed her face. "I think I really need to go now. Next time we see each other, I promise I'll have it together. I'll review these documents and give you a call. I'm sorry. Thank you, Father."

Aurora gathered her things and flew out of the door, out of the parking lot and away down the street.

Frank Hilman sat at the table, feeling rotten. He waited while his pulse slowed. What had he been thinking, arranging to meet with that woman in the Residence, alone? Who was he kidding? What kind of mind games was he playing with himself? He'd set both of them up for that debacle. Would he ever be able to repair the damage and hurt he'd caused? He closed his eyes, saw again the pain in Aurora's face. All of his years of disciplined, rigorous training. How could he have blindsided himself, and her, with such a mistake?

He emptied his water bottle in a few desperate gulps, then went for a long run, past the cemetery and through country lanes to the river.

He ran along the river levee up into the hills of Mount Madonna. Along winding mountain trails he ran, through oak and pine forest. A black-tailed deer and two fawns watched him pass. A blue jay called. A bobcat scrambled under a huckleberry bush as he thundered by. A coyote followed him at a safe distance. Finally, he looped back down out of the mountains, winding along the shining river as sunset colors faded. When he got home, he took a cold shower.

56

AURORA THREW OPEN THE FRONT DOOR TO HER HOUSE, stomped inside, and slammed the door behind her. Blue was there to greet her, but she rushed past him, straight to the bathroom, gulping sobs and hiccupping.

She tore off her despised clothes: the beautiful, expensive, sheer red silk blouse, the Victoria's Secret black spandex lace camisole, the black push-up bra. She yanked off the high-heeled leather boots, peeled off the skin-tight designer jeans, scrambled out of the thong panties as if untangling herself from a Tolkien-esque man-eating spider's web.

She kicked at the discarded items with loathing.

Thong? What was I thinking? I must have lost my mind.

She picked the thing up as if it were a dead rat and threw it in the trash.

She caught a glimpse of herself in the mirror. *Hateful, ugly, vile self. Worthless, stupid, disgusting creature.*

She stepped into a hot, hot shower and scrubbed with a stiff luffa sponge until she was red all over, crying and howling insults at herself. As hard as she tried, she couldn't wash away her shame.

Limp from the hot shower, and drained from the tears she'd shed, she dried herself mercilessly with a scratchy towel, as if she could rub away her humiliation. Blue watched in dismay, flicking the tip of his tail.

She put on cotton panties, sweatpants, and an old baggy T-shirt, and flopped face down on her bed. She pulled a pillow over her head and cried, wanting to disappear from the face of the Earth — no, from the universe.

How can I ever, ever face that man again?

She hated herself so much, she couldn't stand being in the same body with herself another second. She pounded her mattress.

She became aware of watching herself, as if out of her body. Her wallowing self-indulgent self-pity repulsed her. There were so many people in the world with real reason to cry who were, instead, bravely facing their fate. She despised her small, petty self, and began crying for all the heroic beings in the world who were truly suffering. Then, so filled up with frustration, self-loathing, and anger that she felt she might explode, she sat up, scrunched the pillow against her face, and screamed.

Her life was a mess. Down at the bottom of a deep well, trapped in the little cage her mind had become, she raced around in vicious circles searching for an escape.

Alcohol? Yeah, right, and become an alcoholic like my parents. Ice Cream? Ick. Pot? There's probably still a very old joint in the freezer. Forget it! Call a friend? No! There's no one I can talk to about this. No way out. No escape from my disgusting self.

*   *   *

She opened her eyes, suddenly wide awake, and peered at the clock: 10:30am.

Heart thumping, she bolted out of bed. In a panic, she started frantically dressing for school. One arm inside her best permapress blue and white pin-stripe shirt, she remembered that it was Saturday.

Her head throbbed. She undressed, slipped on a robe, and wandered into the kitchen. She felt achy all over and had a sore throat. Blue sat at the sliding glass door, tail flicking. Aurora opened the door, and the roar of enormous waves washed over her. A major winter storm was blasting the California coast with ominous thunder.

Before she realized what she was doing, she found herself in her wetsuit, with her board, in her truck.

West Cliff Drive was flooding with rills of water from the waves crashing over the cliff onto the street. Wind blew sea foam past her windshield.

She slid into a parking space at the lighthouse, jumped out of her truck, and ran to the railing to look over the cliffs.

Unbelievable!

She'd never seen conditions like this in all her years of surfing the Lane. It was like the winter break at North Shore Oahu. Howling offshore winds blew boulder-sized chunks of sea foam and steaming sprays of saltwater all over the lighthouse parking lot.

She could actually feel the cliffs shake under her feet as the waves struck over and over. There were no periods between sets. At the Point break, monstrous peaks steamed and curled into glassy green-jawed tubes that closed out over huge pits, thundering continuously, one on top of the other.

There were only a few people in the water. The waves were forming and breaking far beyond the Point. She could see lines of white water all the way out at Second and Third Reef, where she'd never seen waves break before, even on the biggest days.

A surfer who was just a black dot on the wave disappeared under a twenty-foot wall of white water. She watched someone at the top of a curling peak lose his board and drop through the air down the face of a green wall. It was like watching someone fall out of a three-story building.

Do not do it. A clear voice shouted in her head. *Do not go in!*

She ran back to her truck, grabbed her board, and raced toward the cliff.

At the chest-high guardrail bearing the warning "Extreme Danger! Do Not Go Beyond This Point", she hoisted her board over, then swung herself up and over.

Teeth chattering, she picked her way along the slippery rocks that jutted out from the lighthouse. Her knees felt rubbery. The waves broke in continuous blasts, crashing over the usually dry rock cliff.

At the edge of the precipice, she Velcroed the board's leash around her ankle, concentrating on the waves' crash and surge. As a mountain of white water rose up the cliff, she jumped into the air, throwing her leashed board out in front of her. Her body slapped down into the saltwater monster's jaws.

Scrambling onto her board, she paddled for her life away from the rocky cliffs.

The water attacked her like a live, malevolent beast. She fought to get to the outside of the barreling waves. A gigantic roiling green wall reared up before her, curled overhead, and broke in an avalanche of churning white thunder.

She took a deep breath, grasped the rails of her board and pushed down hard on its nose, plunging it under the ice-cold water, and diving as deep as she could get, praying that she was far enough under the turbulence.

The frigid water griped her head in a vice. Excruciating pain shot through her skull. Saltwater burned up her nose. The cold made her ears ring. She felt the mountainous wave above her. She knew she had to time her rise perfectly if she was going to get a breath before the next wave crashed on top of her. Chest on fire, she swam for air.

Her head popped up through the boiling water. Saltwater streamed down her face and in her eyes. She couldn't see. She gasped for air and sucked in sea foam.

Choking and coughing, she struggled to keep her head above water, wrestled to hold on to her board, wiping at her eyes with one hand. She managed to get one good deep breath just before another twenty-foot wave crashed on top of her.

Again, she dove as deep as she could under the seething sea, fighting panic.

She came up hyperventilating.

Stop it. You can't panic. Take slow, deep breaths.

A piece of someone's broken surfboard bobbed up next to her. She pushed it away, wondering what other potentially lethal, sharp-edged objects were churning around in this gigantic washing machine with her, how many submerged rocks were waiting to cut her and smash her skull.

The boom and crash of cannon thundered all around her. Then she heard the deadly hiss of an enormous fire-breathing dragon racing toward her. A forty-foot green monster loomed up, its hollow dark belly sucking everything into it.

She sucked in air, pushed her board to the side, and swam for the bottom, pulling frantically at the leash around her ankle. She felt a pop as her board leash released. The shock of the wave detonating overhead reverberated through her bones until they rang.

Even though she was far under the wave, the water wrenched, churned and roiled, pushing and twisting her, rolling her over, until she lost track of up and down.

She held her breath as she was spun like a weightless grain of sand. The force of the water yanking her arms one way and legs another felt like it might pull her limbs off, break her neck, maybe even decapitate her.

Desperate for air, she clawed in the direction she hoped was up, expecting her own unleashed board to smash into her face or rip like a missile through her body any second.

Her face broke into the air just as another wave thundered toward her. She was under water again before she could take a breath.

The pressure on her chest burned as if she would explode. With all her concentration she resisted the impulse to inhale. Her legs kicked frantically at the turbulence. She was churned, twisted and bent.

The sound of maniacal laughter filled her head. She opened her eyes under the water. Through the dark indigo blue, she could just make out a shadowy figure standing like an orchestra conductor, waving a baton made of human bone.

No! I don't want to die!

She turned her head away. White bubbles danced and spiraled up through layers of blue toward the light at the translucent surface.

Enormous waves breaking overhead sounded far away, like thunder on distant mountains. The ocean's weight pressed down on her, holding her under.

The frequency of sound shifted and retreated to a great distance, as if she were in an enormous deserted cathedral. She felt entombed in cement. Silence, except for a faraway roar, and the ringing of a distant bell.

Colors swirled behind her eyes. Random moments from her life strobed through her mind.

Surrender.

She stopped fighting and gave in to a feeling of profound timeless peace. Her body began dissolving into an ocean of infinite love. Any second now, she'd black out, and water would rush into her lungs.

"Aurora! Don't give up!" Father Francis' voice circled and eddied, close to her ear. "Keep going. You're going to make it." She felt his arms wrap around her.

Suddenly, as if giving birth, the ocean pushed her out.

Aurora bobbed and gasped on the surface, coughing and sputtering, breathing in great draughts of air, momentarily blinded by the light.

Her board floated next to her like a faithful dog.

Impossible!

There was no way her board could have popped up next to her like this. It was a miracle! She grabbed it, and started paddling for her life.

A perfect swell lifted her board.

The wave gained speed and rose to its full height. She was weightless for a second, then standing on her board, dropping down the glistening face of a twenty-foot nearly vertical slide.

Barreling at a right angle, she cut a hard line across the wall of the massive wave. Wind and water howled in her ears. At the bottom, she dropped her knee, dug in with her back foot, and slammed a deep hard turn, setting her rail for the long-walled blast.

Her board shot back up the face of the behemoth, just ahead of the crumbling white water that chased her like a pack of hell hounds, promising to devour her if she fell.

She carved along the face of the wave as the lip curled and pitched over her with a vengeance. She was a bullet shooting through a shining green tunnel. She danced forward on her board to increase her speed, and shot out of the tube just as it closed out behind her.

Up and down the wave she carved, exhilarated by the adrenaline, the speed, the power and wind, the feeling of dancing on light, and the roar of the avalanche at her back. The cliffs whooshed by in an endless blur.

Another surfer whooped at her as she raced toward shore. She realized she'd surfed all the way to Cowell's Cove, at least a third of a mile.

She cut hard and fast up the face of the wave's last convulsive swell and, just before it broke, kicked her board up and over. She and her board were airborne. Then she splashed down on the calm back of the wave.

She let the white water of the next dying breaker carry her to shore, on her belly all the way onto the beach next to the Santa Cruz wharf.

She staggered out of the water in front of the historic Dream Inn.

Like a drowned beauty queen, with strands of sea grass tangled in her hair, and a trickle of blood dribbling from her nose, Aurora sat on her board in the sand in front of the Dream Inn and lifted her face to a glint of sun shining through an opening in the storm clouds.

Alive. I'm so grateful to be alive.

THE JOURNEY HOME

"You do not become a dissident just because you decide one day to take up the most unusual career. You are thrown into it by your personal sense of responsibility combined with a complex set of external circumstances. You are cast out of the existing structures and placed in a position of conflict with them. It begins with an attempt to do your work well, and ends with being branded an enemy of the establishment."

— Václav Havel.

57

SATURDAY, DECEMBER 3, 1998
Our Lady of Help Church, Valle Verde

FATHER FRANCIS TOSSED AND TURNED MOST OF THE NIGHT. Rising just before dawn, he wandered into the kitchen and noticed a message that Father Ruiz had left next to the phone.

Father Francis, Call Dr. Vogel at the hospital as soon as possible. Urgent.

The priest dialed the number on the memo. He waited a few minutes before the physician came on the line.

"Father Francis. I tried to reach you last night at Victor Lopez' request. Thank you for calling me back. I understand you're a close friend of the family. I'm sorry to have to tell you this, Father. It's about Victor's brother, Juan. He hung himself in his cell at Juvenile Hall."

"Oh no. Dear God."

"Johnny attempted suicide but, by some miracle, he's still alive. He's in ICU and it's iffy. Victor was hoping you would come."

"I'm on my way."

*   *   *

VALLE VERDE COMMUNITY HOSPITAL

"You are here for Johnny Lopez?"

The man standing before them offered his hand.

"I'm Probation Officer Robert James. Johnny's case has been assigned to me."

Victor lifted his anguished face, but ignored the man's outstretched hand. "How could you have let this happen?"

"I'm sorry. You are?"

Father Francis stood and shook the man's hand.

"I'm Father Francis Hilman, a friend of the family. This is Johnny's older brother and primary adult caregiver, Victor Lopez."

"Ah. Good to meet you both. Johnny is still in ICU, but all signs indicate he's going to pull out of this. Once he's stabilized physically, our work together will begin. When the hospital releases him, he'll go into a psychiatric counseling program back at Juvenile Hall. I feel confident that, with your help, we'll be able to get Johnny back on track."

"So, you think he's going to make it?" Victor rubbed his forehead.

"I think we got to him in time. He was refusing to participate in any of the ongoing activities we offer at the Hall: sports, classes, even recreational time. And he was displaying aggressive and potentially violent behavior. We had no other recourse than to place him in an isolation unit. But juveniles who go into isolation at our facility are monitored 24-7. A guard is stationed in the hallway just outside the room at all times."

"Then what the hell happened?" Victor stood and faced the probation officer, clenching and unclenching his fists.

"As I understand it, Johnny managed to be very quiet in his preparations. But when he kicked a chair over, the guard heard the noise, entered the room and found him. When the guard hit the alarm, the response was nearly immediate. They cut Johnny down, administered CPR, got him on a respirator, and to the hospital as quickly as humanly possible."

The probation officer put a hand on Victor's shoulder. Victor shrugged it off.

"I'm very sorry this happened, but maybe it's a blessing in disguise. Sometimes it takes really bottoming out like this before a person can find the will to turn his life around. I have to go now, but I'll be in touch."

Victor slumped down in his chair and buried his face in his hands.

*   *   *

An hour later, a doctor entered the waiting room.

"Victor Lopez?" Victor shot to his feet.

"I'm Doctor Vogel. I've been treating your brother, Juan, since he was admitted. I'm happy to tell you he has stabilized. If all goes well tonight, we'll move him out of Critical Care in the morning."

"Thank God. Will there be any permanent damage, do you think?" asked Father Francis.

"You mean, brain damage? He was without oxygen for a critical period, but young people do tend to be resilient. We've checked his responses, and everything seems normal. In my opinion, the only lasting consequence of this trauma, besides his ongoing psychological issues, will be a scar around his neck. In time, even that will probably fade."

"I need to see my brother, Doctor," said Victor.

"I can take you both in to see him now," she said. "But first, there's one more thing you should know. Sometime in the last twenty-four hours before he was placed in isolation and hung himself, Johnny was raped."

*   *   *

SUNDAY, DECEMBER 4, 1998
GOLDEN BUDDHA RESTAURANT, VALLE VERDE

"Raped?" Charlie Rosa's chopsticks, loaded with Kung Pao chicken, froze midway to his mouth.

Father Francis set his bottle of Tsingtao down on the table. He shook some hot chili sesame oil over his Mongolian beef, then nodded.

"Johnny's been impossible to communicate with since his mother died, nearly two years ago. No one's been able to get through to him. But yesterday, he asked to see me. When we met, he opened up. Said that when he landed in Juvie, some Mara Salvatrucha recruits tried to enlist him. They bragged about all the money he could make as a 'delivery boy,' once he got out of Juvie, driving 'cargo' in their vans. Human 'cargo'."

"Damn." Charlie set down his chopsticks, planted his elbows on the table and leaned forward.

"Johnny told the Truchas he didn't believe them, so they gave him details about a so-called 'package' they 'processed' back in August — a white woman and her little girl. They described the woman as damaged goods. Said she was picked up by a van that takes prostitutes to the fields. But the little white girl was sold for a high price to a man with a yacht. The delivery boys packed the girl in a dog crate and drove her to a dock at Moss Landing."

"Alice's mother and sister?"

"That's what I was thinking." Father Francis rubbed his forehead. "Will we ever find them, Charlie?"

"Don't get your hopes up, Frank. We'll keep the case open, but it's not promising. Either of them could be anywhere in the world by now. And for all we know, that missing Mayan girl could have ended up in one of those dog crates or in a van servicing the fields too. Did Johnny give you names? We've got to question these 'delivery boys'."

"Names, descriptions, even some locations and phone numbers."

"What about Johnny? Did Salvatruchas do the rape?"

"No. Norteños did it. The Truchas made sure Johnny knew too much, then they threatened to shiv him unless he agreed to jump with them. The Norteños got wind of it, and punished Johnny for disloyalty."

"Jesus. No wonder the kid was suicidal."

58

A URORA'S CAR HYDROPLANED. She gripped the wheel, resisted the instinct to slam on the breaks, and focused on keeping the car from spinning into the divider on Highway 1.

Once she'd regained control, she moved to the slow lane and turned her wipers and defroster on high. The rain was coming down so hard she could barely see the taillights of the car in front of her.

Good thing I got an early start. Driving to school this morning is going to take twice as long as usual.

Inching along in the slow lane, her mind wandered.

Winter break flew by! Probably because I spent it with cousin Kathy and family. Accepting the invitation to spend Christmas and New Year's at their Squaw Valley cabin–great decision. Although "cabin" is a silly word to use for that three-story, eight-bedroom winter home Kathy and her husband own at Lake Tahoe.

379

Skiing was the best ever. And the outdoor hot baths at the Squaw Creek Resort have to be one of the most decadent spas in the world — all those outdoor hot pools, engineered to connect and flow into one another as if they're natural, steaming into the night air beneath the snow-covered mountains, giving the illusion of geothermal springs surrounded by mists of enchantment ...

I feel really guilty about the appalling amount of fossil fuel burned to generate all that power for heating and lighting the resort in the snow. But soaking in those tubs after an epic day of skiing followed by a hot river stone massage ... heaven.

Such a strange coincidence that sitting next to me in the manicure chair at Squaw Creek Spa was Malone Baker, of all people. It had been surprisingly easy to talk with her while we were getting our nails done. The champagne no doubt contributed to the relaxed ambiance of our conversation. Malone actually promised she'd talk with her husband about setting up a conservation easement to preserve their ag land!

Then there'd been that very awkward moment later at the bar. Malone wanted to fix me up with her son for the resort's New Year's Eve party.

Malone's son is Billy Baker! Why hadn't I put that together sooner? Thank you Cousin Kath for helping me escape that trap with some semblance of tact.

By the time Aurora pulled into the Prudenciana lot, the rain had slowed to a gentle patter. She pulled the hood of her yellow rain slicker over her head and hustled across the lot to the faculty room.

At the teachers' mail cubbies, she was tossing junk mail into the recycling bin when Katie arrived.

"Happy New Year, Aurora!"

"Hey, Katie. Happy New Year to you too." The teachers hugged.

"Here we go again," said Aurora. "Ready?"

"Yep," Katie replied. "It was wonderful to have a break for a while, but it feels great to get back to work."

"Good vacation?"

"Definitely. Our first Christmas together, as husband and wife, so it was, well — special. Even though we didn't do presents this year, we really enjoyed our time together."

"Why no presents?"

"We're watching our budget carefully, with him still in school, and me on a beginning teacher's salary. We still have my student loans to pay off, so we're being really strict with ourselves about not getting any credit cards. If we don't have the money, we just don't buy it. We must have gotten about five credit card offers a day in the mail over the holidays."

Katie pulled an envelope out of her mail cubby. "Oh, no! Look! Here's another one. A credit card come-along in my professional mailbox at work!"

Katie shredded the offer and dropped it in the recycling bin as if it were a dead rat. "Did you see this message from Ruth? There should be one in your mailbox."

"Here it is. Farm Without Harm meeting next Friday. Are you going?"

"Yep. Definitely."

"Maybe you should skip it, Katie. You know, without tenure, you have no rights. The principal can decide not to ask you back next year, without even giving a reason why."

"What teachers do outside of school, as long as we're not breaking any laws, is our own business. It's my Constitutional right to attend a meeting on my own time if I want to. Besides, how do you think the school administration would even know about the meeting or who attends? Do you think they're going to spy on us or something? Anyway, I can't betray my values, even if it does cost me my job."

"But, you just said yourself that you can't afford …"

"True, it would be a financial disaster for us if I lose my job, but my husband is with me on this. We can't live a lie for the sake of a job. It's how we want to live, to follow our hearts, be true to our ideals, no matter what. Don't worry. I understand the risks."

*   *   *

FRIDAY LATE AFTERNOON, JANUARY 14, 1999
FARM WITHOUT HARM MEETING
UFW OFFICES, DOWNTOWN VALLE VERDE

I'm not going to look at him.

It was the first time Aurora had seen Father Francis since the humiliating meeting at his church. Her face flushed, her heart thudded against her chest, and her head spun as the shame of that encounter washed over her.

Get over yourself. It was crazy poor judgment to dress like that and provoke the poor man into telling you what you already knew. He's a Catholic priest. Celibate. You embarrassed yourself and him. Rise above it and move on. I'm sure he has.

It almost seemed as if he were trying to make eye contact with her.

Don't be stupid. Wishful thinking.

"… to take my son, Danny, to Stanford next Monday for another amputation."

That got Aurora's attention. Guadalupe Santiago, Danny's mom, sat next to third grade teacher May Chang. Mrs. Santiago had lost a lot of weight. She had dark circles under her eyes, and her hair, which had been black and shining at the last Farm Without Harm meeting, was now dull and streaked with grey.

"They were too late removing the foot," said Mrs. Santiago. "We waited too long. Now, they just hope they can keep the bone cancer from spreading any further if they take the whole leg."

Aurora felt sick.

Like a hive of angry bees, the people in the room buzzed with frustration and outrage.

"It's obvious we're in a cancer cluster," said Ruth Redding.

"It seems obvious to us," the Monterey Bay Aquarium marine scientist Sharon Lumina said, "but it takes a whole lot of time, careful documentation and litigation to actually prove the existence of a 'cancer cluster'."

"The burden of proof for this kind of thing shouldn't be on us." Normally soft-spoken, fifth grade teacher Helen Rice was shouting. "It should be on the pesticide manufacturers and users. They're threatening the lives of our whole community."

"When are fumigations scheduled to start up again?" asked Destiny.

"Earlier than usual. We've heard that the methyl bromide distributer, CalGreen, recommended to all the Valle Verde strawberry growers that they start fumigating in early February this year, and do more methyl bromide applications than usual," Jenny Merritt answered. "But we've received assurances from the agricultural commissioner that there will be no fumigations until after the hearing. If the State Department of Pesticide Regulation decides in our favor at the hearing, there won't be any fumigations at all near Prudenciana School this year. So, it's crucial that everyone spread the word about the hearing every way you can. We have to *pack* that hall. The State Department of Pesticide Regulation needs to know that people have had it with being poisoned in their homes and workplaces, having their children poisoned at school, and having their air, water, and food poisoned. We've got a good chance of seeing these pesticide permits revoked. We can do this."

When the meeting ended, Aurora grabbed her raincoat and bag and hurried out through the wrought iron gate of the UFW Offices, desperate to avoid facing Father Francis. All of the shame, loneliness, anger, and confusion she'd felt at his church welled back up.

It was dark. Bright needles of rain strobed in the streetlight. She pulled her raincoat tight and shivered.

She didn't notice the black sedan parked across the street, or the two men in black suits inside the car who were taking photos of her and the other people leaving the UFW offices.

She turned and walked down the deserted side street where she'd parked.

"Aurora!"

She spun around.

Father Francis ran toward her. She held her breath.

He's going to take me in his arms.

He opened his umbrella and held it over her, making a 360° waterfall screen around them. He smiled down at her. His physical power and masculine beauty overwhelmed her. They stood so close she could barely breathe.

I'm in love with a Catholic priest. Why can't I get over this?

"I wanted to check in with you about our ag land conservation project." He raised an eyebrow and smiled. "And I'm not so sure you should be alone on a dark street like this. May I walk you to your car?"

She nodded. They walked side by side and he kept the umbrella over both of them.

"I saw Malone and William Baker over Christmas," said the priest. "We had a concert at Our Lady of Help. The Mount Madonna Choir. Have you heard them?"

Aurora didn't trust herself to speak. She fidgeted with the end of her braid and nodded again.

"Mr. and Mrs. Baker were there. They were married at Our Lady of Help about thirty years ago, and they come to church every now and then. At the reception after the concert, I had a chance to talk with them about the value of preserving their agricultural land. Mr. Baker was especially receptive. He said he's been thinking along the same lines."

A bolt of lightning cut across the sky, illuminating the priest's face.

A loud rumble of thunder reverberated through the night like a gunshot. The rain became a heavy downpour. They moved closer together inside the dome of water pouring off Father Francis' umbrella.

"I talked to Malone Baker over the vacation too," said Aurora. "I thought she seemed receptive. No wonder, since she and her husband had already talked with you. I guess you primed the pump. What do we do next?"

"The seeds have been planted. Now we'll just have to wait and see how things develop."

"Here's my car. I should go." Aurora looked up at the priest's face. She shivered. "I've got to drive all the way back to Santa Cruz tonight, through this rain."

Father Francis held the umbrella over Aurora as she climbed into her car.

"Goodnight. Drive safely."

He shut her car door and turned away, into the dark and the sheeting rain.

59

Agricultural Extension Auditorium, Valle Verde

T HIRTY OR FORTY MEN AND WOMEN holding picket signs walked in circles in the parking lot in front of the Agricultural Extension auditorium where the pesticide permit challenge hearing was about to take place. All the men and some of the women wore AWC caps embroidered with two open hands cupping a big red strawberry.

Aurora made her way through the throng. People were reluctant to give way. Their anger was palpable. She smiled and tried to make eye contact, but most people turned away or glared at her with smoldering black eyes.

Why such hostility?

The Hispanic families she worked with were usually friendly and polite. She was here to help these people, help provide their children with a high-quality education, and help make their schools safe.

Aurora took a closer look at the picket signs in English and Spanish. With a shock, she realized that her name was on some of the signs.

"Why Do You Want To Take Away Our Jobs, Aurora Bourne?"
"Teachers Should Teach, Not Tell Farmers How To Farm, Katie Cooper." "Don't Take Away Our Methyl Bromide, Ruth Redding." "No Methyl Bromide = No Jobs, Helen Rice."

These and similar messages repeated in Spanish and English, named every Prudenciana teacher who had attended a Farm Without Harm meeting.

All of the cardboard posters the picketers carried were stapled to freshly machine-cut pine stakes. Not a single sign was crooked, bent, scuffed, or limp. Aurora knew damn well that the people carrying these signs did not have the resources to pay for the materials the signs were made of.

All of the posters were lettered by the same hand. No grammatical mistakes or spelling errors.

Who made these picket signs, really?

As Aurora entered the auditorium, one of the picketers put a leaflet in her hand. She glanced at it before stuffing it in her bag. *Methyl Bromide Myths vs. Facts.* In Spanish and English. At the bottom of the leaflet was the logo she'd noticed on the hats, plus the words Agricultural Workers' Committee. Below that it read ©Methyl Bromide Working Group, Washington, D.C.

She stood in the back of the already crowded hall, getting her bearings. Almost everyone inside the auditorium was Caucasian. Poor brown outside. Rich white inside.

Democracy in action?

The middle aisle running through the assembly hall cut the crowd into two distinct groups. Permit challenge people sat on the left. Aurora spotted Father Francis in the front row on the permit challenge side. Next to the priest sat Paloma's big brother, Victor, and a row of young men who looked, in spite of their modern clothing and absence of war paint, like American Indian warriors in a western movie.

On the right side of the aisle sat the strawberry growers, the city officials, the school administrators — including both Superintendent Spieler and Principal Deana Wagner — and the men who had presented at the school pesticide assembly — public health commissioner Dr.

Ringer, with his bulbous red nose and clownish bow tie, and Sean Stark, stroking his goatee.

Mr. Choate, the nice grower who had met with the teachers at Prudenciana last October, was sitting next to old Mr. Cowley, whose strawberry field was on the other side of the chain link fence from the Prudenciana Life Lab Garden. Choate leaned over and said something to Mr. Cowley.

Another man flanked old Mr. Cowley on his other side. At least a head taller, and probably a hundred pounds heavier than the old man, all muscle and grit, he was handsome, in a salt-of-the-earth rugged way. His brown hair and moustache were touched with brushes of sun-washed gold, and he had a hint of grey at the temples. He exuded strength and righteousness, reminding Aurora of an old timey Wild West sheriff. The kind of man you want on your side. He looked angry. Aurora recognized him from his newspaper photo. He'd been interviewed after one of the Farm Without Harm demonstrations last month. In the newspaper photo that appeared in all the papers, he wore sunglasses, the protestors at the edge of his strawberry field reflected in his lenses. Gill Garritt. The third grower whose pesticide application permit they were challenging today. Choate, Cowley, and Garritt.

Aurora continued to scan the room. Her body jerked with shock when she saw him. The "I know who you are and I hate you" man in the pinstriped suit. He stood in front of the auditorium, talking to Malone Baker, who sat in the front row. Seated on Malone's left was a barrel-chested grey-haired man, presumably Mr. Baker. On Malone's right was her son, Billy.

Next to Billy sat Yudas Medina, Katie's nemesis. Next to Yudas Medina, at the end of the row, hunched Salvador Luna. He turned to look over his shoulder at Aurora, cheeks glistening with tears.

Aurora's heart ached. *Who could have taken the life of this beautiful, innocent child? Why is he here?*

People approached Malone as if she were a queen.

She's got charisma. Too bad she's not on our side.

On the stage, a long table with chairs had been set up to face the gathering. Attendants arranged water glasses and pitchers of water, and adjusted microphones.

"Have you signed up to speak yet?" Jenny Merritt asked Aurora. "No. I just got here."

"If you want to speak, you need to fill out a card over there."

Butterflies in her stomach, Aurora approached the speakers' sign-up table. She'd written and practiced a speech, timing it so she could deliver it in just under three minutes. As nervous as she felt about speaking in front of all these people, she was determined to tell them they must stop using pesticides around the schools. It was her legal and moral duty to protect her students from harm. Ever since she and Katie had researched and documented exactly what poisons were being used around her school, she'd been one hundred percent certain. This poisoning had to stop, and she'd do whatever she must to make it so.

At an open side door in the front of the auditorium, next to the platform where the Department of Pesticide Regulation officials would sit, men in black suits and black high-gloss leather shoes came in and out. Some stood guard; others carried messages to people inside. In spite of the fading light, all of the men in black wore sunglasses.

What do they think this is, some comic sci-fi movie?

The room spun and shifted. Everything that had felt so menacing and surreal a minute before suddenly seemed absurd.

"I feel like *Alice in Wonderland*," she wanted to shout, "and you're nothing but a pack of cards!"

She marched up to the nearest black-suited man. Almost identical comrades, standing solid as a rock wall, flanked him. She stepped into his personal space. Her nose at his polyester chest, she craned her neck and smiled at her reflection in his sunglasses. He emanated waves of menace. Her body told her to run. She stood her ground. She touched the green river rock in her pocket and visualized a pure light shielding her.

"Hi." She pasted on her sweetest smile. "What's your name?"

He stared over her head.

"Who are you guys, anyway? Are you CIA? Secret Police? FBI? What are you doing here?" She felt like she was poking at a poisonous snake with a stick. A gold pin on the man's lapel with the initials BR and a river logo caught her attention. "Who do you work for?"

Two other black suits stepped forward, surrounding her like the Dark Towers of Mordor. More than a foot taller and well over a hundred fifty pounds heavier than Aurora, they glowered through their dark glasses. One of the men touched his hip, suggesting there might be a gun under his coat.

Ridiculous. Real people don't bring guns into public meetings. That's only in the movies.

"I saw you guys at my school, when we had that pro-pesticide assembly."

"Excuse me, ma'am." A woman who looked like a cop in a waiter's uniform appeared at Aurora's elbow. She was one of the people who'd been setting up the table with glasses and water pitchers. The words "Black River" were monogramed on her collar, along with the same logo as on the lapel pins of the men in black.

"You need to take your seat now, ma'am. The hearing will begin in a few minutes." The woman's tone, backed up by the menacing vibe of the men in black, left no room for argument. Aurora turned.

A group of officials was being escorted into the building through the side door. Ignoring her "orders" to take a seat, she approached the arriving officials.

"Hello." Aurora extended her hand to a tall woman in an expensive-looking red suit.

The woman's legs were shrink-wrapped in nylons and black patent leather high heels. Thin arched eyebrows had been carefully plucked and penciled over a layer of pancake make-up. Her teeth were a little too white. Her shoulder length hair fell in waves of shimmering California gold, a little too shimmering, a little too gold. The hairstyle seemed a little too young for her. The red nail polish on her perfectly manicured fingernails exactly matched her red suit and her lipstick. She wore a double string of large flawless pearls, with matching pearl stud earrings, and thick gold jewelry at her fingers and wrists. Executive Barbie. She almost seemed like a female impersonator.

"You must be with the State Department of Pesticide Regulation. I'm Aurora Bourne, a teacher at Prudenciana Elementary. Thank you so much for coming to review the pesticide permits."

The woman in red ignored Aurora's outstretched hand, looking down on her as if she were a talking cockroach.

Sean Stark and the Santa Cruz County Agricultural Commissioner, Mr. Grumond, rushed up to greet the State Pesticide Regulator like they were old friends. Stark and Grumond ushered the regulator and her entourage away, leaving Aurora standing alone and open-mouthed.

She found a seat on the left side of the aisle, in the back. The hearing was called to order. Everyone rose for the Pledge of Allegiance to the United States of America.

60

WEDNESDAY, FEBRUARY 9, 1999
Prudenciana Elementary

THE TEACHER'S ROOM SMELLED OF FRESHLY BREWED COFFEE. Someone had placed a bouquet of yellow jonquils on the table.

"I couldn't believe those picket signs had our names on them," Aurora said.

"How in the world did those farmworkers get our names?" Helen stood up to get her oatmeal out of the microwave.

"Some of us who speak Spanish talked with the picketers," said Gail Corazone, the bilingual second grade teacher. "We focused on the women with babies. Those poor women. Someone was obviously using them."

"Some of them admitted to me that they were paid to be there," said Katie. "Twenty dollars an hour. Do you realize what a huge amount of money that is for them?"

"Who was paying them?"

"No one would say, but it had to be that so-called union that Yudas Medina is involved with," said Katie. "They had AWC hats on."

Harriet put her hand on Aurora's arm. "Your speech was excellent. So powerful and moving. Could I have a copy?"

"Sorry," said Aurora. "There is no copy; I didn't use what I'd written. It's strange. I've always been terrified of public speaking, but I just opened my mouth and words poured out, almost as if something were speaking through me."

"I can't believe how rude the anti-permit-challenge people in the auditorium were," said Ruth Redding. "Interrupting, jeering. You'd think adults would know better how to conduct themselves in a formal public hearing. Their behavior was completely inappropriate."

"What makes me mad," said Katie, "is that the DPR moderator did nothing to control it. He even let the growers have extra time at the podium, and then cut the pro-permit-challenge speakers short."

"The worst," said Aurora, "was what happened to Mrs. Santiago, the mother of May Chang's student Danny."

"I couldn't make it," said the librarian taking her tea out of the microwave. "What happened?"

"Mrs. Santiago went to the podium holding her son's new prosthetic leg in her hands. She'd just returned from Stanford hospital where they'd amputated Danny's leg to keep the cancer from spreading. She was crying when said she hoped he'd live to wear the prosthesis. People jeered and shouted that her time was up!"

"Unbelievable!"

"It was obscene," said Corky Duncan. "Who in their right mind treats another human being like that?"

Tom Olson arrived with the *Santa Cruz Sentinel*, the *Monterey Herald*, and the *Valle Verde Register* under his arm. He spread them out on the table. All three papers featured front-page articles on the hearing.

Katie picked up the *Valle Verde Register* and skimmed the article.

"Oh, shit. Damn them to hell."

"We lost?"

"Yep. Those dirty rotten bastards. Can you believe it? Listen to this. 'Choate, Cowley, and Garritt have been given the green light by the State Department of Pesticide Regulation. A spokesman from CalGreen, the state's largest distributer and applicator of methyl bromide, stated that they know their practices are perfectly safe, and they're pleased to be getting this affirmation from the DPR. The growers have announced plans to begin their spring cycle of fumigations next week.'"

"Next week! What can we do?"

"We need to make sure all of our parents are notified of the fumigation dates," said Helen.

"I can go by the ag commissioner's office after school today and find out the fumigation schedule," Katie offered.

"Speaking as your union rep, if we're going to notify parents, we need to be very careful to follow district protocol," said Tom. "Remember that we're not allowed to use our class lists to contact people, and we can't use any school district equipment — phones, copy machines, not even paper. We don't want problems from the district about violating our contracts, using school resources for political purposes."

"But —" Katie started to object.

"No, Tom is right," said Helen. "We need to be completely above board on this. We can get phone numbers from the lists of people who signed our petitions. And we can call people from our home phones. For those of us who live in Santa Cruz, it's a toll call to Valle Verde, but better pay the price than have legal issues with the district."

*   *   *

AURORA'S COTTAGE
SANTA CRUZ, THE WESTSIDE

The next Sunday, Aurora sat in her garden with her new cordless phone to her ear, phoning her section of the Prudenciana parent list.

All of the parents Aurora spoke with were very concerned about pesticide exposure and thanked her for notification about the fumigation. Many intended to keep their children out of school tomorrow, and maybe even the next day.

Sunlight danced in and out of billowy charcoal clouds. Yesterday, there had been a light rainstorm. The garden was just beginning to come to life after a barren winter. The fruit trees were showing bud swell, the raspberries were leafing out, and the plum tree was already flowering. Masses of yellow daffodils had sprung up, practically overnight.

The first mockingbird of spring sat in the bare branches of the pear tree, practicing his pond-full-of-frogs and fire alarm symphony, a courting song sure to impress the finest mockingbird females. Aurora gave him a sour glare.

"I bet you'll be having a nice Valentine's Day tomorrow," she told him. "With all your talent and good looks."

The mockingbird flew high into the air. Flashing his handsome black and white tail feathers while doing fancy flips and summersaults, he tumbled down to a branch, not missing a beat of his complex aria.

Should I call in sick tomorrow? I want to stand with the teachers and parents protesting the fumigations. And I hate the thought of exposing myself to yet more toxic chemicals. But unlike Katie, I'm not that stressed out about reproductive harm. I decided a long time ago that I'm definitely not having babies. As much as I love children, the world is just too overpopulated.

The tall cedars behind the pond rustled as if large invisible beings were gliding through the branches. Aurora breathed a silent prayer.

If a lot of kids and teachers are absent tomorrow, the children who do show up are bound to be confused, scared, and anxious. And on top of that, tomorrow's Valentine's Day. That's a big deal for kids. Someone has to be there for them. Okay. I'll go.

*   *   *

**MONDAY, FEBRUARY 14, 1999
(ST. VALENTINE'S DAY)
PRUDENCIANA ELEMENTARY, MORNING RECESS**

Since dawn, a strong wind had been blowing from the bay across the fields onto the Prudenciana campus. The new tarps billowed as high as the rooftops of the school buildings, leaving the freshly fumigated and outgassing soil completely exposed.

The peculiar odor of chloropicrin saturated the air. Aurora recognized that metallic chloropicrin taste on the back of her tongue. Her eyes watered and she felt dizzy, kind of like being stoned. She shook her head, trying to clear her mind. Her two usual yard duty helpers, Beth and Destiny, were absent, as were their children.

"I just got today's attendance data from Bushi," said Tom Olson. "Two hundred and sixty students stayed home today, out of a total enrollment of 650. About half of them say they won't be returning tomorrow, either. Almost a third of the teachers called in sick. Two pregnant faculty members, and almost all of the young, untenured teachers."

"Good for them for having the courage to take a stand," said Aurora. "You don't think there will be any repercussions, do you Tom?"

"What can the district do? "

*　　　*　　　*

VALLE VERDE FIELD

The brown wool blanket on the ground was rough, itchy, and full of burrs. It was so thin rocks poked through.

She lay on her back, knees up, feet on the ground. The cold wind blew dust in her face. Her eyes burned. She closed her eyes.

Head spinning. Feel like throwing up.

She could hear tarps flapping in the wind nearby.

She hadn't bothered to pull her skirt back down from around her waist to cover her nakedness. Blood and semen oozed out of her vagina onto the blanket.

She watched a fat black tick crawl out on a branch of the coyote brush that hid her. The tick dropped onto her thigh. She wondered which direction it would crawl. She could flick it off, but why bother.

She heard the next customer rustling through the bushes, unzipping his pants.

It would still be a long time before they'd come get her, put her back in the van with the other girls.

Maybe tonight, they'd take her somewhere where she could get a bath. But soap would just make the itching and stinging worse.

Maybe they'd leave them in the van tonight, like usual. It didn't matter.

The pretty colored ribbons her mother had woven into her braids had come out weeks ago. Her hair was matted and dirty.

The girl opened her legs and turned her face away from the man on top of her. She cried silently, remembering the last time her mother had braided ribbons in her hair.

61

TUESDAY, FEBRUARY 15, 1999
Prudenciana Elementary

A TEAM OF PEOPLE IN SUITS AND TIES ROVED AROUND CAMPUS. They popped unannounced into classrooms, and even pulled teachers and aides out of classes to speak to them in the little room off the teachers' lunchroom. Aurora caught a glimpse inside, before someone shut the door. It was set up like a police interrogation cell in the movies. She hoped they wouldn't call her in.

*   *   *

THURSDAY, FEBRUARY 17, 1999
PRUDENCIANA ELEMENTARY

On Thursday morning, when Aurora checked her mail, she found that every cubby held a rubber-banded pack of goldenrod-colored papers. There was a memo on top with the superintendent's letterhead, ordering, "These letters must be sent home with your students, today."

Aurora scanned the top letter. In Spanish and English, it read, "The safety of your children is of primary importance to our staff, the District, and the Board of Trustees. This is of a particular concern during the application of methyl bromide near our schools. We assure you that, during and after fumigations in the vicinity of our schools, all proper measures will be implemented to ensure the safety and health of staff and students. Please be assured that there is no need to keep your children out of school. It is in your child's best interests to attend school regularly. Should you have any concerns, please contact our new Safety Officer at (831) 728-6220 x501."

This is nothing but cover-your-ass hypocrisy and lies!

Aurora stuffed the outrage boiling through her. Most of the parents would see this letter for what it was, and she needed to be emotionally clear and positive to teach her fourth graders.

*   *   *

At morning recess, Aurora sat at her desk going over spelling tests. Her fingers wrapped around the handle of a new ceramic mug one of her students had given her, with red hearts and "I Love You" glazed all over it. It steamed with the spicy smell of Good Earth cinnamon tea. A brand new fluffy white teddy bear with a red silk heart stitched to his chest, another gift from a student, leaned against the computer monitor next to a stack of valentines. A half-full bag of pastel-colored, heart-shaped sugar candies with sweet messages sagged on the desk next to the teddy bear, along with a package of Harry Potter's "Bertie Bott's Every Flavor Beans", which Aurora had been using for a math lesson.

Helen Rice and Harriet Ryan entered the room. "Something terrible has happened," said Helen. The fifth grade mentor teachers' faces were grim.

"What's wrong?"

"The school district filed a lawsuit against Tom Olsen," said Helen.

"You're joking, right?"

"No, this is very serious," Harriet answered. "The district administration is furious about our boycott during the fumigation.

Apparently all the unexcused absences cost over $20,000 in loss of state ADA funds."

"What does that have to do with our Union rep? Why are they suing Tom?"

"We think their strategy is to punish one of our leaders. They probably figure if they can silence our Union rep, none of the rest of us will dare to keep fighting."

"What are they suing him for? There's no way he did anything wrong. He's got more integrity than almost anyone else I know."

"Remember those people in suits who were here on Tuesday, snooping around campus?"

Aurora nodded. "Of course. I was relieved they didn't call me in. Who were they?"

"Administrators from the district office," said Harriet. "They were questioning people about how parents found out about the fumigation. The lawsuit claims that Tom used the school telephone and school records to contact parents and tell them not to come to school on the day of the fumigation."

"That's absurd. Tom is the one who cautioned us not to use any school materials or equipment. He's the one who told us we couldn't use our class lists to get phone numbers."

"We agree. And Tom denies that he did any of the things they're accusing him of."

"What's the basis of their assertion?"

Helen and Harriet looked at each other, as if deciding whether or not to tell Aurora what they knew. Then Helen spoke.

"It was Niño, Aurora."

"Our custodian?"

Harriet nodded. "Niño told them that last Friday, after the principal left campus for the night and locked the office, Tom asked to be let in, so he could phone some of his students' parents."

"So what? We have to phone parents all the time. That's what good teachers do, right? If a student's having a problem, you get a hold of the parent right away. Particularly at this time of year, with our big push before standardized testing. Of course he'd stay late to phone parents, and since the District doesn't allow teachers to have phones in their classrooms, there's only the one phone at school — in the office. But Tom cautioned us not to use the school phone or class lists to talk to parents about pesticides, so I'm sure he wouldn't have done it himself. The district is just wrong on this. Niño did that to Tom? What is the matter with that man?"

"We were afraid you might take this badly," said Helen. "Niño probably just answered the questions in all innocence. We hope you won't be angry with him. He's having a really hard time."

"I know. His wife has had a bunch of miscarriages."

"Not only that. Remember, there used to be three daytime custodians and two night men at Prudenciana before all the cutbacks. Now there's only him and one part-time night man. Plus, they've cut back district-wide grounds maintenance crews. So Niño's under pressure to do the work that about five men used to do. He can't question orders or they'll fire him. And he certainly can't afford to lose his job. He's exhausted, stressed, and just plain angry."

Join the club, thought Aurora.

* * *

When Aurora entered the school library that afternoon for the faculty meeting, Superintendent Spieler himself stood in front of the room.

Next to the superintendent, Principal Wagner pursed her thin lips in a scolding frown. On the superintendent's other side was a surprise guest: Billy Baker.

What the hell? What's he doing here?

Aurora closed her eyes. When she looked again, Salvador Luna and Alice's twin stood at the door. Aurora caught Nathena Hamilton's eye. Nathena nodded.

She sees them too.

"I'm here today," said the superintendent, "to introduce our new special consultant, Safety Officer Mr. William Baker."

This can't be happening, Aurora thought.

"Mr. Baker is an expert in the area of methyl bromide fumigations. His close ties to CalGreen, the company that implements all fumigations in the region, will give him special understanding of the procedures involved. If any of you, or any Prudenciana parents, have questions or concerns about the fumigations, contact Mr. Baker directly. Your principal is passing out Mr. Baker's card. Keep it with you and don't hesitate to call him."

The principal passed out Billy's card, plus sheets of paper with the superintendent's letterhead.

"This letter is to provide you with written notification," Superintendent Spieler continued, "there will be another fumigation over Presidents' Day Weekend." The superintendent read the notification aloud.

"On Sunday, February 20th, over the long Presidents' Day weekend, methyl bromide will be applied to a 14-acre parcel behind and alongside Prudenciana School. To ensure the safety and health of staff and students, the following procedures will be implemented at Prudenciana School on the following Tuesday, February 22nd."

The superintendent gestured toward Billy Baker, who read, "The wait time for access to a field where methyl bromide is applied is 48 hours. On Tuesday morning, February 22nd at six am, the District Safety Officer will investigate the school site to determine if methyl bromide or chloropicrin is detected in the area around the school. The Safety Officer will contact the superintendent to notify him of the results of the tests. If substances are detected, we will evacuate staff and students to the cafeteria and gym at Valle Verde High School."

"In any case, the District staff will ventilate rooms on Tuesday morning before school," said the superintendent. "There will be a nurse available on site on Tuesday to draw the blood of all faculty and staff wanting blood tests. The County Health Officer, Dr. Ringer, will provide the tests free of charge to determine levels of methyl bromide in the blood. If there are any questions, please contact the District Safety Officer, Mr. Baker."

Aurora leaned over to whisper to Katie, "This is too elaborate. What are they up to?"

Katie ignored Aurora and raised her hand. The superintendent acknowledged her with a nod. "How will exposure to pesticide drift be monitored?"

"We understand that there has been some talk of independent monitoring of the Prudenciana campus for pesticide drift," said the superintendent. "Let me be very clear that we do not authorize any independent outside agency to access the campus or to set up a monitoring device on campus."

"But," said Katie, "the drift monitoring equipment that the agricultural commissioner uses is out of date and inaccurate. We —"

"That will be all, Miss Cooper." The superintendent glared at Katie.

Aurora was stunned. *There are hundreds of new untenured teachers in the district, but the superintendent knows Katie's name!*

"CalGreen has already installed the drift monitoring equipment in the field to be fumigated," the superintendent continued. "In addition, Mr. Baker here has a new, state-of-the-art, hand-held device that he will be taking through the school on Monday morning to check for airborne pesticide residue. That will give us all the data we need."

The teachers looked shell-shocked. Tom Olsen, across the room, appeared to be in especially bad shape, as if he hadn't slept in days.

Aurora whispered to Helen, "How's Tom doing?"

"The Union attorney has taken his case," Helen answered. "But he'll still have expenses — probably far more than a teacher with a young family can afford. And if they do find him guilty of professional malfeasance, he'll lose his teaching credential, for sure. All those years, money, and time, invested in his education and training to become a teacher, all the years of exemplary teaching, down the drain — gone, ruined, over a malicious and false accusation."

62

Strawberry field, Valle Verde
Byrd River Watershed, Santa Cruz County

T HE MAYAN MAN STRAIGHTENED AND GAZED AT THE GULLS
circling and cawing overhead, appearing and disappearing in and
out of the blue holes in the grey and white clouds. Those clouds
probably held more rain.

He dropped the weeds and spoiled berries he'd cleaned from
around the berry plants into the bag on his back. If they didn't maintain
the field they picked, their pay would be docked. The man stretched his
back and took a moment to watch his wife. She was a skilled picker; her
hands a blur she worked so fast. Yet each strawberry she placed in her
basket was perfect; not one plant was damaged. The *bebé* on her back
slept. Across the fields, beyond the distant eucalyptus grove, rose the
church steeple. A rainbow arced above it.

Thanks to the Blessed Lady they were here, *en Los Estados Unidos*.
They had good work today, an extra day of work this week, because the
strawberries must be harvested fast, on a Sunday, before they molded

403

from the rain. He was grateful for the work. He was grateful that his wife and little girl were here safe beside him today, and that his little girl was doing well, with a good teacher in a good school. Today, he watched over his little one like a bear, keeping her close. He was not going to have another child vanish in the fields. And by the grace of the Virgin, his older daughter would soon be found.

God is good. Under His protection, they had escaped the massacre. The man stooped to resume picking, ignoring the stabbing pain in his back. He recalled that day when he had taken his family into the forest to harvest nuts, *pau rosa* leaves and other medicinal plants. While they were gone, Mexican soldiers came to his village. *Why do the Mexicans hate my people so?* When he and his family returned to their village that evening — he wished his children had never seen what they found. No being left alive. No babies. Not even a dog. So, they had fled. Under the blue cloak of the Blessed Virgin, they'd made the nightmare journey to *El Norte — Los Estados Unidos. A miracle that my family survived.*

A *coyote* had guided his family through a sewage tunnel under the border, through Hell. *At least, going that way, my wife and daughters escaped the Rape Trees.* He'd been blessed to find a clean *coyote*, one of the old ones, not one of those new *polleros* running the Devil's Highway who left people to die in the desert after taking all their money and promising a safe crossing. Or worse, the Devils who trafficked in human flesh — the ones who, it was said, stole women and children for the sex slave trade.

All that is behind us. The man twisted another large, perfect strawberry neatly off at the top of the stem and placed it in the green plastic basket. *My daughter will soon be found, I feel certain. My family will live a good life here, in the Land of the Free. In the Land of Liberty and Justice for all.*

The Mayan man stood and stretched. He squinted across the fields at the church steeple. Gulls circled and cawed, flying in and out of holes in the clouds, and a double rainbow arced over the church.

Queen of Heaven, thank you for watching over us. Tomorrow, we will visit the priest at Our Lady of Help. God willing, Padre Francisco *will have news of our missing daughter.*

*   *   *

OUR LADY OF HELP CHURCH
VALLE VERDE

Yudas Medina strolled out of the church and scanned the sky. Like lost souls, seagulls appeared and disappeared through blue holes in the grey and white clouds.

Mass in English had not been satisfying this morning. That Indian priest, Father Francis, spoiled it. You shouldn't have a dark-skinned Indian offering mass before the most rich and important members of the congregation.

Yudas watched his daughter playing with *los patrónes'* girls.

She is doing very well socially. The children of los anglos ricos *seem to accept her. She is becoming very pretty. I must keep a close eye on her. The boy, though. He looks fine. Straight and growing tall. And he is smart. But he stands away from the other children, all by himself. He makes no effort to meet the sons of these important men. I will have a talk with him, again, when we get home.*

Impatient to go, Yudas scanned the parish hall for his wife. She should be finished soon with helping the other church ladies in the kitchen to serve the cookies, coffee and juice. Yudas did not like that his wife helped in the church kitchen. It made her seem like a servant. He had brought his family to the English mass so that they could mix with the *patrónes* as equals. So his *familia* could hold up their heads and be respected here, *en Los Estados Unidos.*

Yudas pulled the rim of his new Mexican palm cowboy hat over his eyes to block the sun flashing in and out of the clouds. Those clouds looked like they had more rain in them. He adjusted his fancy silver belt buckle, and nodded to an important couple coming down the steps from the church. They were big landowners, friends of the Bakers.

The *patrónes* leaving the church nodded to him like he was one of them. Yudas Medina was an important man. Like all important men, Yudas had connections. Unfortunately, not all of those connections were good people. But they were useful. They helped him to keep his boss happy. Keeping Billy happy meant certain things were necessary for Yudas to do — things he did not like. But all rich and powerful men had to do things they did not feel good about. That was the way of power, and of money, the way the world works, was it not? The trick was not to get caught.

Yudas peered at the sky. The church steeple pointed straight up to those lost souls flying in and out of blue holes in the clouds. He could hear their cries.

Soon, Yudas Medina thought. *Soon, I must go to confession.*

63

Prudenciana Elementary

A T THE MAIL CUBBIES, AURORA CAME ACROSS TOM OLSEN tossing junk mail into the recycle bin. She noticed an odd slackness to the skin around his face and neck, and his eyes didn't seem quite right.

"Morning, Tom. How's it going?" asked Aurora.

"Honestly? Not so good. They're threatening to suspend me — put a sub in my classroom for the rest of the year. My doctor started me on Prozac. It's been hard on my stomach. I just don't feel like myself. I hate the idea of taking antidepressants, but I had to do something. The pressure of this lawsuit is chewing me up. And it's been really hard on my family."

"I'm so sorry, Tom. The whole thing is outrageous."

"The thing is, I was so careful *not* to do what they're accusing me of. Ironic. It's hard not to feel bitter."

*   *   *

407

At morning recess, the Prudenciana teachers waited in line in front of the school office.

Gail Corazone, standing behind Aurora, tapped her on the shoulder. "My eyes aren't watering, are yours?"

"No," said Aurora. "And I don't have that metalicky taste on the back of my tongue, do you?"

"Now that you mention it, I don't either. Maybe since it's so cold, the gas doesn't drift as much. Although I do remember other times when there've been fumigations during cold weather, and still I felt really sick."

"Me too," said Aurora. "Maybe different atmospheric conditions, or something. Oh, it's your turn."

Gail stepped up to the table. The roving school district nurse and two county health nurses were taking blood to be tested for bromine levels. Aurora watched with discomfort while the syringe filled with Gail's blood.

Billy Baker, Dr. Ringer, and Principal Wagner stood shoulder-to-shoulder behind the nurses' table, supervising.

Aurora didn't really want these ghouls to take her blood. It seemed important to go through with it, but something felt wrong. Just as the bell rang, Aurora stepped up to the table and offered her arm.

*   *   *

FRIDAY, FEBRUARY 25, 1999
PRUDENCIANA ELEMENTARY

The next Friday after school, most of the tenured teachers plus Katie were in Helen Rice's room. They'd received the results of their blood tests that morning.

"Do you think she's listening through the intercom?"

Everyone turned to gawk at the loudspeaker under the wall clock. A few teachers laughed self-consciously.

"Right. Well, let's take a look at the map," said Ruth.

Gail Corazone passed out a copy of the school emergency preparedness map. On top of each teacher's classroom drawn on the map, Gail had notated the level of bromide found in that teacher's blood. "As you can see, the numbers correlate exactly with the orientation of the classrooms to the prevailing winds."

Everyone studied the maps.

"Look at this," said Aurora. "The teachers whose rooms directly face the fields all have significantly higher bromide levels than those whose classrooms are in the back of the school, behind other buildings, or to the side, facing away from the fields. It's a perfect map of pesticide drift."

"The only thing is, these numbers are all a little bit below the state's allowable level of exposure. I would have expected the numbers to be higher." Helen's forehead creased as she studied the map.

"Me too," said Katie.

"Gail and I noticed on the day of the fumigation that we didn't have the usual pesticide mental fog and stinging eyes," said Aurora.

"But it was really cold that day," said Gail.

"Maybe it was just less windy than usual, so not as much drift," said Helen.

"Maybe," said Dora Lockhart.

"I think we should find a way to monitor the drift with that new monitoring equipment that Pesticide Action Network offered us," said Esteban.

"But how?" asked Helen. "The superintendent forbade us to set up the monitoring equipment on campus."

"Don't you think that's strange?" asked Nathena.

"It's unconscionable. What is going on, anyway? It almost seems like the school district is colluding with CalGreen," said Aurora.

"What we need is data," said Harriet. "To back up what we're saying, so they can't just dismiss us."

"It's not right that there aren't any records of student illnesses on fumigation days. We send kids up to the office with nosebleeds, headaches, vomiting, rashes, dizziness, breathing difficulties, and they just take their temperature and send them back to class. No one keeps a record of who's been sent to the office, and for what reason. The principal claims they're too busy," said Ruth.

"If they're too busy, then we should start keeping records ourselves. Why don't we ask all teachers to keep a running record in their classrooms of date, time, complaints, and names of sick children they send to the office? We can make a record sheet, and give one to each teacher," said Aurora.

"I bet not many people will do it. What teacher has time for that?" said Corkie.

"It's worth a try. I'll make the data sheet," said Aurora. "And I'll write a cover letter and put it in everyone's mailbox. We can talk to people personally, and encourage them to help out. Let's see what happens."

"I think I have an idea about how we might be able to use the new Summa canister monitors for the next fumigation," said Katie.

*   *   *

A few hours later, Katie popped into Aurora's classroom. "It's all set," Katie said.

Aurora put down a student's story about an imaginary life in Old California during the Gold Rush. "What's all set?"

"Mr. Cowley agreed to let the Pesticide Action Network people set up a Summa canister on his property, on the other side of the fence from our Life Lab Garden. That location should be perfect to monitor the drift in the area where teachers had the highest levels of bromide in their blood, the classrooms that are getting hit by the worst pesticide drift."

"Mr. Cowley agreed to that? Katie, have you been talking to him, even though we were ordered to stay away from the growers?"

"Yep. It's a free country, right? I can talk to whomever I please."

"Okay. Wow. Awesome, Katie."

"He's a really nice old man. I've been telling him how I just got married, and I want to have kids someday, and my classroom is one of the ones getting the worst pesticide drift, and how worried I am about being exposed to reproductive toxins. He told me that the things he heard at the hearing had a big effect on him. He's decided to get out of strawberries. He's putting his fields into raspberries next season, and he's going to try growing them organically."

410

"Really? That's wonderful! So, this Summa canister is for sure a better way to monitor drift?"

"Yep. Even the Department of Pesticide Regulation acknowledges that it's far more accurate for measuring methyl bromide than the charcoal tube monitoring system our ag commissioner still uses. Remember, methyl bromide fumigation is a fairly new technology for growing strawberries. The old way of monitoring air quality just isn't sensitive enough to accurately detect parts per billion of methyl bromide molecules. The new stainless steel Summa canisters have a vacuum pump that continuously monitors the air over a twelve-hour period. Mr. Cowley has agreed to activate the equipment for us when Garritt and Choate do their next fumigations."

"Katie, can we trust Mr. Cowley?"

"I believe we can. He's old. I think he's already knocked on heaven's door; his priorities have shifted. You can see it in his eyes."

64

MONDAY, FEBRUARY 28, 1999
Valle Verde Strawberry Field

S HERIFF CHARLIE ROSA AND THE MEMBERS OF HIS TEAM lay on the
ground behind a berm, focusing their binoculars on a stand of
coyote brush beside the strawberry fields.

"Here comes another one. Are you getting this on camera, Steve?"

"Got it. Listen, Charlie, I think we have more than enough to bust
this thing open. We've been working on this for months. I'm all about
having ducks in a row, but enough is enough. Let's go in."

"Rodger that," said Charlie. "It's a go. On my signal. Take the
driver of the van and the perp collecting money first. Careful. Work
fast. The girls will no doubt try to run. Don't let them. Round them all
up. We've got to bring them in. They'll need medical attention. Most
will probably have to be deported. See that none of the girls are
harmed. Ready. Now!"

*　　　*　　　*

413

PRUDENCIANA ELEMENTARY

By recess, Aurora's eyes were watering. She dismissed her students, went to her desk, and picked up her teacup, put it back down and pushed her thumbnails into the tips of her fingers. Her fingertips were numb. A wave of nausea surged through her. The room spun. She lost her balance. Throwing her hand out just in time, she caught herself on her desk. Leaning with both hands on her desktop, head bent over, she fought down nausea while the room whirled around. Gradually, her head cleared.

Katie peaked inside the door. "Hey, Aurora."

Aurora straightened up carefully.

"Are you alright?" Katie asked, coming all the way in. "You're pale as a ghost."

"I'm really feeling that methyl bromide today."

"Yep, I'm feeling it too. They did warn us that they planned to apply more pesticide than normal, but this is so different than that last fumigation."

"I know. My eyes didn't even water last time," said Aurora.

"Well anyway, I wanted to let you know that Mr. Cowley activated the Summa canisters yesterday, when they fumigated. He's been staying on top of changing out the canisters every twelve hours. He's going to keep monitoring through tomorrow evening. I talked to Jenny Merritt. She'll pick up the canisters from Mr. Cowley and overnight express them to the lab."

"Good news," said Aurora, sitting down and reaching for her water bottle.

"Did you see the papers over the weekend?" Katie asked.

"No. I was too busy."

"Every local newspaper carried articles about our blood tests and the pesticide drift monitoring. The articles made a big deal about how the levels of methyl bromide measured in the air were below the state's allowable limits. And, Aurora, they published our blood test results!"

"Isn't that illegal? A violation of privacy?"

Katie rolled her eyes. "The papers must have received the results of our blood tests even before we did. The newspapers claim that, because our blood bromide levels were below state safety standards, we've been completely discredited. They don't mention that even though our numbers were slightly below the safety standards set by the state, we did have statistically significant bromide levels in our blood. And of course there was no mention about the fact that the map of the classrooms and the teacher's blood bromide levels exactly corresponds to the pattern of drift exposure from the fumigated fields."

"Doesn't it seem kind of fishy to you that the newspapers got private information about our blood tests even before we did?" Aurora resisted the impulse to put her head down on her desk.

"Yep, it's odd."

"You know what? I'm going to have my blood tested again after school today at Doctors on Duty," said Aurora.

"Great idea. I'll go get tested at Salud Para La Gente. We should talk to the other teachers. Some of them will probably want to get a second test, too."

"Katie, do you remember how Dr. Ringer bragged that very few cases of pesticide poisoning have been reported in the county?"

"Yep. Definitely."

"Well, if we have to do all this to get our pesticide exposure accurately measured and reported, as savvy as we are at navigating the bureaucracy with our university degrees and experience with the system, imagine how much harder it is for limited-English newcomers."

"Yep. Very few cases of pesticide poisoning are reported by farmworkers? As my kids would say, '*No duh.*'"

65

SUNDAY, MARCH 13, 1999
(Daylight Savings Time begins)
Opening Day of Salmon Fishing, Monterey Bay

T HE PURPLE HAZE HOOCHIES and the Watermelon Krocodiles had been on fire this morning, the bite hot. The boat had caught its limit early and was heading back in to Moss Landing, Skipper Joe at the helm. Father Francis and Charlie sat on deck with their faces in the sun, eating tuna sandwiches and Frank's mother's homemade cookies.

The sea was calm, with a long, small swell and just a light breeze. Gulls followed the boat, circling and calling overhead. A pod of porpoises played in the boat's wake.

"So, you found her alive. Thank God. Where is she now?" Father Francis asked.

"Valle Verde Community Hospital," said Charlie. "She and the other girls were in pretty bad shape. Malnourished and dehydrated. Cut, bruised, bitten and scratched. All torn up and infected between the legs. About what you'd expect. But they're getting good medical care. And the county is providing rape and abduction counseling and

STD screening. With time, most of them should recover. At least, those who didn't get exposed to HIV, God help them. But I'll tell you what, Padre, it's been hell on wheels trying to figure out who all those girls are, and where they came from."

"Any trace of Alice's mother and sister?"

"The girls we picked up in the van were all dark-skinned Spanish speakers, mostly undocumented. As Johnny told you, they typically send the brown ones out to service the fields. Any white girls they get, like Alice's sister, they sell to high class, big money clients. We did get a line on the little girls' mother, though. Your missing Mayan teen reported seeing an older white woman who fit the mother's description in the van for a few days. The teenager said the woman wouldn't stop crying about missing her baby and her two little girls. The men told her to shut up and threatened to ship her to Mexico, then she disappeared. The woman left a scarf behind. We sent it to the lab and I just got back the report."

"Alice's mother?"

"Looks like it. Everything hooks up. DNA from the woman's scarf matches cheek swabs from Alice and the baby, and also matches blood we found at the meth camp, presumably the mother's. Alice's work with our forensic artist gave us nearly photographic likenesses of her mother, the boyfriend who was stabbed and then eaten by a mountain lion, and the assailants. The drawing of the mother matches the description the trafficked girls gave of the woman in the van."

"Then you're close to finding her?"

"Unfortunately, that woman could be anywhere in the world by now. We're running Alice's DNA through CODIS again. But at this point, I doubt that we'll ever find either the mother or Alice's twin. Sorry, Padre."

"I'll continue praying, and keep my eyes and ears open. I'm grateful that you were able to rescue Sacniete. Have you notified the parents that you found her? Can they see her?"

"We only just figured out we had your Mayan family's kid a day ago," said Charlie. "If you know where the girl's parents are, Frank, by all means tell them we found their daughter. Maybe you can help them get to the hospital. It would no doubt do the girl a world of good to see her mother and father."

"And a relief for the parents too," said Father Francis.

"Of course. But please, before they go to the hospital, make sure they understand that if they do choose to see their daughter, there may be consequences. You get that, right? Once the family engages in the system, I can't make any guarantees that they won't get nailed by immigration, and deported. They'll have to fill out all kinds of official paperwork. Once they do that, and Big Brother has their names and faces, I really don't know how it will roll. If they go to the hospital, they should go with their eyes open. It's a choice they'll have to make."

"I'll be sure they understand. But they are most certainly legitimate asylum seekers so, with a good attorney, they may have a shot at not being deported. Were any of the girls able to I.D. their kidnappers?"

"Not one of them, sad to say. They were all grabbed from behind. Blindfolds and chloroform. But the pimps we rounded up, the *pendejos* running the prostitution ring out of the van, all sang. A few of them fingered a man in a striped suit as head honcho. No one knew his name or anything about him. But I'll give you one guess who the pimps get their girls from."

"Our *adversarios* from the rollercoaster?"

"You got it. The artist's drawings from the pimps' descriptions match what we got from Señora Ramirez. At this point, we're pretty sure that those two Truchas with the tattoos were trying to grab the Luna kid for their sex trade. We figure the deal went down wrong, and the kid got shot. Ballistics on the gun the Truchas dropped at the rollercoaster matched the Luna murder weapon."

"Pieces are fitting together."

"Yeah. The way I see it, this is a nexus of serial abductions, sex and drug trafficking. And it's a lot bigger and more organized than anything we've seen before."

"Globalization?"

"Right. Sort of a World Trade Organization for gangsters."

"The New World Order. What's next, Charlie?"

"We keep looking. Follow cause and effect, tying things together. A leads to B, which leads us to C. It could be that all our leads will eventually dry up, and we'll never hear from those *sucios* with the tattoos again. But I have a feeling that's not how it's gonna go down. I think we'll get lucky. For now, I'm just following the little things. For example, a volunteer from National Marine Fisheries saw our wanted poster and called in that he saw the perps getting into a boat with a guy in a striped suit at the Santa Cruz Harbor a couple of weeks ago. We got a partial boat registration number. And our Beach Flats informants have spotted them a couple of times near the Boardwalk. Those *pinches* are going to turn up again in my radar, sooner or later. And when they do, I'll be ready for them."

"Sounds like you're taking this all personally, Charlie."

"Hell yeah. See Frank, once they took those shots at you, *mi hermano*, and at me — well, that's when it got personal. I hate those two dirty fuckin' scumbags, Frank, to tell you the truth. I'm gonna hook 'em. And I'm gonna make my case. By the time I arrest those pendejos, I'll have enough solid evidence against them to take to the DA, and to stand up in court. We're gonna put 'em away, Padre. I swear I'm gonna protect society from those two, if it's the last thing I ever do."

"Charlie, let's say you catch those two, the men we think shot the Luna boy. Let's say they're actually prosecuted instead of being deported, and that they're convicted of murder. Even if they're sentenced to life without parole, what difference will it actually make?"

"Oh, come on, Frank. You going all existential on me? We have to catch the bad guys and lock 'em up, so they don't do it again. If we can put these fuckers away, maybe we've saved a few kids. Not only that, maybe those two can fill in some more of our missing pieces — like the linkages, if any, between their operation and those three Salvadorans that got deported. Hell, if we get really lucky, maybe they can lead us to the head of the snake. We have to cut off its head, Frank. We have to make our way to the top, and stop this whole thing."

"You know as well as I do, Charlie, that if you catch Salvador Luna's killers, no matter how you interrogate them, they probably won't give up any names, or any information about the structure of their organization. And once you put them away, they'll just carry on their gang life inside prison. Once inside, they'll probably end up big shots. Probably do a lot of recruiting for the Salvatruchas."

"Maybe, maybe not. Inside, prison has its own justice, Padre. Best case scenario, as far as I'm concerned, someone inside has a relative that those two burned, and a vendetta thing develops, and those Truchas meet with a horrific death."

"I agree that we have to catch those two and put them in prison, if we can, Charlie. But, *mi amigo*, I personally can't wish for anyone to meet with a horrific death, not even the men who shot at us."

"How can you not hate them, Frank? Remember what they did to Salvador Luna? Think about the girls and women they've trafficked. People like that are evil, pure evil."

"I'll never forget any of the victims, Charlie. But as horrific as the crimes are, in my view, people are people. We're really all the same. We're all just trying to survive and meet our needs. Each one of us makes choices every day that perpetuate the system that's dehumanizing us. Each and every one of us bears a responsibility to live in a more connected, life affirming way. Some people get twisted, and do evil things, but it's the Evil I hate, Charlie. Not the people who get caught up in it. Those two men, they're lost souls, just drops in the bucket." Father Francis Hilman swept his arm out over the sea. "Just drops in a vast ocean of Evil. It's not a snake we're hunting for, but a hydra with a thousand heads. For every person we cut away in fear and hatred, two new heads grow back on the hydra."

Dark cloud shadows scudded over the vast rolling ocean. Gulls appeared and disappeared through holes in the charcoal clouds.

"So then," Charlie took off his sunglasses and turned to Father Francis. "How can we ever turn the tide on this drug trade and human trafficking? It's getting much worse, now that the Mara Salvatruchas are aligned with the Mexican mafia, and controlling our borders."

"You know something, Charlie? I don't even think that it's Mexican gangs, or Salvadoran gangs or any gangs that are the real problem. I think that as long as we keep trying to go after them, we're fighting shadows."

Charlie shook his head and put his sunglasses back on.

"Know what the real monster is, Charlie? The thing that's causing all this violence and destruction? It's the way we've allowed our system to be structured. It's our basic assumptions about how to live, how to do business, and how to relate with one another. Human beings have become monetized, Charlie, we've become product, commodity to trade, no different than narcotics. Everything and everyone on Earth is being reduced to objects, to be used, bought and sold for profit. We've been brainwashed into believing that we need to consume more and more, faster and faster. It's that belief, that artificially hyped up desire that's driving this relentless appetite to devour everything precious and sacred on Earth — our forests, our oceans, our wilderness, our people — women and children. Those gangsters — are they really much different than the CEOs of transnational corporations who are knowingly poisoning whole communities, for profit? In fact, the reach of the people running the mega corporations is wider than the reach of the biggest, most well-organized gang. So maybe the white-collar corporate criminals are even more dangerous to society."

"Oh, come on, Frank. You're saying CEOs are as bad as gangsters? Do you think the rich are evil?" Charlie stared at his friend over the top of his sunglasses.

"What I think is that the amoral super rich are addicted to greed and power, as much as any drug addict is hooked on his substance of choice. The blind lust and addictions of the rich and powerful are causing great harm. But are those people evil? Again, people do evil, but it's the Evil I hate, not the people. Nevertheless, I believe those people controlling and shaping destructive political and economic policies for their own gain need to be reined in, every bit as much as your Salvatruchas need to be taken down. We can't let either group continue to do the harm they're doing."

"So the question is: How are we going to stop them?"

66

TUESDAY AFTERNOON, MARCH 15, 1999
Prudenciana Elementary

"HEY, KATIE. WHAT'S GOING ON? I just saw Nathena leave your room." Aurora stepped into Katie's classroom and took a seat on top of one of the children's desks.

"They found Iztli's missing sister, Sacniete." Katie was trembling and her eyes glistened with tears. "She's been missing for months and the family never said a word. I can't believe I missed it. No one at the school knew."

"Is she alright?"

"No. It's terrible. She was kidnapped and forced into sexual slavery, in the strawberry fields, right here in Valle Verde. Impossible to believe, right?"

"What? How could that happen here? It's the kind of thing that happens in India or Asia, or the Middle East. Not here in California."

"I know. It's insane."

"Thank God they found her. How's she doing? Was she badly hurt? Where is she now?"

"She was taken to Valle Verde Community along with the other girls who were rescued. Everyone thought she was healing and was going to be okay. Then she cut herself."

"Cut herself? What do you mean?"

"Apparently, she got hold of something sharp in her hospital room and she slashed herself all up and down her inner thighs and all over her breasts, then slashed her wrists."

"Oh, my God!" said Aurora. "Will she be okay?"

"Physically, she'll recover. But the psychological trauma of the whole ordeal will probably scar her for life."

"Imagine the anguish she must have been going through to cut herself like that."

"Definitely. And it was Iztli who found her. The family's been living in a cave. A cave! They learned from that priest, Father Francis, that their daughter had been rescued and, as soon as they found out where she was, they went to the hospital to see her. From what the parents say, everything seemed great. You know, a joyful, tearful reunion. Then the parents went to the cafeteria to get a treat for her, ice cream or something, and while the parents were paying, Iztli went back by herself to her big sister's room, and found her all slashed and bleeding."

"Awful. How is Iztli doing now?"

"She's a basket case. Imagine being a little girl and finding your big sister like that. That was her parents who came to see me just now. They told me everything. You wouldn't believe what those people have been through. Luckily, Nathena was on campus today, and she was able to come down to my room and talk with Iztli's parents. That woman is a Goddess. She took everything in hand, knew just what to do and say. She's already found the family a place to live. And she's getting them an attorney, too."

"Why do they need a lawyer?"

"The authorities are holding Sacniete for seventy-two hours for psychological evaluation. The parents fear that County Mental Health may take her away from them. And on top of that, Immigration may deport them."

424

"The authorities are threatening to take their daughter away?"

"Police tell them one thing, Immigration says another. And now, since the girl cut herself, she's considered a suicide risk. So County Mental Health is threatening to ship her to a juvenile mental health facility over the hill in San Jose, or maybe even to San Francisco."

"That's nuts. Separating her from her family, when she's just been rescued and reunited? That's the worst thing they could possibly do to her."

"Yep. Totally nuts. But Nathena says that a Board of Rich Old White Men just completed a 'trimming the fat' overhaul of the state juvenile mental health facilities. They've shut down the facility on this side of the hill. There's a complete disconnect between the new requirements and what the reality is for people stuck in the system. This poor family is all tangled up in a bureaucratic nightmare. But if anyone can help them, Nathena can. She's like a mama bear, the way she's defending these people. A force of nature."

*   *   *

Malone rolled over in her sleep. Her pink satin pajamas slid smoothly under the fine Egyptian cotton sheets. In the spaciousness of her four-poster canopy bed, she stretched her legs wide. Smiling as she dreamed, she reached her arm across the mattress. Where there should have been the delicious warmth of William's body, it was cold and empty between the sheets. The chill woke her.

She heard a sound, a crash, like something falling over. It came from downstairs.

Malone sat up in the dark and opened the drawer of the bedside table. Her hand groped around in the drawer until she touched the hard metal shape she was searching for. Her fingers closed around the handle of her .38 Special Colt Diamondback. When William was out of town, it was a great comfort to touch the gun he'd bought for her. You never knew when a girl might have to defend herself, or her family.

She pushed a button on the bedside clock radio to illuminate the dial. Two am. The nightlight flared over the revolver's nickel finish.

"Billy?" she called.

"Yeah, Mom. I'm home." His speech was slurred. *He's been drinking.* "Everything's fine, Mom. Go back to bed. Go'night."

Through Malone's window, moonlight glinted off the new black Porsche in the driveway, the replacement for Billy's smashed-up Corvette.

The Strawberry Queen carefully released her fingers from around the gun. She slid her hand out of the drawer, and closed it quietly.

67

Prudenciana Elementary

A URORA WAITED IN LINE FOR THE COPY MACHINE in the teachers' room at lunchtime. Katie sat at the table eating a salad.

"Hey, Katie," said Aurora. "Did you get a chance to read the article in Sunday's paper about the Environmental Working Group's state-wide Summa canister drift monitoring project?"

"Yep. Amazing. The U.S. EPA officially confirms that Summa canisters like the one Pesticide Action gave us to use on Mr. Cowley's field are far more accurate and reliable for measuring pesticide drift than the charcoal filter method our district and the ag commissioner use. Finally, credible data to back up what our senses have been telling us. Irrefutable data that there are ongoing, extremely dangerous toxic exposure violations — far above allowable limits — from methyl bromide drift into 841 schools around the state."

Helen, who was stapling packets of math worksheets, looked up from her project. "Did you notice that they named three schools in our district, including Prudenciana, as among the most dangerously exposed in the whole state?"

"Yep." Katie rolled her eyes.

"I wonder how many people even saw the article," said Corkie, "the way it was buried on page ten in the back of the real estate section."

"Not like the front-page article in our local *Valle Verde Register* about so-called hysterical teachers getting proven wrong after that other fumigation," said Gail, looking up from a stack of papers she was grading.

"At least yesterday's article was syndicated in major papers all around the country," said Harriet.

"It's unbelievable that there isn't a huge public outcry." Helen said. "Why is that? Is everyone asleep, or what?"

"The American people are all drugged is what I think," said Aurora. "Everyone's zoned out on *soma*, like in Aldous Huxley's *Brave New World.*"

"Yep," said Katie. "The drug that takes many forms — shopping, video games, TV sports, casual sex — whatever *soma* we use to distract ourselves from reality."

"Did you get the results of your second blood test?" Ruth asked.

"Yes," said Aurora. "And it was far above OSHA's permissible exposure limit. More than six times higher than that first test they did at school. Anyone else?"

"Mine too," said Gail. "Strange that the results from the two fumigations were so different." Everyone in the room nodded.

"Well if you'll recall," said Aurora, "we already had empirical evidence that something was different between the first and second fumigations. We all felt the difference. None of us had any of the usual pesticide exposure symptoms after the first fumigation, but after the second one, we had that metallic chloropicrin taste on our tongues, our eyes watered, lots of kids had nosebleeds — the usual."

"Pesticide Action Network has been saying all along that the charcoal filter monitoring equipment the ag commissioner uses isn't as sensitive as Summa canisters," said Ruth.

"The charcoal filter method is outdated," said Katie. "It's designed to make gross measurements appropriate for older types of pesticides. It's not reliable for methyl bromide detection."

"Maybe that explains the discrepancy between the two blood tests," said Tom.

"Maybe," said Katie. "But it doesn't explain why the school district and the ag commissioner refuse to use the appropriate monitoring equipment."

*   *   *

WEDNESDAY, MARCH 31, 1999
(CESAR CHAVEZ' BIRTHDAY)
UFW OFFICES, VALLE VERDE

In the UFW plaza, mariachi bands played and Folklorico dancers swirled their colorful skirts. Luis Valdez spoke about the early days of *Teatro Campesino*. People made grand speeches about Chavez, the history of the UFW, and the upcoming union vote in the strawberry fields.

Aurora and Katie sat on the red tiles in the plaza patio with their students and other school groups. Young UFW workers in red *Con Union Se Vive Mejor* T-shirts and blue jeans passed out UFW buttons, which the kids enthusiastically pinned onto their clothes and backpacks.

The folk trio Peter, Paul, and Mary had come out of retirement to perform. Their music was more inspiring than ever. Aurora had been practicing their songs with her class. Her kids knew all the words and sang along with gusto.

When the trio sang out, "It's a hard rain's gonna fall," and then Woody Guthrie's ballad "Deportee", about the plane wreck at Los Gatos, there wasn't an adult to be seen with dry cheeks.

On the way out through the wrought iron gates of the UFW courtyard, Aurora's ears rang with the notes of the last song:

> *I'd sing out danger,*
> *I'd sing out warning,*

I'd sing out love between my brothers and my sisters,
all over this land.

Neither Katie nor Aurora noticed the black sedan in the alley, or the men in black taking photos.

✳   ✳   ✳

THURSDAY, APRIL 1, 1999
PRUDENCIANA ELEMENTARY

First thing Thursday morning, April Fools' Day, Aurora found a white envelope in her mail cubby. The envelope contained a formal reprimand for taking her students to a "political event". Some parents had complained that their children came home from the field trip wearing UFW buttons.

Aurora's mind raced. She'd filed all of the appropriate paperwork well ahead of time, including a letter home with a detailed explanation of the field trip and how it would augment the California State standardized social studies curriculum. In her documentation, she'd even included a copy of the section in her state-adopted fourth grade social studies text that described, on facing pages, the contributions to the civil rights movement of mainstream national heroes Martin Luther King, Jr. and Cesar Chavez. The text implied that the civil rights struggle in the U.S. was ancient history and everything was all better now. Liberty and equal justice for all was a settled matter — no longer controversial or political. Right?

The field trip integrated a state-aligned, best-practice "being there" social studies curriculum with art and a great math lesson on reading bus schedules, planning a route, and telling time. It was exemplary teaching, according to everything Aurora had ever been taught about effective pedagogy.

Her field trip request forms had been approved and signed by the principal and by an administrator at the District Office, and every parent had signed a permission slip. Did no one read her documentation before authorizing the field trip? Why all this recrimination after the fact?

*   *   *

During morning math centers, someone put a whoopee cushion on Aurora's chair. She pretended not to see it, and sat down hard. At the rude sound, she made a surprised and horrified face, which sent all the kids into squeals of laughter. Laughter erupted throughout the day as children found ways to fool one another.

At lunch recess, Aurora showed her letter of reprimand to Katie.

"I got one of those too," Katie laughed. "Of course it's political, Aurora. Don't you know how much this town hates Cesar Chavez? There are still people in Valle Verde who want to commit murder over the whole UFW thing. Chavez was really active here. He stirred things up big time. Valle Verde's hatred of Chavez and the UFW is well-known in agricultural communities all over the world. Even though the UFW's leadership hasn't been very strong since Chavez' death, it's honestly still dangerous to associate with the UFW or evoke the memory of Cesar Chavez around here. By meeting at the UFW offices and going to that birthday celebration, we showed the world that we stand with the UFW. Don't doubt that there are still people in this community who want anyone connected with the UFW to die."

*   *   *

After school, Prudenciana teachers streamed across campus to a classroom in the new portables behind the multipurpose room.

"Can she really require an extra, unscheduled meeting like this?" asked Katie.

"I checked with Tom," said Helen. "He says she's allowed by contract."

Principal Wagner stood at the door of the classroom and scowled. Billy Baker stood by her side, a smarmy grin on his face.

Aurora eyes teared from the strong smell of formaldehyde and other chemicals outgassing in the brand-new portable classroom. Principal Wagner clapped her hands for silence.

"Mr. Baker has some important information for you."

Billy Baker stepped in front of the white board. "The class will now come to attention."

Aurora leaned over and whispered in Katie's ear, "April Fools."

Katie rolled her eyes.

Baker had replaced his usual bad-boy demeanor with a pose of condescension. He puffed himself up and cast a glare importantly around the room.

"Some of you may have read in the paper last weekend," said Billy, "that Pesticide Action Network claims they found higher levels of pesticide drift with their monitoring equipment than we found with the County Agricultural Commissioner's charcoal filter equipment. I've stopped by this afternoon to set the record straight."

Through the open door, Aurora watched the migratory swallows. They had just arrived, and were starting to build their nests of mud and straw under the eaves of the multipurpose room. An awe-inspiring and fascinating feat to observe. She'd bring her students here tomorrow. They'd be enthralled.

"The difference between the two monitoring devices is very technical," Billy was saying. "But we can guarantee that everything is perfectly safe. I have been walking the halls of this school daily with my state-of-the-art hand-held device right here." Billy held up a little black box with a meter that looked like a cheap replica of a *Star Trek* tricorder. He waved the device around.

"If I ever detect anything whatsoever that might present a danger to you or your students, I will immediately inform your principal, the superintendent, the county health officer, and the agricultural commissioner. Your health and safety is my utmost concern."

Baker looked directly at Aurora, leered, and licked his lips.

*   *   *

On the drive home, Aurora thought about how she was going to respond to the reprimand for the Chavez birthday field trip to the UFW plaza. She had the option of writing a response, going in with a union rep to talk to the principal, and having her written response to the reprimand placed in her professional file. But why bother? Was it worth spending her time and life energy writing an angst-ridden reply to this stupid reprimand?

Fuck it.

Strange. Only a few months ago, she would have fallen apart over something like this. Maybe it was Katie's influence, but Aurora found she just didn't care anymore. She no longer respected or feared the bosses.

They can't pull my strings anymore! I'm free.

68

MONDAY, APRIL 5, 1999
Prudenciana Elementary

T HE FIRST BELL RANG just as Aurora met her class on the playground.
"Ms. B! They're gone!" Aurora's students were jumping up and
down in agitation.

"What's gone? What do you mean?"

"The nests! The swallow's nests! They're gone! Last Friday when
you showed us the swallows, you told us they'd probably finish
building their nests over the weekend, and would start laying their
eggs maybe this week. You said we'd get to watch the whole thing. But
the nests are all gone!"

Aurora's heart pounded. "Show me," she said.

She followed her students across campus to the multipurpose
room. There was no sign of a single nest under the eaves. The
pavement under the eaves had been cleaned too.

Niño was emptying trash into the big dumpsters at the corner of
the back parking lot, behind the multipurpose room. Seething, telling

herself to stay controlled and watch what she said, she stalked up to him, her students following.

She forced herself to smile. "Good morning."

Niño's wide shoulders tightened. He had the kind of upper body men get when they lift weights at the gym after work every night. He finished emptying the trashcans, turned around and glanced at Ms. B, then looked away.

"Hey, Niño. I was wondering. Do you happen to know anything about those swallow nests that were in the eaves of the multipurpose room last week?"

He turned his broad back, to lift another heavy trashcan into the dumpster. Over his shoulder, he mumbled. "We cleaned 'em."

"Excuse me?" Aurora's forehead wrinkled.

"We cleaned the nests away," Niño turned to face her. She took a step back. "Those birds make a big mess. They drop their stuff all over the cement. It's not healthy. We cleaned the nests off the eaves. We used a pressure washer."

"So, you just — decided you should do that?"

"The principal told us to. We came in over the weekend to get it done. She arranged for us to get a pressure washer from the district maintenance barn."

Aurora's eyes opened wide. She took a deep breath and bit her tongue.

Without a word, she turned and headed back to her classroom. The children had to run to keep up with her.

What should she do? She'd finally gotten a telephone installed in her classroom, through a grant from Apple, so she could pilot the new internet curriculum being developed to connect STEP classrooms in watersheds up the Pacific coast. But as the only teacher in the school with a phone in her room, she needed to be very responsible about how she used it. Especially after everything that had happened with Tom. Should she make a call during instructional time from her classroom? Was that ethical?

When Aurora got to her room, she started her students on their daily journal writing assignment, set the timer on the overhead projector, then phoned the Santa Cruz County Fish and Wildlife Hotline.

Turning her back on the students and speaking as quietly as possible into the phone, she said, "I'd like to report what I believe may be a wildlife violation."

"What is your situation?"

"I'm a teacher at Prudenciana Elementary in Valle Verde. Every year at this time, swallows build mud nests under the eaves of our school buildings. Last week, they started building their nests. By Friday, the nests were almost all built. But this morning, they're gone. Not a trace left. The custodian just told me that the principal ordered him to come in over the weekend and *clean* the nests off the eaves of the building, with a pressure hose."

"Just a minute. Please hold," said the woman's voice on the other end.

Aurora watched her students write as she waited.

A new voice came on the line. "California State Department of Fish and Wildlife. I understand you are reporting that some swallows nests have been removed?"

"Yes." Aurora repeated her story.

The state official asked for the address and phone number of the school, and the name of the school principal. "How do you spell that? Hold the line a minute, please."

Aurora watched the digital timer she'd set on the overhead projector click away the seconds. Her students still had five minutes left of their daily journal exercise.

"U.S. Fish and Wildlife Service. Special Agent Clark speaking. I understand you are reporting a wildlife violation. Some swallows' nests were taken?"

"Oh. Um, you're with the *federal* fish and wildlife service? I actually phoned the *county* Fish and Wildlife office."

"I understand, ma'am, but the violation you're reporting falls under federal jurisdiction. That's why you were transferred to me. I would like to record this conversation, if you don't mind. Do I have your permission?"

"Yes, of course." Aurora heard a click on the line. Uh oh, she thought.

"Would you please state your name and give your contact information and where you're calling from."

Aurora responded, and then Special Agent Clark said, "Ms. Bourne, please state the name of your school district, your superintendent's name, and the school district phone number and address."

Oh shit.

When she had conveyed the requested information, Special Agent Clark said, "Please describe to me, in your own words, why you are calling."

Aurora repeated her reason for calling. Then she said, "I'm not sure if there are actually any laws protecting these birds, but it just doesn't seem right to me to take their nests down like that."

"Yes, ma'am. It's a good thing you called. You did the right thing. We appreciate it. The birds you describe are protected under the Federal Migratory Bird Act. It is a very serious matter, a federal offense, to destroy their nests while the nests are active. Unfortunately, these birds, which are endangered, expend an enormous amount of energy building their nests. Timing is critical for them. If a nest is destroyed, the nesting pair will most likely attempt to rebuild, but it is very unlikely they will be able to successfully lay and hatch a clutch of young for the season so late. This has a very deleterious effect on the population as a whole. I am going to contact your superintendent and inform him that the district is being fined for the violation. Perhaps, that will encourage him to educate his maintenance personnel to comply with federal law in the future."

Aurora realized she'd fallen into a deep hole full of do-do. She swallowed. "Um, are you going to tell the superintendent who called you?"

"No, ma'am. Your report will remain anonymous. Your privacy will be protected. Thank you again for calling."

*   *   *

That afternoon, Aurora was out on the playground with the kids for PE. Destiny was helping. Aurora told Destiny about the swallows' nests and about the phone call to Fish and Wildlife.

Aurora knelt on the grass, holding down her section of the multicolored parachute for the students whose turn it was to go inside, under the magical dome. The resident pair of golden eagles circled overhead. They had finished this year's remodel of their nest in a heritage Monterey Pine at the school fence line. The nest was ready for this spring's clutch of eaglets.

Aurora felt an upwelling of gratitude for those eagles, and for those pine trees. Besides providing nesting habitat for the eagles, the pines helped to buffer some of the pesticide drift.

A dark shadow loomed over Aurora's head. She looked up, into the furious red face of Principal Wagner.

"Ms. Bourne. I just received a phone call from Superintendent Spieler about some birds' nests. Did you call someone about some birds' nests today?"

Aurora stared at Deana's seething face. She couldn't let go of the parachute tugging in her hands, or the air inside would escape and the dome would collapse on top of the children inside.

She remained on her knees. An eternity passed. The eagles floated in lazy circles high above.

"It was me, Deana," said Destiny.

Destiny stood nose to nose with the principal. Looking more than usual like the federally registered Cherokee that she was, Destiny outweighed Deana Wagner by almost a hundred pounds. It was well known that Destiny and her machinist union organizer husband, Buck, took their Sunday afternoon drives together, when the weather was fine, on their twin Harley Davidson FATBOYS, with their fellow local HOG members. For some reason, Deana always seemed a little intimidated by Destiny.

"I called the Federal Fish and Wildlife Service. You should not have ordered those nests taken down, Deana. It's against the law. Besides the fact that they had tremendous positive educational value for the students, those swallows are a federally protected endangered species. I want you to know that I'll be watching. I'm going to go to every school in the district this spring and monitor the swallows' nests. If I find that any other nests have been tampered with, I will be contacting U.S. Fish and Wildlife again. You and the superintendent can count on it."

All of the students were watching and listening, wide-eyed and open-mouthed.

Principal Wagner's lips thinned to a narrow pencil line. She spun on her heel so hard she cut a hole in the grass, and stormed away.

69

Prudenciana Elementary, Valle Verde
Byrd River Watershed

I T WAS LATE AFTERNOON ON THE LAST DAY OF SCHOOL before Spring Break. Everyone else had already left campus for the holiday. Aurora had stayed late to set up the incubator for the Steelhead eggs that would arrive after vacation. Everything in the classroom was organized and ready for the spring semester Salmon and Trout Education Project. One more walk around the Life Lab Garden to check on the new native plant bed, then she'd go home. Tomorrow, she might just sleep until noon.

*   *   *

Enormous black Cloud Men, straight out of *James and the Giant Peach*, tumbled across the sky. An army of daffodil fairies lifted white Easter lily trumpets into the air and, in the center of each, blazed a yellow torch of hope. Opulent sprays of Chinese wisteria — phthalo blue with a touch of rose madder — hung like thick-limbed Matisse nudes over the Torri gate. The new native plant bed was doing fine. Judging from those clouds, there would be no need to arrange for someone to water over the break.

A district grounds maintenance man driving a John Deere riding mower over the playing field made a large, slow turn, shifted, and mowed a swath toward the Life Lab Garden. Aurora watched the viridian green and cadmium yellow tractor and the figure on board grow larger as it approached.

The grounds man pulled up next to the waist-high redwood garden fence and stopped.

"Howdy."

"Hi," said Aurora from inside the fence. "Think it'll rain?"

The man looked up at the sky. "Yes'm. No question about it. Just a matter of how soon, and how much."

Aurora smiled.

"Getting pretty weedy around this garden of yours, I noticed. Since we're not allowed to use WeedRangler at your school no more, you teachers are s'posed to keep the weeds mowed around this fence. That was the deal."

"I know," said Aurora. "But the teacher who usually takes care of that has been sick."

The man considered Aurora from his tractor. "Guess I could do it, just this once."

"Really? Thank you *so* much. That's really kind of you."

"Don't mention it," he said. "Tell you what: my wife has an organic garden at home. In fact, I picked up a couple a yards of manure from a stable near our place last week, for her garden. She said she can't use it all. Want I should drop some off here? I could leave it right over there, next to your compost bins."

"That would be wonderful! Thank you."

"I been feelin' bad about you teachers over here."

"Why?" asked Aurora.

"Just 'cause o' the way everyone over at the maintenance barn is always making jokes about you all, always laughing about how the district tricked you."

"Tricked us? What's the joke?"

"Well, I shouldn't be tellin' you this, but … you know that fumigation on the field over there, on the other side of the playground? The one that was in all the papers, on account of they monitored the pesticide drift and they hardly found any, so you teachers got turned into a laughing-stock?"

"Yes, I remember."

"Well, the reason the levels of drift measured so low was, there weren't no fumigation that day."

"What?"

"Everyone over in the maintenance barn knew about it, too. They made it look like a fumigation. Those CalGreen folks came in with their applicator trucks and crew and all, and injected something into the soil, and covered it up with plastic tarp, just like a real methyl bromide fumigation. But there wasn't no fumigation at all. It was just water. They injected plain water, steam, into the ground. They didn't use none of the gas, at all."

Aurora couldn't believe what she'd just heard. She struggled to keep a neutral face. "Well, that's a pretty good joke, alright. Are you sure the fumigation was fake?"

"Oh, yeah. I personally heard the superintendent and that Baker fellow talking about it with a guy from CalGreen, some guy with a goatee. Anyway, they were all over at the maintenance barn, yacking about what they were gonna do. Then we saw it in the papers, and we all knew. The guys over at the barn are still laughing about it. But what they did, it jus' wasn't right, is what I think."

"Well, thanks for helping us out with the mowing. And that manure would be just great. What's your name, by the way?"

"Sal. Name's Sal. Glad to help out."

"Thanks, Sal. I'm Aurora. Well, have a good vacation."

"You too, Miss Aurora. Happy Easter Vacation. God bless you."

70

(Passover Begins at Sundown)
Detectives' Bullpen, Santa Cruz County Sheriff's Office
County Government Center, Ocean Street, Santa Cruz
San Lorenzo River Watershed

R AIN BEAT AGAINST CHARLIE'S OFFICE WINDOW. Deep in thought, he stood studying his link board: photos and notes he'd assembled over the past months attached by string and push pins to a map of the county. Red string connected photocopies of the forensic artist's sketches from interviews with Alice, Señora Ramirez, and the Mayan girl, photos of Salvador Luna, Alice, and the baby, the laundromat where the Luna kid was shot and the meth lab, and reports of sightings of the tatted Trucha perps, which people had called in.

The squeal of the teletype machine jarred Charlie out of his reverie. He pulled the printout off the machine and went to his desk to read it.

Finally, a hit. A match with Alice's DNA in the DOJ unidentified persons' database. Charlie skimmed down the page to the details.

445

When a yacht found drifting in the Great Pacific Gyre was towed to dock and processed, investigators found blood and strands of hair matching the DNA profile of Alice's twin. The remains of the ship's skipper, partially eaten by a Great White, were also identified. A wire dog cage entangled in a floating island of plastic debris near the vessel had been retrieved. The cage contained a human leg bone, positively identified as belonging to Alice's missing twin.

"Jesus Christ." Charlie put his hand over his eyes and rubbed his temples. He took a few deep breaths, unwrapped a stick of gum and popped it in his mouth, then pinned the teletype to his link board.

*   *   *

AURORA'S COTTAGE
SANTA CRUZ, THE WESTSIDE
SAN LORENZO RIVER WATERSHED

Aurora sat propped up in her queen bed reading the red *Barons of Bromide* booklet from Pesticide Action Network. It was raining hard, and had been all weekend, without any breaks in the storm. She leaned back against her pillows and enjoyed the sound of droplets tapping the skylight.

Suddenly, the sound got loud, like gravel falling from the sky. *Hail!*

Blue jumped off the bed and bounded to the glass door. Aurora joined him. As they watched the falling hail, the tip of Blue's tail twitched. Frozen white beads bounced on the ground, quickly turning it white.

Aurora thought about what the groundsman had told her.

A fake fumigation? Really? Why would the administration go to such elaborate lengths to discredit the teachers?

The hail subsided, followed by pounding rain. The frozen beads quickly melted. Aurora climbed back into bed.

Who, hidden in the maze of interlocking corporate directorates, are the actual people responsible for methyl bromides' persistence as an agricultural pesticide, in blatant disregard of the legislation requiring its phase-out? How did they get away with simply ignoring the California Birth Defects Prevention Act, a law passed by citizen voter initiative? Who is so powerful they can disregard state and federal laws and international treaties with impunity?

She resumed reading.

"Who Are the Bromide Barons? The global bromine industry is controlled by the Evermal Corporation, 'manufacturer of polymers and fine chemicals.' Evermal, Inc. is the parent of CalGreen Corporation and Dead Sea Bromine, which dominate methyl bromide production and fumigation worldwide."

But who is the wizard behind Evermal's curtain?

Wrapped in her fleece bathrobe decorated with polar bears and penguins, Aurora snuggled into her slippers and headed for the kitchen. Blue padded at her heels.

The cat kibble pouring into the bowl tapped in counterpoint to the rain on the skylight, now a gentle, steady patter.

Aurora turned up the thermostat and the gas heater flamed to life. She sat at her kitchen desk, turned on her new Power Mac, and searched for *Evermal.*

"Evermal began as a U.S. paper manufacturing company in 1887." Paper manufacturing. A highly polluting industry. Aurora's fourth graders had read *A River Ran Wild,* a picture book that told the true story of a paper mill's destruction of the Nashua River in Massachusetts. In the 1960's, the river had been so polluted it was spontaneously catching on fire. This led, after a protracted struggle by the public, to the passage of the U.S. Clean Water Act in '65. Growing public awareness and concerns about the environment had ultimately led to the formation of the U.S. Environmental Protection Agency in 1970.

Aurora read on.

"Under the direction of President and CEO Lawrence Evermal, the little Arkansas paper company became a multinational giant, diversified through conglomerates, holding companies, and corporate affiliates across chemicals, plastics, aluminum, energy, pharma, real estate, financials, fumigants, pesticides, flame retardants, lubricants, and more. Early in its history, it affiliated with the young chemical company, Biogenesis Agrochemical. In 1962, Evermal merged with the Ethyl

Corporation." Aurora typed "Ethyl Corp" and clicked Search. "In 1923, Detroit Motors, DuPoint, and the Rockefellers formed a joint company to manufacture leaded gasoline — the Ethyl Gasoline Corporation."

What's the connection between paper, gasoline, and agricultural pesticides?

"Ethyl 'no knock' Gasoline Corporation merged with Evermal, which, through its affiliate corporations, Dead Sea Bromine and CalGreen, had become the world's largest producer/distributer of methyl bromide. Through a brilliant public relations campaign, methyl bromide, a toxic byproduct of the petrochemical industry, was marketed to agribusiness as an essential pesticide."

A toxic byproduct of the petrochemical industry is marketed as an essential pesticide?

"The multinational conglomerate was broken up during the monopoly-busting era, then pieced back together to become Abaddon Oil and Gas — one of the most powerful petrochemical corporations on the planet."

Petrochemicals — gas, oil, and pesticides. So, this Frankenstein is the wizard behind the curtain, pulling the strings of American agriculture. Cha-ching.

The phone rang. Aurora let the machine take it and listened as the message recorded.

An auto dialer. The fire department was letting everyone know that, due to unusual El Niño conditions, severe storms were expected to continue for the next three days. Flooding was anticipated in most areas. Residents who needed sandbags could pick them up at the nearest fire station. Flood evacuation centers at the following locations … Forecasters predicted this system could develop into a hundred-year storm.

Wind rattled the windows. Rain hammered the roof. While she watched from her front window, a large branch broke off a cedar tree across the street and fell onto the neighbor's yard, barely missing the new Volvo in their driveway. A tall palm tree down the block bent sideways. Huge palm fronds flew through the air. Rain lashed against the front of Aurora's house, blowing in from the ocean at nearly gale force. The street was a muddy, turbulent river. Water was rising up over the sidewalk.

Aurora flopped down on the couch, pulling a blanket over herself and Blue, and soon fell fast fell asleep.

She was underwater, wrestling a giant octopus. It sprayed oily, toxic ink into the water. Through the shadowy muck she could make out many other writhing figures — humans, penguins, polar bears, enormous salmon with human faces — they struggled and suffocated in the tentacles of the monster.

71

San Benito County Emergency Operations Center
Santa Cruz Mountains
Byrd River Watershed, San Benito County

PERCHED HIGH ATOP A BALD PEAK in the Santa Cruz Mountains, the small San Benito County Emergency Operations Center Outpost was lit up like a lighthouse in the storm. Static hissed over the Emergency Ops radio.

"I do not copy," the Sheriff's dispatcher stared through the windows at the storm lashing the mountains below, and shouted again into the mic. "Repeat. Please repeat. Over."

Thunder roared. The Sheriff's dispatcher turned to the EOC chief.

Forked lightning flashed in the dark window frame, followed by another roll of thunder. Rain pinged like bullets on the roof.

"What was that?" asked the EOC chief, who was standing over a large USGS topographical map of the 1,300-square-mile Byrd River watershed, with rivers from four counties converging into the Byrd.

"I said, we've lost contact with the emergency response crew on the upper Byrd, at the San Felipe Reservoir. They've lost power to release water remotely. Wanted authorization for a manual release. It sounds pretty gnarly up there."

"Nothing we can do about it now," said the EOC chief. "They're on their own until they get their radio back online. God only knows what's going on there. All thirty miles of the Pacheco, plus the Santa Ana and Arroyo dos Picachos is coming down on them from the Diablo Range. No way that reservoir's gonna hold. What was the report from the Santa Clara County EOC?"

"Couldn't reach them."

"Jesus. For all we know, the full load from the Llagas and the Uvas are flooding into the upper Byrd at San Felipe, too. God help those men up there. What else?"

"The crew at the Hollister Gaging Station reports that the San Benito is flooding all the way down to the Pinnacles. Tres Piños and Los Muertos Creeks are above the hundred-year flood stage. All that water is converging on Hollister. They want to open the spillways and release the water now. They can't hold back any longer."

The EOC manager glanced up from his map. "Give them the okay. Then contact the crew at Chittenden Gap. Tell them all hell's about to break loose on them. That whole fifty miles of swollen river is coming down the San Benito, with a 5,000-foot head out of the Diablos. It's gonna converge with that mountain of water flooding down from the upper reach of the Byrd, from the San Felipe Reservoir, right there at Chittenden. Tell Chittenden Gap to open their spillways now, or the towns of Hollister and San Juan Bautista are going to be completely under water in a few hours."

"What about Valle Verde? If Chittenden Gap opens their spillways, Valle Verde is going to be washed into the ocean."

"Right now, that's not our problem. Santa Cruz and Monterey Counties will just have to handle it."

The dispatcher turned back to her radio as another branch of lightning flashed in the window.

*   *   *

UPPER BYRD RIVER, SAN FELIPE RESERVOIR
BYRD RIVER WATERSHED, SAN BENITO COUNTY

Despite their yellow rain slickers, the three men could barely see each other in the dark downpour. Raindrops strobed in their flickering headlamps.

"Sam! Over here!"

The men wrestled the spillway manual release lever, their rubber boots slipping and sliding on the muddy bank.

"Jesus, Sam, don't slip on this motherfucker. We'd never find you. There. Good. Hold on to this rebar."

"What did they say, Sam?" shouted the other man. He hung on, with one hand on the spillway lever and the other on a willow branch, and a boot dug into the muddy slope sideways against an embedded boulder. "Did they give us the okay to open it?"

"I lost 'em. Radio crapped out." Sam tried unsuccessfully to wipe the relentless rainwater off his glasses with a wet sleeve, holding on to a piece of rebar cemented into the steep bank with the other hand.

"So we're on our own?"

"Yeah. I think we've gotta pull this son of a bitch now. The whole fuckin' dam's about to fail. If Uvas breaks through, we're dead men."

"It's so fuckin' cold my fingers are numb. Let's get this over with."

"Wait," said Sam. "What if Hollister and Chittenden are opening their spillways too? All that water flooding into Valle Verde without warning, on top of what they've got coming down the Corralitos? We're looking at a major disaster. There's gonna be hell to pay."

"If we don't open her up now, we're gonna die."

"Right. All agreed, then? Okay. On three, everyone pull. One, two ..."

Muddy water came roaring out of the spillway, nearly taking the bank and the men with it.

*   *   *

A tidal wave, a rising wall of black water raced down the thirty-mile-long Byrd River, carving away banks, grabbing whole trees

453

out by the roots, lifting shopping carts, tumbling truck tires, old shoes, bits of plastic, a nest of drowned rats. Four large metal storage barrels marked with a red skull and crossbones slid down an eroded bank and fell into the river, bouncing and rolling downstream. The water tossed giant boulders like they were made of cardboard, bumping them against the metal barrels and dragging rocks and barrels along the river bottom. Hundreds of gallons per minute of swirling water scoured thick sediments laden with pesticides, detergents, motor oil, and estrogens out of the river rocks. Salamander eggs, frog eggs, salmon and trout eggs in the gravel redds washed away. The churning black caldron, rising and boiling in Earth's belly, pushed toward Valle Verde.

*   *   *

PAJARO *BARRIO*, VALLE VERDE
BYRD RIVER WATERSHED, SOUTH SANTA CRUZ COUNTY

The beans came to a boil. Grandmother Ramirez added several cloves of fresh garlic, and turned down the gas flame under the pot of pinto beans that had been soaking since yesterday afternoon. Unable to sleep, she'd decided she might as well get up and start the *frijoles*. The digital clock on the kitchen table read 2:08 am. Maybe she should try to go back to bed. She stared out the window. The rain was still coming down hard.

Her husband and two of her sons had piled sandbags around the front and back doors of the house before they'd left. They'd been gone all night, volunteering with other men from the neighborhood, trying to build a sandbag dam between their houses in the pueblo and the river. The nice priest, Father Francis, was helping.

Yesterday when she'd gone out on the levee to check the river, the water was so high! Ay, *Díos mío*! The men were right to worry that it might come all the way over the top. If it did, the neighborhood would flood, for sure.

Abuelita Ramirez gazed around her snug little house. She was happy here, with her sons and daughters and their families close to her. On the shelf were photographs of her wedding, and of all the children and grandchildren. She smiled at the pictures fondly.

Those young white census takers who'd come to the house last year had seemed disapproving, as if there was something wrong with so many people living in one small house. But Abuelita Ramirez wouldn't have it any other way. *Mi Familia.* Her family was everything. She wanted them close to her. It was a good way for people to live.

She peered out of the kitchen window again, hoping to see the men coming home. Had she done the right thing, telling the policeman about what she'd seen at the laundromat? Ay, that poor child! She wanted to do the right thing under the eyes of God. But by telling, had she put her family in danger? Well, that was behind her. Tonight, it was the storm that had her worrying.

Lightning flashed, illuminating a hideous face in the window.

Abuelita screamed. Her screams were drowned out by a blast of thunder.

She ran into the living room, toppling a glass vase full of flowers. The vase shattered. Ignoring the pains in her joints, she got down on her hands and knees behind the couch. Sharp pain shot through her arm. Her hand felt wet. Blood. She'd cut her hand on a shard from the broken vase. It seemed like someone else's blood. Crouching behind the couch, she began to pray.

Another lightning flash. The horrible face was at the living room window. Had he seen her? It was the men from the laundromat, she knew it. The evil men who had killed the little boy. They had found her. They'd come for her.

What would they do? Would they shoot her? They were going to stab her in the belly, she knew it, for telling the *policía* about them. Her husband would find her like that, with her insides opened up like a butchered pig. What would happen to the children asleep in the back room?

Oh, Lady of Mercy! Help us!

The doorknob rattled. They were pounding on the front door. Would it break?

She could hear a man shouting. What was he saying? She couldn't understand the words. What should she do?

Another flash of lightning. *Ca Vroom!* Thunder rattled the walls of the little house. The lights went out.

The men were at the back door, pounding, shouting.

The old woman crawled on her hands and knees across the floor to the telephone table. Her old knees got tangled in the hem of her apron. It tore. Trying to stay hidden behind a chair, she reached up and grasped the receiver, gulping back sobs. She put the phone to her ear, just as a shotgun blast —

No, it was thunder. Holding the phone with a trembling hand, she waited for the ringing in her ears to stop. She listened. No dial tone! The men must have cut the phone lines. Just like on TV.

A hand grabbed her shoulder. Abuelita screamed. She couldn't stop screaming. Screaming, screaming, as if trapped in a nightmare.

"Grandma. Nani. Grandma."

Abuelita Ramirez looked up into the face of her sleepy teenage granddaughter.

"Abuela, stop. Stop it." The girl patted her grandma on the shoulder. "Shusssh. Abuelita. It's okay. Listen to me, Nani, listen. There's some men at the door. They're firemen. We have to evacuate. We have to leave the house, Grandma. We have to leave, like, right now. We need to let the firemen in and listen to what they're saying. The water's coming. We don't have much time. They're gonna tell us where to go. They're gonna help us get to a place where we can be safe."

*   *   *

UPPER BAKER RANCH PROPERTY
UPSTREAM FROM THE PAJARO *BARRIO*
BYRD RIVER LEVEE BETWEEN MURPHY'S CROSSING AND
HIGHWAY 1
BYRD RIVER WATERSHED, VALLE VERDE

Enormous downed redwood logs pounded the mud banks, tearing out great swaths of dirt and vegetation as they lurched downstream on the swollen brown torrent. Willows and alders, Pacific dogwoods, sycamores, and big leaf maples on the river's corridor whipped and lashed at the wind, whole branches breaking loose and flying off.

River roared, rain and wind hissed and howled. Lightning flashed, briefly spotlighting the faces of two men, drenched to the skin in spite of their waterproof overalls, boots and hooded rain jackets. Their faces were contorted in anger.

Thunder rolled, and another bright fork lit up two John Deere tractors, their oversized tires ready to wrestle the thick mud, motors running, shovels raised as if saluting the river rising just a hundred feet away. One of the arguing men pointed to the tractors as another blast of thunder exploded in their ears.

*   *   *

PAJARO *BARRIO*
BYRD RIVER LEVEE BETWEEN MURPHY'S CROSSING AND HIGHWAY 1

Father Francis, in jeans and a T-shirt, hefted another sandbag onto the dam. Water from his soaked headband ran down his face in rills. A man down the line shouted that they were out of sand bags and the dam was high enough. An older man next to the priest leaned against the dam and held his side.

"Señor Ramirez, are you alright?" Father Francis asked.

"*Sí, Padre.* Just tired. Do you think this will hold it?"

The priest squinted his eyes against the slashing rain and peered at the river levee in the distance. Willow trees whipped in the growling wind, and branches cracked. The barrio of Pajaro, built alongside the river, was below sea level, lower than the river. Historically, the shantytown had flooded many times. But the sandbag wall the men had built between the barrio and the river stood slightly higher than the levee.

"It's possible. As long as the levee holds, even if the river rises over it, I think this dam should keep the pueblo from flooding. We've done what we can, Señor Ramirez. Maybe you should go home now, and see to your family."

"*Sí, Padre. Gracias.* But first, I want to go up to the levee and check on how high the river has risen."

*   *   *

UPPER BAKER RANCH PROPERTY
UPSTREAM FROM THE PAJARO *BARRIO*
BYRD RIVER LEVEE BETWEEN MURPHY'S CROSSING AND
HIGHWAY 1

The two men standing by the tractors in the upper Baker field shouted over the raging storm.

"We can't let the lower fields flood. They've already been planted. We'll lose the whole harvest," Billy screamed into the tortured face of Yudas Medina. "If we breach the levee here, where the fields are still fallow, we can divert a lot of the flood before it takes out the whole berry crop downstream."

"It's too dangerous, Billy. We don't know what the water will do if we release it here. We could drown."

"Just get on the fucking tractor and drive, asshole. Do it now, or we lose everything. I'll be right next to you. We'll go at the levee together, hit it until it's almost breached, then drive uphill like hell."

"Billy, this is against the law. If anyone finds out, we could get in serious trouble."

"Against the law?" Billy laughed maniacally as the lightning flashed on his face. "Who the fuck are you kidding, Medina? Since when did you worry about that? Anyway, we won't be caught. No one's ever gonna know. They'll think that the levee just breached. An act of God. Look! The water's rising fast. Let's hit that son of a bitch. Now!"

The two men climbed on their tractors, levered the gears, and stomped on the accelerator pedals, driving straight for the dirt berm of the levee, with the tractor shovels ready to ram.

*   *   *

PAJARO *BARRIO*
BYRD RIVER LEVEE BETWEEN MURPHY'S CROSSING AND HIGHWAY 1

"It could be dangerous," said Father Francis. "I'll go with you. But we need to be careful."

Grandfather Ramirez and the priest leaned into the rain and wind as they made their way through the *barrio* to the levee. The streets were already flooded ankle high with filthy rushing water, bearing debris and detritus of all kinds down the choked storm drains to the bay.

The two men scrambled up the muddy bank to the concrete walkway along the top of the levee.

"Watch out for falling branches," Father Francis shouted to the old man.

The old man waved his flashlight, signaling that he had heard. Father Francis picked his way upstream along the levee ahead of the old man, observing as much as he could with just a headlamp. The water was rising fast.

*   *   *

UPPER BAKER RANCH PROPERTY
UPSTREAM FROM THE PAJARO *BARRIO*

Over and over again, the tractors hit the berm that held the levee. Yudas felt sick. Water was already pouring over the top. Then, a strike that made the berm shake. It began to crumble. Yudas looked over at Billy.

"Let's get the hell outa here! Now!" Billy yelled above the storm, circling his arm above his head.

The men turned the tractors and sped to higher ground.

*   *   *

Father Francis stood under the overhanging cover of an elderberry, watching with horror as the tractors hit the berm. Lightning illuminated the faces of Yudas Medina and Billy Baker in the drivers' seats. For a split second, Yudas stared directly into the priest's eyes. The levee shook.

The priest shouted and ran toward old man Ramirez.

The levee burst like a bomb detonating.

Father Francis saw the river loom up and take the old man toward the sea, just before he was pushed off his feet and swept away from the river, away from the old man, toward the *barrio*.

The priest put his hands over his head, his knees into his chest, and pointed his feet into the furious flow.

* * *

PAJARO *BARRIO*

The beans on the back of the stove were cold. The gas flame had been turned off. Everyone had left the house. Grandmother Ramirez and her family had been taken to the evacuation center, a tent camp on high ground, in Ramsey Park. The family photos stood on the shelf in the kitchen like sentries, awaiting the family's safe return.

* * *

The river surged through the breached levee and pounded into the sandbag dam around the *barrio*, knocking it away in seconds. The violent waters overturned vehicles, and drowned cats and the dogs who had been abandoned in chains. The rampaging floodwaters smashed windows and broke down doors, vandalizing every piece of furniture and every personal treasure in every house.

Its waters finally spent, the flood subsided into a four-foot thick black ooze of sediment that slowly eased its oily fingers into every cranny of the *barrio*, settling into every nook and crevice of every shop and home. The black mud flopped heavily onto sofas and easy chairs. It poked its greasy fingers into chests of drawers filled with lace panties and great grandma's treasured embroidered linens, dancing shoes and starched uniforms. Legal documents, letters, and hidden cash reserves were irretrievably buried. Artwork ruined. Like a thug with a baseball bat, the heavy mud toppled and smashed TVs, radios, music collections, and computers.

The ooze seeped like a burglar into Señora Ramirez's house. It ran its fingers along the shelf where the family photos were kept, and swept them all onto the floor, smashing the glass in the frames, grinding the photos into the mud.

* * *

RAMSEY PARK EVACUATION CENTER
VALLE VERDE

Her two oldest sons stood over *abuelita*, who was seated on a wooden chair in a large, crowded tent.

"But why didn't your Papa come home with you? Where could he be? *Aye, Díos Mio!* I'm so worried." With a bandaged hand, the old woman wrung the hem of her torn apron.

"He'll come back, Nani." Her teenage granddaughter patted *abuelita's* shoulder. "Don't worry. He'll find us."

72

FRIDAY, APRIL 22, 1999
(Good Friday)
Aurora's Cottage
Santa Cruz, The Westside
San Lorenzo River Watershed
North Monterey Bay Coast

MORNING CARRIED THE SOUND OF BARKING SEALS. A hint of wood smoke smudged the air. Aurora was happy to see that there was no standing water on her decomposed granite garden paths. Great soil percolation. Her fruit trees would do well this year with all that recharged ground water.

The world was yellow. Oxalis, mustard flowers, daffodils — a burst of yellow flowers everywhere. Water hung from leaves in rainbow droplets and glittered like dancing fairies in the grass. Pluto's carriage, carrying Persephone — Goddess of Spring — from her dark winter palace, thundered up, up into the fresh air and warmth of Middle Earth. Deep dormant life forces rose through the ground, quickening every seed and root.

Earth Day. Only three days left of Spring Break. Mother Earth's awakening pulsed through the soles of Aurora's feet and coursed through her body as she walked along the garden path to her bike shed. Blue followed on tiptoe, pausing to shake damp gold granite sand from a paw with an attitude of profound distaste.

Aurora pedaled down Swift Street toward West Cliff Drive. Rainwater still rushed along the gutters toward storm drains.

She had to steer her bike around some large branches that had cracked off the stately Monterey pines and fallen into the street.

At West Cliff Drive, the shimmering bay opened before her. She pedaled slowly along the strand. Kelp flung onto the road by the storm dried in the sun. In every cove she passed, perfect lines of chest-to-shoulder-high waves broke in crumbly sections. The water's surface gleamed as smooth as a mirror, an illusion that masked water poisoned by toxic run-off from streets and overflowing upstream septic tanks.

Aurora stopped to watch a black cormorant with seaweed in its beak fly toward the cliffs where at least twenty breeding pairs were building nests.

All the sandy beaches were piled with driftwood. Not just small pieces, but whole trees and pieces of lumber from buildings and construction sites. Dangerous black shapes of driftwood logs and other flood debris floated in the water.

At the lighthouse, Aurora stopped and straddled her bike to check out the Lane. She didn't need to consult the water quality index on the Surfriders website to know that the *E. coli* count in the bay would be off the charts today. She ached to be riding those glassy waves, but she had no intention of starting back to school with a staph infection … or worse.

On the grass in front of the lighthouse, a loose circle of comfortably clad people mirrored the slow, graceful movements of a local Tai Chi teacher. Aurora joined the circle and flowed as one with the group, like egrets stalking frogs in a marsh.

The heavy blanket of fog looming just offshore ghosted away. Sun spilled gold glitter across the water's surface. Whale sprays spouted all over the bay.

When the Tai Chi session ended, Aurora peddled up the road to the local bakery. She carried her cappuccino, quiche and fruit salad outside and sat in the sun at a little wrought iron and pique assiette table. Surrounded by potted flowering plants and vines in the bakery courtyard, she enjoyed her breakfast, in the company of a group of Spandex-clad bicyclists, a family with a dog and a baby, and an elderly couple, seated at nearby tables. When she finished and her plate had been cleared, she ordered a second cappuccino, opened the morning paper, and read.

CALIFORNIA DECLARED A FEDERAL DISASTER AREA

The Governor has declared a state of emergency in Monterey, Santa Cruz, and other affected counties. President Clinton has declared California a "FEMA designated Major Disaster Area." The severity of the El Niño winter storm took the state by surprise. Rated as a 100-year event, unusually heavy rain fell on already saturated watersheds, resulting in extensive flooding throughout the region. County-wide losses from the flood are estimated at over $38 million. NASA Climate Scientist Dr. John Stevenson warns that storms of increasing severity will be a more frequent occurrence as global warming worsens.

Aurora left the newspaper on the table and pedaled back toward her house, mulling over the news. The impact of the storm was so slight in Santa Cruz compared to the terrible damage wrought in Valle Verde. She worried that many of her students' families would be displaced, staying with relatives or in a shelter and eating Red Cross meals for the next few months. The paper said over eleven thousand people had been affected by the storm. She'd have to be especially sensitive in the next few weeks and do her best to help her students through this.

Bridges, roads, and streetlights were out all over the county. Many stores were closed or running on emergency power. Emergency crews were working day and night to restore power, water, and phone service. Police advised everyone to stay off the streets and close to home.

465

*   *   *

It was Detective Sergeant Charlie Rosa's day off. Knee deep in mud, he shoveled mud into wheelbarrows that others rolled out of Señora Ramirez's ruined house and dumped in the yard. It felt like they'd been at it for a thousand years, and the house was still full of mud. What a mess.

Good thing Señora Ramirez was being cared for by her daughters, back at the evacuation center tent. She was taking the loss of her husband very hard, poor woman.

Charlie put down his shovel and drew the back of his hand across his mud-splattered forehead.

Mud, sweat and tears.

Taking a minute to catch his breath, he leaned on his shovel and watched his friend work. Father Francis Hilman. What a miracle Frank survived getting swept away when the dam breached. The man's got to have some crazy kind of affinity with water.

"You feeling alright, Charlie?" Father Francis asked.

"Yeah. Just thinkin' about Mr. Ramirez."

The priest pinned the detective with an intense look. "Me too. Charlie, I have to talk with you about something I saw on the levee that night. Maybe when we're done here, after we get cleaned up?"

*   *   *

That evening, Charlie Rosa and Father Francis sat at a table in a Mexican restaurant on the north side of Valle Verde, far enough from the river that it was still open for business.

Charlie dipped a tortilla chip in salsa and washed it down with some cold beer. "Jesus, Frank. You sure about that?"

"When that lightning flashed, I saw their faces as clearly as I can see you now, Charlie."

The detective sprinkled shredded cabbage, oregano, and cilantro over the red chili, chicken and hominy *pozolé* in his bowl, then squeezed half a fresh lime over the top. Finally, Charlie met his friend's waiting eyes. "I don't know much about fluid dynamics, Frank, but it seems to

466

me it's very likely that Mr. Ramirez would never have drowned if they hadn't breached that levee. Would you agree?"

Father Francis' jaw clenched. "I think so, yes."

"And the mud covering the Pajaro *barrio*? Think that would have happened if the levee hadn't been breached?"

"Who can say, for sure? But, from what I saw, no. I don't think the river would have flooded over the levee right there, at the *barrio*. It was rising fast, but I think if they hadn't breached it, it would have overflowed the banks of the levee farther downstream, probably around the Baker's lower fields at Highway 1. I'm guessing that's why they did it — to protect the strawberries downstream. Of course, as it turned out, they lost those strawberries anyway."

"There could be a case for manslaughter here, Padre. Not to mention the other laws those two broke. But Frank, with only one witness, in the dark in the middle of a storm like that, I just don't know that I could ever sell it to the DA as a prosecutable case — even with a witness as credible as you. I don't think we have enough to make a case against those idiots. There's not enough to stand up in court."

"I see what you mean. Well, I thought I should tell you. I know you'll do what you can, what is right."

Charlie took a long draw on his bottle of Dos Equis, put the bottle down, and drilled hard eyes into his friend.

"Tell you what, Frank. I think you just got yourself one more reason to watch your back. If Medina clearly saw you, and he knows you witnessed them breaching the levee, it wouldn't surprise me if he and his boss, that Baker idiot, start feeling paranoid. Be careful, *hermano*."

73

A URORA LIFTED ONE MORE FLAT OF PLANTS out of the bed of her truck and carried it into her patio through the side gate, then stood back, hands on hips, and surveyed her purchases.

She'd done it again, bought too many plants.

Too bad there isn't an AA for gardeners.

If she got up early, and worked hard all day tomorrow, she might be able to get everything in the ground before vacation ended.

The phone rang. Aurora ran inside and picked up.

"Oh good. Aurora. You're home. This is Sharon Lumina from Farm Without Harm. I have a big favor to ask. We got a call from Malone Baker. Baker Farms sustained a lot of damage to their strawberries from the flood, so Mrs. Baker has invited people from all the local environmental groups to walk with her along the levee tomorrow, to inspect the flood damage and discuss future river

469

management strategies. It would be great for Farm Without Harm to have a member present, but I can't make it. Are you free?"

Aurora stared out through the glass doors at all of her new plants, still in containers. Her hopes of getting her spring garden in before she had to go back to work sank. But this might be an opportunity to approach Malone again about the Farm Without Harm ag land preservation project she'd promised to work on with Father Francis. She hadn't heard from Father Francis for ages, but the project had been weighing on her mind. A convergence down by the river of growers and local environmentalists seemed like a momentous occasion, full of possibility. Aurora said yes.

*   *   *

She drove down the Highway 1 hill into Byrd River Valley on Easter Sunday. The bay and the plastic on the fields glittered in the delicate April sun.

At Highway 129, she headed northeast up Riverside Drive toward Valle Verde. Wet mud still covered the road. She drove cautiously, inspecting the flood damage. At Main, she turned right and crossed the Byrd River Bridge, relieved that the bridge was intact.

The feeling of the town changed completely on the other side of the river. Entering the *barrio* of Pajaro, it was easy to imagine that you were leaving the U.S. and crossing into Mexico. A crowd of people milled around in the gas station parking lot where she'd been told to meet.

She stepped onto the gooshy brown mud, glad she'd worn her old jeans and Wellington boots. She locked her car and carefully picked her way toward the agitated crowd.

About twenty-five Mexicans holding picket signs glared at her — the same people she'd seen at the DPR pesticide permit challenge hearing.

The messages on their signs were clearly written and perfectly spelled, all in the same well-lettered hand, painted on expensive new poster board, securely stapled onto fresh milled pickets. This time, the signs read, "Clean Our River", "EPA Why Did You Let The River

Flood Our Town?" "Sierra Club, You Are Taking Away Our Jobs", and "People Before Salamanders". The messages didn't make sense. She was certainly in favor of cleaning the river, picking up trash and getting rid of pollution, but there seemed to be something *off* here.

She skirted around the crowd and scrambled up the bank of the levee to get a broader view of what was going on. Had she arrived too late? Maybe Malone's levee walk had already started and she'd missed it. Hoping to catch up with the people she'd come to meet, she hurried along the slippery concrete — hyper-aware of the swollen, black river raging just below. A tangle of fallen trees and flood debris soon blocked her way and she turned back. Standing on the levee above the crowd, she tried to make sense of what was she was seeing.

A palpable current of potential violence flowed through the crowd. Red-faced men surrounded an elderly lady. With a start, Aurora recognized seventy-plus-year-old Louise Daniels, the retired librarian, surrounded by a towering wall of red-faced men.

Even from this distance, the men's body language was frightening. Their dirty shouts defiled the newly washed air.

"Fucking bitch! *Puta*! Fucking cunt!"

Inconceivable.

No sane person in any community on Earth would treat an elderly woman with such disrespect.

Before she knew what she was doing, Aurora slid down the bank, pushed her way through the circle of men, and threw her arms around Louise. A force ran through Aurora like a landslide. She grew twenty feet tall. Her voice sounded in her own ears like the roaring of a hurricane. She opened her mouth and power thundered out of her.

"Stop! Stop it!" she commanded. "What do you think you're doing? Shame on you! Just listen to yourselves. You cannot treat a Grandmother like this. Stop it!"

The men melted away. Aurora and Louise hugged.

"What in the world is going on here?" Aurora whispered, beginning to tremble.

"It seems we've been ambushed. There are a lot of us environmentalists here, but they're keeping us all separated and surrounded. Apparently Malone Baker staged this whole thing as a publicity stunt. She has all the media in the region here today — TV reporters, all the newspapers. I'm not sure exactly what she's up to, but we've definitely been hoodwinked."

Aurora was still processing the information when she realized that Louise had disappeared, and she herself was surrounded. A circle of angry men loomed above her, their energy pushing in on her in red hot waves. Aurora breathed and grounded herself, releasing fear, finding her center of gravity the way her Tai Chi master had taught her.

A TV cameraman aimed his equipment at her, too close to her face. The heavy metal camera felt threatening, poised to smash her in the nose if it didn't like what she said. Bobby Choate's uncle stepped directly in front of her, so close she could smell his sweat.

Pete Choate. So transformed by anger, Aurora almost didn't recognize him. His black beard stubble stood out like spines on his square, clenched jaw; bushy eyebrows bristled across his forehead like charging boars. Aurora watched the veins pulse in his sweating temples and throb in his thick red neck. He bared his teeth and shouted. The TV camera rolled.

Choate pointed a stubby, dirty finger a fraction of an inch from Aurora's nose. She knew he was screaming something, but she couldn't understand his words.

Out of the corner of her eye, she caught a glimpse of those men in black suits she'd seen at the pesticide assembly and the permit challenge hearing, watching her. Her stomach rolled.

"Why are you here?" Choate's words finally pounded into her. "This isn't your home. You don't belong here. Where were you when we were digging the mud out of our farmworkers' houses? Were you down here helping? No. So what right do you have to show up now, and tell us what to do with our river. Go back to Santa Cruz, you fucking bitch."

A burst of masculine laughter made Aurora shrivel. Choate scanned the crowd, seeming to pick up energy from the leering goons. Then he turned his wrath back on Aurora while the TV camera spun.

"I wanted to help," said Aurora. "But I didn't come to Valle Verde earlier because the police and highway patrol told people to stay off the roads."

"You don't belong here. Go back to Santa Cruz, you tree-hugging hippie. Eat your goddamn banana slug!"

Choate grinned at the men again, and they laughed louder.

"Mr. Choate," Aurora raised her voice above the laughter. She chose her words carefully. "Don't you recognize me? I'm Ms. Bourne. I'm your nephew's teacher. I was invited here today. Mrs. Baker asked people from local environmental groups to walk the river levee with her, to figure out together how to best manage the river in the future, for the good of the whole community."

"Bullshit!" Choate snarled. "River? You think this piss stinking channel is a river?" His voice got even louder. "This ain't no fuckin' river. Look around you, baby. The Byrd is just a dirty goddamn drainage ditch."

Aurora's heart cracked open. Her words gushed out like blood. "No, Mr. Choate. Please. The Byrd River is the primary artery of a vast and significant watershed. It *is* a river. It's powerful and ancient, millions of years old. It will live on long after we're gone, when all of us are dust. The river isn't a drainage ditch, Mr. Choate. It's alive. It's the lifeblood of our watershed."

"Santa Cruz County should have cleaned the river! They were negligent. And look what it cost us! Most of our farmworkers lost their houses, their jobs. Look at that field over there. Strawberries buried in four feet of mud. If the county hadn't of let all those plants choke up the river to protect salmon and salamanders, the river wouldn't have flooded! People and jobs are more important than fucking salamanders, or the fucking fish! We need to clean the river! Cut the trees."

"Clean the river!" Others took up the shout, brandishing their picket signs like spears. "Save our jobs! People before salamanders!"

Aurora was beaten. In her heart, she heard the words she wanted to say, but she could no longer speak them.

You don't clean a river by removing its vegetation. It's not the plants that caused the river to flood, it's the levee. People shouldn't build houses and farms on flood plains and then be surprised when the river floods. That's just the river doing its job, depositing nutrient-rich sediments onto the floodplain, bringing life to the whole watershed. The concept is as ancient as the Egyptian Nile.

Aurora sat on the couch in her living room watching the six o'clock news. She wondered how she'd gotten there. She did not remember driving home. Choate's words still pounded in her head.

It's not a river. It's just a goddamn drainage ditch.

She remembered trying to defend the river, but she didn't remember what she'd said. Had she been coherent?

On TV, there was a brief shot of Aurora, looking like a scruffy hippie in her old blue jeans. And then the camera cut to the poor wronged farmer, handsome Mr. Choate. The camera angle didn't show the man's large fist threatening to strike Aurora in the face. The volume of Choate's voice had been adjusted down to a reasonable level.

"Where were you when we were digging the mud out of our farmworkers houses? Were you down here helping? No. You weren't here. So what right do you have to show up now, and tell us what to do with our river?"

Clearly, most viewers would feel sympathetic toward the grower.

The camera cut to the farmworkers. A translator overdubbed English captions as they spoke in Spanish about how the river had buried the strawberries in mud, taking away their livelihood. They said that if the county had done the right thing and kept the river clean, they would still have strawberries to pick, and a paycheck to look forward to. Instead, they were living in evacuation tents and digging mud out of their houses.

The news anchorwoman went on to report that Governor Pat Wilton had declared a state of emergency in the Byrd Valley.

"He has exercised his executive powers to override the Endangered Species Act, and has authorized the immediate clearing of all vegetation from the Byrd River. A coalition of Byrd Valley strawberry growers has filed a lawsuit for criminal negligence against Santa Cruz County for allowing vegetation to accumulate along the river, causing the river to rise over the levee. Environmentalists oppose the river clearing."

A short clip showed the president of the local bird club stating that this was peak nesting season for endangered migratory birds, and that removing riparian vegetation along the river at this time of the year would threaten the already endangered bird populations. The bird club president looked like a stereotypical birdwatcher nerd, not likely to win much viewer sympathy. The news anchorwoman explained that environmentalists asserted that maintaining vegetation along the river is an important habitat management strategy for sustaining the endangered salmon and Steelhead, which migrate along the Byrd River. In addition, several other federally listed endangered species such as the long-toed salamander, the Pacific eel and the Western garter snake depend on riparian vegetation on the river.

The camera panned to a long shot of Governor Wilton walking the levee arm-in-arm with Malone Baker, then to a close-up of a concerned-looking Malone saying, "I'm a tree lover as much as anyone, but these trees along the river have to go. They caused the river to flood our fields. We're not thinking of ourselves. We have a responsibility to our workers. These people depend on the strawberries to support their families."

The scene cut to a shot of the farmworkers holding up their picket signs: "Sierra Club, You Are Taking Away Our Jobs." "People Not Salamanders".

The news anchor continued.

"Work has already begun on the Santa Cruz County side of the river north of Highway 1 to clear all riparian vegetation. During this state of emergency, Wilton has declared the Endangered Species Act null and void."

Now, the messages on the picket signs made sense to Aurora. A well-executed marketing strategy. A photo-op designed specifically to be used as a short so-called news bite, slanted to manipulate the hearts and minds of the TV-watching public. After watching this biased report, how could the viewing public value salamanders over people, or environmental protection over jobs? Playing the "jobs" card could always be counted on to evoke that knee-jerk public reaction, even if the threat was a lie, or too simplistic a portrayal of reality. Someone wanted the public to believe that the bad environmentalists and the bad river had harmed the good strawberry growers and the poor farmworkers. And that someone was powerful enough to persuade the television news director to disseminate their message.

Aurora stared at the TV as the news ran on to the next topic. Another gang-related shooting in Salinas.

Her head swam. Was the river really none of her business? Was she really poking her nose where she didn't belong?

Where did she belong? Anywhere?

Tears ran down her cheeks. Blue jumped onto her lap and ran his sandpaper tongue over the back of her hand. He curled into a ball and began to purr. Aurora held the cat and rocked, her tears dropping onto the blue-black fur, her eyelids growing heavy.

Soon, she fell into a deep sleep.

74

NAADAAYI HÉEN A TAYEE

AURORA WOKE TO SHEETING RAIN pounding against the bedroom window. The sky was ominous and dark. She wasn't sure how long she'd been living in his house, waiting for him to return. She dressed and hurried downstairs, hoping he'd be there.

At the entrance to the kitchen, she stopped short. Three old women sat around the table drinking tea. As if a fog were lifting from her mind, she recognized these women. They were her adopted aunties, and had loved and cared for her since she was a little girl.

"He is ill," said the woman with a streak of white in her hair. "We will take you to him."

Aurora grabbed a rain slicker off the hook by the door and slipped it on.

Although the women were much older than her, she strained to keep up with them.

While she scurried along the muddy red road, images flashed through her mind. She remembered being here with Frank, her companion and dear friend, when they were both young.

She saw herself as a child — lonely, afraid, and newly adopted into the tribe — sitting with young Frank at the village campfire listening to storytellers, walking on the beach and in the woods with him, swimming with him in green forest pools, and praying for him when — his chest pierced and bleeding — he danced the Sun Dance.

As if a veil were being drawn aside, she *remembered* that he had been her friend, and then her belovéd, in this world. She felt his spirit, his *perfection*, and her love for him swelled and exploded like fireworks inside her.

She clearly recalled their bonding ceremony, the promises they'd made to one another at their handfasting.

Icy fear strangled her. She ran with the women through the village and up the hill toward the longhouse. They veered off the main path and hurried along a winding, rock-lined trail to a small structure built of cedar.

One of the hunters who had killed the demon squatted by a smoky fire in front of the hut, his bow and arrows on the ground by his side. He acknowledged Aurora with a nod.

Xigmacse, the elder with white braids — the one Frank had called his doctor — stood in the doorway. He pulled back a blanket curtain so that she could enter. The bone inlaid with abalone shell pieces, which she and Frank had found in the midden, lay on a small table just inside the entrance next to a large abalone shell filled with smoldering sage and other dried herbs.

Aurora blinked as her eyes adjusted to the dark, and breathed in the smells of wood smoke, sage, mullein and mugwort, rosemary, and camphor. Clean medicinal smells. But there was also an odor of putrefaction, and the vile, acrid stink of the beast that had attacked them.

Frank was lying on a cot against the wall. A healer bent over him, chanting softly while changing his bandages. The healer stepped away when Aurora rushed to his side.

Frank wore only a loincloth. His skin had the blue-grey pallor of alabaster, and he'd lost a great deal of weight and muscle mass. His ribs showed through his translucent skin. His skull protruded through the stretched vellum of his face and around his hollowed-out eyes. His beautiful hair was dull and matted. The wound on his chest was open, bleeding anew and festering. And there was a horrific gash on his side, still oozing blood, yet already putrid with infection.

She stifled a cry as she took his hands. He met her eyes and smiled weakly.

"Ah, *ñ'a táayaa*. I'm sorry, my love." His voice was barely a whisper.

"Oh, my God! What happened?"

Frank was so weak he spoke in a breathy whisper. Aurora put her face close to his, to hear him better.

"I joined a hunting party. We found more of the demons and destroyed them, but I was bitten and stung."

His skin was deathly blue all around the wounds. Someone had rubbed ashes on his forehead.

She tenderly kissed his eyes. She kissed his lips, as dry and cracked as autumn leaves, and then she kissed his hands. A tear fell from her cheek onto his.

She turned to the healer. "How can we save him?"

"We know of only one herb that is an antidote. But it is very difficult and dangerous to obtain. I don't know if there is time to gather it."

Frank's eyes were closed now, his breathing shallow, rasping and labored.

"Why hasn't anyone gone to get it? Where is this antidote? We need to have it, now!"

"We believe it will be most effective if it is you who gathers the medicine plant, because of your relationship with *Teheatla*."

"Me? But ... I don't know how. I ... Yes, yes, of course. I'll do it. Please, tell me what to do."

"Aurora." Frank's eyes opened and he reached for her. "No. It's too dangerous. I don't want you to try. Don't."

Aurora turned her back on him and spoke to the healer. "Tell me what to do."

Xigmacse drew her away from her wounded warrior-priest. "The medicine plant is very rare. The only place it grows deep underwater near the rivermouth. It protects itself by filling the mind of anyone who tries to touch it with paralyzing terror. Powerful and treacherous currents surround it. They could sweep you so far out to sea we would never find you. If you get caught in a whirlpool, you may be taken away and never come back. There are giant clams that can clamp onto your foot or hand, and hold you under until you drown. And vicious eels hide in the shadows, with razor sharp, venomous teeth."

Xigmacse described how to find the plant and how to harvest it, and — to the best of his ability — he told her how to survive.

"You must stay in the eddy, where the current curls back upstream against itself, flowing along the riverbank. You will have only a short time, while the tides are changing, when it is possible to gather the medicine plants and survive. At the turning between ebb and flow, the water slows, and changes direction. You must get in and out in the time it takes for the tide to turn."

*   *   *

Through the cold and sleeting rain, Aurora followed the women who had taken her to Frank, and three of the warriors who had hunted the demons with him. They led her to a bathhouse by the rivermouth. The river loomed dark, turbulent, and dangerous.

They showed her to a small room where she put on a wetsuit. They gave her a mask and fins, a mesh sack with back straps to hold the medicine plants, a headlamp, a belt with a sheath, and a sharp knife.

Can I do this?

She'd gone through a scuba certification course, but had never done any serious diving, only resort dives. She was by no means an experienced free diver. No matter. There was no choice. She had to get those medicine plants. She had to.

Savage waves pounded the shore. Wind wailed and whipped icy rain in their faces. Seafoam tumbled over cord grasses. The warriors led her to a place where the river curved.

Ripples snaking upstream through the water marked the eddy. Aurora waded in backwards, looking over her shoulder, shuffling her fins around submerged boulders sharp with barnacles, and balancing as she felt her way over slippery rocks. The dark water grabbed and sucked at her legs. When she was chest deep in the surge, a swell loomed toward her, and she dove.

Freezing cold.

She fought against the undertow. She had to keep close to shore, where the plants grew, to avoid the whirlpools. But she had to stay far enough away from the perilous rocks that she wouldn't be thrown against them and torn to shreds.

When she came up for air, the current almost overwhelmed her. Even at slack tide, the swollen river pulled with a force stronger than she'd ever felt. She fought for her life.

Stay in the eddy or be swept away forever.

She got her bearings, filled her lungs with air, and dove, pulling with all her strength toward the shore against the current. Her headlamp illuminated plants growing underwater along the rocky bank.

Enormous black abalones clung to the rocks. Their shells, raised in feeding position, revealed the soft black bodies of the hungry mollusks, tentacles undulating as they probed the water. Hiding in a crevice behind the abalones, a giant eel coiled, flashing its vicious fangs.

Aurora searched the surging darkness for the medicine plants until her lungs burned. She had to surface and breathe. Then she dove again, and again, growing weaker against the relentless tidal flow.

She surfaced once more, gasping for air.

Too far off shore, just barely at the edge of the eddy.

Desperately, she swam toward shore.

The eddy caught her and carried her upstream toward the bank.

Not too far. Don't ride it too far. Now!

Timing her dive, she plunged down to where she remembered seeing the plants.

Yes. There they are.

The plants glowed from within, seeming to sing as they wavered, stirred by the moving water.

Rumm'e. She heard his voice as clear as if he whispered in her ear. *Rumm'e.* The music of Mother Earth's blood. This was not the soft and joyful water music they'd heard in the mountains, but a violent and passionate dance, dark and menacing; a requiem.

Her lungs filled with fire. As she reached for the plants, they burst into flame. She thrust her hand through the aureole of fire and grabbed a fistful of the medicine plant, chanting the words the old man had taught her. Kicking with all her might to stay in place, she hacked at the base of the plants with her knife and stuffed the medicine in her mesh bag. She might not get another chance, might not find these plants again if she went up for air then dove again. No more time.

She felt the tide turn, but forced herself to keep cutting — fighting panic and pain.

The sound issuing from the plants surged and swelled. A terrifying, chaotic wail filled her being, upwelling like bagpipes, a hundred violins, shofars and kettledrums; glaciers thundering and avalanching into the sea; people wailing, tortured, screaming for help, dying; bellowing and squealing of terrified animals; bombs exploding, armies clashing. She kicked for the surface.

She didn't go anywhere. Searing pain cut into her ankle and stabbed up her leg. She almost lost consciousness. Almost let her knife fall from her hand.

A giant clam had clamped onto her anklebone. Her foot was trapped. With her last strength, she thrust and slashed at the enormous mollusk sucking her foot. It released a spurt of black ink, making it impossible to see. She hoped she wouldn't stab her own leg. She continued to jab, even after conscious thought left her.

And then she was free.

She gasped and choked for air, bobbing on the surface. She no longer had her knife in her hand. She could see that she was about to be pulled out of the eddy and swept out to sea or into a whirlpool. She had no strength left to fight.

Strong arms surrounded her. The three warriors swam her to the bank and carried her to shore.

The women cared for Aurora, while the hunters ran to the cedar hut with the medicine plants.

"Your love is strong," said the women. "With the medicine plants he may live."

75

Prudenciana Elementary, Valle Verde

W HEN FATHER FRANCIS WALKED THROUGH THE OPEN DOOR of the classroom, Aurora was bent over a child seated at a desk. Sun poured through the window at her back. She straightened, and turned toward him, her hair loose and falling in a golden cloud around her face and shoulders. Recognition flashed in her eyes, and she smiled. From across the room, he breathed in the fire in her hair. It stirred him.

In that moment, he realized with certainty that he had loved her forever. He held that knowledge in his heart quietly, tucked it away alongside the certainty that he had made a choice to be born into this world a priest, and he would die with his sacramental vows inviolate.

He set the red and white plastic picnic cooler on the floor and surveyed the room. It had a special feeling, different than most of the classrooms he'd visited. Calm, and happy.

This was not one of those temporary portables he'd seen so many of, but a real classroom, built right, spacious and old-fashioned, with a high ceiling with clearstory windows. In one corner of the room, bookshelves were arranged to make a reading nook, with big pillows on the floor.

Stuffed and painted paper salmon hung from the ceiling, giving the effect of being underwater. Children's artwork was displayed on the walls: fish prints with fluorescent blue and green paint on rice paper; watercolor illustrations of forest, creek, and ocean; ink drawings of native plants, animals, and aquatic insects labeled with scientific names. Under a large, laminated map of the Byrd Valley watershed and posters of the region's indigenous salmonid species, the incubator sat humming away on a countertop. Near the incubator was a lab model of preserved salmon eggs and juvenile salmon at various stages of development, and a selection, preserved in vials, of sensitive aquatic insects.

Aurora crossed the room and stood before him. She offered her hand. He swallowed. Long artistic fingers. He wrapped his hand around hers, prepared for the electrical charge he knew would shoot through him.

"I didn't know you'd be delivering the eggs, Father Francis," Aurora said in a voice soft enough that only he could hear.

"I volunteer at the hatchery. They asked me to do the South County deliveries this year." He hoped she didn't notice the roughness in his voice. "It's nice to see you again, Aurora."

"And you as well." She lifted her face and met his eyes.

The face of an angel.

Aurora turned toward her students. "Boys and girls, the Steelhead eggs have arrived! Raise your hand if you're really excited that we get to raise these precious eggs in our classroom!" All of the children stretched their hands toward the ceiling.

"Ms. B?" Rico waved his hand in the air.

"Yes, Rico?"

"Father Francis was at the beach clean-up at the beginning of the year. Me and Father Francis, we're friends."

Father Francis smiled. "Hey, Rico. Good to see you, *mi'hijo*. How's your Grandma?"

Rico beamed.

Paloma jumped out of her seat, and ran to the priest. She wrapped herself around him like a baby octopus.

He patted her back, while she cried. "Johnny's okay, *mi'hijita*," he whispered. "It's going to be alright. I promise. Your brother's coming home soon."

Paloma let go of the priest, dried her eyes and returned to her seat.

"Yes, River?" Aurora responded to another raised hand.

"Can we see the eggs, Father Francis?"

"Yes, you certainly can," he said. "I have them right here in the cooler. First, though, we need to get them safely into your incubator."

He handed Aurora the license from the Department of Fish and Wildlife authorizing her to rear and transport eggs and fish for classroom education.

"This should be posted somewhere near your incubator," he said. "Now, it would be best for the eggs if we can make it darker in here. Do you mind if we turn out the lights, shut the blinds and close the door?"

Aurora set about dimming the room to the level of a well-shaded river. The students were quiet and attentive, but Father Francis sensed their excitement.

He carried the cooler to the incubator. The aquarium set-up was perfect, the water cold and pristine. He turned off the aerator, then removed a small plastic bag from his cooler. Thirty-six peach-colored Steelhead eggs. Each egg had a small black dot inside. The fish embryos had developed eyes. With great care, he began distributing the eggs into the interstices, the spaces, between the smooth, clean river rocks, floating them up against the glass so the students would be able to watch them develop. When all of the eggs had been transferred into the aquarium, Father Francis switched the aerator back on. He adjusted the power and direction of the stream, so the bubbles gently played over and around the eggs without dislodging them from the rocks.

He was surrounded by children, so quiet he'd hardly noticed that they'd gathered around him.

"Boys and girls, please take your seats," Aurora said. "You can rotate up, one group at a time, when it's your turn to do your first egg observation."

The students returned to their desks, with none of the pushing and shouting he'd seen in other classrooms.

"While you're waiting to do your observation," said Aurora, "we're going to calculate the daily temperature units of our eggs, so we can predict when they will hatch. Here's your DTU worksheet. We'll fill these out now, together. Keep your worksheet in your STEP folder and when our eggs hatch, we'll see how accurate our predictions were."

The first small group of students tiptoed to the incubator to make a careful observation of the eggs.

Father Francis handed Aurora the baggie that had held the eggs. "The DTU your eggs have accumulated so far is marked here," he said, pointing out the number written in black marker on the plastic bag. "And here's your egg progress sheet."

"460 degrees total as of today?" As she took the paper from his hand, their fingers brushed.

Like an eroding cliff, he crumbled into her depths.

"Right. And you can see here the total temperature units required for hatching."

"535 degrees?" Her watched her breasts rise and fall with her breath.

"That's right. And the formula for calculating the DTU's, T, the average daily temperature, minus 32, the Fahrenheit freezing point, equals DTU, is on the worksheet. So, I guess you don't need my help with that?" He swam for shore.

"No. I think we can take it from here, Father Francis. Thank you again, so much."

He checked his watch. On schedule. He still had quite a few deliveries to make. He didn't want to hold the rest of the fragile eggs in bags without oxygen any longer than necessary. He picked up his cooler and, with a nod, left the room.

✳   ✳   ✳

DETECTIVES' BULLPEN
SANTA CRUZ COUNTY SHERIFF'S OFFICE
COUNTY GOVERNMENT CENTER
OCEAN STREET, SANTA CRUZ

"Christ. No. Please no. Not another one."

Detective Sergeant Charlie Rosa's hands shook. He sat at his gunmetal grey desk in the sheriff's office and read the teletype again. The five-year-old daughter of a Corralitos rancher had gone missing. Presumed kidnapped.

He stared at her photo. A little chubby-cheeked, curly-headed blonde.

How long did he have? Where should he start?

76

A T MORNING RECESS AURORA SCANNED THE NEWSPAPER on the table in the faculty room. "City Cleans the River" was the headline on the front page. She skimmed the article.

The California Coastal Commission, which has jurisdiction over the Byrd River on the ocean side of Highway 1, prohibited the clearing of vegetation on both sides of the river from the highway to the ocean. But Valle Verde city workers have already begun the process of removing trees and vegetation along the river on the Santa Cruz County side, from the highway, north to Murphy's Crossing. They will continue regular applications of aquatic WeedRangler to control the vegetation in the river channel.

"WeedRangler? That's glyphosate." Aurora spoke aloud, to no one in particular. "The city plans to regularly poison a wild salmon river with Biogen's herbicide, an endocrine disruptor toxic to wildlife, known to cause birth defects, in order to kill native plants critical to the health of wildlife and the watershed?"

Corkie Duncan looked up from the papers she was correcting and shook her head. "It's the Mad Hatter's Tea Party."

Aurora skimmed the rest of the paper. Malone Baker, whose strawberry fields were buried in mud after the recent flood, was one of the plaintiffs in a multimillion-dollar lawsuit against Santa Cruz and Monterey counties, alleging that they had failed to adequately maintain the river channel.

A sidebar on the front page explained that Santa Cruz County attorneys argued that it was not vegetation in the river, but design capacity of the levee that had caused the flooding. The Army Corps of Engineers' Byrd River Flood Control Project had not been designed to withstand a hundred-year storm. NASA climate scientists warned that unusually severe storm events were going to be occurring with greater frequency and cities should begin upgrading their infrastructure to prepare. A Valle Verde City Council member debunked global warming as an alarmist hoax.

Mrs. Baker stated she was pleased that the City of Valle Verde had acted quickly and decisively to clean the river, even though the work was done too late to save her strawberries and her workers' jobs.

An article on the bottom of the second page reported that overzealous city workers, tasked with clearing riparian vegetation along the riverbank, had removed a privately-owned orchard. The Trask brothers, owners of the historic apple orchard situated on the Valle Verde side of the river, have filed suit against the city on the grounds that, without their knowledge or consent, city workers trespassed onto their property and removed heritage apple trees planted by the Trask's great grandfather. "The trees are irreplaceable," said Cal Trask.

*   *   *

After school, Aurora met with her third, fourth and fifth grade Gifted and Talented students in the kindergarten yard at the front of the school. A scaffold had been set up against the two-story white wall of the kinder building. After months of research, the black outline of the mural depicting Prudenciana Elementary's history had been drawn on the wall, and was finally ready to be brought to life with paint and color.

Aurora's GATE group had been working on the design of the mural with the help of local Ohlone Indian artist Aman Rios. Through their research, Aurora's students had discovered that the school stood on land that had been Ohlone Indian territory for thousands of years. In 1823, the Mexican government granted a vast tract of land, Rancho Los Corralitos, to Prudenciana's husband. As a widow, Prudenciana gave a parcel of the rancho to the community to build a one-room schoolhouse, and donated a nearby parcel to build an orphanage and the first church in the region — Our Lady of Help.

The drawing depicted Prudenciana and her family standing in front of their adobe ranch house during a *quinceañera* fiesta. Alongside the adobe, salmon swam in Corralitos Creek to the Byrd River and out to sea. Hawks and golden eagles flew in the sky above, and a grizzly bear roamed the coastal mountains in the distance. Vaqueros on horseback were riding up into the mountains to capture the grizzly for a Bear and Bull fight, entertainment for the upcoming fiesta. The ghostly faces of an Ohlone family — mother, father, son, and young child — floated in the clouds above the rancho. The Native American mother and father wore Ohlone facial tattoos and basket hats of woven sedge.

Today, finally, the students would begin painting the mural. Aurora had recently invited Alice to join the group. She'd been mute for nearly six months now, since Halloween, but the art and her counseling sessions with Nathena were bringing her out; she was beginning to talk again. She'd been reunited with her baby brother and was now staying weekends with the family in Hollister who were adopting him. Hopefully, they'd decide to adopt Alice, too.

Aurora sat on a bench in the sun watching the students paint. It was very warm. Her eyelids were growing heavy.

"What was the river like when you were a kid?" Sarah asked Aman. Sarah had not had any more seizures since the one early in the year at the pesticide assembly, but she was under a doctor's care, and was being evaluated by a neurologist.

"The Byrd?" Aman put down his paintbrush and a dreamy glaze washed over his eyes. "I remember when I was a boy, there were all kinds of fish in the river. There were chubbies and pretty, colorful sticklebacks, and crawdads as big as lobsters. And there were salmon and trout. They loved the fresh, cool water and fed on insects. We used to climb out on willow branches and swing our fishing lines into the river. Steelhead swam by, easy to see in those clear waters. So plentiful. Silver salmon, and the Coho, too. There were carp, and bluegills, and the little white eels we called who-soo. Frogs abounded. And newts. The river was thick with them. This time of year, we'd find so many frogs' eggs and salamander eggs — big beautiful masses of them, stuck to the rocks. And upstream, we knew there was salmon eggs in the gravels. We'd always be careful not to disturb the eggs, 'cause that's the way our elders taught us."

"What about birds?" asked River as she painted the wings of a red-tailed hawk.

"There were so many birds. There would be kai-kai, or so we called the blue jays. Robins were there and kingfishers diving and little birds hopping through the bushes. There were mockingbirds, meadowlarks, and all kinds of hawks. We used to skinny dip where the water was still and deep. You wouldn't dare swim there now, but the water was clean back then. You could drink it. There were appealing little paths to the river, all gone now. As a boy, the river was a special place for me. I could hide out there in the dense vegetation, so thick and pretty. You could push it aside and make a little house for yourself. We called these places ruks or tule houses."

"Kids went to the river all by themselves?" Sarah asked. "That would be so dangerous now."

"Yes. The river was a place of dreaming and visions. Sitting alone by the river, you could hear voices, like the voices of women as they sang an acorn grinding song: *kay, kayya, ha; ya kay ya, ha.* Once, I heard the voice of my great grandmother, asking me to take care of the river."

"It's terrible that the river is so changed," said Sarah with an angry catch in her voice. "We need to get it back to what it used to be. We need to bring back the wildlife, make the river healthy and beautiful again, and the water pure and good to drink. What can we do?"

From her bench in the afternoon sun, Aurora listened and watched. Her eyelids closed. Sarah's angry voice droned on, but it shifted, as if she'd gone through a tunnel. Aurora stepped into the landscape of the old rancho.

*   *   *

Prudenciana stood at the open door of her adobe casa, gazing out over her land with an air of nobility. Her thick black hair was piled on top of her head in a braided coil, held in place with sterling and tortoise shell combs. She wore a long black gown, tight at the bodice, and a black lace mantilla embroidered with red roses draped over her shoulders. Her fifteen-year-old daughter, Sarah, faced her. Sarah's dark Spanish eyes flashed with fire as she argued with her mama.

"It's wrong to do that to the grizzly bears," Sarah said with heightened emotional timbre, almost a sob. "Dragging them out of the mountains and putting them into a pit to fight the bulls, that's cruel. It's not entertaining, it's terrible. Please, mama, I don't want a bear and bull fight for my quinceañera. Don't let them do it."

Sarah's mama gazed sadly at her daughter.

On the bench where Aurora napped, a cloud shadow passed over. She shivered as she dreamed of the rancho coming to life under the paintbrushes of the muralists.

It was a warm, moonlit night. Prudenciana's daughter, Sarah, lay on a blanket on the bank of the river, in the arms of an Ohlone man only a year older than she. They had just made love, the first time for both, and they were talking in whispers, between kisses.

"I belong to the Bear Clan," he said. "I was chosen by Bear, by Chichayo, when I was born. Now is the season when we dance, now when the bears have come out of hibernation for the winter. Chichayo is our ancestor from the Spirit World. He gives us healing. He is sacred. I wish you could see our Bear Dance. We dance around the fire all night, for the healing of Mother Earth, and all her children. When I dance, wearing Bear's skin, I become Bear. I must be strong, because I eat all the sicknesses of the People and of the World. I take away the pain and hurt, and carry it to the fire, where it is cleansed. There is great power in Bear Medicine. Listen. I will teach you our Bear Song. *He neh yeh he ney yeh he na ye chi-chay-yo.*"

In the moonlight on the river, the water itself seemed to carry voices singing an ancient song. The voices wove through the sound of the river, lapping at the bank as quietly as the soft breeze that rustled the willow branches, as quietly as kisses.

*   *   *

"Ms. B? Ms. B?"

Through Aurora's half-closed eyelids, she could see Sarah. But something was off. Sarah should have olive skin and dark Spanish eyes. Instead, she was as blonde as a Scandinavian milkmaid.

"Ms. B? Did you fall asleep? Look! Look at our mural" said Sarah. "It almost seems like it's alive. Don't you love it?"

Aurora was fully awake now. She stood, stretched in the warm afternoon sun, and walked closer to examine the painting.

"It's wonderful!"

"We were careful about cleaning the brushes in the buckets," said Ben. "We're going to store the paint water until we're all done with the mural, then take it to the public dump's toxic waste disposal, not pour it down the storm drains."

"Ms. B! Aman!" River shouted as she ran toward the group with something large in her arms.

"I found her under the Monterey pines over there next to the fence by the fields." River placed the enormous bird on a table.

"Golden eagle," said Aman. A high-pitched scream pierced the still blue air. A solitary eagle circled above the pine trees. "That makes thirteen dead birds so far since they started the spring fumigations." Aman's eyes glistened. "I will take this one and bury her respectfully, in the Ohlone way. There's going to be a traditional Ohlone prayer ceremony for the river this weekend. It's a ceremony to heal the river, because they're cutting the trees down, and taking away the shade and the hiding places for the fish. All of you and your parents are welcome. Please, join us if you wish," he said. "Next Sunday at dawn. We'll be on the bank of the river at the Trask's orchard, the apple orchard that got cut down. There was once an Ohlone village there. It's a sacred site."

*   *   *

The following Sunday just before dawn, Aurora turned into the Trask driveway and drove down the long farm road to the river. She parked next to the other cars and trucks, stepped out of her roadster into the chilly pre-dawn gloom, and pulled her jean jacket tight around her.

The scene she stepped into looked like a war zone. The destruction of riparian habitat was total, as if bombs had exploded along the river. Not a green plant remained. Splintered shards of tree skeletons reached broken bones into the bleak sky. Across the river on the opposite bank, heavy tree removal equipment was parked, ready for the next phase of tree clearing on Monday morning.

People were gathered around a small fire. Aurora greeted her student, Caleb. Caleb's father, Aaron Trask, stood next to his twin brother Cal, and Cal's Ohlone wife. A few Ohlone men sat around a large drum, beating a rhythm and singing a ululating chant. A native man shook a rattle; another played a melody on a traditional elderberry flute.

The tribal chief of Indian Canyon, Marie Christine, stood at the fire, next to a woman with a white streak in her hair, wearing an abalone shell necklace fit for a queen. The women quietly discussed plans for the Bear Dance, which would be held soon at Indian Canyon.

Despite the pre-dawn chill, a tribal elder with white braids, dressed in a skin loincloth and fur cape, stood barefoot in front of the fire. He held a staff hung with eagle feathers and talons. Fractals of flame shimmering through fog created a halo around him. He chanted prayers in a language Aurora didn't understand.

A man wearing faded jeans and a jean jacket crouched by the fire, his back turned to her, his thick black hair braided with red string. Slowly he rose on long legs, and faced her. *Father Francis.*

He nodded in greeting, his jaw set in a hard line. His glance warmed briefly, but then his eyes shaded like a bird of prey and he turned back to the fire. Her body burned.

A man holding an abalone shell full of smoldering sage approached. Aurora bent her head while he brushed an eagle feather through the purifying blue smoke, sending it swirling over and around her, front and back. She lifted each foot so he could smudge the soles of her feet.

May I walk in Beauty. May I walk in Truth. May I walk in Peace and Love. May I find my way home along the good red road. May all beings …

Tendrils of sage smoke wrapped around her.

The men sitting in a circle around the big drum sang the Bear Song.

Heh na yeh, heh na yeh, heh na yeh chichai-yo.

There followed blessings and prayers for the water, the river, and all the river's relatives.

When the sun rose, the ceremony was complete. Father Francis left hastily, without a word or a backward glance.

Aurora chided herself for feeling sad that he'd ignored her.

This wasn't about you. Move on. There's an epic swell rolling in from the Northwest. Go shred some waves.

77

Corralitos Creek, Santa Cruz Mountains
Byrd River Watershed, South Santa Cruz County

F ISH AND GAME WARDEN KELLI CAVANAUGH drove her truck along the narrow, winding forest road. As the half-ton Dodge 4x4 ascended into the coastal mountains, Warden Cavanaugh kept her eye on the creek that meandered from one side of the road to the other through culverts and under picturesque bridges.

She savored the hint of summer in the warming spring morning, feeling good in spite of the Cal Tip call that had brought her up here.

Someone had allegedly built a dam across the creek and was siphoning off water upstream during salmon egg hatching season — a critical time for maintaining sufficient water flow for the eggs to hatch and the juveniles to survive the summer. The same individuals were allegedly discharging raw sewage and other effluent downstream — a disturbing allegation, and serious violation of county riparian protection ordinance.

Native Coho salmon, a keystone species critical to the overall health and biodiversity of the redwood forest ecosystem, were on the verge of extinction. It was Kelli's job as well as her passion to protect them.

Fish and Game Warden wasn't just a job, but a lifestyle. She put her whole self into being *Guardian of Our Wildlife Heritage* twenty-four seven, in or out of uniform. She considered it her responsibility to be the voice for all of those creatures who couldn't speak for themselves, to explain to people how their everyday activities could — even unintentionally —have profound, far reaching, and sometimes extremely adverse effects on wildlife and habitat. She wanted every person she came in contact with to understand that everyone and everything is interconnected, through the ecology of the land, to the heartbeat of Mother Nature.

Kelli had grown up hunting and fishing in wild California with her parents and grandparents. When she was twelve, on a fishing trip in the High Sierra with her family, she'd had a life-changing encounter with a Fish and Game Warden.

The tall, strong warden had a gun, a badge, and a cool uniform, and had approached her brothers and her with such authority, she'd thought they might be in trouble. But from the first few minutes the warden spoke with them, they'd felt welcomed into the wilderness, and included in a special group of people who loved and cared for nature.

The warden seemed to know everything about the plants and trees, animals, geology, even astronomy … And told such fascinating, and sometimes funny, stories about working in the Sierra that Kelli wished they could hang out for the whole trip.

That meeting had been an epiphany. Up until then, Kelli had assumed that, when she grew up, her only work options would be boring, demeaning, indoor jobs. But this Game Warden was a woman! Meeting a female Game Warden set Kelli free. She knew right then she was going to be a Fish and Game Warden, too.

From that childhood vision, her resolution never faltered. She completed her four-year university degree in Wildlife Biology, Fisheries, and Natural Resources Management at Humboldt State with highest honors, and then went straight into basic training at the Academy. She was proud of the fact that, of all the law enforcement training academies, the Fish and Game Academy in Napa ran the longest, most rigorous and comprehensive program.

And she was proud to be one of the 200 game wardens in the state, responsible for protecting more than 1,000 native fish and wildlife species, more than 6,000 native plant species, and approximately 360 endangered species, in one of the most exquisite natural environments in the world — an environment at risk. With 159,000 square miles of land, 36 million people, 1,100 miles of coastline, about 222,000 square miles of ocean waters, 30,000 miles of rivers and streams, 4,800 lakes and reservoirs and 80 major rivers, in addition to deserts, mountains and, of course, urban areas, California Fish and Game Wardens had a lot on their plates, and were understaffed, underappreciated, and underpaid.

But hey, who's counting?

If she transferred to a job in any other branch of law enforcement, she could earn much more, and she wouldn't be putting her life on the line every day in remote locations without any backup. But she loved the freedom she had as a game warden, and the immersion in nature — food and balm for the soul — that she couldn't find in any other line of work.

Kelli checked her watch: 8:30AM. Not a trace of the coastal fog, which often clung like ghosts to the trees in the mornings.

Maneuvering the green Department truck around a bend in the road, she leaned out of the open window and breathed deeply, drinking in the welcoming smells of the forest: sun-warmed resins of Douglas fir and redwood needles, musty mushrooms nestled in the rich duff of the decomposing forest floor, and the cool freshets of the rapidly flowing creek.

All of Warden Cavanaugh's senses were on high alert, as usual. She wore her duty belt fully equipped today, even though it meant she carried about twenty-three pounds of extra weight. While she steered with one hand, with the other she double-checked each item on the utility belt at her hip: her holstered department issue semi-automatic Glock 22, a magazine pouch with two extra clips for her firearm, two sets of cuffs, pepper spray, a Leatherman utility tool, protective gloves, a folding four-inch Buck Knife, and her portable radio.

She'd tucked a small mag light into her pocket, leaving the department issue eight-inch aluminum flashlight and the 24-inch side-handle baton off her belt. Too uncomfortable and cumbersome, and not mandatory carry. Both the eight-inch and the thirteen-inch department issue Streamlights were in the truck, if needed. And the shotgun on the rack behind her was clean, oiled and ready for bear, so to speak.

Although not overly confident, Kelli did feel competent to defend herself. Since completing the arduous Academy program, she'd continued to sharpen her skills in defensive tactics, and had kept in shape through the physical rigors of a job in the wild. She also made a point of regular workouts on her days off. She trained in martial arts, went to a climbing gym, rowed on the bay, honed her aim on the firing range, and partner practiced using all of the equipment on her belt.

But today felt like a day she needed assistance. Something felt off. She scanned along the sides of the road as she drove, trying to suss out what it was about this investigation that raised the hackles on the back of her neck.

There were often days like today, when the other two field wardens in the county were off duty and, as the only Fish and Game Warden working, she alone was responsible for patrolling not just her own South County beat, but also the entire North County and Marine-Yacht Harbor territories. All three wardens overlapped only three days a week. But even then, she couldn't count on getting backup when she requested it.

I've got to at least try to check in.

Kelli turned the dial on her Pac system, hoping she could still get a signal from a nearby repeater this far up the mountain. She found the signal from the Loma Prieta repeater and contacted CENCOM — the Fish and Game and State Parks dispatch center. She reported her position and destination, and put in a request for backup. Then she went on the sheriff's channel and put in a request for backup, but she didn't have much hope that anyone would respond from the sheriff's office either, with only six Santa Cruz Sheriff's deputies on duty at any given time to cover the entire county.

Kelli tapped her thumb against the steering wheel. Whatever she was heading into, she had a strong feeling she didn't want to go in alone.

She lifted her new Nokia cell phone, the first mobile phone she'd ever owned, off its cradle. Reception for these things was spotty, but no harm in giving it a try. She pushed express dial for the number Sheriff Charlie Rosa had given her.

She got his machine. *At the beep, please leave a message.*

"Sheriff Rosa? This is Warden Cavanaugh. Kelli Cavanaugh. I'm responding to a call about some suspicious activity at 30687 Strider Drive, on Corralitos Creek. The location is close to that abandoned meth lab we found last Fall, where the little girl went missing. Something feels wrong out here today, Charlie. Requesting backup."

The cell phone cut out.

Reception dead zone this far up the mountain. Surprising I got any reception at all.

As she drove, she continued watching the creek meander from one side of the road to the other.

Kelli slowed when she spotted her destination.

Meth House. The warning blinked like a neon sign inside her mind as she cruised by the lot filled with rusted-out, wheel-less cars and trucks, broken glass, tangles of barbed wire, overturned metal barrels, discarded decomposing mattresses, a couch with popping springs, and eroding piles of trash. A loosely nailed-together shack stood falling apart at the waterside.

Kelli parked and locked her truck in a narrow pullout a few feet beyond the driveway, then walked back down the road. She hesitated a moment in front of a "No Trespassing" sign nailed to a redwood tree at the head of the dirt driveway, then stepped onto the property.

Broken glass crunched under her boots. The area felt deserted ... almost. She shivered in the sun.

Nauseatingly strong, bitter ammonia-like fumes burned her eyes and nostrils. Her vision blurred as she teared up and stifled a cough. She pulled a kerchief out of her back pocket and held it over her nose and mouth.

At the end of the drive, Kelli unsnapped her holster, placed her hand on her gun's grip, and cautiously approached a black van parked next to a metal shed.

Motor off. Hood cold. Empty.

The door to the shed slumped open. Inside, wire cages — the kind used to transport large dogs — were stacked to the ceiling against one wall. Marijuana plants hanging upside down to dry filled the rest of the shed. The large outer leaves of the plants had been trimmed away, leaving small bright green serrated leaves and two-foot long resinous flowering colas, as thick as a man's arm.

Prime sensimilla. Probably more than ten thousand dollars' worth. The shed reeked with the skunky smell of drying pot.

Kelli pulled a small digital camera out of her shirt pocket, and took pictures of the cages and marijuana.

She walked around back of the shed, disturbing a swarm of black flies and wasps. The sickly-sweet smell of blood made her gag. Hanging from a tree were two freshly butchered deer carcasses, blood dripping on the dirt.

Poaching. Deer hunting season is six months away.

Flies settled back down on a pile of eviscerated deer organs next to an illegal fire pit. Kelli took photos of the mess.

At the very least, on top of drug charges, these poachers are going to get hit with a $1,000 misdemeanor citation, plus penalty assessments and six-month's jail time, not to mention restriction of their hunting privileges for up to three years.

When she reached the stream bank, she photographed the illicit dam, the pump, and the discharge pipe, the empty cans, flasks, plastic tubing, and cooking vessels.

Just what I expected: meth kitchen. They cooked here, and dumped their waste in the creek. So toxic! It'll probably cost more than $150,000 to clean this HAZMAT site. Gross disregard. Idiots.

Kelli inspected the area for signs of red phosphorous. *One sniff of that stuff can kill you.*

Clear.

But wait. There's something … sweet, pungent odor … eyes tearing up … ethyl ether? Careful.

Hand on Glock, Kelli circled back up to the shed, sensing she might not be alone.

What's going on here?

Well-educated chemists sometimes manufacture meth, but no — their lab would be clean, not filthy like this.

Kelli cautiously approached the dilapidated shed, careful not to trip as she stepped around some empty spray paint cans. She squinted at the tags, her face so close to the old metal siding, she could smell the rust.

Not Hell's Angels.

She turned her head sideways, puzzling out the calligraphy.

MS-13!

Kelli's pulse spiked; her mouth went dry. *Since when have the Mara Salvatrucha been banging in California?*

Stealthily, she side-stepped to the open shed door and peered in. *Okay, I understand the sensimilla, but what are these cages about?*

Hair standing up on the back of her neck, she held still, barely breathing, and listened.

Water running in the creek, nattering squirrel, squawk of a Steller's jay. Normal sounds. No one around?

Kelli returned to the creek, and knelt to get a better look.

Even worse than I feared.

Grieving over the staggering loss, she leaned over the water to take close-up shots of dead salmon smolts and fingerlings floating on the surface.

Red flare. Head exploding!
Pain!
White light
Black tunnel closing in

78

MONDAY, MAY 2, 1999
Corralitos Creek, Santa Cruz Mountains
Byrd River Watershed, South Santa Cruz County

K elli came to with a stabbing headache, curled in a fetal position on a hard, cold surface. She blinked to make sure her eyes were open. Pitch black. She lifted a hand to her face. No blindfold. But she couldn't see her hand.

Am I actually blind, or just in a completely dark space?

When she moved, even slightly, it hurt everywhere.

The smell of stagnation overwhelmed her. She gagged and wretched. Stinging bile burned her throat.

Need water.

She worked some moisture into her mouth with her tongue, spit, and then swallowed.

Little by little, she moved her arms and legs.

Pain on top of pain.

Another wave of nausea.

As she moved, she realized that she was wet where her clothes touched the ground.

Blood?

Painfully sitting up, she explored her body for lacerations. *No wounds.*

A sticky stream of something ran down the left side of her face. The crown of her head was wet. She winced, then sniffed the sticky liquid on her fingertips.

Blood.

Head wound. How bad?

Dizzy. Concussion? Need to stay awake.

The blood on my face is drying, flaking. From the head wound, then — no cuts on my face.

This liquid on the ground — not my blood?

She touched the liquid beneath her, rubbed her fingers together, smelled it. *Something slimy and foul.*

Where am I? She listened hard for several minutes.

A slow water drip. Another sound. Faint. Like a child's whimper.

Painstakingly, she got onto her hands and knees.

Concrete floor. Knees hurt. Head spinning.

Carefully, she stood, rolling up through her spine. Before she could completely straighten, her shoulders hit the ceiling.

Panic and claustrophobia welled up. She took a slow, deep breath and forced herself to stay calm.

Head and shoulders bent, she lifted her arms and felt overhead. The ceiling arched. Her fingers ran into a fuzzy sticky mass.

Spider web.

She took two steps to the right and bumped against a wall. Then four steps to the left and she touched the other wall. The walls seemed to reach forward and back for a considerable distance.

A tunnel? Should I start walking? Which direction?

Suddenly, she remembered her service belt, and her hands flew to her hips. *The belt, with all my equipment.*

Gone!

*　　　*　　　*

BAKER RANCH, VALLE VERDE

Billy poured a hefty glug of Jack Daniel's into his morning coffee. He sat down heavily on his chair, and slammed the mug down hard enough that coffee splashed onto the kitchen table.

Sitting across the table from Billy, his father didn't look up from his bowl of oatmeal. He ate another spoonful, then turned a page of the business section of the San Francisco Chronicle.

Malone's diamond flashed in the morning sun streaming through the kitchen window. She poured herself freshly squeezed orange juice from a blue glass pitcher and joined her men at the breakfast table. She could feel the tension sparking between them. The maid brought her a poached egg and toast.

"It's time to sell, Dad. Everyone says this is the best time in history to sell off our land. If we convert from agriculture to developed property, we'll make millions overnight. The developers are licking their chops. If we try to keep it in strawberries, how're you going to get that mud off the fields? It's dried up hard as cement, at least four or five feet thick. It'll probably cost a fortune to disk through that crust. Besides, on top of the flood damage, some of our wells are pumping saltwater, for Christ's sake. At this rate, saltwater intrusion is only going to get worse. Especially now, since the good people of Valle Verde didn't vote to build a new aqueduct to tie us into the state water project. Now the fuckin' government regulators are putting meters on our wells. It's time to get out of ag, Dad. Time to sell."

William Baker Senior folded his newspaper methodically and put it down on the corner of the table. He took off his reading glasses and scrutinized his son.

"I've told you, Billy. We're not letting developers have this land. We own some of the most fertile agricultural land in the world. That deep black alluvial clay loam out there is the richest soil anywhere. This land is our heritage, Son. It would be a crime to pave over it. A crime against our family, and against humanity. The world needs food, and food comes from the soil."

"But Dad, I—"

"If you're worried about water, think about it, boy. If we let them cover up our soil with parking lots, shopping malls, and streets, the aquifer will be even less able to recharge. All our winter rainwater will just run straight into the bay, instead of soaking into the ground like it's supposed to. I'm a farmer, Billy, like my father and my grandfather. Weather, floods … it all comes with the territory. It's the farmer's way of life. We'll deal with the flood situation, the mud on the field, and the rest of it, just like farmers do — like we always have. We're not selling our land to developers."

"Look at this, would you!" Malone held up the front page of the Valle Verde Register and pointed to an article about the flood.

"Listen to this." Malone poked her red fingernail at the face in the news photo. "It says that this man, Ron Khurie, is a professor of hydrology and water resource engineering at the university. Listen to what he says. 'Floods are a natural process. They help to maintain a healthy river channel by scouring out woody debris and regulating sediment flow. The city should not have removed the trees along the Byrd River. Maintaining riparian vegetation along a stream channel promotes a healthy river system and mediates the effects of flood events. The historical flooding and deposition of sediments in the Byrd and Salinas River valleys, as in river valleys around the world, is what bestows upon these areas their highly fertile soils.'"

"Sounds to me like the guy's a quack," said Billy, pouring another shot of Jack into his coffee. "He doesn't know what he's talking about."

"Oh, don't we know that!" said Malone. "If the city had kept that river channel clear of weeds and willows, we wouldn't have a field full of dried clay this morning. I'm going to phone this Professor Khurie and ask him to come down here to see for himself. Then let him try to claim that flood was good for the farm fields. I want this man to publicly retract these statements. Now that we've got the governor cooperating with us, and the county finally doing something about cleaning that river, I don't want anyone having second thoughts."

"Gotta go, Mom."

Malone studied her son. He was walking straight, in spite of the liquor he'd been pouring into his morning coffee. His clothes were clean and neat, even if his hair was a bit too long and tousled. Her handsome boy.

"Billy, there's going to be a Charity League ball next month, and all the most eligible young women in the Monterey Bay area will be there. Can I make you a reservation?"

"Sure, Mom. Let's talk about it later. The Mexican's waiting for me."

"Hold on a minute, Son," said William. "There was some spillage down in the corporation yard during the storm. About ten barrels of herbicide got knocked over and leaked. That stuff needs to be cleaned up and trucked over to the haz waste disposal site, or we'll be cited. Take care of that as soon as you can."

"Sure, Dad." Billy let the screen door slam as he departed.

Outside, Yudas Medina stood, cowboy hat in hand, waiting by Billy's shiny new black Porsche.

*　　*　　*

Billy's tires squealed as he sped down the winding drive. "Fuck!" He hit the steering wheel with the heel of his hand. "My father's such a fuckin' asshole. What a fool."

Yudas stared at Billy, wondering if there would be an explanation. Billy drove on in silence, speeding to the monthly CalGreen meeting. The Baker's ranch foreman felt like he had ants crawling under his skin.

"Billy, that priest saw us the night of the flood. He saw what we did, breaching the levee, flooding the barrio."

"I've been thinking about that too. But hey, no worries. What the hell can he do? He can't prove a thing."

"What if he tells someone?" Yudas' hand shook as he lit a cigarette. "A person died in that flood. Maybe they will blame us for the death. We could go to prison. My family ..."

"Don't worry about it, ameeego. They can't touch us. I've got your back."

*　　*　　*

CORRALITOS CREEK, SANTA CRUZ MOUNTAINS

Kelli moaned and rolled onto her side. She opened her eyes, sat up and held her hand in front of her face.

Still too dark to see. Or am I blind?

Her heart raced. She focused on her breathing. Her senses woke to the cold stench in the air, and the wet.

Must have passed out again. Did someone hit me, again?

She closed her eyes and tried to recall her last conscious thoughts.

No. No one's been here. I just passed out.

Still feeling a little dizzy, she inched her way over to the wall and leaned back.

Why didn't the attacker just kill me?

With a start, it occurred to her she may have been raped. She felt at her shirt, her pants.

Clothes intact, except for this tear on my shoulder. They ripped my radio mic off my shirt.

No pain down there.

She had to pee. Cautiously, she stood. Head and shoulders bent under the low ceiling, she braced her hand against the wall, listening intently. The sound of her own breathing rasped loud inside her head.

Something else. Water dripping.

She held her breath and listened for a long moment. *Not another sound.*

She had to go, bad. She unfastened her belt, unsnapped and unzipped her pants, pulled down her trousers and panties, squatted, and pissed a long, warm stream. With relief, she noted that it didn't sting.

No one touched me. Thank God for that.

She shook herself dry as best she could and pulled her pants back up.

How long have I been here?

Gingerly she explored her head wound. *Blood still sticky. Hair matted and stiff.*

She remembered her camera and searched her pockets. *Gone. Must have dropped it when I was hit.*

She tried to swallow, but couldn't. The thirst was suffocating. A jolt of fear ran through her. She had to find drinking water, soon. She had to find a way out.

I have to move, or I'll die down here.

Which direction?

She took a small step into the blackness, toward the hollow sound of dripping water. Then another step.

Step again.

Suddenly, the ground fell out from under her.

*   *   *

Kelli tumbled into the darkness, banging, clattering, and pounding against metal. By sheer instinct, her hands grasped for a hold.

She gripped a metal bar with both hands, her feet swinging in nothingness.

She dangled over a void. Her arms ached. She struggled to keep her fingers wrapped tightly around the bar.

Stretching out one finger, she touched concrete.

This bar seems to be solidly pinned into concrete.

She swung, and her feet hit a dirt wall.

Below this bar, then, the wall is dirt, not concrete.

She kicked against it. Chunks of dirt and rock dislodged and fell. The sound cascaded down a very long way before tinkling, pinging, splashing into water.

Kelli swung like a kid on playground bars, and kicked against the wall again. And again, swinging higher. She got purchase. Her feet wedged and took a little pressure off her arms. She knew she didn't have much time before her arms and hands gave out and she dropped like that slide of dirt.

Taking a deep breath, she swung her feet up over her head with everything she had.

She caught the bar with one heel. Holding on for dear life, she worked her foot over the bar until she had one knee hooked around it.

Then, like a contortionist, she worked her other leg up and over the bar. Hanging upside down by hands and knees, she rested and caught her breath.

Blood rushed to her head. A wave of nausea and dizziness swept over her.

Head spinning. Don't black out.

She fought to stay conscious.

Breathe. Hold on.

Water drops echoed inside the cave of her skull.

There's another sound.

79

M ORNING RECESS. Katie sat on a student desk in Aurora's
classroom.

"Fake?" Katie's forehead wrinkled. "The school district colluded
with CalGreen to fake that fumigation so they could discredit us? Are
you sure?"

"The groundsman who told me about it seemed sincere," said
Aurora. "He had no reason to lie."

"There's something I need to tell you too, Aurora. The School
Board met, and has officially determined they will not be renewing my
contract. They fired me."

"No! You're fighting this, right? Is the union backing you up?"

"I had union representation when I went in to talk to Deana. Tom
Olson was with me. But he wasn't much help. The fight's gone out of
him since the district filed that lawsuit. But even if Tom had been a
hundred percent, there's really nothing the union could have done for

513

me. I'm untenured. The district can legally fire me with no explanation and no cause. Officially, I was given ten weeks to improve my so-called teaching performance, but Deana refused to give me any specific information about the problems she sees with my teaching."

"That's because the problem isn't with your teaching; we both know that." Aurora's eyes welled with angry tears. "I'm so, so sorry! What will you do? And what will we do without you?"

"You don't need me. I was just a catalyst. And don't worry about me. I'll be alright. When my husband finishes his B.S. this June, we're moving to Oregon. It's much more affordable there. He's got a great job offer and we're thinking it might be time for us to start our family. Honestly, I'm looking forward to leaving this place."

"You'll be missed. Let's be sure to stay in touch."

"Yep. Meanwhile, we should do something about this fake fumigation thing, don't you think?"

"What do you suggest?"

"First, we need to verify it. Leave it to me. I certainly don't have anything else to lose," said Katie. "I'm going to the ag commissioner's office to request the fumigation records for that date."

"But if they did actually fake the fumigation, they might have faked the records too."

"I'm going to get the truth, no matter what it takes."

*   *   *

CORRALITOS CREEK, SANTA CRUZ MOUNTAINS

The wave of vertigo subsided.

That sound again, like a child crying.

Carefully, she shifted the tension in her muscles from her hands to her legs. She pried one hand, slick with sweat, off the metal bar and wiped it on her clothes. Switching, she wiped the other hand dry, then tightened her grip on the bar with both hands.

For a split second, she imagined herself as a bat hanging upside down in a cave. She almost giggled. Just then, a beam of light flashed on the ceiling overhead.

Light! I'm not blind!
Flashlight beams cut across the cement walls and ceiling.
Men's voices. Someone walking down the tunnel toward me.
Kelli's blood turned to ice.
Sounds like they're about ten feet away.
The echoing footfalls stopped.

"Where the fuck is she? Wha'd you do with her, shithead?" The high-pitched whiney voice made Kelli's skin crawl.

Flashlight beams crisscrossed above Kelli's upside-down perch.

"We brought her down here like you said, *patrón*. She was still knocked out when we left her. I put her right over there myself." *English speaker with a Mexican accent.*

"Did you touch her?"

"No one fucked her, *patrón*, I swear. No one touched her. We left her down here just like you said." *A second Mexican accent.*

"You stupid bastards." *The one called patrón again. No accent, so a native English speaker, but with that weird high-pitched whine.* "A fuckin' game warden. She would've just gone away if you hadn't of whacked her. Now we've got a balled-up mess here."

"*Pardón, Señor,* but you said your *cliente rico* wanted a white woman to go with the *niña blanca*." *A different voice, speaking Spanish.*

"White woman, yeah. But a game warden is like a fuckin' cop. You don't kidnap a cop, you stupid son-of-a-bitch."

"I'm sorry, *Señor*." *The Spanish speaker, again.* "She must of come to and found the way out."

"In the dark, she could've gone that way and fallen over the edge." *Speaking English, with a different accent. Salvadoran?*

"If she did, all our troubles are over." *Spanish speaker.*

Men's laughter.

"If she found the way out, she couldn't of gotten far." *A second Salvadoran.*

"Let's go. We've gotta find that bitch." *Whiney voice again.* "She's gonna have to disappear, for good."

Kelli listened to the echoing footfalls recede.

What incredible luck they didn't shine their flashlight down on me!
She shivered.

Six voices. If I'd gone the other way along the tunnel, I would have run straight into those men.

She dried her sweaty hands on her shirt again, one at time, and counted seconds. Then minutes.

Muscles convulsing. Can't hold on much longer.

A sudden squeal, and a nearby scuffle. *Rats!*

Move! Go for it. Now or never.

Clinging to the metal bar with hands and knees, she tightened her abs, putting everything she had into a crunching sit-up. Straining, she curled her head to her knees. At the same time, fighting dizziness, she let go of the bar with one hand and reached up, slightly touching with her fingertips the next bar she'd gambled would be there. Trembling, she stretched, elongating her torso as much as she could, inching her fingers around the bar. A cramp stabbed her side.

Ignore it. Push through the pain.

Grasping the bar with one hand so hard it hurt, she lunged.

Once she was holding on to the higher bar with both hands and sitting on the lower bar, she carefully worked her right heel up under herself. She wiggled it until her whole foot wedged onto the metal, then shifted all her weight onto that foot, and painfully straightened her knee. Leg muscles cramping and spasming, she pulled up with her hands and pushed with her right leg until she could place her left foot on the bar.

Pieces of dried mud from the soles of her boots broke loose and clattered into the water below. It sounded like a long way down.

Kelli took a deep breath and stabilized herself. She was standing on a vertical ladder made of rebar rods cemented into the side of the drop. Her hands firmly grasped the rung above her feet. From here, it was practically a cakewalk to climb back up to the ledge she'd fallen from.

Thankful for the hours spent lifting weights, rock climbing, and rowing on the bay, Kelli pulled herself up over the ledge and rolled onto the wet cement of the tunnel floor. Lying on her back, she caught her breath, and listened. *Water dripping.*

That other faint sound again, like a child crying. It stopped. Water dripped in black silence.

Something poked her in the hip. She unzipped her back pocket. *The mag light!*

Kelli stood and switched on the flashlight. She swept its strong beam around the concrete tunnel. She'd seen places like this before. A World War II bunker. After the attack on Pearl Harbor, the U.S. government, convinced that Japan was going to bomb California, built underground bunkers in the mountains all over the West Coast. This had to be one of those old military installations.

From where Kelli stood, the cement floor sloped gradually upward, a slimy green trickle running down its center. She started walking.

*   *   *

When Santa Cruz County Sheriff's Detective Sargent Charlie Rosa got the alert, it hadn't taken him long to assemble a tactical team to assist. He wasn't going to let those two tattooed Salvatrucha demons slip through his fingers again.

Another child gone missing. This time it was the five-year-old daughter of a Corralitos apple rancher. He had a pretty good idea what would happen to this child if they didn't find her soon.

While Deputy Jim Jamison drove the curving road along the creek, Detective Rosa, riding shotgun, studied this new missing child's photo again. Blonde curls framed an innocent, cherub-like face. He put the photograph back in the file.

"We're not going to lose this one, Jim."

The young deputy nodded grimly, and checked his rearview mirror. Two vans followed, carrying the tactical SWAT team and dogs.

"I hope Warden Cavanaugh doesn't scare them off, Sir," the deputy said.

"Cavanaugh's a competent law enforcement officer. She knows how to handle herself. But I doubt she has any idea what she's walking into. Hell, we don't even know if our perps are really there, or what else is going on."

"So yeah, Warden Cavanaugh's definitely an extra wild card in play?"

"Yes. I just wish I'd gotten her cell phone message earlier," said Detective Rosa. "I'm not used to these damn things. Didn't think about checking for messages until after we got the missing child alert from dispatch."

"Can't beat yourself up about it, Sir. That's what you always tell me."

Detective Rosa drummed his fingers on the case file in his lap. "Judging from the time of Cavanaugh's call, she must have reached the suspects' hidey-hole hours ago."

"Anything could have happened by now."

"Right. Worst case, everyone's gone, and they took Cavanaugh with them — or left her for dead."

"I sure hope we get there in time. From what I understand about the way these Mara Salvatruchas work, Sir, if they've killed her, she won't be in one piece when we find her."

✳   ✳   ✳

Crying.

The sound grew louder as Kelli cautiously made her way up the tunnel. She kept her flashlight off and edged along the wall.

Her hand touched cold metal. *Feels like prison bars. The crying is coming from inside. Is there a guard?*

Kelli froze, and listened. All her senses strained to detect breathing, any kind of pulse or motion, other than the sound of crying.

Can't be a hundred percent sure.

Tucking into a defensive position, she flicked on her light and swept the area. No goons.

Inside the cell, a child, hardly more than a toddler, lay curled up on a cot. She hugged a teddy bear and stared into Kelli's light with huge eyes. Tears streaked and blotched her chubby cheeks. She had a snotty nose. Otherwise, the child appeared unharmed.

Kelli moved the light out of the child's eyes and shined it on herself. She put a finger up to her lips.

"Shusssssh. My name is Kelli. I'm going to get you out of here, sweetie. I'm going to take you home to your mommy. You just need

518

to wait here a little bit longer. Don't be scared. Stay quiet. I'll be right back."

The child hugged her teddy bear tighter, but said nothing. Kelli turned off the flashlight and moved away, up the tunnel.

In the dark, she could feel the slope getting steeper. The ceiling was higher here. After a few minutes, the toe of her boot hit a ledge. Carefully, she stepped back and merged with the wall. *Listen.*

Silence.

Ahead, she could see a thin rectangle of light. *A door, with daylight seeping around the edges?*

Kelli clicked on her flashlight. Concrete stairs led up to a doorway. Her toe had kicked the bottom step.

Heart racing, she hurried up the stairs.

She stood in front of an old heavy metal door, with a vertical bar handle. *What if they locked it? What if a guard is posted right outside?* Panic rose in her throat. She took a calming breath.

Piercing squeal!

A rat scuttled over her foot.

Her body jerked. She pushed on the door.

It swung open easily. Crouching just inside the bunker, she blinked, momentarily blinded by bright afternoon sun.

Her vision quickly cleared, and she did a visual check of the area. Shoe tracks in the dirt led down toward the creek.

Something rattled in the brush.

She held her breath.

Swainson's Thrush.

Kelli smiled to herself and continued to scan her surroundings.

Built into the side of a hill near the top of the driveway, the bunker was well camouflaged. If you weren't looking for it, you'd never notice it.

Quietly, Kelli closed the heavy door behind her.

Voices. Down by the creek.

Kelli reached for the Glock at her hip, and remembered it was gone.

She tucked and ran out of the driveway. Her truck was still there!

Grabbing the hide-a-key from under the back bumper, she threw open the door and released her shotgun from the rack.

The short barrel 12-gauge pump action, when loaded with double-aught buckshot, kicked back hard against her hundred and fifteen pounds, so she didn't fire it unless she had to.

Now, without hesitation, she loaded the weapon. Cradling it in the crook of her arm, staying close to the dense huckleberry and Manzanita brush that lined the drive, she hustled back toward the voices.

Shouting!

A scream. Then another.

Men screaming!

Horrifying, savage sounds filled the woods!

A growling roar like a hurricane, like thunder.

A roar like an avalanche.

Shouts and screams of primal animal terror, like nothing she'd ever heard before, shook the trees.

80

MONDAY, MAY 2, 1999
Corralitos Creek, Santa Cruz Mountains

S HOULDERING HER SHOTGUN, Kelli stalked toward the uproar.
As she moved through the woods, fog swirled, rapidly engulfing the trees like a rising tide.

Sweet, pungent ethyl ether fumes floated on the fog, stinging her eyes.

If I do have to discharge my weapon, I'll probably blow the whole camp, myself included.

Chilling tentacles of fog wrapped around saplings, vines, fallen logs, and Kelli. The fog quickly grew so thick that everything around her took on an otherworldly quality.

Just as she stepped to the edge of the clearing, a human head went flying by her. Blood from the ragged severed neck sprayed her face and clothes.

A deafening roar shook her to the core.

She crouched behind a tree and peered into the clearing.

Standing on his hind legs, mist swirling around him, loomed the most enormous grizzly bear Kelli had ever seen. Blood clotted his shaggy fur and muzzle. A cord of intestine dangled from his mouth. Behind the monstrous behemoth, one of the deer carcasses lay on the ground, partially eaten.

In front of the grizzly, the torso of a man splayed out, its head and both arms missing. One leg had landed some distance away; the other twisted behind the torso at an impossible angle. The beast had opened the man's gut with sharp, powerful claws and had scooped out a mass of intestines. The stench of the grizzly overwhelmed the smell of blood and spilled bowels.

With the heightened perception that comes from shock, Kelli studied a disembodied arm near her feet, its dead skin decorated with tattoos of spiders, skeletons, and skulls. A broken rifle lay in the redwood duff nearby.

Other bodies bled out in the dirt.

Kelli tried to sort out which ones belonged to the voices she'd heard in the tunnel. Two corpses were eviscerated, dismembered and decapitated. One body still had a head, but was missing an arm and part of a leg. The dead men's blood pooled and mingled with the drying blood of the hanging deer. Among the broken weapons scattered near the bodies, Kelli recognized her own Glock.

Another blood-curdling scream.

Settling the butt of her shotgun snugly against her shoulder Kelli clicked off the safety and, sighting down the barrel, took aim.

The grizzly, on his hind feet, stood at least fifteen feet tall. He held a tattooed man in his front paws. The man was bleeding profusely. One tattooed arm dangled from a torn shoulder by tendons. The beast roared again, an inch from the man's face.

Kelli could feel the wind of the monster's breath. The trees around her shook.

Through thick, dreamlike fog, the scene unfolded in slow motion. The grizzly opened his mouth wide, exposing huge, carnivorous teeth and a vivid red tongue.

The bear roared again, shaking the ground.

Kelli felt the man's screams inside her own body. His face contorted in a mask of such horror it didn't look human.

As if viewing the strobing frames of an old-time picture show, Kelli watched the bear's mouth envelope the tattooed man's entire face. Muffled screams. Crunch of bone and tendon. Spurt of bright red blood.

The bear's jaw pulled away with a juicy sucking sound, taking the man's whole face with it.

The grizzly released the limp body from his claws. The body dropped to the ground in a heap of blue ink and crimson blood.

Roaring again, the behemoth turned around. He sniffed the air, then looked straight at Warden Cavanaugh. His eyes shone with an ancient, eerie intelligence.

Suddenly, he turned his shaggy back on the game warden and, with one swipe of his great paw, knocked the second deer carcass to the ground. Dropping on all fours, the grizzly seized the deer meat in his mouth and disappeared into the mist-shrouded forest.

Kelli stood as if turned to stone for what seemed like an eternity.

Gradually, she became aware of sirens, of men shouting, lights flashing and dogs barking. She clicked the safety back on her shotgun and lowered it to the ground. Then she vomited, trembling uncontrollably.

∗   ∗   ∗

The SWAT team swarmed the area.

"Over here, Captain!"

"Jesus Christ! This one's still alive."

"Get a medic over here. Don't let him bleed out. Keep him breathing. We've gotta find out what he knows."

"Alert Medivac. They're standing by. We need to get him to the hospital fast! Hurry!"

"The dogs are going nuts! What the hell was that? Did you see it?"

"Hold the dogs! Don't let them go after that thing."

"Don't fire your weapons, for God's sake, or we'll have an explosion!"

"Find the girl. Search the premises."

"Kelli! Warden Cavanaugh! Are you hurt? Talk to me. Kelli!"

The smell of blood was so overwhelming, Kelli felt as if she were drowning in it. She threw up again. A strong arm held her shoulders.

Someone gently wiped her face with a cool damp cloth. It smelled like fresh laundry.

"It's not her blood, Sergeant Rosa. No cuts on the face or neck. She appears to be uninjured, just in shock. Oh, wait. There's a nasty wound on the top of her head. It's stopped bleeding, though."

Someone held a water bottle up to her mouth. She took the bottle and, with help, filled her mouth with cold fresh water. She swirled it and spit blood. Blood that had sprayed her from the severed head.

Don't look at it.

Again, and again, she swished fresh, clean water, gargled, spit. Finally, she drank.

She met Detective Rosa's eyes.

"Charlie, I know where the little girl is. I can show you."

✳ ✳ ✳

The child was rescued from her cell and taken down the mountain to her parents.

The Medivac helicopter stirred the treetops as it sped away, carrying the lone survivor of the mauling, unconscious and barely holding on to life, minus an arm and leg.

The fog cleared.

The team secured the area. They photographed body parts from various angles, and made plaster casts of tracks. With professional precision, they collected fingerprints and DNA samples from the wire dog cages and the van, and scoured the grounds for other evidence.

Once the forensics team had completed their work, and the human remains had been bagged and removed, the county HAZMAT team would begin cleaning up the meth kitchen and restoring the creek habitat. Back at the crime lab, they were going to have a hell of a job putting all the pieces together again.

*   *   *

Kelli sat in her truck with Detective Rosa. He'd finished taking her formal statement.

"We won't be getting a statement out of our two tattooed shooting suspects now," said Charlie. "But I think a forensics investigation of their remains will prove we found our perps for the Salvador Luna murder. We don't have to worry about those killers getting the justice they deserve."

Kelli squeezed an emergency cold pack to activate it, and held it to her forehead. "With any luck that scum bag who's still alive will hang on long enough to fill us in on all the other abductions."

"Sorry, Kelli, but sex traffic is a black hole. Those other kids could be anywhere in the world by now, if they're still alive — which is unlikely. At least we saved one child today, thanks to you."

"Plus we cleared out a nest of vermin," said Kelli.

"Think we've accounted for all the voices you heard in the bunker? Did we just cut the whole cancer out?"

Kelli closed her eyes. "There were six men. Two were Salvadorans."

"Salvadorans? You sure?"

"Distinctive accent. Those tatted Salvadorans are definitely dead. Yes. It seems like there's a body to go with each of the other voices I heard, except ... Wait. One's missing. I think the one they called *patrón*, with a whiney voice." Kelli opened her eyes and stared into the forest. "Earlier, during all the screaming, I thought I saw a white man in a striped suit running into the woods."

"None of the bodies we found were dressed in a suit."

Kelli moved the cold pack to the back of her neck. "I think we'll find human tracks leading away from camp, running in the opposite direction from that — that beast. Maybe *patrón* got away."

"And the 'beast'? What the hell was that thing?" Detective Sargent Rosa's eyebrows pulled together. "Did you get a good look at it?"

"I've been trying to make sense of what I saw, Charlie. I was close enough to see everything. Too close. But what I think I saw just doesn't compute."

"It was a bear, right?"

"It was the biggest bear I've ever seen."

"But ... we don't have bears here in the Santa Cruz Mountains. Do we?"

"As a matter of fact, although sightings are still rare, the core population of black bears in the state has been expanding over the last few years. Most of them are in the High Sierra, but we know there are also a few in the Southern Coast Mountain Range. They've been moving into habitat that, a hundred years ago, was grizzly territory. To date, I haven't heard of any bears as far north as the Santa Cruz Mountains, but, of course, anything is possible."

"So, it really could have been a bear, then."

"Well, yes, and no." Kelli's forehead furrowed. "If a black bear had made its way into this area, it certainly would have been drawn to the camp by the scent of those deer carcasses. But Charlie, that was no black bear."

"What do you mean?"

"What I saw ..." Kelli answered, "The bear I think I saw was, well ... It had that characteristic hump on its back. Charlie, that beast definitely looked like a California grizzly. But it was far larger than any other grizzly I've ever heard of, except for maybe Monarch."

"Monarch?"

"The mythical 'Big Bear of Tallac' — the captive grizzly whose picture is on the California Republic flag."

Sargent Rosa shook his head.

"California grizzlies were systematically extirpated in the nineteenth century. William Randolph Hearst hired a journalist, Allen Kelley, to capture one of the last known wild grizzlies in the 1880s, as a publicity stunt. Kelley caught the famous Monarch bear on Samhain, Halloween of 1889, and brought him to San Francisco. They kept Monarch on exhibit at Woodwards Gardens, and he lived in captivity for twenty-two years. Then, one day, he just vanished. Without a trace. It's said he embodies the heart, soul, and spirit of California."

"So then you're saying the monster that mauled our suspects was a California grizzly?"

"Well ... what I'm saying is: it looked like a grizzly. But ... our beast couldn't possibly have been a grizzly bear, Charlie."

"Why's that?"

"The last California grizzly was shot and killed in Tulare County, near what is now Sequoia National Park, in the summer of 1924. *Ursus arctos californicus* has been extinct for nearly a hundred years."

81

CalGreen Headquarters, Hollister, California
Byrd River Watershed, San Benito County

S EAN STARK PUT DOWN THE PHONE. He stroked his goatee. Good
news. They had their federal exemption allowing them to continue
methyl bromide fumigations for another year. And it hadn't cost as
much as he'd anticipated. A couple of million in well-placed political
donations, and a little favor to an influential man.

He buzzed his secretary and told her to get Billy Baker on the phone.

Though annoying, Baker was a useful tool. Offering the greedy
dimwit stock options in CalGreen had been a smart move. Over his head
in day trading, Baker had been easily hooked. Now he was completely
dependent on the success of his CalGreen options to survive.

Those little favors Baker had arranged for CalGreen's business
associates over these last years had the pitiful son of a bitch so enmeshed
in complicity, he'd never get free. Billy Baker was Stark's boy.

Stark thumbed the point of an ornate silver letter opener on his
desk. A drop of blood shimmered on the tip.

He smeared the blood across his appointment calendar. Golf at Pebble next weekend. Soon, he'd be getting away from the wife and her drinking problem. Between the clean, white sheets of The Grove, he'd be plowing the slick little cunt of Shibu Yayoi, Arita Chemical's rising star.

Flying her over from Japan for a few days was her reward for coming up with that gem of a methyl bromide alternative, methyl iodide. Arita's research facility had found methyl iodide to be a potent biocide in experimental trials inducing cancer in lab rats. It should do just fine as a pesticide. Shibu was a good little chemist. She'd given him exactly what he needed. This year, they had their methyl bromide exemption. But there would come a time. And thanks to Ms. Yayoi, CalGreen would be ready to roll out an alternative when needed.

Stark's secretary buzzed. "Mr. Baker on the line."

"Put him through." Stark picked up the phone.

"Good news, Baker. Our exemption is just about in the bag for another year. It all depends on you, my man. Our — eh — sponsor just requires a little favor, to sweeten the deal. That's alright. No. Just give him the mother of the little one you arranged for our deceased sailor friend. Your, ah — associates still have her, right? He wants to pick up the merchandise out on West Beach Road by the railroad tracks, behind the abandoned frozen food plant. Call me when you've made the arrangements."

*   *   *

LOWER BAKER RANCH PROPERTY
BYRD RIVER LEVEE
BYRD RIVER WATERSHED, VALLE VERDE
SOUTH SANTA CRUZ COUNTY

"So, now that you're here, Ron, isn't it obvious that the county should have kept the channel clear?" Malone's diamond ring sparked as she raised her hand to condemn the river. "Do you see these trees and bushes growing right in the middle? No wonder all that mud overtopped the levee and flooded our fields."

Professor Ron Khurie glanced sideways at the woman walking the levee next to him. Malone's eyes flashed in the sunlight, and those red fingernails made her look predatory. He knew the type. Pushy blonde. Cunning. The kind that always gets what she wants, one way or another.

He stopped to consider the river, then turned toward the Bakers' strawberry field, covered in more than three feet of hard-caked clay. He was going to do a soil test for her, but he didn't need to see the results to know that this mud was full of toxins, pesticides, petrochemicals, and coagulants that were bad news for the environment and for farmland. The stuff shouldn't be disked in. They'd need heavy equipment to crack it up, and then it should be taken to a hazmat waste disposal site.

"Listen, Ron." Malone batted her heavily mascaraed eyelashes and put her red-tipped fingers on his sleeve. "I'm as much a nature lover as anyone else, but this river has caused our community too much harm. Our workers are suffering. We have to clean this river, now. And in the future, the county needs to do its due diligence to maintain this channel. They've agreed to use regular applications of aquatic WeedRangler to keep the channel clean. Now that you're here, surely you can see that your statements in the paper about flooding being good for farm fields were wrong. Those statements hurt us, Ron. The Byrd is a flood control channel. It needs to be properly maintained."

"At this point in time, you're correct in calling it a flood control channel, Mrs. Baker. But that's only part of the story. Historically that was not the case. And going forward, the answers about how to most effectively manage the Byrd are complex."

How was he going to explain the intricacies of hydrology and water resource engineering to this woman in a few minutes, out here on the levee? It had taken him a lifetime to begin to understand the mysterious dynamics of watersheds.

"I have to agree with you that the mature willow trees and other vegetation growing in the middle of the channel did greatly reduce the levee's capacity during this recent flood and should be removed."

Malone smiled like the cat that ate the canary.

"But, there's much more to it than that. It helps to know something about the geological and cultural history of the river." The Professor pushed on. He might never get another chance to educate this woman about her land. "This whole area was a *vega* — a natural wetland — in early California history. The Spaniards grazed their cattle here. The river flooded regularly. High flood flows washed fertile sediments down from the mountains, bleeding off and depositing the productive soils out over the *vega*. The Byrd River used to meander, like a living organism. Picture a live snake winding through the valley, connecting all the sloughs."

Professor Khurie was passionate about his subject, but Malone was standing on one foot and then the other and fidgeting with her big diamond ring. Clearly, she found him tedious. The fact that she was hearing him out told him she had an ulterior motive. What did she want?

"At one time," the professor continued, "Byrd River actually flowed through Elkhorn Slough. But the natural wetlands have been diked, filled, levied, pushed, distorted and channelized, until now nature's system of controlling sediment flow, scouring the river's spawning rocks and gravels, maintaining a healthy salmon habitat, and recharging the aquifer no longer functions as it should."

"We certainly agree that the Byrd is not functioning as it should," said Malone. "But go ahead and continue your history lesson, Professor."

"These levees were put in by the army in the 1940s. During the war, it was feared that the Japanese might attack our prime West Coast agricultural area to jeopardize our nation's food security. It was believed that the levees would protect our food production system."

"And we still need to protect our food production system," said Malone. "That hasn't changed. But the levee didn't do its job during this flood. We need to clean the channel so it can function like it's supposed to."

This woman's rage against the river was a childish temper tantrum. She wanted to lash out at the bad river for hurting her strawberries by cutting down its trees. And like dysfunctional parents in knee-jerk reaction, the governor and the city and county officials were giving her what she demanded. Removing trees along the banks

532

of the river was a bad idea, as anyone with even a rudimentary understanding of watersheds understood. But he couldn't alienate this influential woman. He needed to work with her.

"You're right, Mrs. Baker. The flood control project failed this time. But with these 'hundred-year floods' coming more frequently now that climate change is starting to affect California, some in-stream riparian vegetation will be necessary to slow the water coming down the channel, so that it can sink in, and recharge the aquifer. The saltwater intrusion we have here in the valley is the real disaster. We need sustainable watershed management practices that will recharge our aquifer."

"My husband and my son have been talking about the saltwater intrusion. But I don't believe in climate change, and I don't see what all this has to do with cleaning the river."

"Well, again, hydrology is a complex science, Mrs. Baker. But here's the connection: in order to prevent saltwater intrusion, we have to recharge the aquifer, the underground water table, with fresh water. To do that, we need to slow the water flowing downstream during heavy rains. Riparian vegetation does that. My advice for the future is not to clear vegetation. Instead, reduce the sediment load coming from upstream."

"How do we do that?"

"Consider the fact that the Byrd River extends into four counties. The responsibility for overseeing the river as a flood control project lies not just with Santa Cruz and Monterey. We need to have cooperation with the San Benito and Santa Clara County water agencies in the upper reaches of the Byrd. If San Benito hadn't opened the spillway at Chittenden Gap, your fields and the barrio of Pajaro probably would not have flooded. Cooperation and communication need to be improved between the counties. We need to establish a four-county river management board and encourage all stakeholders to participate in the newly-formed Coastal Watershed Council."

Malone took off her sunglasses and turned her gaze upstream. Khurie could hear the gears clicking in the woman's brain, connecting the people she knew who could make a four-county river management board happen.

"San Benito currently operates a sewage treatment facility in the upper Byrd floodplain, and allows a gravel mine to operate right on the banks of the river," Professor Khurie continued. "Those are big problems that need to be corrected if the river is going to function properly. Ideally, land should be set aside on the upstream reaches of the river, along the floodplain, to establish a riparian forest that can reduce the sediment load before it gets washed downstream."

"You really know your hydrology, Professor Khurie. I'd like to hire you to be our consultant, to help us deal with this situation." Malone swept her arm out across her mud-encrusted strawberry fields.

The woman was actually listening to him. He wanted to tell her that strawberries should not be grown here, that it wasn't a sustainable crop for this river valley. That in the face of extended periods of drought predicted by climate scientists, the luxury of enormous, artificially produced, perfect, year-round strawberries was too water-intensive for this depleted aquifer. He wanted to tell her that the Bakers and the other farmers who owned fields along the river should give up strips along its banks, so that the current out-of-date levee could be removed and widened, and the channel restored to a more natural system that would be able to withstand the increasingly severe storms that were inevitable in the near future. And he also wanted to say that the entire barrio of Pajaro should be resettled, because it was insanity to build housing on a floodplain. But he bit his tongue. He'd learned that you couldn't come at a woman like this head on. Had to approach them sideways. By chance, he'd been given a tremendous opportunity here. He would work with her. Little by little, he would try to teach these people how rivers work. Maybe he'd succeed, in the long run.

82

WEDNESDAY, MAY 4, 1999
Corralitos Creek, Santa Cruz Mountains

AURORA CLOSED UP HER CLASSROOM as soon as the last bell rang, and cruised with the top down along winding country roads toward Corralitos Village. It was a glorious day for her annual sojourn to the creek to scope out the site for her upcoming salmon release field trip.

Agricultural fields gave way to apple orchards. At the Corralitos Market, she turned north up Eureka Canyon Mountain Road. In a few minutes, she was driving under a thick redwood forest canopy. The creek meandered through culverts from one side of the road to the other.

A faint inner voice reminded her that she hadn't told anyone where she was going. She recalled seeing gang tags spray-painted on the culvert of her release site last time she'd visited. She pictured a lone woman scrambling down a steep cliff to a deserted stream and poking around in a dark culvert. Her inner lens panned to the woman's mangled body being pulled out of the creek.

I'll definitely take that self-defense class next summer.

When she arrived at the pullout and climbed down to the creek, she was relieved to find Dr. Scott, the hatchery biologist, with a Conservation Corps crew, painting over the gang tags. She spotted Johnny working with other youths from Juvenile Hall, a police monitor on his ankle and a nasty red scar around his neck. He turned his back on her, but she was glad to see he looked well, and was out in the sunshine doing good work under Dr. Scott's excellent supervision.

Aurora and Dr. Scott talked about the progress of her Salmon and Trout Project and made arrangements to meet back at the creek on May 16th for her class's salmon release.

It was five-thirty when Aurora pulled into a parking space in front of the Corralitos Market. She was hungry and looking forward to a couple of smoked cheesy Bavarian sausages on a five-seed bakery bun, with ketchup, pickle relish, mayo and mustard, and sauerkraut on the side. Maybe she'd even have a slice of Gizdich Ranch olallieberry pie. It had become a private tradition for her to treat herself to a famous Corralitos Market smoked sausage sandwich after her scope-out of the creek each Spring.

Head down, spinning with thoughts, questions, and plans for the last weeks of school, she rounded an aisle too fast and crashed into a man carrying a grocery bag in each hand.

He dropped the bags and caught her in his arms, smiling down at her, one eyebrow cocked, eyes twinkling.

"Well, haven't run into you for a while." He released her and stepped back.

"Father Francis!" Aurora blushed in embarrassment. "Sorry!"

"You seem to be in a big hurry."

"I was thinking about a sausage sandwich."

The priest laughed. "I understand your urgency, then. I was planning to have one of those for dinner myself. I just have to put my salmon in the car first. The market smokes it for me." He picked up his shopping bags. "Care to have a picnic? We could sit across the street in that little park and talk. I think we should bring each other up to date on our progress with the ag land preservation project."

"Sounds like a great idea."

Don't be stupid, Aurora told her pounding heart.

*   *   *

THURSDAY, MAY 5, 1999
BYRD RIVER, VALLE VERDE

Just a few days after the trauma of being held hostage by traffickers, Kelli Cavanaugh had received clearance to resume her full duties. Friday morning, she drove down to the Byrd River to survey the flood damage.

She'd heard about Malone Baker's ambush of the environmentalists. Malone had managed to use the publicity from that stunt to manipulate the governor into overriding the endangered species act. Removing riparian trees during prime migratory bird nesting season? Outrageous!

Kelli climbed up the riverbank to the levee. It was ugly — like the aftermath of a battle. A war had been waged here against the "bad, bad river." Clearly, the community had a lot to learn about their watershed.

Kelli had accessed the levee a good ways upstream of the Trasks' demolished apple orchard and was walking downstream to get perspective on the damage. Later, she'd arrange with the president of the bird club to do a survey out here. They should collect data on the effect of this tree removal on the threatened and endangered birds that nested here this time of year.

As she approached a bend in the river, a faint mechanical hum grew louder. She rounded the bend and discovered the source of the sound: a truck with a huge tank on its flatbed. A pump was spraying something into the river. Whatever was in there, it couldn't be good. Kelli pulled her new digital camera out of her pocket and took photos.

"Stop right there, miss. This is private property. You need to leave."

The *click-click* of cocking rifles echoed inside her head.

A covey of quail startled into the sky.

Kelli swung around to face two men with rifles pointed at her heart.

"Hi, there." Kelli put on her best smile. This wasn't the first time she'd encountered men with guns in remote areas.

The Latino man facing her down wore a sombrero, the type farm foremen wore, and a big silver belt buckle. The white guy looked kind of like a golf pro. But instead of a 3-wood, he gripped an AK-47 in his hands.

Kelli knew that the entire reach of the Byrd River levee, all the way to the bay, was a public right-of-way, but she wasn't going to argue the point.

A pick-up trailing a cloud of dust raced toward them along the farm road and squealed to a stop below her. An older, barrel-chested man jumped out of the truck and scrambled up the bank of the levee.

"Billy! What the hell? Is this the material I told you to dispose of?"

"They already cut the trees down anyway, Dad. We figured this would just speed along the process. Kill off the weeds and clean the river that much faster. It's a lot cheaper than what you had in mind." The golf-pro look-alike grinned.

"Oh, good afternoon, Miss." The older man tipped his hat to Kelli, then turned back to the men with rifles. "Billy, go shut off that pump. You and Yudas wait for me by the truck. I'll be over to talk with you just as soon as I have a chat with this young lady here."

The two rifles departed.

"Sorry if my boys scared you, Miss. My name is Baker. William Baker. And you are?"

Kelli offered her hand. "County Fish and Wildlife Warden Kelli Cavanaugh."

"This is private property, Kelli. We've had some terrible losses down here recently, and we're just trying to get ourselves back together. We're a little sensitive right now about outsiders coming around. We don't want any hippie environmentalists monkey-wrenching our tree removal operation. What can I do for you?"

"The Byrd is within my jurisdiction, sir. I just came down to assess the flood damage."

"To be honest, sweetheart, we don't want you government do-gooders coming around here and sticking your noses in our business. I think you'd better get along, and let us take care of our own."

Taking care of this watershed *was* her business. But Kelli knew how to pick her battles. She'd go downstream and collect water samples, which should enable her to identify what was in that tank, then write up a report. Depending on her findings, she might pay Mr. Baker a visit later, with a citation in hand. She treated Mr. Baker to another sample of her best smile, turned around, and retreated.

83

FRIDAY, MAY 6, 1999
Prudenciana Elementary, Valle Verde

IN THE TEACHER'S ROOM BEFORE SCHOOL, Aurora waited for her coffee to reheat in the microwave.

Bushi rushed into the room. "Everyone, I've just had terrible news. Our librarian has been diagnosed with stage four cancer. She will not be coming back. The school board is closing our library permanently. They plan to use the space for storage."

Aurora shook her head and retrieved her coffee from the microwave. Stage four. They'd all seen this coming for a while, but still, it was almost more than Aurora could bear. She'd often wondered why people with jobs or homes in suspected cancer clusters didn't just leave. Now she knew. It was complicated.

What next?

Numb, she picked up the newspaper someone had left on the table.

On the front page of the *Valle Verde Register* was an article about various weekend festivities going on around town in honor of Cinco de Mayo. She skimmed through to the back pages.

A group of Catholic priests brought out to Valle Verde last fall by Bay Berry to observe conditions in the fields released a statement criticizing the company for its low wages, working conditions and intimidation of UFW supporters.

Last weekend, the Agricultural Workers Committee had held what organizers dubbed a "March for Truth". Several hundred people marched through the streets of Valle Verde, holding signs denouncing UFW leaders Arturo Rodriguez and Dolores Huerta as *hijos del diablo*, children of the devil, and calling for the UFW to get out of the fields. But this morning, the UFW announced its victory in the Bay Berry union vote. The UFW is filing suit against AWC, calling them a fake "company union" and alleging that they violated the 1975 California Agricultural Labor Relations Act.

Aurora skimmed a story next to the "March for Truth" article about the California Rural Assistance League filing a civil rights lawsuit with the EPA for failing to address the dangerous levels of pesticides Latino children are exposed to in public schools, and a landmark lawsuit, on behalf of farmworkers, against the California Department of Pesticide Regulation, the Methyl Bromide Coalition, and the Monterey Bay Strawberry Growers Association.

The suits alleged that working in fields where the pesticide have been applied endangers the health and safety of the laborers. The strawberry growers countered that, "lowering levels of methyl bromide use would cause loss of hundreds of millions of dollars to the industry — with concomitant job losses, and increases in consumer prices."

"Look at this," Aurora handed the paper to Katie, pointing out the article about the lawsuit.

Katie glanced at the article and rolled her eyes. "Yep. Same old specious threats. Consumer protection — your job or your health, what will you choose? This suit will probably go on for years. I predict that once it's finally settled, nothing will change. Does anybody have the Cinco de Mayo Folklorico dance assembly schedule for this afternoon?"

"You can have mine," said Corky Duncan, putting her lunch in the refrigerator. "It's on top of my stack of mail on the table."

Third grade teacher Mrs. Chang burst into the teachers' room, sobbing. "What's the matter, May?" asked Nathena.

"It's Danny Santiago." She spoke with difficulty. "My student who's been battling bone cancer. He died last night."

*　　*　　*

In Aurora's classroom after lunch, during science circles, River shouted, "Ms. B! The eggs are hatching! We just saw an alevin wriggle out of its egg! It's hiding in the spaces between the pebbles. It looks kind of like a tadpole. Look! Another one just hatched!"

Aurora's students spent the afternoon making birthday cards for their salmon and Mother's Day cards to take home for next weekend.

On the front of Alice's Mother's Day card, she had painted a woman with a pink butterfly tattoo. Inside the card Alice wrote, "I miss you Mommy."

84

S ATURDAY EVENING, YUDAS MEDINA SAT IN HIS CAR, parked in the shadow of a gnarled pepper tree in the far corner of Our Lady of Help parking lot.

He couldn't put this off any longer. Father Francis was alone in the church tonight.

The UFW had won the Bay Berry Union vote. AWC was finished, but it didn't matter anymore. AWC had never been a real union for the workers anyway, just a fake, controlled by the owners. Might as well be honest with himself. AWC was just one more dirty thing he'd done for his boss.

No other cars left in the lot. For the last fifteen minutes, no one had come up or down the stairs through the front doors of the church.

It was getting dark. The time for confession was almost over. Father Francis would be leaving soon.

Yudas slipped out of his car, closed the door quietly, and scanned the area.

He didn't notice the silhouettes of two men in black standing as still as gravestones in the cemetery.

He turned up his jacket collar and adjusted his AWC cap to shadow his eyes, then slid his hand in his pocket, wrapping his fingers around the cold metal object he carried there.

Stealthily, he approached the church. Like a rat, he scuttled up the stairs and into the deserted narthex.

In the silent church, candles flickered at the feet of the statue of Our Lady of Help.

*   *   *

An indigo Mercedes 4WD SUV, almost invisible in the dark, pulled up behind the abandoned frozen food plant by the railroad tracks. Hidden by Benz privacy glass, the occupant held his crotch and rocked while he waited for the van to arrive with his little gift.

*   *   *

Father Francis, dressed in his vestments, knelt inside the confessional praying — in a transcendental state, unaware of time, or even of his own body.

Huph, huph, huph, huph. Bears dance through the dusk in a circle, their eyes reflecting angry red flames that blaze incandescent at the center of the arbor. Men sitting in darkness under the oak trees drum, play rattles and flutes, and sing.

Hen'na yeh hen'na yeh hey'na yeh chi'chai-yo.

Father Francis dances in the inner circle of warriors. Cloaked in bearskins, he and the other the warriors have become Bears, dancing ancient healing medicine.

All the People standing in the outer circle pray and chant. When a Bear lumbers near, hands of the People seeking healing reach out to touch, to wrap fingers in the warmth of primordial fur. Through touch, those who have Journeyed to attend the ancient ceremony take in sacred Bear energy, into the body, into Spirit.

The Bears absorb all pain, wounds, disease of the People who touch them. The Bears eat the People's sins, transform all sorrow, so that the People can be Healed, Strengthened, and given Courage for accomplishing the Great Work, the work of Healing Mother Earth, and Caring for the Her Children.

Huph, h' uh uh. The Bears huff, shuffling heavily in the dirt. Their claws shimmer in the moonlight.

*   *   *

The driver of the Mercedes strokes himself in anticipation, planning the route he'll take with his cargo to a remote cabin in the High Sierra. In a week or two, when he's finished, he'll leave the cargo behind in a rocky area of the mountains known only to him, high above the timberline. Pumas will pick the bones clean in no time.

*   *   *

It was so quiet inside the church. Yudas panicked and held his breath.

Has the priest already left? No. The green light above the oratory is on.

Father Francis is inside the booth. Alone.

Yudas slithered up the side aisle and skulked behind a pillar. He waited for several minutes, sweating, mouth dry, fingers wrapped around the cold metal in his jacket pocket.

Finally, he stalked toward the confessional.

*   *   *

A sound jolted Father Francis out of his meditation.

The doorknob to the confessional turned.

Slowly, the door opened.

Father Francis could not see the person on the other side of the oratory screen.

A blast of breaking glass shattered the peace of the sanctuary. The priest's head snapped back and struck the wall.

*   *   *

The man in the Mercedes unzipped his pants, wrapped his fingers around his cock and closed his eyes. After a few minutes, he groaned.

While he cleaned himself, disappointment washed over him. They'd informed him this morning that he'd be getting only half of his order. There'd been a snafu — no little ones available. He'd have to make do with just a woman. But next time, they'd deliver double, as promised, or else. He'd warned them. He was prepared to blow the whistle. He'd send an anonymous tip to the press. Leak everything he'd done, as accountant for the superintendent. Imagine what would happen when the public found out that Superintendent Spieler was embezzling school district funds and channeling them through a global trafficking cartel with ties to crooked congressmen and a multinational development scheme.

A black van pulled up next to the Mercedes. The accountant pushed a button to unlock his rear door. A man in a striped suit stepped out of the van.

Striped suit's voice was high-pitched and whiney. "Sorry but I'm gonna need you to help me with this. I don't have my usual assistants tonight, and this crate is fuckin' heavy."

The accountant and the man in the striped suit hefted the covered crate into the back of the waiting Mercedes.

The accountant lifted a corner of the blanket covering the wire dog crate and peered inside. A naked woman, gagged and bound, stared at him with eyes opened wide. On her breast was a pink butterfly tattoo.

*   *   *

In the confessional, Yudas bent down and picked up the framed copy of the Act of Contrition. A few pieces of broken glass tinkled to the ground.

*　　　*　　　*

In a well-appointed bedroom in Pebble Beach, Sean Stark thrust over and over again into the tight, silky pussy of Shibu Yayoi.

Beads of sweat from his forehead dropped onto her face. He ground his chest into her small pink and white breasts. She cried out. He raised her hips with his hands and stuffed a pillow under her, banging her harder, thrusting deeper. He knew he was hurting her; that aroused him.

*　　　*　　　*

Hands shaking, Yudas hung the framed Act of Contrition, with its broken glass, back on the wall. That sound — like a gunshot — the glass shattering. His shame — that he could be so clumsy, knocking the Act of Contrition off the wall — magnified the guilt and grief he already carried. Yudas knelt under the crucifix hanging above the grille.

He put his hand in his pocket and pulled out his rosary, a string of beads attached to a heavy metal crucifix.

*　　　*　　　*

In the small compartment on the other side of the grille, Father Francis rubbed his head where a goose egg was forming. Careless of him to have been startled by the noise, bumping his head on the wall like that.

The priest got off of his knees and took a seat facing the penitent. He made the Sign of the Cross to open the way for the Sacrament of Reconciliation.

"Bless me Father, for I have sinned," came the emotion-strangled voice on the other side of the grille. "It has been five years since my last confession. I was not born an evil man, Father. But I did not want to die a poor man. Because of that, I have sinned. I have lied more times than I remember. I have committed many mortal sins, Father."

The man began to cry. He described in detail how he had procured drugs, women, and children from the Mara Salvatruchas for his *patrón*.

"God celebrates the return of his prodigal son, my child. God loves you and forgives you unconditionally. But when our sins wrong our neighbors, one must do what is possible in order to repair the harm, my son. Absolution takes away sin, but it does not remedy all the disorders sin has caused. Therefore, in addition to a penance of prayer and fasting, which I will give you, I also urge you to go to the authorities, my son. Tell them what you know about these crimes being committed in our midst. Thus may you bring forth fruits worthy of Penance, which insofar as it is done in and through Christ, and offered by Him to the Father, you will find peace".

On his knees, weeping, Yudas recited the Act of Contrition.

"God the Father of Mercies," responded the priest, "May the Grace of Christ, which has set you free from all of your sins, be with you now and forever. Amen."

*   *   *

Viagra erection stiff as a gun barrel ... Not bad for a man of sixty-two.

Sticky fluids trickled onto pristine white sheets.

Need to call Bentley and Vera ... Blackriver's working out well ... Keep an eye on things ... Most important — control the message ...

In one swift movement, he flipped Shibu over and drove hard into her ass. She struggled and cried out, exciting him more. Holding her tight around the hips, forcing her face and shoulders down into the sheets, he lifted and tilted her.

Uh uh uh uh.

Harder and faster he plunged into her.

*   *   *

High in the mountains, a Puma screamed.

85

Seascape Beach Resort, Aptos
Santa Cruz County

"I now pronounce you man and wife. You may kiss the bride."
The groom, in white linen shirt and pants, with a Maile-style Ti leaf *lei* draped over his shoulders, lifted the bride's veil. They kissed under an arbor covered with plumeria, tuber rose, and jasmine.

"What a beautiful place for a wedding," said a stout matron in purple silk with a gardenia corsage pinned at her chest. She daubed tears from her eyes with a lace handkerchief.

"Yes, I love the Seascape Resort. What a magnificent view."

Malone gazed out over the rolling grass lawn, beyond a grove of eucalyptus trees, to the sparkling bay. In the distance, a lone surfer cut up and down the face of a wave.

"When my son finally chooses the right girl, I want them to have their wedding here."

*   *   *

Father Francis retired to a private room reserved for his use inside the hotel, where he kissed his stole and prayerfully removed his vestments. With practiced efficiency, he packed away the liturgical objects used for the wedding mass and completed his paperwork. Then, dressed in black and wearing his clerical collar, he joined the wedding party at the reception.

Momentarily blinded by the sun as he stepped outside onto the patio, he couldn't see the person who put a glass of champagne into his hand. He turned to find Malone Baker smiling at him.

"Father Francis," Malone said. "So nice to see you again. I know you're expected to meet and greet all the wedding guests, but do you suppose I could persuade you to join William and I at our table for a little while? We're sitting right over there."

"Thank you, Mrs. Baker. It would be a pleasure. Lead on." The priest, champagne glass in hand, followed Malone to one of the outdoor tables.

"Father Francis," said William Baker, standing to shake the priest's hand. "Nice to see you again."

The party of three settled themselves at the table.

A waitress placed a platter of sashimi and ginger, and another heaped with calamari — with thinly sliced lemon, fresh dill, and garlic aioli — in the center of the table. There was a small plate in front of each guest.

"Haven't laid eyes on you since the Christmas concert at the church," said William.

"Yes," said Father Francis. "I hope we'll see you at church more often in the future." William and Malone Baker smiled at each other. Malone patted her husband's hand. A waiter came by to refill champagne glasses.

The priest placed slices of sashimi and pickled ginger on his plate, poured soy sauce in a little dish, and added a smudge of wasabi.

"We didn't get a chance to chat with you much after the concert, Father. But as I recall you mentioned that you're involved with a land conservancy committee bent on saving Byrd Valley farmland." William wiped his hands on his linen napkin and put the cloth down on the table. He pushed his empty plate away and gave the priest a hard look. "That interests me."

Malone set down her fork, shaded her eyes, and stared out over the bay. Father Francis followed her gaze. A lone surfer paddled to shore, planted her board like a spear in the sand, and stood, hands on hips, at the water's edge.

Malone turned to Father Francis. "I've learned to understand and appreciate our farmland much more deeply since we hired Professor Khurie, the hydrologist, as a consultant after the flood." Malone rested her hand on William's arm. "William and I have spent a good deal of time lately talking about the future. I see now the great value our land has for posterity, far beyond short-term financial gain."

"We just hope our son Billy will understand once he matures," William continued. "Tell us more about your farmland conservation scheme."

The priest nodded. "There's a coalition of environmental groups in the Monterey Bay area working to support the preservation of agricultural land in the South County. We all come together under the umbrella of the Open Space Alliance. The idea is to use the National Marine Sanctuary as a model, to create a Farmland Sanctuary, so to speak, in the Byrd Valley. Preserving agricultural lands here could serve as a resource and an inspiration for communities everywhere."

"Just how do you propose to do that, Father?" William Baker dipped a piece of warm French bread in rosemary olive oil and balsamic.

"We have some very astute policy makers and planners on board," the priest answered. "Our committee includes a prominent environmental attorney who's working pro bono. She's taking care of the legal aspects of creating conservation easements and land trusts tailored to each property owner's personal situation."

The small plates were cleared, and salads arrived.

"What I want," said Baker, "is to make sure that the goddamn developers don't ever turn my grandfather's farmland into shopping malls and filling stations. Pardon my French, Father."

"I understand your concern, William. That's exactly our goal. Our attorney can create a binding conservation easement that would enable you to continue to own your property, with all of the rights you currently enjoy, but assure that it will remain agricultural in perpetuity."

"Exactly what is a conservation easement, Father?" asked Malone.

The priest put down his fork and leaned forward, elbows on the table. "In this case, it would create a legally enforceable land preservation agreement between the landowner and our land conservation organization. The agreement would restrict real estate development, commercial, and industrial uses on the property, forever. But in all other matters, the landowner would maintain full control over the acreage, and all private property rights under the law."

Malone looked at William. He nodded, and turned his attention to his salad.

A waiter came by offering a choice of beverages. "Would you happen to have a chilled bottle of Kongsgaard Napa Valley chardonnay?" asked Malone.

The waiter checked his wine list. "Yes, ma'am."

"Bring us some of that, please, and three glasses." Malone turned to the priest. "I'm very picky about my chardonnay, Father. I think you'll enjoy this one. John Kongsgaard harvests his grapes from a small, rocky vineyard and leaves the wine alone in its barrel — a practice he likes to call 'death and resurrection'. It's an absolutely opulent wine."

Father Francis watched the surfer carry her board up the path. *Aurora.*

Her shining braid made him think of a burnished golden chalice.

She followed the meandering trail below the patio just below where he sat, her wetsuit peeled off her chest and arms, exposing her bikini top. Beads of water flashed on bare skin. Her wetsuit swung like a hula skirt around feminine curves of belly and hips, so ripe it made him ache.

"Oh, there's that teacher," said Malone. "Beautiful girl, isn't she? She's been a thorn in our sides, with all that nuisance about pesticides, but I admit I've become much more open-minded about you environmentalists since we've been working with Professor Khurie."

Malone watched Aurora round a bend in the path and disappear. She reappeared at the lower edge of the rolling lawn, below the patio where the wedding guests sat.

"A charming girl. I've actually been hoping my son Billy might take an interest in her. What do you think, Father?"

Father Francis forced himself to take his eyes off Aurora. "Charming. I agree."

William cleared his throat. "So if I'm understanding you right about this conservation easement thing, we would sign papers stating that our land will always be used for agriculture. Even if it goes to our son one day, he could never sell it to a developer?"

"That's right." The priest leaned back so the waiter could clear away salad plates and brush breadcrumbs off the tablecloth with a silver handled brush. "The restrictions of the easement, once set in place, run with the land and are binding on all future owners of the property in perpetuity. Everything is spelled out in a legal document that's recorded in the local land records, and the easement becomes a part of the chain of title for the property."

The sommelier arrived with a bucket of ice and the bottle of chardonnay. It was opened with a flourish. Malone tasted it and gave her approval for glasses to be filled. The bottle was nestled in the ice bucket.

Father Francis lifted his glass. He swirled the amber liquid in the light, watched the wine's viscous "legs" ooze down the sides of the glass, then tipped the rim to his nose to appreciate the bouquet.

He sipped, then nodded to Malone. "Very nice."

"Please," said Malone, "continue with what you were saying."

"Well, beyond what's already been discussed, you'll also receive significant state and federal tax advantages. Even better, you'll have the pride of knowing you've contributed to the public good by preserving the conservation values associated with your land for future generations. As you know, the Byrd Valley is some of the best agricultural land in the world. We can't afford to lose it."

"I thought an easement meant that the public was granted access to our land. I certainly don't want that." Malone's eyes flashed.

"Not at all," Father Francis paused while a luncheon plate with fresh-caught local halibut was set before him. "Some conservation easements do allow public access of land, but the type we're offering only prohibits development. It absolutely does not make your property public. The details are all spelled out in the legal document that creates the trust. Of course, if you decide to pursue this, our attorney will make all pertinent documents available to your legal counsel for review."

"I'm liking the sound of this," William said.

To Father Francis' surprise, Malone was smiling and nodding her head in agreement.

By the time the priest had a chance to glance back toward the path, Aurora was gone.

86

TUESDAY, MAY 10, 1999
Prudenciana Elementary School

I N THE LIFE LAB GARDEN, Aurora and her students were practicing
using transects for insect collection, in preparation for the macro
invertebrate water quality study they would do on their salmon release
field trip. She was proud of how well her students recorded their data
and handled the math.

Where the protective row of heritage Monterey pines had stood
until last weekend, there was now a gaping ruin. This was so out of the
blue. The principal had completed paperwork and obtained district and
county approval for heritage tree removal, without letting anyone know
what she was planning. She'd claimed the trees were diseased and had
become a safety hazard. She feared they might fall and injure a child.
Aurora certainly didn't want any children hurt, but the principal had
made no attempt to find out if the trees could be saved. Now they were
gone forever, no longer standing sentry as a buffer between the school
and the toxic acres of gleaming plastic.

The silent sky was a vacant blue field. The golden eagle pair no longer carved their infinite figure eights in the air.

Ruth Redding, wearing a wide-brimmed straw hat and carrying a basket over her arm, seemed to float, like one of the good witches of Oz, across the playground toward the garden. Her seventeen first graders followed like a fluffle of bunnies, with tripping, stumbling and flapping of ears.

"Good morning." Aurora greeted the little ones. "What are you guys doing in the garden today?"

"First, we're going to do the Hokey Pokey, then we're picking mulberry leaves for our silkworms."

The children formed a circle in the center of the garden, and they sang and danced.

"Put your whole self in, take your whole self out, put your whole self in and shake it all about. Do the Hokey Pokey and turn yourself around. That's what it's all about!"

Once the children were busy harvesting leaves, Ruth turned to Aurora.

"Have you heard?" she asked.

"What?"

"Deana is force transferring me."

"No way!"

"She's getting rid of us, Aurora. Anyone who's challenged her authority, who's been involved in questioning the pesticides. She wants us gone."

"She's making you leave Prudenciana?"

"They're transferring me to a year-round school. I'll have no summer break at all."

"Oh, Ruth! I'm so sorry. What are you going to do?"

"I don't know. I'm heartbroken to leave Prudenciana. I love this school. I've been here over thirty years. I was planning to teach here until I retire next year."

"Have you talked to Tom?"

"That was the first thing I did. But honestly, he's just a shell of his old self. The man has been tortured by the district's trumped-up lawsuit. He has tremendous integrity, I have to say. In spite of everything, he

556

continues to put his whole heart and soul into teaching. But in terms of his union work, the fight's just gone out of him. I'm sure it's partly the antidepressants he's on. He says he feels empty. He's decided he won't be coming back next year. He submitted his resignation. They beat him."

"What about the lawsuit?"

"The district is dropping their spurious suit. But Tom says the experience has made him face the fact that he can't support a family as a teacher. He's pretty bitter about the way public education is going. Over in Silicon Valley in the computer industry, he can at least double the $40,000 a year he makes teaching, and that's just at entry level. He has a job offer, and he's accepted."

"What a loss for education. What about you? Are you going to fight the transfer?"

"There's nothing I can do, Aurora. The district can't fire me without grounds since I'm tenured, but they can transfer me anywhere they want. You can count on one thing, though."

"What's that?"

"I'm not giving up on this pesticide war. I plan to organize the teachers and parents at my new school. I'm going to bring them into Farm Without Harm, and persuade them to opt-in to becoming a pesticide-free school, under our district's new Cal EPA grant."

"You're truly an inspiration, Ruth."

Ruth chucked. "I try to set an example, like my parents did before me. I've been an activist all my life, you know. When Rachel Carson's *Silent Spring* came out in the '60s, I was a Mother Against DDT. I was breastfeeding my daughter, had my breast milk tested and results came back with high levels of DDT, so I joined other breastfeeding mothers, and we organized and helped to get the pesticide banned. I'll never stop fighting this insanity. Not until my last breath." Ruth took Aurora's hands and looked deeply into her eyes. "Together, we have power. Believe it, Aurora. But watch out."

"What do you mean?"

"Don't be surprised if they go after you, next."

Aurora studied the children in the garden, then gazed out over the strawberry fields. Finally, she took a deep breath and turned back to Ruth.

"You know what, Ruth? I'm all in, all the way, with my whole self. I can't possibly go back now. Bring it on. I don't care what they try to do to me. I'm not afraid. I'll never give up."

87

"THINK THIS IS GANG RELATED?" asked Detective Rosa. Deputy Jamison knelt over the bloated body that had just been pulled out of the river. "Maybe Salvatrucha? Maybe this vic has a connection with the trafficking ring we busted up at Corralitos Creek, those guys that got mauled by the bear."

"In a case like this," said Rosa, "never rule out a possible nexus. Always stay alert for clues and connections. But no. Not Salvatrucha; not this time. Look again. Not the right MO."

"The body is intact."

"Right. MS-13 dismember their victims. If this was Trucha's work, the vic's hands and feet would be severed, maybe also his head."

"And his dick would be stuffed in his mouth," said Deputy Jamison.

"This guy's got nothing but the one clean bullet hole in the forehead, as far as I can see. Nasty exit wound though."

"Maybe a suicide? Looks like a wallet in his back pocket. Should we check for an ID?"

"Wait a minute." Rosa held his deputy off while the forensic team worked. The victim's face was pretty badly decomposed, but the detective had a feeling he already knew what the I.D. would say. When the M.E. and forensic photographer finished, Rosa gave Jamison the go-ahead.

With a gloved hand, Jamison withdrew a driver's license from the dead man's soggy billfold.

"Hey, I recognize this man from the newspapers," said the deputy. "Yudas Medina. He's president of AWC. A vocal opponent of the UFW. Maybe this has something to do with the union vote they just held at Bay Berry. AWC lost."

Charlie Rosa bent down for a closer inspection of the entry wound. "Strange wound. Can't quite identify the type of bullet. Too much decomposition. Might be suicide. Could be murder, maybe connected to strawberry politics. We'll know more once we get the coroner's report."

*　　*　　*

FRIDAY EVENING, MAY 13, 1999
PRUDENCIANA ELEMENTARY OPEN HOUSE

The Amah-Ka-Tura dancers of the Byrd Valley Ohlone Indian Council — about fifteen children and adults in face and body paint, wearing the feathers, shells, and animal skins of traditional regalia — beat clacker sticks and drums, shook rattles, sang and danced to bless the new mural.

After the ceremony, children led their families and guests to their classrooms to share the year's work.

In Aurora's room, slender inch-long silver arrows darted through the bubbling water of the fish incubator tank. All the Steelhead had buttoned up their little yolk bellies, swum up out of the rock interstices and graduated to the developmental stage called "fry".

In the History corner of the room, student models of California missions were displayed, along with relief maps of the state, and a model of an Ohlone village with real tule huts.

Arranged on bulletin boards were book reports and reports about the Gold Rush, the Donner Party, the building of the intercontinental railroad, and the Three L's of Santa Cruz history: leather, lumber, and limestone. Each student's genealogy report was proudly displayed on the student's desk, with information about the historical periods students' family members had immigrated from everywhere in the world to California. A world map with place of origin flags illustrated the diverse heritage of Aurora's students.

Student artwork, creative writing, and samples of best work in all subjects decorated the walls. With cardboard, colored paper, and *papier-mâché* they had transformed the center of the classroom into an interactive salmon habitat — from the redwood forest of a high mountain stream, down river to the estuary and ocean tide pools, kelp forest, and deep ocean.

Over the year, Aurora had taken her students on a field trip to each habitat. A videotape looped with clips of student activities and field trips.

Families tried out favorite hands-on science experiments from the Salmon and Trout Education Program. A bulging student STEP folder was displayed on each desk.

At the end of the evening, everyone left Open House with smiles on their faces.

Aurora and Katie locked up and walked to the parking lot together.

"How did it go tonight, Katie?"

"Strangely," said Katie, "it was great. I figured Mr. Medina would do his usual mean stunt and ruin my Open House. But, he didn't show up. And Antonio, his little boy, has been absent, too. I don't know what's going on, and I hope Antonio's okay, but it was great not having mean Yudas Medina in my face. Everyone had a fantastic time, including me."

*   *   *

SUNDAY MORNING, MAY 15, 1999
SANTA CRUZ, THE WESTSIDE

Aurora relaxed in her patio, bathing in the delicious warmth of spring sunshine on her skin, sipping a cappuccino and turning the pages of the Sunday paper. Blue rolled on his back under the lavender bush, paws in the air, and purred.

An Anna's hummingbird flashed his iridescent throat collar, *tich tich tich'ing* as he landed on the feeder. A recently arrived migrant, the black-chinned *Archilochus alexandri,* charged the Anna's with the "zzzzzzrl" of high-speed wings. The migrant and the resident went at it fiercely, battling for territorial dominance with a brilliant flash of their sapphire, violet, and fiery red throat feathers and iridescent emerald backs. The small warriors flew high into the air and together, balls of twisting sparking color, tumbled and spun down from the sky. With angry clicks and ps*stcheeeew's,* they veered off into the kiwi thicket at the last moment.

Ripening kiwi fruit hung on vines twining along the fence. A profusion of old-fashioned sweet pea blossoms perfumed the air. The Meyer lemon, pear, plum, apple, Chinese persimmon, guava, passion vine and fig tree had all set fruit, and the snow peas and spring salad greens were ready to harvest.

In Section D on the second to last page of the paper, Aurora read a short article about a body found in the Byrd River. The body was identified as a Mr. Yudas Medina. Suspected cause of death: suicide.

*   *   *

OUR LADY OF HELP CHURCH
VALLE VERDE

Father Francis read the article in the paper on Sunday afternoon, after mass. He said a prayer for Señor Medina and for his family, and special prayers for the redemption of a soul lost to suicide.

He had hoped that Yudas Medina would go to Detective Rosa and give up everything he'd revealed in confession. Father Francis was bound by the seal of the confessional never to disclose what Yudas had told him. Now, all of Medina's information — names, details of the drug and sex trafficking network were lost.

Suicide? Really?

✳   ✳   ✳

SANTA CRUZ, THE WESTSIDE

The man in a black suit and dark sunglasses put his paper coffee cup down on top of the vending machine. He dropped coins in the slot and pulled out a Sunday paper, carried the newspaper and his coffee cup to the outdoor table in front of the bakery, sat, and slid the paper across to his almost identical associate. The second man in black thumbed through the paper, while the first sipped his coffee.

"Did you get the memo from Headquarters?" asked the first man.

"The recruitment flyer for a new Blackriver dark op in the 'Stan? Nah, I didn't give it much notice. I'm done with the sandbox. Stateside with CalGreen suits me fine."

The first man in black nodded and sipped his coffee.

The second man turned to the last page of Section D, read, folded the paper in a neat square, and slid it across the table.

The first man read, then lifted his eyes from the page, with a hard squint behind his dark glasses. He lit a cigarette, took a deep draw and exhaled a spiral of blue smoke, then leaned back in his chair and stretched out his legs.

"Suicide?"

The second man's lip curled, revealing pointed white canines. "Let nature take its course."

They laughed softly, a hissing sound, more hyena than human.

88

FRIDAY, MAY 27, 1999
(The Salmon Release)
Corralitos Creek, Santa Cruz Mountains
Byrd River Watershed

DESTINY AND AURORA USED A SMALL NET to transfer the delicate salmon fry from their incubator to a plastic container full of chilled water, then placed the sealed container inside an ice chest for transport.

Excited students, dressed for a day at the creek, helped load science field study equipment into Destiny's van, and then piled into their chaperones' waiting cars.

As Destiny led the caravan of chaperone-drivers up the winding Eureka Canyon Road, Aurora, riding shotgun, reviewed her list of chaperones and their groups. Bobby Choate's uncle, the strawberry grower Pete Choate, was coming along. Aurora had no idea what to expect from that.

At a roadside pullout just before the four-mile marker, Dr. Scott, the hatchery biologist, met the caravan. He and Mr. Choate carried the cooler with young steelhead down a steep path to a staging area on a sandy beach and secured the container in a cold, shaded rock pool. The other chaperones pitched in to relay the rest of the equipment, while Destiny and Aurora helped the most adventurous students climb down the steepest path, holding on to a rope tied around a tree.

Standing on the bank in his knee-high rubber boots, Dr. Scott addressed the students. "When you're looking for a place to safely release your salmon, what are some of the things you need to keep in mind?"

Students readily answered.

"Cold water 45° to 62° Fahrenheit." "High quality, pollution-free, flowing water." "A high dissolved oxygen content." "The water has to be within a healthy pH and nitrogen range." "Shade and woody debris for the fish to hide in." "Waterfalls, deep pools, riffles, eddies, meanders, undisturbed spawning gravel." "Aquatic insects for food."

Dr. Scott looked pleased. "As you make your measurements, remember that all the data you collect on water and habitat quality today will be sent to Cal Fish and Game. After you release your fish, you're going to be helping our habitat restoration project by clearing the fish ladder under the road culvert. You are making a difference here, boys and girls. Thank you."

Students listened with big eyes.

Finally, the release ceremony began. Students lined up and Aurora handed each child a clear plastic cup filled with creek water. Dr. Scott netted a tiny wriggling fish to drop in each cup, and then every child carried a personal shining sliver of hope to a safe release spot along the creek.

During the release, television and newspaper crews arrived. One of the parents had notified the press again this year. Aurora knew it was important to inform the public about this wonderful and important project, but she felt embarrassed that her class was getting all the publicity, once again. She asked the reporters to point out that Aurora's class represented only one of 171 schools in California — from Half-Moon Bay to the Carmel River — participating in the Salmon and Trout Education Project.

A man balancing a Channel 8 TV News camera as big as a child on his shoulder filmed the event, while he picked his way over slippery river rocks. Reporters interviewed students and chaperones.

Rico spoke to the camera. "I thought that kids couldn't do nothin' about big things, like saving endangered animals, but now I know we can. We don't have to wait 'til we're grown up to make a difference. This is how school's supposed to be."

After the release, students conducted a biodiversity survey. They found, identified, counted and recorded caddis fly larvae, mayfly, dragonfly and stonefly nymphs, dragonfly casings, freshwater crayfish, salamanders, and salamander and frog egg masses. One group of kids found a Western skink with a bright turquoise tail.

Happy squeals echoed through the narrow canyon when children spotted a snake undulating through the water. Dr. Scott reached into the stream, swooped up the small, slender reptile, and held it by its head. It coiled around his arm — a dark jade Egyptian bracelet with topaz highlights, a golden stripe along its back, and a scarlet tongue that flicked in and out. Dr. Scott introduced the students to the non-venomous and docile Santa Cruz garter snake and, when everyone who wanted to had petted it, he put his hand into the water and the snake slid off and slithered away.

Water rushed and bubbled, birds called, trees rustled as if stirred by unseen spirits. Students measured current flow, surveyed the number of sensitive aquatic insects found, did tests of sediment, pH, nitrates, and dissolved oxygen. All data confirmed previous Department of Fish and Wildlife creek studies. In May of 1999, according to the EPA macro invertebrate protocol for water quality assessment, the upper watershed of Byrd River on Corralitos Creek measured at the highest quality on the scale, despite pollution downstream.

Dr. Scott and Aurora led everyone into the ankle-deep water rushing through the culvert tunnel that channeled the creek under a two-lane mountain road. The twenty-foot tunnel was cool, dark, mysterious and exciting. Children's shouts bounced off the corrugated metal sides of the tunnel as chaperones helped kids clear the winter accumulation of boulders and debris out of the fish ladder.

When they came out the other side, everyone blinked in the bright sunlight and stood awed before the waterfall grotto. At the mouth of the culvert where the creek veered ninety degrees to make its way upstream, a twenty-foot waterfall gushed from a hidden spring and tumbled down to a forest pool.

Aurora led her kids into the chest-high water. The mountain-cold cascade surrounded them with mist. Splashes of fire and ice sparkled in the sun. The pool shimmered with shadows and reflections of moss and ferns.

*   *   *

Once they'd made their way back through the culvert, everyone settled down on the sandy beach for a picnic. During lunch, Pete Choate found an opportunity to speak privately with Aurora.

"I want to apologize for my behavior after the flood, when we ambushed you with the press at the levee."

What?

Aurora certainly hadn't expected that.

"We were all blindsided by that flood, and the damage it did. We just lashed out. It was inexcusable. I hope you'll forgive me." The man's face was earnest. "I honestly hope my kids will be in your class when they get to fourth grade, Ms. Bourne."

"Thank you very much, Mr. Choate. I consider that an honor. And please, call me Aurora."

"One more thing I want you to know, Aurora. After I met with you teachers at the school last Fall, I talked with my family about everything you said. You really got me to take a hard look at what I've been doing to the environment, and the consequences that could have for my children's future. We've given it a lot of thought. It's not going to be easy — it's going to take years to get certified, and I know we'll have a hard time staying afloat financially during the transition. But as difficult as it will be, I'm getting out of strawberries and going into organic salad greens."

"That's wonderful! Congratulations, Mr. Choate. That's really, really good news."

*   *   *

On the way home, it was quiet in Destiny's van. Most of the children had fallen asleep. Aurora's eyes grew heavy.

She knew that out of twenty-five hundred eggs, an average of only two salmon would reach adulthood, make it down to the sea and back again to the creek to spawn. But she also knew that, for the rest of their lives, each one of her students would be an advocate and steward for the protection and preservation of the salmon and the watershed.

Aurora's head lolled against the cold window glass. Her eyelids closed.

Behind her eyes was a field of indigo. Out of the deep blue, a vortex of glowing violet lights swirled toward her. In the center of the vortex a golden flower opened. Brilliant silver spears emerged from the flower and swam toward Aurora. The front-most spear became a human-sized Silver Salmon, standing upright on her tail as if she had feet. Behind her stood legions of powerful warriors in shining fish suits of maille.

Wilghtnee, the Salmon Queen, and her tribe.

All at once, the Salmon Queen and her army lifted up their fish faces like helms, revealing human faces underneath. *Wilghtnee* removed her helmet; her long black hair floated around her face like sea grass. As she began to speak, iridescent bubbles rose from her mouth and floated through the liminal blue.

89

FRIDAY, JUNE 3, 1999
Prudenciana Elementary

F RIDAY, THE LAST DAY OF SCHOOL, WAS A MINIMUM DAY. By one
o'clock, Aurora had said goodbye to all of her students and picked
up the last pencil and scrap of paper off the floor. She collapsed in a
chair at her round reading table. A brown teddy bear wearing a red
ribbon collar and a red satin heart inscribed "Hug Me" sat atop a box
of chocolates. Piled around the teddy bear were other gifts from
students and their parents.

Aurora rested her elbow on the table and dropped her forehead
on her hand. She knew this feeling. It was the usual last-day-of-school
let down. She barely had enough energy to haul the gifts out to her car
and drive home. The principal had scheduled her final check-out for
1:10 pm. Aurora watched the wall clock.

At precisely 1:10 pm, Principal Wagner darkened the door. She
entered without a word, clipboard in hand, and stalked around the
room, opening cupboards and making notes.

Aurora lifted her head and observed, but stayed seated.

Finally, the principal pulled out a chair and sat across from Aurora, her back ramrod straight. She glared at the gifts piled on the table and wrinkled her nose as if they smelled bad.

"Do you have your form?"

Aurora handed the principal her check-out form. Mrs. Wagner scrutinized the document, then checked and initialed the very last box.

"Give me your key."

"Sorry, what did you say? Returning teachers customarily keep their keys over the summer."

"I am collecting all keys this year. If you wish to come in to work in your classroom over the summer, you will have to make an appointment for Bushi or Niño to let you in."

Aurora spun the key off her keychain and handed it over. Principal Wagner clipped it onto her key ring and made a notation on the top page of her clipboard.

Aurora thought that would finish it, but Deana Wagner continued to sit at the table in silence, glaring.

By the time the principal spoke again, Aurora was quite uncomfortable.

"Don't think this is over, Ms. Bourne," the principal hissed through tightly drawn lips. "Your little storm drain fiasco cost me dearly. You professionally humiliated me, and I intend to return the favor. I have spent my whole career striving to become a principal. Now that I've finally attained my goal, you are not going to ruin it for me. I was personally picked by the superintendent to rein you teachers in. Next year, I will be watching your every move. You will make mistakes. Be assured I will document your incompetence until I have a rock-solid case for your termination."

The room spun.

"And don't think you can get away from me by transferring to another school, or another district, or even another line of work. I plan to make sure that anyone interested in hiring you knows what a troublemaker you are."

With that, Deana Wagner rose and stomped out of the room.

Aurora gathered the teddy bear into her arms and buried her face in its fleece. She felt numb; her mind a blank. She sat and rocked for a long time. She did not cry.

∗　　∗　　∗

SATURDAY, JUNE 4, 1999
OCEANVIEW CONTINUATION HIGH SCHOOL, VALLE VERDE

The young men circled around Father Francis on the Oceanview Continuation High School basketball court, sweating and panting. Some doubled over, holding their sides, trying to catch their breath, while others took great gulps of water from their bottles, and poured water over their heads.

Father Francis wiped away a rill of sweat that had escaped the bandana tied around his forehead.

"Good work, men. That was an outstanding defensive shell drill. Strong, clean passes in the triple-threat position, Pancho. Congratulations on refraining from stealing the ball, this time, Jaime."

Pancho beamed. Jaime scratched an itch under his ankle bracelet and his friends laughed at Coach's reference to stealing.

"Don't forget the importance of rotating quickly when you're sprinting in and out of helpside. No lazy players on this team, men. We're here to play a go game, right?"

"Right!" the young men shouted.

Some of the boys shoved one another, laughing.

"Respect, gentlemen. Keep your discipline." The boys focused their attention back on their coach. "Alright. We have twenty minutes for a full-court, man-on-man pressure defense game. Let's go."

The young warriors put everything they had into the game; Father Francis played hard at their side.

When the game was over, the players drank Gatorade, poured water over themselves and each other, and toweled off. Some boys punched others in the biceps; a few knocked together knuckles and locked thumbs in the handshake of the initiated. Everyone thanked the coach.

"Hey, Padre. You comin' to our graduation?"

The priest surveyed the earnest faces. His basketball team had had a good season; even now that the season was over, the boys still met weekly for practice. They'd developed a love for the game and a sense of good sportsmanship and teamwork. When they'd started the year together, some of these kids had claimed Norteños cliques, and some Sureños. Yet here on the court, they'd managed to transcend their gang rivalries, to come together as a team.

Victor's gold crucifix caught the sunlight. His mustache was now more than just a smudge of coal dust over his lip. He was filling out, becoming a man — a good man. Soon he'd have his high school diploma, the first in his family. Next fall, he'd enter the university with a full scholarship. No doubt Paloma would follow his example. Maybe even Johnny would get through school, in time. Johnny, angry red scar around his neck and prison bracelet around his ankle, sat on a bench by himself drinking a soda. He'd returned home just last week, and would attend Oceanview next year, with an ankle monitor. Hopefully, he'd stick with the team.

"Am I coming to your graduation? Of course, *m'hijos*. I wouldn't miss it for the world. I'm so proud of you. You men are the real deal. Wherever you go, no matter what happens, I've got your back one hundred percent. I'll always be there for you."

*　　*　　*

NEW BRIGHTON STATE BEACH
SANTA CRUZ

Saturday, first day of summer vacation. Aurora sidestepped down the steep, well-worn locals path and crossed the railroad tracks. Then — using the roots of an old Monterey Pine as handholds — she lowered herself down the sandstone cliff. The gnarled roots were polished as smooth as a fine banister by years of beachgoers' hands. At the bottom of the cliff, she ran across the state beach parking lot to the top of the wooden stairs.

Before her was a seascape of infinite beauty. The bay opened its arms to the vast ocean — nothing on the horizon but the Pacific all the way to Japan. Flat water shimmered in tints of blue, lavender, abalone green and pink. A radiant blue sky illuminated white sand stretching out in two directions.

To the northwest, a short reach of sand ended in tidepools teeming with life, where beachcombers found fossils millions of years old preserved in the rocks.

To the southeast, toward Monterey, hot air wavering above sand and water created mirages that transformed distant cliffs into fantastical castles in the sky. The white sand beach swept around the arc of the bay until it dissolved in a hazy gradient of pale rose and blue-violet foothills melting into opalescent water.

There were days when fast, glassy, long rolling waves made this beach an epic bodysurfing and boogie-boarding break. But this afternoon, it was *Lago Pacifico*, Lake Pacific out there. A small ruffle of wave lapped gently at the sand, the water's quicksilver surface as still as a mirror.

Aurora ran down the stairs and into the sea.

Two dolphins seemed to appear out of nowhere. They swam side-by-side below her. One of them blew a perfect torus ring bubble that floated up toward her. The other blew small bubbles into the ring. In an instant, the two were gone. She raised her head above the water to look for them. They leapt out of the sea behind her, landing with a loud splash, as playful as children. Aurora laughed with joy, feeling the angst of her terrible school year wash away.

A dolphin mother and baby swam nearby. Aurora's heart swelled with love. She watched through her goggles as they glided away into the dark deep green.

As quickly as they had appeared, the dolphins were gone. Scissor-kicking, she raised her shoulders above the waterline, pushed up her goggles, and scanned the sea. Far off in the middle of the bay, hundreds of dolphins leapt, twisted, splashed and porpoised across the water, racing toward the south.

*　　　*　　　*

MANRESA BEACH

The last of the boys had departed. The afternoon was still hot. The tires of Father Francis' Honda crunched gravel as he drove out of the school parking lot and headed along San Andreas Road. He turned on Sand Dollar Drive, and then into the entrance to Manresa Beach.

After such a hot workout on the court with the kids, a swim was going to feel fantastic.

Father Francis stripped down to his swim shorts and ran barefoot across the black asphalt parking lot, pausing at the top of the stairway leading down to the sand.

Manresa was a wild and beautiful stretch of beach. White sand reached around the curve of the Monterey Bay in both directions. Northwest, toward Santa Cruz, the water tended to be calmer. But here, along the South County beaches, the currents were strong and tricky, even on a calm day. He smiled at the thought. He loved swimming against the current. He enjoyed the sensation of his muscles pulling hard against the water, and the way he could feel how to navigate complex fluid flows. Sometimes it was almost as if he could breathe under water.

Father Francis gazed toward the horizon. In the distance, far out on the bay, hundreds of dolphins leapt, spun and twisted in the air.

A wave of bittersweet sadness washed over the priest. Overcome by a deep longing, he watched the dolphins, wondering at the ache in his heart.

Chiding himself for his weakness, he ran down the stairs, across the sand, and dove into the icy water.

90

MONDAY, JUNE 6, 1999
Our Lady of Help Church

FATHER FRANCIS PICKED UP THE PHONE ON THE SECOND RING.
"Glad you called, Charlie. I hear you're investigating Yudas Medina's death as a homicide. He's been on my mind. Any leads yet?"

"We got an anonymous tip. Someone claimed they saw that teacher, Katie Cooper, with Yudas down by the river. We thought she looked like a good suspect. The way Medina publicly harassed her all year definitely gave her motive. So we brought her in and questioned her, but it turned out she had a solid alibi for time of death. That's not why I called, though, Frank."

"I'm listening."

"We've been running the DNA from Alice and the baby through CODIS for months, and we finally got a hit on the mother."

"Thank God. You found her?"

"Well, what was left of her. Mountain lion researchers near Crystal Lake discovered remains. They ran the DNA and notified us when a match turned up."

"Crystal Lake … that remote area of Mineral King in the High Sierra? How in the world did the woman end up there?"

"Figuring that out turned out to be a cakewalk. A mountain lion ate parts of her after she died, but — just like that incident earlier this year — cause of death was not cougar attack. We tracked the remains back to an old miner's cabin near the lake. That's where the woman died. Multiple broken bones, ligature marks, lacerations, abrasions, and contusions — her body was beaten nearly to jelly. Ultimate COD was strangulation. We found prints and semen all over the cabin. The perp's DNA was in the system."

"Who killed her?"

"You ready for this? He's an accountant for the school district here in Valle Verde. Name's Uriah Howard. When we brought him into custody, he gave up everything in exchange for us taking lethal injection off the table."

"How did Howard get a hold of Alice's mother?"

"He helped Superintendent Spieler embezzle millions of dollars from the school district. The woman was Howard's bonus from Spieler for a job well done."

Father Francis raised an eyebrow. "Wait a minute. You're saying that the superintendent is not only an embezzler, he's also involved in sex trafficking?"

"Tangentially, yes," said Charlie. "Remember the man in the striped suit?"

"Ms. Bourne mentioned him," said Father Francis.

"We finally ID'd him. He's used multiple identities, but his real name is Sergei Kovalev. He's a big-time real estate broker under investigation for fraud and tax evasion. Property isn't the only thing he's been brokering, though."

"He sells people?"

"Yes. He's been moving trafficked women and children from MS-13 to rich clients for years. When we cleared out that MS-13 rats' nest with the help of Warden Cavanaugh, Kovalev ran into the woods and got away. We couldn't ID him at the time. But now we've got him."

"What led you to him?"

"Uriah Howard gave him up. With no one left to help him with his dirty work, Kovalev had to start taking care of his trafficking business on his own. He personally met Uriah Howard behind the abandoned frozen food plant by the railroad tracks to deliver Alice's mother in a dog cage. Howard drove the woman up to his cabin by Crystal Lake, violated her until she died, and left her remains for the mountain lions."

"That poor woman. I'll offer up a mass for her and her little girl. Have you arrested Kovalev?"

"Oh yeah. We nailed him," said Charlie. "We have solid evidence to make our case. We're going to put him away. And we have a warrant out for the superintendent, too."

"A real estate broker and a school superintendent — what's the connection?"

"Kovalev is Superintendent Spieler's brother-in-law."

Father Francis shook his head. "What about Yudas Medina? Do you have any theories to explain why he was shot?"

"We're working on the trafficking angle. Could be Yudas was tangled up in it somehow, and that's what got him killed. We're talking to anyone who was connected to him. We're planning to bring in Yudas's boss, Billy Baker, for questioning. Also that pesticide mogul, Sean Stark. Maybe they can shed some light."

Father Francis steepled his hands in front of his mouth and nodded his head. Bound by the Seal of Confession, he could say no more.

91

TUESDAY, JUNE 7, 1999
Aurora's Cottage
Santa Cruz, The Westside

AURORA STEPPED AWAY FROM THE EASEL next to her koi pond and squinted, considering the juxtaposition of lights and darks on her canvas. She blended a few drops of linseed oil into a daub of rose madder on her palette. As she painted, she mused about her teaching colleagues.

Dear Ruth Redding, over sixty and so close to retirement. The Monday after the Prudenciana school year ended, she'd been forced to start a whole new class at a year-round school. Setting up a new classroom is as big a job as moving a household, and Ruth wasn't even given custodial support. No one realized what she was going through until it was too late. Climbing a ladder to put a heavy box up on a shelf, she fell and broke her hip. Recovery from surgery and then rehab was going to take many painful months.

Tom Olson. Moved to Silicon Valley and getting a divorce.
What a loss!

Katie Cooper and her husband. Moved out of state without leaving a forwarding address or a phone number.

Can't blame her. She needed a clean break from what was no doubt the worst year of her life.

Aurora could still hear in her mind her last conversation with Katie. "Aurora, why are you so hard on yourself? You're amazing. Please believe in yourself. You're a strong, competent, independent woman. You don't need to be alone the rest of your life to prove that — to yourself or to anyone else. Everybody needs love. It's not a sign of weakness. You act like you believe you're not worthy of love. But you are. You should have lots of love in your life. 'All of this and passionate kisses', like the song says! You deserve to be happy."

The waterfall shushed a soothing sound. A dragonfly dipped the tip of its curved abdomen into the pond, laying eggs on a water lily's heart-shaped leaf. Aurora slipped her hand in her pocket and thumbed her green river rock.

A twig snapped and Aurora looked up. Three children smiled at Aurora from under the shadow of a nearby fig tree — Salvador Luna; Alice's twin, Miriam; and one-legged Danny Santiago, the boy who'd died of bone cancer. Danny leaned on a twisted madrone crutch. A woman resembling Alice stood with the children, her arm around Miriam's shoulder. The group appeared to be prepared for a journey. The children wore backpacks, and the woman held a suitcase decorated with pink butterfly tattoo decals. Salvador wistfully raised his hand in a goodbye.

"I love you," Aurora said. "I'll never forget you. Go in peace."

The little group turned and walked across the water of the koi pond, into the deep shade of the incense cedar grove in the corner of the garden. A misty light surged around them and then they were gone. Aurora had a feeling she wouldn't see them again.

*   *   *

The next day at sunrise, she met some members of the Santa Cruz Bird Club in the parking lot of the County Government Building. They drove down to the Byrd River together to take a census. The club had done a study earlier in the spring. Today they were following up, collecting more data on the impact of post-flood riparian vegetation removal on the bird populations.

By late morning, it was clear that removal of nesting habitat after the flood, at the height of breeding season, had severely impacted both resident and migrant birds. Numbers of individuals and diversity of species were far lower than any previously recorded on the Byrd River. Nest-robbing cowbirds, starlings, and crows proliferated.

Along a reach of the riverbank not visible from the road, Aurora found herself staring at a shantytown built of trash. She picked her way through the brush, careful to avoid wads of used toilet paper and heaps of human feces.

At the survey zone's uppermost reach, along the edge of an arroyo willow thicket, Aurora listened for bird song. Above the pale violet Gabilan Mountain Range, sunrise colors had given way to brilliant cerulean blue. A flash of yellow caught her attention. A series of descending notes, slurred and abrupt, bubbled out of the tangled brush. Wilson's warbler. She made a tick mark on her data card and watched the bright yellow bird flit upstream.

The river was a solid ribbon of molten silver. It wound through grey-green fields cut with dark furrows. The furrows converged at the distant horizon, pointing like an arrow to the chalky lavender mountains of the north. Silhouetted at the foot of the mountains was the steeple of Father Francis' church.

Aurora's heart reached for him. She thought about how she'd changed since they'd first met nearly a year ago. She would probably always have to struggle with her inner critic, but her confidence and self-esteem had grown, and she'd awakened fully to her life purpose. She'd found her voice, and would never again be bullied or shamed into silence.

Still, she was alone, and hopelessly in love with Father Francis. Aurora's breath caught on that ever-present bittersweet ache. Why couldn't she shake it? She couldn't imagine ever caring for anyone else, even though her relationship with Father Francis could never be more than platonic. So be it. That would have to be enough. She sighed, accepting the ache in her heart. She just needed to practice being grateful and at peace with herself, and putting her whole self into living the life she'd been given. It was an honor to be associated with him, and with of all the other people who were working so hard to protect Mother Earth and keep hope alive.

She turned to rejoin her companions and finish the census. On her way home, she'd visit Ruth at the hospital.

Bushwhacking through the dense willow thicket, she was greeted by a loud chorus of frogs.

She pushed aside a tangle of branches, and stepped onto a red dirt road.

She rubbed her eyes. Ahead, a familiar garden gate and craftsman's cottage beckoned.

*   *   *

NAADAAYI HÉEN A TAYEE

She awoke in her bed, naked. The curtains were open, the sky grey and drizzling.

Where is he? Did the medicine plants save him?

Aurora rushed to the wardrobe — empty except for an eyelet-trimmed white shift with pearl buttons up the bodice. She grabbed it off the hanger and pulled it over her head. Not bothering to brush her wild hair or fasten the buttons, she burst out of her room and down the hall. When she reached his bedroom, she threw open the door.

He was sitting up in bed. His chest was bare. From the hips down, a white comforter covered him. His skin had regained its healthy color and his physique was completely restored — sculpted and muscular, more powerful and vibrant than she'd ever seen him. A small scar on his breast just above his heart and a fading red welt along his side remained where the demons had slashed and stung him. His clean and shining hair hung loose around his shoulders. A cozy fire burned in the fireplace.

He smiled, melting all her fear.

She ran across the room and threw herself on top of him. He wrapped his arms around her, strong and certain.

She raised her face to his. His kiss was hungry and wet. She moaned. He stroked her hair, and ran the tip of his finger over the curve of her ear. Pleasure stabbed down to her curling toes. He kissed her eyes and nose and chin and throat, nuzzled the crook of her neck, and gently bit her earlobe.

She arched her back. He ran his hand over her bottom and under her shift. She held her breath as he softly teased up along her inner thighs. When he parted her with fingers that wriggled and tickled like sea grasses, she cried out.

Unremitting in his attentions under her shift, he palmed her breast with his other hand, tracing her sensitive areola in feather-soft circles.

She kissed down the muscled curves of his torso, inhaling his scent, then plunged her hand under the comforter to his cock, hard and erect. Her breath caught. She gripped the silky ridged skin. He made a sound, part growl, part moan, threw his head back, and kicked away the covers.

With only her shift between them, they rolled and kissed until he was on top of her. She squeezed her thighs tight around him, feeling his erection push against her belly, needing him to enter her.

With trembling hands, he lifted her gown over her head, and put his mouth to her breast. Aurora's desperate hips pushed and circled against the naked length of him.

With a deep-throated chuckle, he thrust his fingers into her. Waves of ecstasy crashed and broke through her. She called his name and shuddered. His mouth found hers.

Panting, she reached again for his pulsing cock, caressed its veined ridges and smooth wide crown, its opening wet and sticky. She lifted and arched, straining to guide him into her.

His body stiffened. He rolled off.

She begged him not to stop.

Propped on an elbow, he brushed a curl away from her face, and kissed her on the tip of the nose.

"Wait," he said. "Wait, *ñ'a táayaa.*"

Aurora threw her arm over her eyes, her heart roaring in her ears as waves of desire thundered through her.

He slid out of the bed and lifted her in his arms. Gently, he released her onto the floor, squarely on her own two feet. He reached for a blue silk robe draped over a chair and helped her put it on. They stood face to face — she in his robe, he naked and hard. His cockstand twitched ferociously, a glistening drop of moisture on the tip.

He pulled her into his arms and kissed her on top of her head, breathing her in. She strained her hips against him, wanting him, needing him. With a gentle touch, he raised her chin and held her with his eyes.

"We need to wait, Aurora. First I'm going to marry you."

She buried her head against his chest and sobbed. He picked her up and sat down on the bed with her on his lap.

He rocked her, nuzzling and kissing her softly, immersing her in his scent, enfolding her in the powerful and comforting essence of his being. Gently stroking her back, he spoke to her tenderly in a language she didn't understand. Through the silk robe she felt his desire, still strong and hard. She ached to have him. But she was certain he would do no more than hold her, for now.

When he set her back down on the floor, she stood barefoot and shivering, her emotions yo-yoing between need, shame, and anger.

He wiped a tear off her cheek. "I'm sorry, *ñ'a táayaa*. I shouldn't have let things get so far. Will you forgive me?"

She nodded. He gave her fur-lined slippers, and wrapped her in a soft, warm blanket. Then she watched him dress in sweat pants, a sweatshirt, and moccasins. His eyes were sapphire blue fire; their usual grey-green hue burned away, his pupils intense and enlarged.

"What we both need right now," he said, "is something nourishing to eat."

In the kitchen, Frank held Aurora's chair for her. Once they were both seated and had begun to eat, Frank spoke.

"You've been through a lot, *ñ'a táayaa*. I know what you did to get the medicine plants for me." His eyes were so full of love she blushed.

She put down her fork and wrinkled her forehead. "Exactly who is taking care of us, Frank? Who's doing all of this cooking and housekeeping? Why are they doing it?"

"Everyone in the tribe is taking a turn. It's fundamental to our culture that we help and care for one another. We're family."

"When the old women came to tell me you were hurt, I thought I remembered them. And as I was rushing to you, I had visions of having been here with you long ago, when we were both young. And … some of the words in the language you speak are beginning to make sense. Are these actual memories?"

"Yes. When you were about eight, you had an accident UpRiver. Remember?"

Aurora closed her eyes. "It was summer. I was at a lake with my parents. I slipped and fell off a pier, hit my head and almost drowned. I've been told that I was unconscious for over twenty-four hours."

"You fell through Frog Woman's Pond and came up here, in *Naadaayi Héen a Tayee*. You were so young, so lost and frightened. We didn't think you'd ever be able to go back UpRiver, so the tribe adopted you. You and I became inseparable friends. Our People love you, Aurora. But you insisted that you had to return UpRiver, and eventually you found a way." Frank reached for her hand. "And now, *ñ'a táayaa*, you've found your way back to me."

*   *   *

WEDNESDAY, JUNE 8, 1999
AURORA'S COTTAGE
SANTA CRUZ, THE WESTSIDE

Blue was waiting at the front door for Aurora when she returned from the bird survey. His purr in high gear, he circled her, arching his back and rubbing against her ankles. He followed her into the house and wouldn't let her rest, demanding to be fed.

She filled his bowl and he shook the kibble as if it were prey, crunching its bones in gastronomic delight. Aurora slumped into her chair and stared into space. After some time, she noticed the answering machine blinking. She hit the play button.

"Hello. Aurora. This is Father Francis." She sat up straight, heart racing. "I hope you are well, and enjoying your summer vacation. I have good news. The Bakers contacted me. They want a meeting with our committee to finalize putting their property into an agricultural conservation easement. They've already met with our attorney, Mrs. Petrakis. They've requested that our whole group convene with them and their lawyer at their beach house this Friday evening, June 10th. Mrs. Baker specifically expressed interest in having you join us. Number 1386 Pelican Dunes Condos. Seven o'clock. You've been a part of this project from the beginning, so I hope you can make it. Please give me a call and let me know."

Aurora listened to her heart drum against her chest. She dialed his number and left a message confirming that she'd attend the meeting at the Baker's.

92

T HE NEXT FRIDAY, AURORA DROVE DOWN THE COAST just after 6:00pm. The sun was still high in the sky. Her radio wailed out "Scar Tissue" by the Red Hot Chili Peppers, the summer's big hit. She crested the Mar Monte hill and looked out over the wide Byrd River Valley below. Sun flashed on a patch of azure blue ocean to her right. A big swell was due to hit the coast this evening. There'd be great surfing tomorrow. Her heart soared.

She turned up the radio to drown out inappropriate thoughts of Father Francis Hilman. She felt sexy in her brand new, matching blue bra and panties and her pretty summer rayon dress — a floral print with pearl buttons, a low, scooped neckline and princess cap sleeves. She loved the way the hem of the skirt fell with a graceful swing just above her knees. She'd arranged her hair in a chignon, and had even put on a little make-up — mascara and light lipstick, a spritz of tuberose and gardenia perfume, and she'd painted her toenails in a hot new summer color.

Should she have worn something more professional? She didn't want to do or say anything that would distract from the important purpose of this meeting. The Bakers were actually going to sign an agreement to put their property into an agricultural trust in perpetuity! What an incredible break-through! Finally, after all the suffering and setbacks of this past year, here was a victory — one shining light, a beacon of hope. Mr. Baker even seemed interested in eventually transitioning to organic farming. The Bakers were influential. If they could be convinced to abandon chemical-intensive agriculture, the rest of the valley might follow.

Aurora pulled into the gatehouse of Pelican Dunes Estates and rolled down her window. The thunder of breaking waves told her that the huge southern swell she'd been anticipating had hit the coast. The guard gave Aurora a guest permit and a map, with a circle drawn around the Bakers' beach house.

She navigated through the complex of large and unique homes, parked and found her way along a path meandering through native sand verbena and lupine. Catching glimpses of the rivermouth as she walked, she realized she was not far from the placed she'd been assaulted nearly a year ago. A shiver ran down her spine. She promised herself again that this summer she'd finally get around to taking that women's self-defense class she'd been putting off all year.

Aurora arrived at the Baker's modern three-story beach house and knocked at an imposing carved wooden door. A maid welcomed her.

Father Francis and the environmental attorney, Mrs. Petrakis, had just arrived and were standing in the foyer. When Father Francis turned toward Aurora and smiled, her emotions climbed, dipped, and whiplashed like a rollercoaster. His eyes lingered on her — her face, her dress, her breasts ... She blushed.

"Aurora, I believe you've met Mrs. Petrakis, haven't you?" asked Father Francis.

Aurora and the environmental attorney shook hands, and the maid escorted the guests into a dining room with white walls and high-vaulted ceilings. Tall windows opened to a dramatic view of the ocean. The Bakers and their lawyer were seated around a table.

William Baker rose when Aurora, Father Francis, and Mrs. Petrakis entered the room.

Mr. Baker held a chair for Aurora, next to Malone. It was the first time Aurora had seen Malone since the media ambush debacle after the flood at the river levee. She looked haggard, her face pale and her hands trembling. Was she having a hard time signing away, in perpetuity, rights to develop her land?

Malone leaned close to Aurora and patted her hand. "Glad you could come tonight. Billy should be here soon. He's looking forward to seeing you." Her breath smelled of liquor.

The maid circulated, offering dark chocolate truffles and port. Aurora felt awkward for so many reasons.

When she was sure he wasn't looking in her direction, she risked a glance at Father Francis. His hair was neatly braided and tied with leather. He licked a spot of chocolate off his lip. His white-on-white Hawaiian-style fish-print shirt was stunning against the cinnamon tone of his skin. A cloud slid across the sun shining through the window, and a shadow pattern resembling fish scales flickered over his arms.

Mrs. Petrakis led the Bakers through a review of the contract. When the review was finally completed and all details found acceptable, Malone and William Baker signed their conservation easement papers, legally guaranteeing that their land would remain agricultural, never to be paved or developed, forever.

The documents were notarized and flurry of hand shaking and congratulations all around followed. It was done!

Aurora, along with the rest of the committee, found herself being escorted out of the Bakers' door on a surge of mutual congratulations.

Outside, Aurora froze in place and stared upward into the living canvas of an impressionist painting by one Aurora's favorite painters — a California colorist from the Society of Six. The setting sun had impastoed the sky with raw color. Jagged, thick brush strokes of magenta, Bellini blue, orange madder, and Indian yellow blazed across the western horizon.

She glanced over her shoulder. The priest and the attorney, absorbed in conversation, were walking away up the path. Aurora turned again to the sky — a lightshow of kaleidoscopic color changes. She had to go to the beach to watch.

A trickle of fear ran through her veins. The faces of those deranged men in the dunes flashed in her mind.

No. It's a beautiful beach, a beautiful night. I refuse to be afraid.

She slipped off her sandals and headed toward the water.

Sitting on the sand above the water's edge, she savored the fading colors. A few stars were already visible. Line after line of enormous breakers rolled in, rooster tails spraying off their backs. The surf was rising. Waves with eight-foot faces pounded the shore. Down the beach at the rivermouth, hundreds of sea birds circled in the air, waded in the shallows, mewled and called.

"Aurora!" The shout pierced the twilight. She recognized that voice.

93

TWILIGHT, FRIDAY, JUNE 10, 1999
Pelican Dunes, On the Beach

AURORA WATCHED BILLY STAGGER TOWARD HER over the sand. He loomed above her, feet apart, hands in his pockets, swaying slightly.

"Go'devening, gorshous. 'magine meeting you here."

A gust picked up the hem of Aurora's dress and flipped it, uncovering her legs to the hips.

Billy leered. He sat down heavily beside her, with an exhaled *ump* of alcoholic fumes, and slung his heavy arm over her shoulder. She shrunk away from him.

"So was'sis 'bout you talking with my par'nts? You wanna stop us from developing our property, shweetheart?"

"They invited us to meet with them, Billy."

"Yeah. Mother told me you were coming." Billy's laugh sounded odd. "She thinks you and I should get together."

He leaned over and put his face just inches from hers. A ring of blood crusted around the rim of his nostril. He was more than drunk. Billy Baker had that cocaine look.

Aurora knew better than to be confrontational with a coked-out drunk. She smiled at him as sweetly as she could.

"I need to go now, Billy. I'm already late. Someone is expecting me," she bluffed. She tried to rise.

He grabbed her. "Wait a minute. Wha'cher hurry?"

"Really, I have to go now."

She struggled against him in earnest, panic rising.

He swung onto his knees, straddling her, and shoved her shoulders into the sand with both of his hands. His face came close. His breath was sour. His lips were fat and slimy. A lock of greasy blonde hair fell across his forehead. Fear heightened her perception of his bloodshot eyes, and the beads of sweat on his upper lip. She turned her face away, fighting waves of panic and nausea.

He grabbed her chin and kissed her roughly, biting her lip, making it bleed.

She twisted frantically under him.

"No! Stop it! Get off me!"

She bucked and writhed, trying to get free. A hard ridge pressed like iron against her pubic bone.

"Oh, yeah, sweet pie. Tha's good. Umm. I wan'ed ta ball you since the firs' time I saw you."

Billy wedged his knee between her legs, forcing them apart. He grabbed the top of her dress and yanked. The pearl buttons ripped off all the way to her waist. He forced his hand down the top of her bra, grabbed her breast, and pinched her nipple hard. She cried out.

"Get off."

A powerful male voice cut through the pounding of the surf.

"What the fuck?"

"Get off her, Billy."

The weight of Billy's body lifted and Aurora was able to breathe. She pushed herself onto her elbows.

Father Francis yanked Billy to his feet. The men glared at one another, fists clenching, neck tendons bunching.

"What? Son of a bitch. You! Oh this'iz good. You fuckin' piece of shit priest. Leave me alone."

"You need to leave Ms. Bourne alone, Billy. How about if you just go on home now."

"This'iz none of your fucking business, *Father*." Billy took a swing at the priest, who easily ducked the blow. Billy stumbled as Father Francis danced aside.

Aurora scuttled like a crab away from the men, scrambled to her feet, and brushed sand off. She covered her breasts and stood with her arms across her chest, sucking her stinging, throbbing lip and watching the men, horrified.

Billy and Father Francis were close to the water's edge. She moved near enough to hear what they were saying over the crash of big waves.

"You meddling son of a bitch. Shtay away from my fam'ly. Our property'sh none of your god'amn bishness. Keep away from me and my par'nts."

Billy charged the priest, landing a glancing blow to the shoulder.

Father Francis gracefully sidestepped, putting his hands in the air in a gesture of nonviolence.

"Okay, Billy. I hear you. I'm just going to take Ms. Bourne and go now."

"Ha! Take Ms. Bourne and go? Oh, yeah. I bet you wanna take her, don't you. You pathetic bastard. Think I don't know you wanna *do* her? I've seen how you look at her. All your motherfucking priest bullshit. You're hiding, Hilman. You're kidding yourself. You wanna do her, bad. Jus' like me. But yer not man enough."

"Okay, Billy. Be that as it may, we're going to go, now. Maybe we can talk about all this later, when you're sober."

Father Francis, hands still in the air, stepped backward into the water. The full moon shone on the men's faces and on the waves. The inexorable tide was rising higher. Surging water swirled around the men's ankles.

"Sober my big dick. I'm perfectly cogni— coa— I'm perfect'ly clear. I know exac'ly what's going on. You gotta go mucking 'round in everybody else's business, 'cause you're not man enough to get it up on your own."

Billy charged the priest again.

Father Francis stepped back, open palms up. The two men stood calf-deep in the moonlit lace edge of sea foam. The water hissed and boiled over sand and shells.

"Look, Billy, I —"

Billy's right shoulder dipped. His arm reached across his body. He drew something out from under his shirt at his left hip and raised the object over his head. In the fading light, it gleamed like a torch.

Aurora stood at the water's edge, her body quaking uncontrollably. *A gun!*

*   *   *

Billy leveled the weapon at the priest.

"Stay away from my mother, you son of a bitch."

"Billy, put the gun down," said Father Francis. "If you shoot me, you'll ruin your life."

"Ruin my life?" Billy's high-pitched laughter startled a flock of gulls into the air. "My life is already ruined, *Father.*" Billy waved the revolver. "It doesn't matter if I kill you or not. It's already over."

"No, Billy. Your life isn't over. You've got plenty going for you. A good life to look forward to."

"You don't know anything, Father. I'm finished."

"Why would you say that?"

Billy waved the weapon at the priest. "This is the gun that shot Yudas Medina."

"Wait." Father Francis took several steps toward Billy, holding out his hands. The rising water whirled around him. "There's still hope. Stop this, Billy. Come with me to the Church, now. Let me hear your confession tonight."

Billy laughed again. "You want to hear my confession? Okay let's do this. Here and now." He steadied the gun with two hands, pointing it at the priest. "Forgive me Father for I have sinned. I fucked up bad. Day trading, I lost everything. About a million dollars. Borrowed from Stark against my CalGreen options, but I needed more, then more again. Stark gave me everything I asked for, then held the debt over my head. Threatened to tell my par'nts, said he'd force them to pay, unless I did what he wan'ed. I did it all. Bad things. Real bad. I hustled drugs an' women an' — kids, for his clients. I made Yudas Medina my go-between with the cartels. But that pansy-ass Medina lost his nerve. The idiot wan'ed ta tell the cops everything. Even tried to get me to take the fall with him." Billy's laugh rang through the twilight.

"You shot him so he wouldn't expose you?"

"Shut up. This'iz my confession. Jus' listen. We were in my par'nts' livingroom, arguing." Billy's shoulders slumped and he lowered the gun. He swayed as the water twisted and eddied around his knees. "Yudas says he's decided to go to the police, tells me I should turn myself in too. Jesus Christ. What a loser." Billy raised the revolver and aimed at the priest's face. "I tell him I'll drive him to the police station. But it's a trick. I head for the river instead. When we get out of the car we're standing on the riverbank, shouting at each other."

"Then you shot him?"

"No. No. I heard a gun go off. Bullet went right through Yudas' forehead. He fell." Billy waved his gun toward the priest's heart.

"Someone else shot Yudas?"

"I turn around. There's Mother, her Colt in her hand."

"Malone?"

"Yes. She must of heard us, followed us from the house. She's always trying to protect me from everything."

"Your mother shot Yudas?"

"Yes. Yes. My mother." Billy, trembling and crying, shouted over the thundering waves. "I pried the gun out of her hand. Told her I'd take care of it. Sent her home. Then I rolled Yudas' body into the river. That's it. I have sinned, Father." Billy cocked the gun. "And now I'm going to hell."

Father Francis raised his hand and made the sign of the cross. "God loves you and forgives you unconditionally, Billy. May God the Father of Mercies and the Grace of Christ set you free from all of your sins."

"No! No. It's too late."

Even before she heard the shot, Aurora watched a black stain spread over the front of Father Francis' white shirt.

Pain contorted his face. He put a hand to his chest, stumbled backward.

A mountainous wave crashed over him, engulfed him.

He disappeared under the churning black sea.

Without hesitation, Aurora dove into the surf. The shock of cold saltwater cut her through and through. Underwater, her hands groped for his body. Seaweed tangled around her arms and legs. She kicked and came up for air, then dove again.

She raked the black water frantically, hoping that if she touched something, it would be human, not a shark lusting for blood.

She came up for another breath. The waves avalanched overhead. He would surely drown soon. She dove again.

*   *   *

Billy staggered in the surge and dropped the gun. The tide took it. Open-mouthed, he stared over the empty black water sucking at his legs.

The ground shook. He felt the shockwave rumble like a locomotive racing toward him under the Earth.

Jesus Christ. Earthquake.

The sand liquefied under Billy's feet. He fell. The Earth kept shaking. He got to his feet and stumbled backwards. Kelp coiled around his ankles. The churning water pulled him over. His head struck a rock.

*   *   *

They watched from the dunes, unconcerned by the little quake. Dressed in black, the two men were nearly invisible, except for the moonlight glinting off a rifle.

"One shot, three kills," said the first man. "Nice work."

The second man lowered his modified Barrett M82 sniper rifle and snorted scornfully. "My bullet hits the priest, he falls in the water, the bitch dives in after him, and Billy trips and whacks his head on a rock." He rolled his shoulders. "But I can't claim confirmed kills unless we recover the bodies."

The Men in Black peered out over the dark ocean, then watched Billy's unconscious body wash back and forth over the sand.

"Did you see Billy's face?" The second man softly snorted again.

"He thought his bullet hit the priest." The first man's upper lip raised in a snarling grin.

"Just like Malone when we took out Yudas," sneered the second man.

"My Yudas kill was much more technical."

"I'll give you that."

The men's laughter hissed through the dune grasses.

✱   ✱   ✱

Aurora's lungs burned. Spots swam behind her closed eyes. The surf thundered above. She'd have to surface soon, or drown. Her hands flailed in the dark caldron.

There. What was that?

It brushed against her again. She lunged, and struck him with her head. She grabbed, wrapped her arms around his body, rolled him to get her hand under his armpit, and kicked hard for the surface.

She hit air.

Breathe.

Hand under his chin, she lifted his face above the roiling water, then kneed the unconscious man in the rear, so he floated on his back.

In the moonlight, she could see that they were outside the breaking waves. She shivered violently as she floated, her right arm over his right shoulder and across his chest, her right hand gripping his left armpit. It was too dark to tell how much he was bleeding.

Is he alive?

She placed her middle fingers on his neck and searched for a pulse. Yes. There it was, like a butterfly in her hand. In spite of her shivering, she could feel his chest move up and down.

He lifted his left arm out of the water, dropped his hand over hers, and squeezed weakly.

Her whole being went out to this man in her arms. With that gentle squeeze of the hand, they were welded as if two sides of the same

599

penny. What she was made of blazed and melted into the incandescent metal of his soul and she knew she could never let go of him, no matter what.

The water surged and splashed around them. His lips touched her ear. "Aurora, I love you. Don't give up. It's not over."

Aurora looked out to sea. An enormous outsider hissed and crackled toward them.

As the wave crested overhead, Father Francis' voice rang through her. "We're going home, *Ña' táayaa.*"

The wave curled and started to break.

"Breathe!" she screamed.

She wrapped her arms and legs around him and pulled him down under the breaker.

They were deep, but still they tumbled and rolled. She held on to him with all her strength.

A whirlpool caught them. They were spun around, around. She couldn't fight against it. It pulled them down into the depths.

Her chest was about to explode. Still, they clung to one another.

A curtain drew across her mind, absolute black, devoid of sound or light. A swirl of blue light appeared out of the dark and spiraled toward them. In the center of the blue, a point of white light opened and closed like a flower, coming closer.

Out of the flower came forth forms — silver, shimmering, luminous, circling.

THE VILLAGE ON THE RIVER
UNDER THE RIVER

"My bounty is as boundless as the sea, My love as deep; the more I give to thee, The more I have, for both are infinite."

— William Shakespeare, *Romeo and Juliet*

94

3RD YEAR OF RESTORATION AFTER GLOBAL WARMING
DELUGE
Recording #56-b from the archives of Dr. Melody A. Escobar,
Anthropologist
Narrator: *Yáahl*, a Storyteller

NAADAAYI HÉEN A TAYEE, AN AREA NOT LOCATABLE ON GPS

*W*E PULLED THEM OUT OF THE SEA. *Two pathetic, drowned beings. Ah, she was beautiful. Her thin dress torn and clinging to that mermaid body. Hair like melted gold fell on her cheek, her arms, and the rise of her breast.*

He was bleeding from the bullet wound just above his heart.

I helped carry them to a blanket on the shore and our healers set to work.

We made a bonfire on the beach. The wood cracked and smoked. Hot flames warmed their poor cold bodies.

The bullet went through and through. We were lucky it missed heart and lungs. Our healers staunched his bleeding with a compress of medicine plants.

We stripped off the torn rags of their clothes and wrapped them in our blankets, woven with medicine patterns.

While some rubbed their hands and feet with herbs, others pushed hard on their chests, and breathed for them, until the water they had swallowed came up and they choked and vomited and started to breathe on their own.

Warriors beat the lodge drum, hit the clapper sticks, and sang. I danced a medicine dance around the fire. In this way, we thanked the Great Mystery for the return of Salmon Boy and his mate.

Their eyes fluttered open. Their shivering blue lips parted to swallow hot tea. Life flushed their skin with color. Salmon Boy sat up and grinned at us. Were those tears in his eyes? His woman fainted.

He smiled down at her, gently touched her cheek. Then he looked at us, and his eyes rolled back in his head. We lowered him down to the blanket. And then we carried them both up to the house we had made ready for Salmon Boy and his ñ'a táayaa.

95

AURORA WOKE, SUNLIGHT WARMING HER FACE.
Father Francis stood at the window, the gauzy curtain billowing gently around him. Sun played over his wounded, bandaged back.

He turned toward her. Blood seeped through the dressing covering the bullet wound above his heart; dark blood, not fresh. Relief and joy surged through her.

He's alive.

She raised herself on one elbow so she could see all of him. Faded blue jeans hung low on his hips. She inhaled deeply then, realizing she'd been holding her breath, thinking he might be naked.

As he approached, she pulled the sheet up to her chin.

He leaned close, his brow creased. She felt more than naked.

"How do you feel?" he asked.

"I — ah ..."

He sat down on the edge of the bed. The mattress sank under his weight. Tenderly, he took her hands in his. "I don't know what you remember. We were rescued by our people. We're in our home village, in *Naadaayi Héen a Tayee*. You're safe, Aurora. Nothing will harm you here."

The ceiling spun. Aurora tugged her hands out of his and let her head fall back on the pillows. She covered her eyes.

"Are you dizzy?"

"Mmn."

"The dizziness will pass. It's better if you sit up. Let me help you."

He put his arms around her. His stubble rasped her cheek. Her face pressed into the curve of his neck. He smelled of wood smoke and the ocean. Her mind fluttered wildly. Her eyes fixed on the muscles flexing in his arms.

Wincing, he lifted her to a sitting position. He fluffed the pillows behind her. The sheets fell down around her waist.

With a pained look, he pulled the sheets back up to cover her breasts.

"Here, drink this."

He put a glass of water to her lips and she drank. The water was ice cold, as if it had flowed over granite.

His physical proximity engulfed her. The man was beautiful. She could barely resist the urge to smooth her fingers over his skin. She couldn't stop staring at his bare chest and hard stomach.

"Aurora?"

She felt her face flush again, and lowered her eyes.

"I apologize for not wearing a shirt this morning. It's just that it hurts to get my arm in a sleeve. But if I'm making you uncomfortable, I'll go put something on."

"No, of course not. I don't mind. To be honest, I like seeing you shirtless." Aurora blushed again. "And to answer your question about what I remember, our time together here as children is still a bit foggy, but I do recall everything that's happened since we met on that physics hike UpRiver last summer. And Frank, I — I need to a make confession."

He arched an eyebrow in surprise and did an almost comical double take. "Confession?"

Aurora looked at her hands. "When I was here alone while you were hunting demons, I explored your library and I, um, I discovered your Kama Sutra and your books on Tantra yoga."

Frank threw his head back and laughed. "I was hoping you'd find those!" He winced and put his hand on his chest.

"Does it hurt badly?" Aurora asked.

"Don't worry. I heal fast."

"I feel so badly that you were shot. I never imagined Billy had a gun, or that he'd actually shoot you. It's my fault. It's a miracle either of us survived."

"You have no reason to feel guilty. What happened was inevitable. There's nothing you could have done to change it. You saved my life, Aurora. The bullet was nearly fatal. If you hadn't held onto me in the surf, the vortex would surely have been too much for me. I would have drowned. You saved me again, Aurora. With your strength and courage, and your beautiful loving heart."

The fire in Frank's eyes made Aurora burn. Before she could think of something to say, he rose.

"I'll leave you now, *ñ'a táayaa*. I didn't want you to wake up alone. But now that you're awake, you'll want some privacy. When you're ready, meet me in the kitchen." He smiled and closed the door firmly behind him.

Aurora could still feel the weight of him sitting next to her on the bed.

*   *   *

In the kitchen, chili verde simmered on the stove. There was also a salad, a pot of black beans and a pan of Mexican rice. Cheese enchiladas warmed in the oven. On the kitchen counter, they found a covered basket of fry bread, a bowl of guacamole, and another of salsa fresca.

They ate in companionable silence.

Aurora finally spoke. "Why do you call me *ñ'a táayaa*? What does it mean?"

Frank pushed away his plate. "UpRiver, it would be identified as the Haida language. Here, a much older language is spoken, the origin of many of the UpRiver tongues. *Ñ'a táayaa* means, well, simply put, it means my sweetheart."

Frank wrapped Aurora's hands in his. "You are my sweetheart, Aurora. My desire, my own heart. I love you with every atom of my being. I will love you forever."

Aurora closed her eyes for a moment. When she opened them again, he was still watching her. She slipped her hands out of his.

"Frank, the last time we were here together, you said you were going to marry me."

Frank smiled and nodded. "Yes." He reached out to touch her face. She pulled away.

"I think, well, aren't you supposed to ask me first? I mean, is this the kind of place where women don't have any say in who they marry?"

Frank raised his brow again, with a glint in his eyes. "Ah, *ñ'a táayaa.* You've forgotten?"

Aurora shook her head.

"I proposed to you before we were handfasted. You accepted me, then. But, of course … Please, forgive me for being so presumptuous."

He scraped his chair out of the way and knelt before her. Again taking her hands in his, he said, "My beautiful, cherished Ms. Aurora Bourne, I adore you with every fiber of my being. I will love you forever. I long to marry you, and finally become one with you, in every way. Please, will you consent to be my wife?"

Aurora's heart beat in his hands. The man kneeling before her seemed god-like. It was inconceivable to her that she could be worthy of marriage to such a magnificent being.

"Aurora, you don't fully realize who you are yet. You have more power than you dream of, and more beauty. Not just physical beauty but inner beauty of the mind, heart, and spirit. To look at you, to be with you, unsettles me to the core. I want you more than I can say. I have wanted to wed you for eons. Please, don't make me wait any longer. Marry me, *ñ'a táayaa.*"

Trembling, she whispered, "Yes."

He stood and helped her to her feet, then wrapped his arms around her. She lifted her face to his, and they kissed with great tenderness. She closed her eyes and they were floating, the glorious ringing music of Rumm'e rippling all around them. Love and light flooded through her, forever dispelling the old ache in her heart. She was finally truly home. No matter what happened, she'd never feel alone again.

When the kiss ended, he took a step back, holding her at arm's length, his forehead wrinkled.

"I have to go away for a few days, Aurora."

A wave of panic surged through her. She stared at him, wide-eyed. "No!"

"I can't be in the same house with you right now, *ñ'a táayaa*. I don't think I can control myself any longer. I'm going away until our wedding."

"How — how long?"

"I will be away for three days. Ever since we were handfasted, last time we were here together, our people have been preparing for a wedding upon our return. You will be taken care of, and initiated into the wedding rites while I'm gone. There's something I need to do."

"But, last time you went away ..." She couldn't finish what she wanted to say.

"I am not going into danger. Don't worry, *ñ'a táayaa*." He grinned suggestively, lasciviously. "When I marry you, in three days' time, I will be intact."

96

THE WEDDING OF
TEHÉATLA SAGRADO **AND HIS** *Ñ'A TÁAYAA*

O N THE THIRD DAY, women who Aurora now remembered and cherished as family sang as they helped her prepare for her wedding.

Well before dawn, they bathed her with fragrant herbs and washed her hair, all the while offering advice, some of it playful and ribald, some serious and solemn, about how to have a successful and happy marriage. Amidst much laughter, they informed her that the men were instructing her groom in a similar manner.

They wrapped her in his silk robe and brushed her hair until it shimmered like gold. Then they tied feathers into the strands with slender colored ribbons.

Finally they slipped off the robe and covered her nakedness with a white doeskin dress they had taken from the wardrobe. The doeskin fit perfectly and felt astonishingly soft and warm.

The dress was decorated with shells — which tinkled like delicate bells when she moved — and colored glass beads that glowed like drops of fused starlight, casting rainbows all around her.

When Aurora stretched out her arms, her fringed sleeves looked like wings. On her feet, her bridesmaids slipped white deerskin moccasins beaded with the same shimmering crystals as her dress.

Clothed in bridal regalia, Aurora was led downstairs. A clatter of pots and pans, happy, chattering voices, and delicious aromas issued from the kitchen where the wedding feast was being readied.

A beautiful little girl placed a bouquet of white lilies, wildflowers, and lobelia in Aurora's arms.

As she passed through the house, women stopped to pat her hands and shoulders, and touch her hair. Men looked at her admiringly, and children bestowed upon her stares of awe, which she accepted as a bride's due.

Aurora recognized many people by name, flashes of memory coming to her from the other time she'd lived here and had known the Salmon People — her People — as teachers, friends, and adopted family.

The women of her bridal party led Aurora through the parlor and out the front door.

Pale predawn light, augmented by torchlight, revealed a large blanket spread out on the grass in the front yard. Colored prayer flags had been staked into the ground at each of the four corners of the blanket. People were leaving gifts for the couple on the blanket: fire wood, a buffalo skin, a fan of eagle feathers, an abalone shell necklace, a basket of smoked salmon wrapped in seaweed ...

Guests streamed across the meadow toward a ceremonial arbor at the river's edge. In the dim light, Aurora could just make out the structure, constructed in a traditional manner. Cut branches, hung with colored ribbons and feathers, formed a corral-like fence around a large circular space. At the east side of the enclosure, a chute led under an archway of flowering branches into the ceremonial space. In the center, at the base of a totem pole, a bonfire burned in a rock-lined pit.

Firekeepers stood at the entrance, smudging the wedding guests with smoke from smoldering bundles of dried sweetgrass and sage.

The women in Aurora's bridal party bid her to stop under a grove of elderberry trees some distance away, where she could see but not be seen.

Aurora observed as the inner circle of guests entered the arbor. Hundreds more guests congregated in a ring outside the fence. Aurora wondered at the multitude of people, at the diversity of races and styles of dress.

"Tribes and clans of Salmon People and their relatives from all the rivers of Earth have come to celebrate the wedding," said Grandmother Nokemes, the woman with the white streak in her hair. "The great Gathering will last for at least seven days."

A high-pitched ululating call issued forth. The ceremonial drum began its rhythmic beat.

"It is time," said Nokemes sister, Grandmother Agaskw.

Aurora's heart beat louder than the ceremonial drum as her bridal attendants led her toward the arbor circle.

When she reached the entrance, she was smudged with sweetgrass, then escorted through the chute and under the flowering arch. Her bridal party led her to the left, sunwise around the circle, so that she passed in front of each of the inner circle of guests: clan and tribal chiefs, healers, elders, family and closest friends. Many hands touched her and offered blessings as she walked by. When she had come full circle, she was conducted toward the fire in the center.

Suddenly he was there, facing her, with the leaping flames at his back, surrounded by a fiery radiance. His skin glistened. Over a white buckskin breechcloth, gathered between his legs in a manner that left no doubt about the nature of his manhood, he wore fringed white buckskin chaps, fastened with silver conchos, cut wide and flared open from the thigh down to his bare feet. The amulet against his chest flashed firelight. Long black hair, adorned with a single eagle feather tied with red string, hung loose around his shoulders.

The fire in his eyes flared through her, and her knees went weak. A sister's strong hand at each of Aurora's elbows supported her and urged her forward.

At the groom's right hand stood a chieftain, as powerful and tall as he. Clothed in a magnificent feathered cape, the chief held a long staff. He was surrounded by an aura of spectral colors wavering and glowing as brightly as the bridegroom's. The two men's auric fields merged along the edge where their shoulders met.

The bridegroom and the chief stood flanked on either side by twenty warriors, wearing only loincloths, with bows and quivers full of arrows slung over their backs.

Aurora trembled as she stepped into this force field of male power.

A handmaiden took the bouquet from her arms and another removed Aurora's moccasins. The bride and groom stood barefoot, facing one another. Frank stepped forward and took her hands in his.

The chief faced the sun just rising over the river and held up his staff, which glowed with magic in the first light. He offered prayers of blessing and thanksgiving to the spirits of the four directions, to Mother Earth and Father Sky, and to the ancestors.

Two women — daughters of Nokemes and Agaskw, and two men — the storyteller Yáahl and Cheveyo, one of the demon slayers — stepped forward. These four people identified themselves as the bride and groom's sponsors, and pledged to help, support, and guide the couple through life, to the best of their abilities.

A bowl of water was brought forward and blessed by an elder. Then the sponsors washed the hands of the bride and groom. Old Xigmacse, the healer with the long white braids, made a small cut in the palm of Frank's hand, on the mound of Venus just under his thumb, and then cut Aurora's palm in the same manner, deep enough so that blood flowed freely. The couple's hands were joined, their blood commingled. Then their hands were bound with herbs inside a clean cloth, and tied together at the wrists, while prayers were said in the old language.

Hands bound, they stood side by side facing the new morning sun sparkling on the river. Singing, handmaidens braided his and her hair together, shining gold and shimmering black strands intertwining, while the couple was smudged with smoky sweetgrass, cedar, and sage.

Nokemes stepped forward, the white streak in her hair glowing as if formed from distant galaxies. She presented the folded shawl that Aurora had received from Salvador Luna and the other children. Aurora and Frank's sponsors shook open the material. It glistened like

614

spun starlight. Fresh roses tumbled out of the folds and rose petals fell at the couple's feet, enveloping everyone in a fragrance of ethereal beauty. Aurora's skin tingled. The sponsors draped the shawl over the bride and groom, covering them head to toe, as if they were together inside a cave.

The chief spoke. "From today forward, you will feel no rain, for each of you will be shelter for the other. Now you will feel no cold, for each of you will be warmth to the other. Now there will be no loneliness, for each of you will be companion to the other, giving your whole selves, forever faithful and true. May all of your days together be filled with happiness, may beauty surround you, and the Creator light your way."

Frank whispered in Aurora's ear. "I love you, Aurora. I adore you." He kissed her softly on the temple. "Take seven steps with me, *ñ'a táayaa*, then stop."

Hands and hair entwined, they walked together under the starry shawl, sunwise around the fire for seven steps.

The chieftain standing in front of the fire raised his staff. His eyes seared through Aurora, seeing into her soul. He turned and spoke to Frank.

"Do you swear before the Creator, before your ancestors and before these people gathered here that you wish to take this woman as your wife, to declare her as your mate, to be known as her husband, to go with her as One, from this time forward, forever along the river of life, death, redemption, and return, bound by blood and love, of one body, one heart, one mind, and one spirit? Do you commit that you will faithfully and unconditionally love, respect, and care for her, with courage, strength and honor, sharing the responsibilities as well as the joys of the Turning Wheel, forever?"

"Yes. I do so swear," Frank declared in a strong and steady voice. "*Noso'n.*"

She felt him urge her forward. Her hand, cut and bound to his, throbbed and burned.

Together, they took seven more steps around the fire. Again, the chieftain raised his staff and spoke the words, this time to her.

"Yes," said Aurora. "Yes, I do so swear. *Noso'n.*"

They took seven more steps, and stopped. The priest raised his staff and spoke to the whole gathering about the reciprocal responsibilities of the couple and the community. The people shouted a response.

Once again, Frank urged her to walk. Seven more steps brought them full circle.

The chief raised his staff and intoned, "May the sun bless you by day, may the moon restore you by night, may the rain wash away your worries, and the breeze blow new strength into your being, and all the days of your life, may you walk in beauty through the worlds with gentleness and compassion. If difficulties, fear or sacrifice assail you, remember to give one another the unconditional trust, honesty, respect, care and kindness your love deserves. Have faith that your love will endure forever."

Frank slipped a circlet of gold, worked with filigree, onto Aurora's left ring finger.

Aurora wished she had a ring for him.

A woman leaned forward and put a gold ring in Aurora's hand, whispering, "This is the ring you designed for him when you were handfasted, the last time you were here."

Engraved with mysterious markings, the heavy circlet was warm, and emanated a vibration that grounded Aurora in feelings of safety and peace. She slipped it onto Frank's ring finger and met his eyes.

The chief struck his staff on the ground four times, evoking a preternatural roaring sound like thunder.

"The Creator has blessed your union. You are husband and wife."

Before Aurora had time to think, Frank was holding her close, kissing her with waves of infinite love deeper than the ocean and more vast than the sky. A joyful noise of whooping voices, clacker sticks, bells, drums, flutes, and uilleann pipes rose up to the heavens.

Someone removed the shawl from the couple's heads, folded it, and carried it away. Someone else slipped the moccasins back on Aurora's feet. All the while, she felt a powerful love and life force growing as it passed back and forth between herself and her belovéd through their cut and bound hands, and through their hearts.

"I do feel as if I've become one with you," she whispered, in awe of the sensations she was experiencing.

"From this day on, I will always be a part of you, my *ñ'a táayaa*. And you will always be part of me. No matter what distances may separate us, we will never again be alone, belovéd. These last three days away from you have been torture."

He pulled her into a strong embrace and kissed her again, this time wet, and hot, with a promise of what they would do when they were alone.

When he released her, she caught her breath, trying to stay on her feet while the Earth and sky spun. Her head cleared. They stood alone by the smoldering fire.

"Do you feel pain in your hand, Aurora?"

With surprise, she realized she did not.

"No. I only feel this surging love between us, through our hands and …" she blushed and cast her eyes down. "And through my whole body."

"Good. I'm going to unwrap the bindings, then. But know that, even when these bindings are removed, the sacred bonds of blood and spirit that join us will never come undone. Remember this, Aurora, my love. Never forget this feeling. From this day forward, we will always be One."

When he lifted the cloth and the herbs fell away from her cut, Aurora gasped in astonishment. Only a bit of dried blood and a small red line crossing her mound of Venus remained. She flexed her fingers and felt no stiffness or pain. She stroked his open palm, along a faint red welt where his cut had been, then raised questioning eyes to his.

"A small scar will remain on both of our hands, to remind us. If one or the other of us is ever in danger, the wound may reopen in the other's hand. But faith in our love will always heal us."

With a warrior's fierce and gentle strength, he kissed her palm. Then, raising his hand to cup her cheek, he searched her eyes. "Now, *ñ'a táayaa*, unbind our braids. But know that I'll always carry this feeling with me, the way our hair is entwined — our lives and destinies are forever woven together."

When she had finished unbraiding, he took her in his arms again and kissed her passionately.

She arched against him. His hands slid below her waist and he pulled her closer. She whimpered and rolled her hips, feeling him rise beneath his buckskin.

He put his hands on her hips, holding her still, and laughed softly. "Shusssh. Not yet, *ñ'a táayaa.*"

He ran his finger over her lips, then kissed her gently — a kiss full of promise.

"Come with me, my *wife.*" He drew her hand through the crook of his elbow and escorted her out of the arbor.

Feasting, revelry, and dancing had broken out in every direction. As Aurora walked with her husband across the meadow, she heard many different languages and accents: Scottish and Irish, Norwegian and Swedish, Canadian and American English, the long vowels of Maine and New England and the many dialects of the indigenous peoples of the Pacific Northwest Coast and the North Atlantic.

Guests were dressed in their best native costumes. Some wore the furs of bear, fox, puma, and wolf. Others were clothed in feathers and skins, and woven fabrics of many colors and patterns. It was true. The Salmon People and their relatives, all of the clans and tribes from around the world, were gathered here for Teheatla Sagrado's wedding.

A tangle of excited people watched as men dug a whole roast pig out of a pit, where it had been cooking for hours.

Aurora and Frank made their way to a buffet and filled their plates. They found a place at a table with friends who drank to their health and happiness and made toasts to love.

Frank placed a small piece of wedding cake in Aurora's mouth, and she in his. The cake dissolved in a burst of sweetness, and they kissed.

The music started. Frank took Aurora's hand and led her to the dancing area set up by the river. Musicians on a stage above the dance platform played fiddles, guitars, mandolins, clapper sticks, concertinas, drums, uilleann pipes, and flutes. When Aurora and Frank arrived, the musicians began a waltz. All of the other dancers parted.

Frank caught Aurora around the waist and pulled her to him. His flushed face looked dangerous. Aurora touched his cheek, and he smiled down on her. He reached for her hand and placed it over his heart, under the buckskin shirt he'd slipped on after the ceremony. His skin felt hot; she could feel his heart beating against her hand.

They waltzed dizzyingly around and around. With a graceful intimacy that made her knees wobble, he slid his thigh between her legs and held her tight, his arousal undeniable between them. Aurora closed her eyes. Their bodies fit together perfectly as they floated in the timeless music of the river. *Rumm'e.*

Just when Aurora had begun to feel too tired to dance any more, a grey-haired man wearing a green tweed wool cap stepped to the center of the stage. The dancers sat and listened while he sang a ballad about the river and the sea and his own true love. Other singers followed, men and women, with first a romantic song, then a sea shanty, a bawdy, and another ballad, and songs in languages Aurora had never heard before.

At twilight, Frank led Aurora away from all the people, along the river to the small wooden dock where she'd spent her afternoons during those strange and lonely first days in *Naadaayi Heén a Tayee.*

Vivid sunset colors washed across the sky. The little island on the other side of the inlet hovered rose pink in the mist. Water lapping against the rowboat played percussion with the distant music of the wedding guests.

"Do you trust me, Aurora?"

"Yes, of course I do."

"Good. Then get into the boat, *ñ'a táayaa.* I'll row."

97

THE CROSSING

R OWING FELT GOOD TO HIM. His pent-up body needed a physical outlet. He pulled hard through the calm water, breathing in the cool evening air that flowed over the inlet to the sea. He studied his bride, imagining how he would take her. The beads on her dress caught the fading light, creating a shimmering aurora all around her. His blood thickened.

He shook himself, took a deep breath, and pulled harder through the silken water — pink, orange and violet with the colors of sunset. *Almost there.*

He rowed around the fishing boats and sailboats anchored near shore, gliding his skiff smoothly up to the dock. Jumping ashore, he tied off and helped her out.

The temperature had begun to drop now that the sun had set. Aurora shivered in the breeze. He put an arm around her and pulled her tight against him. His own body was like a furnace. She snuggled in closer under his arm.

"It's not far now, Aurora. Come this way."

He led her up the gangplank to the wharf. A few paces along the wharf, they came to a wooden stairway. He took her by the hand, and they climbed up to the impossibly crooked little structure where old Chinvat, the Owl Woman, kept her store.

When he opened the door to the shop, a bell rang overhead. They entered, he blinked and his eyes grew accustomed to the dim light inside.

Chinvat greeted them at her counter. Behind her, and all around the small room, items of every imaginable size, shape, and use were stacked and crowded onto shelves. Owl Woman handed him a backpack, grinning her gap-toothed smile and cackling knowingly.

"Here's what you need, Dear. Go quickly, while there's still enough light so she can see where you're taking her."

He thanked the Old One, slumped the pack over his shoulder, and nodded to Aurora to follow him. She had a dazed look on her face.

"This way now."

They set off on a trail made of planks built over the marshy ground. The trail stretched away from the inlet into the rainforest.

"Stay on these planks," he warned. "There are some places along here where the ground is so soft that if you tried to walk on it, you'd sink up to your chest. It would be hard to pull you out."

Aurora nodded. "That was a strange shop," she said.

"The store and Old Chinvat have been there forever. The store is built on a Gateway. Even though it seems small, she has access to anything in the Universe a customer might want or need."

Aurora took in this new information in silence.

As they hiked, they basked in the beauty of the emerald forest. They heard birdcalls, and several times glanced up to see a great blue heron or a bald eagle gliding overhead. The trail skirted along the edge of the island. Through gaps in the towering red cedar and spruce trees, they caught frequent glimpses of the aquamarine sea. The farther along the trail they walked, the more a sense of peace deepened around them.

Finally, they reached the end of the plank trail and stepped onto a limestone outcrop.

Here, the path curved around a sulphur spring that steamed and bubbled out of the ground to form a small rocky pool. The pool overflowed, its hot water snaking alongside the path in a silver thread until it dropped over a rock ledge.

"Oh!" Aurora's delight roused his blood.

"Follow me." He led her down the path a short way to stairs carved in the limestone.

At the bottom of the stairs, they found themselves alone in an intimate fern grotto, warmed by its proximity to the hot springs, with open sky above them.

Frank took candles and matches from a rock shelf and lit the candles against the gloaming twilight. Flames danced, reflected in veins of natural crystals embedded in the stone. Ethereal lights flickered over the two of them and on the ferns and grotto walls.

A travertine step led down into an elongated pool of intense azure water carving between massive green boulders to the ocean. Steam rose from the pool.

At the near end, hot water from the spring above fell in a steamy waterfall onto a smooth throne-sized boulder of jade.

At the pool's far end, silhouetted in the gloaming, monumental standing stones thrust into the sky at angles — sentries before the open ocean. Powerful waves crashed and broke harmlessly against the stones. Gentle flows of cold seawater rushed up the slot cavern to mix with the hot spring waterfall, creating a temperature gradient that bathers could float along to find that perfect sweet spot.

Frank dropped his backpack on the dry, moss-covered ground, and smiled at his bride.

"If you'd like to, we can have a hot soak later," said Frank. His own voice surprised him — a deep rumbling purr. "Now, *ñ'a táayaa*. Come here."

98

THE CAVE OF *TEHÉATLA SAGRADO*

H E TOOK HER HAND and pulled her through a cave mouth that opened in the rock wall next to the pool. The cave was warm and dry.

He struck a match, and lit a torch mounted in a simple iron wall sconce. The torchlight burned clean, with a pleasing cedar scent and warm orange flame that cast sensuous shadows over walls veined with gold, crystals, and jade.

Handwoven rugs covered the natural marble of the cave floor. A simple wooden table and two chairs sat to one side, next to a plain wooden hutch. A thick, king-sized futon on a raised platform took up the far wall. Blankets, furs and pillows covered the futon.

He stood at her back, arms around her waist, while she adjusted to her surroundings.

"What is this place?" she whispered.

"This cave was given to me when I first came to *Naadaayi Héen a Tayee*, long ago. I use it for retreat and meditation. I sweat in a vapor cave nearby, and soak in the hot pool. This place is sacred to me. I've never shared it with anyone. I spent these last few days preparing it so you'd feel comfortable here."

He pressed himself against her backside and buried his face in the curve of her neck. She arched against him with a sound that sent the blood roaring in his ears.

He turned her around and kissed her lips, full and moist and yielding. His tongue entered her. She went limp in his arms, pulling a deep growl out of him. He supported her easily, pressing her hips against his with one hand, while with the other hand untying the lacing at the front of her dress. The laces came free, opening the soft doeskin down to her navel.

He caressed her breasts, warm and soft and heavy, and suckled her nipples, hard and erect.

He would take his time to open her, give her more pleasure than she'd ever dreamed of. Then he would take her further.

His hand slid down the doe hide and under the hem of her dress. He explored her bare skin, which grew warmer as he reached toward her opening. She quivered like a small animal under his touch. He stopped short, his hand resting on her inner thigh.

Tease her.

He watched her face.

"Please, Frank. Please." She tried to pull his hand higher.

He remained immoveable. With a moan, she surrendered. He slowly proceeded upward.

When his fingers reached their intimate destination, he lightly touched her. She cried out. His mouth covered hers; she yielded to his kiss. He was going to torture her with pleasure.

He picked her up and carried her to his bed, laying her down on her back. Her face was innocent, yet full of voluptuous desire. She raised her knees. He knelt between her legs and parted her.

"You're beautiful." His voice was deep and gravelly.

He ran his finger along her cleft. Her breath caught and her eyelids fluttered closed. She arched upward and her breasts swelled.

He grasped her legs, opening them wider, and rasped the stubble of his chin along her inner thigh. She cried out and lashed her head from side to side, lifting her hips.

He covered her with his mouth, and found the spot that made her quiver and call his name. Her hands clutched at the furs, her hips moving in urgent circles.

He had infinite time to pleasure her. He kissed and licked her, tasting her in infinite loops. When she thrust her hips, he eased his finger inside her.

She whimpered, begging him.

Her shudders grew violent. He raked over her sex with his tongue. She rippled like a ship coming apart in a storm. At her peak, he growled and worked his fingers deeper in, his tongue never relenting. She pulsed with shattering contractions in sweet waves.

When she lay still and limp, throbbing and panting, he lifted her to a sitting position and pulled her dress over her head. Gently, he set her back down and stared hard and long at her nakedness. She blushed and turned her head away.

"Don't be embarrassed to look at me, Aurora, or to let me see you. I'm your husband. I need to know everything about you, every part of you. Are you alright?"

She nodded and smiled up at him with shining eyes.

"I love you, *ñ'a táayaa*. I adore you, and I adore your body. I will love you forever. I'm going to take you and give myself to you, until neither of us can tell any longer where one of us begins and the other ends. Come here, my wife."

He pulled her into his arms and lay with her. When he felt her relax, he began to move his hands over her, slowly coaxing her desire to flame once more. With his mouth and hands, he possessed every inch of her, rousing her to climax again and again, until she screamed and writhed in ecstasy.

He watched her rest, her hair tousled and her skin flushed. Neither of them knew nor cared how long they'd been in one another's embrace.

"I need to touch you," she said in a husky whisper.

Trembling, he took her hand and put it on his loincloth, over his erection. She ran her finger lightly along his length and he shuddered.

She rose to her knees and straddled him, pushing him back when he tried to sit up.

"No," she said. "Lie still."

She gently took a strand of his hair between her fingers, kissed it, then kissed his lips, nibbled along his chin and kissed his throat.

"Now sit up," she said, pulling on his arms. He obeyed and she slipped his buckskin shirt over his head. He held his breath as she kissed his scars, licked his nipples, and rubbed her breasts against him.

Suddenly her hands were under his leather chaps, and she was lightly tickling the sensitive skin of his inner thighs. Her fingers curved up and inward and he shivered, a low groan escaping from his depths.

She unfastened the straps and conchos that held his chaps and they fell away from his legs.

"Stand up," she demanded.

Slowly, he rose. Hands at his sides, he watched her, his cockstand quivering under his loincloth.

She climbed cat-like off the futon and stood in front of him with a sultry look, then drew his loincloth aside and stared. His cock twitched and his balls drew up.

"Frank, I, um …"

"I'll be careful, *ñ'a táayaa.*"

He unfastened the deerhide and let it drop to the floor, and flopped heavily into her hands. She cupped his balls, bowed her head and gently breathed her warmth over them.

He threw his head back. She stood on tiptoe and kissed his throat, then covered him with kisses — making little mewling sounds, sucking, and licking from his chest to the V of his low belly. He ached to push her head down to his cock but resisted. She raised her face, looked in his eyes, and smiled.

She bent over him again and grabbed his cock in her hands, giving him soft kisses along his shaft, then suddenly a long lick up to the head of his cock.

He groaned and twined his fingers in her hair, heart racing.

She smiled up at him again. "Does this feel good?"

He could only softly moan in answer. She played with him, licking and swirling her tongue up and down while exquisitely working his shaft and balls with her hands. Without warning, she took his cock all the way into her mouth.

Fire and ice. Slashes and arrows of pleasure almost too intense to bear.

Struggling for control, he put his hand on top of her soft curls.

"Stop, *ñ'a táayaa*. Wait. Not yet."

She released him with a delicious sucking sound that made him draw in his breath through his teeth. Holding him by the hips, she guided him to the edge of the futon. "I love you."

He sat down on the bed panting for air and reaching for control with the breath of fire.

She pushed him onto his back, straddled him with her bottom facing him, and took him in her warm, wet mouth again.

Like feathers her tongue circled him, lifting him into the clouds. He closed his eyes and softly stroked her while she sucked and flicked the tip of his cock.

Suddenly his animal instincts claimed him, surging through him like a tidal wave. He rose up, rolled her onto her back, pushed her knees apart and wedged himself between her legs.

She opened. He rolled the crown of his cock along her cleft and she shuddered beneath him.

He rose to his knees and thrust, pushing all the way into her. He pulled out, then thrust again, going deeper.

The sounds she made drove him wild. Reaching for control, slow and sure, he circled his hips, working in and out until he was buried to the root.

He barely heard her screams of ecstasy, or his own.

He forced his hands under her and raised her so he could take her deeper. She squeezed her legs tight around his waist.

"Breathe with me, *ñ'a táayaa*." He put her hand over his chest. "Match your breaths with mine. Follow me."

He slowed until her breathing synched with his, then drove into her faster.

He jammed a pillow under her, lifted her legs over his shoulders, and plunged deeper. His balls rhythmically slapping against her made an erotic sound. He found the trigger that unlocked her floodwaters, her very essence, and she released with a scream of pure abandon, expanding and contracting around him.

He pumped faster, panting and grunting, pressure building until a convulsive shudder racked his being.

He exploded and crashed into her depths. Wave after thundering wave rolled and broke over them, towering heat waves of liminal energy reverberated to their core, washing through them, flooding cities, drowning flocks, sinking highways, inundating fields, tractors, train stations and clock towers, bridges and armies, knocking down tall skyscrapers constructed in their minds.

Crashing tidal waves of infinite unconditional love, without beginning or end, rolled and rent them, tore off their flesh, flinging their bones to the stars at the far ends of the Universe. He broke and shattered and dissolved with her into a billion shimmering drops, falling, tumbling, a kaleidoscope of endless beauty. The music of Rumm'e rang through them like temple bells.

They lay in the afterglow a long while still joined, tangled in one another's love.

Finally Frank rose and lit the wall sconces. Crystals in the cave walls sparkled. He led Aurora through an arch and down a short tunnel to another chamber warmed by the hot springs. It had a pleasant scent of lavender, cedar, pine, and chocolate. Flickering flames illuminated a shower with natural serpentine walls and a smooth rock bench. In another small antechamber, a bag of cocoa bean husks leaned against the wall next to a sink and a composting toilet. At the far side of the chamber, a Dutch door fitted to the cave mouth opened onto a clearing in the forest, under the stars.

In the steamy shower, Frank made soap circles around Aurora's breasts and belly, then turned her and washed her back, lingering over the curves of her bottom. Gently, he soaped between her legs, then rinsed her from head to toe.

He stood still while she slowly washed him, learning every inch of his body, playing with him, driving him wild with pleasure, until he was rising and reaching for her again.

When they stepped out of the shower, they dried one another with thick, fragrant towels. He wrapped her in a sarong and then, hand in hand, they returned to the main room of the cave. He ducked outside momentarily and returned with his backpack.

He pulled plates and utensils down from the hutch shelves, and withdrew surprising things from the pack. Soon, the table was set with a bottle of sparkling wine, a crusty loaf of bread, cheese, smoked salmon, watercress, apples, walnuts, and dried cranberries.

"I can't remember when I've ever felt so happy and content," Aurora said.

"Me too." Frank reached out to hold her hand.

When they finished their meal, Frank rose from the table.

"Ready for the hot springs?"

*   *   *

Aurora found herself standing again in the fern grotto outside the cave, barefoot and naked. It seemed like a million years had passed since she'd gone into the cave with him. The night sky was black velvet, pierced by stars. Candlelight, reflected off crystals embedded in the grotto walls, lit their way down a travertine step to the pool.

"It's so beautiful," said Aurora. "Why is the water glowing?"

"The unique minerals in the spring and the color of the travertine bedrock create this otherworldly topaz blue glow. It's believed that the water has healing properties."

Frank held Aurora's hand and helped her into the pool. The water was hot enough to make her draw in a sharp breath. The travertine felt almost spongy to her feet, with just enough grit to keep her from slipping. She waded deeper, until the hot water lapped around her hips, then eased herself into the slightly salty, very soft water down to her shoulders.

She floated on her back as Frank pulled her through the pool. Her eyes closed and she surrendered to the soothing sensations of hot liquid rippling all around her.

He glided her to a large piece of jade that had been carved into a bench by the falling water, then sat down and lifted her onto his lap, his erection bobbing between them like a strange sea creature with a life of its own. The sight of it made them both laugh.

Straddling him, she put her arms around his shoulders and tried to guide him into her.

"Shhhh, *ñ'a táayaa*, let me." He shifted her hips and slipped inside her, then buried his face in the curve of her neck and laughed again, a low deep liquid rumbling. "Be still, my love."

As water pulsed over them, between them, over backs, chests, bellies, Aurora became aware of the sound of his breathing, and the stars sparkling and strobing in the water droplets. His hands on her body seemed to melt into her flesh.

Wild ocean waves thundered harmlessly against the sentinel stones at the mouth of the pool. The ocean surge gently rocked them as it mixed, cold and salty, with hot water falling from the spring above.

Aurora's eyelids grew heavy. She heard a faint twinkling sound coming from far away, beautiful and strange.

"*Ñ'a táayaa*." His breath was sweet and warm. "Open your eyes. Look up."

A curtain of neon colors floated through the sky, flowing and rippling like a dancer's veil, reaching, searching, fluttering, transforming into unworldly shapes and colors of infinite beauty.

They watched the aurora borealis until they could stay awake no longer. Then the warrior priest carried his bride to bed.

They stayed alone at the cave for seven joyful and deeply peaceful days, steaming in the vapor caves, soaking in the hot springs, walking in the forest, sharing laughter and wondrous meals from the bottomless backpack. Their lovemaking was outside of time, as if they were the only people left in the world.

Some evenings, in the clearing behind the cave, they built a bonfire in the stone fire ring. There, they made love under the stars on blankets spread out by the fire, and talked and told each other stories until dawn. Most nights, the aurora borealis appeared in the sky in an ever-changing display of wonders.

Every day, Aurora remembered more about other times they had been together. Their friendship deepened, along with their love.

*   *   *

One afternoon while steaming in a vapor cave, the lover's conversation turned to the events UpRiver that had propelled them into *Naadaayi Héen a Tayee.*

"Do you think Malone actually murdered Yudas Medina?" Aurora asked.

"Both Billy and Malone believed she killed Yudas," said Frank. "That's why Billy shot me. He was trying to protect his mother. But Malone's bullet didn't actually kill Yudas. And Billy's shot isn't the one that wounded me."

"Billy missed? Then who?"

"The Men in Black."

"The Men in Black killed Yudas and shot you?" Aurora frowned. "I always had a feeling they weren't what they seemed. Who are they, really?"

"UpRiver it's believed that they're mercenaries — dark soldiers in a private paramilitary. Sean Stark, head honcho of CalGreen Pesticide Company, thought they worked for him. He hired them to spy on Farm without Harm, the UFW, and on you and me."

"Why us?"

"Stark sensed correctly that our efforts to raise public awareness against pesticides could actually end up transforming agriculture. The kind of agricultural transformation we envisioned, if it spread around the Earth, would be profound. Such a transformation, coupled with a shift to sustainable energy systems, could truly alter the fate of the worlds."

Aurora nodded. "I can see that. But if the Men in Black weren't really working for Stark, who do they work for?"

"They are not of the UpRiver world, but of a much darker dimension. The Men in Black are spawn of the Black Snake."

"The Black Snake?" Aurora shook her head.

"An ancient legend," said Frank. "The Black Snake is a Hydra, a many-headed monster of pure evil. It is foretold that the Black Snake will destroy all the worlds, unless there are enough people pure and true of heart to stop it."

"It has to be stopped! What can we do?"

Frank's eyes clouded with sadness. "There is a way, *Ña táayaa*, but it would require great sacrifice."

Aurora placed her hand over Frank's mouth. "Wait. Stop. Not now. Please. I'm not ready to hear anymore."

*　　*　　*

The next morning, they stood hip deep at the ocean end of the pool, where the water was cold. Chilling white threads of seawater surged around them.

"We must go back to the village now, my Aurora."

Tears welled in Aurora's eyes. "No! So soon? Why?"

"I think you already know. I've been Called."

"Called where? What do you have to do?" She pushed on his chest as if she could force him to stay. "How long will you be gone? When will you come back? Please, Frank. Please don't leave."

"Slow down, *ñ'a táayaa*. We must talk seriously now, my love."

Tears rolled down Aurora's cheeks and dropped onto her breast. He kissed away her tears, brushed a wisp of hair out of her eyes, and tucked it behind her ear.

"Shussh. Don't cry. I love you forever. We are One, my Aurora. We can never be separated, not by distance, time, or even quantum boundaries between worlds. Always remember that, my love."

"But ..."

"You've seen that our world here is deconstructing, dissolving. *Naadaayi Héen a Tayee* and the Salmon People will soon disappear, if we don't act. The dark disease infecting all the worlds is shaking the Pattern apart to the roots. We're running out of time."

"Yes, but ..." She twined her fingers in his hair, leaned close, breathed in his scent, and searched his eyes.

"I'm a warrior, a shamanic priest, Aurora. You know that. I've been summoned to the borderlands between dimensions, to fight and defend, and to help reconstruct the Sacred Geometry. I must go. I don't know when I'll be able to return."

Aurora placed her hands over his heart. She felt his sadness and longing, his love for her — a love she knew was true and would never end. But she also felt determination beating in his blood — a commitment strong and pure and fierce, an indomitable love for all of Creation, which he was bound to protect.

She took a deep breath. "I need to help too. What can I do?"

A cloud of fear crossed his face. Then he smiled with a warmth meant to reassure her.

"You don't have to *do* anything, *ñ'a táayaa*. Just *be*. I want you to stay safe. Stay in our home in the village and wait for me. It will help me survive and succeed, knowing you are safe."

"I can't stay home and do nothing, Frank." Aurora felt no hesitation or doubt. "You know me well enough to accept that. I need to help. I can't possibly just expect others to take care of this. It requires everyone, every being of good heart and good will, here in *Naadaayi Héen a Tayee*, and UpRiver, and in all the worlds, giving our whole selves, to heal the damage and restore the sacred balance. We must stop the Black Snake and its spawn. I *must* help."

"I was afraid you'd feel like this. Xigmacse and the other elders warned me. They reminded me you have a warrior spirit. I will tell you the path they revealed to me, the path that is your destiny, if you are determined to help."

Aurora shivered.

"You have a choice, Aurora. Are you sure?"

She nodded. "Yes."

"This will be more difficult and dangerous than anything we've yet done, *ñ'a táayaa*." His eyes were green and infinite. His cheeks were wet with tears. "If you want to help ..." She held his gaze, and held her breath. "You must go back."

"*What?*"

"If you want to help, your only path is to return UpRiver."

"Is that even possible? What would I do there? Tell me everything."

"Once we return to the village, we'll have some days to adjust and say goodbye. When the time comes, you'll swim to the middle of the river where the current is swift and treacherous. If you make it without being swept out to sea, and the vortex catches you, it will take you through the portal. If you don't drown, you'll probably return to the place where I was shot."

"Come with me, Frank. Come back UpRiver with me, please?"

"It's not possible, *ñ'a táayaa*. At least not now. As you know, there are immutable codes that hold the Pattern together and determine the probable course of our evolution. You have a choice. But if you choose the path of Service and Healing, destiny requires that you return UpRiver. I myself committed to the path of the Formless Warrior long ago. That path, for now, requires that I take a different way."

"What will happen when I go back?"

"We cannot know those details now. We can't yet know if, or how, each of the infinite strands of possibility will be re-woven into the Pattern."

"Will I remember any of this? Will I remember — what you and I — that we ..."

He shook his head. "I don't know, Belovéd."

They held one another and cried.

"Once I'm UpRiver again, how will I know what I should do?"

"You will be guided, I promise. Pray, meditate, do your yoga, practice right livelihood, and follow your intuition. Trust your beautiful, courageous heart, *ñ'a táayaa*. You will know, with certainty, what actions to take, what direction to go, when the time comes. You'll know, even if you're not sure why you know. Be brave. Make bold choices. Our love is strong; trust that it will light your way."

"Will I ever see you again?" Aurora sobbed.

"Aurora, *ñ'a táayaa*, my belovéd wife, blood of my blood, my soulmate ... Someday, we will be reunited. Even if all the worlds end, I will find you. Together we will make our way back Home. I promise."

His words stabbed her heart. She wanted to stay alone with him here forever. But when he spoke, she knew it would be futile to argue. They couldn't hide from their destinies. They had worlds to save.

Morning sun scattered gold foil circles over the surface of the topaz pool. She took his hand and pulled him up toward the hot end of the springs, and there she made love to him under the waterfall.

I love you forever.

AFTERWORD

QUEEN SALMON'S LAMENT

We were so many once
The sea itself would churn with the wake of our endless schools.
When we turned, in our great gyres, the head of the school
Would be half way down to Kodiak while our tail
would still be deep in Siberian Waters, pecked at by Aleut hunters
 brave enough to pursue us in flimsy skinboats.
From frigid Kamchatka to the balmy southern coasts,
we were known as The Providers ...
who guaranteed meat to bear and eagle, and raven
and human And a multitude of others.
When we entered the rivers,
compelled by the sacred, fatal urgings of our loins,
a huge wave preceded us to let the hunters know we were coming.
The rivers swelled and the fishermen roared with glee
at our spirit churning the Water to foam.
We were royalty visiting from a larger, more exotic realm,
charging Each valley from Siberia to Point Conception
with the power of the deep, and The exaltation of purest sex.
And when that was over, our carcasses sent to the Peaks
 a stench that sickened
even the skunk people
but spoke of oceanic riches
Being returned to the rivers, and the land,

to put spine in the green growth and Recharge the cycle of life.

We were the mortar and thong that bound river and ocean, Land and sea.

We were the Lifebringers.

And now, the animals who ate us have almost forgotten our taste.

Only the oldest humans can remember the last of our glory.

This cursed age

When all of nature is made so small, so diminished. When all that stand

Of size or greatness or is so tiny and fine as to go unnoticed,

is punished for its Very existence by losing it.

Oh how has the world been so reduced?

We, the Salmon People are few now in so many places where we were once

a multitude. What was glorious is now furtive and quick,

no longer a din filled with the thundering Power of Creation.

We seem a tattered remnant.

The barren shadow of a once brilliant shimmering.

Why? Is it humans?

They were part of the scheme once,

  native to The land, brave and humble players.

What is this curse we all suffer through Them?

Why must it be so?

Do our people have to go down to dim perdition

Never to show our brilliant silver sides

to any eyes anywhere in the universe?

Will not even the humans lament our passing?

WHAT NOW?

During its 35 years of operation, the **Monterey Bay Salmon & Trout Education Program (STEP)** inspired nearly 100,000 young people to become watershed stewards and champions of the environment. In the 1980s, Santa Cruz County STEP students helped to initiate the federal listing of Monterey Bay Coho as an endangered species. But by 2000, the Monterey Bay Coho ("Silver Salmon") was considered extinct in the Corralitos Creek watershed. In 2014, due to the low numbers of Steelhead ("Rainbow Trout") returning to spawn, California Department of Fish and Wildlife determined that they could no longer permit Steelhead eggs to be incubated in classrooms. The Monterey Bay STEP program was terminated. Although conservation measures continue, and it is hoped that the MBSTEP program can one day return, all Monterey Bay salmonids, critical to the overall biodiversity of the Pacific Salmon population, are currently considered to be at high risk.

http://planetwatchradio.com/salmon-restoring-an-endangered-species/

The Earth is currently on the precipice of the **Sixth Great Extinction**, the start of a new geologic era — **the Anthropocene** — during which it's probable we will lose three-quarters of all species on Earth, due to human-caused disruptions of natural cycles. It is essential that we make every effort to preserve the **biodiversity of life** on this planet.

The **California Birth Defects Prevention Act (SB 950)** legally passed by voter initiative in 1984, "… required DPR to acquire certain toxicological data for registered pesticide active ingredients in order to make a scientific determination that their continued uses will not cause significant adverse health effects." Satisfactory data was never provided by the industry for methyl bromide, yet the EPA continues to allow agricultural use of the chemical into the twenty-first century, in complete disregard of California citizens' legal mandate. Follow-up is needed.

As of 2017, **methyl bromide** was finally {mostly} phased out as a field fumigant in California, after receiving years of federal exemptions from the international ban. The strawberry industry still relies on the pesticides Chloropicrin and 1,3-Dichloropropenene — along with a toxic brew of other estrogen, reproductive, endocrine, and immune system disruptors; neurotoxins; and carcinogens. It is well-known that there are synergistic effects to combining these pesticides, but so far, no systematic studies have been made.

New research from UC Berkeley and UC Davis, including the now famous **CHAMACOS Study**, links exposure to these brain-harming pesticides with lower IQ, autism spectrum disorders, and learning disabilities. *Yet by 2019, the problem of toxic pesticide drift into the schools had still not been addressed.* In the first year of Trump's presidency, his **EPA** Chief Scott Pruitt swept aside seventeen years of research and the scientific concerns from his own agency about the brain-harming chemical **chlorpyrifos**, produced by DowDuPont, ruling that farmers can continue to use the chemical. However, California, Hawaii, and New York have implemented state-wide bans on the neurotoxin. See more at:
pulse.ncpolicywatch.org/2017/04/03/state-ag-commissioner-troxler-ple ased-epas-ruling-allow-brain-damaging-pesticide-crops/

On April 24, 2019, Audet & Partners, LLP filed the first widespread class action lawsuit against **Monsanto** based on the established link between **Roundup weed killer and non-Hodgkin's lymphoma**. On May 13, 2019, a California jury awarded the plaintiffs a verdict of over $1 billion each in punitive damages against Monsanto.

A new generation of dedicated Santa Cruz and Monterey county **school teachers** have reinvigorated the struggle to protect the more than 500,000 California school children who spend their days within a quarter mile of hazardous pesticide applications. See more about the group carrying on **Farm Without Harm's work — Safe Ag SafeSchools ("SASS")** — on the web at *http://safeagsafeschools.org* and on Facebook at *https://facebook.com/safeagsafeschools*.

In 2014, according to the United Nations Commission on Human Rights, 1.2 million **children were trafficked worldwide for sexual exploitation.**

From April to June of 2018, U.S. President Trump ordered border patrol officers to **forcibly take nearly 2,500 immigrant children** — breastfeeding infants to seventeen-year-olds — away from their parents. The children were imprisoned (some of them in cages) in makeshift facilities in various border locations, and have since been secretly shipped to unknown locations around the U.S. **A billion-dollar private prison industry** has quickly developed to construct permanent internment camps for the children, the location of the facilities shrouded in secrecy. No adequate records of the children's identity, the location of the facilities where they're being held, or the identity and whereabouts of their parents has been kept. Parents of many of the children have been deported to untraceable rural locations in Central and South America, while their children continue to be held in U.S. "tender age" prisons. Many of these children will never see their parents again. Whistle blowers have begun leaking troubling images and first-hand reports about the condition of the children, which show them being drugged, beaten, and abused. As of June 2019, at least seven children under the age of 10 have died of neglect in captivity.

The larger issue of **Juvenile Justice** must be addressed in our country. One organization working to assist gang-involved youth and young adults is **Homeboy Industries**, founded by Father Gregory Boyle.

Public cries for **immigration reform** have gone unheeded, and as 2019 draws to a close, legislation put forth by the Democratic House of Representatives has been ignored by Senate Majority Leader Mitch McConnell.

Colonialism and genocide against **Native Americans**, are not only part of our country's history, but continue to this day. Yet our indigenous First Peoples persist and stand strong against assaults to

Mother Earth, such as the **Standing Rock** occupation to resist a **dangerous oil pipeline** that threatens to poison a vital artery of our country's **water. Water is Life.**

The **free, public, high-quality educational system in the U.S. — vital to the health of our nation's democracy** — is being systematically dismantled under the Trump Administration by Department of Education appointee Betsy DeVos. Her appointment was widely contested by parents, teachers, unions, and highly qualified educational experts and researchers, and was only approved when Vice President Pence stepped in to cast a deciding vote.

An unqualified billionaire with no experience in public education, DeVos has demonstrated her ignorance of basic math, and her **rejection of scientific data** on school policies and performance. She has worked for decades to **undermine teachers unions** and has long supported unaccountable, Christian-motivated, for-profit charter schools and vouchers, which drain public schools of critical resources and offer no choice for the most vulnerable students — those with special needs, those who don't speak English, and those living in poverty. She is an enemy of **intellectual freedom, freedom of religion, gender and racial parity, , and respect for diversity**. DeVos and her family have contributed billions to promote their elitist, racist agenda by **interfering in U.S. elections**. DeVos' brother, Erik Prince, founded the **Private Mercenary Army — Blackwater**. According to some sources, Blackwater has contributed at least a million dollars to the **NRA**, known to be heavily funding extreme right-wing election campaigns.

Plastic debris in the oceans is a growing threat. As of 2018, the Great Pacific Garbage Patch, a collection of floating plastic trash — primarily suspended, often microscopic, particles in the upper water column — has grown, by some estimates, to more than 600,000 square miles — twice the size of Texas and three times the size of France, with a similar area of man-made marine debris within the North Atlantic Gyre. Cities around the country are responding to this threat to our oceans' health by passing ordinances to ban plastic grocery bags, plastic straws, and restaurant take-out containers. Scientists, inventors, and entrepreneurs are developing initiatives to clear and repurpose the debris. **"No More Mermaid Tears"**, one such project, is a **youth-led initiative** with the goal of empowering young people as ocean defenders capable of addressing coastal plastic pollution. *http://planetwatchradio.com/no-more-mermaid-tears.*

Other **significant youth-led initiatives** have emerged around the urgency of climate change. See **Greta Thunberg** and **Our Children's Trust** landmark legal case.

The consequences of **climate chaos** are being felt around the globe. Climate scientists now predict that your grandchildren may never get to walk in an old growth redwood forest, or see a wild salmon or a whale. The 2015 Paris Accord was a hopeful signal that the world's governments will take effective action to reduce carbon emissions and mitigate the **consequences of global warming**. Although President Trump has formally rescinded the United States' commitment to the terms of the Paris Accord, citizens in communities everywhere are taking matters into their own hands, working locally to rein in pollution, curb social injustices, and transition their food, water, transportation, education, health, and energy systems for a sustainable future.

Your help is needed. Dive in!

GRATITUDE

There's not enough space on this page to mention all of the people who encouraged and helped me to tell this story. You know who you are. Thank you. *Muchas Gracias. Maholo nui loa.*

To my dear life partner, Joseph Bell Jordan, Jr. ("Cosmic Joe") my inspiration and sure shining light. And my deeply loved spirit animal, Sarah Bella the Siberian husky, who camped out at my feet day after day, while I worked on this manuscript.

My dearly esteemed **teaching colleagues**, my amazing **students** and **their parents,** especially the ones who lived this true story with me.

Father Gregory Boyle of Homeboy Industries, who was doing the real work before Father Francis was conceived.

Fearless Editors: Elizabeth Lyon, Leonard Tourney, Maria Grusauskas, and Heather Lazare

Subject matter consultants: Santa Cruz Police Department Lieutenant (retired) Tom Vlassis; Father Al Mengon and Father Marc Rougeau of Our Lady of Help of Christians Church-Watsonville CA; Woman Surfing Champion Kimberly Mayer; Monterey Bay Salmon and Trout Project Education Coordinator Barry Burt; Monterey Bay Salmon and Trout Project Co-Founder Matt McCaslin; Coastal Watershed Council Founder Donna Meyers; Santa Cruz County Riparian Habitat Resource Officer Dave Hope; Carmel-by-the-Sea Central Coast Fly Fishing shop owner/fly fisherman Geoff Malloway; Deep Sea Fisherman Miochael B. Schell; California Fish & Wildlife Captain Don Kelly, for whom Kelli Cavanaugh is named.

Most wonderful teacher/mentors: Dr. Kenneth S. Norris - UCSC Environmental Studies (Whoof!), Dr. Arthur Pearl - UCSC Education, Professor Al Johnsen - UCSC Art, Professor Jennifer Anderson - UCSC

645

Environmental Interpretation, Dr. Steven R. Gliessman - UCSC Agroecology, Professor Roberta Jaffe-Founding Director Lifelab Science school gardens program, Professor Don Rothman - UCSC Writing Project, Professor Sandy Lydon - Cabrillo College History, Muralist Guillermo Aranda, Dr. William H. Friedland - UCSC Community Studies, Dr. William Domhoff - UCSC Sociology, Dr. Robert R. Curry - UCSC Environmental Geology, Dr. Craig Schindler - UCSC Interfaith Council, Dr. Jerome Kirk - UCI Sociology, Ohlone Tribal Chair of Indian Canyon Anne Marie Sayers, Florence Richardson Wyckoff (1905-1997) - artist, historian, and life-long grassroots social activist — my STEP mother.

Valuable feedback, support, and expertise: Professor T. Mike Walker, Don Monkerud - photography, Michael Larsen and Elizabeth Pomada - San Francisco Writers Conference, Gar Anthony Haywood - Santa Barbara Writers' Conference, Nancy Wood - who introduced me to Paper Angel Press; *Fruit of the Devil* story midwife Sarah Rabkin - editor of *Cultivating a Movement: Sustainable Agriculture and Organic Farming on California's Central Coast*; and Bruce Neuburger - author of *Lettuce Wars,* who came up with the title, *Fruit of the Devil.*

Generous and Astute Early Readers and Critique Partners: Jamie Jefferies, Barry Burt, Jim Scott-Behrends, Dr. Dvera Saxton, Vinnie Hansen, Micah Keeley, Chris Goddard, Rick Parfitt, Rachel Pfotenhauer, Lynda Scott, Cheri Wells, Kaethe Sullivan, Dr. Ann López , James "Wolf" Starkewolf, Janet Kreitzer, Jean Thomas, Kathy Ellis, Kate Hitt, Laura Shaw Van Zandt, Fred and Roberta McPherson, Mary Mansir, Trish Unruh, Becky Blythe, Lois Robin, Eugene Beer, and Lily Lightbridge

My brilliant publisher, Steven Radecki of Paper Angel Press, who — with courage and vision — pulled this book out of the RiverUnderTheRiver and into the light of day.

ABOUT THE AUTHOR

After earning a teaching credential with an emphasis in Environmental Education, Mary Flodin worked as a naturalist in an Outdoor Science School for two years before moving into the classroom. From the mid-1980s until 2000, she taught in an elementary school surrounded by strawberry fields. Mary became involved in the struggle to protect her students from pesticide drift, and help found the environmental group Farm Without Harm, now known as Safe Ag Safe Schools (*SafeAgSafeSchools.org*).

Fruit of the Devil, her first novel, was a finalist for the PEN/Bellwether Award for Socially Engaged Fiction and for the Pacific Northwest Writers' Competition. She was awarded a fellowship to the Squaw Valley Community of Writers, and has participated in numerous writers' conferences, including BreadLoaf Orion and the Association for the Study of Literature and Environment (ASLE).

Mary lives in a cottage on the Central California Coast with her husband — a retired NASA climate scientist— and their dog, koi, chickens, and gopher herd. You can learn more about her world and works at *maryflodin.com.*

Made in the USA
Columbia, SC
12 November 2019